A History of African American Theatre

This is the first definitive history of African American theatre. The text embraces a wide geography investigating companies from coast to coast as well as the Anglophone Caribbean and African American companies touring Europe, Australia, and Africa. This history represents a catholicity of styles – from African ritual born out of slavery to European forms, from amateur to professional. It covers nearly two and a half centuries of black performance and production with issues of gender, class, and race ever in attendance. The volume encompasses aspects of performance such as minstrel, vaudeville, cabaret acts, musicals, and opera. Shows by white playwrights that used black casts, particularly in music and dance, are included, as are productions of western classics and a host of Shakespeare plays. The breadth and vitality of black theatre history, from the individual performance to large-scale company productions, from political nationalism to integration, are conveyed in this volume.

ERROL G. HILL is Professor Emeritus at Dartmouth College, Hanover, New Hampshire. He taught at the University of the West Indies and Ibadan University, Nigeria, before taking up a post at Dartmouth in 1968. His publications include *The Trinidad Carnival* (1972), *The Theatre of Black Americans* (1980), *Shakespeare in Sable* (1984), *The Jamaican Stage, 1655–1900* (1992), and *The Cambridge Guide to African and Caribbean Theatre* (with Martin Banham and George Woodyard, 1994); and he has been contributing editor of several collections of Caribbean plays. He was awarded the Gold Medal for Drama from the Government of Trinidad and Tobago, the Barnard Hewitt Award for Outstanding Research in Theatre History, the Robert Lewis Medal for Lifetime Achievement in Theatre Research, the Presidential Medal for Outstanding Leadership and Achievement from Dartmouth College, and an Honorary Doctor of Letters from the University of the West Indies.

JAMES V. HATCH is Professor Emeritus in the Graduate Theatre Program at the City University of New York. He is author of several books on African American theatre, including *Black Theater USA* (coedited with Ted Shine, 1996) and the prize-winning biography *Sorrow is the Only Faithful One: The Life of Owen Dodson* (1993). With his wife, Camille Billops, he founded the Hatch–Billops Collection, an archive of black cultural materials that has published twenty-one annual volumes of *Artist and Influence*. His recognitions include the Skowhegan Award (with Camille Billops) for contributions to the arts, the Winona Fletcher Award for Outstanding Achievement in Black Theatre, the Life Achievement Award from the American Theatre in Higher Education, and two Obie Awards for contributions to off-Broadway Theatre.

The American theatre and its literature are attracting, after long neglect, the crucial attention of historians, theoreticians, and critics of the arts. Long a field for isolated research yet too frequently marginalized in the academy, the American theatre has always been a sensitive gauge of social pressures and public issues. Investigations into its myriad shapes and manifestations are relevant to students of drama, theatre, literature, cultural experience, and political development.

The primary intent of this series is to set up a forum of important and original scholarship in and criticism of American theatre and drama in a cultural and social context. Inclusive by design, the series accommodates leading work in areas ranging from the study of drama as literature to theatre histories, theoretical explorations, production histories and readings of more popular or paratheatrical forms. While maintaining a specific emphasis on theatre in the United States, the series welcomes work grounded broadly in cultural studies and narratives with interdisciplinary reach. Cambridge Studies in American Theatre and Drama thus provides a crossroads where historical, theoretical, literary, and biographical approaches meet and combine, promoting imaginative research in theatre and drama from a variety of new perspectives.

A History of African American Theatre

ERROL G. HILL
Dartmouth College

and

JAMES V. HATCH
City University of New York

CAMBRIDGE
UNIVERSITY PRESS

PUBLISHED BY THE PRESS SYNDICATE OF THE UNIVERSITY OF CAMBRIDGE
The Pitt Building, Trumpington Street, Cambridge CB2 IRP, United Kingdom

CAMBRIDGE UNIVERSITY PRESS
The Edinburgh Building, Cambridge, CB2 2RU, UK
40 West 20th Street, New York, NY 10011–4211, USA
477 Williamstown Road, Port Melbourne, VIC 3207, Australia
Ruiz de Alarcón 13, 28014 Madrid, Spain
Dock House, The Waterfront, Cape Town 8001, South Africa

http://www.cambridge.org

First published 2003
Reprinted 2004 (twice)

Printed in the United Kingdom at the University Press, Cambridge

Typeface Adobe Caslon 10.5/13 pt.   *System* LaTeX 2$_\varepsilon$ [TB]

A catalogue record for this book is available from the British Library

ISBN 0 521 62443 6 hardback

Contents

Illustrations

Foreword

Lloyd G. Richards

History is made in four ways. First, by those who participate in the event. Second, by those who observe the event and will pass their version on by word of mouth, embellishing, forgetting, or adjusting as the circumstances demand. Third, by the professional observer who writes and whose accounts end up in a chronicle in the library. And fourth, by those who do not write. Much of history is lost because it was not written about either accidentally or purposefully. Much of the history of Blacks in America simply was not written about, certainly from a black point of view. That applies to the history of Blacks in American theatre.

I came to the United States from Canada at the age of 4. All my education through university has been in America. The theatre was not discussed around our dinner table, for we didn't go. Why should we? The stories were not about us, nor did we have an opportunity to speak our mind. I went to the movies a lot. I saw events of history and of human existence. I never saw two black people kiss. The films also taught me that black people did not walk down the streets in New York, or anywhere else for that matter. I never saw a cotton field without a black person in it or a red cap without a black face under it. I was being educated. This was reality. This was history. Were it not for the strength of character of my family, my education would have been left to Epaminondas and Little Black Sambo.

I certainly never read a chapter in a theatre history book on the black theatre in America. Nor did it appear on any of the required or suggested reading lists that I encountered. Purposefully or carelessly we were being educated toward the fact that we did not count. It is a wonder that I survived my education to spend my life in the theatre.

Wondrously, in the last decade more volumes have begun to appear to augment those pitiful few on the library shelves. And now Errol G. Hill and James V. Hatch have brought tireless research and writing skill to address this question. One of their most important discoveries is that they have just begun to tap the vein. There is much more to be discovered.

Every black person who aspires to a life in the theatre should be fortified with a knowledge of his/her past as his or her rite of passage. And every white child should have knowledge of the vigor and diversity of the theatre in America as we join in creating a true American theatre.

Preface

James V. Hatch

Black Manhattan (1930) may have been the first attempt to chronicle the history of African American theatre; its author, James Weldon Johnson, focused on the theatre he knew best, the New York commercial stage. Fifteen years later Fannin Saffore Belcher Jr. wrote a more comprehensive history entitled *The Place of the Negro in the Evolution of the American Theatre, 1767 to 1940*, his 1945 dissertation at Yale University. It was never published. Another decade passed before Tom Fletcher published his memoirs, *One Hundred Years of the Negro in Show Business* (1954). Fletcher performed professionally until his death in 1954 while his book was still in press. Loften Mitchell, a professional New York playwright, published *Black Drama* in 1967, again an important volume because Mitchell had known and worked with many of the artists he wrote about; however, the major focus of his book was Harlem and New York City theatre. In the three decades since Mitchell's history, African American theatre's styles and locales have changed radically, emerging as a widely recognized world theatre.

This *History of African American Theatre* makes a concerted effort to embrace a wide geography, investigating companies from coast to coast as well as their travels abroad. The book presents a catholicity of styles from African ritual to European forms, from amateur to professional, and from political nationalism to integration. It chronicles nearly two-and-a-half centuries of black performance and production, with issues of gender, class, and race ever in attendance.

In order to define the boundaries of African American theatre the authors asked: what is Black theatre? The easy answer appeared to be that it is an art created by black people, but that definition raised more questions. Should the immigrants and migrants born in the Caribbean, in Africa, or in South America be included? Or should only those born in the United States be included? For the purposes of this book we have attempted to limit the geography to continental North America, while recognizing migrant playwrights and actors from the Anglophone Caribbean, as well as African American companies touring Europe, Australia, and Africa. This global aspect has stretched the book's boundaries to include such diversity as minstrelsy, Ira Aldridge, the Negro Ensemble Company, and many others who often took their talents abroad.

What, then, are the criteria for selection? We have chosen to write about companies, productions, actors, managers, and technicians who achieved national reputations, who exhibited pioneering courage and endurance, who represented a larger number of like theatre artists or companies, who exemplified movements or fashions, or who changed the form or essence of African American theatre. The authors knowingly have omitted names of many theatre practitioners, a painful excision compelled by space limitations.

Whether boastfully virulent or shamefully camouflaged, America's changing racial climates and policies over the years are noted. The cultural exchanges between Blacks and Whites, although never constant, have been continuous throughout both segregation and integration. In this vein, the authors have set down instances when the races "borrowed" performance and culture from each other in order to create a distinctive branch of American theatre.

In recent years definitions of theatre have expanded beyond performances on the traditional stage. Half-time displays at football games, marching bands at funerals, even public executions have been added to performance ritual. One has only to think of the jitterbug contests at the Savoy Ballroom in Harlem or the step dance contests in historically black colleges and universities to be reminded that African Americans have often celebrated themselves on nontraditional stages – streets, lodges, schools, nightclubs, cabarets, and churches. To embrace the full diversity of black performance would be to write a second volume; nonetheless, we have selectively included some minstrel, vaudeville, and cabaret acts pertinent to the development of American theatre, particularly music and dance.

While our history focuses on black theatre, it was not possible to exclude white. For example, we have included *Porgy and Bess* (1935), a show written, produced and directed by Whites. A white-conceived musical such as *Carmen Jones* (1943), with its all-black cast, is pertinent. Even shows that opened with white casts and which were later recast black, such as *Hello Dolly* (1967), deserve to be recognized because their stars should not be ignored. Jean Genet's *The Blacks* (1960) and a host of Shakespearian productions, as well as other classics by white authors – but acted by Blacks – were germane because they were steps on the ladder of black achievement.

Although Donald Bogle, Phyllis Klotman, Edward Mapp, and others have already written the histories of black television shows and films, on occasion when a stage play like *A Raisin in the Sun* was developed into a film, we noted it, especially if the actors were known for their theatre tenure. Token black actors in white theatre companies, along with performers in mixed media such as dance, poetry, and music, have necessarily been omitted.

Some problems in assembling this history are pertinent: first, the scarcity of certain written, oral, and photographic records. Africans came in chains, their cultures, rituals, and languages having no validity in a hostile environment. As they settled into the routine of southern plantation life, or became northern freemen, accounts of their music and dance begin to appear in newspapers and journals, albeit always filtered through a white racial gaze. Even when African Americans in the nineteenth century began to set down their own histories, the biographers unabashedly selected individuals from their own class, preserving those aspects of black life that they thought Whites might approve of. For this reason, one may pore over many bio-dictionaries of black "achievement" and find few women and no theatre folk unless that artist had already won the approbation of white audiences, as Bert Williams had.

Theatre history has always depended upon subjective memory, biography, and reviews. Compared to the mountainous theatre archives of Whites, early African American records are often scarce and sometimes contradictory. Nonetheless, with persistence and hard digging one may uncover treasures such as those in the National Archives, where the United States Food Administration in World War One set down the names of 104 theatres, cinemas, and cabarets in Chicago that catered to Blacks. This is to say that until recent times theatre archives, be they libraries, newspapers, or books, have not served African Americans well, except, perhaps, when they noted Blacks appearing before white audiences.

In matters of documentation, we have placed our asides and references in endnotes. Our bibliography lists those books and periodicals referred to in these notes. In matters of style, we have chosen to use the terms *Black* and *African American* interchangeably. We have capitalized Black and White when they appear as nouns, but not as adjectives. African, Colored, Negro, Afro-American, Afri-American, and People of Color appear when quoted or when appropriate to the period under discussion. Ironically at the beginning of the twentieth century during the "melting pot movement" the children of immigrants chose to be "hyphenated" as a means of asserting "We, too, sing America," an idea that triumphed in the working-class Festival of Nations movement of the 1920s and 1930s. However, by the 1980s hyphenation meant someone other than a "genuine" American. For this reason, we have omitted the hyphen between *African* and *American*.

Both authors of this book, although long familiar with black theatre history, were amazed at the breadth and variety of materials that they uncovered. We were not able to set it all down in this text. But other African American theatre histories will follow, uncovering fresh treasures, reinterpreting a difficult terrain, and, yes, improving on our inadequacies. We welcome them. We have done our best.

Acknowledgments

We wish to express our gratitude for the generous assistance received from the institutions and individuals listed below. It enabled us not only to undertake travel, research, and consultation needed in preparing the text, but also offered substantial help and encouragement in establishing the factual record, both historical and contemporary. The following are among the various means of support.

To Errol G. Hill: a grant from the National Endowment for the Humanities, and a winter term 1999 residency at the Getty Research Institute, Los Angeles, California (nominated by the African Grove Institute for the Arts). Professor Hill writes: research visits were made to several collections, namely, the Harry Ransom Humanities Research Center, University of Texas, Austin, Texas; the Countee Cullen/Harold Jackman Memorial Collection, 1881–1995, at the Robert W. Woodruff Library of Atlanta University Center, Atlanta, Georgia; in New Orleans, Louisiana, (i) the Amistad Research Center, (ii) the Howard-Tilton Memorial Library at Tulane University, (iii) the Historic New Orleans Collection at Williams Research Center, and (iv) the Huntington Library in San Marino, California.

I am grateful to the following scholars from whom I have quoted relevant extracts from an earlier work that I published under the title *The Theatre of Black Americans*. The writers quoted are Shelby Steele, Eleanor Traylor, Eileen Southern, Robert Farris Thompson, and my coauthor, James V. Hatch. Others in academia from whose research and insights I have profited include John Graziano, Samuel Hay, Tisch Jones, Bernth Lindfors, Thomas Pawley, Eric Ledell Smith, George A. Thompson Jr., and Sylvia Wynter. Dr. Jewel Plummer Cobb, a relative of the multitalented Bob Cole, generously allowed me to inspect family owned papers about him.

Caribbean-inspired theatre in America has a history dating back to the early twentieth century but it was only in the mid-1970s that an attempt was made to form a resident Caribbean American Repertory Theatre (CART) in New York. That endeavor still exists along with a West Coast branch known as CART/West. Data on the work of these companies have been provided chiefly by leading participants Austin Stoker, Olivier Stephenson, and Rudolf Shaw, to whom I extend thanks. More recent playwrights and theatre workers from the Caribbean, as well as collectors abroad who have contributed to the present study, include Lennox Brown, Ray Funk, William Norris, and Mizan Nunes. In addition, bare-boned professional theatre troupes based mainly in Jamaica have begun traveling to America to present their productions. Information on these and other Caribbean-related theatre activities has been furnished by Jean Small of the Philip Sherlock Centre for the Creative Arts at the University of the West Indies, Mona, Jamaica, and by David Edgecombe, director of the Reichhold Center of the Arts on St. Thomas, Virgin Islands.

At Dartmouth College, librarians Patricia Carter and Bonnie Wallin were most helpful in tracking down information sources; Susan Bibeau and Otmar Foelsche of humanities resources repeatedly rescued me from computer woes; the theatre department provided a quiet office at a crucial time when, due to reconstruction, faculty offices in the Baker Library were unavailable, and theatre staff gave unstinted assistance at all times. Special thanks are due to emeritus professor Caldwell Titcomb of Brandeis University for faithfully supplying copies of his theatre reviews published in the *Bay State Banner* and elsewhere. Richard and Jennifer Joseph graciously opened their home to my wife and myself when lodgings in Atlanta proved inhospitable.

I acknowledge with appreciation the help of my sister Jean Sue-Wing in Trinidad, for her ready response to many inquiries. To my coauthor, James V. Hatch, I am immensely indebted for his willingness to assume responsibility for a much larger portion of the history than was initially assigned, when at a critical point in the writing I experienced serious health problems that required surgery and prolonged treatment. Finally, I acknowledge with gratitude the material assistance of my wife, Grace, and our grown children, whose care and concern for the completion of this project have been truly humbling.

To James V. Hatch: a fellowship from the National Endowment for the Humanities, and travel and research funds from the Research Foundation of the City University of New York. Next, he extends his appreciation to the editor of the *Cambridge Studies in American Theatre and Drama*, Don B. Wilmeth of Brown University, for encouragement in writing this history. Professor Hatch writes: the following librarians were most helpful – Nancy Burkett of the Antiquarian Society; Randall K. Burkett, Woodruff Library, Emory University; Rosemary Cullen, Brown University; Andrew Davis, Museum of the City of New York; Richard H. Engleman, Sayre-Carkeek Collection, special collection and preservation division, University of Washington; Annette Fern and Michael Dumas, Harvard Theatre Collection; Liz Fugate, Theatre Arts, University of Washington; Kathy Harvey, Theatre and Performance Sayre-Carkeek Collection, Seattle Public Library; Diana Lachatanere, Schomburg Center for Research in Black Culture, New York City; Robert N. Matuozzi, Butler Collection, Holland Library, State University Pullman; Melissa Minette Miller, Theatre Arts Collection, Harry Ransom Humanities Center, University of Texas; Bernard L. Peterson Jr., Bibliographer, Elizabeth, North Carolina; Theatre Collection, Free Library of Philadelphia; George Thompson Jr., Research, Bobbs Library, New York University; and Beth Turner, Editor, *Black Masks*, New York University.

This work has benefited from the generosity of many scholars who shared their research. I thank Addell and Gary Anderson, Wayne State University, Detroit; Annemarie Bean, Theatre, Williams College, Massachusetts; Oscar Brockett, University of Texas; Professor Beth Cleary, Macalester College, St. Paul; Winona Fletcher, Indiana University, Bloomington; Brenda Dixon Gottschild, Temple University, Philadelphia; John Graziano, Music Department, City University of New York; Leo Hamalian, English, City College of New York City; Tisch Jones, State University of Iowa; Woodie King Jr., New Federal Theatre, New York City; Brooks McNamara, Performance Studies, New York University; Thomas D. Pawley Jr., Lincoln University, Jefferson City, Missouri; Kathy Perkins, University of Illinois; William R. Reardon, University of California, Santa Barbara; Peter Rachleff, Macalester College, St. Paul; Leslie Catherine Sanders, York University, North York, Canada; Ted Shine, Theatre Department, Prairie View, Texas; Judith L. Stevens, Penn State University, Orwigsburg; Dana R. Sutton, City University of New York; Vanita Vactor, Illinois State University; Margaret Wilkerson, Ford Foundation; Bob West, National Conference of African American Theatre, Washington, DC.

For finding and providing photographs I thank Celeste Beatty, Parker Smith, Nadine George-Graves, and Brenda Thompson. For personal correspondence, interviews, and telephone conversations I acknowledge assistance from Douglas Q. Barnett, Black Arts West; Lou Bellamy,

Director, Penumbra Theatre; Camille Billops, Hatch–Billops Collection; Susan Blankenship, research assistant, Spokane; Walter Dallas, Freedom Theatre, Philadelphia; Zerita Dotson, Oakland Ensemble Theatre; Ricardo Khan, Crossroads Theatre; Ernestine Lucas; O. Vernon Matisse, University of California, Los Angeles; Joan Maynard; Mona Scott, Berkeley Black Repertory Theatre; George C. Wolfe, Joseph Papp Public Theatre; Barbara Lewis, research assistant, City University of New York; and India Amos, who prepared the manuscript.

Abbreviations

AEA	Actors' Equity Association
AETA	American Educational Theatre Association
AGIA	African Grove Institute for the Arts
AME	African Methodist Episcopal
ANT	American Negro Theater
ANTA	American National Theatre and Academy
AUDELCO	Audience Development Committee
BARTS	Black Arts Repertory Theatre School
BBR	Berkeley Black Repertory
BTA	Black Theatre Alliance
BTN	Black Theatre Network
CAFE	Caribbean Arts Festival Ensemble
CAMP	Central Area Motivation Program
CART	Caribbean American Repertory Theatre
CAU	Colored Actors Union
CCC	Civilian Conservation Corps
CET	Concept East Theatre
CETA	Comprehensive Employment Training Act
CHT	Council on Harlem Theatres
CNA	Committee for the Negro in the Arts
CNAT	Chicago Negro Art Theatre
CUNY	City University of New York
ELT	Equity Library Theatre
ETC	Experimental Theatre Club
FST	Free Southern Theatre
FSWW	Frank Silvera Writers' Workshop
FTP	Federal Theatre Project

HADLEY	Harlem Artistic Developmental League Especially for You
HARYOU	Harlem Youth Opportunities Unlimited
HBC	Hatch–Billops Collection
HBCUs	Historical Black Colleges and Universities
HCTC	Harlem Children's Theatre Company
HET	Harlem Experimental Theatre
ICCC	Inner City Cultural Center
KRIGWA	Crisis Guild of Writers and Actors
LORT	League of Resident Theatres
MTV	Music Television
NAACP	National Association for the Advancement of Colored People
NADSA	National Association of Dramatics and Speech Arts
NAG	Negro Actors Guild
NBAF	National Black Arts Festival
NBPC	National Black Political Convention
NBT	National Black Theatre
NBTC	National Black Touring Circuit
NBTF	National Black Theatre Festival
NCBRC	North Carolina Black Repertory Company
NCCC	Network of Cultural Centers of Color
NEA	National Endowment for the Arts
NEC	Negro Ensemble Company
NEH	National Endowment for the Humanities
NFT	New Federal Theatre
NIDA	Negro Intercollegiate Dramatic Association
NLT	New Lafayette Theatre
NNT	New Negro Theatre
NPC	Negro Playwrights Company
NRC	Negro Repertory Company
NTCP	Non-Traditional Casting Project
NVA	National Vaudeville Artists
NYSF	New York Shakespeare Festival
PAH	Postmodern Afro-American Homosexuals
PASLA	Performing Arts Society of Los Angeles
PEN	International Association of Poets, Playwrights, Editors, Essayists, and Novelists
PMA	Producing Managers Association

RACCA	Richard Allen Center for Culture and Art
RAM	Revolutionary African Movement
RPC	Repertory Playhouse Company
SADSA	Southern Association of Dramatic and Speech Arts
SCLC	Southern Christian Leadership Conference
SNCC	Student Nonviolent Coordinating Committee
SSCPA	South Side Community Performing Arts
TOBA	Theatre Owners' Booking Association
TTW	Trinidad Theatre Workshop
UBW	Urban Bush Women
UNIA	Universal Negro Improvement Association
USAA	United Scenic Artists Association
USO	United Service Organization
UVI	University of the Virgin Islands
UWI	University of the West Indies
WCF	Working Capital Fund
WCT	Wild Crazy Things
WPA	Works Progress Administration
YMCA	Young Men's Christian Association
YMHA	Young Men's Hebrew Association

Introduction

Errol G. Hill

In the march of human history few topics have generated as much controversy as "race." Now, at the dawn of the third millennium AD, all such disputes can be put to rest, scientists having conclusively established that human beings are biologically the same under the skin. "We all evolved in the last hundred thousand years from the same small number of tribes that migrated out of Africa and colonized the world," said research scientist J. Craig Venter; adding, "race is a social concept, not a scientific one."[1] Socially then, or perhaps "culturally" would be more appropriate, differences do exist among the descendants of those earliest African migrants, doubtless caused by changing environments and the many ways – physical, mental, emotional and, yes, spiritual – that humans strove to survive through control of those harsh environments. That regardless of outward appearance we are all part of the same family has been acknowledged and proclaimed by saints and savants from time immemorial. Hence a history of the African American theatre is a human story worthy of study and review by all peoples in view of the unique conditions in which that theatre was created and sustained.

By "unique conditions" we refer to the slave trade that brought to America millions of black Africans who remain the only minority group forcibly transported to the United States and enslaved. Yet, in spite of and through this experience, African Americans over time have created and maintained a theatre of their own. Accordingly, it is fitting to provide a brief sketch in this introduction of the background to the trade in African people to the New World, in order to place in perspective some of the issues that confronted (and consumed) Blacks, free and enslaved, as they began a new life in America.

It started well before Christopher Columbus. Throughout recorded history mass movements of people from one region or country to another have resulted from catastrophes, natural or man-made, including war. Nothing, however, has equaled in scale, longevity, and horror what has been called "the rape of Africa" that followed Europe's first contact with the Americas. For a period of well over three hundred years, from the early sixteenth to the mid-nineteenth century, black Africans were seized, bound, shipped across the Atlantic Ocean and sold to labor in the territories of the New World. Their numbers defy logic: 12 to 15 million Blacks were reliably estimated to have survived the horror. How many did not remains debatable.[2] That African chiefs were complicit in the capture and sale of their fellowmen (whether felons, prisoners of war, or tribal enemies) compounds the guilt but does not mitigate the tragedy. At the start of the twenty-first century the long-term effects of that forced migration continue to haunt the most powerful and prosperous nation the world has known.

Slavery has been a common human phenomenon for countless years, but not until the modern era was it limited to people of any particular racial group. Ancient slavery often resulted from warfare and was governed by the rules of war and carried no ignominy; hence the Greek philosopher Plato could suggest that every man had slaves among his ancestors. To Christian Europe, the rise of Islam added a new dimension to the institution of slavery by making religious persuasion a central issue. Members of the two faiths saw each other as infidels who deserved to be enslaved. "The same rationale served both groups when economic interests and improved technology focused world attention on Africa."[3]

As early as the 1420s Prince Henry of Portugal (who was later given the honorific title "the Navigator") had heard stories of Africa's wealth and ordered his captains to explore the Guinea coast. By 1444, having made contact with settlements of Moors, the Portuguese captured some 235 men, women and children; others perished or were killed. The captives were promptly baptized and enslaved. In less than a decade Portugal was importing a thousand baptized Africans a year to serve on the docks, in the fields, and in the homes. Since there was at the time no marked color line, "the two races mingled freely, resulting eventually in Negroid physical characteristics in the Portuguese nation."[4] The racial situation would change drastically after Europe "discovered" the existence of a new world and extended its assault upon Africa to the native peoples of the Americas.

Enter Columbus: "From the moment he signed the articles of agreement with the Catholic Kings," wrote Germán Arciniegas, "he promised them gold. He was obsessed by the idea... And so in the account of his first ten days in the islands the word *gold* appears twenty-one times."[5] That was not all. Arciniegas, who apparently had access to the relevant documents of the period, explained that when the people of the New World gazed at the beard of Columbus and believed he was Heaven-sent, the explorer thought of ways "in which this may be turned to advantage to enslave them. Even before he took ship, Columbus was thinking of gold and slaves... He was the forerunner of the gold-hunters."[6]

Black Christian converts from Portugal and Spain joined the early explorers of the New World. Pedro Alonso Niño, pilot of one of Columbus' ships (possibly the *Niña*) was allegedly of African descent. Other Blacks, whether servants or slaves, were assigned various duties whose proper execution was essential for the safety of all. In this way life aboard ship tended to circumscribe recognition of status and favor effective working relationships. The Negro Estevan, a scout for the explorer Narváez, was in 1527 the first foreigner to penetrate what is now Arizona and New Mexico. Much later, as the Jesuits led French parties into Canada, one of the many Blacks among them, Jean Baptiste Point du Sable by name, would become the founder of Chicago.

Portuguese mariners who held a virtual monopoly over the *asiento*,[7] an authority ultimately sanctioned by the Papacy, were among the first in the post-Columbian era to carry Blacks out of Africa to the New World. By 1500 Portugal had laid claim to Brazil, established in 1532 a permanent settlement in São Paulo, and repulsed all attempts by other adventurers to invade its sphere of influence. Portuguese traders imported Africans to work in the cane-fields as slaves, an institution that would endure in Brazil for some 350 years until it was totally abolished in 1888. That black slavery under Portuguese settlers may have been more tolerant than elsewhere in the Americas is witnessed in the founding by 1630 of the black republic of Palmares in northeastern Brazil. It exists today as a town 60 miles south of Recife.

Other maritime nations of Europe soon carved out their own colonies. Spain, an early contender in the search for rumored gold, established overseas settlements around the western arc of the Caribbean Sea in regions known today as Florida, Mexico, and Central America, and extended its reach to Colombia and Venezuela in northern South America. The island of Cuba and part of Hispaniola were also appropriated by Spain. The seafaring nations of Holland and Denmark joined the colonial rampage by sending raiding parties to Africa and by setting up outposts in coastal areas such as Surinam (also called Dutch Guiana) and the smaller Antillean islands. England and France also joined the pillage, transferring their historic rivalry in Europe across the Atlantic to North America and the Caribbean.[8]

In discussing the European exploration of the Americas, one ought not to leave the impression by one's silence that the new lands were devoid of people or inhabited by bands of savages. The opposite is true. From the fourth century AD until the European invasion began in the late fifteenth and early sixteenth centuries, several highly developed and structured civilizations existed in parts of today's Mexico, in Central America and in northwestern South America. Their people were known as the Maya, the Toltec, the Aztec, and the Inca; the latter two empires received the brunt of contact with European explorers and adventurers. In addition there were in North and South America and throughout the Caribbean islands distinct ethnic groups in the lowlands and river valleys who lived by farming, fishing, hunting, and gathering, each regional group possessing its own beliefs, its unique arts, crafts, and ways of being.

"Spain," wrote the Jamaican scholar Sylvia Wynter, "sent two kinds of conquistadors to the New World: the conquistadors of the flesh; and those of the spirit. Those who came to conquer with the gun, and those who came to conquer with the Cross of Christ." Ms. Wynter concluded dolefully that while both types of conquerors bolstered and supported each other, "the time would come when the Cross would take it for granted that it would survive in the gun's shadow."[9] And so in the early sixteenth century the Aztecs under Emperor Montezuma II (ruled 1502–20) were utterly destroyed by Hernando Cortés, leader of the invading Spanish armies. While professing friendship Cortés used treachery, broken promises, and stirred up revolt among subject peoples to undermine the authority of the emperor and his military general. The Aztec treasury, much of it exacted in a fraudulent deal that contained a promise to spare the emperor's life, was stolen and the sovereign executed. That the treasury was lost at sea on the voyage back to Spain is an irrelevant footnote.[10]

The actions of Cortés were closely mirrored by Francisco Pizarro, another Spanish general who learned of fabled wealth at the Inca's capital of Cuzco, located in the mountains of modern Peru. With the approval of the Spanish king who had decorated him and made him governor of a Central American province not yet colonized, Pizarro in 1531 traveled with his three brothers back to Panama, his ship resupplied with soldiers and arms for the journey to Cuzco. Learning that the sovereign Inca, Atahualpa, was then at Cajamarca, Pizarro sought and gained an audience with him at the great square in the city, having first deployed armed soldiers nearby but out of sight. The emperor eventually arrived with a retinue of several thousand men, apparently unarmed or with no arms to match those of the Spaniards.

At the first opportunity and without provocation,[11] Pizarro summoned his troops, who seized the emperor and slaughtered the surprised Incas. Imprisoned in a cell, Atahualpa agreed to fill it with gold in exchange for his life. This he did but was then falsely accused of plotting to overthrow the Spaniards and was strangled to death. The centuries' old Inca empire and its satellites were no more.

This epic tale, brilliantly dramatized as *The Royal Hunt of the Sun* by British playwright Peter Shaffer, showed on Broadway in the 1965/66 season. It was, in its author's view, "a kind of total theatre, involving not only words but rites, mimes, masks, and magics." Shaffer conceded that the villains of the play were "the neurotic allegiances of Europe, the Churches and flags, the armies and parties," but he hesitated to name a hero unless it was by a curious paradox Pizarro himself who "recovers joy by finding real grief." The play was staged at Dartmouth College in 1969, with black students as the Incas and white students the Spaniards, and proved a memorable event for the newly appointed faculty director.[12]

As European nations began to establish colonies throughout the circum-Caribbean basin, the native Amerindian peoples were displaced.[13] They faced two dangers: the superior firepower of the invading armies and strange diseases brought by the foreigners, which could also be fatal. These pre-Columbian indigenes called by different and often overlapping names – the Ciboney, Lucayo, Taino, Arawak, and Carib[14] – originally inhabited lowland forests and grasslands adjacent to the Amazon and Orinoco rivers in northeastern South America. In the distant past these "Amerindians," as they came to be called, traveled up through the Caribbean islands in rudimentary canoes and piraguas, pushing ever farther northward. At the time of their first contact with the European settlers, the Tainos or island Arawaks, a gentle agrarian people, occupied most of the Greater Antilles, while the warlike Caribs[15] were largely based in and around the Windward Islands of St. Vincent and Dominica.

Meanwhile the Spanish, in their insatiable lust for gold, had forced the indigenes to work in the minefields of Hispaniola, where an early colony had been established. In 1502 Bartolomé de Las Casas of Seville arrived in Hispaniola to join his merchant father, who, having sailed with Columbus on his second voyage, had brought back an Indian slave to be his son's personal attendant. Eight years later Bartolomé became a Roman Catholic priest in the Dominican order, but he continued to support the enslavement of American Indians as necessary to provide a steady labor force until he experienced a conversion in 1514 and realized that the enforced work system

Figure 1. Errol G. Hill's Dartmouth College production of *Royal Hunt of the Sun* by Peter Shaffer, 1969

was "unjust and tyrannical."[16] In his assumed new role as "protector of the Indians," Las Casas appealed to Rome against their harsh treatment by the Spaniards and suggested, in the course of his plea, that it would be better to replace the Indians with hardy African slaves. What till that time had been a steady trickle of Africans to the Americas would soon become a flood tide.[17]

What the victims endured in their forced transfer from Africa to the Americas, especially during the Middle Passage, should be neither forgotten nor cheapened.[18] Captured Africans – men, women, sturdy youths – were chained together and trekked over long distances to holding pens that might be open-air stockades or damp dungeons in seaside forts owned by Europeans, or might be kept on floating "barracoons" (abandoned hulks of vessels), all to await the arrival of the slave ship. These ships would ply up and down the west coast of Africa picking up their cargo of Blacks at different points along the coast until the vessels were full to capacity.

The second leg of the journey was the dread "Middle Passage" aboard ship. Africans were shackled together and, except for limited periods of exercise on deck, were kept below in confined areas with women on the upper and men on the lower levels. Stacked like sardines,[19] their diet unaccustomed, their conditions unsanitary, on a crossing that often took several weeks, black captives were prone to disease including dysentery. The death rate on seventeenth-century ships soared to 24 percent.[20] The third and final stage of the journey began after the surviving Blacks arrived in the Americas. Washed, fed, put on sale and branded, they traveled to the estates of their new owners, where they were housed in slave cabins or huts. They were now the property of the master who purchased them, their future dependent on his every whim and that of his family, his overseer, and his slave driver.

The American poet and playwright LeRoi Jones (aka Amiri Baraka) attempted to dramatize the Passage in his short play *Slaveship* (1969), staged at the Academy of Music in Brooklyn's Chelsea Theatre Center, under the direction of Gilbert Moses on a set designed by Eugene Lee. Characters listed were Old Tom (slave), New Tom (preacher), Captain, Sailor, Plantation Owner (eternal oppressor), Dancers, Musicians, Children, Voices and Bodies in the ship.[21] Since captive Africans spoke little or no English, the action was mostly choreographed (by Oliver Jones) to sounds of creaking timbers, rattling chains, and occasional voices uttering a few words in Yoruba, calling on deities – Shango, Ogun, Obatala, the Orishas – for deliverance. Voices hummed and groaned in anguish. Children wailed; a disembodied white voice reported nonchalantly that a slave woman had killed her child and strangled herself with her chains. Similar voices talked sneeringly of "black savages," avidly of "riches"; indistinguishable dark skins muttered "white beasts" and "devils." Using a director's prerogative, Gilbert Moses introduced atmospheric background music by jazz saxophonist Archie Shepp; distant drums beat in the mind. For sensitive members of the audience, the experience must have been devastating.

From the slave merchant's perspective, his "Triangular Trade" paralleled the three stages of the African's journey into slavery. The ship left its home port in Europe, Britain, or North America stocked with guns, ammunition and chains used in the capture of Africans as well as with rum, cloth, pans, beads, and other baubles that could be bartered for them. At the second stage the ship would pick up its human cargo and sail to the Americas. Finally, having delivered its cargo, the sanitized vessel would load up with staple produce from the plantation: coffee, tobacco, rice, molasses, rum, or cotton and return to its home port, where the produce would be marketed and the cycle would start again.

The essential difference between slavery in former times and as it latterly developed in the Americas was the concept that the individual person was a piece of property to be bought and sold at will, broken or repaired, without recourse to law or higher authority. Naming the new captives "slaves" before they left Africa promptly changed their status from human to nonhuman; as "black slaves" they unwittingly conferred the stigma of inferiority to free Blacks on the basis of skin color. Thus in 1753, at the height of the slave trade, the Scottish philosopher and historian David Hume, in supreme ignorance of or callous disregard for the great African civilizations of Ghana, Mali, and Songhay, as well as traditional African arts and letters, could write: "There never was a civilized nation of any other complexion than white nor even any individual eminent in action or speculation. No ingenious manufactures amongst them, no arts, no sciences."[22] More than one hundred years later a similar sentiment would be expressed in America some months following the defeat of southern confederate states that sought to withdraw from the Union over the issue of slavery. Writing in the Richmond (Virginia) *Whig* newspaper on 15 November 1865, the correspondent declared: "That the negro is or can be made equal to the white man, the world will never be convinced... The negro's happiness and safety are best promoted by... conformity to his manifest destiny and that is social and political inferiority to whites."[23] It would be comforting to report, as the nation enters the twenty-first century, that such benighted sentiments have long been

Figure 2. Amiri Baraka, author of *The Slaveship*

banished from public discourse in America. Sadly this is not the case. Extremist hate groups or individuals, often protected by law or by a lack of law enforcement, still spread their venom, leading at times, as recent history has demonstrated, to acts of extreme cruelty against black Americans. Only then can the perpetrators be prosecuted and brought to justice; by which time the victims are already maimed or dead.

I

Slavery and conquest: background to black theatre

Errol G. Hill

The ghost ship known as *The Flying Dutchman* is an obverse metaphor for the horror of black slavery. We need only change the spectral vessel to a Dutch man-of-war; the venue from the Cape of Good Hope to Jamestown, Virginia; the date from eternity to the year 1619; and for the criminal white captain doomed to sail perpetually without ever reaching port we have a cargo of innocent starving Africans whose only crime was to be born black. The true story of that arrival may never be fully known, but a few essential details will suffice:

> The English ship *Treasurer* left Virginia to acquire provisions for the colony. It "came into contact" with a Dutch man-of-war and the two ships then "happened upon" a Spanish frigate with a cargo of African slaves. Crews from the *Treasurer* and man-of-war relieved the frigate of its human cargo but were separated and delayed by bad weather. Many slaves died from starvation. When the Dutch man-of-war arrived at Jamestown only twenty survived of the one hundred slaves taken aboard. The *Treasurer* landed one person, a woman her captors called Angela.[1]

Since slavery was not yet legalized in Virginia, the twenty and odd victims were more likely to have been employed as indentured servants than as lifetime slaves. So too many Whites, facing deportation from their home country for debt or for some infringement of the law, would contract themselves to work in the colonies for a period of years, after which they would be free to pursue their lives as they wished. In the 1650s, for instance, several free Blacks in Virginia were granted acres of land for farming and development on the basis of having imported indentured workers from abroad.[2] Despite these signs of progress, laws were enacted to recognize the institution of slavery and increasingly to put restrictions on the liberty of Blacks, slave and free. The net result was a series of slave revolts accompanied by the loss of life and the hanging of those involved in the plots.[3]

When the English colonists in America felt the yoke of an imperious home government and began to voice their dissatisfaction, King George III instructed colonial lawmakers in 1770 to pass no laws that obstructed the importation of slaves to America. Thomas Jefferson, assigned by Congress to draft the document proclaiming the colonists' independence from Britain, was quick to add this indictment to a score of charges against the king:

> He has waged a cruel war against human nature itself, violating its most sacred rights of life and liberty in the persons of a distant people who never offended him, captivating and carrying them into slavery in another hemisphere or to incur miserable death in their transportation thither... Determined to keep open a market where Men should be bought and sold, he has prostituted his negative for suppressing every legislative attempt to prohibit or restrain this execrable commerce.[4]

Delegates to the Continental Congress from South Carolina and Georgia stoutly resisted the inclusion of this clause and threatened to secede from Congress if it were retained. Moreover, Jefferson sensed that "our northern brethren" were also concerned about the censure because, while they held comparatively few slaves themselves, they owned many of the vessels that carried the trade. In the interests of unanimity the offending charge was removed from the Declaration of Independence and a compromise clause inserted that trading in slaves should not be prohibited by Congress before the year 1808.

In fact, antislavery sentiment ran high among some separatist leaders. Tom Paine thought it was hypocritical to fight for freedom from Britain while continuing to hold slaves. John Adams refused to own slaves but admitted that free labor cost him thousands of dollars. Patrick Henry allowed that it was inconvenient to live without slaves, but said he could not and would not justify slavery. Although favoring the Declaration, Jefferson owned slaves and believed Blacks were inferior to Whites in mind and in body. He expressed regret that their difference in color and perhaps of faculty were powerful obstacles to their emancipation.[5]

Two-and-a-quarter centuries passed when white descendants of Jefferson, knowing of the rumored affair between their admired progenitor and the slave woman, Sally Hemings, became aware that genetic proof of issue from the relationship had taken place. The group, named the Monticello Association after Jefferson's plantation home in Virginia, invited their presumed black cousins to attend the eighty-sixth annual reunion at "Monticello." Thirty-five members of the Hemings' line showed up. As reported in the *New York Times*, evidence from the tests revealed that Jefferson probably fathered one of Hemings' three sons. On the other hand, offspring of the other two sons had placed emphasis on oral histories passed down by their families. At a heated business meeting the association voted to postpone a decision for a year, allowing more substantial evidence to be assembled. A year later, however, there was still no agreement, except for the suggestion to name a street Hemings Way in recognition of Sally Hemings.[6] The theatre's treatment of this peccadillo by one of the nation's "founding fathers" preceded the events described above. On 16 January 1999 the musical *Sally and Tom* opened for a six-week run at the Castillo Theatre off off-Broadway. With book and lyrics by Fred Newman and music that "sometimes soars with lyrical beauty" by Annie Roboff, the role of Jefferson was taken by Lee Lofton while Andrea Lockett played Sally.[7]

War with Britain proved inevitable. Skirmishes had already begun by 1770 when Crispus Attucks, an African American, became the first patriot to be killed in what is called the Boston Massacre. Fearing a general clamor for full emancipation if Blacks were permitted to participate, General George Washington issued an order prohibiting the recruitment of Negroes or vagabonds into the American forces. However, when the British promised to free all slaves of rebellious colonists and an estimated sixty-five thousand bondsmen from the southern colonies moved to their side, Washington rescinded his order and allowed the enlistment of free Blacks, many of whom had already been involved in battles. Then, as the course of war brought reverses to the patriots, black slaves were enlisted in the army and navy, except those from South Carolina and Georgia, whose governments were adamant against the recruitment of slaves.

Eventually, in 1781 the British forces under Lord Cornwallis were defeated at Yorktown, Virginia, by the Americans with the support of French troops. The British evacuated their positions, withdrawing from ports in Savannah, Charleston, and New York. Blacks leaving with them numbered around twenty thousand, of whom portions were landed on the British Caribbean islands of Jamaica, the Bahamas, and St. Lucia. As part of the general exodus, many slaves who had joined the British forces crossed into Canada. From this group a contingent of almost twelve hundred left Halifax in fifteen ships on 15 January 1792 to settle in Sierra Leone, West Africa. The dispersal of black freemen and slaves to and from the Caribbean and beyond underscores the need for a wider view of black performance beyond the territorial United States, in order to produce an accurate history of African American theatre.

In England, meanwhile, the antislavery movement was gaining ground. In 1772 the Lord Chief Justice ruled that a slave became free the moment he set foot on English soil, a decision that enabled several prominent runaways to find safe refuge from bounty hunters in America in the coming century. English abolitionists launched a two-pronged attack on slavery. They aimed first to stop the trade in slaves by alerting the public to the heavy loss of life sustained by English sailors on a single voyage across the Atlantic. They then planned to attack the institution of slavery itself.[8] However, it was not until a new government was installed under the antislavery liberal George Fox that Parliament abolished slave trading as from 1 May 1807 and stipulated that no slave could land in a British-governed country after 1 March 1808.

In America the successful end to the revolutionary war bolstered sentiment among the northern states for an end to the trade in slaves. Several of these states had been principally engaged in the carrying trade with seaports in Newport and Bristol (in Rhode Island), Boston and New York being major departure points for slaving vessels, along with Charleston in the south. Following Vermont's 1777 example, northern states began the process of abolishing slavery, either outright or gradually in stages. When Congress finally acted in 1807 to ban the slave trade, it was a weak law that prohibited "the importation of slaves into the United States or territories thereof" after 1 January 1808. The law did not prohibit the sale of slaves between states, nor was it enforced through patrol boats ready to challenge ships suspected of carrying contraband cargo.

For the slaves themselves the lesson taught by the revolutionary war was salutary. Freedom was worth fighting for, whatever the cost. They had joined both sides in the conflict and regardless of the outcome thousands of bondsmen had gained their liberty; there was virtue in struggle. Two events of the 1790s profoundly reinforced the determination to end their bondage. First, the Canadian government passed laws prohibiting the importation or sale of slaves and declared that every child born of a slave mother would be free at the age of 25. By 1800 slavery was a dying institution in Canada, a neighboring country that had become both a beacon and a haven for runaway slaves mostly from southern plantations. Then in 1791 the Haitian revolution broke out, two short years after France itself (of which Haiti was a thriving colony) had suffered a similar convulsion. Black slaves threw off their shackles, set fire to plantations, organized their attacks, and under desperately fearless leaders repulsed attempts by the French, the Spanish, and even the British imperial forces to reenslave them. On 1 January 1804 Haiti became an independent black republic.[9]

The new mood among slaves is reflected in a study entitled *Runaway Slaves: Rebels on the Plantation* by John Hope Franklin and Loren Schweninger. From many instances of collective resistance cited in their study I offer the following examples. The expressed concern of Governor Pinckey of South Carolina to the legislature of "armed fugitive slaves... carrying on guerilla warfare." In Virginia and the Carolinas runaways hid in woods and swamps during the day and emerged at night to commit "various depredations on farms and plantations." After the acquisition of Florida from Spain "great numbers of Negroes availing themselves of existing disorder" ran away and took refuge among the Indians while some escaped to Cuba. Georgia braced for an attack by hostile Creek Indians who "were collecting all the force they can among themselves and from the negroes." Major General Irwin wrote to the Alabama governor of his fears that "large bodies of them [Negroes]... have had uninterrupted intercourse with the Indians... and may have matured some plan of cooperation." When a farmer in North Carolina from whom runaways were stealing organized a hunt for their capture, the runaways responded defiantly by taking seventy-five of his hogs and warning him "if he would not hunt for them again – they would not kill any more of his hogs – but if he did, they should kill him."[10]

The prospect of a final end to the African slave trade spurred a frantic drive to capture and ship from African ports as many Blacks as possible before the prohibition date of 1808. Urgency was partly due to the invention of Eli Whitney's cotton gin, which enabled picked cotton to be cleaned fifty times faster than by hand, thus increasing its profitability. In the Southland the demand for slaves to prepare virgin territory to plant, tend, and harvest the growing cotton was insistent. In addition, opening new farmland in the south and west following the 1803 Louisiana Purchase heightened the need for a substantial infusion of slave labor. The supply was met partly by increased domestic trade with states such as Virginia, where an oversupply of Blacks resulted from a fecundity among the slave population.[11] And although Britain sought to enforce the abolition of slave trading by having its frigates patrol the sea-lanes from West Africa, the bulk of that trade had simply moved from western to eastern Africa, with ports in Madagascar, Mogadishu, Mozambique, and Zanzibar being well positioned to replace the slaveholding pens that dotted the Guinea coast. That there was no shortage of black slave labor to meet the demand is reflected in the census figures. From 1800 to 1810 the slave population in America rose in round figures to more than 1,191,000, representing an increase of 33.3 percent over the previous census count.

Despite the ban on foreign slave importation, measures legal and illegal were employed by southern states to acquire the additional able-bodied bondsmen needed for the flourishing cotton industry. At the same time, and with the instance of Haiti's revolution providing a much-feared reminder,[12] the treatment of slaves became more repressive: teaching them to read and write was forbidden; bounty hunters were hired to track down runaways and bring them back; the South was rife with rumors of slave conspiracies, mutinies, revolts, and rebellions.[13] When leaders were caught, either through betrayal, lack of vigilance, or poor planning, they were hanged: Gabriel Prosser (1800), Denmark Vesey (1822), Nat Turner (1831), John Brown (1859). Joseph Cinque and his fellow mutineers on the *Amistad* (1839) were freed eventually and returned to Africa;[14] those on the *Creole* (1841), led by the slave Madison Washington, seized control of the ship with the loss of only one sailor and compelled the crew to sail to Nassau in the Bahamas, where the mutineers were protected by British law.

In the struggle for liberty leaders, who face tremendous odds, are apt to become heroes regardless of the outcome. Thus in the 1920s when African American playwrights began to write serious dramas for performance in black schools and colleges and turned to history, they found sustenance in the determination of racial ancestors to be free whatever the cost. An important pioneer in the effort to dramatize history was Professor Randolph Edmonds, who published three collections of his plays, among which were two short dramas on Denmark Vesey and Nat Turner. Professor Edmonds' work will be discussed more fully in chapter 8.

The white abolitionist John Brown was a visionary. Believing he was "destined to be the deliverer of slaves, the same as Moses had delivered the children of Israel," Brown moved to Kansas, where he fought a single-family battle against proslavery forces determined to introduce slaves in the newly settled territory. Following this encounter, John Brown made plans for a broader assault on slaveholders in the South and sought to enlist the support of 42-year-old Frederick Douglass, a prominent black leader and former slave runaway. Brown decided to attack the federal arsenal at Harper's Ferry, Virginia, and seize arms for a protracted war against all those who held slaves. But Douglass demurred, considering the plan too dangerous and impractical. Brown, however, would not be swayed and at the head of eighteen men, including five free Blacks, his two sons Oliver and Owen, and eleven other Whites he marched on the arsenal and into history.[15]

Of the events in this tragic story, dramatist William B. Branch in his three-act play *In Splendid Error* (1954) focused on the meeting between Brown and Douglass, which the author placed at Douglass' home in Rochester, New York, that served as a way station on the Underground Railroad to Canada. At first Douglass seemed partial to the idea of a guerrilla war against the plantation owners, who, Brown argued, would be forced to rid themselves of slaves if keeping them proved more costly than setting them free. But when Brown outlined his plan to seize the federal arsenal for weapons, Douglass protested that such action would be tantamount to treason against the United States government and would likely lose all sympathy for the rebels and for the slaves themselves. John Brown refused to wait. With his band of supporters he marched on Harper's Ferry, was captured, charged, found guilty, and hanged along with his followers.

In the final scene Douglass, having received mementos from John Brown's widow, questions whether he was right to withhold support, for "there are times when the soul's need to unite with men in splendid error tangles agonizingly with cold wisdom and judgment." Of the play's relevance one hundred years after John Brown's rebellion took place, playwright Branch has stated:

> in Douglass' dilemma I saw uncanny parallels between the pre-Civil War racial-political struggles of the 1850s and the post-World War racial-political climate of the 1950s. Thus in subsequent drafts, the play became more and more of a personal statement as to the differing roles people could play in a revolutionary movement.[16]

The play was first produced at the Greenwich Mews theatre off Broadway in October 1954. Reviews were mixed; critics were pleased with the acting of Alfred Sanders as John Brown and William Marshall as an eloquent Douglass; however the writing was considered prolix and at times ponderous.

Probably the most heroic of all nineteenth-century runaway slaves was Harriet Tubman. Having escaped from bondage in Maryland, she repeatedly went back to the Southland to lead more than three hundred slaves to freedom. No less than three playwrights, all female, have written of this indomitable woman. The first was May Miller, who, in the one-act play *Harriet Tubman* (published 1935),[17] has her heroine narrowly avoid being caught on one of her raids by taking a boat at flood tide instead of traveling overland with her runaways. The well-respected dramatist Alice Childress also wrote of Tubman in a children's play entitled *When the Rattlesnake Sounds* (1975). The third drama, *Harriet's Return* (1998), a moving portrait in two acts – "Slavery" and "Freedom" – was first developed by actress and playwright Karen Jones Meadows as a one-woman show. It was later enlarged with the addition of four bodied characters that represented "Harriet's Voices." They humanized the title character by presenting the various options and challenges she must face, all involving considerable risk. Staged at the Geffen Playhouse in Los Angeles, the production, with the multitalented Debbie Allen as Harriet, was an exalting experience for those fortunate enough to view it.[18]

Apart from runaways who lived in northern slave-free states or who linked up with native American clans in southern regions,[19] there existed a legitimate free black population in the United States. The first census of 1790 gave the number representing the "free colored population" as 59,557. This count may well be suspect; an authoritative estimate for the year 1750 put the number of African Americans at 220,000.[20] Many Blacks would be reluctant to identify themselves for fear of being captured by bounty hunters who were known to seize free Blacks and on flimsy evidence accuse them of being runaways. There were in fact Blacks born of free parents; others by extraordinary industry and thrift earned enough money either to purchase their freedom outright or to pay off their master in installments over a period of years. Others could be bought by a sympathetic humanitarian and then set free. Slave masters would often free their children born to enslaved mothers, and sometimes free the mothers as well. Also, slaves might be liberated when they were too old to work, or, occasionally, for faithful service over many years. Legally, any child born of a free mother, even if fathered by a slave, was declared to be free.[21] By the time of the next census, in 1800, free Blacks amounted to 108,435, a substantial increase of just over 82 percent on the previous tabulation.

There was another category of Blacks in addition to those who were indentured, enslaved, or free (whether by purchase, escape, or emancipation). These were the so-called "free-slaves," a phenomenon that numbered

> many thousands, living in nearly every region of the South (though especially in urban centers) and attaining a remarkable degree of upward mobility within the caste system, they came and went as they pleased, earned their own living, hired out and ran their own businesses, and lived outside the purview, and sometimes the control, of their master.[22]

In order to explain how this group of bonds men and women have in the past received scant attention, author Schweninger traced the career of one such free-slave named James P. Thomas through slave letters, notes, and autobiographical reminiscences. A summary of his findings is not without

interest, exemplifying as it does the bizarre nature of what has been eu-
phemistically called "the peculiar institution."

Born in 1827, James was a mulatto, the son of a well-known Tennessee
judge, John Catron, and a resourceful slave woman called Sally. As property,
they were inherited by a young man in Virginia, who promptly put them
up for sale with the result that they eventually were returned to Nashville to
the house where James was born. When at age 8 James was again advertised
to be sold, his mother acted quickly. She had already averted the sale of her
two older sons by hiring one to a Mississippi barge captain and helping the
other escape to New York, and now she appealed to a prominent lawyer,
Colonel Foster, for assistance. She had saved up money by hiring herself out
as a cleaning woman in her free time and wished to know how much her
son's master would take for him. Being $50 short of the required amount,
she pleaded with the colonel to make up the balance and to hold James (as
collateral) until she was able to repay him. Foster agreed and Sally received
a bill of sale, although her son James was legally not free.

James performed a variety of chores for his slave mother but he was able
to attend school – without paper, pencils, books, or proper clothing – where
he was taught surreptitiously by free black instructors who risked their lives
to teach their young racial brothers.[23] At the age of 14 James was hired out
as an apprentice barber to another free-slave, Frank Parrish, earning about
$12 a month. He also began violin lessons with a local musician. At age 19 he
opened his own barbershop in the same house where his mother operated
her cleaning business. His reputation spread and he received an offer from
plantation owner Andrew Jackson Polk to serve as his barber on a trip to New
York. Reluctant to leave his new business he politely demurred, but speedily
changed his mind when Polk retorted: "Don't tell me about your business;
I'll buy it and shut it up." The trip by stage coach, river-packet, canal barge,
railroad, and steamboat was 1,100 miles, and an enormous challenge. James
was constantly questioned by strangers and slave traders, urged to leave his
master, greeted by jeers and hoots, denied accommodation on buses, asked
to leave museums, and refused admission to the theatre. He was stunned
at the hypocrisy of northerners, who were supposed to be the black man's
friend. On his return to Nashville, James Thomas built up a flourishing
business and in 1853 when the city's first business directory was published, it
carried an advertisement in boldface print for "Jas. Thomas, Barber Shop,
10 Deaderick Street."

Despite legal barriers to Blacks in bondage owning personal property,
earning money, or managing a business, and the requirement that freed

Blacks must immediately leave the state, James, with the help of influential friends, was able to expand his business, purchase real estate, and gain his freedom and residency. In time he moved to St. Louis, bought a number of barbershops, got married, and at the height of his business career in 1882 was reported to control an estate valued at $400,000. Schweninger admits that James Thomas was exceedingly fortunate. He had a permissive master, lived in an urban environment (as did fewer than 10 percent of southern Blacks), and grew up with a determined and loving mother. Yet he was not singular:

> In every region of the South slaves hired their own time, chose their own employers, made their own housing arrangements, and lived as *de facto* free blacks. The constant demand for laborers (both skilled and unskilled) allowed bondsmen to profitably peddle their skills...In some instances, they lived completely outside the regulation of the master...city officials [in Mobile, New Orleans, St. Louis, and Baltimore] constantly complained about "virtually free negroes" and masterless slaves moving about the streets seemingly oblivious to any law or regulation.[24]

In a collection of critical essays published under the title *The Theatre of Black Americans*,[25] several writers contributed to the first section labeled "Roots and Rituals: The Search for Identity." They wrestled with the question of origins, of defining the essential quality and purpose of black performance as expressed in word, song, music, mime, and dance. How that culture may have been transformed with the passage of time and tragic circumstance will remain debatable. The contributions of five of the writers should be noted in summary form as evidence of a beginning in a performance culture that has matured into what is rightly called African American theatre.

In his "Notes on Ritual in the New Black Theatre" Shelby Steele affirmed: "art must be functional; it must serve an end beyond itself. Functional art becomes a means to an end rather than an end in itself." As applied to theatre, Professor Steele explained that unlike black American music such as the blues, spirituals, and jazz, which were wholly created out of African American culture, black drama has had to "take the dramatic form and reshape it to meet the particular needs of the black community." He acknowledged that ritual may seem inimical to the requirements of dramatic suspense and thematic variety, but he believed that ritual could be achieved "through the repetition of patterns, symbols, and values from drama to drama rather than the traditional religious method of repeating a single ceremony until it becomes ritual... The message is the same but the form through which it is communicated varies from play to play."[26]

Eleanor Traylor's essay "Two Afro-American Contributions to Dramatic Form" contended that "the *source* of all that can be called representative American theatre is [to use James Weldon Johnson's term] Aframerican." Citing a passage from Henry Louis Gates on the mask as the most compelling African artifact, Professor Traylor maintained that "when the lore, songs, dance, and masking rituals of African slaves made their entrance on the stage, a native American dramatic form was born." The authentic minstrel show (rather than the caricature created by white comedians) was a masking-miming ritual "born out of plantation playtimes around the Negro cabins." The second contribution to dramatic form, in Professor Traylor's view, were the oral accounts of runaway slaves that "by 1845 had become a powerful literary mode no better practiced than by Frederick Douglass" and by 1858 a distinctive literary device first employed by William Wells Brown in his play *Escape; or, A Leap for Freedom.*[27]

Eileen Southern has written extensively on the music of black Americans. In her article entitled "An Origin for the Negro Spiritual" Professor Southern defined the spiritual as "the religious musical expression of black folk in the United States" and reminded readers that in the eighteenth century

> black folk sang songs in their native African languages and danced to the accompaniment of home-made instruments... In the northern colonies, the celebration of Pinkster holidays (the week following Pentecost Sunday) was turned over almost entirely to the Blacks, slave and free, who revived African festivals as they had performed them in the countries of West Africa, the ancestral lands of most black Americans. In New England, Blacks sang and danced in the African manner during their so-called 'Lection Day festivities.

In discussing the culture of black slaves in America we are reminded that among the demands made of African captives who survived the harrowing Middle Passage was the adoption of a new and strange language. New arrivals needed to communicate not only with white masters but also with other slaves whose native African tongue may have been different from their own. When in the early nineteenth century southern slaveholders, fearing rebellion if slaves were able to consult together, disallowed the teaching of English, it stiffened the newcomers' resistance, making them even more desperate to be free. Professor Southern explained that up to the last decades of the eighteenth century Blacks worshipped in churches (in segregated pews), where their fondness for singing psalms and hymns was noted with approval until they created a distinctive repertory of religious folk music. This development so shocked a Methodist cleric of Philadelphia that in 1819 he wrote disparagingly of it in words that might provide "a clue to the time and place of the origin of the Negro spiritual": "We have too, a growing evil, in the practice of singing in our places of public and society worship, *merry* airs, adapted from old songs, to hymns of our composing . . . and most frequently composed and first sung by the illiterate *blacks* of the society." In a further comment, Southern debunked the myth that spirituals were invented by slaves as they labored in the cottonfields; instead, she affirmed, the evidence suggested that "the song type originated in the black churches of the North where black congregations, freed from the supervision of white clergymen, could conduct their religious services as they wished."[28]

Robert Farris Thompson in "An Aesthetic of the Cool: West African Dance" analyzed the drumming and dance of West African peoples whose culture he designated as "percussive," since in his view that quality dominated their concept of performance. The dancer in West Africa, he argued, would be expected to respond kinetically to every rhythmic subtlety of the master drummer, rising on his toes as the level of pitch rose or becoming explosive in gesture in accord with drumming that signified the presence of the hot-tempered Yoruba, God of Iron. A second trait of West African music was multiple meter when several time signatures were performed simultaneously, while the dancer chose one or more rhythms to be danced by different parts of the body. A third trait was identified as "apart playing and dancing," during which West African musicians danced to their own music, each drummer being intent on his contribution to a polymetric whole. Similarly, apart dancing, a recognized choreographic custom of West Africa, is a noteworthy phenomenon in modern dance-halls.

Two other features of West African music and dance were noted by Professor Thompson. First, the call-and-response format by soloist and chorus found a similar pattern in dance, where two single individuals or groups move alternately. Though antiphonal singing is fairly widespread, Thompson found the African variety unusual in its consistent use of overlapping phrases by leader and respondents, as if each were seeking to outdo the other. The final trait – more moral than musical – comprised satiric song and its parallel in derisive dance; one dependent on sharpened wit and the other on pungent mime.[29]

I close discussion of this topic by referencing the essay "Some African Influences on the Afro-American Theatre" by James Hatch. Working down from recognized black plays and musicals of an earlier time to then contemporary plays of the 1960s and 1970s, Professor Hatch urged us to read between the lines and discover hidden meanings that lay below the surface comedy. As an example I borrow the verse he quoted that came originally from the early twentieth-century songwriters Bob Cole and Rosamond Johnson:

> Dere ain't no use in try'n to rise up in de social scale,
> 'Les you kin trace yo' name back to de flood.
> You got to have ancestral halls an' den you mu'nt fail
> To prove dere's indigo mixed in you blood.
> I done found out dat I come down from ole chief Bungaboo,
> My great gran'daddy was his great gran'chile,
> An' so I'm going to sail away across de waters blue
> To occupy my castle on de Nile.

As sung by the superb sad comedian Bert Williams in the musical comedy *The Sons of Ham* (1900–02), beneath the comic pose of social climbing lay a deep if muffled cry for a legitimate homeland for black people. Hatch's final comment is salutary: "For the last 150 years Afro-American theatre has been drawing energies from both sides of the hyphen, sometimes consciously, sometimes intuitively. As acquaintance with things African grows, as the essential and difficult work of tracing Africanisms in American culture continues, we will come to know how really vast and invisible the African influence on all American theatre has been."[30]

2

The African Theatre *to* Uncle Tom's Cabin

Errol G. Hill

At the beginning of the nineteenth century African Americans in New York City numbered around six thousand, half of whom were slaves. By 1820 the slave population had dropped to some five hundred while free Blacks in the city increased to more than ten thousand. This demographic shift reflected awareness that, as voted by the Legislature, slavery would be abolished throughout the state no later than 4 July 1827. For the city, abolition would hardly be noticed since slaves were dwindling in number, were not germane to the economy, and most had acquired skills that gave them a sense of selfhood. Besides, New York had become the most important port on the country's eastern seaboard. It was, and would continue to be, the major entry point for immigrants from Europe and the Caribbean.

Among the latter group were black seamen who had learned seafaring skills and sought work in the relatively free and equitable environment aboard ship. From captain to cook, each sailor had his appointed task, the proper performance of which was essential to the well-being of the entire crew and the passengers. These merchant vessels plied from New York to Liverpool, then to western Europe and back across the Atlantic to the Caribbean, completing the round trip by sailing north to New York. From the ranks of this intrepid group of seamen in the port city came the founder of the first known black theatre company in North America. His name was William Alexander Brown.[1]

During the hot summer months, it was customary in the city to open pleasure gardens (known also as "tea gardens") where residents could spend their leisure time out-of-doors and be entertained by musicians, dancers, gymnasts, magicians, and various other performers, while refreshing their appetites with beer, mead, ice cream, cake, tea, and other delicacies. Although there were several of these venues, such as Vauxhall, Chatham, and Castle Gardens, black folk were denied admission to them. To redress this inequity and provide similar entertainment for Blacks, William Brown created a facility that he called the African Grove. It was situated at the back of his dwelling-house at 38 Thomas Street, west of Broadway, and it opened for three or four summers prior to 1821.[2] The Grove had promenades for patrons to walk about, separate stalls furnished with tables and chairs where guests could recline for refreshment, a bar or service area, and possibly an al fresco platform for performers. Originally the Grove might have opened only on weekends, and Sunday patrons would dress nattily for the occasion. The novelty of having their own pleasure garden would have attracted an eager clientele from the city's black community.

The African Grove did not last long. Situated in a housing area where neighborhood residents would have to contend with noisy crowds on a regular basis, the Grove prompted complaints to the police and by the summer of 1821 Brown was required to close down his garden entertainments. The resourceful manager was not, however, discouraged. It seems as if he had been planning all along to start a dramatic company and was using performances at the Grove as a subtle form of audition for possible recruits to the stage. Conscious of the need to retain his patrons for a year-round operation, Brown promptly converted rooms upstairs of his Thomas Street dwelling into a small theatre, picked a play, recruited a cast, and posted bills announcing an opening performance on Monday, 17 September 1821. He called the enterprise "The African Theatre" and chose for its inaugural production Shakespeare's *Richard III*.[3]

William Brown apparently came from the West Indies. He had been a steward on a merchant vessel registered in Liverpool and on retirement set up shop in New York, where he worked as a tailor. By his own account he had had first-hand experience of the 1795–97 war between the British and the Black Caribs on the Caribbean island of St. Vincent. The Black Caribs were so named to distinguish them from yellow Caribs, one of the waves of aboriginal Indian peoples from South America who had migrated north to the Caribbean. The origin of the Black Caribs will be discussed presently. Brown would later write and produce a play about the Carib war for his theatre. Judging by the tenacity with which he pursued his brief tenure as African Theatre manager, as well as by the subject matter of the plays he produced, it is safe to say that Brown was truly "a race man," one who stood firmly and fearlessly for the rights of people of African descent.

The leading establishment playhouse in New York City at this time was the Park Theatre. Located on Park Row, it was owned and managed by the lawyer Stephen Price, an Anglophile who had acquired a reputation for hard dealing and who was referred to in a respected biography of a nineteenth-century actor as "avaricious, boastful and unpopular."[4] The Park had been destroyed by fire in 1820 and the restored playhouse was slated to reopen on 1 September 1821, just over two weeks before the African Theatre made its bow to the public. Price belonged to a well-known New York family and was a formidable antagonist accustomed to having his way. He is credited with introducing the star system to American theatre, by luring to his playhouse prominent English actors such as George Frederick Cooke and Edmund Kean. He was destined to play a fateful role in the fortunes of the African Theatre.

In attempting to summarize the activities of this theatre, it must be acknowledged that the known record remains incomplete. Manager Brown did not usually advertise performances in the New York newspapers, which may have been too costly for his budget and probably also because the papers were seldom read by the black community. Instead, Brown posted playbills around town and distributed handouts. Being more ephemeral than press notices, these flyers were less likely to be preserved for future generations. Moreover, at first African Theatre productions were not taken seriously by journalists and critics of the principal newspapers, with the result that its productions were largely ignored by the press. Hence, editor Mordecai Noah of the *National Advocate* found it necessary to advise readers that his criticism of the African Theatre's staging of *Richard III* was not a satiric fable, but that the production actually took place. Clearly, his subscribers could not believe that Blacks were capable of staging a play by Shakespeare and assumed his critique was written in jest.[5] Finally, following its first performance on Thomas Street, the African Theatre changed its location several times, often under duress. Company members and Brown himself were harassed by police, physically assaulted by white roughnecks during performance, and victimized without compensatory redress in the law courts. With such caveats in mind, I now proceed to assess the work of this historic theatre troupe.

The African Theatre survived for only three seasons, from its inception in September 1821 to its demise by the summer of 1824, although its name continued to be associated, beyond its closure, with mostly one-man performances given by its leading actor, James Hewlett. From the known record, during its existence the African Theatre mounted at least ten major productions, most of them receiving several performances either on the first run or in later revivals. Among the ten, Shakespeare accounted for two majors, namely, *Richard III* and *Othello*. Additionally, there were two productions that included scenes from these plays, as well as from *Macbeth*, *Julius Caesar*, and possibly *Romeo and Juliet*. Other dramas included such plays as John Home's *Douglas* and Richard Sheridan's *Pizarro*. A more complete staging of *Pizarro* was apparently directed by Mr. Brown in the city of Albany in December 1823.

Brown also produced in New York two dramas entitled *The Fortress of Sorrento* and *She Would Be a Soldier*, both written by editor Mordecai Noah, who served as a sheriff of the city. A Tamany Hall democrat, Noah was vehemently opposed to extending voting rights to Blacks, who generally favored the opposition Republicans.[6] Although Noah's reviews were often condescending, mention of the African Theatre in his paper probably had the unintended effect of attracting Whites to the shows; thus manager Brown thought it prudent to indulge Noah with a production. For summertime fare the African Theatre offered the pantomime *Don Juan* twice, coupling it in one instance with the comic opera *The Poor Soldier*, by John O'Keeffe, and another time with John Fawcett's melodrama *Obi; or, Three-Finger'd Jack*. The two remaining major productions were William Moncrieff's operatic extravaganza *Tom and Jerry; or, Life in London* and Mr. Brown's own historical play, *The Drama of King Shotaway*.

The emphasis on Shakespeare in the foregoing list of productions reflects the popularity of his plays in America, especially as they were performed by celebrated English actors who toured the United States playing in New York and other theatre towns. Indeed, stagestruck youths and adults from the city's black community would frequent the segregated upper gallery of the Park Theatre to keenly observe the manner in which these admired English stage veterans presented Shakespeare's heroes. Black patrons who applied for and received appointments as dressers to the star actors were deemed most fortunate. When, therefore, the African Theatre decided to begin its first season with *Richard III*, it was not only choosing a play of known appeal but, ludicrous as it may seem, it was inviting comparison with performances at the Park.[7]

Brown began his theatre by offering the well-known plays of Shakespeare but he quickly moved beyond such fare. It seems the crafty manager, who directed many if not all of the African Theatre productions, had a special agenda in view. Most of the plays had an element of revolt about them, or at least a capacity for struggle with the underdog triumphant, often at the cost of his life. And so midway through his first season Brown presented his own play about the Black Carib war in St. Vincent against both English and French settlers backed by their home governments. Then in his adaptation of the musical extravaganza *Tom and Jerry*, he inserted an entirely new scene depicting a slave market in the city of Charleston, South Carolina. The wanton sale of enslaved human beings that often separated children from parents, wives from husbands, and one sibling from another is one of the searing memories from the slave experience. Finally, with *Obi; or, Three-Finger'd Jack*, Brown staged a play set in Jamaica about a runaway slave who chose to live in the mountains rather than submit to the cruel indignities of chattel slavery.

Admittedly, Brown's nascent company did not have the resources to present full-scale productions of these plays. Texts were heavily cut, improvisation accepted, yet these performers took their work seriously. At least some perceptive spectators, allowing for the newness of the event, the lack of formal training or apprenticeship, and the minimal theatrical furnishings surrounding the performance, were willing to give the company credit for trying. And if the main dramatic production was truncated to fit the company's limited resources in personnel and material, the evening's offering would compensate for any shortcoming in the main fare by filling out the program with a variety of lighter items that might include song recitals, a hornpipe dance or ballet, a fencing match, or a light comedy or farce requiring a small cast.

At the start of his theatre and in keeping with the clientele he attracted, manager Brown addressed his playbills primarily "to the Ladies and Gentlemen of Color." By his second production, however, the shows were exciting such interest among white playgoers that Brown had to erect a partition at the back of the theatre to accommodate them. Still later, as the white audience grew in number, Brown found it necessary to reserve a portion of the house near the stage for his loyal black patrons. The enthusiasm evinced at the production of *Richard III* encouraged Brown to offer the play on three successive Mondays, but the excited crowd in attendance on opening night and leaving the theatre late that evening were more disturbing to neighbors than the African Grove patrons had been. As a result, Brown had no option but to move his theatre, after its first performance, to another location where the noise factor was less troublesome. He found an empty building in an undeveloped area at the corner of Mercer and Bleecker Streets, over a mile away from his previous quarters. He rented the building, moved in with his family, fitted up the necessary stage appurtenances, and was ready to continue performing the following week.

The theatre's new location was less than ideal. Isolated, in a district devoid of other buildings, with unpaved streets and no street lighting, it was inconvenient for playgoers to get there and unsafe for them to return home at night after a performance. Brown's second production, presumably *Othello*, and his third, *She Would Be a Soldier*, must have taken place at Mercer Street, but for his next offering he devised an audacious plan. He decided to move the location of his theatre once again, from its current inauspicious setting to a more favorable spot. He rented a hall in the Hampton Hotel that stood in the business district opposite City Hall. The site was accessible to the public and already frequented by playgoers since the hotel was next door to the rebuilt Park Theatre. Here Brown opened the African Theatre's fourth known production, a medley of acting scenes from Sheridan's *Pizarro* and from Shakespeare, interspersed with songs by James Hewlett, his leading actor. By January 1822 the company had increased its playing time to three performances a week. The entrance fee remained at 50 cents but as an added attraction, "a grand historic painting" was exhibited at the end of each performance for an additional fee of a shilling.[8] To ensure strong support from fellow Blacks, the performance was advertised as a benefit for James Hewlett, the principal actor of the African Theatre, a sailor and professional tailor (as was Brown himself), and a prominent member of the city's black community.

William Brown had reckoned without the forceful opposition of Stephen Price, the Park Theatre's irascible manager, who promptly acted to get rid of what he felt was an unacceptable intrusion on his turf by a mischievous interloper. Price would recall that Brown had opened his theatre with *Richard III* just two weeks after the Park had staged the same play with its English star. Now Brown had brought his black company next door to the Park in a program of scenes from Shakespeare, prior to the rumored appearance of Edmund Kean, the most celebrated if controversial English actor of the age. In fact, the African Theatre's playbill had announced a scene from *Richard III* that James Hewlett would perform "in imitation of Mr. Kean."[9] Such insolence was not to be tolerated. Price promptly hired a group of white hecklers to disrupt performances at the African Theatre and when the troupe persisted in playing, Price arranged for the night watch to crash the theatre during a performance and arrest the actors. They were taken to the watch-house, warned to cease playing Shakespeare, and released at a late hour.

The press report of this incident gave added publicity to the African Theatre, but it was not in the interests of the Hampton Hotel, where the performance was held, to allow the production to continue. Thus, for the third time in its first season Brown's theatre was forced to move. Brown took his company back to the former inhospitable Mercer Street building, which, he promised playgoers, would now be provided with an exterior lantern to guide them on their journey from Broadway. But Brown did not submit to Price's rebuke in silence. He posted a bill, respectfully informing the public that his "theatrical establishment" (at the Hampton Hotel) had been broken-up "through the influence of his brother managers of the Park Theatre."

Quite possibly, Brown may have suspended the activities of the company for a short spell in order to focus his attention on constructing a new theatre facility. Despite continued difficulty in finding a permanent home for his theatre, the enterprise seemed to be potentially lucrative, as it attracted a wider and more diverse audience than had at first been expected. If he was to be confined to the Mercer Street area, Brown wished to provide the best affordable facilities. He leased a plot of land at 103 Mercer Street, "to the rear of one-mile stone" on Broadway, a block south of his present location, and began to build a permanent small theatre. An eyewitness who had watched the building under construction and who attended an early performance in the new house on Friday, 9 August 1822 described some of the theatre's features.

It was built of wood and its auditorium consisted of a pit below stage level, tiered house seating not partitioned into boxes so as to enhance the flow of air, and a gallery whose ceiling was too low to permit hats and bonnets to be worn by spectators. Separate entrances led to each of the seating areas. A four-piece music band was in attendance and a front curtain rose "one end at a time" to reveal a woodland scene at the back, while the sides of the stage showed cottages, alehouses, gothic windows and ruins – a composite setting. In advertising his new playhouse, manager Brown called it the "American Theatre,"[10] although the troupe was still referred to as the "African Company." To open his second season that summer Brown chose light popular fare: the pantomime of *Don Juan* followed by a comic opera in two acts entitled *The Poor Soldier*. Between the pantomime and the afterpiece, a hornpipe was danced with vigor by a young lady.[11]

Apparently, the fracas initiated by hecklers at the Hampton Hotel prior to the African Theatre's closing had left old sores. The youth Ira Aldridge, then approaching his fifteenth birthday and already a theatre buff, may have been involved in the incident. Court records show that on 19 July 1822, a few days before Brown's new theatre opened, Aldridge was assaulted on the street and severely beaten by James Bellmont, a circus performer. This attack was a mere prelude to the riot, instigated by a band of white hoodlums on

10 August at the Saturday evening's performance of the African company in their newly built theatre. Leading the rioters was George Bellmont, brother of James. According to a newspaper report by an outraged observer, a gang of fifteen or twenty ruffians, including some riders from the circus in town, entered the theatre with regular tickets, extinguished the lights, and proceeded "to demolish and destroy everything in the shape of furniture, scenery, &c. &c. it contained." Actors and actresses were stripped, their apparel torn to pieces, and manager Brown was soundly beaten. The report spoke of the persecutions, including "virtual exclusion from our theatres," that were meted out to members of "that wretched race." Yet when they devised their own amusements "they have been hunted with a malice as mean as it seems to be unmitigable, in every attempt they have made to form a permanent establishment."[12]

As perpetrators of the riot, eleven men were arrested and brought before the special justices. Ringleader George Bellmont was particularly vicious in his attack on manager Brown, who swore out a warrant against him. In September Bellmont pleaded "not guilty" to assault and battery charges. Although he was never so identified, the villain behind this wanton and malevolent act could well have been Stephen Price, the Park Theatre's manager, whom author George Thompson with commendable restraint called "an unprincipled, grasping man," one who "was certainly not above such a piece of villainy."[13] Price was known to be merciless in stifling any challenge to his monopoly of the New York stage, a position he achieved by employing devious means to destroy all rivals or nullify their effectiveness. He controlled the importation of English star actors; he bought out and closed down a theatre that had given him competition; he had recently used an elephant from the circus on the stage of the Park and was negotiating to purchase the circus itself, since its program had begun to include specialty acts that had become popular with the public.

Though Price was never formally charged with having instigated the riot, at the very least he bore responsibility for creating the conditions, through his harassment of the African Theatre, where ignorant white thugs could feel justified in attacking and destroying a black-run enterprise and injuring its employees. In view of the relative influence with the law of the opposing parties, it is not surprising that the case lay dormant for over seven months and no evidence exists that the perpetrators were ever punished. For all its misfortune, the riot afforded one advantage to the researcher; it provided the only known contemporary reference that indirectly linked Ira Aldridge with the African Theatre, of which he was destined to become its most famous alumnus.

In October 1822 Brown reportedly took a group of his actors to Albany, New York.[14] Escaping from the city after the harrowing experiences of the past year must have come as a welcome respite. Moreover, with the city suffering a yellow fever epidemic from August to October, company members would be eager to join the tour. And if they were previously compensated marginally in New York, where they could also hold daytime jobs, they would now have to be paid as professionals in order to cover room, board, and other expenses on tour. Regrettably, there is no further information about this visit: the length of their stay in Albany, what plays were staged from their repertoire, or the kind of public response they received. It is significant, however, that for the next five months the only performance at the African Theatre in New York was a one-man "At Home" show by James Hewlett on 24 March 1823. Hewlett obviously did not travel to Albany with the company and may have resumed touring on his own to present solo performances of songs, character sketches, and imitations of well-known actors in their favorite roles.

The African Company returned to Brown's restored theatre on Mercer Street on Saturday, 7 June 1823, in the musical extravaganza *Tom and Jerry; or, Life in London.* Written by William Moncrieff and based on a serial novel by Pierce Egan, this musical play had swept London a year earlier with productions at no less than six theatres simultaneously.[15] In New York, the Park Theatre first staged the musical in March 1823. Once again the African Theatre was showing its mettle by emulating the Park, except that their production, directed by Brown and with new scenery, included the previously noted slave auction scene in Charleston. The afterpiece was even more pertinent. For his concluding item Brown chose to present *Obi; or, Three-Finger'd Jack,* a dramatization by John Fawcett of the true story of a runaway slave on the island of Jamaica in the years 1780–81. Using the rumored magical powers of his "Obi" or talisman, Jack terrorized the island colony for two years from his mountain hideout with a price of £200 on his head. Eventually he was hunted down, captured and slain by three Blacks, who claimed the ransom money. That is factual; but when the play was premiered at London's Haymarket Theatre in 1800 the production, despite its serious theme, was treated as a "pantomimical drama," with the first-act finale taking the form of a grand Jonkanoo (masquerade) ball.

Brown's next New York production was a reprise of his own play, *The Drama of King Shotaway,* on 20 and 21 June 1823. It was first announced for January 1822 but lacked performance data, which are available for its revival. Quite possibly, Brown was inspired to write his version of the Black Carib war after seeing a production of *The Carib Chief*, a revenge tragedy in five acts by Horace Twiss, which was performed at the New York Theatre in November 1819.[16] Since Brown's drama has not been found, an outline of the play that most likely influenced him to write his own is not without interest. Twiss' play is fictional and set on the island of Dominica, still the Caribbean home of the fast-disappearing aboriginal Caribs. However, Twiss placed the dramatic action back in the sixteenth century at the start of Queen Elizabeth's reign when, according to the author, both English and French soldiers were vying for control of the island.

Briefly, the plot involves two Carib princes, Maloch and Omreah, who rule the northern and southern parts of the country respectively. To preserve his territory Maloch sent sixty slaves as a gift to France; Omreah, however, resisted the Europeans, was overthrown and sold into bondage. Now he is back, vowing to avenge the death of his family and to reclaim both his people and appropriated Carib lands. Also seeking to regain control of the island are English forces led by General Trefusis, who is opposed by Montalbert, the French garrison commander. As the conflict begins, the French advance guard are taken prisoner but Omreah refuses to collaborate with the victorious English. Still defiant, he tells Maloch, the dissembling chief:

> I will not do it.
> You, if you will, may wear a double face,
> For you've so long been leagued with these deceivers,
> Taking their stamp, speech, customs, arts and seemings,
> (As might indeed behove their subject king).
> But I, whose only converse with their tribe
> Has been disgrace and torture ...
> I will not palter with my honest hate
> By stooping, even in show, to treat with bandits.

After many twists and turns in the plot, Omreah's army is ascendant but the Carib priest has been killed. Omreah insists that Montalbert must die with his bride, Claudina, as a sacrifice for the dead priest:

> I have pronounced it
> We are the masters now; and, when we've clear'd
> These white pests from our land, and made it sure
> With our own forts, and all those arts of war
> The experience of your murderous tribe has taught us,
> We'll keep our native isle, or losing, die for 't.

But in an unexpected discovery, just as Claudina has been mortally cut for the sacrifice she is identified as Omreah's own child, who had been saved from slaughter. Desolate, Omreah attempts to stab Montalbert, and failing, he turns the weapon on himself. The English general has the last word: after the funerals, the English will leave the island "to its own heirs, the children of the soil." This fictional promise was never fully realized. Dominica remained a British colony for some two hundred years until 1978, when it gained self-government, by which time the Caribs were marginal forest dwellers.

Returning to *King Shotaway*, it is understandable why Brown would wish to present a more correct version of the Black Carib struggle for survival and why, in advertising the play, he would claim that it was historically authentic. In fact, several crucial features make this drama an appropriate choice to close out Brown's career as manager and artistic director of New York's African Theatre. First, the script stands alone at the threshold of plays written by black Americans. Second, the playbill, addressed to "the Gentlemen and Ladies of this city," on whom the African Theatre would depend for future support, suggests that Brown now considered the potential audience for such plays to come from both the colored and Caucasian publics. Third, as with the first announcement of this drama eighteen months earlier, its revival was billed as a benefit performance by the African Theatre company for their manager, Mr. Brown. Fourth, and most important, the play is said to be "founded on facts taken from the Insurrection of the Caravs [Caribs] in the Island of St. Vincent, Written from experience by Mr. Brown."[17] With this statement Brown attests to the historical veracity of the drama he is about to stage by asserting that he was present as the events unfolded.

We can but speculate on the nature of Brown's "experience" and the extent of his involvement in a conflict that arose when English and French colonists decided to expand their settlements into Black Carib communities and the Caribs resolved to repulse them. A century earlier St. Vincent, which was considered to be "the center of the Carib Republic," also contained a great number of Blacks.[18] They were either runaway slaves from nearby Barbados, slaves rescued from wrecked ships, or slaves stolen by the Caribs on their frequent raids to neighboring islands. Over time, cohabitation between Blacks and Caribs had produced a new strain known as Black Caribs. Noted for their courage and independence, they had formed communities under local chiefs, all bearing allegiance to their paramount chief, Chatoyer (King Shotaway in Brown's drama.) The conflict, known as the Second Carib

War, began in March 1795 and ended in the fall of 1796 with the defeat of the Black Caribs and their banishment to small islands off the coast of Honduras.[19]

It is unlikely that Brown was a Black Carib.[20] The Garifuna, as they are known in Honduras, spoke their own language and were more allied to the French colonists than to the English. Even if he spoke English, it was unlikely that a Black Carib would be employed on a Liverpool vessel so soon after the war. Brown could have been a free Black serving with the English forces at sea. In casting the play, Brown had his star actor, James Hewlett, in the title role; Bates took the part of Shotaway's brother, Prince Duvalls, while Misses Hicks and Lavatt were Shotaway's wives, Queen Margaretta and Queen Caroline. The full evening's program included a group of songs by several soloists, appropriate speeches about war and the passions, a hornpipe danced by Bates, a grand combat between Shotaway and the prince, and an Indian war dance.

On Friday, 8 August 1823 the African Theatre presented two summer stand-bys, the *Don Juan* pantomime and a revived *Obi; or, Three-Finger'd Jack.* Sandwiched between them was William Barnes' one-act burlesque tragic opera in rhymed couplets, *Bombastes Furioso.* Filling out the summer's evening program were the usual songs by individual company members, hornpipe dances by Miss Shaw, and a *pas de deux* by Misses Hicks and Lavatt. The printed bill credits the African Company with this performance and promises a new production of *The Forty Thieves* on the following Monday, but in a singular omission the bill fails to name the company's manager, thus presaging the end of Brown's tenure. Having built his playhouse and watched it destroyed, having taken his troupe to Albany while the building and properties were being restored, Mr. Brown must have faced a serious depletion of his savings. He may well have been the William Brown whose petition for bankruptcy was finalized in July 1823, precluding his continuance as owner-manager of a theatre in the city.[21]

Brown's departure effectively marks the end of the African Theatre's existence in New York. However, the resolute manager very probably took a nucleus of his company and moved to another town, as witnessed by the following extract from a record of the Albany stage for the year 1823: "A house opposite the Columbian Hotel was also fitted up by a Mr. Brown, for an African theatrical company which opened on December 19 with *Pizarro*."[22] The record makes no further reference to this company, but Albany Directories list a William Brown in residence at "rear 42 State Street" in the years 1823 to 1825 but not for 1822 or 1826.[23] Albany at this time had approximately fifteen thousand inhabitants and two other theatres in operation beside Brown's.

James Hewlett

Back in New York, the Mercer Street Theatre did not immediately close its doors. On Monday, 19 January 1824 Hewlett gave a one-man performance, listing himself on the playbill as "Manager of the Theatre" with Mr. Benedict as his assistant. Offered as a benefit for the Greek people to support their independence war against Turkey, the show imitated the English comedian Charles Mathews, who mimicked various character types in his humorous "At Home" performances. On a trip to America in 1822–23 Mathews had visited the African Theatre and was shown around by Hewlett. But when he returned to England, Mathews parodied the black company as incompetent would-be Shakespearians, a caricature galling to the sensitive Hewlett, who, copying Edmund Kean, saw himself as "Shakespeare's proud representative." Hewlett addressed a public letter to Mathews denouncing his actions, then traveled to England in the fall of 1824 to challenge Mathews, but the two never met. Hewlett came home bitterly disappointed.

In 1824 one more performance took place at the African Theatre on Mercer Street before the playhouse was finally closed and the property sold. Called "Hewlett at Home," it was largely a solo performance with the actor singing, dancing, and reciting scenes from Shakespeare, assisted by Bates in items such as the sword fight. A consummate entertainer, Hewlett dazzled spectators with magic tricks and to round out the evening, "the audience and Hewlett had a right good jig together [and] we all started away in high spirits."[24] With the theatre for Blacks gone, Hewlett spent most of the next year, 1825, as a ship's steward, traveling to the Caribbean and the Mediterranean. However, on his return to New York he again began to present one-man shows, performing in a variety of public halls and in neighboring towns and cities, such as Albany, Baltimore, Boston, Brooklyn, Philadelphia, Saratoga, and York (PN). He sang, danced, and gave imitations of established British actors and of the new American star, Edwin Forrest. In all, he imitated some thirty actors and singers, male and female. His acting repertoire totaled over forty roles, including twelve from Shakespeare, and his song list numbered close to forty.

From a traveler's report, it seems that a black theatre group existed in New York during the 1828/29 season, when *Julius Caesar* was one of the plays presented. Hewlett might well have taken a leading role with this company, but we cannot be certain as no further details are given in the report, nor is the troupe mentioned in available newspapers of the time.[25] Hewlett next appears in Virginia (town unknown), where his performance was advertised in a novel manner. He received passing mention among a catalogue of items called out by a street crier around midyear 1831. Ringing his handbell to attract attention, the crier offered for sale frying pans, gridirons, a book, oyster knives, and then added in his unschooled vernacular: "by 'tickler desire, Mr. Hewlett will gib imitations ober again."[26] Hewlett, a light-skinned mulatto, was born in Rockaway, Nassau County, New York, and was a permanent resident of the city. Judging from the long letter he wrote to Mathews about the latter's "At Home" caricature of African Theatre actors, Hewlett seemed fairly well educated, with a knowledge of Shakespeare's plays from which he would quote appropriate passages as occasion warranted.

Hewlett was also a familiar and respected figure in his community. Therefore, it is puzzling to understand his actions over the next few years that twice landed him in jail for stealing. Had he become impoverished and was too proud to seek assistance from friends, or had he sunk into a depression and was not in full control of his actions? Touring a one-person show while having to arrange for new venues and publicity, as Hewlett did for most of his appearances, can be wearying to the artist. At one of his performances at the New York Museum in July 1831, Hewlett was reduced to the hazardous novelty of inhaling ether on stage to heighten the effect of his actions. As a contemporary report explained: "This gas produces great exhilaration, an irresistible propensity to laughter, a rapid flow of vivid ideas, and an unusual fitness for muscular exertion... those that have inhaled it once generally wish to inhale it again."[27] Had Hewlett become addicted to this sort of experience?

In June 1834 Hewlett signed on as steward to a ship in port and allegedly stole a variety of articles such as tablecloths, copper sheets, a carpet, and bottles of wine before decamping. Brought before the magistrate, he did not flatly deny the accusation but instead asked the official if he could believe him guilty of such a crime. On receiving an affirmative reply, Hewlett resorted to play-acting: "Where's my dungeon; lead me to my straw... I have slept hard to do the state service." He was sentenced to six months in prison. Three years later, Hewlett was again charged with petty larceny for stealing a watch from a home where an inquest was in progress, to which he had invited himself. He accounted for having the watch in his pocket by asserting that it had been handed to him for safe keeping by an attendant and that he had no intention of stealing it. Once again, "Hewlett defended himself in mock heroic style to the great delight of the audience, but his eloquence was of no avail." He was sent to jail for two years "amid shouts of laughter and applause from the audience as well as the Court."[28] He had turned what should have been a solemn conviction of a twice apprehended thief into an occasion for theatrical farce.

On his release, Hewlett must have thought it advisable to go abroad for a spell. He is last heard of in Trinidad in the West Indies, in December 1839, through notices placed in that island's newspapers. Claiming to be from the Royal Coburg Theatre in London,[29] he announces that he will open the Royal Victoria Theatre on Cambridge Street, Port-of-Spain, on Saturday, 14 December, to present Imitations, Recitations, and Songs. For his second appearance, he offers selections from *Richard III*, *Pizarro*, the opera *Almavira*, Othello in song, and other items, with *Mazeppa* in preparation. While no review of any performance has been found in the available Trinidad newspapers, there was published a tongue-in-cheek bluster on Hewlett's playwriting ("he is great in all he undertakes") and acting ("positively superior to Kean"), followed by an illiterate letter supposedly signed by Hewlett, thanking the island's governor for purchasing tickets to one of his shows. The letter was so inept that it was reprinted as a gag in the prestigious *Sunday Times* of London under the caption "A New Tragic Actor."[30]

The letter, it turns out, was fraudulent, inserted by Trinidad newspaper compositors whom Hewlett had offended by suggesting they had importuned him for tickets to his performance. Hewlett was known for his mordant wit, which increasingly got him in trouble, particularly among strangers unfamiliar with his quirky brand of humor. The following tribute written in 1826 by "A Friend to Merit" may serve as a fitting closure to Hewlett's quixotic career. The anonymous writer described him as "a young man who, notwithstanding the thousand obstacles which the circumstance of complexion must have thrown in the way of improvement, has ... risen to successful competition with some of the first actors of the day. Those who have witnessed his imitations ... must have been convinced by the accuracy and tact of his performance, that they were listening to no common individual."[31]

Judging from the performers named in its playbills during its short existence, the African Theatre employed no less than thirty actors, equally split between adult male and female, and two male youths. Several of them had special skills as singers, hornpipe or ballet dancers, or as swordsmen. In addition, there was a group of three or four musicians, which at times was

HEWLETT, NEGRO ACTOR, AS RICHARD III

Figure 3. James Hewlett in costume as Richard III

racially mixed. Beside Hewlett, one other actor was convicted of stealing. This was Charles Taft, also known as Charles Beers, the first Richard III at the African Theatre but who was supplanted from the second performance when Hewlett became available. Taft had been a slave but was at the time unemployed. His former owner, named Hodgkinson, for whom he worked as a waiter at the City Hotel, had turned him out of doors for neglecting his duties (probably in order to attend rehearsals). After playing Richard for a single performance in a rather shabby costume stitched together from the discarded ballroom draperies of the hotel, Taft was cast as Othello in the theatre's second production. Needing desperately to repair his image as an actor of tragedy by wearing finer clothes on and off the stage, Taft stole money and clothing valued at $100. He was arrested and charged with grand larceny, found guilty, and sentenced to serve ten years in prison, a seemingly harsh sentence but one conditioned by the fact that Taft had recently been granted his freedom.[32]

Despite the shortness of his tenure with the African Company, William Brown's achievement was unique. He founded and managed for three seasons the first black theatre enterprise in the United States; he recruited a black professional company, adding white musicians when he needed them; he built and owned a black theatre facility; he inspired, wrote, and produced (or collaborated in writing) the earliest black play of record, although no text has apparently survived. As for his character, he was courageous, persistent yet flexible, and encouraged talent wherever it appeared. He employed an out of work ex-slave and gave him the role of Othello. To have pioneered as a black theatre artist in either writing, building, owning, recruiting, founding or managing, in the first quarter of the nineteenth century would suffice to make one memorable. To have done them all under the most trying circumstances requires that we humbly recognize William Alexander Brown as the true father of African American theatre.

Ira Aldridge

Of all the African Theatre players, one achieved international fame. This was Ira Aldridge (the youth beaten on the street by the circus rider), who had an amazing career as a professional actor in England and Europe for over forty years. Had Mr. Brown's African Theatre produced only Aldridge, its legacy would be secure. Ira Aldridge attended the African Free School in New York, where he won prizes for declamation and became attracted to the stage. He reputedly appeared as Rolla in the African Theatre's production of *Pizarro*, and may also have attempted Romeo, as reported later in an 1860 memoir by his schoolfellow, Dr. James McCune Smith.[33] Being close to Mr. Brown, Aldridge would have witnessed the difficulties encountered by the theatre manager. He would be aware that little opportunity existed at the time for a black performer to pursue a serious acting career in America. By then a committed and ambitious young player, his only hope of success would be to seek employment outside the United States. Thus in 1824 he left for England on the same ship as the English actor James Wallack, who would serve to introduce Aldridge to the English theatre scene.[34] However, when Wallack arrived in England and announced that Aldridge was his servant, a breach ensued in their relationship and the young actor at age 17 was left to fend for himself in a strange country.

Aldridge could not have reached Britain at a more propitious time. The industrial revolution had begun, bringing about radical economic change. An emergent middle class sought to establish its new-found influence while the working class, having organized the first trade unions in 1824, grew ever more vigilant. It was also a time when proslavery and antislavery lobbies in London were actively promoting their separate positions, Parliament, having already outlawed the slave trade, now being confronted with the prospect of abolishing slavery itself in the British colonies. These developments affected the theatre, where a new and vociferous audience with sympathies favoring the underdog had supplanted the old, staid aristocracy. In 1800 only ten theatres were open in London, but by mid-century that number had increased to twenty-two. All that remained sacrosanct was a residual pride in the two patent playhouses of Drury Lane and Covent Garden, which, through the Theatre Licensing Act of 1737, maintained a monopoly on the presentation of "legitimate drama." The prospect of a black actor suddenly entering the scene and attempting to perform the works of England's most revered dramatist, Shakespeare, was cause for no little consternation. His mere presence on the English stage was proof of the ability of Blacks to achieve parity with Whites in the performing arts, and by extension in all areas of endeavor, given the necessary education and training. This argument strongly repudiated that of the slave-mongers who remained adamant that Africans, whether enslaved or free, were by definition inferior to Whites.

Aldridge had prepared carefully for his introduction to the British public. Having limited onstage experience and lacking name recognition, he concocted a story of his African lineage, claiming to have descended from the Fulani princely line. Moreover, he cannily adopted the name of Keene, a homonym for the then popular British actor, Edmund Kean, to snare playgoers attracted by the familiar sounding name into reading his playbill. He was also known as the African Roscius, after the famous Roman actor of the first century BC. By 1831 Aldridge had taken the name F. W. Keene Aldridge and still later he would be called the African Roscius, Ira Aldridge. His first recorded London engagement occurred at the Coburg Theatre in October 1825, when he took the principal role in *The Revolt of Surinam; or, A Slave's Revenge*. This play, adapted from Thomas Southerne's popular drama *Oroonoko*, was based on Aphra Behn's novel about an African prince who has been kidnapped and brought as a slave to Surinam (formerly Dutch Guiana). Mrs. Behn had become acquainted with Oroonoko when she lived with her family in Surinam, where her father served as lieutenant-general. Because Southerne's drama was actually owned by the London patent theatres it could only be performed in a so-called minor theatre under another title and diluted by adding music, singing, and other "nonlegitimate" elements.

As one of the popular minor theatres, the Coburg extended Aldridge's engagement to seven weeks. He appeared in five plays, all concerned with the racial issue and the quest for freedom from slavery. Three were set in the Caribbean; in addition to *Oroonoko* there was "a new and beautiful melodrama founded on fact" entitled *Obi; or, Three-Fingered Jack* (1830) by new author J. Murray, and *The Death of Christophe, King of Haiti* by J. H. Amherst. Press reviews of Aldridge's performances were mixed and often contradictory. For the *London Times* he was "baker-kneed and narrow-chested," with lips so shaped that "it is utterly impossible for him to pronounce English"; the *Globe* found his conception of Oroonoko to be "very judicious" and his enunciation "distinct and sonorous"; and the *Drama* described him as "tall and tolerably well proportioned" with a weak voice that "gabbles apace."[35] None could deny, however, that theatre audiences at the Coburg gave Aldridge an enthusiastic and rousing reception.

At the end of the season Aldridge married an English lady nine years his senior, whom he had earlier met. He next appeared at a theatre in Brighton as Othello, which he alternated with Oroonoko. It was his first performance of Shakespeare in the bard's own country and, at age 18, he probably felt his inadequacy in a role that was certain to become a staple of his career. The next year found him quiescent. He may have traveled to Glasgow for further studies, but by September 1826 he was having difficulty securing an engagement in the English provinces, if we can trust the authenticity of a report copied from an Exeter newspaper and captioned "Keene in

Distress." It urged members of the profession to support a subscription that was proposed "to free him [i.e., "the celebrated American Roscius, Mr. Keene"] from immediate want, [and] supply him with funds wherewith to return to his native country with his wife who now shares her husband's wretchedness."[36]

However destitute Aldridge may or may not have been, his financial troubles were surely transitory for he never returned to America. Instead, by 1827 he began an extended period of touring throughout Britain and Ireland that lasted for twenty-seven years, followed by periodic visits to Europe, including Poland, Sweden, and Russia to the north and as far east as Constantinople in Turkey. All told he appeared in over forty-five different roles, seven of which were from Shakespeare, namely, Othello, Macbeth, King Lear, Hamlet, Richard III, Shylock, and Aaron the Moor. In addition to Shakespeare and a plethora of black roles like the previously mentioned Oroonoko, the Haitian King Christophe, and Fabian in *The Black Doctor* (1847), Aldridge, in search of new and suitable material, also appeared occasionally as white European characters, for which he would be appropriately made up with greasepaint and wig. Examples of these are Captain Hatteraick, a Dutch sea captain in the dramatization of Sir Walter Scott's novel *Guy Mannering* (1830), and the title role of a count turned pirate in the Reverend C. R. Maturin's *Bertram; or, The Castle of St. Aldobrand* (1831). Another innovation Aldridge introduced early in his career was a direct address to the audience on the closing night of his engagement at a given theatre. Especially in the years leading up to the emancipation of all slaves in the British colonies (effective 1 August 1834), he would speak of the injustice of slavery and the passionate desire for freedom of those held in bondage.

When Aldridge performed in a country where English was little known, he would speak in English while the rest of the cast spoke their native tongue, an arrangement that probably made special demands on his mimetic ability. He was equally adept in comedy as in tragedy, his favorite comedic roles being Mungo in Isaac Bickerstaffe's comic opera *The Padlock*, and Ginger Blue in *The Virginian Mummy*. In the words of a present-day scholar: "Indeed, his versatility was absolutely stunning."[37] The former play, often performed as an afterpiece to *Othello*, has the time-honored plot of an ageing husband-to-be, in this case a rich West Indian planter called Don Diego, who locks up his young intended spouse and leaves the key to her door with his house slave, the impertinent and mischievous Mungo, with strict instructions to allow no one to enter the house while he is away. As soon as his master leaves the house, Mungo helps himself to a bottle of liquor, sings antislavery songs, and admits the lady's lover to her room, where Don Diego finds them on his return.

When his tours of Europe commenced, Aldridge was already a seasoned actor, poised and self-confident. He had refined his performances, drawing on his observations and experiences as a black American, and his interpretations were often incisively original. From several eyewitness accounts it is clear that he was ahead of the usually acclaimed actors in portraying the tragic hero "speaking and walking like a common mortal, void of exaggeration either in posture [or] exclamation."[38] Not only was he honored with distinguished titles and medals from European heads of state in countries where he appeared, but often members of the public would wait on him after a performance to express their satisfaction and to thank him for representing the common folk so sensitively.

The question has been raised why Aldridge, despite his triumphs in provincial theatres and abroad, was seldom invited to appear at the major theatres of London, the theatrical capital of the English-speaking world. His exclusion persisted, it is argued, even after the 1843 repeal of the Licensing Act that had restricted productions of legitimate drama to the two royal theatres.[39] Aldridge actually appeared in approved West End dramatic theatres on three occasions. The first occurred at the Covent Garden Theatre in April 1833, as a result of a tragic circumstance. The famed Edmund Kean, playing Othello to the Iago of his son, Charles Kean, and with admired Ellen Tree as Desdemona, collapsed on stage on the opening night and died within weeks. Sixteen days later, Aldridge was invited to assume the role with the rest of the company intact, except for the grieving Charles Kean, who was replaced. When that announcement was made, some influential London critics expressed outrage and condemned the choice of Aldridge prior to his performance. The burden of their ire could be summed up in the *Athenaeum*'s remark that it was "monstrous" for an authentic Black to appear in an English national theatre.[40]

However, the reviews were not all unanimous. The evening *Globe* noted Aldridge's inadequacies yet with commendable impartiality concluded: "there are beauties throughout which more than compensate for these"; the *National Omnibus and General Advertiser* in a revealing statement wrote:

> This gentleman is, beyond all doubt, a good actor. In all the dialogue of the character he is unobjectionable; it is only in the high poetic parts that he disappoints ... he is equal to any on the stage ... there are characters

in which he would have given more satisfaction, and we were looking forward to his performance of some of them in the expectation of giving him our unqualified praise, when we heard that in consequence of the ill-natured critique of the drunken reporter of a daily Paper, the manager had put an end to the engagement.[41]

Due to the negative reviews the revival was allowed only two performances. The year 1833 was one of the most contentious between proslavery and anti-slavery forces in England. Parliament had determined to abolish slavery in all British colonies the following year and decisions on proper compensation for slave-owners, with a guarantee of adequate labor for their estates, were unresolved issues that excited passionate feelings.

Aldridge's other two West End appearances took place at the Lyceum Theatre in 1858 and at the Haymarket Theatre in 1865. By then he was a seasoned actor and played *Othello* on both occasions. Moreover, times had changed; the political climate was vastly different and it was no longer necessary for London critics to denigrate the black actor in order to justify slavery in the colonies. The *Athenaeum* that had once castigated him for daring to perform in a national theatre now produced a long, upbeat report declaring that he spoke not only "distinctly and correctly, but with elocutional emphasis and propriety ... his general action [being] marked with elegance and ease." The review commended "the sweetness and softness of his voice which ... is both pleasing and effective"; and it admitted that Aldridge had left a favorable impression of his talents, that he was an intelligent man who had studied his art earnestly and gained facility in its exercise.[42] Commenting on the performance at the Haymarket Theatre seven years later, the same paper exudes satisfaction. Aldridge played with feeling, intelligence, and finish; he was well received and his merits acknowledged by a numerous audience; yes, the Negro intellect is human and demands respect. The review concluded: "Altogether we have seldom witnessed a representation of this great tragedy which pleases us more."[43]

Aldridge finally began to plan for his return to America. While on tour in Europe he wrote from Paris authorizing theatrical agents in New York to arrange for his appearance "in such cities and towns which you think it will be prudent for me to visit."[44] A tentative date was set and Aldridge was expected to leave for New York on 16 August 1867. From France he went to Poland and eventually arrived in the city of Lodz, where he was scheduled to perform on 25 July. However, his opening was postponed due to illness, which proved to be fatal. On 7 August 1867 Ira Aldridge died of a

Figure 4. Ira Aldridge, lithograph, 1853

lung infection and was buried in a memorable and fitting ceremony at the Evangelical Cemetery in Lodz.

African Theatre productions and those emanating from the careers of its two alumni, Hewlett and Aldridge, were not the only theatre activities of black Americans at home and abroad in the decades leading up to the Civil War. From early in the nineteenth century Blacks, whether slave or free, had been admitted to special sections of playhouses in both the North and the South.[45] Indeed, in 1833 lessees of the Washington Theatre in the district of Columbia appealed to the city fathers for relief from the law authorizing constables to arrest colored people found on the street without a pass after nine o'clock. The lessees contended that "a great number of our audience consists of persons of this caste, and they are consequently deterred from giving us that support that they would otherwise do." And in the case of performances that appeal strongly to the gallery gods, "it is not unusual for the Black gods to be in the great majority."[46] Minstrelsy had come into vogue as a unique form of American theatre that presented unflattering and clownish images of black folk, and this is dealt with in a separate chapter. But there were other attempts by African Americans to stage regular plays, although evidence of such activity is fragmentary and reports are often couched in such disparaging terms that we are left to wonder whether a reported event was factual or a humorous invention of the writer.

In New Orleans a playhouse was opened and operated especially for the colored population in 1830. White patrons were also admitted, with discounted tickets for slaves and servants accompanying them. Despite the city's polyglot population, segregation was practiced among the coloreds themselves, with mulattoes and quadroons being seated apart from other Blacks.[47] Also in New Orleans, a free man of color named E. V. Mathieu received permission in 1838 to establish a theatre for people of color. Called the Marigny Theatre, it was located on the corner of Champs Elysée and Bon Enfans (equivalent today to Elysian Field and St. Claude). By vote of the town council, the theatre was exempt from taxes usually imposed on cabarets, taverns, and ballrooms, provided the manager furnished free of charge a box for use by the mayor and other city dignitaries. From 3 April to 30 June the Marigny produced an average of one play a week, in French, although revivals often allowed a second play to be presented on the same bill. Playwrights included Beaumarchais, Duval, Etienne, Picard, Voltaire, and others. In July the theatre was up for sale and a new director, named

Vitalis, was installed for the season beginning in September. It is not known what became of this enterprise.[48]

From Baltimore comes a passing reference to a "theatrical exhibition" by eight colored men, near the corner of Sharp and Pratt Streets, presumably in May 1853. These actors, having failed to make the required security deposit prior to their performance, were arrested, taken to the Southern Watch House and sent to jail by Justice Yoe. In reporting the incident the *Baltimore Sun* had merely this comment: "their queer costumes and drollery, and the general *tout ensemble* are said to have presented one of the richest scenes in police annals."[49]

The next report of a black theatre production is fictitious. It appeared in an 1855 publication written by Q. K. Philander Doesticks, a pseudonym for the American humorist Mortimer Thomson. In the years 1854–55 Thomson ran a column in certain newspapers where he published, under his cognomen, a series of satiric letters on various topics. He then collected and printed some of the letters as chapters in a book entitled *Doesticks: What he Says* (1855). Four letters recounted vists to the theatre, the last visit to see 'Shakespeare darkenized – Macbeth in high colors." I cite parts of this report as much for its invention as for the attitude revealed regarding black productions of Shakespeare.

The author describes a performance he attended at the Church Street Theatre built in New York by colored folk and situated some four miles from City Hall.[50] *Macbeth* was offered as part of a grand Shakespearian festival and Doesticks set out "to witness the unusual spectacle of a Bowery darkey representing a Scotch king." Inside the theatre, the stage drop curtain showed three figures: "a thick-lipped lady of dark complexion" represented Tragedy, "a woolly headed brunette in short skirts" stood for Comedy, and between them was a portrait of the African Roscius "attired in a swallow-tailed coat with brass buttons and a red velvet collar." The orchestra consisted of a bass drum, one violin, and a cornet.

Macbeth was a fat gentleman of jetty hue dressed in a cook's apron; he wore a paper cap with a turkey feather stuck in it, his steel by his side, a butcher knife in hand, and the cover of the soup pot for a shield. Macduff looked more like a Lake Superior Indian, with a superfluity of red flannel fringe and silver rings in his ears and nose, while Lady Macbeth rejoiced in a tin crown with seven points, each one with a crescent on top, brass-heeled gaiters, a green baize train, kid gloves and jewelry. Much of the action was decidedly original: the removal of Birnam Wood was accomplished by opening a back scene to reveal "four darkies carrying pine kindling wood from a wagon with a jackass team, down cellar into a coal-hole." For the final duel between Macbeth and Macduff, one flourished a long toasting fork and the other wielded a rolling pin. They fought furiously until Macbeth was killed and Macduff, with his rolling pin, stood over him "in a grand saw-buck attitude of victory and triumph."[51]

Around mid-century three writers emerged whose impact on African American theatre and society was markedly varied. One writer, a French-speaking mulatto from New Orleans, was sent to France to be educated and stayed there. A second writer, born a slave in Kentucky, escaped to the North, educated himself, and settled in Boston. The third, a Caucasian female author of strong Christian faith, eschewed the theatre. Yet, when once her story of southern slavery was, against her wishes, successfully transferred to the stage, it swept the nation and countries abroad, was copiously and egregiously adapted in inferior versions, and occupied the American theatre for some seventy years.

On 2 June 1821 Victor Séjour was born, the illegitimate son of a white man from Santo Domingo and a quadroon woman of New Orleans.[52] Sent to Paris to further his education, Séjour attracted the attention of the literati with the publication in 1841 of his heroic poem, "Le Retour de Napoléon." Among his new associates were two playwrights, the mulatto Alexandre Dumas, *père*, and Emile Augier, the latter having encouraged Séjour to write for the stage. In the ensuing thirty years from 1844 to 1874, Séjour wrote twenty-two plays, all but two having been produced in Paris during his lifetime. Four of his pieces were presented at the New Orleans Theatre while he lived, but although he had become one of the most popular dramatists in nineteenth-century France, he wrote no plays about Blacks or mulattoes, or on an American theme, and only one of his plays, *Le Martyre du cœur* (1858), includes a black character, who is Jamaican. A trusted servant whose master is dying, he is sent to Paris to deliver an inheritance to his master's estranged daughter.[53] Séjour received the honorary title of Chevalier and became a member of the Légion d'Honneur in 1860, but when at age 53 he died of tuberculosis, on 10 September 1874, he was in a charity hospital in Paris.

William Wells Brown, fugitive slave, wrote two plays that were not staged during his lifetime. The first was a satire directed at the Reverend Dr. Nehemiah Adams, a Boston preacher who, after spending three months in the Southland, had in 1854 published what amounted to a defence of slavery. In response, Brown ridiculed Adams, pointing out that since he, Brown, had spent twenty years as a slave he knew as much about the "peculiar

institution" as Adams did. Brown wrote his first play, entitled *Experience;
or, How to Give a Northern Man Backbone*, in 1856. In it, his fictional cleric is
mistakenly sold into slavery and experiences it first hand. When he is eventually freed, a much chastened preacher has a completely different view of
life as a slave. Wells Brown read the play on his lecture circuit on behalf
of the American Anti-Slavery Society. When some time later a colleague
objected to his reading a play instead of delivering a lecture, Wells Brown
explained that in certain places the reading was in fact more effective than a
lecture, because "people will pay to hear the Drama... that would not give
a cent in an anti-slavery meeting."[54]

Wells Brown's second play (the one that exists) is *The Escape; or, A Leap for
Freedom*. Also written in 1856, it dealt with the problems runaway slaves faced
as they made their way to Canada and freedom. As fugitives in America,
they were subject to arrest and could be returned to even harsher treatment
by their former owners. Wells Brown considered this second play to be far
superior to his first. In a short preface to the published version, he explained
that "the main features of the drama are true. Glenn and Melinda are actual
characters, and still reside in Canada. Many of the incidents are drawn from
my own experience of eighteen years in the South." He felt the ignorance
of the slave was a common phenomenon wherever chattel slavery existed
and mentioned the difficulties created in the household by the presence of
beautiful slave women. Such situations were exemplified in his play. Wells
Brown concluded his preface by admitting to defects in the playscript, but
added: "as I was born in slavery, and never had a day's schooling in my life,
I owe the public no apology for errors."[55]

Most critics found the playscript to be inadequate, an unruly hodgepodge
of different scenes, with language that is artificial, but they are prepared to
excuse the author since he did not expect his play to be staged. However,
as the playwright himself asserts in his short preface, many of the incidents are authentic reporting of the slave experience, such as "jumping the
broomstick" to confirm marriage between slaves and the abuse of beautiful
slave women by their masters and field overseers. Moreover, while the play
may be somewhat flawed in structure, a completely satisfying experience is
likely to be the judgment of anyone fortunate enough to have seen either
of two modern productions: at Emerson College, Boston, in December
1971, or at Boston University Theatre in February 1977, both directed by
James Spruill. Of the former staging, one reviewer applauded Spruill for his
"inspired direction," noting that the play was produced only after careful and
considerable research. She added: "this production proved that a resourceful

and imaginative director can make a drama designed for another period and audience, even for another purpose, come alive for us today."[56]

William Wells Brown was born a slave near Lexington, Kentucky, in around 1814. Unsure of his age, he explained that slave owners preferred to keep the ages of their slaves secret so that old hands could be sold as younger slaves after dyeing their hair. His father was a white man and his mother an attractive field hand who produced seven children, each one for a different father. Wells Brown's maternal grandfather, a mulatto slave in Virginia, had served in the Continental Army, expecting to gain freedom in reward for his service. However, after the war he was honorably discharged and sent back to his master to die as a field slave. Wells Brown was only 10 years old when he witnessed an overseer, reputed for his cruelty, beat his mother for being a few minutes late for work in the field; "the cold chills ran over me," he wrote, "and I wept aloud." He had three different owners and during the last six years of enslavement he was hired out to white employers, working variously in a hotel, for a newspaper (where he learned to read), on a steamboat, as a doctor's aide, and as a general factotum. Later on, when he was about 50 years old, he began to practice medicine, though he had no formal training as a physician.

Wells Brown made three attempts to escape from bondage, succeeding on the last. He experienced being chased by bloodhounds and, after his recapture, being whipped and locked in a smokehouse to inhale burning tobacco stalks while his mother, who had accompanied him on the second attempt, was sold into the deep South. Eventually, he succeeded in running away when, traveling only at night and half-frozen in a January winter, he was aided by a Quaker family that helped him recover from fever and restore his body for the journey north to Cleveland. He acquired the name Wells Brown from his Quaker rescuers. One of his early paying jobs was as a steward on a Lake Erie steamer, where he helped to carry fugitive slaves to Canada. By 1836 he had married, begun a systematic self-education program of reading books and newspapers, attended antislavery meetings and became a practicing abolitionist.

Wells Brown moved from Cleveland to Buffalo, then to Farmington, New York, finally settling in Boston in 1847. His public addresses on behalf of the Anti-Slavery Society were legendary. In July 1849 he went to Paris to attend the International Peace Congress, moving to London to rally support for the abolitionist cause. But enactment of the Fugitive Slave Law in 1850 forced him to remain abroad in order to avoid capture and reenslavement on his return to America. Having to earn his keep in Britain for the next few years, he became a regular contributor to several London newspapers, and, in addition to lecturing, began to write and publish books, including *Clotel; or, The President's Daughter; A Narrative of Slave Life in the United States* (1853).[57] In 1854, after friends in England had purchased his freedom, Wells Brown returned to Boston and continued to work as an antislavery agent until the end of the Civil War. Upon his death in 1884, the *Cleveland Gazette* wrote: "No man of the race commanded a higher regard, or was more widely known among active workers for the welfare of humanity than he...when the history of the men [and women] who have stood by the race shall be written, that of the late Wm. Wells Brown will stand out boldly as par excellence."[58]

By mid-century, then, ominous tensions had developed between the northern states that had abolished slavery and the southern states where slavery was entrenched. As the country expanded westward, the question of whether slavery should be permitted in newly settled territories was a source of acrimonious wrangling in the United States Congress. Facing repeated threats by southern states to secede and in order to maintain national unity, compromises were reached that guaranteed the continuance of slavery. In 1850, for instance, one of the more invidious of these concessions permitted slave catchers to hunt down fugitive slaves, regardless of how long they had been free, and return them to southern bondage. This new law encouraged the kidnapping of any black individual who could be seized and charged on dubious evidence as a runaway. Since Blacks had no legal standing against Whites in a court of law, many sought safety by moving to Canada, where slavery no longer existed. In addition, militant abolitionists were known to invade northern courtrooms in order to rescue Blacks charged as fugitives but who were of good standing in their communities.

In this widening rift between North and South, the theatre played a role in fashioning public attitudes toward race. On the one hand, the popular minstrel stage presented degrading images of Blacks over many decades; on the other, the issue of slavery formed a serious undercurrent in productions by the African Theatre and in the plays of Wells Brown. These productions were but a small quota of the number of plays staged in theatres across the country dealing with aspects of the slave experience.[59] Even a play as historically remote as Robert Montgomery Bird's *The Gladiator* (1831) could be viewed with alarm in southern states when Spartacus, the Roman gladiator and insurrectionist, rallied his comrades-in-arms with the words:

> Ho, slaves, arise! it is your hour to kill!
> Kill and spare not – For wrath and liberty.
> Freedom for bondsmen – freedom and revenge![60]

Of the antislavery dramas seen in America, one play proved to be the greatest theatrical hit in the annals of the English-speaking stage. It started out as a series of fifty episodes in narrative form written by Harriet Beecher Stowe and published during 1851–52 in the Washington, DC, abolitionist newspaper, the *National Era*. These episodes were then collected by Stowe and published as a novel under the title *Uncle Tom's Cabin*. It was an immediate success. The first edition, consisting of 5,000 copies, was bought out in just two days, while first-year sales amounted to some three hundred thousand. It is estimated that about 3 million copies have been purchased in the United States. Foreign sales were similarly phenomenal. In one year, forty pirated editions were printed in Great Britain and its colonies, with total sales estimated at 1.5 million. The book was translated into some forty different languages and dialects; three newspapers in Paris carried installments simultaneously. Germany issued seventy-five editions, and in Italy, despite being banned by the Pope, every available copy of the book was surreptitiously read by the public.[61]

Viewed as a sure-fire vehicle for the stage, the novel was immediately pounced on by playwrights and permission sought to dramatize the story. But Mrs. Stowe, daughter and wife of Presbyterian ministers and sister to half-a-dozen preachers, rejected any such offer outright, fearing that "any attempt on the part of Christians to identify themselves with them [i.e., theatrical performances] will be productive of danger to the individual character and to the general cause."[62] However, as copyright laws did not then exist to protect the work, several unauthorized stage versions quickly appeared in the United States and abroad. Initial attempts in America to dramatize the narrative failed on stage, but the third adaptation, that by George L. Aiken, was a resounding success, playing at the Troy Museum in Troy, New York, for 100 performances from 27 September to 1 December 1852, before moving to the National Theatre in New York City in July 1853. From then on, "Tom troupes" proliferated throughout the country for the next eighty years, except for a decade-long interregnum caused by the Civil War and its immediate aftermath. By 1900 there were twelve different playscripts in print and probably many more pirated and adapted versions were staged but never published.

A history of the African American theatre would not normally pay attention to a drama emanating from a Caucasian view of black slavery in the United States. But Mrs. Stowe's intentions were beyond reproach. Her prefatory note to the novel stated her object in writing "to awaken sympathy and feeling for the African race as they exist among us, to show their wrongs and sorrows" under a cruel and unjust system. Stowe admitted that what she had written of the evils of slavery "is not the half that could be told of the unspeakable whole." Indeed, initial reaction to the novel by African American leaders was highly favorable. Speaking at the Colored National Convention of 1853 Frederick Douglass called it "plainly marked by the finger of God," and William Wells Brown wrote that it "had come down upon the dark abodes of slavery like a morning's sunlight, unfolding to view its enormities." Having spent a short time in the Southland, Stowe's experience of plantation slavery was limited, but she had read a number of published slaves' narratives and this knowledge gave her story a ring of authenticity.[63]

Congress had banned the importation of slaves in 1807 but it was a ban more honored in the breach than the observance, since the last slave ship, the *Clothilde*, discharged its cargo in Mobile, Alabama, as late as 1859. This blatant infringement of the law and other notable events had repeatedly prepared the ground for the inevitable conflict between a free North and a South that saw black slavery as a permanent way of life. Beginning in 1800 there had been no less than four major conspiracies to end slavery by armed rebellion; there were also two successful mutinies by slaves aboard ship; two public appeals encouraging slaves to revolt; the establishment of an abolitionist newspaper, the *Liberator*, in 1831; the formation of the American Anti-Slavery Society in 1833; and in 1849 the gallant Harriet Tubman, having escaped from slavery in Maryland, returned repeatedly to the Southland and led some three hundred slaves to freedom.[64]

The story of Uncle Tom, in brief, is that of an ageing house slave imbued with true Christian virtues for which he suffers not only deprivation but physical injury and death. When other slaves escape to avoid being sold in the deep South, Tom declines to join them, believing it is his duty to submit to his superiors. On the journey South by riverboat he saves Eva, a saintly child, from a watery grave by plunging in after her when she was accidentally pushed into the water. In return, Tom is bought by her father, St. Clare, and becomes her slave companion. Having promised to give Tom his freedom, St. Clare dies of a stab wound before doing so and Tom is again sold, this time to a sadistic slaver, Legree. When Tom refuses Legree's orders to whip a teenage female slave, he is severely beaten on orders from Legree and dies a martyr to his Christian beliefs. Apart from Tom, Blacks prominent in the novel and subsequent drama are the runaways George Harris and his wife, Eliza; a mischievous waif taken into the St. Clare household and called Topsy, who had been bought as an infant by a speculator and raised for the slave market knowing neither mother nor father but "just growed"; Legree's mistress, the octoroon Cassy, whom he fears; and sundry others including Tom's wife and children, who were left behind when he was shipped away to be auctioned.

Adapting a novel to the requirements of the stage is fraught with difficulty. A book that may be read at leisure over many days has to be compressed into two or three hours of performance. Characters that come and go blissfully in the narrative have to justify their existence in the life of a play and at every appearance on stage. The more times they appear, the more important they are likely to seem. In an epic drama, the number of significant characters is usually reduced to a handful in order to retain focus on them and to avoid confusion in the minds of the audience. Place descriptions that give color and texture to a narrative become painted scenery and sound effects in the live theatre. Apart from soliloquies, seldom found in realistic drama, reflective passages in the novel that reveal the innermost thoughts and feelings of characters have to be expressed in forceful dialogue and physical action. Scene endings often require striking visual tableaux or other memorable climaxes to maintain interest while stage settings are being changed. Moreover, when a theatre finds itself competing for a mass audience it is hard for a writer or producer to resist the temptation to appeal to the generality by means of caricature, spectacle, and emotionality.

Nevertheless, *Uncle Tom's Cabin* deserves careful consideration for several reasons: as drama, it had a profound impact on the country as a whole and especially affected the lives of African Americans; it provided opportunities for black performers to participate in productions, initially as jubilee choruses or extras in crowd scenes, and eventually as characters in the play, including the title role; it brought about racially integrated theatre with Blacks and Whites participating in the same production; in some instances it countered the debased image of black folk perpetrated in minstrel shows by creating in Uncle Tom a Christ-like figure who cared for others more than himself; and finally, it demonstrated how easily a popular success in nineteenth-century American theatre could sink into a travesty of itself by catering to the baser instincts of its audience.

In 1855 the showman P. T. Barnum brought a new adaptation of the novel to New York to compete with the Aiken version. It offered a "Grand

Panorama of a Portion of the Mississippi River Down to New Orleans" with many song-and-dance numbers. The scene of the slave auction included a plantation jig with banjo accompaniment. Eight years later there were four rival productions in New York, "all stuck full of banjos, cakewalks, and tin-pan-alley coon songs with no relation to either the action or the character singing."[65] Following the hard-earned successful tour of the Fisk Jubilee Singers of the early 1870s, most full-scale productions of the drama carried a chorus of authentic Blacks to sing and dance plantation and jubilee songs and to perform so-called Negro specialities. Animals including a donkey for Lawyer Marks, a horse for Legree, bloodhounds chasing the runaway Eliza as she crossed the Ohio River on a slab of ice, cradling her infant son in her arms, and even a swamp alligator were incorporated into the show. In one performance at Haverly's Brooklyn Theatre in 1883, "a terrible fight started on stage among the bloodhounds pursuing Eliza. Some of the animals fell into the orchestra pit, scattering the musicians and spreading panic in the audience."[66]

In the circus-like atmosphere created by these superfluities, legitimate actors eschewed the Tom-shows or played them only out of dire necessity. Characters, black and white, became stereotypes, including Uncle Tom, whose resistance to tyranny began to seem piteous, a mere foil for Legree's ranting and raving. When one of the regular road companies went bankrupt, the manager came up with the idea for a "novelty." He would stage a Tom-show and get a real Black to play Uncle Tom, since hitherto all actors in productions were White. He chose Sam Lucas, a well-known minstrel trouper who became the first African American to play Tom, twenty-five years after the role was initially performed. As it turned out, casting Lucas was determined less by his color or acting credentials, though he was clearly suited in both respects. Rather, he had a propensity for wearing diamonds, which were used to bail out the company from its debt. Lucas would later become the only black actor to play Uncle Tom in the movies – a dubious honor since it cost him his life. He was already 72 years old and in the scene where he had to leap into the frigid waters of the Mississippi to save little Eva, he caught pneumonia and never recovered.

One writer has argued that Tom-shows "even accentuated Mrs. Stowe's notions of the superiority of 'white blood' by playing Eliza, George Harris and Cassie [sic] – the slave characters of energy and enterprise – with white actors using little if any dark makeup and eschewing Negro dialect. Only Tom [eventually], Topsy, and the chuckleheaded minor characters were played as identifiable Negroes."[67] One result of this debasement of the

"Uncle Tom" drama was to fix in the public mind for decades the black performer's role on the professional stage as a song-and-dance entertainer or a comic buffoon. Many serious artists and actors resented this stereotyping and attempted to set up their own black theatre companies, where they would be free to play dramatic roles. When they succeeded in doing so, the problems of securing a proper playhouse and of attracting a literate and supportive audience proved overwhelming. In their frustration, resentment festered against the Tom-show as the principal cause of their troubles.

Also crucial in producing black disillusionment with the Uncle Tom character was the experience of Blacks after the Civil War. The success of Union forces against the rebellious slave-owning states had preserved the republic, a victory achieved with the direct and often decisive participation of thousands of African Americans. Some two hundred thousand of them had enlisted in the Union Army, thirty thousand in the navy, while another quarter of a million had worked as support personnel for the troops. When the war finally ended, an all-too-brief period of reconstruction followed during which the federal government assumed responsibility for protecting the rights of former slaves. But this protection soon deteriorated under a reign of terror perpetrated against Blacks by hardline white supremacists in the South, of which the murderous Ku Klux Klan was the most blatant offender.

By 1876 when republican President Rutherford Hayes, newly elected by means of a deal with southern democrats, declared that "absolute justice and fair play to the Negro" could best be achieved "by trusting the honorable and influential Whites," Blacks knew they would have to fight for their survival and human dignity against the injustices of the so-called "Jim Crow era." An 1880 editorial in the *Chicago Conservator*, a black newspaper, summed up the mood of African Americans: "President Hayes has plainly told the colored people they must make peace at any price. We repeat it, but with a different signification – they must make peace at any price. It may cost treasure, it may cost blood, it may cost lives, but make it, be the cost what it may."[68] More explicit and revolutionary was the advice given in an October 1889 speech by a leading black journalist, John E. Bruce:

> Let the Negro require at the hands of every white murderer in the South or elsewhere a life for a life. If they burn our houses, burn theirs; if they kill our wives and children, kill theirs ... If they demand blood, exchange it with them until they are satisfied. By a vigorous adherence to this course, the shedding of human blood by white men will soon become a thing of the past.[69]

These desperate counsels by African American leaders of the time are quoted
to emphasize the militant mood of responsible black opinion in the closing
decades of the nineteenth century, a militancy provoked by the severe reversal of hard-won victories in the struggle for equal justice. As the editor of
the *Indianapolis Freeman* wrote in an article captioned "Let My People Go":
"Slavery is no more, but in its stead stalks race, caste, business and commercial ostracism, civil oppression and debarment, political persecution, and all
the brood of evils that survived the demise of the parent evil."[70]

Ironically enough, this period coincided with the ascendancy of Tom-
shows, some four to five hundred troupes being in existence. Thus, while
the forty-year-old relic of antebellum days was roaming the nation extolling
the virtues of the long-suffering, compliant, forgiving and fictional Uncle
Tom, often played by blacked-up white actors, Blacks throughout the land,
having at last gained freedom from slavery, were facing the reality of Simon
Legree and were determined not to submit without a struggle. Clearly,
their former regard for the saintly Tom would turn sour. In a masterly
essay published in 1903, W. E. B. Du Bois attempted to explain the now
repugnant phenomenon of the submissive black slave:

> The long system of repression and degradation of the Negro tended to em-
> phasize the elements in his character which made him a valuable chattel:
> courtesy became humility, moral strength degenerated into submission
> and the exquisite native appreciation of the beautiful became an infinite
> capacity for dumb suffering.[71]

It was, however, in 1919, just one year after 100,000 black Americans had
once again risked their lives in defence of the republic and to make the world
safe for democracy, that the image of the docile Uncle Tom was publicly and
passionately denounced. That year a wave of lynchings and other violent acts
against black citizens engulfed the nation, inspired by fear among insecure
Whites that returning black soldiers would demand the equal treatment
they had long been denied. Among the victims of rampaging white mobs
were discharged black veterans, some still in uniform. In response to these
new outrages, black leaders declared the advent of the New Negro, whose
militancy would finally obliterate the notion of the impotent Tom, resigned
to persecution and second-class citizenship.

Whether as literature or theatre, the time had come for a reassessment
of the quality and influence of Mrs. Stowe's novel. *The New Negro*, an
anthology of writings by black Americans collected by Alain Locke and
published in 1925, contained several reevaluations of *Uncle Tom's Cabin*. The

lead-off essay by the editor, a Rhodes scholar and philosophy professor at Howard University in Washington, DC, affirmed that "the day of 'aunties,' 'uncles,' and 'mammies,' is equally gone. Uncle Tom and Sambo have passed on...The popular melodrama has about played itself out and it is time to scrap the fictions, garret the bogeys and settle down to a realistic facing of facts."[72] Another contributor, the poet and journalist William Stanley Brathwaite, argued that the moral and historical effect of Uncle Tom was an artistic loss and setback, since "the treatment of Negro life and character, overlaid with these forceful stereotypes, could not develop into artistically satisfying portraiture."[73] Yet a third writer, Montgomery Gregory, a then recently retired English professor at Howard University, turned his attention to the character of Topsy:

> she has given us a fearful progeny. With her, popular dramatic interest in the Negro changed from serious moralistic drama to the comic phase...The earliest expression of Topsy's baneful influence is to be found in the minstrels...These comedians, made up into grotesque caricatures of the Negro race, fixed in the public taste a dramatic stereotype of the race that has been almost fatal to a sincere and authentic Negro drama.[74]

This outpouring of sentiment against *Uncle Tom's Cabin* came at a time when touring Tom-shows were already in decline. In January 1931, *Theatre Guild Magazine* carried an article entitled "Uncle Tom is Dead," alleging that for the first time in more than three-quarters of a century there was no company performing the play in all of America. The obituary was in fact premature. Letters promptly poured in to the magazine's mailbox from all parts of the country testifying that the play was alive and well on provincial boards. As if to confirm these reports the prestigious Players Club in New York, for its twelfth annual revival of a classic American play, chose *Uncle Tom's Cabin* and gave it a handsome production.

With Whites in blackface playing the leads (Otis Skinner was Tom, having first played the role in 1877, and Fay Bainter was Topsy), the production opened at the Alvin Theatre on 29 May 1933 for a limited run. In a straightforward and dignified reading of the script, Skinner's portrayal of the "holy slave," according to a report, "was a profoundly pathetic study in Negro nobility"[75] and there was hardly a dry eye in the house. The play topped box-office receipts in the city, had its run extended by three weeks, and then went on tour. Three years later George Abbott attempted a racially integrated musical version under the title *Sweet River*. Written from the point of view of the slaves, the book apparently lacked the vitality of the original story and although the production was deemed to be "probably the best looking *Uncle Tom's Cabin* yet devised...the attempt to dress Mrs. Stowe's classic in fine style and give it dignity and good manners" was a failure and the play was withdrawn after five performances.[76] Traditions die hard.

With the noblest intention, Harriet Beecher Stowe had created a Jekyll-and-Hyde character that contained the seeds of its own destruction. Earnestly seeking to lift the burden of chattel slavery that had been imposed on Blacks, she produced in Uncle Tom a character who persuaded white racists that Blacks would accept the intolerable conditions of serfdom without fighting back. This was a clear calumny on the race, no less damaging because it was unintentional. As far as black people are concerned Mrs. Stowe's novel, particularly in its stage trappings, did as much harm as good. For as the abolitionist and Civil War general Thomas Wentworth Higginson wrote more than a century ago: "If it be the normal tendency of bondage to produce saints like Uncle Tom, let us all offer ourselves at auction immediately."[77]

3

The Civil War to The Creole Show

Errol G. Hill

The American Civil War began when a group of southern states, ultimately eleven in number and calling themselves the Confederate States of America, attempted to secede from the Union. On 12 April 1861 they attacked the federal Fort Sumter in South Carolina and forced its occupants to surrender. After four grueling years the war ended on 9 April 1865 with the surrender of southern general Robert E. Lee to General Ulysses S. Grant at Appomattox, Virginia. Five days later President Abraham Lincoln, attending a performance at Ford's Theatre in Washington, DC, was assassinated by an unstable actor, John Wilkes Booth, brother to Edwin Booth, who would become the highly acclaimed American tragedian of the nineteenth century. Although several factors led to the internecine conflict, as far as African Americans were concerned all causes could be reduced to one single overriding issue – slavery.

In the decade leading up to the war, the United States Congress had passed substantial legislation in an effort to appease the slaveholding states. I have mentioned the Fugitive Slave Act of 1850 that permitted bounty hunters to seize runaway slaves and return them to former owners. In 1854 Congress passed the Kansas-Nebraska Act, repealing the Missouri Compromise of 1820 that restricted slavery in the Midwest to the southern boundary of Missouri. The South argued such restriction was illegal for publicly owned land and the Supreme Court agreed; the result was armed conflict in the state of Kansas between the opponents and the supporters of slavery. Finally, in 1857 the Supreme Court handed down the Dred Scott decision that effectively made Blacks noncitizens bereft of civil rights that Whites should respect. Despite these concessions, southern states led by South Carolina set up their own government, elected a provisional president of their confederacy, appointed an army commander, established their capitol at Richmond, Virginia, and, with the capture of Fort Sumter, took control of federal property in the South. These actions challenged the authority of the duly constituted government of the United States, forcing President Lincoln to issue a call for troops to put down the rebellion.

Initially, free Blacks were not accepted into the army, but as Union troops suffered one defeat after another in the first year of the war, field generals began to organize black regiments without waiting for formal approval. Fifteen months into the conflict Congress authorized the recruitment of Blacks; it took two more years before they received equality with white troops in pay, arms, equipment, and medical services. Eventually some 185,000 black soldiers and 29,500 black sailors fought for the Union, while an additional 200,000 Blacks were employed in nonmilitary support. The Confederate response branded as criminals black troops and their white officers, who could face execution if captured. In one notorious Tennessee case, when in 1864 rebel forces overcame Fort Pillow, manned mostly by Blacks, the Confederate general, Nathan Bedford Forrest, massacred some three hundred defenders, sparing neither soldier nor civilian, male or female, Black or White.

Citizen Abe Lincoln was convinced slavery was wrong. He wrote as much in 1842, when he hoped to see "not one slave or one drunkard" on God's green earth. In his 1858 debate with Stephen Douglas for the presidency, Lincoln condemned slavery as "a moral, social, and political evil."[1] As president, however, Lincoln considered it his solemn duty to preserve the Union at all costs. In the first two years of the war he twice recommended to Congress that slaveholding states should be compensated for agreeing to abolish slavery gradually. Twice also he revoked proclamations by his generals freeing slaves in regions that they had conquered. He even met with black leaders to urge support for a plan to send free Blacks back to Africa or to a new all-black state in Central America, leaving the United States a mostly white nation (presumably with black slaves). Black leaders roundly rejected the proposal.

Unable to find a viable compromise, Lincoln issued a preliminary proclamation in which he warned the Confederacy he would free all slaves in states that were still in rebellion on 1 January 1863. The proclamation was duly signed on the announced date, but it had little immediate effect as slaves wisely chose not to leave southern plantations or domiciles without the protection of conquering Union troops. However, once Union soldiers took charge of an area, slaves left their bondage in droves to join the war effort. In fact Lincoln's "Emancipation Proclamation" did not free all slaves in the United States. To avoid offending the so-called "Border States" adjoining the eleven in rebellion, Lincoln excluded them from his proclamation, leaving thousands of slaves in bondage in nonrebel country. Full freedom came in January 1865 after Congress passed the Thirteenth Amendment to the Constitution, ratified in December, that put an end to slavery in America.[2]

Once the war was over, the new freedmen and -women set about ordering their lives. Their needs were basic and urgent: food, shelter, the chance to earn a living and to have a family of their own in a supportive community. Equally as important was the desire to be educated, since in southern states teaching slaves to read and write had been prohibited.[3] Many were aware of Field Order no. 15, issued in January 1865 by Union general William Sherman, whose army had marched victoriously through Georgia and South Carolina. Concerned about the plight of the former slaves, Sherman required that abandoned southern plantations for a stretch of thirty miles inland from the sea should be apportioned to Blacks, with each family receiving not more than 40 acres of tillable ground. Settlers were to be protected by military authorities and the newly created Freedmen's Bureau would be responsible for carrying out the terms of the order. As a result some forty thousand Blacks were settled on 40-acre lots in South Carolina and given provisional titles pending final action on the abandoned lands of Confederate rebels.

It was not to be. With the assassination of Lincoln and the ascendancy of vice-president and southerner Andrew Johnson to the presidency, the new administration not only revoked the policy of distributing land to ex-slaves but also required that land already apportioned should be returned to its owners. Three-quarters of a century later Theodore Ward would write a searing drama, *Our Lan'*, about a company of freedmen and -women who laid claim to their promised 40 acres per family of abandoned land on an island off the coast of Georgia. They cleared and tilled the land, planted food crops, suffered through a harsh winter, and refused to surrender the property when federal troops moved in to enforce Johnson's order. In the ensuing struggle their leader was shot and killed. Once again Blacks would be sacrificed at the altar of political expediency in order to win back the loyalty of southern states that had acted to destroy the Union.

Black theatre after the war

Ira Aldridge was planning to return to America when he died at Lodz, Poland, in 1867. That his return might have been premature is evident in the careers of two younger aspirants for histrionic honors, Samuel

Morgan Smith and Paul Molyneaux Hewlett. Learning of Aldridge's success overseas, they too went to England hoping to hone their skills and
gain the recognition denied at home. Morgan Smith arrived in England a
year before Aldridge died. Born in Philadelphia on 20 June 1832, he must
have received a good basic education for he wrote and published a lengthy
monograph rebutting the allegation in a speech by lawyer Charles O'Conor
that slavery was not unjust but benign and of divine origin.[4]

Morgan Smith worked as a barber and hairdresser, but he was passionately devoted to the stage. Like others before him, he not only observed
professional actors from the upper gallery of theatres, but also helped to dress
them for performances. One of these actors was the distinguished Philadel-
phian James Murdoch, whom Morgan Smith attended at the Chestnut
Street Theatre.[5] Smith had been giving public readings and recitals as early
as 1863, when he invited Murdoch to a performance. By 1865 he decided
on a stage career, moved to Boston and New York, where he sought and
obtained training under professional actors, but when he applied for permission to visit backstage in order to learn about production techniques
he was denied admittance at the Boston and Continental Theatres "on account of his color." Undaunted, Smith sailed for England with his wife
and infant child, arriving there in May 1866. He had carefully studied the
plays of Shakespeare and other popular dramatists and was ready to perform
them.

That Morgan Smith was a "talented, courageous, enterprising, and resourceful" individual was immediately evident upon his arrival in England.[6]
Within three days he had contracted to manage for a month a little theatre
at Gravesend and had announced *Othello* for its opening. Having never before appeared in a full-length play, he assumed the title role and for the rest
of the month he successfully took leading parts as Richard III, Macbeth,
Hamlet, and Shylock, appearing on twenty-one nights in all. In addition
to Shakespeare he also presented Bulwer-Lytton's *The Lady of Lyons* and
Richelieu, Morton's *The Slave*, Southerne's *Oroonoko*, and Scott's *Rob Roy*.
At the end of his Gravesend season, Morgan Smith advertised his availability, citing excerpts from flattering reviews and calling himself "the coloured
American tragedian." His repertoire consisted of the above-named plays
as well as *The Revenge* by Edward Young and *The Black Doctor*, adapted
from the French original by Ira Aldridge. More than half of his roles were
nonblack, for which he appeared in whiteface. Although the season was not
a financial success, he had attained his major objective of showcasing his
talent and gaining favorable press notices.

Morgan Smith apparently had little difficulty in securing engagements, both in the minor London theatres and in the provinces. During his first year in Britain he appeared in no fewer than twenty-nine different cities and towns in England, Scotland, Wales, and Ireland. He played a different role every night of the week and would then change venues and perform with a new company, often on a weekly basis and occasionally for two weeks. This was a taxing schedule, not only for him but also for his wife, who, presumably, was left alone much of the time in a strange city to care for their child. After less than eighteen months since his arrival in England, Mary Eliza Smith died, on 7 October 1867, at age 27.[7] Two weeks later Smith was back on tour, filling engagements. He appeared at the Theatre Royal, Barnstaple, for six nights in the characters of Othello, Hamlet, Richard III, Shylock, Macbeth, and Richelieu.

When Smith remarried, his new wife, Harriet, was an actress and apparently Caucasian. She appeared with him in several of Shakespeare's dramas, playing the roles of Desdemona, Ophelia, Lady Macbeth, and Juliet, as well as in other non-Shakespearian plays that were already in her husband's repertoire. This arrangement enabled Smith to share with his second wife some of the challenges that beset the peripatetic star actor and to enlist her support in expanding his repertoire. In the ensuing months Smith added five new plays to his roster. These included a new and scenically spectacular version of *The Black Doctor*, staged under the title *The Rising of the Tide* and received with wild enthusiasm; then came *Child of the Sun; or, The Bondsmen Brothers*, a romantic drama written expressly for Smith, in which he took the role of the Chevalier St. George;[8] next, *All But Love*, a drama set in Canada in 1757 with Smith as Uncas, a Mohican chieftain loved by a retired British officer's daughter (obviously a role for wife Harriet). There followed *The Fall of Magdala; or, The Death of King Theodore*, a historic drama of Ethiopia with Smith as the ruling monarch; finally, *War* by Charles Daly, set against the background of the Franco-Prussian war of 1870, Smith taking the role of a freed South American slave. In a decade of touring, Morgan Smith's repertoire reached thirty-five different roles. Playing a different role every night on tour called for a prodigiously retentive memory.

As summer approached, Smith sought engagements in or near London.[9] In 1873 he was at the Surrey Theatre in *Richard III*, *Othello*, *The Slave*, and *Dred*, the last-named being a dramatization by C. W. Taylor of Mrs. Stowe's second antislavery novel. Reviewing Smith's performances, the *Era* of 25 May 1873 found that *The Slave* was hardly an adequate test of his numerous powers, which it described as "good reading, unexaggerated

action, a clear, powerful voice, a correct memory, and an intelligent appre-
hension of dramatic requirements." Of special note was Smith's "natural
delivery and accompanying deportment." This last-mentioned quality was
important to Smith. He viewed acting as a high art and chose his roles
carefully to present characters that were unfairly victimized or who suffered
for a noble cause. Accordingly, few of his roles were comedic. Whereas Ira
Aldridge excelled in both comedy and tragedy and had been an irrepressible
Mungo in *The Padlock*, Smith never once played this role. It was some years
after he remarried that Smith first appeared in a comedy, doubtless urged
by a desire to provide his spouse with appropriate parts in his productions.
In the single instance that Smith appeared in the then popular *Uncle Tom's
Cabin*, he declined to take the title role of the compliant slave, preferring
instead to appear as George Harris, the proud Black who detested slavery
and escaped with his wife, Eliza, and their infant child.

On 22 March 1882 at his home in Sheffield, England, Morgan Smith
died of pneumonia. He was 49 years of age and had been in retirement. He
had suffered "a severe accident" in December 1875 but was able to resume
touring a month later. The year 1877 was a good one for engagements, but
in 1878/79 there was a substantial decline in the number of his appearances
recorded in the press. We are left to wonder whether his health had become
impaired. Morgan Smith was a superior performer, an actor of intelligence,
good judgment, and proper deportment. For some thirteen years he had
appeared in the British provinces, often performing with modest companies
bypassed by named stars. He encouraged the staging of Shakespeare's plays,
taking the lead roles himself. Although he may not be ranked equally with
Ira Aldridge in his range of parts or in the reach and length of his career,
he deserves to be recognized as a worthy successor to Aldridge.

The third nineteenth-century African American dramatic actor to seek
his fortunes in Britain was Paul Molyneaux, who had dropped his family
name of Hewlett.[10] He was born in 1856 in Cambridge, Massachusetts,
the son of Aaron M. Hewlett, a boxing coach and gymnasium director at
Harvard College. Having inherited his father's athletic build and boxing
skill, Paul assisted in coaching, although his preference leaned towards a
stage career. When his father died in 1871, he began training under the
retired Shakespearian actor Wyzeman Marshall of Boston. Then he applied
for a position with Boston managers, offering to start at a low level, but was
turned away because "of the ill-favored accident of color." He then decided
to test himself by undertaking on stage a major role – Othello, no less. He
recruited a supporting company of actors, "all white and of good ability."

The production took place in Boston in 1880 before a friendly and racially mixed audience that gave Molyneaux a generous reception. He was well aware that he needed further training on stage, but he also knew it would be difficult in America to gain that opportunity at a professional level. So he packed his bags, found a vessel, and worked his way across the Atlantic.

Aldridge had reached England at a time of heated debate over the freeing of slaves in the British colonies. He quickly came to represent what free Blacks could achieve given education and training. Likewise, Morgan Smith arrived in England a year after the end of the American Civil War and he, too, came to symbolize black potential once freedom was attained. Molyneaux's arrival in England in the early 1880s did not coincide with such public debate, which could capture the public interest and bring curious audiences to the theatre. Moreover, authentic black minstrel troupes, which were much in vogue in Britain, siphoned off members of the playgoing public who might normally have attended dramatic productions. As a result, Molyneaux found it difficult to secure bookings. The previously cited *New York Globe* report of 1883 quoted two reviews of his performance as Othello in England, without identifying place, date, supporting company, or the source of the reviews. One journal wrote, "His impersonation was at all times careful and conscientious; it was occasionally very impressive"; the other review gushed, "Mr. Paul Molyneaux gave one of the best, if not the best, impersonations of the Moor we ever saw... the whole heart and soul of the actor were thrown into the character and the result was perfection."[11]

More to the point was the news that Molyneaux had lately composed and sent back to Boston a small volume styled "The Curse of Prejudice; or, A Struggle for Fame," in which the young actor still in his twenties described his trials and tribulations in America and in England as he sought to advance his career in the theatre. Indeed the reporter for the *Globe* admitted that in pursuing his goal, Molyneaux found the path "sometimes smooth, but oftener very rough." Not surprisingly, by 1889 Molyneaux had returned disheartened to America and was living with his lawyer brother in Washington, DC, where he died two years later "from brain trouble." Superb athlete though he was, his constitution seemed to lack the emotional resilience necessary to cope with the changing times.

In the decades immediately following the Civil War black theatre groups proliferated in cities and towns across America. Mostly amateur in rank, they could be formed by members of a church, school, or community organization, who would come together to produce a play in order to raise funds for an announced need. Occasionally, persons interested in the theatre might coalesce around an actor or actress of talent, who would lead the group and might be compensated for their services from box-office receipts. Possibly the stimulus for a production might come from a playwright, who, having spent considerable time constructing his or her drama, was able to persuade a group of actors to undertake its production. There also existed a small number of professional troupes that presented plays with some regularity. Finally, there were solo readers and reciters, in the tradition of James Hewlett of the African Theatre, who traveled the country presenting scenes and monologues from plays, reciting poems, or reading prose passages. Since it is not necessary to detail all recorded dramatic presentations, examples will be chosen to illustrate the variety of performance and locale, with a steady thrust towards professionalism.

Some of the earliest theatre groups to become established in the aftermath of the Civil War were in northern California, far away from the sound of battle. Based in San Francisco, they were mainly amateur and centered around two individuals, Mrs. Cecelia V. Williams, a leading player, and George W. Bell, newspaper editor and keen thespian. These two actors appeared together in several productions, primarily nineteenth-century romances and melodramas written by English authors. As editor of the San Francisco weekly newspaper *The Elevator*, Bell ensured that productions were well advertised and reviewed. A second theatre ensemble developed from the careers of two talented young vocalists known as the Hyers Sisters, whose hometown was Sacramento and who traveled extensively across the country as professional troupers. Of the four major productions with which they were associated, the locales of three were in America and the fourth in black Africa.

George Bell first appeared in the title role of the melodrama *Michael Erle, the Maniac Lover* by Thomas Wilks, with a group calling itself the Union Exhibition Association. The performance took place on 24 December 1868 at the Turn Verein Hall in San Francisco and must have been well received, for it was repeated the next month on 13 January at Mozart Hall in the city. Cecelia Williams was apparently not part of this production until the play was again presented with George Bell on 2 and 9 November 1870. By this time Williams and Bell were combining their talents in other dramatic presentations. One was Richard Sheil's *Evadne; or, The Statue*, the initial production on 12 March 1869 credited to the Langston (Colored) Amateur Association. Williams played the lead faultlessly and with her rich, musical voice was judged to be "the great feature of the evening." The play was revived on 12 September 1870 with Bell and Williams again sharing honors.

It was still popular in 1877 when Williams presented it with her own Colored Dramatic Troupe at Platt's Hall on 17 December.

Another drama featuring these two actors in 1870 was Euripides' *Ion*, in Woodhull's English translation. At the initial performance P. A. Bell took the part of Adrastus, the tyrant king,[12] with Williams starring in the male role of Ion. Several features helped to make this production by the Colored Amateur Company memorable. First, it was presented at Maguire's Opera House, an unusual venue for a "genuine colored dramatic performance." The audience was about evenly composed of colored and white patrons. And finally, the proceeds were given as a benefit for *The Elevator* newspaper and a repeat performance at the Metropolitan Theatre on 31 December was announced as a benefit for Cecelia Williams.[13]

A few additional productions recorded in San Francisco in this early period may be noted. On 13 April 1869 George Bell was "just passable" as the hero in *Ugolino*, a tragedy by Junius Brutus Booth the elder, staged by the Union Exhibition Association. For its next offering and despite a refreshing name change to the San Francisco Drama Association, this group fared no better presenting two unidentified farces that the reviewer dubbed "decided failures," except again for Mrs. Williams, who was the only "correct" actor. Several in the cast forgot their lines and called for the prompter's assistance, to which the audience responded with hisses and imprecations. In 1871 *Pizarro* was offered at Maguire's Opera House with Bell as the General and Williams doing double-duty as Elvira and the production manager. A summary review of her acting career claimed she was "brilliant" in this and other plays.

In January 1872 the dormant Langston Dramatic Company came alive long enough to announce a forthcoming production of *Therese; or, The Orphan of Geneva*, but there is no confirmation that it was actually staged. The last recorded production of this period worth mentioning is Sheridan Knowles' *The Wife; or, A Tale of Mantua* (the last three acts) combined with scenes from Shakespeare's *Macbeth*, staged by the Amateur Dramatic Company at Platt's Hall on 28 March 1876. Playing the female leads in both plays, Williams was supported by newcomer Mr. O. Sampson of the National Theatre, Albany, while other actors from New York joined the locals. Stating that on the whole "this was one of the best amateur performances which has been given in this city," the reviewer nevertheless expressed surprise that Sampson did not live up to expectations as a seasoned stock actor, and even Williams was considered deficient in portraying all the emotions her characters required. As Lady Macbeth in her nightgown, she spoiled the effect by whitening her face with so much powder that she seemed like a ghost instead of a demented, horrified woman.[14]

It is not necessary to report all amateur performances in the Bay area through the end of the decade. Mrs. Cecelia Williams left the city by rail for New York and New Haven in September 1874 and did not reappear on the San Francisco stage until March 1876. In the interim, theatre activity diminished. Instead, colored citizens were disturbed by a court case involving Charles Green and Thomas Maguire, the opera house manager who had refused Green a seat in the dress circle although he had bought a ticket for $1 and was entitled to it. A public meeting was called by colored citizens when they learned that on 2 June 1876 United States circuit judge Sawyer ruled against Green, contending that since Maguire managed a private enterprise for profit, he was free to decide how that enterprise should be conducted. Colored patrons viewed Maguire's action as discriminatory and particularly egregious in light of a decision taken several years earlier by the California Theatre on Bush Street, San Francisco. For a spectacular production of *The Count of Monte Cristo* at that theatre in 1870, "respectable" Blacks for a small price increase had been allowed to sit in the balcony immediately over the dress circle and in the tier below the gallery to which they had previously been denied entry. Maguire's action was therefore deemed recalcitrant and deserving of protest.[15]

The Hyers Sisters were important performers of musical theatre in northern California.[16] They lived in Sacramento and started out as musical prodigies. Anna Madah was 12 years old and Emma Louise 10 (although they were billed as aged 10 and 8 years respectively) at their concert début in 1867 at the Metropolitan Theatre in Sacramento. Their parents, Samuel B. Hyers and Annie E. Hyers (née Cryer), had come west from New York. As singers themselves, they had first trained their daughters before sending them for instruction to a German professor, Hugo Frank, and then to the opera singer Josephine D'Ormy. Anna was a soprano; Emma a contralto and gifted comedienne noted for her character songs. They performed for several years in the San Francisco and Oakland areas before embarking on their first transcontinental tour in 1871, under their father's management. For their east coast performances, including an appearance at the Steinway Hall in New York, Samuel Hyers engaged the services of Wallace King, tenor, and John Luca, baritone. Mr. A. C. Taylor, pianist of San Francisco, traveled with the sisters as accompanist.

Early in their repertoire the sisters had included "dialogues in character" and were said to possess "great dramatic ability." It was no surprise, therefore, when on 26 March 1876 at the Academy of Music in Lynn, Massachusetts, they presented a musical drama entitled *Out of the Wilderness*, which had been written for them by Joseph Bradford of Boston. For this show the quartet of singers was joined by Sam Lucas, a sometime minstrel actor slated to become a veteran comedian of the African American stage. Billed as the Hyers Sisters Combination, the troupe toured their show to New England towns, playing mostly one-night stands. In June the play's title was changed to *Out of Bondage*. It was a simple tale of a slave family before and after the Civil War. Four younger slaves go North as older folk hold back when Union troops arrive to liberate the South. In the end the family is reunited as the elders, who had stayed behind, visit their children, who have become professional vocalists. The dialect text contained slices of homespun humor, as in the following dialogue between Kaloolah, a young woman played by Emma Hyers, and Uncle Eph, an older man acted by Lucas:[17]

> KAL: I say, Uncle Eph, wuz Adam a black man or a white man?
> EPH: Why, a black man of course. What makes you ask such foolish questions.
> KAL: Den whar did all de white folks come from?
> EPH: Well one day de Lord got down on some ob de cullud people, an he white-washed 'em as a terrible example to ebil-doers.
> KAL: Den whenever de Lord gets down on a cullud pusson, he white-washes dem?
> EPH: Yes, indeed, chile.
> KAL: I jus wish he'd get down on me for a while.

The final act took the form of a concert with the sisters singing selections from their regular repertoire. When years later this show was offered by the sisters at the Los Angeles Theatre, in 1890, the critic found the lines given to characters were

> very few and those quite ineffective. Not one of the six people who make up the chief persons in the cast has any idea of acting ... But the moment they strike into song they show themselves at home, and most of their melodies are of the expected quaint and interesting kind. The third act is occupied in displaying the gifts of the singers in more ambitious selections, and among others the "Tower Scene" from *Trovatore* is given by the Hyers Sisters with considerable *empressement*.[18]

With a scenario flexible enough to allow local vocalists to be invited to join the singers on stage – a tradition in black musical theatre that still exists in productions on the Chitlin' Circuit – the show retained its popularity with

Figure 5. Sheet music with Sam Lucas and Emma Hyers in *Out of Bondage*

audiences and remained in the Hyers Sisters' repertoire for some fifteen years.

A second musical drama or *opera buffa* entitled *Urlina, the African Princess*, by E. S. Getchell, was introduced by the sisters at the Grand Opera House, Indianapolis, on 13 January 1879, on their return trip to California. In the plot the usurping king of an African nation has banished Urlina, the rightful successor to the throne. When the usurper's son sees a picture of the princess, he falls in love with her and attempts her rescue with his ally, Kekolah. As they stealthily return to the kingdom they are seized by the king's soldiers, imprisoned, and left to die. Kekolah in disguise escapes imprisonment and with the help of friends succeeds in overthrowing the usurper. In the cast of fourteen, Madah Hyers played the princess while her sister Emma Louise, in the tradition of English pantomime, was the prince. Willie Lyle as the maid was a female impersonator and Billy Kersands played an array of humorous characters. Warning that the show could not be judged by legitimate rules of criticism, one commentator acknowledged that "there is much in the performance which pleases, amuses, and even touches the tender sympathies of the audience. *Urlina* combines harmoniously the elements of comedy, burlesque, and pathos."[19]

The third major production of the Hyers Sisters Combination was their version of *Uncle Tom's Cabin*. It was staged at the Gaiety Theatre, Boston, in March 1880. Black performers had been incorporated into Tom-shows some years earlier, but only as plantation choruses, and Sam Lucas was singular when in 1878 he was picked to play the title role in an otherwise white company on condition that he brought his diamonds.[20] For their production, the sisters recruited a racially mixed cast, with Blacks playing black characters and white actors taking roles intended for Whites. This first fully interracial casting of record on the American stage is indicative of the respect accorded the sisters by members of the theatrical profession. Lucas again appeared as Tom and recited a new prologue written by Mrs. Stowe. Emma Louise was a natural for Topsy, while Anna Madah played Eliza Harris and sometimes a second Topsy. The sisters took their production around to six New England states. In 1883 they persuaded the two separate Callender's Minstrel Festival companies (one Black, the other White) to combine their actors in a spectacular production of the play in San Francisco, and in 1891 the Hyers Combination were still playing a version of it under their own auspices at the Bijou Opera House in Milwaukee, when they were assisted by one of the companies of Nashville Students.[21]

The Hyers Sisters also took part in the musical drama *Peculiar Sam; or, The Underground Railroad* written by the novelist Pauline Hopkins and presented by her Colored Troubadours at the Oakland Garden, Boston, for a one-week run beginning on 5 July 1880.[22] Although Sam Lucas joined the sisters in the cast, they were featured separately, neither integrated into the action nor did they attempt a subsequent revival of the play. Writing of this

Figure 6. Emma Hyers and Anna Madah Hyers in *African Princess, c.* 1879

experience years later, Lucas commented that "the piece failed as the time was not propitious for producing such a play."[23]

In 1883 the sisters decided to leave their father's management. Their parents had long been estranged, mother Annie Hyers having moved away from the family home in Sacramento, first to San Francisco then to Stockton. The breach with their father came in 1881 when he admitted into the company a young woman, "little more than a teenager," named Mary C. Reynolds, whom he married two years later. He was then 53. Reynolds, billed as Mrs. May Hyers, was also a contralto and competed with Emma Louise for roles. As the situation became untenable and likely to generate controversy, the sisters felt it incumbent on them to leave. At ages 17 and 19, they chose to be on their own. Meanwhile Samuel Hyers revamped his company, adding the Harper Sisters, Billy Banks, William Morris, and others. It became known as the S. B. Hyers Colored Musical Comedy Company (often shortened in press notices to the Hyers Comedy Company) and opened at the Criterion Theatre in Chicago on 3 September 1883, in Scott Marble's three-act musical drama *The Blackville Twins*. This play became a staple of the Hyers Comedy Company and for the next ten years two professional Hyers groups existed, which must initially have caused confusion among theatregoers.

The sisters found new engagements for their combination of vocalists, at times in league with other managements, at other times contributing special items in companies of so-called minstrels. Both sisters entered first marriages in 1883: Anna Madah to cornet player Henderson Smith and Emma Louise to bandleader George Freeman.[24] The latter wedding took place in full view of the audience on the stage of the Baldwin Theatre in San Francisco during a performance of *Uncle Tom's Cabin* by Callender's Minstrels.[25] For the 1886/87 season the sisters teamed up with manager L. H. Donavin to revive their first major show, *Out of Bondage*. They opened to a crowded house in Marion, Ohio, on 23 August and proceeded to tour the Midwest before moving to the eastern cities. Traveling by rail to Des Moines, Iowa, on 24 November the rear coach of their train derailed and hurtled down an embankment, inflicting broken and bruised arms, legs, and heads on troupe members. After several days' rest and repair the tour resumed with the company playing in Chicago for two weeks beginning on 7 January 1887 and planning to arrive in the eastern cities by 1 February.

By the start of the 1890s the sisters were once more back in San Francisco. They had been performing professionally for more than twenty years and had won recognition and respect for their skill and deportment, but now they seemed to have little more to offer. They had gone back and forth across the country and had even split up occasionally. In 1894 Emma played Topsy to the Uncle Tom of Walter Espy at the Lyceum Theatre in Cleveland and the next year Anna Madah sang operatic finales with Isham's Octoroons in New York. Emma joined the company in 1896 and appeared in an opening skit called "The Blackville Derby," while Madah contributed "vocal gems." On tour the production played at the Empire Theatre in Philadelphia. It would be the last known time that the sisters were together in the same show, for Emma died in 1899 and Madah traveled to Australia and New Zealand with M. B. Curtis' Afro-American Minstrels.

Ernest Hogan acquired the show after Curtis declared bankruptcy and apparently fled the country. Hogan took the company to the Theatre Royal in Brisbane, where Madah Hyers was still singing her heart out to rapturous applause. A contemporary report called her "about the most cultured operatic star it has ever been our lot to hear" and affirmed that "she is nightly bringing down the house."[26] On her return to America, Madah Hyers took the role of Miss Clorindah Tattles in the skit "Coontown Four Hundred," which formed part of the *Colored Aristocracy* presentation on 13 to 19 January 1901 at the Grand Opera House in Seattle, Washington. Her final recorded performance was as Aunt Beck in the Williams and Walker hit musical *In Dahomey* (1902), after which she retired to Sacramento, where she was visited by Delilah Beasley in 1919. The date of her death is not known.

Making their concert début just two years after the Civil War, the Hyers Sisters under the guidance of their father had a clear mission in view. Despite their youth, they would demonstrate to the country at large that African American performers – and by extrapolation Blacks in general – could equal Whites in any field of endeavor, given the desired training, opportunity, and application. The sisters' chosen field was lyric theatre and their singing received uniformly high praise throughout their careers, even from those critics who were less enamored with their acting ability or with the quality of the material they presented. But the Hyers women also had a message for Blacks, which was that even with superior talent such as theirs, excellence is not achieved and sustained without arduous labor and study. When Uncle Eph in *Out of Bondage* grumbled that "freedom's a fraud" because black freedmen had to work just as hard as when they were slaves, Narcisse replied that freedom does not mean idleness but labor. They all had a responsibility to humankind, she declared, because "neither man nor woman has any right to live in the world without striving to make it better."[27]

In choosing their supporting players, the Hyers Sisters Combination selected the best among the race, names synonymous with achievement:

Wallace King, tenor, and John Luca, baritone; Sam Lucas and Billy Kersands, gifted mirth-makers; James Bland, renowned composer. Other consistent performers were Dora King and Grace Overall, comediennes, Joseph Hagerman, a character actor, and Willie Lyle, a female imperson-ator. In their choice of material the sisters likewise fulfilled their mission. Starting out as classically trained vocalists, they extended their repertoire to include black music such as spirituals, camp songs, and sentimental ballads. Their lyric theatre productions focused on the rapid improvement of the race from slavery to freedom or from the slave cabin to the concert stage, a potential they demonstrated by inviting Blacks from the communities where they appeared to join them on stage during performances.

The Hyers Sisters were apparently the earliest black theatre ensemble to stage a musical set in Africa, a trend that would be frequently emulated by other black companies; nor were the sisters reticent in promoting pro-ductions that were racially integrated when it seemed appropriate to do so. A critic reviewing *Urlina, the African Princess* faulted the sisters for taking themselves too seriously, contending that "dead earnest is not exactly the spirit in which to approach burlesque." The Hyers Sisters, however, sought a higher purpose than that assumed by the flippant critic. A writer in a Chicago newspaper came nearer the truth when he wrote:

> There is an indescribable charm, an originality and feeling of reality about the songs of these dark-skinned artists which is positive relief from the hackneyed rubbish of the bogus, cork-grimed variety man. The music of these vocalists seems to swell up spontaneously from a reservoir of sensibility somewhere near the heart, and makes evident to the listener the fruitfulness of the saying that "those who would make others feel, must feel themselves."[28]

Above all, the Hyers Sisters were models of propriety and discretion, they worked hard, achieved much, and were admired by all with whom they col-laborated. They were truly precursors to black musical theatre in America.

Crossing the continent in search of east coast black drama companies, we find an entry in the *New York Clipper* dated 5 August 1876. It reproduced a bill, first published four years earlier, of the first performance in the city of L'Africaine Dramatic Association. The play offered was John Tobin's romantic comedy *The Honeymoon*, the venue was Pythagoras Hall at 134–136 Canal Street, and the date Monday evening 1 July 1872 at 8 p.m. Managers of "the great event" were Edwin Rupert and John Pendy, who advised the public that their troupe, having had several months of careful preparation, hoped to meet with liberal support from the colored class. A cast composed of eight males and four females, plus extras, made its first appearance and select music was promised, all at a cost of 50 cents admission. The bill concluded with an announcement that the company's next presentation, on 8 July, would be Lytton's *The Lady of Lyons* followed by the farce *A Kiss in the Dark*. Assuming the bill was legitimate, the managers obviously expected to stay in business. However, no further mention of this apparently well-organized troupe appears in the records searched.

Mention of three other productions and their principal participants will draw to a close black theatre events initiated during the 1870s. Two of the three have the distinction of being original compositions, although not enough is known to permit an evaluation of their quality. The third production, however, was that most popular of historical dramas, Shakespeare's *Richard III*. The title role was entrusted to a hotel waiter named Benjamin Ford, founder of a loosely organized New York troupe that would become the basis for the most prominent company on the theatrical scene in the next decade. But first, the originals. On 2 July 1876 the Louisiana Colored Troupe presented at the Third Avenue Theatre in New York the play *Under the Yoke; or, Bond and Free*, written by actor-playwright John S. Ladue. Called at the time "the companion play to *Uncle Tom's Cabin*," the drama was also given in New Haven and revived in May 1888 at the Brooklyn Grand Opera House with a cast of sixty, comprised of both colored and white performers, "including supernumeraries, specialists, banjoists, and jubilee singers."[29] A further revival of the play was announced on 15 March 1890 by the previously mentioned Benjamin Ford, to take place at a city theatre with Miss Maggie Watts of New Bedford supported by a company of amateurs.

John Ladue was born in New York City in 1842. He attended public schools and at age 9 was brought into a production of *Uncle Tom's Cabin* to play the child with whom Eliza escapes by crossing the ice-bound Ohio River. As an actor, Ladue was said to be good at comedy, although showing a penchant for tragedy. Eight years after writing *Bond and Free* he authored another script, *Deceived; or, All Alone*, a play that showed the results of a daughter's disobedience to and deception of her father. This drama, produced at Adelphi Hall in New York on 25 and 26 March 1884, was written for the stage début of Miss Sadie Roselle, with Ladue taking the part of her heartbroken father. A reviewer found the drama to be "a mass of meaningless phrases." Conceding that Ladue himself was a fair actor whose performance as the grieving father was excellent and deserving of high praise, the critic advised Ladue not to direct and act in the same production: "we lay the fact of his failure in this instance at the door of his ambition to encompass too much."³⁰

Less is known of the second original play of the 1870s, which might have been more pageant than drama. It was mentioned in the form of an advertisement in Chicago's *Inter Ocean* newspaper of 11 May 1878, which simply announced that a performance of *Servitude and Freedom* by a troupe of colored dramatic artists was scheduled to take place "this evening" with a matinée on Sunday. Of importance for these two early original theatre pieces is that both addressed the enormity of the task facing some 4 million newly freed Americans. Citizens for little more than a decade, they were supposedly entitled to the rights, responsibilities, and opportunities accorded to all Americans, but they knew in their hearts that such privileges would be a long time coming.

On 8 April 1878 a production of Shakespeare's *Richard III* played at the Lyric Theatre at 723 Sixth Avenue, New York City. Benjamin J. Ford had the title role and Hattie E. Hill was Lady Anne among an all-colored cast. No further mention of Ford or Miss Hill appears in the records searched for the next six years until 1884, although it is more than likely that either or both were actively involved in stage performance in the intervening period. On 5 April 1884 the *New York Globe* reported that John A. Arneaux had joined Benjamin Ford to prepare a production of *Othello* in which Ford would play the Moor and Arneaux, a mulatto from Georgia, would be the implacable Iago. Called the Astor Place Company of Colored Tragedians, the new group planned to open shortly at a city theatre in New York. The Manhattan performance actually occurred at Thompson's Eighth Street Theatre on 30 June, by which time the show had already made its début at the Brooklyn Atheneum. From Eighth Street the production moved to the Cosmopolitan Theatre, giving it, for its time, a reasonably long run in the city. In addition to Arneaux and Ford, other principals in the cast were the octoroon Alice Brooks as Desdemona, Marie Lavere as Emilia, B. C. Devereaux as Cassio, and R. R. Cranvell as Brabantio.³¹

Arneaux was born in 1855 of a Parisian father and a mother "of French descent" who died when he was 12 years old. He attended public and private schools in Georgia before enrolling at the Beach Institute in Savannah, Georgia, from which he graduated after four years' study. He then moved to New York to find a job, but continued to read the classics and began preliminary work in German and Latin. Arneaux then entered the Berlitz School of Languages in Providence, Rhode Island, to study French. Assisted by his father, he enrolled a year later at the Paris Institute, in France, where he completed two courses before returning to the United States to pursue a career in the theatre. He began in vaudeville and at age 21 appeared on the legitimate stage in New York as a southern planter in Ladue's drama *Under the Yoke; or, Bond and Free*. Next, he attempted his first Shakespearian role as Iago in the already mentioned 1884 *Othello* production. He scored an instant success, the *New York World* reporting: "he possesses a keen perception of the cunning and craft necessary to a faithful copy of the accomplished villain. The whole play was Iago, and Mr. Arneaux's interpretation the best and truest in the entire cast."[32]

Buoyed by success in its first effort, the Astor Place Company next presented John Banim's nineteenth-century tragedy *Damon and Pythias* at the Academy of Music in November 1884. For this offering, manager Arneaux (as he had become) was Pythias to Ford's Damon, and had recruited some new talent as supporting players. As Dionysus, John Ladue's performance was declared "the worst of all the kings ever seen on the American stage."[33] The esteemed elocutionist Henrietta Vinton Davis of Washington, DC, played Calanthe, and Belle Martin was Hermion. Arneaux was considered weak in his part. In April 1885 the company produced *Richard III* at the Adelphi Hall, accepted an engagement in Providence, Rhode Island, then returned to join with other drama groups in Manhattan and Brooklyn for a Grand Gala Night of theatre, the details of which remain unknown. In fall 1885, "Arneaux and Company in concert" offered scenes from *Richard III* in which Benjamin Lightfoot was seen as Richmond and Henry VI, and Hattie Williams (née Hill, presumably) returned as Lady Anne. On 10 November the Astor Place Company revived *Othello* at Steinway Hall in the city as a benefit performance for the Grant Memorial Fund. The only significant change from the earlier cast was a different Emilia in the person of Eloise Molineaux.

When Alice Franklin of Middletown, Connecticut, decided to attend the Paris Conservatory to further her acting studies, a testimonial benefit was arranged for her and Arneaux generously agreed to be Romeo to her Juliet. The event took place on 17 May 1886 at the Lyric Hall on Sixth Avenue in New York. Arneaux's gallantry was highly appreciated as Miss Franklin was a newcomer to the professional stage, having made her début in a scene from the play a mere eight months earlier. But of all Shakespeare's heroes and villains, the role Arneaux most enjoyed playing was the crookback Duke of Gloucester who became King Richard III. He had developed an unusual manner of using the character's infirmity to sharpen his roguery, as described in a review published in the *North American*:

His walk, for instance, was something peculiarly his own … its rather flip-pant step was in accordance with his well-sustained theory that Richard was a villain whose humors rapidly changed from wicked to jocose. It was in this spirit of merriment that Mr. Arneaux made Richard take the audience in his confidence by a lightness of phrasing after each of his gravest deeds that showed the insincerity of Richard's good professions. The idea is a novel one and most effective.[34]

Arneaux took the part once more at New York's Lexington Avenue Opera House in October 1886, when Miss Bertie Toney played Lady Anne and Ladue was King Henry. The production was repeated the following January at the Academy of Music in Philadelphia. By this time Arneaux's perfor-mance in the role was being compared favorably with that of Edwin Booth, Lawrence Barrett, and John McCullough, shining lights of the American tragic stage.[35]

Arneaux had been a journalist and a newspaper editor, as well as an actor-manager. He was, however, increasingly drawn to the theatre and early in 1887 announced his intention to retire from the stage for two years of further study. To mark his impending retirement a benefit performance was arranged in which he appeared as Macbeth in scenes with Henrietta Vinton Davis as Lady Macbeth and Thomas Symmons doubling as Macduff and Duncan. This production, billed for 29 April at Clarendon Hall in the city, was supposed to be Arneaux's farewell gesture, but that year he prepared a version of *Richard III* "specially adapted for the drawing-room and rendered less difficult for amateurs to perform." It was published and sold at 25 cents a copy. On 3 January 1888 Arneaux made yet another stage appearance in scenes from *Othello* and *Macbeth* with the support of Hurle Bavardo, a sometime unreliable actor, and Alice Franklin, who had returned from Paris the previous month. This final performance was held at the Wilson Post Hall in Baltimore.

A report in the *Cleveland Gazette* of 14 April 1888 indicated that Arneaux "had been suffering the past year from vertigo" and had gone to Canada for a change of climate. He still wrote for various newspapers and planned to remain in Montreal until midyear, when he would return to New York to prepare for his trip to France. Once there he intended to devote himself to the study of languages and the drama. Arneaux apparently did travel to Paris later in the year, but little is known of his activities there, nor was any record found of his return to America. For a period of some ten years John A. Arneaux had joined and energized the activities of para-professional black actors in New York and nearby states. Being well educated and articulate, he instilled their efforts with a panache that filtered through the ranks of players. His predilection for Shakespeare encouraged others to match his ability by seeking to understand and speak the Shakespearian lines with forceful intelligence. Arneaux's willingness to work with less experienced actors would be missed when he left America and apparently retired from the theatre. Although he was still in Paris a decade later, no record of further stage appearances, either in France or America, has been traced.

Further mention may be made at this point of Benjamin J. Ford with whom Arneaux first collaborated when he launched his whirlwind career in New York. Ford remained in the shadows as Arneaux stole the limelight, but in May 1889 he turned up in Albany, New York, where for the next three years at least he appeared in several dramas with a company of amateurs. A listing of play titles and dates of production should do him justice: *Don Caesar de Bazin* in May 1889 for the benefit of the AME Church; Ladue's *Under the Yoke* in March 1890; *Deception* by "a San Francisco lady" in September 1890; *Ingomar* at Albany's Academy of Music in March 1891 to benefit the Afro-American League; and finally *Damon and Pythias* at Bleecker Hall in November 1891, as the annual entertainment of the Abraham Lincoln Lodge.

The 1880s showed a marked increase in dramatic activity among African Americans. This increase was partly due to continued production efforts by earlier theatre companies, both amateur and professional. There was also a healthy number of newly formed groups, an increase of new black playwrights, and a growing cadre of actors and elocutionists who sought professional stage careers. Of some eighty-six recorded productions by African American troupes during the decade, about one-third were devoted to Shakespeare, mostly *Richard III* and *Othello*.[36] Another forty productions were of plays written mostly by white nineteenth-century dramatists and some twenty by black writers. Ten additional plays written by Blacks but not produced help to increase the total number of new playscripts by African Americans to thirty for the decade under review.

While it is not possible, in the absence of scripts, to assess the quality of these plays,[37] brief comments on a select few will serve to introduce the authors and suggest the range of topic and type of treatment covered in new black plays of this period. In 1880, Powhatan Beaty of Cincinnati, Ohio, a decorated Civil War veteran, wrote *Delmar; or, Scenes in Southland*, which he staged privately and successfully in January 1881 with himself in the title role of a rich southern planter, old Delmar. The action takes place in the years 1860 to 1875, a critical period for Blacks in transition from slavery to freedom, with scenes in Kentucky, Mississippi, and Massachusetts. A newspaper comment prior to staging found that the script "abounds in fine, dramatic situations," but lacking a review of the actual production it is not possible to confirm this impression. As an actor, Beaty had been an impressive Spartacus, the Roman slave in Robert Montgomery Bird's blank-verse melodrama *The Gladiator*. He had also performed with the talented Henrietta Vinton Davis in Cincinnati, Washington, DC, and in Philadelphia. In 1888 Beaty became the drama director of the Literary and Dramatic Club of Cincinnati, which he had helped to form.

A. A. Anderson of Kansas City had a minor part in a traveling production of *Richard III* when he came to New York in 1885 as a mere 20-year-old. He had with him a script of his play *Gio, the Tyrian Armorer*, which he hoped to put in rehearsal. Set in the year 340 BC on the island of Tyre, the drama told of Gio, king of Egypt, who traveled to Tyre disguised as an armorer to search for his daughter. She had been stolen away by a Tyrian prince intent on making her his wife. Having found his daughter, Gio is caught escaping with her and sentenced to death. He appeals to the gods for justice and is saved by the oracle of Hercules. Gio then leads a revolt against the tyrant king of Tyre and his son; they are defeated and the people of Tyre hail Gio as their new sovereign.

Anderson recruited a cast with himself as Gio and Alice Franklin as the Princess Marino. Rehearsals were problematic; Anderson complained of lack of cooperation and cancelled them. Then he announced a preview performance of the first three acts of *Gio* to take place at the Lyric Hall on Sixth Avenue on 31 May 1888. He may well have been hoping to impress a potential sponsor for the show. If so, nothing came of his strategy and his name drops from the records. Anderson had previously shown himself to be short-tempered. A year after he arrived in New York he produced the highly favored play *The Lady of Lyons* at Chickering Hall in December 1886, having cast himself as the leading male character, Claude Melnotte. Attendance on opening night was disappointing and once the play began, Anderson became so incensed at the low turnout that he stopped the show and berated the audience for their lack of support.

Louise A. Smith and Emma Hatcher were two playwrights of very different skill. Smith, hailing from the nation's capital in the District of Columbia, was a teacher and practiced writer. Several plays are attributed to her, including *The Little Mountain Fairies*, a children's play in prose and verse that she produced in Chickering Hall, New York, on 23 December 1887. On the same bill with this production were two scenes from her more recent piece, *The East Indian Princess*. Smith also wrote *Zilla, the Gypsy Queen*, which was presented at Newport, Rhode Island, to a crowded house in September 1889 and revived by the Providence Ideal Dramatic Company on 4 December. By this time Smith had apparently married and relocated, for the play was attributed to Mrs. Louise Mars of Providence, Rhode Island. One review in the *New York Age* referred to her as "the talented dramatic writer" whose plays were "creditable in the extreme."[38]

Emma Hatcher came originally from Sonora, Mexico, where she was known as Ogarita Honrodez. She acquired the name Hatcher from an estranged husband. Orphaned as a child, Emma was raised by "a colored lady" from Louisville, Kentucky, with whom she resided long enough to be considered native to that state. She was still in her teens when in 1887 she made her stage début as a reader and received an ovation. A year later she had not only expanded her repertoire to standard plays such as *Ingomar, the Barbarian*, in which she appeared as Parthenia and surprised audiences with her "rare dramatic power... and a voice sweet and sympathetic", but had also written and appeared in her own play *Lizette*, "a sparkling domestic drama" that was presented by a company of mostly white actors. At the time of the report the production was playing in Iowa on its way to the eastern states. A contributor to the *New York Age* wrote of Miss Hatcher: "The lady is young, untiring and ambitious, most conscientious in her work and a favorite artistically and socially wherever she goes. One can safely predict for her a most brilliant future."[39] Despite this welcoming introduction, Emma Hatcher soon vanished from the records that are available to us today.

Soldier, pastor, journalist, lawyer, legislator, and activist against the colonization of the Congo Free States, George Washington Williams in a relatively short life still found the time to write a morality play, entitled *Panda*, on the subject of slavery. The plot is straightforward in its simplicity. A raiding party in Africa has seized the royal family of an African court and shipped them to America. These formerly privileged Africans are suddenly thrust into the most humiliating conditions, first aboard ship and then on a plantation, where they experience all the suffering and indignity of slave life. "The objective," wrote the author, "is to present the horrors of slavery as it existed before the [Civil] War."[40] What story line was chosen to present these horrors remains unknown for no copy of the playscript has surfaced, nor a record of its production. When Williams died in 1891 in Blackpool, England, he was just 41 years old.

Another playwright, Robert E. Ford, went to the Old Testament for the source of his so-called historical drama *Ham, the Accursed*. In this play the author aimed to show that the curse placed on Ham by his father, Noah, was the cause of his wife's desertion and the discovery of her infidelity, from which Ham fled to Africa with his son, Nimrod. His elder brother, Shem, had promised that when the world became peopled again (after the Flood), Ham would be remembered. After many years Shem fulfills his promise by relating Ham's story to his niece, the beautiful Dimonah, and permitting her to go in search of her uncle. In her travels she encounters Nimrod, who brings her to Ham, and the two are married. Reconciliation and the ability to make a fresh start are important reminders for people torn from their native land and forced into servitude, owning nothing but the skin on their backs. The drama, consisting of five acts, was written "in the heroic measure."[41]

The next two plays were apparently written in the comic vein. Little is known of their plots or treatment beyond the bare essentials. In April 1886 Professor John P. Sampson, an American Methodist Episcopal churchman, lecturer, and writer from Hightstown, New Jersey, produced a play entitled *The Disappointed Bride; or, Love at First Sight* at the Opera House, with a repeat performance at a public hall. Apart from the terse comment that the play produced "quite a sensation, eliciting highest praise" from the audience, and the fact that it was not only staged publicly but also published by the Hampton Institute, Virginia, its merit as comedy remains unknown. The other writer of comedy was C. W. Anderson, a *New York Age* drama critic whose pen name was "The Rounder." Anderson had already dramatized several popular novels for amateur performance and his "new and original comedy in four acts entitled *A Stranger at Home*," completed in September 1888, was being readied for touring. Anderson came originally from Oxford, Ohio, and was well-educated. He read, wrote, and spoke French and German fluently and was considered to be somewhat severe in his criticism of "colored artists," yet in so doing he felt he had, arguably, elevated the standard of art among African Americans.[42]

The news of Ira Aldridge's death in Poland and the record of his achievement as an actor reached the American black community slowly. When it did, several amateur groups sought to honor his memory by adopting his name for their companies. In the late nineteenth century Aldridge-titled troupes existed in Washington, DC, in Philadelphia, and in New Haven, their respective productions at the time being an adaptation of Kotzebue's *Pizarro* by Sheridan in 1883, *School* by Tom Robertson in 1885, and George

Baker's *Comrades* in 1889. The practice of naming groups after Aldridge continued into the early twentieth century, with amateur companies in Harlem, St. Louis, and Baltimore respectively. In 1920 a playhouse in Oklahoma City was called the Aldridge Theatre.

No less than six other early African American troupes have honored theatre notables by adopting their names. One chose the British actor Henry Irving, who, in reply to an 1884 request from a New York group, was pleased to permit the use of his name by their dramatic club. Their inaugural production that year was Charles Mathews' comedy, *Married for Money*. Another individual, long dead, whose name was appropriated for naming three groups was the French playwright Alexandre Dumas, *père*, who, unlike Irving, was a man of color. In 1886 the Dumas Company of Louisville, Kentucky, staged *The Rough Diamond* and *Above the Clouds* in separate productions and the next year announced *Broken Ties* as their forthcoming play. Then, in 1902, the Dumas Dramatic Club of St. Louis, Missouri, produced the melodrama *Bound by an Oath* at the Fourteenth Street Theatre on 21 April. As late as 1916 the Settlement House started by the Jelliffes in Cleveland (and later renamed Karamu House) sponsored the Dumas Players before a name change to the Gilpin Players in 1922, when they were visited by the actor Charles Gilpin (1878–1930), who was then at the height of his powers. Finally, in Louisville, the Booth–Barrett Amateurs honored two American tragedians and actor-managers, Edwin Booth and Lawrence Barrett. They had often worked together and were respectful of each other's talent, even alternating the roles of Othello and Iago at the Booth Theatre in 1872. In 1888 this amateur company announced an ambitious production program that included *Richard III*, *Othello*, *Macbeth*, and Bulwer-Lytton's *Richelieu*, but no record of performance, presuming one did occur, has survived.

In its issue of 2 January 1887 the New York *World* carried a long essay under the caption "Our Colored Star Actors" and signed "Gloster." It was most likely written by the actor John Arneaux, whose favorite role, I recalled earlier, was Richard III, former Duke of Gloucester. Black-and-white sketches accompanied each of the eight actors profiled in the article, among whom were, in alphabetical order: Arneaux himself, then Hurle Bavardo, Henrietta Vinton Davis, Alice Franklin, Martin Henderson, John Ladue, Henri Strange, and Charles Winter Wood. From this list, I have already introduced and summarized the careers of Arneaux and Ladue. Bavardo and Henderson were of little consequence as time progressed, the former being increasingly unreliable on stage and the latter appearing but seldom.

Within a short time after she returned from training in Paris, France, Alice Franklin appeared briefly in Baltimore, then traveled to Kingston, Jamaica, in June 1890 to join the Tennessee Jubilee Concert Company. In August she returned from Kingston thoroughly discouraged and claiming that the climate was not congenial. By 19 September 1891 the *New York Age* reported that Miss Franklin tried to make a living in the theatre "but became disgusted with the precarious nature of the work" and had abandoned the field. Of the eight star actors originally named, only Davis, Strange, and Wood remain for further report.[43]

Henrietta Vinton Davis was probably the premier actor of all nineteenth-century black performers on the dramatic stage, yet she was denied the opportunity to fulfill her enormous potential. Eventually she abandoned the theatre to become a political activist, leaving her country poorer for the waste of her singular talent. She was born in Baltimore, Maryland, in 1860. Her father was a gifted musician, who died during her infancy. She attended school in Washington, DC, graduated at age 15, then passed the required examination and became a teacher, first in Maryland then in Louisiana. But with an ailing mother, Miss Davis returned to Washington to be near her and took a job as copyist in the office of the Recorder of Deeds. From an early age she had shown an aptitude for elocution and now decided to prepare for a career in the theatre.

She began serious studies with reputable teachers in Washington and New York, rounding off her training with a spell at the Boston School of Oratory. Her début as a public reciter occurred at Marini's Hall in Washington, DC, on 25 April 1883, when she was introduced by one of the finest public speakers of the age, the incomparable Frederick Douglass, under whom she worked in the Recorder's Office. According to the local newspaper, her performance was a complete success: "from the time she said her first line to the close of the last sentence, she wrapped the whole audience so close to her that she became a queen of the stage in their eyes ... she will in due season become our star on the stage of tragedy and the drama."[44]

Miss Davis acquired professional managers and arranged a touring schedule that began in Boston and covered towns and cities in the eastern states. She electrified audiences with her acting and was applauded "to the very echo." Her programs included appropriate speeches from Shakespeare's women – Rosalind, Juliet, Lady Macbeth, and Cleopatra – as well as scenes involving another actor or actors, in such plays as *Richard III* and *Ingomar, the Barbarian*. In a scene from the latter play when Ingomar, played by Powhatan Beaty arrayed in a wolf-skin lap robe, "cast himself at the feet of

Parthenia and in heavy tones implored her to tell him what love was like, there wasn't a dry eye in the house."[45] For the next ten years Miss Davis presented concert performances to an ever-widening circuit of cities, touring the south and west in addition to eastern states. A mostly white audience in Evansville, Illinois, was held "spellbound" by her dramatic truthfulness; the Goldsboro *Argus* of North Carolina considered her "the greatest living genius of her race." Calls were renewed for her to be accepted into a regular company presenting Shakespeare and other dramatic classics; all in vain.

In a career that spanned well over thirty years, Miss Davis appeared in only four full-length dramas and one pageant. One of the dramas was a touring production and two were later revived, each for a single performance. The first complete play in which she participated was the perennial nineteenth-century favorite *Damon and Pythias*. It was staged by the Astor Place Company in November 1884, some eighteen months after Miss Davis' professional début, and was a rather indifferent production that did not improve the reputations of its principal players. Her next full-fledged production occurred nine years later. She had by then separated from an abusive husband and gone to live in Chicago, where, in 1893, the World's Columbian Exposition (or World Fair) was being held. Because the managers had at first deliberately excluded American Blacks from planning or presenting anything at the fair,[46] Miss Davis privately staged and performed in a production of an original play, *Dessalines*, written by William Easton about the black Haitian emperor. Years later, in 1912, she would also direct and act in Easton's companion drama on the next Haitian monarch, *Henri Christophe*. In the period between these two productions, she collaborated on writing and staging a Civil War drama, *Our Old Kentucky Home* (1898), and went to Indianapolis to participate in Charles Sager's pageant *The Negro*. These productions will be discussed in a succeeding chapter. Most notable is that, at the close of the nineteenth century and beyond, for the leading black actress in America to secure a major stage appearance in reputable plays of her race, she had either to direct the plays herself and act in them, or help to write and direct the plays as well as to take a major role. With such limited access to full-scale dramatic productions, Miss Davis can be forgiven for seeking other avenues in which to make her mark.

Since the days when she clerked for Frederick Douglass, Miss Davis had been interested in politics. Later she supported the Populist Party and offered to lecture on its behalf. In 1912–13 she traveled to parts of Central America and the Caribbean to give readings and assist in benevolent social work with the local populace. She joined and held important offices in the

Universal Negro Improvement Association founded by Marcus Garvey in New York in 1917, and traveled to Jamaica and Liberia on its behalf. Her work with the movement spanned twelve years and included a pageant entitled *Ethiopia at the Bar of Justice* by the Reverend Edward McCoo, which she staged in December 1927 at the Ward Theatre in Kingston, Jamaica.

R. Henri Strange was one of the actors to be classed a "star" in the 1880s. He was born a Virginian in 1860, but his parents, seeking better educational advantages, chose to settle in Philadelphia, where he was educated. In 1880 he became valedictorian of his high school class. He had evinced a talent for elocution and on leaving school began to study for the stage under a retired actor named Kelly. He next attended the National School of Elocution in Philadelphia and graduated with honors. By January 1887, when he was "an exceptionally good Richmond" to Arneaux's Richard III at the Academy of Music, he had appeared in a number of different roles. During that year's summer he initiated an annual tour of the Jersey coast, offering Othello to the Iago of B. Franklin Webb at Atlantic City, his Desdemona being Hélène Gorham. His performance was considered to be "a very fine piece of work in all its parts," one which won much applause from audiences. Fourteen years later his summer company was still very active.

Over the years Strange added the characters of Hamlet, Macbeth, Shylock, and Cassius (in *Julius Caesar*) to his repertoire, and also appeared in leading roles, in an English version of Victor Hugo's popular *Ruy Blas* and in *The Lady of Lyons*. For his concert appearances, he prepared the poems of Paul Laurence Dunbar, which he included on his program to the delight of audiences. In 1911 he was assigned the role of King Meneleh in the Williams and Walker musical comedy *Abyssinia*, and in 1912 he took the title role in Henrietta Vinton Davis' production of *Henri Christophe*. In a professional career spanning more than a quarter of a century, wrote a contemporary columnist, R. Henri, Strange "has done more than any one man to develop [this] city's taste for the classical drama"; on the concert stage he "stands without a rival."[47]

A tale of uncommon originality surrounds the emergence of Charles Winter Wood as actor and college teacher.[48] Wood was born in Nashville, Tennessee, in 1870, moved with his widowed mother to Chicago at age 9, and shined shoes for a living. When one of his clients heard him mumbling Shakespeare's lines and challenged him to recite the ghost scene from *Hamlet* for a few friends, they were so impressed with his performance that they made arrangements for him to receive training in elocution. By 1886, at age 16, he had organized a company and presented Shakespeare's *Othello* and

Richard III at the Madison Street Theatre and at Freiberg's Opera House in
Chicago, receiving favorable reviews for his performances in the title roles.
Partnered in these shows by Ada O. Brown, Wood took his company on a
tour of theatres in the area, garnering press notices that referred to him as
"the distinguished boy tragedian of Chicago." Eventually, a wealthy Chicago
businessman, at whose home Wood had given a reading, offered to send him
to college after the necessary preparatory schooling. Wood entered Beloit
College in 1891 and graduated in 1895 with a bachelor's degree in Greek, the
college having at that time an outstanding program of annual productions
of Greek plays in English translation. In college Wood had appeared as
Heracles in *The Alcestis* and as the king in *Oedipus Rex*. His performance in
the latter role was "greeted with tears as well as with bursts of applause."

In accord with his sponsor's expressed wish, Wood next attended the
Chicago Theological Seminary and gained a doctorate in divinity. He became a college professor at Booker T. Washington's Tuskegee Institute,
where he taught English, drama, and public speaking, and where he directed
the Tuskegee Players. During his tenure at Tuskegee he traveled regularly,
giving speeches and recitals on behalf of the institute. In his appearances he
incorporated southern folktales as well as passages from Shakespeare, billing
himself as "the celebrated impersonator, humorist, orator and scholar." Once
in the 1930s, while still employed as a college professor, he was called upon
to understudy the lead in an important new black play on Broadway, to be
discussed later. At the end of this assignment he returned to teaching at
Tuskegee, then moved to Bennett College in North Carolina, and finally
to Florida Agricultural and Mechanical College, where a newly built theatre was named after him. Wood devoted the latter years of his career to
organizing and developing dramatic clubs in southern black colleges in con-
junction with Professor Randolph Edmonds and others. His professional
teaching and acting career, which spanned more than fifty years, came to
an end with retirement in 1949, followed by his death four years later at his
home in Queens, New York.

As the century entered its closing decade, the involvement of African
Americans in the theatre as a profession could no longer be officially ignored.
For the first time the national decennial census included Blacks in the performing arts, the enumeration for 1890 showing 1,881 musicians and music
teachers, 1,310 showmen and theatrical managers, but only 180 designated as
actors,[49] probably because most straight actors held second jobs that could
provide a living wage when they were "resting" between shows. Nevertheless, the decade witnessed giant strides toward confirming the view that in

theatre, no less than in other forms of endeavor, Blacks were determined to play their part. The long-reigning dominance of blackface minstrelsy was losing ground and would eventually be replaced by an exemplary array of authentic black actors, dancers, singers, and musicians of quality, authors and composers both creative and skillful, company managers, and even by an attempt to displace the virtual white monopoly in booking shows at theatres across the country. In fact, shows would be presented in a greater variety than hitherto, resulting in a concomitant search for new skills and a proliferation of specialty acts by individuals or teams of duos, trios, or quartets.

The demand for new and different kinds of talent meant that performers were constantly on the move, frequently inventing new acts, seeking more advantageous contracts, and hoping to gain wide exposure, including visits to countries overseas. They traveled to Britain and Europe as expected, to the Caribbean and South America as hitherto, but also journeyed to Russia and Scandinavia, and as far away as Hawaii, Australia, New Zealand, and the Far East. Blackface minstrelsy might be losing ground but some features of plantation life were being reintroduced by Blacks as showbiz items in a cavalier exploitation of the slave experience. In particular, the 1890s brought to theatrical prominence several specific types of slave entertainment: the singing of traditional Negro spirituals and of musically arranged spirituals called "jubilees";[50] the buck-and-wing dance; the cakewalk strutting contest; and, finally, the composition and performance of "coon [raccoon] songs." Indeed, the apparent currency accorded the term *coon* by most of the leading black entertainers of the period requires and will receive further explanation.[51]

In 1890 manager Sam T. Jack, acting on a suggestion from minstrel-turned-vaudevillian Sam Lucas, installed a small group of veteran black performers as an added attraction to one of his regular white road companies. The new addition proved to be so popular with audiences that the manager decided to expand the group to a full-scale company offering burlesque entertainment that featured lavishly costumed black women in lead roles, supported by other talented male and female troupers. Manager Jack called the combination *The Creole Show*; he took charge of business and finance and was content to leave the show's conception, production, and staging to Lucas. It turned out to be transitional, following the conventional minstrel format of three distinct parts comprised of an introductory semicircle but with a smartly attired female chorus at center and a female interlocutor. The olio consisted of specialty acts by various song-and-dance performers.

The finale might be an original sketch or a company dance number. Thus, opportunities were offered to composers, choreographers, and writers of short comic sketches to contribute original material that would usually be introduced at the start of each season.

The Creole Show premiered in Haverhill, Massachusetts, then played briefly at the Howard Theatre in Boston prior to opening at Proctor's Theatre in New York City on 25 August. In the second year the show opened in Chicago and toured vaudeville houses across the country, becoming noted during its run for the outstanding theatre artists it employed, such as Bob Cole and Stella Wiley, Charles Johnson and Laura Dean, Tom and Hattie McIntosh, Billy and Cordelia McClain, the Mallory Brothers, and many others. "The first-third of the 1890s was one of the most dynamic periods in the history of black entertainment," wrote Henry T. Sampson, "and it set the stage for the revolution in black music and dance that was to come in the remaining part of this decade."[52] Having an open format that allowed for a variety of performing talent, featuring a finely dressed female chorus, and playing for seven successive years, *The Creole Show* had a major influence on the black musical theatre of the early twentieth century. It did not replace blackface minstrelsy – it would be a long time before something did that – but it did offer alternatives to the tiresome caricature of black folk, while its chorus of vivacious colored beauties opened possibilities for bigger and brighter black musical comedy productions in the years ahead. *The Creole Show* eventually closed in 1897 and within two years manager Sam Jack had died from a liver ailment. He was 46 years old.

4

American minstrelsy in black and white

James V. Hatch

Wheel about and turn about
An' do jist so –
An' ebery time I wheel about
I jump Jim Crow ...

The weave of racial cultures

From an embryonic performance at New York's Bowery Amphitheater in 1843, minstrelsy blossomed into the nation's first popular entertainment, developing from one evening's improvisation by four white men into a thriving business for hundreds of companies, black and white. Beginning as a working-class recreation, minstrelsy's jokes, dance, and music eventually entertained all classes, including American presidents, British royalty, and Indian rajahs. Its resonance echoes around the world today. Evidence suggests that minstrelsy's origins were mostly African American and Irish.

Even before the war of 1812 many Irish had fled English persecution, although it was between 1845 and 1849 that 1–1.5 million potato famine refugees arrived in Boston, Baltimore, New York, and traveled as far inland as California. Suffering poverty and discrimination, the Irish found themselves living in urban slums with Blacks, some of whom had come from the Caribbean but most of whom were either northern freedmen or "contraband slaves" escaped from the South. Blacks and Irish shared a love of music, dance, and verbal virtuosity. The Irish soon appropriated black music and dance, and Blacks returned the compliment by learning to jig and to sing Irish songs.[1] To cite a single example: Lafcadio Hearn, an American journalist of Irish-Greek heritage, in the 1870s wrote a series of newspaper articles on Cincinnati's Bucktown, a rough district of Irish and Blacks who worked on the levees and riverboats. Hearn's descriptions of random performances at Pickett's Tavern detail intimate exchanges between the two groups. Black singers mimicked the Irish accent "to a degree of perfection." Hearn witnessed African Americans dancing jigs and Irish dancing break- downs. Showman Leni Sloan in an interview in 1982 claimed that even after one hundred years, "It is impossible to know where the Irish leaves off and the African actually begins. Or vice-versa... Afro-Ibernian!"[2]

The commercial origins of blackface minstrelsy are precisely placed. On 6 February 1843 the Virginia Minstrels – Billy Whitlock on banjo, Dan Emmett on fiddle, Frank Pelham on tambourine, and Frank Brower on bones, each of whom were experienced blackfaced circus clowns – came together for the first time to present a full evening's entertainment. Naming themselves "minstrels" (possibly after the successful 1839 tour of the Tyrolese Minstrel Family[3]), and dishonestly "Virginia," they suggested that their ma- terial was "real southern Negro." In choosing the name Virginia Minstrels, the group piggybacked upon the success of earlier "Virginny" farces and comedies.[4] These shows had given a total of 308 blackface performances in New York City before the Virginia Minstrels premiered with their jumble of songs, banjo solos, jigs, and jokes. In 1846 Edward P. Christy brought order out of the chaos by developing the three-part minstrel pattern with two blackface end-men and a central white interlocutor, but initially on that first evening, all four men functioned as interlocutors and as end-men. The evening's raucous chaos delighted its audience.

What did early minstrel performances look like?[5] Newspaper engravings portray a semicircle of white males, their faces black, their eyes and mouths outlined in white, red, or both. Trousers were striped or checkered, as were their vests and jackets. Tattered straw hats, if they had them, were perched uncertainly on their woolly wigs. In the center of the ensemble sat Mr. Interlocutor, elegantly attired, often in a tuxedo and top hat. As master of ceremonies in the English music hall style, Mr. Interlocutor served as the straight man to the jokes and horseplay of the end-men, who were costumed theatrically as plantation "darkies." Tambo sat stage right with his tambourine and stage left with his rhythm-clacking ribs sat Bones.

The troupe would march on to the stage, perhaps singing a lively Stephen Foster tune – "Oh! Susanna"(1847) or "Ring, Ring the Banjo" (1851) – and parade around the chairs arranged in a semicircle until Mr. Interlocutor commanded, "Gentlemen, be seated." Part one might feature a jig later called a *breakdown*, followed by a sentimental ballad, all interspersed with rapid repartee, riddles, and jokes between the end-men and interlocutor. The first section might end with the banjo and bones playing "Dixie" for a "walk around" by the entire company, in which each member performed his specialty, much as a jazz band might give a chorus to its musicians. This feature of the show may well have been inspired by slaves singing and dancing the African ring-shout, which also moved counterclockwise and in which individual dancers were challenged to display their special steps.

Thomas W. Talley recalled the African ring-shout from his boyhood in Tennessee:

> Usually one or two individuals "star" danced at a time [took center stage for solo performance]. The others of the crowd (which was usually large) formed a circle [and] repeated the Rhyme, clapping their hands together, and patting their feet in rhythmic time with these words. It was the task of the dancers in the middle of the circle to execute some graceful dance in such a manner that their feet would beat a tattoo upon the ground answering to every word [of the song], and sometimes to every syllable of the Rhyme. There were many such Rhymes. "Possum up the Gum Stump" and "Jawbone."[6]

The circle or challenge dance that Talley had observed was similar to that described in the nineteenth century by G. W. Cable, who, along with other writers, witnessed the dancing in Congo Square, New Orleans. By the 1840s Whites had observed not only plantation ring-shouts but also similar dances at Pinkster as well as Governors Election Day celebrations in New York State and New England.

Part two of the minstrel show was called an *olio*, which might either feature a man dressed as a "wench," sporting wig, bustle, and skirts, or as a professor or doctor, replete with pince-nez. Sprinkled with malapropisms, and delivered in a "darky" dialect, the lecture might burlesque suffragettes, doctors, lawyers, professors, or politicians, all those the working class perceived as exploiters. The minstrel man doubled the fun by assuming the personae of Blacks and women, thereby, seemingly, making his victims mock themselves. After the olio came part three, a sketch or short one-act play, often a burlesque of an opera or a Shakespearian tragedy. It closed the show. All this for an admission of 25 or 50 cents, perhaps one-third of a day's wages for a working man.

Following the Virginia Minstrels' début, minstrels multiplied into some hundred professional troupes whose company members might number six, twelve, fifteen, or twenty. After the Civil War, black or white company members might number eighty or a hundred. Over the decades the songs and dances changed radically. From the 1870s onward, acrobats, dog shows, and all sorts of specialty acts crept into minstrelsy. As early as the 1870s women joined men on stage, and minstrelsy drifted into burlesque, variety shows, and revues.

In the early nineteenth century American audiences had welcomed several new types of comedy character to the stage: frontiersmen, Native Americans, riverboatmen, Broadway b'hoys, New England Yankees – all speaking regional dialects, all with idiosyncrasies peculiar to their ethnicity, occupations, and geography. Dale Cockrell in his study *Demons of Disorder: Early Blackface Minstrels and their World* states that long before the first performance of the Virginia Minstrels, an estimated twenty-five hundred blackface presentations, legitimate and otherwise, preceded minstrelsy. They ranged from comedies and lampoons to dramas. Leading the list was *Othello*, with 425 presentations.[7] Cockrell, along with William Mahar, suggests that in the early days blackfaced characters may not have been caricatures of African Americans, but simply clowns of various sorts.[8] Perhaps. The long and convoluted use of blackface on the English stage from medieval Christmas pageants, through the Elizabethan revenge tragedies, and then the Harlequins and Fridays of the pantomimes, cannot be taken up here. However, it is fairly clear that after two hundred years of black slavery, American eyes no longer looked upon a white actor in blackface without beholding a "darky."

By the 1850s half the population of Pittsburgh had been born abroad. The white poor of Europe flooded into New York, the city where black-cork minstrelsy began. Slum housing, disease, despicable wages, all justified the immigrant poor in naming themselves "wage slaves."[9] These Whites sought to escape their misery, some in evangelical religion, some in alcohol, others in minstrel laughter, music, and mockery. In the flush of this stimulant, the immigrant's status was lightened by the knowledge that he was "free, White, and twenty-one."

Still burning in the memory of New Yorkers was the 1791 Haitian revolution, which had brought Creoles, declassé aristocrats, and former slave-owners to New York City. By 1824 twenty branches of the American Colonization Society (founded in 1816 by white Presbyterian ministers) had been formed to send Blacks back to Africa. The 1822 conspiracy of Denmark Vesey and the 1831 revolt of Nat Turner threatened white power, but in those same years a series of slave narratives describing whippings, rape, and black families torn apart at the auction block, propelled the anti-slavery movement.[10] Led by the verbal militancy of William Lloyd Garrison of the *Liberator* (1832–65), abolitionists demanded the end of slavery in all the states. In 1827 New York State manumitted its slaves. Black freedom scared Whites, especially the poor, whose jobs were already insecure. In 1834 Whites carried their fears onto New York City streets, erupting into three days of rioting, burning the homes of white and black abolitionists. The *Washington (DC) Telegraph* offered the opinion that the violence had occurred "in consequence of the competition between the free white labor and the black labor of the North." The depression of 1837, exacerbated by sweatshops with their concomitant breakdown of the apprenticeship system, fueled the disorder.[11] While abolitionists had increased public awareness of slavery's abuses, many working people preferred the alternate, sentimental version provided by minstrelsy – Blacks were happy in bondage.

The living incarnation of this myth was Thomas Dartmouth "Daddy" Rice (1808–60), a dancing demon who "jumped Jim Crow" at the Bowery Theatre. An 1833 etching pictures Jim Crow, a blackfaced prancing tatterde-malion holding one hand to his hip while waving the other in the air, as he kicks with his left foot while balancing on his right foot, which peeks from the toe of his wornout shoe. As he "jumps" like a crippled bird, he sings, "Wheel about and turn about / An' do jist so – / An' ebery time I wheel about / I jump Jim Crow." The stage is jammed with men, hardly allowing room for Rice to dance. For two hours working-class males vicariously en-joyed Jim Crow's insouciance, singing his version of "I got Plenty of Nothin' and Nothin' is Plenty for Me," while at the same time they themselves en-dured ten- and twelve-hour shifts for pittance wages. The audience was able to embrace this contradiction only because Daddy Rice was white. Had he been a Black, the audience would have resented him. From ignorance and fear, the white self-designated "wage slave" had joined the southerner in opposing abolition, and Jim Crow soon had become generic for the social and economic segregation of Blacks.

For a time minstrelsy's foot-tapping vigor, the moist tear evoked by the ballads, the cracking skill of its dancers, the wit of its comics absorbed and perhaps redirected the raw passions of racism. To populist delight, the masked demons derided women, sassed the government, and ridiculed the art, music, speech, and dress of the upper classes. The wedding of blackfaced performer and audience was a love match based on social passions not fully understood but deeply felt by both partners.

What was the white hunger for performing blackness? Eric Lott, minstrel historian, named two powerful forces – "love and theft." He could have added "fear."[12] Lott's reexamination of minstrelsy, *Love and Theft*, raised the question: what was stolen and by whom? Some preferred to let sleeping dogs lie, for what was to be gained by pawing through the old racist bones? Others were intent upon identifying those unique qualities that Africans had brought to American theatre, an entertainment that was not solely a European creation. Black energy and talent had infused it from minstrelsy's first days, so it is necessary at this point to look briefly at the origins of minstrelsy's music, song, verbal virtuosity, and, of course, dance.

One of the prime specialty acts of the minstrel show were the English and Irish jig or clog dances usually performed in straight lines with the back and shoulders rigid, the hips straight forward with heel and toe, bringing the shoe into percussion with the floor. However, as has already been shown, Americans had observed Africans dancing in a very different style – crouching, bending the knees, rolling the hips and shoulders, the gliding shuffle in the ring-shout with bare feet flat to the ground. Dance historian Brenda Dixon Gottschild notes that the Irish jig and the West African *gioube* mutated into minstrel juba dancing.

> It is a fused Afro-Irish jig in which the Irish influence was absorbed and transformed into an Africanist context, so much so that soon the jig became associated primarily with African Americans... The jig became so closely associated with Africanist expressive forms that early twentieth-century white rural carnivals... had a segregated section for African American performers call the "jig top."[13]

Indeed, Blacks performed the dances so well that "jigaboo" became an opprobrium for "Negro." Blacks danced in parks, saloons, brothels, in streets around the "Old Brewery," a cruel New York City tenement, and at Five Points, which housed hundreds of poor Irish and Blacks. The first black dancer to be widely recognized and the greatest to emerge from Five Points was William Henry Lane, who was known professionally as Juba. Born *circa* 1825, at the age of 14 Juba began dancing for his supper – a dish of fried eel and ale. He "had supposedly learned much of his art from Uncle Jim Lowe, a Negro and reel dancer of exceptional skill."[14] Juba danced and played tambourine with the Georgia Champion Minstrels and had several engagements with Charley White's Minstrels in New York. Charles Dickens, the English novelist, on his visit to America made a special trip to Five Points to see Juba, and his description published in *American Notes* (1842) caught something of Juba's skill.

> Single shuffle, double shuffle, cut and cross-cut; snapping his fingers, rolling his eyes, turning his knees, presenting the backs of his legs in front, spinning about on toes and heels like nothing but the man's fingers on the tambourine; dancing with two left legs, two right legs, two wooden legs, two wire legs, two spring legs – all sorts of legs and no legs – *what is this to him?* (emphasis added)

Dickens' comment "what is this to him?" suggests Lane demonstrated "cool," the African trait of grace under pressure. By 1845, newspapers had crowned Master Juba the best in the profession. He received top billing over four white minstrel men, an unprecedented distinction. Lane's mastery was described on a handbill: "Master Juba's Imitation Dance in which he will give correct Imitation dances of all the principal Ethiopian [blackface] Dancers in the United States. After which he will give an imitation of himself."[15]

The reader will recall that actor James Hewlett, too, was lauded for his impersonations as well as for his stunning sense of humor when confronted with jeopardy in court. The quality, noted above, Robert Farris Thompson named the "aesthetic of the cool." The ability to remain "cool" under pressure may well be one of the qualities brought to the jig by Lane in a series of challenge dances with the Irish-American champion John Diamond. Lane won every time. In 1848 he sailed to London and soon drew raves in the British press. Dancing from 1839 to 1852, he died in London at the age of 27, possibly from exhaustion, but his influence did not die with him. Marion Winter writes: "In America it was Juba's influence primarily which kept the minstrel show dance ... in touch with the integrity of Negro source material. There was almost a 'school after Juba.'"[16] Dance historian Jacqui Malone concurred: "Every tap dancer after Juba is in some sense a student of the William Henry Lane School. The ability of twentieth-century rhythm tap dancers to play the floor with their feet reaches back to Lane's ability to use his body as a musical instrument."[17] As one critic wrote, his dancing was equivalent to a musical instrument.

While the influences of the Irish jig remained, Blacks gave minstrel dance its creative excitement. The Buck-and-Wing and the Virginia Essence were indisputably black. The Virginia Essence evolved into the soft shoe, in which the dancer glides slowly across the floor by subtle movement of the heels and the toes without changing the position of his/her legs, giving the appearance of motion without movement. The post-Civil War performer Billy Kersands perfected the dance to the point that many thought he had created it. Jim Dandy's strut and Jim Crow's shuffle with all their variations emerged from black dance.

Many white performers boasted that they had obtained their materials from "real plantation Negroes." While these boasts were promotional and laced with hyperbole, some contained shreds of truth. Many musicians did not read music and could not transcribe their creations. Unprotected by copyright, black music could be expropriated with impunity. A classic debate of music's paternity is who wrote "Dixie," the South's Civil War "anthem." Was it white minstrel Dan Emmett who held the copyright,

"JUBA," AT VAUXHALL GARDENS.

Figure 7. William Lane, known as Juba, London, 1848

or was it the Snowdens, an African American family who were Emmett's Ohio neighbors? "Dixie," a lively quickstep march used widely in minstrel shows, may have surfaced commercially in 1859 in New Orleans.[18] The audience upon hearing "I'll take my stand to live and die in Dixie" went wild, demanding seven encores. When war was declared in 1861, "Dixie" became the South's rallying song. Because of the tune's intimate identification with the Confederacy, few suspected it might have been written by two black musicians, who had their tombstones engraved with "taught Dixie to Dan Emmett."[19]

Were the minstrel tunes found on southern plantations composed by African Americans? In some cases, yes. Other adaptations of English, Irish, and Scottish melodies were given African syncopations. As the business of minstrelsy moved into its second decade, Blacks and Whites made money by writing simple songs that could be hummed by everybody. Lyrics often served slavery by creating nostalgia for the ol' plantation days. Two of the most popular composers in this genre were Stephen Foster, who wrote "Old Folks at Home" and "Old Black Joe," and James Bland, a Long Island born Black who composed "In the Evening by the Moonlight" and "Oh Dem Golden Slippers." Both men captured and perhaps helped create a longing for the plantation days. Homesickness had a special appeal for immigrants, who keened their own homesick laments, "My Bonnie Lies Over the Ocean," and "Take me Home again, Kathleen." Other remnants of southern nostalgia were the "uncles" and "aunties." These benign extended family creatures made their way through folklore and on to the minstrel stage even before Harriet Beecher Stowe published *Uncle Tom's Cabin* (1852). Tenors crooned "Old Folks at Home," "Old Uncle Ned," "Old Black Joe" – Bland's "Carry me Back to Old Virginny" fed into this nostalgia and was adopted as Virginia's state song in 1940.[20] Although Bland's and Foster's songs sold widely and each man gained a national reputation, both died in poverty.

Minstrelsy encouraged the growth of popular music. As publishers made songs available to young pianists in their own living-rooms, black composers and songsters competed for the market. By the end of the century Blacks had emerged as important competition to white composers.

If the sources of minstrel music have been controversial, so have the origins of the musical instruments used in minstrelsy; the banjo, bones, tambourine, and fiddle all allowed a musician to simultaneously dance and sing. Because the banjo was originally an African instrument, an assumption followed that it was widely played by slaves. Stephen Foster's songs promoted it: "Oh! Susanna" (with a banjo on my knee), and "Ring, Ring the Banjo" (I like dat good ol' song). However, southerner Joel Chandler Harris (1848–1906), creator of Uncle Remus, contended that he had seen Negro people play fiddles, blow flutes, beat triangles and drums, but "I have never heard one play on the banjo." Another southerner, George W. Cable (1844–1925) added that although the banjo was to be heard occasionally on a plantation, it was far less frequently seen than the violin.[21] The claims made by white minstrels that they had learned their banjo techniques from plantation "darkies" were often self-promotional. An outstanding example of maintaining those myths can be found in the 1880s, when the black Bohee brothers, James and George, arrived in London with Haverly's Genuine Colored Minstrels. Historian Harry Reynolds singled out the Bohees: "Their entertainment consisted of ballads, banjo songs, and dance in orthodox costume of velvet coats, knee breeches, and jockey caps, a smartly worked number this."[22] The brothers remained in England to form the Bohee Operatic Minstrels, with their own thirty black and white musicians playing nine performances a week. "They usually had a street parade in which James in gorgeous costume rode on horseback at the head of the procession." Apparently, three of the performers were "coloured ladies," De Simoncourt, Georgina Barlee (ballad singers), and Carr Lyon, who had a "remarkable double voice" (possibly all three were female impersonators). James Bohee manufactured banjos, "without exception, the finest yet made." Their theatrical agent wrote: "It is pretty generally understood that it was from them the Prince of Wales took his first Banjo lesson." It was true. Their delicate style of finger-picking, advertised as "novel, refined, pathetic, and amusing," appealed to the British. Their publicity photos reveal the Bohees dressed in tuxedos, and at other times costumed in Tyrolean lederhosen, but always plucking their banjos as they danced. The Bohees wrote in their London program:

> the banjo is essentially a home instrument and among the Negroes of the South of the United States, that is to say amongst probably the most domesticity loving community in the world – the banjo is at once a solace and a joy. It is even more to the humble "darky" than the pipe is to the British working man; for not only does it keep him company when he is alone, but it is the national instrument of mirth and festivity. (n.d., n.p.)

Both Bohee brothers had been born in Indian Town, Massachusetts, and attended school in Boston; their southern "darky" images were minstrel memories they had concocted while abroad. Nonetheless, for a time the

Bohees created a craze among the élite for plucking the "darky's" instrument in the English drawing-room.

It is proper, if not ironic, that the acknowledged king of banjo players was Horace Weston (1825–90). Born to a black dancing-school master in Derby, Connecticut, his professional career began in Boston with a minstrel troupe, Buckley's Serenaders. After brief service in the Union military during the Civil War, Weston traveled to England in 1867 with Charles Hicks' Georgia Minstrels (described later.) Upon his return, Weston worked three seasons on the showboat *Plymouth Rock*. In 1873 he toured the United States and in 1878 he returned to England with Jarrett and Palmer's *Uncle Tom's Cabin* Company. He appeared before Queen Victoria and so entertained her with his pluckery that she presented him with a gold medal. When an Uncle Tom troupe played at Booth's Theatre in New York in 1878, Weston was the star attraction, receiving thirty minutes out of the drama to feature his banjo playing. His wife also played banjo and sometimes performed with him.

Weston was highly regarded by his contemporaries for his banjo compositions; as late as 1969 one of his pieces, "Minor Jig," was performed at a concert in New York. In addition, he was known to be an excellent dancer. His obituary in the *New York Morning Journal* read in part that Weston "was perhaps the greatest banjoist the world has ever heard. He did not learn on the southern plantation the magic touch that drew the witchery from the strings. He was born of free parents in the nutmeg state of Connecticut."[23]

Every minstrel troupe had a man who played bones, two pairs of ribs or wooden sticks fashioned to simulate ribs that were manipulated by the fingers of both hands to provide a clacker rhythm, and when played by an expert, ribs might become a virtuoso performance. Their origins are misty and disputed, but they are mentioned in Shakespeare's *Midsummer Night's Dream*, act 4, scene 1, where Bottom speaks "I have a reasonable good ear in music. Let's have the tongs and the bones." They were played much as the Irish played their "spoons," that is, held between the fingers and clacked together. It seems probable, given the overwhelming presence of Irish in minstrelsy, that the bones were more European than African.[24] The European violin became the American fiddle, used widely in the South for dancing Scottish and Irish reels. Slaves not only learned to fiddle but were hired out to play for plantation holidays and parties; however, on stage the fiddle never rivaled the popularity of the tambourine, banjo, and bones.

In 1810 New York City's population numbered 96,373, Blacks numbering 9,823, or slightly more than 10 percent. From this total, only 1,686 were slaves, leaving the vast majority of 8,137 free. Many with entrepreneurial ambitions and skills had immigrated from the West Indies. William A. Brown, with James Hewlett as his star, had opened the African Theatre, which attracted a rising black middle class discussed earlier in this history. Ira Aldridge had attended the African Free School, whose graduates by the 1830s numbered in the hundreds. Already in 1827 black literacy was common enough for Samuel Cornish and John Russworm to establish *Freedom's Journal*, the first African American newspaper. Yet, minstrelsy insisted that "niggars" were incapable of mastering the English language. Here are the opening lines of "A Black Lecture on Language," delivered by a "professor" in burnt cork.

> BELOBED BLACK BRODREN, Me tend to dress my scorce to you dis nite on de all imported subject of Language, an de warious tongues ob difern nations and niggars, libbin and dead, known and unknown...[25]

Again, we have an ersatz Black testifying against himself. Within ten years of the Virginia Minstrels début in 1843, minstrel dialect had dissolved into near gibberish, with distortions so pronounced that *Witmark's Amateur Minstrel Guild* recommended that companies should "not use dialect, nor allow it to be used, as it spoils the stories and is often unintelligible to the audience."[26] White minstrels must share responsibility for perpetuating images of black illiteracy.[27]

An English visitor wrote in the 1820s: "One striking feature [of New York] consists in the number of Blacks, many of whom are finely dressed."[28] Social class, like race, divided people, and the walls between rich and poor were high, indeed. Poor Whites could not suffer a man of color who "put on airs," one whose attire placed him a class above them. In a number of instances, white ruffians attacked Blacks for riding in a carriage or for dressing well. The minstrel stage joined the mockery of Blacks who had risen "above their station." Dandy Jim or Jim Dandy (still an expression of quality), a figure of sartorial splendor stood in contrast to tatterdemalion Jim Crow. Dandy sported opera glasses in his gloved hand; a gold chain swept across his flowered vest; his neck was hidden by a cravat and a high, ruffled collar. He attracted women. Whites in blackface promoted audience envy of Dandy's style and sensuality, and at the same time they mocked his pretentious foppery. Some seventy years following Dandy's minstrel début, Williams and Walker appropriated Dandy for their musical *In Dahomey* (1902), transforming him into the *nouveau riche* Cicero Lightfoot, who sang "Society," a patter song not unlike Gilbert and Sullivan's

> Cicero: To get in high society
> You need a great reputation,
> Don't cultivate sobriety
> But rather ostentation,
> A lot of gold lay'd by in gilt-edge stocks,
> A few town lots, let's say a dozen blocks,
> A high-toned house that's builded upon rocks.
> Then you're in society.

The evolution of Jim Dandy as he moved from white minstrelsy into black operetta provides yet another example of Blacks in the 1890s recasting white stereotypes.[29] In the Williams and Walker operetta, Jim Dandy lost his dialect and malapropisms. He became secure enough to be cynical about his own social position. He retained his slave name and in the play sips expensive liquors; he married, had a daughter, and no longer bragged that he was irresistible to women – a quality given him by white writers and removed by black Victorians.[30] Jim Dandy in the person of Cicero had become a black millionaire.[31]

In the Victorian era an American woman's place was in the home, but alas, her husband's wages could not sustain her and his children. Forced into sweatshops, often in the garment industry, the wife not only competed with her husband for a job, but had the potential freedom of her wages and close association with other men. Male jealousy, fear, and anger found expression on the minstrel stage.

Males cross-dressed as women. In stump speech after stump speech the men dressed as feminists to mock women's participation in politics, and chided them for abandoning their natural roles of wife and mother. As more women entered the workplace and pressed for equality, the greater grew male fears.

> When woman's rights is stirred a bit
> De first reform she bitches on
> Is how she can wid least delay
> Just draw a pair ob britches on.

The question "Who wears the pants in your family?" was a challenge to male egos. A typical end-man's joke: "Why is a woman like an umbrella? Because she is accustomed to reign."

Some middle-class women fought back. In 1837, a year of economic depression, seventy-one women, black and white, met in New York in the first Antislavery Convention of American Women, a bold move for a gender

Figure 8. Sheet music for "Jim Dandy from Caroline," 1844

that would not obtain the vote for another seventy years. They declared slavery a *sin* and petitioned Congress to abolish it. As the second part of this chapter will show black males, too, cross-dressed as women. Finally, I shall examine in chapter 13 the unforgiving presence of white minstrelsy's ghost in the next millennium.

Black minstrelsy

Before the Civil War Blacks organized a half-dozen transient companies, none lasting more than a few weeks – among them, the Mocking Bird Minstrels, Apollo Minstrels, an anonymous troupe in New Hampshire, and the Seven Slaves from Alabama, "who are now earning their freedom by giving concerts under the guidance of their northern friends." Their songs, they emphasized, were authentic southern plantation music, but alas, it was discovered the songsters were northern freedmen who had been earning small change by singing in Philadelphia's bars.[32]

After the war Blacks entered minstrelsy in large numbers. Northerners were curious to see and hear the "authentic" former slaves, about whom they had read so much. Thus, the white managers who formed the first companies advertised Blacks as being the genuine article, singing their "cabin songs," but by the late 1870s Blacks slipped the opprobrious designation of "former slaves" and "contraband" and organized their own companies. By the 1890s black minstrelsy would evolve into ragtime operetta. Indeed, the term "the New Negro" did not wait for the 1920s, but appeared in 1900, "to measure and represent the distance that African Americans had come from the institution of slavery."[33]

Middle-class black newspapers and periodicals steadfastly refused to review minstrelsy or to place its stars in their biographical dictionaries of race progress. There were exceptions. New Englander James Monroe Trotter, who wrote the first survey of American music, black or white, disliked minstrelsy. In the name of fairness he suppressed his distaste and in 1878 he attended an African American performance of the Georgia Minstrels and found "educated musicians and performers of high merit."[34]

The Ira Aldridge Troupe performed in Franklin Hall in Philadelphia in June 1863.[35] Ira Aldridge himself had sailed for Europe in 1824, never returning to the country of his birth, but his reputation had. Although the company advertised itself as a contraband group (fugitive slaves), their program eschewed the southern genre of old "darkies" longing for the plantation. The exclusion of southern nostalgia may have been in deference to a majority black audience, whom the *New York Clipper* reported as "A more incorrigible set of cusses we never saw; they beat our Bowery gods all to pieces." In contrast, "The whites were orderly in their demeanor...but the blacks behaved very bad, making all sorts of fun of the performers, and openly criticizing everything that was done." The decorum of the Whites is especially surprising since they were the Irish members of the Weccacoe Hose, one of the local fire brigades, groups known to be raucous.

In lieu of southern sentiment, the Ira Aldridge Troupe presented Miss S. Burton singing "When the Cruel War is Over," a popular song that framed a dying soldier's wish to see his true love once more – a song that pleased both the Irish and the Blacks. As Miss Burton sang her encore, she slipped "into a regular Methodist style, keeping up a movement with her body to the air of the song, collapsing at last into a regular camp meeting breakdown." Another popular item with the audience was a Mr. Brown playing a character called Pat O'Callahan. The reporter noted "'the nagur' mixing up a rich Irish brogue promiscuously with the sweet nigger accent."

The Ira Aldridge Troupe appearing during the war made it "unique in the annals of minstrelsy,"[36] first, because the *Clipper* thought it important enough to review; second, because it occurred before a mixed audience; and third, because a black troupe presented a program designed to appeal to their black audience.

Theatre historians have routinely excused black minstrel troupes in the 1860s and 1870s for wearing blackface, using "darky" dialect, and presenting southern stereotypes, but black resistance to minstrelsy's "darkydom" occurred early, and a man at the forefront was Charles B. Hicks.

The Civil War had introduced many northerners to "authentic" southern black culture. Colonel W. Higginson from Massachusetts wrote: "The war brought to some of us, besides its direct experiences, many a strange fulfillment of dreams of other days."[37] His dream had been to hear authentic Negro spirituals, and when he did, he was astounded at their beauty. In April 1865 a similar dream must have seized Captain W. H. Lee of the Union Army, for he organized a musical company comprised of former slaves.[38] Lee named them the Georgia Slave Troupe and hired G. W. Simpson as his business agent; they staged a 4 July concert in Macon, Georgia. Lee hired African American Charles "Barney" Hicks as company manager and called his singers a minstrel troupe. By tracing Hicks' career, it is possible to glimpse many of the other African American stars in minstrelsy.

Hicks claimed to have been born a slave in Baltimore *circa* 1840, but the personal history of his early years is shadowy. J. T. Utling, a reporter, once described Hicks as "a very fine specimen of an Octoroon; is almost white; has a Caucasian head and face; and is possessed of great intelligence."[39] Because of his considerable skills as a singer, interlocutor, and comic, he may have previously been employed by a white minstrel company. Such a performance history is indicated in 1861 by a notice in the *Clipper*, which reported a competition between Hicks and J. Lewis of the Belroy Ethiopian Troupe. The loser was to present the winner with a set of silver-mounted bones. In any case, by the time of his death Hicks had earned the reputation of being one of the best press agents and managers in the business. He was a born showman, a hustler. Faced with a weather disaster at an opening in Philadelphia, he notified the *New York Globe* that he opened to a big business in a pouring rain. "Scored a great success; house is full and big sale for the week."[40] In his memoirs, Ike Simonds reported that Hicks was feared by his competitors.

Hicks' story is sometimes contradictory, often baffling. In the last year of his life he wrote in a letter to the *Indianapolis Freeman*: "From Indianapolis in 1865, I started the first company of genuine Negro minstrels that had been successful in touring America – the Original Georgia Minstrels."[41] He may have been referring to becoming both manager and coproprietor with W. H. Lee and later with Brooker and the Clayton Georgia Minstrels. In September 1865, only five months after General Lee's surrender at Appomattox, Hicks advertised the troupe as former slaves from Macon, Georgia, performing "plantation life in all its broad and mirthful phases." At this point, Hicks apparently replaced some of the company with professionals. Multitalented, Hicks acted as manager, proprietor, balladeer, and comedian. His troupe headed north to Michigan, opening in Detroit on 9 October 1865 as the "real nigs," but they failed at the box office. He promptly renamed the troupe Hicks' Original Georgia Minstrels and billed them as "The Only Simon Pure Negro Troupe in the World."[42] The *New York Clipper* reported that two days before Christmas, they played Boston's Tremont Temple and did well. One reviewer writing in retrospect assayed that the troupe was "the best of its kind ever seen here." Audiences flocked to see "genuine," "bona fide," "real" ex-slaves perform.

Hicks played the small towns, with occasional forays into Boston, New York, and Philadelphia. His success contributed to changing minstrelsy in several ways. First, other black companies were formed, rushing to cash in on Hicks' success. Among them were Lew Johnson's Minstrels, the Tennessee Contrabands, Smallwood's Great Contraband Minstrels, the Georgia Slave Brothers, and many others. Second, Hicks' success prodded the large residential companies in New York and Boston into touring their second companies to small towns, where money could be made. Third, the word *Georgia* in the name of a minstrel troupe became a generic code for "Black" and "ex-slave." Fourth, Hicks fought the white syndicate that forced black troupes to use white managers and owners. Finally, the popularity of African Americans provoked white minstrels to drop their plantation material and substitute variety acts – trained dogs, acrobats, female drill teams – pushing them toward vaudeville because their audiences no longer believed their plantation acts were authentic. In 1884, after viewing a white troupe performing in Norwich, Connecticut, a reviewer noted that the whites were passable, but "they were unfortunate in following so closely a competing company of genuine negroes. It became painfully apparent that there is as much difference between a bona fide 'nigger' show and the best counterfeit as there is between genuine dairy butter and the best Olio margarine ever made."[43]

In 1866, while playing in Utica, New York, Hicks met an Englishman, Samuel Hague, who had been a clog dancer in white minstrelsy. Hague negotiated with Hicks and the owner, Captain Lee, for a tour of the British Isles; however, Hicks himself did not go, but remained behind to form his own troupe. A British historian narrates a variant tale concerning the fate of the black troupers who left with Hague. It is worth quoting, in part to illustrate how contradictory minstrel history can be.

> Sam Hague left New York with his company of twenty-six emancipated slaves on June 16, 1866, and they gave their first performance at the Theatre Royal, Liverpool on July 9, 1866. It was a success, but for one night only. The public compared this crude representation of real Negro life with the educated, refined [white?] minstrel companies that were then so popular in England and naturally the troupe suffered by the comparison. There was not a man who could read or write, or tell a note of music from a horseshoe.[44]

After box-office failure, Hague returned some Blacks to Georgia "at great expense to himself and engaged a number of white men in their stead." According to Reynolds, the Blacks who remained in England fell into dissipation and in spite of Hague's efforts to take care of them, "they soon killed themselves." Published in 1928, more than sixty years after the purported events took place, the memoirs are questionable. Reynolds does note that the best of the real colored comedians were Aaron Banks, Abe Cox, and Neil Soloman. Banks became known for his enthusiastic rendition of

"Emancipation Day." Abe Cox's great song was the "'Hen Convention' introducing vocal imitation of the farmyard." Reynolds then noted that "Coloured comedians frequently excel at eccentric dancing." Hague, after his initial failure to interest the British in a black troupe, changed his program to include white singers with their more classical repertory. In Liverpool, on 31 October 1870 Hague rented St. James Hall with three "real nigs," and for the following eighteen years played the same theatre with his "integrated" troupe, an entertainment attraction not then possible in the United States.

Charles Hicks, who had remained in America to organize his own company, acquired top talents: Horace Weston, banjoist; George Danforth, bones player; and Bob Height, a comedian who later would be favorably compared to Bert Williams. He also hired a white business manager, probably because that was the only way he could get bookings. He commenced his second season on 3 September 1866 in Chicago with a strong cast.[45]

In the heat of July 1867 Hicks invaded the heart of minstreldom, opening at the Broadway Opera House only four blocks from Mechanics Hall, where the Christy Minstrels had once held the stage for nearly ten years. Hicks' troupe included Lew Johnson, bones player, who over the next twenty years would establish his own touring companies. Dick Little played banjo and Hicks himself sang ballads. In 1868 they were on the road again, dipping down to Panama for a short stay. Evidently Hicks had learned that the best way to retain management of his own company was to go abroad for a time. Upon his return he toured smaller towns, with a sally into New York's Third Avenue Theatre before taking his company to Germany. He disembarked in Hamburg in February 1870 with nine members of his so-named "Slave Troupe." Hicks placed an ad:

> Starting Thursday, February 10, every night: a show of the Macon Georgia Negro slave minstrel troupe consisting of Negroes, mulattos, octoroons, and quadroons which have become so famous in America. Scenes from the house of the slave-owner, funny songs, ballads, hunting and clog dances of the negroes. Essence of Old Virginia and Georgia dance, performed by the best American Negro dancer, Aaron Banks. Parodies of the mocking bird performed by the unrivalled mulatto George Jones.[46]

Only two other newspaper notices for the Slave Troupe appeared in Germany. Their last, on 21 February, announced that "Due to unexpected obstacles" the nine members could not perform as promised. The troupe was competing against two-dozen alternatives, including operas, symphonic and military concerts, but the use of dialect may have been the major obstacle to German enjoyment. The audience simply failed to understand the words. The troupe may have traveled to Prussia, but in any case, the tour was a box-office disaster, and a financially strapped Hicks brought his company to Liverpool. Several members, including Hicks himself, then sought employment with Sam Hague's American Slave Serenaders, with whom Hicks worked as a comic with Japanese Tommy.

Back in New York in 1871 Hicks reorganized the Georgia Minstrels, billing them as "the Great Slave Troupe, having returned from their great European tour where they have appeared before the Royal Families of Great Britain and Germany."[47] True or not, appearances before royalty in Europe sold tickets in England and America.[48] In July 1872 Hicks sold his interest in the company to N. D. Roberts, but remained as a performer who had to endure a reviewer's praise: "The success of this troupe goes to disprove the saying that the Negro cannot act the 'nigger.'"[49] That same September, Charles Callender, a white tavern owner, bought the troupe. Keeping Hicks as manager, Callender added new and stronger talent, the best in the business – comics Bob Height, Pete Devonear, Tom McIntosh, Billy Kersands, and Sam Lucas. After Callender enlisted Sam Lucas, the troupe was renamed the Georgia Colored Minstrels. In October 1873 the company of fourteen played the Midwest and South, with Hicks serving as advance man. In New Orleans they drew a largely colored audience, curious to see black performers. Within a year, Hicks formed his own troupe, the King Laughmakers, but soon changed the name to the Georgia Minstrels. In the early 1870s at least two other black companies named themselves the Georgia Minstrels, making a total of four in that season (1874) using similar names. For a time, Hicks toured Canada and the Midwest, avoiding the larger cities where Callender's Georgia Minstrels played. Before pursuing the remainder of Hicks' career, it is necessary to pay tribute to the "Dean of the colored theatrical profession," Sam Lucas.

Born 7 August 1840 or 1848, in the town of Court House Washington, Ohio, Sam Lucas left at age 19 for Cincinnati, where he became a barber. He taught himself guitar, served in the US Army during the Civil War, spent a year at Wilberforce University, and taught school in Louisiana before obtaining his first show business job as a guitar player and caller for Hamilton's Celebrated Colored Quadrille Band. He joined Lew Johnson's Plantation Minstrels in 1871 and after two years moved to Callender's Georgia Minstrels as a ballad singer. An 1878 anecdote about the wealth of his personal jewelry became a legend in his own lifetime. He told vaudevillian

Tom Fletcher, "You see this diamond ring and gold watch? I pawned them in Cincinnati so the stranded Frohman company could be bailed out."[50]

How had Lucas acquired diamonds and a gold watch? It was a tradition in minstrelsy, black and white, to award popular performers jewelry, knowing that they would probably have to pawn it sometime or other. Lucas received his first gold medal in St. Louis with Hart's Colored Minstrels in 1874. He acquired a gold-headed cane after his performance with Haverly's Minstrels in London. As I will show later, the 1890s brought Lucas a series of good roles. He also published two books of minstrel songs and claimed to have written his most popular numbers, "Grandfather's Clock," "Carve dat Possum," and "Turnip Greens." Music historian Eileen Southern questions whether he actually wrote the songs for which he was famous. In his last years he was called "Dad," a title that pleased him. Lucas toured in Ernest Hogan's show *Rufus Rastus* (1905). He never had to look for an engagement, but worked every year. In his last show, *The Red Moon* (1909), he was able to play the barber he had started out to be. Lucas retired in 1912, but returned to play Uncle Tom for a film. In one of the scenes he had to jump in a river and rescue Little Eva. Lucas never finished the film but caught pneumonia and died 15 January 1916.

On 6 October 1871 a new entertainment had first crept and then swept through minstrelsy – jubilee singers – although the original choir, the Fisk Singers, never dreamed that their songs would become popular on the minstrel stage. Eleven black students had set out to tour the eastern states to raise money for their college. The mixed group of males and females attracted national attention. Large audiences came to hear them sing "genuine" slave spirituals, and within a month the group had changed their name to the "Jubilee Singers," a reference to the biblical "Jubilee," a year of celebration when the slaves were set free. Two years later, the Hampton Institute fielded a group of seventeen singers (thirteen of which were ex-slaves) presenting a similar program they called "cabin" (folk) songs. The public made it very clear they preferred "cabin songs," that is, spirituals that had not been composed but had, like Topsy, "jis' grew." To attract women and church congregations, managers quoted reviews praising "the absence of vulgarity or anything which would be shocking to the most refined lady." In January 1875, to exploit the craze, Callender added a second black troupe, the Jubilee Minstrels. Black troupes hurried to add quasi-religious music to their programs. When the Kentucky Jubilee Singers of eleven colored men and women – including a Chinese impersonator – sang in Seattle at Yesler's Hall, the reviewer noted, "Performance good throughout and far superior to the average minstrel show."[51] For a successful program, spirituals and other religious songs became essential.[52]

On their way to Philadelphia in 1876, America's centennial year, the Jubilee Singers, by then named the Centennialites, numbered "thirty colored ladies and gentlemen." They booked Tammany Hall in New York City for the Fourth of July celebration. James Bohee, a member of the company and a famous banjoist, issued a challenge that he would offer $1,000 to any man in America who could play sacred airs up against him.[53]

Black minstrelsy was ready to move abroad into the South Pacific, where, earlier in 1854, Commodore Dewey had opened two Japanese ports to western trade. Dewey had entertained Japanese officials aboard his flagship by presenting a minstrel show performed by his crew. G. B. Sansom reported: "It was a most hilarious occasion. The Japanese guests can scarcely have appreciated the finer points of wit between Mr. Bones and his colleagues; but though this exhibition of western culture was something quite beyond their own aesthetic experience, they laughed heartily at the costumes and antics of the performers."[54]

Charles Barney Hicks, sensing that a black troupe could make money in Australia and knowing that he would have a greater chance to retain control of his company abroad, persuaded nineteen members from the black Haverly company to sail with him on 23 March 1877 to New Zealand, an English-speaking nation freer from race prejudice and not yet weary of minstrelsy. Charles Hicks, as manager, had worked with nearly all nineteen in earlier companies, and nine of the men as recently as the previous year. At their first port of call, Dunedin in New Zealand, Hicks advertised his seasoned crew as "The Far-famed Original Georgias." On 7 July 1877 the critic in the *Saturday Advertiser* exclaimed:

> If crowded houses, enthusiastic applause, and loud laughter are indica-
> tions of success, then the Georgias have made a tremendous hit in our
> city, for since their arrival in Dunedin a week ago, the theatre has been
> packed by appreciative audiences. We have never witnessed anything in
> the "corner" business [the British term for end-men] to equal the tambo
> and bones performances of Messrs. Wilson, Brown, Caruso (Crusoe),
> and Mills. Two of the gentlemen have mouths which, when expanded,
> present an exhibition well worth the entrance money alone.

Saturday Advertiser reporter J. T. Utling arranged an interview. Hicks, like Barnum, knowing that exotica sold tickets, accentuated the troupe's racial differences. He averred that the entire troupe had been slaves, himself included. Utling's article concludes: "I asked Mr. Hicks if he would tell me the composition of the troupe under his charge. He then informed me that he was an Octoroon; that Messrs Mills, Matlock, Keenan, Jackson, Caruso (Crusoe), and Thomas were Mulattos; and that the rest were full blooded Niggers."[55]

Opening his show in Hobart, Australia, in late July 1877, Hicks toured the cities and hamlets of Australia and Tasmania for three years. The Georgias, he insisted, had played before the royalty of Europe. Borrowing from his former boss, Callender, Hicks used four end-men instead of two, and took credit for originating the idea. Perhaps *he had* given Callender the idea back in 1872.

Although Hicks played on the slave origins of his troupe throughout the three years of their tour, programs with Stephen Foster's songs about darkies longing for the good ol' days were scarce. Hicks placed a realistic sketch in the program, "The Cotton Field Scene; or, Our Alabama Home 'Fore de War," which he claimed represented "a realistic picture of slave days." Hicks himself sang nonracial ballads such as "See that my Grave's Kept Green." Although his show appealed to all classes, it was the laboring people who filled his theatres. It is reported that Hicks charmed even the gallery gods into admiration.

His second year in Australia topped the success of the first when he joined his Georgia Minstrels with L. M. Bayless' Dramatic Company, who were touring a version of *Uncle Tom's Cabin*. Hosea Easton in the role of Uncle Tom was widely praised for his naturalness. According to Waterhouse, the Hicks–Bayless version of the antislavery play was the "most successful version ever staged in Australia," possibly because of the combination of minstrelsy and melodrama, a wedding long popular in the United States.

By the beginning of the third year, Hicks had wearied his audiences. Attendances fell. Some members of the tired troupe returned to America, including the mainstay Charles A. Crusoe. Although Hicks supplemented his company by taking on white vaudevillians, his box office did not improve. Then Hicks himself withdrew from his own company and joined R. B. Lewis' company to act in *The Slave's Revenge* and *The Octoroon*. In late May 1880 Hicks departed for America, "leaving his partners to settle creditors."[56] Eight years later he would return to Australia with a new minstrel troupe.

Although Hicks may have been the most adventuresome manager among African Americans, he was not the only entrepreneur to venture into *terra incognita*. Lew Johnson, with a troupe that numbered only a dozen or so, could not compete in the big cities, so he pioneered into rugged terrain, playing small towns, first in the Midwest and later mining camps in the Far West and Canada. Johnson boasted that his company was the first to play the Utah, Wyoming, Idaho, and the Montana territories. Born in Chicago (c. 1840s), he organized the Lew Johnson's Plantation Minstrels in 1870 and began a touring career that lasted twenty-eight years.[57] Like other managers, Johnson changed the name of his group to fit audience expectation. When he observed in 1875 that "original slave" troupes were popular, he adopted the name Plantation Minstrel Slave Troupe, and when in 1877 jubilee spirituals commanded big box office, Lew Johnson's Original Tennessee Jubilee Singers traveled the circuit. He followed these with Lew Johnson's Combination in 1881, the Black Baby Boy Minstrels in 1886, and the Refined Colored Minstrels and Electric Brass Band in 1890.[58] By the 1880s Johnson toured the Far West exclusively, moving up and down the coast from Los Angeles to British Columbia. Booker T. Washington claimed that during this period Johnson hired a young, unknown performer:

> One day a colored man named Lew Johnson, who kept a barber shop in San Francisco, asked Bert Williams if he did not want to join a little company that he intended to take up along the coast to play the lumber camps between San Francisco and Eureka, and then come back by way of the mining camps at the western edge of the mountains.[59]

Washington went on to write that Williams came back from the tour in rags and reported: "It was then that I [Williams] first ran up against the humiliation and persecution that have to be faced by every person of colored blood, no matter what his brains, education or the integrity of his conduct." Ann Charters presents a contradictory account, saying that Williams enjoyed the tour and resolved to start a career in popular entertainment. Of interest here is the note that Johnson owned a barber shop, no doubt earning an income during the off-season. In January 1887 he published in the *New York Clipper* an account of his fifteen-week tour through the Rocky Mountains, Idaho and Washington Territory. His "hard work and good management" netted a total of $10,978, certainly a good sum in those days. Johnson played Seattle twice, once in February 1899 and again in September, albeit under a different name. Two reviews of his troupe in San Francisco provide a glimpse of how minstrel programs changed by the addition of more and more novelty acts. The Summaries below are from programs that are two years apart and well illustrate the trend away from blackface minstrelsy.

In 1888 Lew Johnson's Black Baby Boy Minstrels still employed banjo specialties, "darky" impersonations, an "impersonation of a Chinaman," and jigging.[60] Two years later, on 13 April 1890, Johnson's program for his Refined Minstrels at the Los Angeles Theatre reflected his rush toward vaudeville. Part one concluded with Professor Gilmore's Musical Carnival. Part two began with The Boy Wonder in Baton Exercises; A Marvelous Knife Throwing Act, and Aerial Juggling on the Invisible Wire and introducing a flock of trained pigeons. This was followed by the Shadowgraph Emperors, in their comic pantomime and grand naval combat; a Dogs' Carnival, introducing his troupe of trained French poodles, and an afterpiece entitled "Somnambulism, or He's in the Asylum Now."[61]

Near the end of his career and still filled with creative energy, Johnson toured California with his own *Uncle Tom's Cabin* company, "carrying twenty people, all white with the exception of Mr. and Mrs. Johnson." Lew Johnson retired to Grand Forks, British Columbia, where he assumed ownership of a dye store. His last years were spent as the manager and lessee of the opera house there. He died on 27 February 1910.

Lew Johnson should be remembered as one of the first managers to carry a brass band on a road tour. A reviewer in Redding, California, wrote: "Lew Johnson's minstrel band . . . is the best band that has traveled through here for years."[62] Johnson's was not the only black company to tour the west and northwest. From the 149 visits by minstrel troupes to Seattle between 1864 and 1911, at least one-third or fifty visits were by some fifteen colored troupes. With the completion of the transcontinental railroad in 1867, brass bands toured and advertised their presence very much as circuses paraded their elephants. To attract an audience, a company would disembark from the train in their uniforms, playing as they marched to the theatre, a practice called "dragging the town." The larger troupes had both a band and an orchestra. Soon marching bands were incorporated into the shows as precision drill teams. White troupes had used gauche military marching to lampoon black soldiers in classic drills of confusion and chaos. In the 1875/76 season Callender cast comedian Billy Kersands in "Georgia Brigadiers," a sketch designed to mock the black soldiers. Ten years later, in 1886, when Kersands managed his own troupe, he slipped the yoke and changed the joke by offering a prize of $1,000 to any minstrel unit that could better his own company's precision drilling.[63] The bands played on. In November 1879 Haverly's Georgia Colored Minstrels astonished the citizens of Shreveport, Louisiana, by giving a parade with two brass bands, "the company being divided, each band going in opposite directions, and after coming together on the main street, both playing the same tune in perfect unison."[64]

The success of comic drumming acts was not lost on the comedian Tom McIntosh, who took it to England in 1881 with Haverly's Genuine Colored Minstrels. A reviewer noted that "T. McIntosh made excellent comedy with a big drum with which he got terribly entangled. First he dived right over it, then underneath it. He was all over it, everywhere in fact but inside it, but he always came up just in time for his beat."[65]

McIntosh is remembered as the people's comic – rough, obvious, and good-humored. At various times he had his own company, but usually he worked for others, changing troupes every year or two. He and his wife Hattie parlayed their act "The King of Bavaria" into Sam T. Jack's *The Creole Show* (1890). He toured with Black Patti on the Keith vaudeville circuit. The *Freeman* reviewed the McIntoshes in John Isham's Octoroons (1895): "Mr. and Mrs. Tom McIntosh are easily the leaders. Both have an intelligent idea of low comedy, and their act is full of new and original humor."[66] Later, Hattie became a regular in all the Williams and Walkers shows. The *Indianapolis Freeman* published the comic's obituary: "Tom McIntosh is best remembered as the man with the unusually large mouth who used to put an entire newspaper in it to make people laugh, and he usually succeeded," a feat for which he received $300 a week. He wrote farces in which he starred: *Down Among the Cypress*, and *A Hot Time in Dixie*, the latter featuring songwriter Gussie Davis and dancer May Bohee. Reviews of McIntosh were typically: "McIntosh was irresistibly funny." In 1904 McIntosh died as he had lived – on tour.

Except for large companies like the Christy Minstrels or the Bryant, most troupes toured small cities and towns, sometimes moving every night or two. A typical company contract is offered in the endnotes.[67] For smaller black troupes, unless they traveled in their own railway cars, as W. C. Handy did with the white-owned Mahara's Minstrels, lodging was a problem because all of America was Jim Crow. On the road, agents reported frequent humiliation: "The Georgia Minstrels were unable to secure accommodations at any hotels in Decatur, Illinois, on their arrival to perform on the 10th. They insisted that their agent had made arrangements for their accommodations at one of the hotels, but on their arrival the manager claimed that he had not the necessary rooms."[68] Booking agents arranged venues weeks in advance, in the hope the troupe could meet the date. Transportation even by train was uncertain. Talent was often stranded without salary payment. What compensation, what hopes, lured these men to risk their health? Certainly

not a typical $25 per week paid jointly to two acrobats. Management con-
tracts were merciless. Performers could be fined for lateness, stage waits,
mud on their shoes, dirty shirt fronts, drunkenness, or "mashing" women
within two blocks of the theatre. One-night stands were the rule; trains
reeked of coal gas. Musical instruments and costumes often were crushed
into a single suitcase.

Life on the road could be dangerous. In 1894, while the train was on
the siding in Missouri, Jack Mahara, advance agent for Mahara's Minstrels,
pulled his pistol and returned shots with five masked men during a holdup on
the express. When the shooting stopped, the car windows were smashed and
Mr. Mahara was wounded in the head. He recovered. On other occasions
the minstrel railroad car would be left stranded. In May 1897, McCabe,
owner and manager of the Black Trilby Company, filed a $20,000 damage
suit against the North Carolina and St. Louis Railroad for refusing to haul
the company's Palace Car over its line. In his autobiography, W. C. Handy,
band leader for Mahara's Minstrels, wrote of several harrowing accounts.
"Orange was the Texas town we dreaded most. Whenever it became known
to the home town mob that our show was routed their way, they would sit
up all night waiting for the train to pass. Their conception of wild, he-man
fun was to riddle our car with bullets as it sped through their town."[69]

Diets were poor, health problems endemic. The *New York Clipper* regularly published minstrel obituaries: Lewis Pierson, balladist and interlocutor,
died in Washington, DC, of consumption. Robert Turner, age 32, leader
of a brass band, died in St. Louis of smallpox. Most of the men traveled
without family; some resorted to prostitutes in an era when syphilis killed.
Among the fatalities were Ernest Hogan, George Walker, Bob Cole, and
Scott Joplin.

In an opposite vein, many were family men who seriously saved money,
as this letter from a Mahara minstrel to the *Freeman* testified:

> At Rogers, Arkansas, where no Negroes are allowed to stop, they permit-
> ted our show to play. When many of the company went to send money
> by express, the agent remarked, "You have some great crap games, don't
> you?" He soon found that eight orders went to our wives, some to help
> in business enterprises, and that some of the single boys were helping to
> take care of parents and school their brothers and sisters; that our salaries
> were equal to agents, clerks, and cashiers.[70]

A further word about the Mahara's Minstrels. Owned by three Irish brothers – William, Jack, and Frank – they traveled "from ocean to ocean,"

their circuits being Southern, Midwestern, and Northwestern. There were twenty-five members in the troupe, of which twelve were women. To see their parade from the railway to the theatre was to believe their claim that they were "the greatest colored troupe in existence":

> W. A. Mahara's Minstrels opened the season at Belvidere, Illinois with a new wardrobe. The suits for the first part consist of satin coats, silk vests, and velvet knee pants. The six end-men wear full satin suits and the orchestra is dressed in satin suits with lace sleeves. The street parade is in full dress, silk hats, and eight silk banners, bearing various designs, with six Mexican-dressed drum majors and pickaninny drum corps, six walking gents with white Prince Albert suits and white silk hats, kid gloves and canes with W. A. Mahara (the only White in sight) and his St. Bernard dog, Sport in a carriage in the lead of the parade.[71]

William, the elder Mahara, had learned the trade when he was manager for Hicks' Georgia Minstrels in 1875. Although the Mahara brothers managed both colored and white companies, the colored were superior, with top talents – W. C. Handy, band leader, and Attrus Hughes, orchestra leader. As the nineteenth century progressed, the band and its parade grew in importance. McCabe and Young's Minstrels replaced the bones and tambourine with brass horns, and they carried three sets of costumes for the street parade. For the drilling teams, comic or serious, no uniforms were more colorful and theatrical than those of the French Army in from Algeria, the Zouaves, uniforms known for their exotic embroidered vests, pantaloon trousers, and their tasseled fezes and turbans.[72]

Although minstrelsy always had its specialty acts, the number and variety increased as minstrelsy melded into vaudeville and ragtime musical. A half-dozen talented specialty acts must represent the hundreds not named in this history. Thomas Dilward, a.k.a Japanese Tommy, who was known as African Dwarf Tommy, impersonated women. While with Hague's minstrels in 1870, Japanese Tommy assumed the role of a prima donna. He became one of the few African Americans to work regularly with white minstrel companies. Pearl Woods, whom the Australian *Observer* called "the greatest acrobatic artist for a lady ever seen in this city, is an artistic dancer and high kicker of rare merit, and her work is one of strongest turns of the entire show."[73] Harry Krayton (Kraton) "the hoop roller was a favorite. Some of his manipulations of hoops were little short of marvelous. He keeps twenty-four of them in motion at once."[74] In 1909 Sylvester

Figure 9. McCabe Minstrel Band, *c.* 1910

Russell described Kraton "dressed in white duck pants and white shoes with plum colored shirt, and a high collar to catch the sweat, with nice hair parted near the middle, the partly self-esteemed boy wonder controlled hoops careless enough to convince the average novice that he is perfection unsophisticated."[75]

Black Carl (Carl Dante), a.k.a the Creole Mahatma, the Hoo-doo Magician, was generally reviewed as "a marvel, and one of the best magicians of the age, the color line apart."[76] Sometimes his act partook of spiritualism, when he performed his tricks in the atmosphere of a "seance." Carl introduced a technique of circumventing racism in the audience that sometimes surfaced when Whites felt that the black magician on stage was smarter than they were. Carl instructed his black assistant to stand wide-eyed and open mouthed, making the audience laugh at his stupidity instead of their own. One may speculate that he was called "Black Carl" because of his "dark" art; however, many artists of the period promoted themselves by adopting shadow names – Black Patti, after the Italian singer, Adelina Patti; Susie Anderson advertised herself as the Black Melba; John W. Brewer as the Black Eddie Foy; and Black Herman, after Alexander Hermann the Great, a popular magician. These performers did not see their racial sobriquets as demeaning, but rather they profited by using a name already made popular in the theatre.[77] "The Black Napoleon," ventriloquist John Walcott Cooper (1873–1966), earned his title in 1902 after performing with a cast of five dummies requiring the use of six voices in a playlet he had written, *Fun in the Barbershop.*

Following the death of his parents, at age 13 Cooper joined the Southern Jubilee Singers. By 1897 he had learned ventriloquism, made his own dummy – the Prince of Madagascar – and signed on with Pringle's Georgia Minstrels. Advertising his as "The Cleanest and Most Wholesome Profession on Earth," he toured with Black Patti, Flora Batson, and Henry Strange. After a long period in the vaudeville, he coached others in the art. He died at the age of 93.[78]

Amid minstrelsy's raucous laughter, the working classes enjoyed misty-eyed moments when they might tearfully recall the loss of loved ones. The tradition of the silver-voiced male tenor began with the Irish domination of minstrelsy and lasted a hundred years, ending with John McCormack and Nelson Eddie. African American minstrels joined the tradition of lamenting lost loves, longing for distant homelands, as well as sorrowing eternally for dying children and dead mothers. Possibly the greatest tenor was Wallace King. Born in Newark, New Jersey, in 1840, he had studied with Peter O'Fake, an African American who was a society band leader. The *Boston Journal* discovered that Mr. Wallace King, while singing with the Hyers Sisters in 1871, had "a pure, sweet tenor voice of remarkable compass, and sings with excellent taste." The audience was so delighted with the singing of Wallace King that they showered him with silver dollars while he was on the stage. Although he sang for both the Callender and Haverly troupes, King seemed to prefer the more serious music of the Hyers Sisters, who signed him in 1879 to be the tenor in their quartet. King sailed to Australia with Hicks' Georgia Minstrels and remained there most of his life, singing and playing parts in minstrel skits. He became so familiar to Australian audiences that his producers billed him as "Australia's favorite tenor." In 1903 the *Freeman* reported a telegram from San Francisco that stated King had arrived there from Australia completely demented.[79] Shortly after his return to San Francisco, Wallace King died.

As companies grew larger, J. H. Haverly began a flamboyant advertising campaign in the manner of P. T. Barnum. He let it be known that when his Colored Georgia Minstrels gave a brass band concert at Stillwater Prison in Minnesota, they received thanks from several famous outlaws, including the three "Younger Brothers" (once members of the Jesse James outlaw band). Haverly labeled his new company "The Black One Hundred," and he put

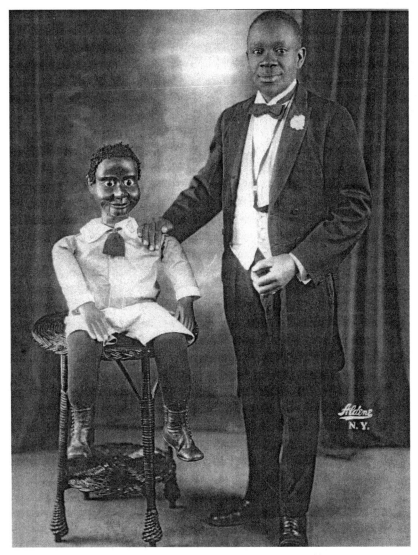

Figure 10. Ventriloquist John Cooper and his dummy "Sam," 1897

reviews like this one from the *Baltimore American* to good use: "Nothing like it was ever heard in Baltimore. The theory that only an Irishman in burnt cork can transmit the flavor of the plantation "darky" is a mistake. These genuine sons of Africa kept the house in a continual roar and scored a grand success."

By 14 June 1880, when Haverly played Niblo's Garden Theatre in Boston, his Grand Colored Minstrel Carnival boasted the Black One Hundred – sixty male, forty female. This figure included ten end-men (the best in the business), as well as the Bohee Brothers, the Blackville Jubilee Singers, and Billy Kersands. By October, when they played the Haverly Theatre in Chicago, the troupe was considerably augmented, and comprised in the first part twenty end-men. *"Yes, count 'em. Twenty!"*

The next year, Haverly's Colored Minstrels sailed to England for a year's tour. A London reviewer reported he had counted "sixty-five real Negroes, male and female, coal black to the light brown, all ages, ancient Uncle Toms and Aunt Chlöes, smart young coons and wenches down to the little pickaninny a few months old nestling in its mother's lap."[80] For years, Bob Mack had been tickling audiences with his "Hen Conversations," an act he had borrowed from Abe Cox of the Original Georgia Minstrels. In London, Mack added a novelty, a real bantam rooster. Dressed as a big rooster, Mack held mock combat with the bantam, "Little Dick." If imitation is the most sincere form of flattery, three decades later Bert Williams borrowed the rooster act for the Ziegfeld Follies. While all show folk imitate successful acts, and Whites regularly stole routines from Blacks, the African American tradition of passing along "crowd pleasers" has always been strong, so strong the Harlem Hoofer's Club, with tongue-in-cheek, admonished, "a member must never copy another member's routine...exactly."

By the 1880s minstrelsy had become a poker game where owners and managers gambled, winning and losing their companies as they tried to drive their competitors from the boards.[81] Whites used Barney Hicks' talents and shrewdness, rehiring him again and again even after he had betrayed them by carrying their stars off to Australia. One is reminded of a comment attributed to Samuel Goldwyn when he fired Otto Preminger from the filming of *Porgy and Bess*. "I'll never use that man again until I need him." And the white managers needed Hicks.

In 1885 Hicks had left Haverly to manage Billy Kersands' new troupe, which he led on a "Grand Southern Tour." His instinct for public relations and self-aggrandizement was reflected in a letter published in the *New York Clipper* on 10 April 1886:

> The advent of Brains has carried our Banner to Victory, through the Greatest Southern Tour ever made by a colored company...The only company that has played six weeks in New Orleans for the past twenty years, and our Grand Parade Band given the place of Honor, and requested by Rex, Carnival King, to escort his State Carriage at the Mardi-Gras.

Billy Kersands was one of the few black comics that historians have written about, possibly because of his large mouth, in which he could place a cup of tea on its saucer or several billiard balls. In the next century, white comics Joe E. Brown and Martha Ray in similar fashion exploited their big mouths. Kersands had other talents. He danced the Virginia Essence to perfection, maneuvering his 200 pounds in airy suspension to the tune of "Swanee River."

Born in Baton Rouge, Louisiana, in 1842, Kersands never learned to read and write, but had all his songs taught to him by others, frequently by Sam Lucas. He moved to New York City at an early age, and played with every major black company, including his own, Kersands' Colored Minstrels (1885). Sam Lucas, who wrote Kersands' obituary, recalled:

> His main specialty was dance, "The Essence of Old Virginia." In that dance he would lie flat on his stomach and beat first his head and then his toes against the stage to keep time with the orchestra. He would look at his feet to see how they were keeping time, and then looking out at the audience, he would say, "Ain't this nice? I get seventy-five dollars a week for doing this."[82]

Kersands performed with the Hyers Sisters in their musical *Out of Bondage* (1875), and made several worldwide tours, the last one to Australia in 1912. He lived to play in vaudeville at the age of 73. While doing the biggest business of the season in 1915 with his own troupe in Artesia, New Mexico, he returned as usual to his private railroad car, and had just seated himself for a short chat before retiring when he fell over dead.

In 1885 Hicks left Kersands to form the Hicks and Sawyer's Minstrels, another all-black troupe. Initially, the reviews were solid. "That minstrelsy still retains a strong hold on the public was clearly proven by the immense houses that witnessed both performances of Hicks and Sawyer's Minstrels yesterday. The company is, if anything, superior to the late Haverly and strictly of a refined, pleasing nature."[83] But something more powerful than the box office was driving Charles Hicks. In 1887 he again sailed to Australia, this time absconding with the Hicks and Sawyer company name and some of its members. A. D. Sawyer, properly upset, placed a notice in the *New York Clipper* warning managers to beware of parties advertising and calling themselves Hicks–Sawyer Colored Minstrels. "I will prosecute anyone attempting to trade on my name or use that title." In Australia, safe on the other side of the globe, Hicks sometimes used the name and sometimes reassumed his old company name, the Hicks Georgia Minstrels. Several former members of his troupe who had stayed in Australia, married, and had families, rejoined him.[84]

After eight years' absence, "down under" creditors had either forgiven Hicks, or forgotten him, at least in Adelaide where he chose to open at the Gardner's Room "to a house packed in every part." Nestled into his own company of thirty-three, Hicks served as interlocutor. "Almost every item in the entertainment was entirely new," wrote the *South Adelaide Register*. While the Black Zouaves, a smart drill team, "elicited the heartiest applause," the whole evening glowed with success, and Hicks settled in for a ten-month run. How sweet it must have been for him to once again command his own African American company. His houses were jammed. Hicks changed the program every week, holding the community's attention by playing baseball with the local teams and by securing public affection with a benefit performance for the inmates of the North-Terrance Lunatic Asylum. He kept his competitors envious by sending long cablegrams to the *New York Clipper* detailing his triumphs.

In October Hicks moved to Sydney and changed the company's name to the American Coloured Minstrels. Within four months he had stricken nearly all the plantation material; even the coon songs that had opened his tour were no longer listed on the program. In the second part he had added women to the troupe, as "The Pictures of Loveliness, the Frietas Sisters in their artistic song and dance entitled 'Prettiest Little Song of All.'" Did these moves toward vaudeville include black women? We do not know.

In January 1890 Hicks took his troupe to New Zealand, where the company repeated its triumphs. In May he sent a cable to the *New York Clipper* announcing that they would be sailing home in a few months. He never did. Possibly he never intended to, but only wished to keep his name on the lips of folks back home. In August, Hicks launched his boldest experiment. He cast his company in dramas from the legitimate theatre, a dream not possible in America, where company owners were mainly white and audiences were intolerant of African Americans as serious actors. The *Brisbane Queenslander* received Hicks' Dramatic and Minstrel Combination positively: "The sensational drama, *Across the Continent*, [was] presented for the first time. The drama was staged very carefully, and it was received with a good deal of favor. The piece has been running through the week." Within a fortnight Hicks mounted two more dramas, *Uncle Tom's Cabin*, with Hosea Easton again in the starring role he had played twelve years before, and a popular mystery, *The Thicket-of-Leaves*.[85] The *Queenslander* critic wrote:

"The characters were, without exception, well cast, and the performance was, on the whole, a very effective one." The cast included three women, probably white – Hicks did not abandon minstrelsy entirely, but joined his American Coloured Minstrels with the company of Slade Murray playing the Gaiety Theatre as the Burlesque Combination. At this point Hicks had managed his own troupe for nearly three years, and successfully. Even his latest adventure, the Combination, drew big houses. Nonetheless, he again abandoned his troupe and in 1898 embarked on a tour of India as manager with Harriston's Circus. For the next ten years he toured the Penang Straits, Batavia, Singapore, Calcutta, and Bombay as well as occasionally sailing back to New Zealand and Australia. One of his last communications was a lengthy letter to the *Freeman* attacking its editor, McCorker, for demeaning the talents and characters of Billy Kersands and Tom McIntosh. In December 1902 the *Freeman* reported Hicks' death from cholera in Surabaja, Java (now Indonesia), where he had been managing Harmston's [probably Harriston's] Circus. The *Freeman's* brief obituary closed with "Mr. Hicks was of such light complexion that he could easily have passed for a white man."[86]

Hicks' passing left Orpheus Myron McAdoo and his wife, billed as "Madame Mattie Allen McAdoo," as the major black company in Australia. A graduate of Hampton Institute with a classical education in music, McAdoo had joined the Fisk Jubilee Singers in 1886 as a baritone. After touring the world with them for three years, he returned to the United States to organize his own group, the Virginia Jubilee Singers, composed of former Hampton students, including his brother, Eugene. McAdoo arrived in Australia following a five-year tour of South Africa, where his company had distinguished itself by becoming the first African Americans to perform the cakewalk in Cape Town.[87] The reviews glowed.

> An excellent variety show was given, which introduced some marvelously clever juggling and some high kicking, the like of which has not been seen in Cape Town before. "The Grand Cake Walk," the Negro minuet, proved a most interesting novelty. This performance consisted of the company promenading in couples, the audience awarding the cake to the most graceful couple.[88]

Earlier, in 1862, the Christy Minstrels had captivated Cape Town. When McAdoo arrived in 1890 with his Virginia Jubilee Singers harmonizing in four-part arrangements, Cape Town burst with welcome. McAdoo stayed for two years, left, and returned in 1895 to stay another three. His long tenure in Cape Town insured a blackface tradition: his troupe inspired a New Year's celebration, the Cape Town "Coon Carnival," with blackface troupes singing and dancing in competitive styles.[89] McAdoo sailed from Cape Town to Melbourne with two companies: the McAdoo Jubilee Singers, named after the emancipation day celebrations (but suggesting that they were celebrating Queen Victoria's jubilee); and McAdoo's Original Colored American Minstrel and Vaudeville Company, a secular unit using jugglers and acrobats. After a successful year in Australia and New Zealand, McAdoo leased the Palace Theatre in Sydney as a home for his "colored stock company" and invited black artists in America to join his troupe. Among those who came were Flora Batson, concert singer, Henderson Smith, band leader, and Wallace King, tenor.

Although female impersonators had appeared as early as the Christy Minstrels in the 1840s, the latter years of the nineteenth century saw several notable cross-dressers. "Mr. William [Willis] Ganze, a female impersonator, completely mystified the audience, obtaining grotesque effects by suddenly lowering his vocal range to his own man's voice," a common device that allowed an audience to discover they were male.[90] In 1871, T. Drewette with the Georgia Minstrels sang "Sweet Spirit Hear my Prayers" "with a wonderfully sweet falsetto, letting down to gruff baritone at the close in a laughable way."[91] In 1889, for Richards and Pringle, Ganze played the role of a female twin in "The Blackville Twins," and on the same bill he impersonated Black Patti "in voice, dress, and actions."[92] For a year, Ganze worked as a "him and her" team in vaudeville with the great comic Tom McIntosh. Their act broke up when McIntosh married.

Perhaps the greatest of all the female impersonators was Andrew Tribble, who worked for forty years in the trade. Born in 1879, Tribble attended school in Richmond, Kentucky, and toured as a member of a pickaninny band *In Old Kentucky*. Then he grew too tall to be a "pick." In 1904 Robert Motts discovered Tribble singing and dancing in a State Street music hall in Chicago. Motts booked him into the Pekin Theatre.

> One night in an afterpiece, Tribble slipped on a dress and the audience screamed at his performance. He found his dress-wearing characterization so effective that he began to dress in drag at the Pekin where Cole and Johnson found and cast Tribble in their musical *Shoo-Fly Regiment*. It was there he created his most successful character, Ophelia Snow, a single-minded woman, careless, kindly, tough, and above all desirous for an affair of the heart just the same as her sisters blessed with more beauty.[93]

As Ophelia the spinster, he sang "Who Do You Love?" to Matt Marshall playing Napoleon. A reviewer in Dallas, Texas, found Tribble "screamingly funny, as well rendered as anything which has been seen here in many moons." Tribble's most popular creation was Lilly White, a washerwoman featured in Cole and Johnson's *The Red Moon* (1908). By this time he had a claque. "Andy Tribble, the Chicago favorite, was well-received on every entrance."[94] In around 1908 at the Lincoln Theatre in Harlem he played "Subway Sal" in blackface. The next year, his female impersonation in *His Honor the Barber* (1909), a musical comedy, reached Broadway. The *Freeman* reviewer wrote: "Hello, here's Andrew Tribble, playing Babe Johnson with a line of the funniest talk ever. You all know Tribble is funny anyway."[95] Audiences now expected Tribble to be both in drag and funny.

Sylvester Russell, easily the most severe black critic of the era, wrote in the *Freeman*: "Mr. Andrew Tribble [is] the greatest protean artist his race has ever produced . . . 'Watermelon Time' was a perfect fit of a song, in which Mr. Tribble wore salmon silk, something wonderful in quality, that outshone anything in the female contingent."[96] In the 1920s Tribble played in vaudeville and in musical revues that toured. In 1928 he had his own star act, *Ophelia Snow from Baltimo'*, a vaudeville piece. He died in 1935.

Female impersonation had originated, in part, because women had not been admitted on to the minstrel stage, but, nonetheless, male parody was often preferred over women playing themselves. Although women had impersonated men in English theatre since the eighteenth century, in minstrelsy black women began male impersonation in the 1890s. Florence Hines, who was billed as the Black Vesta Tilley (after the British music hall impersonator), traveled with Richards and Pringle-Rusco and Holland's Big Minstrel Festival, where she sang "I'm a Millionaire's Son."[97] The *Freeman* wrote: "as a male impersonator, Miss Hines is fine." The same newspaper reviewed her in Sam T. Jack's *The Creole Show* (1890) as "the greatest living song and dance artist." Ada Overton Walker took over her husband George's role in *Bandana Land* (1907–09) when he became too ill to perform. Alberta of the Whitman sisters billed herself as "'Bert,' cut her hair short, dressed as a man, and became one of the best male impersonators."[98] Her dance specialty was the strut. A generation later, Moms Mabley and Gladys Bentley impersonated males for cabaret audiences. In the 1960s black comic Flip Wilson engendered the same androgynous pleasures by cross-dressing on television skits in the character of Geraldine, whose "What you see is what you get" became that generation's byword.

Children, too, by the 1880s had been pushed on to minstrel stages. Topsy, a perennial favorite, the naughty pickaninny in *Uncle Tom's Cabin* (1852), was played by white women in blackface. Genuine African American children, then called "picks," found their way into plays requiring plantation settings. They sang, they danced, their "innocence" delighted the audience. In 1881, when the Callender Spectacular Minstrels played in New York City, the Society for the Prevention of Cruelty to Children stopped the performance of the Alabama Pickaninnies.

The last of the big black professional companies, the Rabbit's Foot Minstrels founded by Pat Chappelle in 1900, had fifty-five performers and a brass band that traveled in their own private railway cars. As a promotion gimmick, they fielded a baseball team that challenged local teams in towns where they performed. When Chapelle died in 1911, the F. S. Walcott Carnival Corporation bought the Rabbit's Foot Company and continued to play towns in the South until well into the 1940s. Small companies also kept playing at carnivals and fairs. Minstrel comic Pigmeat Markham remembered touring in 1919: "I started in a little carnival called a gilly with a little minstrel show. In those days we didn't have no band. We only had about six people, and we clapped our hands and would hum the music. At that time I was getting a dollar a week."[99] After the Second World War Pigmeat Markham reluctantly gave up wearing cork because after twenty-five years it was difficult for him to perform without it.

A history of black minstrelsy must include two of its premiere actors and innovators – Billy McClain and Ernest Hogan. The funny, outrageous, and often controversial comic Ernest Hogan was born Reuben Crowder at the end of the Civil War in Bowling Green, Kentucky. Like Hicks, he was a man of contradictions. Hogan began as a pickaninny touring with an *Uncle Tom's Cabin* company, where he may have acquired his smiling-in-your-face style. For a white show, *Widow Jones* (1896), Hogan wrote a song, "All Coons Look Alike to Me." The combination of the word *coon* and the new ragtime syncopation created a sensation. In the song, a woman rejects her former lover with the chorus: "All coons look alike to me, / I've got another beau, you see, / and he's just as good to me / as you, nig! ever tried to be..." It was a tremendous hit. Coon songs became the rage.

In retrospect, Hogan may have intended the lyrics simply as a character song. On the other hand, he may have intended, consciously or not, an "in-your-face" use of white racism, for Hogan could be a fighter. He once knocked down a white box-office attendant in the Deep South for insulting him. He then had to be smuggled out of town, and immediately joined the

Curtis Minstrels leaving for Australia. In any case, the criticism for writing "All Coons Look Alike to Me" followed him the remainder of his life. Yet the coon song and the cakewalk significantly influenced the trend of popular song and dance in the United States before the phalanx of the black middle class finally drove the word *coon* from the theatre.

Hogan toured with the Georgia Graduate Students and later wrote and starred in his musical skit, *At Jolly Coon-ey Island* (1898). He starred in Will Marion Cook's *Clorindy; or, The Origin of the Cakewalk* (1898), where he sang "Hottest Coon in Dixie," his own composition. In 1899 he was the only Black in the all-white Captain Kidd Company. Hogan was the hit of the Curtis Company in Australia, where among many acts, "his imitation of a Negro preacher's speech sent the house into uproarious laughter."[100] In New York, both he and Bert Williams separately escaped death at the hands of a mob, which, ironically, did not recognize Hogan. He was the highest paid performer in vaudeville, $300 a week in 1901, while most first-class performers earned $12–$15 a week.

In 1905 Hogan and his wife Louise are credited with staging the first "syncopated music" concert in history. Using the "new" ragtime music, he organized the Memphis Students to star himself, Abbie Mitchell, wife of the show's composer, Will Marion Cook, and the featured dancer, Ida Forsyne (Hubbard), billed as "Miss Topsy, the girl who was not born, but just growed." They played at Hammerstein's Victoria Theatre on Broadway for one hundred performances. Hogan and Billy McClain danced with the Smart Set Company on waves of raves. In 1905 Hogan starred in his own production of *Rufus Rastus*, originally named *Birth of a Minstrel*. An often fussy critic, Sylvester Russell, approved.

> His greatest achievement was the quaint song, "Oh Wouldn't it be a Dream," responded by an invisible chorus what was most excellent. "Is Everybody Happy?" [his signature greeting] was something that can never be duplicated by white comedians, and this comes as a refreshing treat to white people in New York where genuine colored minstrel shows are generally crowded out.[101]

In 1896, in the *Freeman*, Hogan commented on the status of Blacks in show business: "In my troupe there is not a man or woman who cannot read and write intelligently and grammatically." As Hogan wrote and rehearsed *The Oyster Man* (1907), his strength began to give way. When the show opened, he could perform but once a week. It closed in March. On the first day of summer, 1908, a grand testimonial put together by his peers – Williams and Walker, Jesse Shipp, Alex Rogers, Cole and Johnson, and Lester Walton – was held at the West End Theatre. A seriously ill Ernest Hogan could not attend. He died of paresis at the age of 44.[102]

Billy McClain may have been the greatest talent black minstrelsy produced. Unlike Williams and Walker or Cole and Johnson, his name has been obscured, possibly because he spent many of his most prolific years in Europe. Born in Indianapolis on 12 October 1866, he entered minstrelsy in 1883, playing cornet in Lew Johnson's Minstrels. Over the next decade he, like his colleagues, worked as a comic for a variety of managers, including Black Patti's Troubadours. In 1899 he sailed with M. B. Curtis to Australia, where the troupe foundered. McClain joined Orpheus McAdoo's Jubilee Singers and Concert Company. Upon his return to America three years later, he conceived and wrote *The Smart Set* (1901), which ran through various versions until 1924. The original starred Ernest Hogan and included McClain's wife, Cordelia.

McClain's hunger for knowledge sent him on many adventures. In Washington, DC, he was known as "Doctor" McClain – he had received a diploma in osteopathy on account of the sprains and fractures of acrobats and dancers that he had attended to. He took boxing lessons, and later in 1910 trained Sam McVey for his fights in France and Belgium. An unidentified clipping from a French newspaper reveals his passion for motor cars. "Billy McClain since his sojourn in Paris, has become quite an expert chauffeur. On a 40 h.p. De Dion, the other day, he created a record between Paris and Monte Carlo for touring cars."[103] In an unconfirmed report, Billy McClain, known as the "Diamond King," was arrested in Kansas City for having "too much jewelry for a colored man." He was eventually released after he proved ownership. At the time McClain was wearing diamonds worth about $7,000 and a gold nugget weighing 14 ounces [*sic*] and valued at $523. He was also traveling with 37 trunks, 13 hat boxes, 24 rugs, 14 brass instruments, 3 typewriters, 9 birdcages, 7 dogs, and a private secretary.[104]

He wrote music and lyrics in profusion: "The Roll Call," "Priscilla Eloped with a Coon," "Don't You Think So," "Mother's Last Letter to Me," and "Shake, Rattle, and Roll." In October 1902, when Hogan and McClain opened their Smart Set company with "Enchantment," a Philadelphia critic raved that it surpassed all Negro comedy companies.[105]

In Honolulu his acting talents in *My Friend from Georgia* (1902) were noted. "McClain is an actor. He is not only a dancer, the best in Negro minstrelsy that has been seen here in years, but he has made some strides along the way and his poise, his quiet demeanor and his command of a situation show real dramatic instinct."[106] Other critics agreed.

> The attraction of Crawford's theatre this week contains some features somewhat out of the ordinary as theatrical features generally go. A remarkable achievement is Billy McClain's rendition of old "Uncle Tom's Cabin" in the play there this week. He has earned the title of being the foremost colored actor on the stage today. So long has he been identified with comedy and minstrelsy that it will seem incredible to the American public to learn of him playing "Svengali" in Trilby and "Tom" in *Uncle Tom's Cabin* for four consecutive months.[107]

His directing and production talents appeared early. McClain is credited with having conceived the idea of producing *The South Before the War* (1891) by persuading Whallen and Martell to finance the show, which toured with a mixed cast. He claimed credit (as did so many others) for being the first to introduce the cakewalk on the stage. He named the dance a "walk around." Sam Jack had hired McClain as talent scout and stage manager for his *The Creole Show* (1890). He also organized and rehearsed sixty Blacks to perform in the spectacle *The Siege of Vicksburg*. With this success behind him, Nate Salsbury, known as Buffalo Bill Cody's partner in the Wild West Exhibition, hired McClain to produce *Black America* (1895) in Ambrose Park, South Brooklyn. The spectacle employed a cast of over 365 black entertainers, including the 9th US Cavalry Band. In London and Paris, McClain was able to indulge his taste for theatrical spectacle, as this excerpt from a letter to the *Freeman* indicates:

> I finish my Paris engagement November 30, and open on Moss and Stoll, London December 17, continuing until October. I have purchased fifteen evening gowns for Madame Cordelia (his actress wife) and five each for my girls, making a total of forty dresses, and twenty suits for my boys. My people change four times a night, and never wear the same gown the second time during the week's engagement. I have just received a letter asking me if I would assist in producing the Drury Lane Pantomime. My troupe is a big success. Every step I have made has been successful. Now I am turning money away.[108]

He also claimed to have been the first to produce a black vaudeville show in French. Amid all of his triumphs, he never forgot, or possibly Europe never allowed him to forget, he was black. In a letter to the *Freeman* postmarked 20 October 1906, from Southampton, England: "There is just as much prejudice here in England as in America, and you will find it out if you stay long enough." The story of McClain's years between 1910 and 1950 have yet to be told. His retirement was spent in Los Angeles, living in a trailer house. The trailer caught fire, and McClain burned to death on the night of 19 January 1950.[109]

After World War One, the soul of minstrelsy had died; but for another twenty years, amateurs kept the corpse twitching. Amateurs' Guild Books had appeared as early as the 1850s. As the new century progressed, for 10, 25, or 50 cents, more and more guidebooks, skits, and music became available. Small-town minstrelsy became ubiquitous. On 29 May 1935, at the Golden State Theatre in Oakland, California, the NAACP promoted an all-black minstrel show as a fund-raiser. At that point, whiteface minstrelsy moved to radio with *Amos 'n' Andy*, and then managed a rebirth in the 1950s on television. As chapter 13 will show, even in the millennium, minstrelsy's ghost still lingers in the white American soul.

From 1843, when four white males sang, danced, and created merry chaos, minstrelsy evolved in forty years to a cast of one hundred with the Mastodon Minstrels (1880s). Then, in the 1890s, minstrelsy slipped into burlesque, variety, and vaudeville. According to Brander Mathews, minstrelsy's decline stemmed from three causes: minstrelsy did not devote itself to developing the character and qualities of the real Blacks; by the end of the nineteenth century audiences wanted to see women singing and dancing on stage; and ragtime and the variety shows were gradually replacing the tired minstrel cliché.[110] Mathews could have added a fourth cause. Blacks simply provided a fresh and superior alternative entertainment, labeled variously as "combination," "operetta," "opera," "musical comedy," "song play," "revue," and "musical farce." These changes took place over a long period of time, but the trend was already evident by the mid-1880s. Blacks abandoned the pejorative label, but the public had grown up with "minstrel." The old name sold tickets and most troupes continued to use it. Among the hundreds of African American performers who graced the stages between 1865 and 1930, four led the way in shattering the old Jim Crow and Zip Coon images. In their various ways Sam Lucas, Charles Hicks, Ernest Hogan, and Billy McClain forced the changes that became so evident in the 1890s.

5

New vistas: plays, spectacles, musicals, and opera

Errol G. Hill

The Creole Show proved that there was indeed a popular audience in America for black musical theatre other than shows labeled "minstrel" or spurious variants of *Uncle Tom's Cabin.* New combinations including spectacles of different size and effect were tried with varying success. From 1891 to 1893 three new productions shared similar characteristics: they were set in the South, they were produced by Whites, and their companies comprised both black and white players. Each show consisted of multiple separate acts, as in vaudeville, and black items displayed an honest attempt to exhibit aspects of black culture in music, dance, song, humor, and fighting spirit without using the parodic blackface.[1]

South Before the War (1891) was the first of these productions. It was brought up from Louisville, Kentucky, to New York City by its two managers, John Whalen and Henry Martell, who had been approached with the idea for the show by Billy McClain. The program comprised plantation scenes with songs, dances, and other specialties and it toured the burlesque circuit around the country omitting the Southland. McClain led the black corps in the company, wrote some of the original songs, and served for a spell as stage manager. His contribution was acknowledged when in 1893 the producers presented him with a gold key during the run of the show at the Arch Street Theatre in Philadelphia.

McClain's wife, Cordelia, a soloist and actress of merit, was a company member, as was J. Ed. Green, whose Black Diamond Quartet remained with the show for more than two years. Green would later play a pivotal role as director of the Pekin Stock Company of Chicago. By 1897 the western company of *South Before the War*, now owned solely by Martell and managed by George Chennell, was reported to have closed in St. Louis without the usual two weeks' notice, leaving its artistes stranded. In 1899 the parent company, under Martell, was at the New Burbank Theatre in Los Angeles, with a program which began with a presentation of "*The Passion Play* by the Animated Picture Machine"; the movies had arrived. After an intermission the interracial drama as announced was performed. Then came specialty acts, including appearances by the soprano Flora Batson, buck-and-wing dancers, and, finally, a grand cakewalk contest. This show survived for eight seasons, finally closing in 1899.

Slavery Days (1893) was the second of the three productions under review. Little is known of this venture beyond a few elementary facts.[2] It opened at Brockton, Massachusetts, in September 1893 with a company consisting of some ten men, twelve women, and two quartets, under the management of Major Ben Payne. In October, Al Anderson is credited with introducing a new four-song-and-dance piece called "Four Night Ramblers," to be performed by Jerry Mills, Henry Winfred, Frank Sutton, and Anderson himself. This production was designed to tour, as the following May the troupe was visiting "the British provinces" (in Canada, presumably) when two lady members, Rosa Anderson and Ida Winfred, left the group and sailed home to Boston. The company's last mention in the available records is in October 1894, when John Stokes is listed as manager and proprietor and Clara West as musical director.

The third production is seemingly an attempt to reenact in theatrical terms an episode from the Civil War, when General Grant set out to capture a key port city on the Mississippi River. After direct attacks failed, the general laid siege to the city, which held out for six weeks against constant bombardment but which in the end was forced to surrender. The single entry in the records regarding this show is dated 24 June 1893. It advised that Billy McClain was rehearsing sixty black performers, who would participate in Pain's [*sic*] spectacular production of *The Siege of Vicksburg*, scheduled to open at Manhattan Beach, Coney Island, on 26 June.[3] No further details are available about the author or the producer. One assumes that with a large mixed cast involved in a "spectacular production," the performance may have been closer to a pageant than a drama, and it probably took place in an open-air arena. Of particular note is the fact that all three companies here discussed consisted of black and white performers. It is a matter of record that the decade of the 1890s witnessed the emergence of several such companies, possibly indicating a greater degree of racial tolerance among theatre folk than existed in the general public.

To mark the four-hundredth anniversary of the arrival of Columbus in the Americas, a world's fair, World's Columbian Exposition, was held in 1893 in Chicago. Planning began when President Benjamin Harrison appointed a national commission consisting of 208 members. However, disregarding petitions from black leaders addressed to him and to Congress, Harrison refused to name African Americans to serve on the commission, the net result being that Blacks would have no voice regarding whether or how they would be portrayed at the fair. On the other hand, fair officials were persuaded by one Xavier Péné, a French labor contractor and ivory trader in West Africa, to award him a concession to exhibit an African village, as had been done in previous expositions in Europe. The village would be peopled with Africans and, Péné promised, would include the famous Dahomey women warriors. Invitations were sent to countries around the world to participate in the exhibition, which was slated to open for six months from 1 May to 31 October.

In addition to Péné's village group, two African states responded to the invitation. Liberia and Cape Coast province sent exhibits but no representatives. Péné recruited sixty-seven Africans, who came from the French Congo, French Guinea, and mostly from Benin. Installed as "Dahomeyans" in a village setting constructed at the far end of the Midway Plaisance, they were a mile away from the main fairgrounds. White observers found the Africans to be savage and threatening. One correspondent wrote: "blacker than buried midnight and as degraded as the animals which prowl the jungles of their dark land...In these wild people we easily detect many characteristics of the American negro."[4] From the Caribbean, Haiti provided a pavilion and invited the 75-year-old Frederick Douglass, who had served as Minister to Haiti in 1889, to be that country's official commissioner. There were also exhibits, but no representatives, from Jamaica and Curaçao.

On dedication day no black American sat on the dais for dignitaries. The director-general of the fair and the Lady Managers chose not to appoint Blacks to any responsible positions. Only after repeated protests and calls by black-owned newspapers for a boycott of the fair was a colored St. Louis school principal belatedly added (as an alternate) to the commission and a controversial Colored People's Day scheduled on 25 August. While many African Americans stayed away, Douglass embraced the occasion to speak on the Race Problem in America, affirming that the exposition "bore witness to a moral regression – the reconciliation of the North and the South at the expense of Negroes."[5] Apart from Douglass' oration, the program for Colored American Day, arranged by the young composer Will Marion Cook, consisted of musical selections from the classics performed by soloists and instrumentalists, slave songs by the Fisk Jubilee Singers, readings by elocutionist Hallie Q. Brown, and readings of his own poems by Paul Laurence Dunbar. White supporters also gave short addresses.

Probably the most noteworthy African American event during the exposition did not occur on the fairgrounds. This was the production of William Edgar Easton's four-act play, *Dessalines*, directed by Henrietta Vinton Davis at Freiberg's Opera House in Chicago. A romantic melodrama written in blank verse, the play focused on Jean Jacques Dessalines, the first Haitian emperor. Having actively engaged in the overthrow of slavery, Dessalines declared his country to be a free republic, which he ruled over briefly from 1804 until he was assassinated in 1806. In the title role was Professor Thomas C. Scottron, a dramatic reader with "a majestic presence and a deep, sonorous voice" so controlled that from it he could draw "the tenderest and most pathetic tones."[6] Miss Davis took the role of Clarisse, sister of Rigaud, a mulatto general in the French colonial army. Abducted by renegade Blacks, she is saved from death by the ferocious Dessalines, who, tamed by her innocence, falls in love with her. The play was revived years later in 1909 at Trinity Congregational Church, Pittsburgh, when Miss Davis not only directed but also performed two roles: the flower girl, Zingarella, and the comic, Dominique. In this revival Henry Lewis played Dessalines. The only other production on record took place at the Fine Arts Theatre, Boston, on 15 May 1930 by the Allied Arts Players, whose general director was the pianist and *Crisis* columnist Maud Cuney-Hare. Granville Stewart took the title role while Avon Long played the Papaloi or voodoo priest.

In its issue of 2 March 1889, the *Indianapolis Freeman* commented that stage portrayals of the colored man as an illiterate, contented servant were becoming monotonous. The paper asked: "Why has there never been a drama showing the manly and heroic side of the Negro's life? There is no dearth of material." Had William Easton read this challenge it may well have spurred him to complete his play on Dessalines, followed after several years by his second original drama entitled *Christophe: A Tragedy in Prose of Imperial Haiti*. In this play General Henri Christophe chafes under the harsh rule of Dessalines, craftily plots his assassination, and replaces him as Haitian monarch, only to become as autocratic as his victim. Having built the impregnable mountaintop fortress of Sans Souci with its secret underground entrance, Christophe withdraws to its safety with the remnants of his troops when attacked by superior forces under the mulatto, General Boyer. But Christophe is betrayed by his confidant, the false priest Père L'Avenge (in reality the Lady Valerie), who seeks vengeance for the murder of her fiancé by one of Christophe's officers in act 1. Playwright Easton revealed that he wrote the drama for Miss Davis, whom he had in mind for the role of Valerie.

The play was produced by Miss Davis at the Lenox Casino in New York City for a 21 March 1912 opening, when she performed the dual roles of Valerie and Père L'Avenge, appearing opposite to R. Henri Strange, who played Christophe. In a 1975 essay, Robert Fehrenbach found a new angle from which to judge Easton's Haitian plays. Of *Dessalines* he wrote: "Whichever short-comings Easton's play has because he was unable to avoid sentimentality and preachment . . . and because he imitated a heroic dramatic form from white Europe, *Dessalines* nonetheless remains a remarkable expression of one man's pride in his race and a significant attempt to convey that pride to his people."[7]

As Easton's mother was descended from one of the generals of the Haitian revolution, the subject of Haiti's survival must have been close to his heart. Easton was born in 1861 in New York[8] and was well educated, having attended the La Salle Academy in Providence, Rhode Island, and college in Canada. He then moved to Texas, where he became first a public school teacher, then by turns a newspaper editor and customs officer, and was engaged for twelve years in political work as secretary for the Republican Central Committee in Austin, Texas. In 1901 he relocated to Los Angeles and held jobs in both private industry and state government. He was also a newspaper correspondent and publicity man for the illustrated weekly journal *New Age*. In addition to his historical dramas, Easton wrote two one-act sketches, namely, *Is She a Lady in the Underworld?* and *Misery in Bohemia*, for which no performance record has been traced.

The 1890s witnessed several more straight dramas – at least by intention, if not in fact. One of particular interest was the premiere production of a new play entitled *Marcus, a Story of the South* that was "performed by a selected company of colored and white artists." Written by Messrs. Richings and Strange with R. Henri Strange in the title role, it was staged at the Academy of Music in Philadelphia on 12 November 1896; it told the story of Marcus (played by Strange), who "rises from a ragged colored boy to become a prominent lawyer." The last act, however, clung to tradition by introducing a number of so-called special features, including vocalists Flora Batson and Theodore Drury, as well as a violin soloist, Joseph H. Douglass, the grandson of Frederick Douglass.[9]

Another dramatic production that opened in the fall of 1898 and which played in northern cities was the four-act Civil War play, *Our Old Kentucky Home*, written by the journalist John E. Bruce in collaboration with

Henrietta Vinton Davis. Miss Davis also directed the play and took the principal role of the Creole slave Clothilde who, disguised as a man, attacks an enemy fort at midnight and helps her lover, Basil, to escape. She is then reunited with Basil, a freed slave who had enlisted in the Union army prior to his capture. In a 1903 revival[10] at the East Turner Hall in Denver, Colorado, under the title *Clothilde the Creole; or, Our Old Kentucky Home*, the role of Basil was assigned to Albert Young and the play deemed to be the most successful melodrama ever staged in Denver.

In its issue of 19 March 1898 the *Colored American* of Washington, DC, reported that a young dramatic author named Charles Sager of St. Paul had recently 'produced' an original play entitled *The South in Slavery*. No further data regarding the play or its fate appeared at the time or later.[11] However, the following year Sager was responsible for another dramatic production in which the indefatigable Miss Davis also played a role. Billed as a spectacular pageant called *The Negro*, it was first presented in August 1899 at the Park Theatre in Hannibal, Missouri, to mark the city's Emancipation Day celebration, of which Sager had been appointed manager. Scenes included the South at the time freedom was proclaimed and the royal court of Dahomey in West Africa, where the queen (presumably the role played by Miss Davis) presented an entertainment in honor of the visiting American ambassador. The production in Hannibal was seen as a fitting finale to a day of great celebration. Sager toured his play to cities in the Midwest, including St. Paul, St. Louis, Kansas City, and Indianapolis, as well as to centers in Illinois and Ohio. Albert Young must have worked well alongside Miss Davis in *Our Old Kentucky Home*, for he was engaged to join the tour of *The Negro*. We will encounter Charles Sager again in the new century in connection with Robert Motts' black Pekin Theatre in Chicago.

In January 1899 the *Freeman* reported that Ernest Hogan had written a play that "will be the first legitimate colored production that has ever been on the boards [combining] opera with farce and comedy with pathos... through it all will run a pretty love story."[12] Ignoring the proverbial blurb about the *first* this or that, which is seldom true and often unprovable, I will summarize the plot before raising a thorny issue. Of two rival black politicians in New Orleans, one was backed by Scrub Ashby, known as "The King" (and played by Hogan). When the candidates fight a duel, a preacher intervenes and is accidentally shot. Ashby's candidate is chosen, but is so impoverished by the campaign that his daughter, a musician, takes to the stage. She becomes a sensation, restores her father's wealth, and marries "the King." Now to the issue. It is identified by the play's title: *King of Coon Town*.[13]

In black theatre history it is common knowledge that by 1896 Ernest Hogan had composed an immensely popular song entitled "All Coons Look Alike to Me" that was later condemned as so reprehensible that he was never allowed to forget his infamy. In fairness, Hogan was neither the first nor the last to use the term *coon* in reference to people. Nor was its use at the time considered derogatory. A brief history of the term is illuminating.[14] In 1741 it was used as a short form for "raccoon." By 1832 it meant a frontier rustic and by 1840 it referred to a member of the Whig Party (1834–55), which had been formed to oppose the Democrats and which was eventually renamed the Republican Party. The song "Zip Coon" (1834), for instance, did not refer specifically to either Black or White, and in the 1840s and 1850s "coon songs" were Whig political songs.

According to Stuart Flexner, by 1862 *coon* had come to mean a Black person but one of the earliest surviving texts of a coon song by a black writer is dated more than twenty years later. Entitled "De Coon Dat Had de Razor," its lyrics were attributed to "Prof. Wm. F. Quown," supposedly a pseudonym for Sam Lucas, who also composed the music. In three verse-and-choruses it told the story of a quarrel between two men at a Negro ball, "where dem coons all carry razors," and how one cut up the other. Each verse and chorus ended with a refrain that echoed the song's title. Of particular interest is the final verse, in which old policeman Haiser, when called to the scene, declared: "I ain't gwine to touch dat coon / For he has got a razor." Other than the use of *coon* to signify African American, the song might well be deemed a cautionary ballad in line with many other ballads that speak of a violent act committed hastily under the influence of wine or another such stimulant. There is also the implied threat to civic authority when the policeman declines to arrest the slasher, who is still in possession of his razor.[15]

By the 1880s, in a list of 130 most successful popular songs compiled by Edward B. Marks, seven – all written by Whites – were identified as "coon songs." Of the seven, only one, "New Coon in Town" (1883), employed enough syncopation "to foreshadow the true, shouting, ragtime school."[16] By this time the real coon song became musically identified with the exciting syncopated music of African Americans that had entered show business. Thereafter, the term "coon" was frequently used in play and song titles, for example, in 1897 *A Trip to Coontown* by Cole and Johnson; in 1898 Hogan's "Hottest Coon in Dixie," composed for Cook's operetta *Clorindy*; Isham's *A Tenderloin Coon*; Williams and Walker's *Lucky Coon Company*; and in later years there were such absurdities as *the Coontown Four Hundred* Company (1899) and *the Coontown Golf Club* Company (1902–03), featuring

the comedian, producer, and stage manager, S. H. Dudley. Black lyricists
and musicians had written some one hundred "coon songs" until about the
year 1905, when, probably stung by a strong rebuke from the colored middle
class, retractions were in order and the genre's popularity declined.

Ironically, one of the forces that led to a new theatre was the nearly complete segregation of black minstrel performers until the 1880s. Racism had
become a centripetal force spinning African American musicians, actors,
dancers, and writers closer together, for as I shall show, nearly all the shows
at the turn of the century were the products of several talents that fed and
inspired each another. Clearly, black music and dance as represented by
ragtime and the cakewalk drove the new entertainment engine. The magic
for both had been syncopation, a musical term for shifting the accented beat
in 4/4 marches to an unstressed position. One of the first published versions of syncopation was Ernest Hogan's chorus (not verse) of "All Coons
Look Alike to Me." He kindled a fad that became a firestorm of ragtime
compositions.

The earliest documented performance of Hogan's song was by the actress May Irwin, who appeared in John McNally's farce-comedy *Courted Into
Court*, first presented at the Bijou Theatre in New York on 29 December
1896.[17] Nothing in the all-white play, or in Hogan's song (assuming the lyrics
were the same), was explicitly degrading to African Americans. Since there
were no Blacks in the cast or in the world of the play, the chorus "All Coons
Look Alike to Me" could only refer to three men in the comedy who were involved with Dottie Dimple, the character played by Miss Irwin. These were
the judge, her husband, and her husband's father – all of whom were white.
Of course, the implication might be that they were all acting like lower-class
black men, hence the phrase "all coons look alike." Or it might just have
been an early unrecognized feminist play!

The rubric "Spectacles" is introduced by one of the most stupendous
productions on record in the history of African American entertainment.
Entitled *Black America*, it was assembled by the owner and producer of
Buffalo Bill's Wild West show, Nate Salsbury. His stated purpose mentioned
on the playbill was to reveal "the lovable, bright side of the true southern
Negro, presented in a series of animated scenes of rural simplicity." His
plans followed the pattern set in his earlier production. He would open and
run the show for some months in the northeastern states, then transfer it
to Europe, where *Buffalo Bill* was an outstanding success and still showing.
Having an all-black cast numbering some five hundred men, women, and
children, *Black America* opened at Ambrose Park in Brooklyn, New York,

on 25 May 1895. It played at the 7,000-seat open air theatre twice daily, every day, for seven weeks; then it moved to a 7,500-seat amphitheatre, also outdoors, at Huntington Avenue Grounds in Boston for another seven weeks. Next, it toured to several towns in the northeast, played a two-week stint at Madison Square Garden, and had further bookings in Philadelphia and in Washington, DC. Then, six months after it opened, the show closed and the company dispersed. The promise of a European tour was denied.[18]

Black America comprised two main parts beside an introduction and a finale. For the introduction, an orchestra regaled spectators with popular music of the day. In one program copy this item was performed by Herr Ascher's Transatlantic Military Band directed by Professor Emil Ascher. Following the band concert the chorus made a grand entrance from behind a huge painted backdrop that depicted a steamboat landing beside the Mississippi River: "when the line of Negroes, men and women, filed out from behind the scene ... it seemed it would never end; and when the 500 plantation hands in their ornate costumes, assembled in front of the grandstand and began to sing their grand old plantation melodies, the effect was most startling in the spectators."[19]

The second part of the program consisted of specialty numbers, such as a drill by black soldiers, hundred-yard flat races for men and fifty-yard races for women, acrobatic displays, contortionists, barrel-boxing, buck-and-wing dancers, breakdowns, banjo players, and colored jockeys on thoroughbreds. As events proved unpopular or unseemly, they were promptly discarded and replaced by more suitable acts, special attention being paid to their educational, historical, and moral value. The finale constituted an "historical apotheosis." As the company took part in various drills while the chorus sang appropriate songs, huge 20-foot high portraits appeared of individuals whose actions had furthered the cause of Blacks in America, namely, John Brown, Frederick Douglass, General Grant, Abraham Lincoln, General Sherman, and Harriet Beecher Stowe.

This production was unique in several respects. It was, at the time, the largest assembly of Blacks ever to participate in a theatrical production. Set outdoors in Brooklyn and Boston, it introduced spectators to a recreated pre-Civil War slave village of 150 log cabins actually built to house the cast. Nearby was planted a cotton field and the black cast were first observed working at various chores in imitation of plantation life. All this activity took place before the show formally began. However, when the company went on tour and played in more restricted areas indoors, the village setting was excluded and the cast reduced by as many as two hundred or more members. On such occasions the large cast would be housed in a special train carrying twelve railroad cars. Moreover, in an effort to keep performances fresh and seeming spontaneous, the program was frequently changed, both in content and in structure.

Despite its impressive size and the desire to be "natural" and "authentic," elements of the old-fashioned minstrel stereotype crept into the performance. One such item was a mad scramble for watermelons brought in on a cart while the chorus sang "Watermelon Smiling on the Vine"; another was a cakewalk contest when twenty to thirty couples dressed in gaudy outfits paraded up and down through the aisles. A generally supportive press acknowledged that *Black America* was strikingly original, entertaining, and instructive. The *Washington Post* found it "unique in character, abundant in merriment, grotesque in some of its features and pathetic in others, and from beginning to end absolutely free from anything approaching vulgarity."[20]

Roger Hall's previously cited essay offers three possible reasons why *Black America* did not go to Europe as originally intended. First, producer Salsbury had been unwell during preparations for the show and may have suffered a relapse. Second, despite reasonably good reviews the production did not generate sufficient income to offset the cost of retaining such a huge company. Third, Salsbury was experiencing a good deal of trouble with the star of the *Wild West* show, Bill Cody, whose notorious conduct as a drunkard and womanizer caused endless worries to an already ailing producer. Not mentioned but worth considering is that *Black America* had its own built-in paradoxes. It pretended to be an authentic picture of slave life but showed nothing of the horrors of slavery. It aimed to demonstrate black progress and achievement but apart from two or three notables, such as Billy and Cordelia McClain and the soprano Mamie Flowers, it employed none of the nation's top black performers, preferring instead to rely on the so-called natural ability of the unskilled masses. For all his apparent altruism in mounting this stupendous pageant, Salsbury himself, judging from his press statement, held a limited view of African American potential: "The white man can imitate the Negro, but no Negro that I've ever seen was a success as an actor. Singing and dancing are the Negro specialties; and they would do well to stick to them as closely as possible."[21]

By the mid-1890s recognizable features of a new type of programing had surfaced for the burgeoning number of black road shows. In three or occasionally four acts, most productions would include comedy skits, sketches, or playlets with which a show might open or close. Another feature could be a group of operatic selections to be sung by principal soloists backed by a vocal chorus. The show's midsection, still referred to as the *olio*, continued to be reserved for novelties and specialty acts from jugglers to gymnasts, dancers, comedians, and the like. The majority of productions also found a place on the program for a cakewalk contest, which had become exceedingly popular, especially when audiences were invited to take part in judging the contest and picking the winning couple by acclamation.

For the season that commenced in September 1896, the impresario Al G. Field produced a new show whose title, *Darkest America*, was obviously chosen to capitalize on its similarity to the prodigious *Black America* of the previous year. On this occasion, however, a normal-sized troupe of around fifty artistes was hired, along with a brass band and orchestra, both led by black conductors. According to the printed program for a February 1897 performance, the scaled-back production was no less ambitious than its predecessor, its intention being to provide snapshots of black progress "from Plantation to Palace," with little concern for historical accuracy. The first act began with life on the plantation, followed by a proclamation to end slavery and the parting of master and slaves. Act 2 covered life on the levee, with steamboat songs sung by roustabouts. In a realistic-looking race between steamships, "a thrilling catastrophe" occurred when Uncle Amos was thrown into the river. The third act unveiled "the vicious side of Darkey Life" in a visit to a gambling den, whose ramshackle building caught fire and from which children had to be rescued. How these catastrophes and pyrotechnics were presented on stage is not disclosed. The last act was an "operatic kinetoscope" that placed the colored society of Washington, DC, in attendance at a high-class concert, probably at the Palace Theatre. This final scene was added somewhat later by the same Billy McClain who had been director of *Black America*.[22]

Along with the ubiquitous McClains, *Darkest America* did engage a number of prominent professionals, including the revered comedian Sam Lucas and his wife Carrie Lucas, a contralto singer, the admirable tenor Lawrence Chenault, versatile John Rucker in the role of Uncle Amos, male impersonator Florence Hines, and several others. However, the growing number of new entertainments, varying in type and quality, provided opportunities for experienced black troupers to bargain their way in and out of contracts with remarkable agility. The most talented among them were constantly on the move from one show to the next, a condition that kept the program of any individual production in a state of flux. By the end of the first year, the perceptive manager, John W. Vogel, had leased the rights to *Darkest America* and bought it over completely the next year. One review credited him "with the possession of a company of real artists capable of giving as finished and enjoyable a performance that is a delight to see and hear."[23] The production would run for four years until April 1899.

The attraction of the ethnographic title in show business was given a new twist when the colored producer John W. Isham launched his Oriental America Company at Palmer's Theatre in New York City on 3 August 1897. Having a very fair complexion, Isham was often assumed to be white,[24] which gave him a decided advantage in gaining responsible employment, booking shows, or dealing with agents and managers. Having been an advance man for Sam T. Jack's *Creole Show*, Isham decided to form his own company, *Isham's Octoroons*, which opened at the Olympic Theatre in New York in August 1895. Following Jack's lead, Isham installed a chorus of attractive women, emphasized singing, including operatic selections in the first part of the program and dancing towards the end, with the inescapable cakewalk featured. The central portion was filled by a burlesque sketch that was changed from time to time. Isham's strong corps of performers was so successful that he formed a second *Octoroons* company that the *Freeman* judged to be well equipped, thoroughly enjoyable, and superior to the average white performer.[25]

Striving for innovation and excellence, Isham next organized the *Oriental America* troupe, which was heralded as bigger and better than his other shows. Despite its name, the show contained little of the Orient and was, in fact, composed entirely of colored artistes, some of whom were transferred from the Octoroon companies. The only items lending credence to the show's title were a Japanese dance by four females and the march of the Oriental Huzzars (*sic*) led by Belle Davis. Nevertheless, there was much to be admired in the performance, reported in the *Washington (DC) Morning Times*:

> From the rise of the curtains on the opening chorus, the audience, which filled the house to the doors, were first surprised, then pleased, then delighted, and reached a climax of enthusiasm in rounds of applause when the last curtain fell on the magnificent rendition of the bridal chorus sextet from "Lucia di Lammermoor" in which all the stars appeared. Mr. Isham has certainly eclipsed all his former efforts in this line.[26]

Among the stellar performers were: Mattie Wilkes, leading soprano; Billy Eldridge, comedian; Jesse Shipp and Edward Winn, descriptive vocalists; and J. Rosamond Johnson singing in costume the armorer's song from De Koven's opera *Robin Hood*. This was a show of high quality but perhaps a little ahead of the popular audience. Isham took the production to Britain, where it played in Scotland and England for several months. However, by May the following year he was forced to file a petition for bankruptcy and retire from theatrical management.

His brother, Will Isham, who had worked with him in the past, made a final effort in the 1900/01 season to succeed with a farcical vaudeville production called *King Rastus*. Featuring veteran minstrel player Billy Kersands, the Mallory Brothers, and other old-timers, the show peddled many stereotypical jokes at the expense of Blacks and was castigated by a critic writing for the *Freeman* of 30 March 1901, as "a slander on the Negro of America." It was the antithesis of everything brother John had stood for. Some years earlier, in a thoughtful article on the progress of the Negro in the theatre, R. W. Thompson of Washington, DC, had written of John Isham:

> With just a leavening of low comedy, Mr. Isham constructed a composite musical extravaganza, clean, crisp, and up-to-date, abounding in popular music and climaxing with a series of the finest operatic gems... He scoured the country and drew together the most representative aggregation of colored artists yet developed, costumed them richly... spared no expense... eschewed the plantation idea of the Negro and painted him as he has grown to be. As a result, Mr. Isham's three companies are the best paying investments of the season.[27]

The best investment it may have been for a limited period of time; it was also, in the long run, a costly one since the appeal was clearly not to the generality and a price had to be paid for aiming too high.

At the time Isham organized *Oriental America* (his third road company), the managing partnership of Voelckel and Nolan decided it was time to give him some competition. In 1896 they signed a contract with the concert singer Mme. Sissieretta Jones, known professionally as "the Black Patti," to create a variety show in which she would be the star attraction among a cluster of other items, such as a sketch and the usual specialty acts. The managers also engaged two exciting young theatre artistes, Bob Cole and Billy Johnson, who were gaining a reputation for their original musical compositions and comic sketches, as well as for their stage performances. They would write songs and stage the show, which the managers undertook to promote under the title *Black Patti Troubadours*.[28] By this time, Mme. Jones had already gained an enviable career on the concert stage.

Sissieretta Jones was born in Portsmouth, Virginia, on 5 January 1868 and given the name Matilda Joyner.[29] Her father Jeremiah Joyner was a carpenter by trade. Assisted by his wife Mary, he served as choirmaster and may also have been a lay preacher at the Afro-American Methodist Church in the city. By 1876, when the family moved to Providence, Rhode Island, the parents were estranged and living apart, with the youthful Sissieretta joining her mother. Sissieretta was only a teenager when she married David Jones and bore a daughter, who died in infancy. The young woman had developed a singing voice of such exceptional quality for its clearness and brilliancy that she was often pressed to give concerts at area churches. At age 18 she began studies at the Boston Conservatory of Music for about two years, followed, it is believed, by further study at the New England Conservatory and with recognized private tutors.

In April 1888 Mme. M. S. Jones, as she was referred to in the press,[30] first appeared in New York at a Bergen Star Concert at Steinway Hall. On that occasion the prima donna soprano was Flora Batson, her senior by five years. A month later Mme. Jones made her début at the Academy of Music in Philadelphia and that summer embarked on a six-month tour of the Caribbean area, supported by the tenor Will A. Pierce and an adequate chorus of singers. Countries visited included Jamaica, Panama, Surinam, Demerara (now called Guyana), Trinidad, and Barbados. The visit proved so successful that a second year-long trip was made in 1891, beginning with Haiti and returning to the countries where Mme. Jones had previously sung. On these overseas trips Professor A. K. LaRue was her piano "accompanist and teacher" and Mme. Jones was supported on stage by a chorus of six singers, three of whom were soloists. Her husband also joined the tour as company manager.

The early 1890s was a period of great advancement for Mme. Jones, who began to be called the Black Patti in deference to her vocal qualities, which matched those of the reigning diva of concert singers, Adelina Patti. In February 1892, Mme. Jones was invited to appear at the White House in a private concert for President Harrison and his family; in April she was the featured singer at New York's Madison Square Garden for a "Grand Negro Jubilee." That year her appearance at the Pittsburgh Exposition was so well received that she was engaged for a week the following year and also appeared at the Chicago world's fair.[31] At the height of her powers Mme. Jones was interviewed in February 1893 by a reporter of the *Detroit Tribune*. She expressed a fond wish to sing in Meyerbeer's opera, *L'Africaine*, with the Metropolitan Opera Company, but doubted it would ever take place:

"They tell me my color is against me," she added ruefully. Then in 1895 Morris Reno, president of the Carnegie Music Hall Association of New York, engaged Mme. Jones for a concert tour of European cities under the management of his associate, Rudolph Voelckel. Beginning in late spring 1895 and for the next eighteen months Mme. Jones visited and sang in London, Paris, Berlin, Cologne, Munich, Milan, and St. Petersburg. The tour was a triumph and included a command performance for England's Prince of Wales, the future King Edward VII.[32]

It was at this point in Mme. Jones' career that manager Voelckel, now in partnership with John J. Nolan, introduced the proposal for a vaudeville company called the *Black Patti Troubadours*. Bolstered by the revered Black Patti name linked to the exciting troupers Bob Cole and Billy Johnson, the *Troubadours'* first New York performance, on 26 September 1896, played to a packed house at Proctor's Theatre. Leading the mirth-makers, Tom McIntosh was a hit in the burlesque "Reuben Green" written by Cole, but within a month he and Mrs. McIntosh had left the company, to be replaced by a 40-minute skit, also created by Cole, that opened the show. The complete program, promising "three hours of mirth and melody," comprised three parts. Part one, a musical skit entitled "At Jolly Coon-ey Island," showed the boardwalk of the well-known resort with the different character types for which it was noted. Among them were the tramp Willie Wayside, played by Cole, a bathing girl, a bicycle woman, a coon singer, a buck dancer, and the "Couchee Couchee" girls. During the action musical pieces were rendered, several being original. A chorus of forty trained voices supported the soloists. Part two consisted of the "Vaudeville Olio." The DeWolf Sisters sang duets; Cole and Stella Wiley offered a terpsichorean review; Billy Johnson sang his latest "descriptive songs"; the chorus, in toreador costume, formed letters in a series of maneuvers; and Grant and Rastus executed comical acrobatics. Part three was labeled the "Operatic Kaleidoscope." It introduced Black Patti assisted by three leading singers – contralto, tenor, and baritone – and a chorus of forty voices. They sang selections from grand and light opera, along with popular items such as a medley of national airs.

Essentially this would be the format used by *Black Patti Troubadours* as they toured across the country for the next thirteen years. During that time there were at least ten different opening skits, while individual specialties in the olio changed frequently as artistes came and went. In 1897 a breach occurred between Cole and the managers over salary. Cole withdrew as stage director, taking his script and music with him. Sued for larceny, he was found "not guilty," thus establishing ownership of his material. Ernest Hogan replaced Cole as stage director and promptly produced a new edition of the Coney Island script over which he claimed authorship.[33] In the olio he added a competitive cakewalk, a feature then enjoying considerable popularity with audiences, and he sang a number of original coon songs prior to the appearance of Mme. Jones and chorus in opera selections.

In 1909 Voelckel and Nolan, owner-managers of the Troubadours, dissolved their partnership, causing a name change in the troupe to the Black Patti Musical Comedy Company. The company had, in fact, been moving steadily over the years in the direction of musical comedy, as the sketch writers became more skillful in developing plots and characters. For instance, the opening presentation in 1902 of "A Filipino Misfit," described as "a farcical skit in one act," introduced musical numbers "during the unraveling of the plot."[34] For the 1904/05 season the critic of the *Freeman* credited scriptwriter Bob Cole with "having presented a musical Negro comedy quite as genuine as white comedies of the same class." Finally, in 1908 "The Prince of Bongaboo" sketch was deemed "a show that puts real significance in that much-abused term, musical comedy."[35]

The reorganized *Original Black Patti Musical Comedy* Company first presented *A Trip to Africa* written by Jolly John Larkins, in which a group from an American college journeyed to Africa to rescue a favorite instructress who had been abducted by a tribe of natives and installed as their Princess Lulu. The role of Lulu was assigned to Mme. Jones, who remained the featured singer of the company but who had small speaking roles. Other musicals followed: *Captain Jasper*, *In the Jungles*, and *Lucky Sam from Alabam'*, but for Mme. Jones the new format proved less than hospitable. With the Troubadours, whatever else may have preceded her appearance, Mme. Jones had a segment of the show reserved primarily for her concert singing with support from other soloists and chorus. In the revised format, though her voice retained its freshness and richness of tone, it had to contend with the racy and sometimes raucous musical comedy setting, hardly ideal for the display of her unique vocal talent, now subordinated to plot and the comic moment. The company disbanded during the 1916/17 season, and Mme. Jones retired and returned to her home in Providence, Rhode Island, where she lived quietly and frugally until her death in 1933.

When Will Marion Cook composed the operetta *Clorindy; or, The Origin of the Cakewalk*, at around 1897, and persuaded the poet Paul Laurence Dunbar to collaborate in writing the libretto and lyrics, he little dreamed there would be much difficulty in promoting it. He intended to offer it to the Williams and Walker team, but they were on tour on the west coast.

Figure 11. Bob Cole, standing, and Rosamond Johnson, seated, *c.* 1898

So Cook traveled from his home in Washington, DC, to New York City to offer it to white promoters, one of whom remarked that he was crazy to believe any Broadway audience would listen to Negroes singing a Negro opera. Undeterred, Cook gained the support of veteran comedian Ernest Hogan, who agreed to train more than a score of singers and dancers for an audition that won them an engagement at the Casino Roof Garden in the city. Cook conducted the orchestra at the 1898 premiere and what occurred is best told in his own words:

> the show downstairs in the Casino Theatre was just letting out. The big audience heard those heavenly Negro voices and took to the elevators. At the finish of the opening chorus, the applause and cheering were so tumultuous that I simply stood there transfixed, my hand in the air, unable to move until Hogan rushed down to the footlights and shouted: "What's the matter, son? Let's go!"...My chorus sang like Russians, dancing meanwhile like Negroes, and cakewalking like angels, black angels! When the last note was sounded, the audience stood and cheered for at least ten minutes.[36]

The hour-long show, ending with a cakewalk against the background of a rousing chorus, was an unqualified success, but it served to intensify a growing controversy among black folk. Some felt the cakewalk was a degrading reminder of slavery and should not be staged; others defended its performance as a unique high-stepping dance created by African Americans. Some claimed the distinction of being the first to present it on stage, among them Billy McClain, who affirmed he introduced it in an unidentified Hyers Sisters' show in the mid-1870s when the dance was called a "walk around." No such performance with the sisters has emerged in the records, although McClain did later acquire an enviable reputation for staging impressive cakewalks, as instanced in his production of *Darkest America*, when fifty genuine colored people participated in the event. Finally, questions remained over the true origin and purpose of the cakewalk. A report copied from the New Orleans *Times-Democrat* newspaper in 1897 indicated that the event was a type of wooing ritual, originated more than a century ago among French Negroes of Louisiana, whence it spread across the entire South. It replaced the prohibited marriage ceremony among slaves, by allowing a man legitimately to show his preference for a woman and thus to publicly claim her as wife.[37]

One of the earliest cakewalk exhibitions was given in 1876 as part of the Centennial of American Independence celebration that took place in

Le Trans-Atlantic
Nouvelle Danse américaine au NOUVEAU CIRQUE
1ͬͤ Figure (aller)

Figure 12. Children performing the cakewalk in France, *c.* 1900

Philadelphia. According to Tom Fletcher, the dance was also known as the "chalk-line walk" or the "walk around," and the prize was an enormous cake for the winning couple.[38] Whatever its origin, there is no question of the cakewalk's immense popularity in the theatre, beginning probably around 1887 and continuing unabated through the 1890s and into the new century for a total run of almost twenty years. On 18 January 1887 McCabe and Young's Black Trilby Company, performing at the Opera House in Huntsville, Alabama, invited couples in the audience to join the professionals in a cakewalk competition, which was won by locals.[39] That ploy was certain to bring out dance enthusiasts and their friends in great numbers.

Thereafter few companies failed to include a cakewalk on their program, even tacking it on to a production of the perennial *Uncle Tom's Cabin*.[40] High-stepping was only one feature of the dance. Style in dress and grace of movement were also essential, the feet keeping time with the music throughout. Turns were especially important. "They must be made square at right angles ... when you start from a turn, the left foot must always lead."[41] I close discussion of the topic with a poetic description of the winners of a cakewalk contest at Madison Square Garden in January 1897:

> It was a great walk; it was a dusky carnival of grace, merriment and poetry of motion. These images ... clad in array that blinded the eye and benumbed the senses, swept by like a river bearing upon its bosom flowers fair to look upon – Billy Farrell and, by his side, graceful as ever, his wife glided, and they were declared first prize winners.[42]

Will Marion Cook was an impeccably trained musician. Born 27 January 1869 in Washington, DC, where his father was a Howard University law professor, Cook at age 13 was enrolled at the Oberlin Conservatory in Ohio. After two years there he won a scholarship to study the violin under Josef Joachim in Berlin, Germany. Later, in 1894–95 he also attended the National Conservatory of Music in New York for further training with director Antonin Dvorak and John White, among others. He began playing the violin professionally while still a student at Oberlin, but his début as a concert violinist took place in his home city in December 1889, after his return to the United States. Within a year Cook was named director of a new orchestra, with which he toured selected cities such as Boston and Chicago.

When Cook went to New York in the mid-1890s contact with vaudeville and ragtime completely changed his outlook. From a classically trained musician and orchestra conductor, he became a composer of songs and music

for the stage, occasionally mounting the conductor's podium to lead the theatre orchestra himself. The success of *Clorindy* having won the attention of
music publishers, Cook was assured his songs would gain wide distribution
among theatre folk, black and white. He had become acquainted with the
comedy team of Bert Williams and George Walker, destined in the ensuing
decade to be international stars in big ragtime musical comedy productions.
Cook would compose songs and music for most of their major shows from
1898 to 1907, and he was happy to have Paul Laurence Dunbar as lyricist for
two productions before Dunbar declined to write further for him.[43]

The highly successful tour of *In Dahomey* to London included a command performance for royalty that ensured Cook's reputation would be enhanced internationally. The *London Sunday Dispatch* of 20 May 1903 wrote
that Cook's music was of the highest class and that his technique, "racy of
the soil," contained finales that would be acceptable in the English opera
house of Covent Garden. Cook also composed music for the comic opera
The Cannibal King (1901) staged by Bob Cole and Rosamond Johnson. In
June 1905 he wrote all the songs for a specialty number entitled "Songs
of Black Folk," which was presented at the Paradise Garden on the roof
of New York's Victoria Theatre. Featured performers were Ernest Hogan,
Cook's spouse Abbie Mitchell, "a comely mulatto with a sweet soprano
voice," and twenty-five others serving as chorus and orchestra. The roof
garden reeked with melody, according to the review, barbershop harmony
and broken melody mingling in fantastic confusion. There was a fervor in
rendering the songs and choruses that, in the writer's opinion, could never
have been supplied by white singers.[44] The show was a hit and completed
more than a hundred performances on the roof garden that summer.

The chorus had come from the Memphis Students Company and Cook
then arranged to take seventeen company members, his wife, and the
dancer Ida Forsyne to London, where they opened at the Palace Theatre in
December for a stay of several months. The company returned to America
in May 1906. Moving to Chicago, Cook joined the production team of
Motts' Pekin Theatre, writing music with Joe Jordan for such shows as *My
Friend From Georgia* (1906) and *In Zululand* (1907), as well as Miller and
Lyle's first major musical comedy, *Darkydom* (1915), on which Cook worked
in tandem with James Reese Europe. In 1919 Cook embarked for Europe
with his New York Syncopated Orchestra, returning to the United States in
1922. For the rest of his working life Cook primarily toured with orchestras
and promoted concerts for notable singers, such as Paul Robeson. His last
known stage offering was a collaboration with the composer Will Vodery

to write and produce the musical *Swing Along* (1929) that premiered at Harlem's Lafayette Theatre. Cook died in July 1944, having made a lasting contribution to the music of African Americans from his adopted city of New York.

The work of Bob Cole and his collaborators, on the one hand, and of the Bert Williams–George Walker duo on the other, represent solid achievements in the growth of American musical comedy as the nineteenth century drew to a close and the twentieth dawned. Robert Allen Cole Jr. (1868–1911), another multitalented showman, was an all-round performer, composer, director, producer, and scenarist. A recognized leader in his day, "his presence," in the opinion of a modern scholar, "was important, perhaps even critical, to the development of black musical theater."[45] Cole was born in Athens, Georgia, of parents who had been slaves. His father was a carpenter, prudent and thrifty. All six children were musically inclined and Bob (the eldest and only boy) played banjo, guitar, piano, and cello. He attended public schools but not college, was employed for a spell at Atlanta University and eventually moved north, where he found work at summer resorts, in hotels and clubs. He became known as "the singing bellboy" with his guitar, original compositions and comedy routines. Moving from the northeast to Chicago, Cole joined with Lew Henry and produced vaudeville acts. When success eluded them Cole shifted into solo work consisting mainly of comic monologues and songs he had written. Unlike many others who gained early experience as blackface clowns, Cole "never seems to have joined a medicine show or circus ... and did not use blackface makeup (as even 'genuine' black minstrels had done)."[46] In fact, in what may seem a gesture of defiance, Cole created in whiteface the character of a ragged and humorous tramp called Willy Wayside, who appeared in two of his productions.

By the mid-1890s Cole was in New York working in Sam T. Jack's *Creole Show* as comedian and stage manager. There he met the clever soubrette and dancer Stella Wiley, with whom he teamed to play vaudeville and later married; a union that lasted only a few years. In New York, too, there was a loosely organized group of some fourteen African American performers who called themselves the All-Star Stock Company. They met in the auditorium of Worth's Museum[47] to discuss their needs, including training. Cole joined this group, which included Gussie Davis, Ben Hunn, Billy Johnson, Stella Wiley, Hen Wise, and others. Will Marion Cook was musical director. Little more is known of the group's activities, although it is likely Cole wrote skits for training sessions. Only two play titles are associated with the company: *Georgia 49* is cited as its first production,[48] and a notice in the

Raleigh (North Carolina) *Theatre Gazette* of 31 October 1896 advises that "The All-Star Dramatic Concert Troupe will render their great play *A Pair of Spectacles* very soon." In fact the All-Star Stock Company was short-lived. Members were busy pursuing their individual careers and in the absence of proper management the company folded.

Cole had found a new partner in Billy Johnson, with whom he produced for the *Black Patti Troubadours* an hour-long farce, "Jolly Coon-ey Island," which he later withdrew in a quarrel with manager Voelckel over salary and working conditions. The quarrel had initiated a number of other disputes between black artistes and white managers. Adding fuel to the fire, the Cole–Johnson team decided to promote their new musical *A Trip to Coontown* (1897) under black management, thus mounting a serious challenge to white impresarios and agents who normally booked shows into both white- and black-managed playhouses. When the musical was ready, in fall 1897, a boycott instigated by Voelckel and Nolan (managers for the Troubadours) forced it to open in eastern Canada and to play in the worst theatres in every American city visited during its first year. Despite this difficulty audiences liked the show, as may be judged from published reviews – mostly undated and unattributed – in newspaper clippings in the Cole family papers. They appear to range from late 1897 to spring 1898. One review covered a performance at the Academy of Music in Halifax, Nova Scotia; another was at the Grand Opera House (no location given); and one other at the little-known Third Avenue Theatre in New York. Short excerpts from these clippings suggest how the musical was received:[49]

> The audience was alternately in roars of laughter and in sensations of delight as fun or music pervaded the stage...little plot but plenty of action and life... (Academy of Music, Halifax)

> enjoy two hours and a half of fun...the large audience was kept in a constant uproar. Bob Cole as Willie Wayside, a tramp, makes him one of the funniest creatures ever seen on a local stage. (Grand Opera House)

> One of the most artistic farce comedy shows that New York has seen in a long time...they are such delicious dancers and such fine actors that the first half of the performance is one long rollicking frolic. There are many white comedians who could sit at the feet of these negro actors and learn a thing or two. (Third Avenue Theatre, New York)

There was money to be made in handling the show and a leading New York firm of promoters, Klaw and Erlanger, disregarded the ban and sponsored it. *A Trip to Coontown* toured for three seasons, but an emotionally drained Cole had to retire from the cast, leaving Billy Johnson in charge. When the show closed in 1900, Cole, it is said, accused Johnson of financial disloyalty and they separated.[50]

Bob Cole's meeting with the brothers James Weldon and J. Rosamond Johnson was in many ways fortuitous. They had come up from Jacksonville, Florida, hoping to interest New York producers in a musical comedy they had written and composed. James was author of the playscript and lyrics while Rosamond wrote the music. He was an accomplished pianist, who had attended the New England conservatory in Boston and studied composition in London under Samuel Coleridge-Taylor. A joint venture with the experienced and ambitious trouper Bob Cole seemed desirable and when James Weldon joined the US consular service Rosamond and Cole continued as partners until Cole's final illness in 1910–11. An article in the *Colored American* of 1 November 1902 hailed the new partnership: "their primary ambition is to develop a distinct school of music from the primitive melodies of our race and to do for Negro music in this country what Coleridge Taylor is doing for it in England."

A year later the team was making waves in musical theatre: "In New York there is scarcely a playhouse, big or little, which caters to the popular taste in which the songs of the Johnson brothers and Bob Cole are not heard every night," wrote one critic. Their compositions were heard in shows white and black, and there were requests from leading players for particular songs suited to their act. The effect on Cole was transforming; coon songs were gone, his favorite whiteface tramp character vanished for an evening dress suit as he and Rosamond Johnson appeared in a high-class vaudeville song-and-dance act. "Between 1900 and 1910," wrote Thomas Riis, "Cole and Rosamond Johnson, frequently assisted by James Weldon Johnson, produced some 150 individual songs. Many were used in their vaudeville act. Many more were written for interpolation into larger shows produced by Klaw and Erlanger, the leading moguls of the day." Riis specified the major changes: lyrics no longer refer to aggressive, thieving, or violent Blacks nor to broad farcical situations; songs are sentimental and romantic, at times melancholy; if humorous they were not racially oriented. As may be expected with a highly trained composer on board, the music was more polished, with richer chords and smoother progressions. These changes first occurred when songs were commissioned for performance in white shows, but their popularity grew until they became generally fashionable.[51]

In addition to writing songs and appearing in vaudeville acts that included singing and soft-shoe dancing, Cole and the Johnson brothers prepared a

new musical comedy entitled *The Shoo-Fly Regiment* (1906). It opened in
the fall 1906 at the Majestic Theatre in Washington, DC, with a cast of
fifty, including ten named characters and a chorus. It was also staged at the
Park Theatre in Indianapolis that winter; was booked for a week in May
1907 at the Girard Theatre in Philadelphia; and in early June 1907 it was at
the Grand Opera House in New York, doubling back to Philadelphia for a
week at the Casino Theatre, and then on to the Bijou Theatre on Broadway.
But after two weeks there the engagement was terminated because Johnson
had become ill. By October 1907 the production was installed at the Folly
Theatre in Brooklyn. Clearly all was not well with the show. The plot dealt
with a young Tuskegee graduate (played by Rosamond Johnson), who is
about to become an instructor at Lincolnville Institute when war breaks out
in the Philippines. He joins the army, leaving behind a distressed fiancée
(Fannie Wise), who hands back her engagement ring. The young man
distinguishes himself overseas and comes back to straighten things out.
Bob Cole took the role of an eccentric janitor at the school who signs up
as an army cook. Additional characters were Brother Doolittle and Brother
Doless, members of the Bode of Edj'cashun (played by the redoubtable Sam
Lucas paired with Wesley Jenkins) and sundry others.

As black musical comedy the production was breaking new ground and
audiences were confused: "Those who came to see the ordinary buffoonery
of the average Negro company remained to wonder at, to be entertained by,
and to ponder over a most delightful entertainment," wrote the supportive
Lester Walton of the *New York Age*. Walton pleaded with African Americans
to help Cole and Rosamond Johnson remain on Broadway, by proper behavior at the Bijou Theatre. Quite possibly, however, the production may
not have been ready for opening. Fourteen months after its premiere and
noting that the show had acquired a new set of managers (its third), Walton
reported that fresh songs had been interpolated, dull and unnecessary dialogue excised, and more action added: "*Shoo-Fly Regiment* is now full of
ginger," he wrote, it "has more comedy as well as more melody."[52]

While Rosamond Johnson's music was of the usual high order, he was
apparently miscast in the leading "straight" role. As an actor he "waded
through the dramatic lines and situations with a great deal of earnestness, if
not much skill," trying to act when he needed to be still. On the other hand,
Cole, a consummate craftsman, appeared to do little but kept the audience
in stitches of laughter. The sequence of scenes added to the confusion. Lucas
and Allen as members of the "Bode of Edj'cashun" (one of the hit songs)
appeared early in the show suggesting to the audience that they were the
principal mirth-makers, thus undercutting Cole's entry. Despite these flaws

the *New York Telegraph* in its review found Cole "immensely entertaining in everything he attempted," turning in "a smooth and rollicking performance" of which the mixed audience heartily approved.[53]

More than five years had passed since Cole appeared in a full evening's show and the reception accorded his latest effort must have been keenly disappointing. Plainly, they had bombed on Broadway and advance bookings were poor. Moreover with a fairly large company in tow, it would be uneconomic to travel from one city to another for a few performances at each venue and with no guarantee of full houses. Especially galling was the success of the rival black troupe led by Williams and Walker that had produced a number of hit musicals in recent years, including a trip to England with a command performance for royalty. In retrospect the thematic thrust of *Shoo-Fly* was a nonstarter, being serious about promoting education, loyalty to country and to marriage vows, while the audience came expecting levity.[54]

Just prior to the show Cole and the Johnsons had been engaged by Klaw and Erlanger to write new songs and music for the English pantomime *Humpty Dumpty* (1906) that had been adapted for American audiences, after which they had successfully performed their vaudeville act in England. On the quality of their work for the pantomime, the *Freeman* of 14 November 1905 had written: "Messrs. Cole and the Johnson brothers have...contributed music equal to a first class musical comedy and in so doing rise a step or two above the requirements of a pantomime." They had the credentials to produce a memorable show. It was time to get back to work.

With the truly talented, failure can be a test not only of resilience but also of renewed creativity. In May and June 1908 Cole and Rosamond Johnson reverted to vaudeville surrounded by a chorus of ten and "rendering songs that are whistled and hummed after everyone has left the theatre," but they must already have begun work on their next show and were determined to learn from their errors.[55] One was to avoid lofty well-meaning themes for their own sake and the other to pair Cole with Rosamond Johnson in order to nurture the latter's acting skills. By mid-September a new musical was ready for an extensive try-out touring schedule before braving Broadway. It was called *The Red Moon*, with book and lyrics by Cole and music by Johnson. Early reviews from Philadelphia were ecstatic: "a brilliant success... best work of its kind ever presented...chockful of fun and music...tuneful and picturesque with an abundance of rare comedy..."[56] Similar plaudits came from other cities visited. What was the show about? Would Broadway buy it?

For the African American, a red moon signifies bad luck, while for the Native American, it is a call to war. Minnehaha, daughter of an Indian chief and a colored woman, was deserted by her father. He returns to Swamptown, site of the government school for Indians and Blacks, to claim his child for her classmate, "Red Feather." The chief prevails and Minnehaha is taken away to the reservation. Two rascals, an indigent impresario named Slim Brown (Cole) and a has-been pianist called Plunk Green (Johnson), posing as lawyer and doctor respectively, set out to rescue her. After many comic adventures their efforts are successful and Minnehaha is brought back to the best parlor in Swamptown, where in gratitude she agrees to marry the pianist. Minnehaha was played by Abbie Mitchell, the Indian chief by Arthur Talbot, and "Red Feather" by Theodore Pankey. Additional fun makers included Sam Lucas, Fanny Wise, and Wesley Jenkins. When in February 1909 George Walker fell ill, causing a suspension of the Williams and Walker shows, a considerate Cole invited Aida Walker to join *The Red Moon* production, where she both sang and performed her aboriginal "Wildfire" dance to prolonged applause.

Critics wrote approvingly of the stage settings, especially for the impressive second act, which portrayed the towering cliffs and deep canyons of Indian territory away to the west. The previously quoted *Inquirer* observed that the best and catchiest music was placed in this act from the "Bleeding Moon" chorus at the opening to the "War Dance of the Braves" at its close. For the *Freeman* of 21 November 1908, the best-received songs were "On the Road to Monterey," "Big Red Shawl," "I Ain't Had No Lovin' in a Long Time," and "Pathway to Love." The same newspaper asserted that the show "might be justly called a full-fledged and well-constructed comic opera, deserving presentation in the better class of houses." The reminder is important since in first-class theatres ticket prices were higher and big expensive shows had a better chance to make a profit on the road by being booked into them. To be relegated to second-class houses or worse meant certain financial disaster for expensively mounted productions.

By the time *The Red Moon* arrived at New York's Majestic Theatre for a short run towards the end of December 1908, Broadway's vaunted imprimatur seemed almost irrelevant. Word had got around of the show's success and audiences clamored to see it. The *Telegraph* of 29 December admitted that lyrics and music were both "excellent" and that all three acts were "magnificently staged," while the impersonation of Red Indians was praiseworthy, with some actors showing a real grasp of character work. Even the modest *Toledo Blade* newspaper of 14 December felt secure enough to urge white producers of musical comedy to take a lesson from the show's chorus, whose "snap, ginger, life and evolution ... are absolutely refreshing." When the show returned to the Majestic Theatre in May 1909, the *New York Dramatic News* stated that the company were received with open arms and would remain for an indefinite period.

Bob Cole's genius had finally flowered, but it was almost too late. At the end of the 1909/10 season Cole and Johnson announced their retirement from musical comedy, stating that large productions could no longer survive by playing only in popular-priced theatres.[57] The team returned to vaudeville, receiving $750 a week for their services at Keith's Fifth Avenue Theatre. At the close of their engagement in fall 1910, Bob Cole suffered a mental breakdown that steadily grew worse, leading to his tragic suicide by drowning in the Catskills on 2 August 1911.[58] Penning a lengthy eulogy in the *New York Age* of 10 August 1911, Lester Walton concluded:

> He was a man whose mind was rich with imagination and pregnant with ideas; an omnivorous reader and a lover of debate; a man who did not fear to express his convictions; a Negro who believed in his race and in the equality of mankind; a dutiful son and a devoted brother; one who was liked, admired and respected for his ability and force of character; a man who died by his own genius, fiery overwork of brain and unquenchable ambition.

After Cole's death Rosamond Johnson continued for a time to work in vaudeville with other partners and in 1912 became musical director of Oscar Hammerstein's Grand Opera House in London. His next appointment, in 1914, was as director of the Music School for Colored People in New York, where he increased the enrollment to more than two thousand students. In later years he did return to the theatre spasmodically. During the bustling 1920s he took part in a few black shows; he also appeared in *Porgy and Bess* in 1935 and in *Cabin in the Sky* in 1941. He died in his adopted city of New York in 1954.

The team of Bert Williams and George Walker, contemporaries of Cole and the Johnsons, overcame initial problems of exclusion to gain laudatory recognition from audiences and critics at home and abroad. In one respect the teams were markedly different: Cole from the start opposed wearing blackface while Williams, a mulatto of light skin, created such a lovable burnt-cork "coon" figure that it proved impossible to conceive his stage persona in any other form. He was, in fact, branded with it for the rest of his professional life. Williams was born in Nassau, New Providence, in the

Figure 13. "The Cake Walk No. 2", originally a tobacco ad for Old Virginia Cheroots, suggested the likenesses of four popular dancers – George and Aida Walker with Bert Williams and Stella Wiley.

Bahamas,[59] around 12 November 1874, and in 1885 moved with his parents to Riverside, California, where his father worked as a railroad conductor. About age 16 Bert left school and, moving to San Francisco, sought a career in show business. There he met George Walker, a young man from Lawrence, Kansas, and his senior by one or two years. Walker had been performing in a medicine show and was hoping to find work with a regular troupe. The two formed a partnership and after various adventures touring in the west with minstrel-type shows they moved east by stages, reputedly stopping at Chicago during the 1893 world's fair.[60]

For their specialty act, Williams and Walker had worked up a duet with Bert strumming on the banjo and George singing a coon song. Walker, the flashier of the two, began as a dancer and stooge to Williams' "straight man." However, it was only when they reversed roles that the act worked surprisingly well. Williams, naturally tall, straight, handsome, light complexioned and of good diction, became the blackfaced, slouching, lazy, dialect-speaking and unlucky Negro for whom everything went wrong – the Jonah man. The sharp and sprightly Walker, on the other hand, played the dandy, sporting Black dressed in a tailored suit, wearing spats, high silk hat, gloves, and monocle, and carrying a malacca cane. He was generous to a fault, mostly with the Jonah man's money. With heightened confidence the duo readily agreed to join Victor Herbert's *The Gold Bug* (1896) at the Casino Theatre on Broadway, New York, even though the operetta had opened to unflattering reviews. In a desperate bid to save the show, producer George Lederer decided to add their act to the variety section. The production closed in a week, but they were a decided hit: "The second night's show...proved as spiritless as the premiere," said Lederer afterwards in an interview, "but the audience couldn't get enough of Williams and Walker...they stopped *The Gold Bug* that night until they eventually gave out physically."[61]

After two more aborted engagements, Williams and Walker began to despair of finding substantial employment on stage. Lederer encouraged them to try vaudeville and gave them a contact at Koster and Bial's in New York.[62] It was timely and productive. They opened in late fall 1896 and were immediately successful. "The dude" Walker did a number of so-called funny walks while Williams, described as "the common everyday nigger [who] had only to open his mouth to bring laughs," offered a song entitled "Oh, I Don't Know, You Ain't So Warm." Noting that the act was "rather crude," one critic predicted it could be an immense hit if properly fixed by an expert farce writer.[63] In December Williams and Walker left the vaudeville house to join a troupe at Proctor's Theatre in New York, but within a month they were back at Koster and Bial's for what would be an unprecedented run. Their next billing was at the Bijou Theatre in Philadelphia, where they were hailed as "the greatest comedy act ever witnessed in this city."[64] The Empire Theatre, a music hall in London, was next on the roster. They opened for a week's run, were placed after the ballet item, "and promptly died." Too late they realized that black American humor might not seem quite so risible to staid British audiences.

Beginning 29 August 1898 and for almost a decade, the Williams and Walker team, along with their professional associates,[65] mounted no fewer than seven full-scale musical productions that toured the country, with one show also playing successfully in England. The company started out in mundane fashion; their first three productions had vaguely similar plots that were notably weak in invention. Early July 1898 had witnessed Will Marion Cook's *The Origin of the Cakewalk* (initially meant for Williams and Walker) and the two troupers had already staged their comic version of the dance to cap their vaudeville act. Now they would revive it in full as the second part of a two-act musical novelty called *Senegambian Carnival* that was scheduled to open in Boston on 29 August. The first part introduced the principal characters: a rich miner from the Klondike called "Dollar Bill" (Bert Williams) and his buddy, a natural-born confidence man named "Silver King" (George Walker). This "King" had arranged an excursion for family and friends from their plantation setting in the Southland to a northern city, and they gathered at sunset to sing and dance in celebration of the coming trip. In act 2 the visitors were guests of a wealthy hostess in New York, where they introduced a grand cakewalk dance.

This first effort at self-contained musical comedy fell far short of expectations, being merely a variety show of specialties with a strong minstrel flavor. The next two productions, *A Lucky Coon* (January 1899) and *The Policy Players* (October 1899), showed a marginal improvement. In the first, Williams and Walker retained their previous characters, but a winning lottery ticket replaced Klondike gold. In the second the gambling game of "Policy" provided the means for a gathering of "the Colored Four Hundred." Williams, butler to a wealthy family that lived on the Hudson, is persuaded by Happy Hotstuff (Walker) to impersonate a fictitious ex-president of Haiti and grace the assembly. To modern ears these plots sound naïve as they doubtless were even in their day. Conscious or not, it was part of the strategy to be nonthreatening to preponderant white audiences who were highly entertained by the singing, dancing, and fun-making of the clever "real black coons." Meantime, Williams and Walker were perfecting their craft and if their dialogue occasionally contained hidden jibes about racial inequities, Blacks in the audience would likely spot them to their increased satisfaction.

For their fourth production Williams and Walker expanded the theme of mistaken identity in *Sons of Ham*, written by Jesse Shipp and Stephen Cassin. The drifters Tobias Wormwood (Williams) and Harty Lafter (Walker) show up in Swampville, Tennessee, pretending to be the long-absent sons of Hampton Flam, an aging black man. In fact his two sons have been away at college and are due back imminently. On arrival, they turn out to be accomplished acrobats with predictable consequences to the imposters. The production opened in upstate New York in September 1900 and after a short tour arrived in Manhattan a month later. It proved a great success, having attractive scenery, lively music, clever lyrics, and with principal players each contributing popular items. In the last scene of act 1 a ballad by Bert Williams dressed in a Zulu warrior's costume received many encores:

> In my castle on the river Nile
> I am gwinter live in elegant style
> Inlaid diamonds on de flo'
> A baboon butler at my do'
> When I wed 'dat princess Anna Mazzoo
> Den my blood will change from red to blue
> Entertaining royalty all the while
> In my castle on the river Nile.[66]

There was no logic in the sudden scene change to Africa, but the song clearly touched a nerve in parts of the audience and probably led to African settings in the next two productions, when Williams and Walker were at the top of their form. But first, a word on their spouses, who were a crucial part of the team.

Sometime during 1899 George Walker married Ada Overton (who subsequently changed her first name to Aida) at a home ceremony. Born in New York City on 14 February 1880, Ms. Walker was an exquisite nymph-like performer who had studied dance from an early age. She spent a short time with the Black Patti Troubadours but left the troupe over the controversy with Bob Cole. She became the resident choreographer and dancer for the Williams and Walker productions and was considered the third most important company member after the principals. "During her lifetime," says Eric Ledell Smith, "she was regarded as the best black female dancer in the United States," and as well she was the first black female choreographer.[67] Ms. Walker was also a soloist and became a tolerably good actor, who played leading roles in Cole and Johnson's *The Red Moon* (1908) and in S. H. Dudley's *His Honor the Barber* (1911). After her husband's death in 1911, Ms. Walker plunged into work in vaudeville and engaged in social events to benefit Blacks. In 1913 a week-long appearance with her own company at the Pekin Theatre in Chicago elicited the comment that she is "the only colored lady that has ever been accepted as a danseuse of the classics in reference to her performance of the dance 'Salome.'"[68] She did not long survive her husband, being but 34 years old when she died in New York in 1914.

Figure 14. Aida Walker, Queen of the Cakewalk, 1890s

Lottie Thompson was a recent widow and eight years senior to Bert Williams when she moved from Chicago to New York about the time Bert was in rehearsal for *Senegambian Carnival*. She appeared in the Boston production of the show under the Thompson name and continued to be so listed until November 1901, when she was billed as Lottie Williams. She sang and danced in several shows to good if not rave notices, but apparently her major role was to provide emotional support for her husband, whom she adored and who was desolate when in December 1908 Lottie announced her retirement from the company due to exhaustion. They had no children of their own and when sometime in 1913 her sister in Chicago died leaving three daughters, Lottie brought them to New York and took care of them. From all accounts she and Bert were a devoted couple and Lottie continued to be his soul mate for the rest of his career.

Musical theatre productions by the Williams and Walker company in its heyday were *In Dahomey* (1902–05), *Abyssinia* (1906–07), and *Bandanna Land* (1907–09). *In Dahomey* opened at Stamford, Connecticut, on 8 September 1902 with book by Jesse Shipp (who also served as stage manager and was a good supporting actor), lyrics by Paul Laurence Dunbar, and music composed by Will Marion Cook. The critic Sylvester Russell thought the script was too reminiscent of comic situations from past seasons. Bert Williams was "something wonderful" in his new dance, while his song "Everything Goin' Out an' Nothin' Comin' In" created a furor. In the second act Walker was a crowd-pleaser with his "rich new talk," but Aida Walker owned the stage for too short a spasm of time. Russell was particularly aggrieved with the musical's structure. He found that the first act dragged, the second was well written but long, and the third a dramatic fiasco since only then did the visitors from America reach Dahomey.[69] Attending a performance in Brooklyn a month later, Russell noted "a wonderful change" consonant with his suggestions. When the production arrived on Broadway it was further improved, prompting his remark: "few comedy teams of any race shine more brightly in the eyes of New Yorkers than Williams and Walker... Their dialogue was clever and witty throughout." Russell waxed poetic in describing Aida Walker's appearance: "A clear stage – no stars in the way – everybody breathless, choking in the throat; no music – not even any signs of having a song – nothing but a wheelbarrow and a looking glass to see herself in; we behold, all full of female whimsicalities, the greatest coming female comedy star of her race, Aida Overton Walker."[70]

With encomiums ringing in their ears, Williams and Walker determined once again to win over English audiences. On 16 May 1903 they opened at the Shaftesbury Theatre in London and though next day the *New York Herald* reported they were "irresistible," the British public remained aloof until it was learned that a command performance for royalty had been scheduled.[71] Ticket sales soared. Of Bert Williams, hit of the show, the London *Sunday Dispatch* pronounced: "There is not a white comedian on our stage who could not profit by watching his methods. His singing of 'I'm a Jonah Man' is the quintessence of art."[72] The company played in London for several months, then toured other major cities in England and Scotland, finally returning home in triumph. They had been abroad more than a year; proudly adding "The Royal Comedians" to their billing, they toured the show across the United States for another forty weeks.

Emboldened by success, Walker took the lead in planning their next show – "a new musical oddity" called *Abyssinia* that would be bigger and better than the last. He changed managers who balked at the proposed size and cost of an enlarged company, arguing persuasively that tour bookings should in future be exclusively at first-class theatres that charged higher admission prices. When disputes arose over broken contracts and caused further delay, Walker found a single backer, businessman Melville Raymond, for the show and began rehearsals. From all of this preproduction activity Bert Williams remained aloof, prompting rumors of a rift between the two principals that was never confirmed. Walker simply charged ahead and proved his business acuity.

Settings required for the show were: (i) on the way to the city; (ii) outside its walls; and (iii) within the city of Addis Ababa, capital of Abyssinia, where a party of black Americans from Kansas arrive on a visit to the ancient African kingdom. They are escorted by the two promoters, Jasmine Jenkins and Rastus Johnson (played by Williams and Walker respectively), who are mistakenly arrested as a market thief and a rebel chieftain, the penalty for the former infraction being dismemberment of the offending hand. In the end, the emperor's daughter declared their arrest was a case of mistaken identities and the freed prisoners were reunited with the visiting party as they prepare to leave the country.

The musical opened at the Majestic Theatre in New York City on 20 February 1906. Jesse Shipp wrote the book while Bill Williams joined Will Marion Cook in composing the music and Alex Rogers contributed most of the lyrics. Williams produced music for six nonchoral numbers and was again featured in the crucial scene, when he sang a new hard-luck song, "Here it Comes Again," as he awaited the sounding gong that would indicate guilt or innocence. Before the end of the season, Williams would sign a lifetime contract with Columbia Records to record his popular songs. Meanwhile, having expended enormous energy in managing and staging the show, George Walker saw his own performance lose its edge, as reviewers urged that he shorten his stage appearance to allow more time for Williams' sad-sack humor. As dancer and choreographer, Aida Walker found favor with the critics wherever the company played. Typical was the *Chicago Tribune*'s comment that her dancing chorus "move[d] with a grace and a swiftness that makes watching them a pleasure." And as for Ms. Walker herself, "the absolute grace, the abandon, and the modesty with which she does the most intricate steps, make her without a rival."[73]

Abyssinia was the proverbial critical success that forced its producer to declare bankruptcy and placed the production into receivership. Yet losses could hardly have been disastrous as the show closed with a credit balance rather than a loss. However, it was prudent to find a more stable financier for the next production, so Williams and Walker signed with F. Ray Comstock, the Shuberts' business associate whose company was itself a branch of the Shubert Corporation. The contract required that Williams and Walker be responsible for everything concerning selection and staging of the new production and that they would retain control of the stage management of the play, for which they would jointly receive $500 a week salary. Comstock would advance money to cover the costs of rehearsals and first production of the play; he would book the play for a season of not less than thirty-five weeks and would be reimbursed from the show's profits. Finally Williams, Walker and Comstock would collectively agree on a touring itinerary and the company would be booked only in first-class theatres with seat prices ranging from 25 cents to $1.50.[74]

The new play, *Bandana Land*, retained the established characters of dimwit Williams and smart aleck Walker, although Walker's usual role as a goad for Williams seemed to be shared by two characters. The play's action occurred in a small southern American town where Blacks formed a syndicate to buy a farm before a railway company acquired it for restricted use as a park. Led by the scheming lawyer Mose Blackstone (Jesse Shipp) the syndicate raised money for the purchase but was still short of cash. Blackstone approached the slow-witted heir to a legacy, a young man named Skunton Bowser (Bert Williams), whose self-appointed guardian was the extravagant Bud Jenkins (George Walker).[75] Bud helped the syndicate by urging Bowser to lend them the required sum. They bought the land and sold half of it to the railway. Then Blackstone revealed his plan to turn the other half of the farm into "Bandanna Land," a park for colored people who, encouraged to make as much noise as possible, soon forced the white railway company to pay any price to be rid of them. The plan was successful; the railway paid handsomely for the rest of the site just as Skunton decided it was time he took charge of all business dealings, so the syndicate got nothing for its pains.

Bandanna Land enjoyed a successful first season and began its second, which would prove the last for the Williams and Walker partnership.

Among highlights of the show were: (i) the pantomime poker game by Williams, considered by many to be his most memorable stage act which was included in the 1916 movie, *A Natural Born Gambler*; (ii) the hit song "Bon-Bon Buddie" sung by Walker that captured his cocky nature with Will Marion Cook's music and lyrics by Alex Rogers; and (iii) Aida Walker's sanitized version of the "Salome" dance as well as her prophetic ballad of unrequited love, "It's Hard to Love Somebody":

> It's hard to love somebody, when somebody don't love you
> When you keep doing little things and proving
> That your love is on the level too
> Instead of wooing, it's a-fussing and a-stewing
> 'Til you almost lose your health
> It's hard to love somebody, when that somebody
> Is loving somebody else.[76]

Early in the show's second season, Walker became ill on stage and was diagnosed with paresis, a form of syphilis for which there was then no known cure, penicillin being not yet available. Bravely he continued performing for some months but by February 1909 in Louisville, Kentucky, it was evident he could no longer appear on stage. He was sent to a sanitarium and steadily declined in health over some two years before expiring on 6 January 1911 in Islip, New York, at age 38. In its obituary notice the *Boston Guardian* called the team of Walker, his wife Aida Overton, and Bert Williams "the most popular trio of colored actors in the world."[77]

At first Bert Williams nourished the hope that his partner would recover. Realizing that even with a reduced onstage appearance he could not cope as Walker had done with the business end of a full-scale production, he closed the show and sought a new three-year contract from Ray Comstock, with a clause permitting the return of Walker should his health be restored. Williams spent the summer in vaudeville and received the unwelcome news that Aida Overton Walker had left the company to accept a major role with Bob Cole's troupe. Replacements were recruited and with a totally original script by Shipp and Rogers, the Williams' company opened its new musical play, *Mr. Lode of Koal*, in Toledo, Ohio, on 29 August 1909. The setting was mythical, the characters of no particular race comprised a kidnapped king, a fortune teller, four convicts, bandits, a monkey, and other fantasies – in short, a children's play. It moved into New York's Majestic Theatre on 1 November and, despite earlier flattering reviews *en route* to the big city, the production played a mere forty performances at the off-Broadway house – a poor record for the metropolis. All told the production recorded a loss of more than $11,000. Williams blamed Comstock for failing to advertise the show effectively and for consistently booking it into second-class theatres where ticket prices were low. Williams had demonstrated his ability to carry a major show without a partner, but he also knew that his company would invariably suffer with no one on board to vigorously promote its business interests.[78]

Recoiling from the financial disaster, Bert Williams signed up for a season of vaudeville at Hammerstein's Victoria Theatre in New York, where he headlined the bill and ran into more trouble. This time The White Rats labor union had decided that no colored artist should head a bill over a white vaudevillian and they pressured the managers to cease promoting Williams as the star. However, by printing his name larger than others and giving him bigger publicity pictures, the managers made it obvious whom they considered to be the top drawing card and highest earning showman on their bill. By the fourth week Williams was playing at two theatres: he appeared in early afternoon at the Victoria and then took his act uptown to the Alhambra at 126th Street and Seventh Avenue for an evening show.

About this time Florenz Ziegfeld Jr. invited Williams to join his variety show known as *The Follies* on a three-year contract. The show normally started in early June each year and played through August on the Roof Garden of a New York Theatre, then toured the country in the fall and winter. The company then returned to New York to recuperate and begin preparations for a new show to open in June. First staged in 1907, *The Follies* had acquired a reputation for high-class entertainment and the offer to join a reputable show where he would be free from managerial duties was tempting except for a major obstacle: the cast was entirely white and had always been Caucasian. There was a chorus line of fifty women specially selected for their figure and personality, and Williams' appearances would be strictly limited to special scenes where he could recite in his inimitable way an original comic monologue, sing one or more of his hard-luck ballads and, with a supporting actor or two, perform a burlesque or travesty of a popular production that was still on the boards.

It was also generally understood that women would not appear in scenes with Williams, a rule that was occasionally relaxed in later years. Moreover black audiences were certainly not admitted to any part of the house but, in regular theatres as opposed to summertime rooftops, they were confined to the topmost gallery, known as "nigger heaven." As a result Williams could expect to be criticized for appearing with a company that segregated black folk. What may not have been expected, however, was the reaction of cast members, who threatened to leave and boycott the show if a Black were employed. In response Ziegfeld was adamant, saying he could replace everyone of the cast except the one person they wanted him to fire. Eventually no one left the company, but Williams would remain an outcast to the other (white) players once the performance was over.

Bert Williams was a member of the renamed *Ziegfeld Follies* from 1910 to 1919, except for the years 1913 and 1918. At the time Lottie took charge of her nieces when their mother died, Bert elected to stay at home the first year and help her raise the girls. However, an invitation from his theatre club, the Frogs, to perform for charity in its summer variety *Frolic* could hardly be declined, even though it required a series of one-night stands at eastern coastal cities. With Sherman Dudley as his escort, Williams appeared "for the first time in his career in the role of a dusky damsel, who was all dressed up in a slit skirt and other female toggery... They sang an old song, 'Goo Goo Eyes' and then proceeded to tickle the funny bone of all present in a grotesque dance."[79] The second occasion was more problematic. Soon after he joined the *Follies*, Williams had been in touch with the playwright-producer and director David Belasco, who seemed interested in working with the colored comedian when the timing was right. Williams even considered that his first stage appearance without blackface should occur in London to allow American audiences to get used to the notion of their chief fun maker in a straight dramatic role. Of course, war in Europe (1914–18) put all such plans on indefinite hold, especially after the United States joined the conflict on the side of the Allies on 2 April 1917.

The truth is that Bert Williams was becoming tired of constant ostracism. He was in the *Follies* but was not part of it. He did not eat or travel with the company; he had to find his own accommodations while on tour; use backroom elevators in hotels; and, moreover, having cast his lot with the all-white company, he was unable to take an active part in the creative changes currently occurring in black theatre. Being a celebrated black actor whose skills were defined by wearing a comic blackface was frustrating. He had done all that could be expected of him in creating an array of entertaining ditties and skits: there was his signature song "Nobody" that audiences never tired of hearing him render; he was cabman to a besotted Leon Errol, circling the stage and returning him to the pick-up point; or working with him atop a skyscraper and watching him tumble off; playing a serious pantomimed poker game with imagined players; parodying the Russian ballet dancer Nijinsky and the fearless Mexican bandit Pancho Villa; and on the occasion of Shakespeare's tercentenary in 1916, depicting a travesty of tragic heroes that in the final analysis evoked laughter but no real tears. To crown it all, the writers hired by Ziegfeld no longer produced interesting scripts or situations that Williams could develop.[80]

Lacking proper material, Williams decided not to appear in the 1918 *Follies* but instead to take part in the *Ziegfeld Midnite Frolic* at the roof garden of the New Amsterdam Theatre in New York. This was really a training ground for chorus girls and comedians who hoped to be chosen for the regular *Follies*. A relaxed audience gave him a rousing ovation. By playing the late-night show Williams reclaimed past successes, avoided competing with other comedy stars such as W. C. Fields, Will Rogers, and Eddie Cantor, was free to play the occasional week of vaudeville, and, best of all, did not have to contend with onerous touring conditions but could remain close to home, with Lottie and her nieces. A further boon was his availability to record his songs and stories for Columbia Studios, which he increasingly did.

One of the truly painful incidents that typified Williams' continuing alienation from the Follies company occurred the following year, in 1919, during the run of what became his last *Follies* show. The Actors' Equity Association (AEA), formed in 1913, was heading for strike action against show producers newly reorganized as the Producing Managers Association (PMA). As a producer of musical comedy, Ziegfeld considered his show to be exempt from the controversy and was incensed when sections of his company voted to walk out in support of their actor-comrades. He promptly filed a court action against them for breach of contract. How did the strike affect Bert Williams, the nonequity star performer? This is how Williams explained it to W. C. Fields:

> I went to the theatre as usual, made-up and dressed. Then I came out of my dressing room and found the stage deserted and dark, the big auditorium empty and the strike on. I knew nothing of it: I had not been told. You see, I just didn't belong. So then I went back to my dressing room, washed up, dressed, and went up on the roof. It all seemed a nightmare.

Retelling the story Fields added his own comment: "It was one of the saddest things I ever listened to and felt ashamed that such a thing could happen to so fine an artist."[81]

In the long run the frequent slights, insults, and other indignities meted out at that time to people of color, regardless of their status or calling, took their toll on Williams. He drank heavily, usually at night so as to avoid affecting his performance, but surely deleterious to his health. The *Follies* had spawned any number of revues in New York and Bert Williams agreed to join some of the former Ziegfeld players, such as Eddie Cantor and George LeMaire, in a new show called *Broadway Brevities of 1920* that was installed in the Winter Garden theatre. Williams, still wearing blackface, appeared in a couple of scenes in each of two acts and received polite notices for his turn, but the hit of the show was a clever dance-pantomime entitled "The Kiss" conceived by Williams and performed by a dance couple to music he had composed. Overall the production managed to stay alive for a respectable one hundred and five performances, despite the critics' censure of "vulgarity" in certain other areas of the revue.

Since this last show did nothing to enhance his image as a serious actor under the comic blackface, Bert Williams would try again. He had already surmised that playing comedy did not allow the actor the time needed to develop a serious or solemn emotion since comedy essentially relied on the unexpected turn of events while tragedy was often a piling on or deepening of grievous circumstances. Moreover, the stunning achievement of Charles Gilpin as the haunted Emperor Jones in Eugene O'Neill's melodrama that opened a month after *Broadway Brevities* was both an inspiration of what could be achieved with the right material and a challenge to Williams finally to cast off the Jonah-man image if he wished to win respect as a straight actor.

For his next and last stage show, Williams starred in what was thought to be a proper musical comedy, *The Pink Slip*, later retitled *Under the Bamboo Tree*.[82] Except for Williams in trademark blackface the company was white, with the main players coming from vaudeville. The trite plot tells of an eccentric old gentleman who, prior to his death, buries treasure on the grounds of a resort hotel and writes its location on a pink slip of paper that he cuts into six pieces and hides. The hotel's porter, played by Williams, hopes to find the treasure himself and plants phony pink slips about the hotel; when suspected of duplicity, he goes into hiding. In the second act the porter becomes paranoid; he talks to a puppy dog (a real one) in whose collar he has hidden a slip and decides to get rid of the puppy. In the end he confesses to his trickery and the guests pardon him, realizing that money should not, after all, be the only measure of a man.

The production opened at the Shubert Theatre in Cincinnati, Ohio, on 4 December 1922 with the expectation of moving to New York after try-outs. The reviews were polite, even kind, and Williams was commended for his performance. The show next played in Chicago, where the critics were less enthusiastic, though respectful of Williams' performance. The truth is that gate receipts were much less than expected. The comedy lost more than $2,000 during the first week and more than $7,000 the second week, with the result that the Shuberts allegedly withheld paying royalties to the writers and peremptorily reduced by some $200 weekly the salary due to Williams.[83] Other changes were made with the staff that disturbed Williams, who, as those close to him could see, was a sick man. He had caught a cold in Chicago that developed into pneumonia and there had been a heart problem. But he insisted on going to Detroit, the next stop. What happened there is best told by Robert Evans, the show's manager:

> His valet and I dressed and undressed him all the time like a baby. The mere effort of moving enough for us to adjust his collar, tired and winded him ... Finally came Saturday with its two performances – this was the last straw. Bert Williams gave the evening performance even against his own better judgment and halfway through he collapsed. In the wings I caught him as he fell and together with another man, carried him to his dressing room. Still in the harness of burnt cork and the comic clothes, Bert Williams gave his farewell performance ... he would never act again. He had just finished singing "Puppy Dog" – that song which had been recognized as his masterpiece.[84]

On Tuesday, 28 February 1922, Bert Williams was taken by train to New York, where he was met by his wife Lottie, driven home, and put to bed. Doctors were called in, but to no avail. He expired on Saturday, 4 March, aged 46, survived by his mother, his wife Lottie, and their three nieces. The director, playwright and manager David Belasco, who had hoped to present Williams to the public, wrote of him: "He was one of the simplest, kindest, most amiable and most likeable men that I have ever known ... a delightful entertainer ... a sincere and careful artist ... a genuine comedian ... he made this world a happier, brighter place to live in than it would have been without him."[85]

The musical talent of Blacks in the late nineteenth century was not confined to musical comedy and operetta. Some boldly attempted to compose, produce, and perform in European-style operas. As theatre, opera combines the elements of stage action, appropriate settings, dress, and other accoutrements with characters and chorus whose thoughts and feelings are expressed primarily through song and recitative rather than through speech. In opera the emotional content of a scene resides largely in the power of its music rather than in overt physical action. Opera began in Italy in the late sixteenth century as an attempt to recapture the choric chant of ancient Greek theatre, and in the first half of the seventeenth century it spread to other European countries. Because of its artificial form and association with the literati and privileged classes, opera remained the last bastion of American professional theatre from which Blacks were excluded, regardless of their proven competence, training, and talent.

In America musical theatre can be reduced to four basic types: grand opera, light opera (including ballad opera, comic opera, and operetta), folk opera, and musical comedy. To conclude this chapter I cite a number of African American pioneers[86] in the late nineteenth and early twentieth century who found ways of exposing their vocal and musical skills by either (i) forming their own rudimentary opera troupes, (ii) giving concert performances that included operatic airs and accepting engagements to appear in opera on foreign boards, or (iii) composing and staging their own operas. By such strategies Blacks sought to demonstrate their competence until in America "the walls [of opera] came tumbling down."

The earlier mentioned African Theatre of New York deserves credit for introducing elements of operatic performance by Blacks among its offerings. Primarily responsible for staging scenes and songs from opera as part of the theatre's program was its leading actor, the multitalented maverick James Hewlett.[87] That there were never more than three instruments available for accompaniment – violin, clarinet, and bass fiddle – deterred neither the performers nor apparently their audience's appreciation. Three instances of song performance will suffice. For his benefit on 1 October 1821, Hewlett preceded his version of *Richard III* with "An Opera," consisting of seven songs by himself and three by other company members. Some months later, at another benefit performance, Hewlett inserted, between scenes from *Pizarro* and *Macbeth*, eight songs "to be sung in the character of Count Bellino" (from the opera *The Devil's Bridge*). A final example occurred on 9 August 1822, when the African Theatre presented *The Poor Soldier*, a comic opera by John O'Keeffe with music by William Shield, in which Hewlett and two actresses were featured.[88] None of this work approached grand opera; it did, however, demonstrate a penchant for sung drama by black actors and a tolerance for it on the part of their audience. When the African Theatre closed Hewlett continued to give one-man performances during which he would imitate well-known actors and opera singers during a tour of towns along the eastern seaboard.

Another antebellum soloist of repute was Elizabeth Taylor Greenfield (1809–76), whom the critics dubbed "the Black Swan." She was born in

Natchez, Mississippi, and was a mere infant when she was taken to Philadelphia and adopted by a Quaker, Mrs. Greenfield. Observing in the child an aptitude for singing, Mrs. Greenfield arranged for her to study music. In time Elizabeth began to entertain friends and eventually established a reputation as a professional soloist in an 1851 appearance before the Buffalo Music Association. Over the next two years Ms. Greenfield toured the northern states and in 1854 visited England, where her remarkable achievement was rewarded by a command performance at Buckingham Palace for Queen Victoria. A review in the Toronto *Globe* of 12–15 May 1852 describes the singer's artistry: "The amazing power of the voice, the flexibility, and the ease of execution took the hearers by surprise...The higher passages of the air were given with clearness and fullness...It is said she can strike thirty-one full, clear notes; and we could readily believe it." Despite critical acclaim Ms. Greenfield's singing career was brief. As her concerts in America failed to win wide public support she was forced to retire from performing and instead opened a voice studio in Philadelphia.

A few opera companies were organized by "colored folk" in northern states during the last third of the nineteenth century. Though production details are often inadequate, the instances are cited to indicate interest and intent among Blacks to participate in all forms of musical expression. In 1872 the Colored American Opera Company was formed in Washington, DC, composed of some thirty-five to forty choir members of St. Catherine's (Catholic) Church. The musical director was Professor J. Esputa, the church organist. In March the next year the company gave performances in Philadelphia and Washington of Julius Eichberg's *The Doctor of Alcantara* to warm applause, despite playing to a small audience in the much too large Horticultural Hall in Philadelphia. No further productions by this company have been traced.

The year 1884 witnessed the American premiere of an opera entitled *Il Guarany* by the Brazilian composer Carlos Gomes and considered to be his most successful work for the stage. Presented at the Start Theatre in New York, the opera is based on a novel by a Brazilian Indian writer and deals with heroes of the native Guarany Indians. It was staged at La Scala, Milan, in 1870, and, upon hearing it in Ferrara, Verdi wrote it was the work of a "truly musical genius." Three passing and teasingly incomplete references to colored opera companies come next. In 1886 the Colored Opera Company of Chicago announced its first performance would take place in February at the Opera House in that city. No further details were given, nor has the promised production been traced. Then, in 1891, Signor A. Farini's Grand

Creole and Colored Opera Company staged Verdi's *Il Trovatore* in New York with the mezzo-soprano Desseria Plato (Broadley) receiving plaudits for her acting and singing in the role of the gypsy Azucena, who had stolen away the Troubadour as a baby and reared him as her own child. And, in 1896 the Afro-American Opera Company made its first (and only recorded) appearance at Freiberg's Opera House, Chicago, in Planquette's *The Bells of Cornville*, with full orchestra, a chorus of seventy-five voices, elaborate costumes, and scenery.

So far operatic productions involving African Americans lacked continuity. They were singular events of two or at most three performances before the company disbanded. Possibly the complex nature of opera production required a greater degree of managerial and physical resources than most fledgling troupes could afford. Actually, one company, first mentioned in 1889, survived for well over twenty years, largely because it was, in essence, a single individual, who, devoted to operatic performance, would recruit singers as and when he was ready to begin rehearsals. His name was Theodore Drury (*c.* 1860s–1940s).

In October 1889 the Theodore Drury Opera Company announced a concert performance for two nights at Clarendon Hall in New York City. The program consisted of a scene from Verdi's *Il Trovatore* that included the "Gypsy Chorus" and the "Miserere," as well as the Drinking Song from Lecocq's light opera *Girofle Girofla* and other solos. The director was Professor Sol Thompson, while J. Stanton as Manrico and Maggie Scott as Leonora were the principal singers. Drury was apparently not part of this production. The *New York Age* of 19 October 1889 praised the excellent voices of the troupe, noting that their costumes were owned by the company. The *Il Trovatore* scene was revived at the Bridge Street Church on 26 December. The company then played to a full house, bill unknown, at New York's Adelphi Hall in February 1892, after which it dropped from the records until 1900,[89] when it began to stage an annual production of a grand opera with occasional visits to churches and other venues in neighboring states.

Operas presented with revivals over the next decade included Bizet's *Carmen*, Gomes' *Il Guarany*, Gounod's *Faust*, Verdi's *Aida*, Mascagni's *Cavalleria Rusticana*, and Leoncavallo's *I Pagliacci*. Drury, a baritone, played many of the leading male roles assisted by Stanley Gilbert, George Ruffin, George Taylor, and James Worsham. Among the female cast were, most often, Daisy Allen, Estelle Clough, Desseria Plato, Margaret Randall, Marie Rovelto, and Mary Terrell. Although the company was reputedly African American, Drury did not refrain from recruiting white talent,

especially in an emergency, as occurred in *Aida* when the individual cast as
Amneris withdrew during rehearsal and was replaced by Genevieve Motley,
a white prima donna. Similarly, Drury would utilize an all-white or a racially
mixed orchestra when it proved difficult to recruit a black one.

In December 1911 he produced Handel's *Messiah* in Boston, where he
had moved from New York and founded the Drury Musical Arts Club.
He reportedly went abroad for further study some time after May 1912,
returning to the United States in 1918. He then toured the country singing,
before resettling in Boston as a voice teacher and coach. Twice he produced
what must have been his favorite operas: *Faust* was staged in Providence,
Rhode Island, in October 1928 and ten years later *Carmen* was presented in
Philadelphia, where Drury had made his home. That he had died is noted
in an *Amsterdam News* article of 5 May 1945, but the actual date of his passing
is unknown.[90]

In his essay on "Opera" in *Africana* (1999), Peter Hudson calls African
American opera singers of the nineteenth century "crossover artists" who,
barred from major American stages, "transgressed the boundaries between
high and low culture by playing the marginal American concert stages...
as well as minstrel and vaudeville shows."[91] The designation is a perfect fit
for the Hyers Sisters, already discussed, and to some extent it also applies
to Sissieretta Jones, who, as I have shown, was denied the opportunity to
appear with recognized opera companies.

Mme. Jones, along with Marie Selika (Mrs. Sampson Williams, *c.* 1849–
1937) and Flora Batson Bergen (1864–1906) were considered to be "the three
leading black singers of the late nineteenth century."[92] Mme. Selika was
certainly one of the earliest professional sopranos. According to a *Cleveland
Gazette* report of 28 April 1888, Mme. Selika was asked back in 1878 to
substitute for soprano Etelka Gerster at a concert in Boston, Massachusetts,
where she gave such a fine performance she was later engaged to sing the
title role in a stage production of Meyerbeer's *L'Africaine* at the Academy
of Music in Philadelphia. Mme. Selika went twice to England and Europe
for study or to sing professionally from 1882 to 1885 and again from 1887 to
1892. She sang in most of the large cities and reportedly gave a command
performance for Queen Victoria on her first visit.

Flora Batson Bergen grew up in Providence, Rhode Island, where she
sang in concerts as a teenager before becoming a member of the Bergen Star
Concert Company in 1885. So impressed was manager James Bergen with
his latest acquisition (her vocal range was from mezzo-soprano to baritone)
that he took over her management, made her the leading prima donna

of his company, and, in 1887, married her. Début performances in New York and Philadelphia were followed by worldwide tours, with appearances before Queen Victoria, the Pope, and other heads of state. In 1896 Mme. Bergen dissolved her marriage and formed a partnership with basso Gerald Miller. They appeared in "Operatic Specialties" with the South Before the War troupe and other companies. Although regarded as one of the most successful African American soprano vocalists of the nineteenth century, Mme. Bergen did not appear in a complete opera production in America.

There were, however, two colored sopranos who made their operatic débuts in Europe and were later engaged by recognized companies at home. Lillian Evanti (née Lillian Evans), a 1917 graduate in music of Howard University, Washington, DC, began her career by touring as a concert artist prior to further study abroad, in France and Italy, in the period 1925–30. At this time she sang with opera companies, assuming the title role in Delibe's *Lakmé* in Nice and repeating the performance in Paris in 1927. On her return to America, Ms. Evanti began a rigorous touring schedule that took her across the United States and on to South America, the Caribbean, and back to Europe. She reportedly knew some twenty-four operas and was especially hailed for her performance as Violetta in Verdi's *La Traviata*, staged in 1943 by Mary Cardwell Dawson for the National Negro Opera Company at Washington, DC.

The other singer to gain operatic experience in Europe was Caterina Jarboro (née Catherine Yarborough), whose musical training began at Catholic schools in North Carolina and was furthered in New York, where for a time she sang in Broadway musicals, such as *Shuffle Along* (1921). In 1926, however, Ms. Jarboro traveled abroad for additional study and in 1930 made her début in grand opera, singing the title role of Verdi's *Aida* at the Puccini Theatre in Milan. Engagements with other European opera companies occurred until 1932, when she returned to the United States. The next year marked her American début in *Aida* with the Chicago Civic Opera in July, followed in the fall by the lead role of Selika in Meyerbeer's *L'Africaine* at New York's Hippodrome Theatre. Concert touring in the United States proved unsatisfying and Ms. Jarboro relocated to Brussels, Belgium, from which city she was able to accept operatic roles throughout Europe.

Among several male equivalents to the lady opera vocalists noted above, I have selected for commentary three outstanding singers who were born towards the end of the nineteenth century. They are Roland Hayes, tenor, Jules Bledsoe, baritone, and Paul Robeson, bass-baritone. Hayes (1887–1976) came from Georgia but moved to Chattanooga, Tennessee, where in his early teens he sang in a church choir and listened to musical recordings. He studied music at Fisk University in Nashville, joined the Fisk Jubilee Singers and by 1911 had traveled around the country with a professional Fisk quartet, settling eventually in Boston. In the period 1912–19 Hayes continued touring and sang at Carnegie Hall concerts in New York and at the Colored Musical Festival Concerts in Atlanta. In 1920 he was financially able to go overseas for further study and concertizing in European capitals, where he won considerable recognition for the limpid quality of his voice. His varied repertoire admitted lieder but ranged from the Renaissance to the current day, including Negro spirituals. On his return to America in 1923 Hayes sang with the Boston Symphony, was appointed to Boston University's music faculty in 1950, and "was undoubtedly the leading concert tenor in the world during the 1920s–40s."[93]

Despite his acknowledged ability, Roland Hayes was born too soon and did not receive a call to sing with one of the leading opera companies in his homeland. His younger contemporary by eleven years, Jules Bledsoe (1898–1943), was more fortunate. Born in Waco, Texas, and a graduate of that state's Bishop College, with further studies at Virginia Union College in Richmond, Bledsoe had sung at church concerts and studied the piano as a child, but was expected to enter the medical profession and had actually enrolled at the school of medicine at Columbia University in New York (1919–24). While in the city, he also pursued his interest in singing by studying with professional tutors and giving concert appearances. These proved so successful that he abandoned a medical career, débuted as a concert baritone in 1924, and spent two more years in voice training before creating the role of Tizah in Frank Harling's opera *Deep River* (1926). Other major operatic parts sung by Bledsoe include the title role in Gruenberg's *The Emperor Jones* (1934) that played in Europe and New York; Amonasro in Verdi's *Aida* (1932) at Cleveland's Summer Opera in Ohio; and the title role of Moussorgsky's *Boris Godounov* (1933) at the Italian Opera in Holland. Bledsoe enjoyed an active career in musical plays (e.g., Ziegfeld's *Show Boat*), in concert appearances, in opera, and on radio for twenty years as a worthy successor to Roland Hayes.

To many renowned, by others reviled, Paul Robeson (1898–1976), actor, concert singer, and civil rights activist, sang in his high-school chorus and as a student at Rutgers University, but, being black, he could not join the college glee club. After graduating from college, he took his law degree at Columbia University, New York, while gravitating to the theatre by accepting roles that required him to act, as in *Simon the Cyrenian* and *The Emperor Jones*, to sing, as in Hall Johnson's choruses and the musical *Show Boat*, and to concertize, as in his unique song program of Negro spirituals, which he promoted over the more conventional and artificial opera derived from Europe. He believed that the spiritual was the supreme artistic manifestation of the American and West Indian Negro and considered it an appropriate means for the worship of God.[94] To this exaltation of the Negro spiritual must be added Robeson's commitment to social justice, or, as he put it, "The artist must elect to fight for Freedom or for Slavery. I have made my choice."[95]

His choice, which included singing for troops defending democracy in Spain (1937) or embracing socialism during the Cold War (1948), embarrassed the Truman government into revoking his passport (1950–58), thus cutting him off from engagements outside America. Meanwhile much publicized concerts at home were repeatedly disrupted by thugs posing as "patriots." Robeson resumed traveling in 1958 for a few years until he retired due to ill health in 1961. His numerous and prestigious awards worldwide are a testimony both to his art and to his heart; in the words of Eileen Southern, "his best-known performances were associated with his struggle for human rights and dignity of all peoples – the Negro spirituals, the labor song 'Joe Hill,' 'Old Man River' from *Show Boat*, and the cantata *Ballad for Americans*."[96]

I turn now to three early African American opera composers, along with mention of their work, either in concert form or as full stage productions, provided the performance occurred during the composer's active years. Selected for discussion are H. Lawrence Freeman, Scott Joplin, and William Grant Still, all born in the last third of the nineteenth century.

H. Lawrence Freeman (1869–1954): born in Cleveland, Ohio, Freeman was a child pianist, assistant church organist at age 10, and in 1893 composed his first opera, *The Martyr*, about an Egyptian nobleman put to death for accepting the religion of Jehovah. The work was produced during the same year by the Freeman Grand Opera Company at the Deutsches Theater in Denver, with additional performances in Chicago, Cleveland, and at Wilberforce, Ohio. Scenes from his second opera, *Nada* (1898, later revised and entitled *Zuliki*) were performed by the Cleveland Symphony in March 1900. Freeman next composed music for stage shows in Chicago and New York, then once again organized the Freeman Grand Opera Company that produced *Valdo* (1906), a tragedy named after his son, Valdo Freeman, and performed at Weisberger Hall in Cleveland, and *The Tryst* (1909), a tragedy of mistaken identity that was staged at the Crescent Theatre in New York. *Vendetta* (1923), on the rivalry between a nobleman and a toreador for a woman's love, was presented at the Lafayette Theatre in Harlem, and *Voodoo* (1928), considered by some to be Freeman's best-known work, dealing with cultic practices in Louisiana, was presented in a tent theatre in New York's Broadway district. In all, Freeman wrote no fewer than fifteen grand operas (not including a tetralogy of four one-act operas), in which his wife, the actress and singer Carlotta Freeman, was prima donna of those performed while his son, Valdo Freeman (1900–72), a baritone, produced and directed certain operas and sang leading roles.

Scott Joplin (1868–1917) wrote and composed two ragtime operas, the first one being unaccountably lost. Entitled *A Guest of Honor* (1903), it was actually performed in St. Louis by a group called Scott Joplin's Ragtime Opera Company, which had planned a tour of Midwestern towns. Then, for no apparent reason, the score simply vanished. One presumption is that Joplin himself might have become dissatisfied with the work and destroyed the score.[97] His second attempt was the ragtime folk opera, *Treemonisha* (1907), about a young woman who, abandoned as a child and found by a childless couple, is educated by Whites and becomes eager to start teaching her own people. She is abducted by a voodoo conjurer and eventually rescued to begin her career. Joplin preserved his second opera by publishing the 230-page manuscript himself and seeking a producer. Yet, despite encouraging reviews of the score and announcements of forthcoming productions, nothing materialized. In 1915 at a Harlem rehearsal hall Joplin held an informal audition of the score for an invited audience without attracting backers. Only in 1972 was the opera presented in a concert version by the music department of Morehouse College, Atlanta, supported by the Atlanta Symphony Orchestra. The opera's first full-scale production was given in May 1975 by the Houston Grand Opera and taken in October to the Palace Theatre on Broadway, New York, for an eight-week run. Carmen Balthrop alternating with Kathleen Battle played Treemonisha.

William Grant Still (1895–1978) lived a musically productive life. He was surrounded by music first played by his parents, then in public school and college, at the Oberlin Conservatory of Music, and under private tutors. He was, in fact, prepared for professional music *performance* at age 19, when he played with a dance orchestra; for music *arrangement* two years later as W. C. Handy's assistant; and for music *composition* that began in his college years and became established by 1926 with a performance of his *Levee Land*, a work for orchestra and soloist that "blended jazz idioms with traditional European elements."[98] In his creative work Still explored different musical forms: operas, symphonies, ballets, chamber groups, suites for piano and accordion, and a variety of songs. In much of this work he consciously introduced black folk elements.

Three of Still's operas were performed in his lifetime and merit comment. *Troubled Island* (1949) with libretto by Langston Hughes was based on Hughes' drama originally entitled *Drums of Haiti* (1936). The work deals with the rise and fall of Dessalines, the slave leader of the Haitian revolution who became the country's first black emperor. The opera was performed at the City Center by the New York City Opera to mark the group's fifth anniversary. Hughes reported that the leading roles were sung by Whites in blackface; they looked odd but sang beautifully.[99] The second of Still's operas to be staged was the one-acter *Highway No. 1, USA* (1963), with libretto by Verna Arvey (Still's wife). It showed the effect of stress on a young couple who operate a gas station close to a major highway, and was premiered at the University of Miami's Festival of American Music. Still's third opera, *A Bayou Legend*, was based on a Mississippi legend about a man who falls in love with a spirit. Composed in 1941 it was first staged only in 1974, by Opera/South in Jackson, Mississippi. A film version was telecast by PBS in 1981.

Indisputably, the work accomplished by artistes mentioned herein, both creative and interpretative, represents merely a small fraction of the output of African Americans in the field of music and theatre towards the end of the nineteenth century and the first part of the twentieth. That these achievements were made despite exclusionary practices in the North and vicious attacks in parts of the South is a matter of history, no less important because they were instigated either by socialites or hoodlums. When in 1939 Marian Anderson – to whom Toscanini declared after hearing her sing: "Yours is a voice such as one hears once in a hundred years" – was denied permission by the august Daughters of the American Revolution to give a concert in Constitution Hall because of her color, public protest was so vehement that the White House (read Eleanor Roosevelt) intervened. Ms. Anderson was invited to give an open-air concert on the steps of the Lincoln Memorial in Washington, DC, and on Easter Sunday morning she sang before an assembled audience of seventy-five thousand. Eighteen years later, the Metropolitan Opera Company saw fit to schedule her as the first Black to sing with the company, her role being that of Ulrica in Verdi's *Un Ballo in maschera*. The walls had finally collapsed.

6

The struggle continues

Errol G. Hill and James V. Hatch

When the Negro Theatre of Tomorrow becomes a reality, someone might mention my name and note that the Lafayette once existed.

Lester A. Walton

As the nation prepared to enter a new century tensions between Blacks and Whites, not limited to the former breakaway states of the confederacy, loomed ominously. Thirty-five years after the Civil War, the wanton shedding of human blood remained a safe and proven means to enforce white supremacy. It restored a sense of power over life and limb that slavery's end had eliminated. The list of African Americans lynched by white mobs in the South during 1900 reached an all-time high of 103.[1] These victims had merely been *accused* of wrong-doing, according to the press release; there had been no jury trial, no defense, no proof furnished. How these conditions affected black performers as they practiced their profession in southern regions of the country can only be imagined; players were even more at risk when they attempted to establish resident troupes in the Southland. Along with these risks were other perennial challenges, such as (i) being forced to use separate public facilities, (ii) being denied service at public restaurants, and (iii) for troupes traveling by public railway and needing overnight hotels, being required to use back stairways if they were admitted at all.

In New York in the summer of 1900 a fracas involving a colored man named Arthur Harris, his wife, and an overzealous white cop in plain clothes resulted in the cop's death. As described by James Weldon Johnson, Harris had left his wife for a moment to buy a cigar and when he returned he found her struggling with a white man. Harris rushed at the man, was struck by him over the head with a club, and retaliated with his pocketknife, inflicting a wound that proved fatal.

Then Harris ran away. The cop claimed he had arrested the woman for soliciting. He died and was buried three days later. The evening of the funeral witnessed one of New York's great race riots. To quote Johnson: "Negroes were seized wherever they were found, and brutally beaten. Men and women were dragged from streetcars and assaulted . . . The police themselves beat many Negroes as cruelly as did the mob . . . During the height of the riot the cry went out to 'get Ernest Hogan and Williams and Walker and Cole and Johnson,'"[2] names familiar to the bloodthirsty crowd. Hogan, playing at the Winter Garden in Times Square, was allowed for his safety to stay all night at the theatre. George Walker had a narrow escape when he was pulled from a streetcar and just managed to find sanctuary by running into the nearby Marlborough Hotel. It is a fact of history that the lynching of colored folk in America continued into the 1950s as a cancer on the nation's honor.[3] In his autobiography, James Weldon Johnson recalls an incident when, as an officer of the National Association for the Advancement of Colored People (NAACP), he investigated the burning alive in Memphis of a Negro named Ell Persons, who had been charged with being an "axe murderer." Johnson could find no positive evidence that Persons was guilty of the crimes committed. Of his visit to the site where the burning took place, Johnson wrote:

> While the ashes were yet hot, the bones had been scrambled for as souvenirs by the mobs. I reassembled the picture in my mind: a lone Negro in the hands of his accusers, who for the time are no longer human; he is chained to a stake, wood is piled under and around him, and five thousand men and women, women with babies in their arms and women with babies in their wombs, look on with pitiless anticipation, with sadistic satisfaction while he is baptized with gasoline and set afire. The mob disperses, many of them complaining, "They burned him too fast." I tried to balance the sufferings of the miserable victim against the moral degradation of Memphis, and the truth flashed over me that in large measure the race question involves the saving of black America's body and white America's soul.[4]

The impotence of government at the highest level to stop the atrocity of lynching was never more evident than in the 1898 response of United States President William McKinley to a Chicago delegation that presented him with resolutions from a mass meeting. The resolutions urged the President "as chief magistrate of this great nation" to take action to apprehend and punish the lynchers of Postmaster Baker of Lake City, South Carolina.

Baker and his infant child had been shot and killed, his wife and three daughters were shot and maimed for life, a son was wounded, and the family home set on fire. Why? Because Baker, appointed postmaster three months earlier by the Postmaster General in Washington, was black and not wanted in Lake City. The delegation spokesperson was Ida B. Wells-Barnett,[5] a fearless antilynching crusader who respectfully urged (i) that the President should have the lynchers of Postmaster Baker apprehended and punished, (ii) that the widow and children who lost a husband and father, as well as sustained injuries themselves, should be fully compensated, and (iii) that national legislation should be enacted to suppress the crime of lynching. She ended her appeal by reminding the President that the United States government had recently indemnified Italy and China for the lynching of their citizens on US soil and she hoped that the government would do as much for its own citizens. In response, President McKinley said he was in full accord with the petition and that "the attorney general...had been instructed to see what could be done by the government." At this point in the text a footnote indicated "Nothing was done."[6]

When the United States entered World War Two, W. E. B. Du Bois raised the question in his *Crisis* editorials: why should Blacks serve in the military of a nation that turned a blind eye to mobs lynching Blacks? When the editors of the *Messenger* asked the same question, the US government, under power given it by the Espionage Act, arrested the editors when they encouraged Blacks to resist. Du Bois, under pressure from his own NAACP, withdrew the no-democracy-no-military-service stance. However, the question did not go away, but marched on to the stage.

Alice Dunbar-Nelson (1875–1935)

Widow of the poet Paul Laurence Dunbar, Alice Dunbar-Nelson wrote and staged a short protest play entitled *Mine Eyes Have Seen* (1918) that asks if African American soldiers should defend a "democracy" that has been denied them. The play leaves the final decision squarely in the minds of the audience. The remnants of a small family are living in squalid circumstances in a northern industrial town, having been driven from their comfortable home in the South, their father killed defending it, and their house burnt to the ground. Their mother did not long survive relocation in the North; the elder brother, Dan, has been crippled in a factory accident, a sister tries to keep the family together, and now, to cap all their troubles, the younger brother, Chris, has been drafted for the war. He decides he owes no allegiance to a nation that has not protected them from violent racists, and therefore he will not go to war. With the question posed, it is argued back and forth by the family and their close friends – an Irish neighbor, a Jewish lad, Chris' fiancée Julia, and others who come to the house, having heard the news of his call-up. Eventually, Chris' resolve weakens, especially when Julia who has defended his stand, begins to talk of loyalty to country and to race while outside the music from a passing band is heard. The music becomes gradually louder until it is recognized as "The Battle Hymn of the Republic."

In the house individuals of the assembled group begin to sing softly or recite lines from the hymn, and as the music grows louder they run to the window to watch the parade. Chris "remains in the center of the floor, rigidly at attention, a rapt look on his face." Produced at the Dunbar High School in Washington, DC, on 10 April 1918, while American soldiers, black and white, were in the trenches in France "fighting to keep the world safe for democracy," the play's message could not be more pertinent to its audiences.

Mary Burrill (1884–1946)

The one-act play *Aftermath* brought the black serviceman home, in this instance to his South Carolina farm family. Burrill's play focuses on the homecoming from France of soldier John, the family's hero son. He had received the French War Cross for gallantry by saving the lives of his company during World War One. John's moment of joyous reunion with his family is shattered when he learns that the father he has loved so dearly has been burnt to death by Whites for striking a white man who, in an argument over the price of cotton, had called his father a liar and struck at him. John's sister had kept this news from him, believing that John already had much to contend with in the war. John asks who led the lynchers and is told. Then, with smoldering determination, he begins to load up his two revolvers. Thrusting one in the hands of his timid younger brother and keeping the other himself, he goes off to find the gang responsible for lynching his father. (See chapter 7 for the genre of lynch plays.)

World War One brought further protests to the stage. Billy King, a comedian and vaudevillian producer, in 1919 wrote and staged a musical, *Over the Top* (title drawn from a war term for climbing out of the trenches to charge the Germans). In the bare-bones plot, a black sea captain is denied admission to the Paris Peace Conference because of his color. Returning to the United States, the Captain makes several speeches about the mistreatment of Blacks in America. After opening at the Grand Theatre in Chicago, the musical toured, including the Lafayette Theater in New York City. The cast included top talents – comedian Billy Higgins, singer Gertrude Sanders, and dancers Ida Forsyne Hubbard and Olga Burgoyne. The latter two had had their careers in Europe aborted by the war. Burgoyne, an entertainer with a company of fourteen, had worked in St. Petersburg, Russia, where she owned a lingerie shop (1904) that employed twenty women. When the Russian revolution came, Burgoyne returned to the States "with only pocket money."

In a nursing home in Brooklyn, Ida Forsyne at age 90 unfolded her similar story of fleeing Russia during the war. She began her account in 1893, when at the age of 10 she was taken to the World's Columbian Exposition in Chicago.

> I was always frisky and I had to do the cakewalk with a little boy at the Fair. A woman wanted me to dance the cakewalk. My momma said I didn't know it, but the woman said, "I saw your child doing something out there on the sidewalk." So the woman persuaded Mamma, who was looking for the dollar. I did the cakewalk from then on. Everybody that could prance a bit and smile – you had to smile in those days; they didn't accept people that looked like they were mad.

After telling how she had gone to Europe with Abbie Mitchell, and how she was admired in Russia, she told how she was forced to return to America.

> I speak French, I speak German, I speak Russian. I speak some Norwegian because I've been to all those places. I know the words to all those fashionable songs that people were singing during that era. I know [she sings in Russian]

> > I'm neither a soubrette
> > nor a chansonnette
> > I'm neither English nor Parisian.
> > I just speak Russian
> > and wait for what comes to me.

Forsyne stated she had encountered no racial prejudice in Europe, but when she returned to the United States "I never got to the top... there's something about my skin that gives me away." Late in her life, Jerome Robbins consulted her on how to choreograph the cakewalk for the New York City Ballet.[7]

Ida B. Wells-Barnett (1862–1931) and the Pekin Theatre

Committed to helping Blacks from all walks of life, Ida B. Wells-Barnett had worked in Chicago with a white Unitarian minister in establishing the Frederick Douglass Center, where colored and white people could meet and become better acquainted with one another. To help raise funds for the center, Mrs. Wells-Barnett made a deal with Robert T. Motts, proprietor of the Pekin Theatre, that if he would allow his renovated theatre to be used for a benefit show for the Douglass Center, she would in turn undertake to improve the size and quality of audiences attending his shows. Since Motts' reputation as former manager of a liquor shop and gambling saloon was repugnant among the city's colored religious leaders, several of them highly disapproved of the planned performance and withdrew their support of the venture. However, Mrs. Wells-Barnett countered that since Motts had apparently reformed and was providing a proper theatre for the race, he should be encouraged, not spurned. She affirmed her resolve to cooperate with Motts to their mutual advantage and succeeded in making more than $500 for the Douglass Center.

Robert Motts, originally from Washington, Iowa, had come to Chicago as a young man. He worked at odd jobs before securing steady employment as a watchman, which enabled him to save enough money to buy part interest in a saloon at 2700 State Street in the colored section of the city. Motts then became interested in politics, organized workers to "get out to vote" and in return secured jobs for Blacks. As his influence grew he bought out his partners and expanded his saloon to include a gambling section. In 1901 he visited Europe and became interested in the *Cafès chantants* or music halls of Paris. On his return to Chicago, to quote his own words, "I had my mind made up to change the nature of my business and build up something that would be a credit to the race."[8] Adjacent to his business quarters, Motts established in 1904 an amusement hall that he advertised as "The Pekin Temple of Music,"[9] offering high-class vaudeville entertainment and being "The only theatre in America playing colored artists exclusively." Motts engaged the services of Charles Sager as stage manager, but soon thereafter a fire ruined the interior of the theatre, giving Motts the opportunity to enlarge the stage and auditorium, install a fire curtain, a balcony surround and boxes, and to redecorate the interior attractively, thus turning the theatre into a proper establishment seating more than one thousand patrons.

More important, Motts was persuaded to bring on board a talented and experienced group of theatre operatives to produce his shows. In addition to Sager as stage manager, J. Ed. Green was appointed producing director, Joe

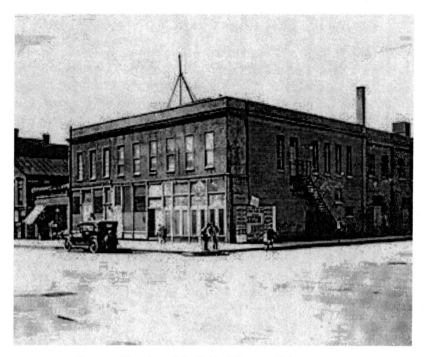

Figure 15. Exterior of the Pekin Theatre, Chicago, *c.* 1906

Jordan was resident director of music, and Will Marion Cook was retained for some musical shows. The scenic artist was R. J. Moxley, and other staffers included Tim Brymn (of S. H. Dudley's Smart Set Company), and H. Lawrence Freeman, a practiced musician and director who had worked with the *Rufus Rastus* troupe that starred Ernest Hogan. Further, the Pekin Theatre employed a press agent, a treasurer, and even a house physician among a staff of eighteen. The acting company (including staffers Green and Freeman) numbered thirty-four. Of this impressive line-up for a spanking new theatre, the *Chicago American* boasted that the Pekin was "the only theatre in the country, probably the only regular playhouse in the world, owned, managed and conducted by colored people, presenting with a stock company of colored artistes, original musical comedies, farces and plays written and composed by colored men is in this city."[10]

The new Pekin Theatre, located at the corner of Twenty-Seventh and State Streets, opened its doors on Saturday, 31 March 1906, and, for the first time on any stage, presented the three-act musical comedy *The Man From 'Bam* – book by Collin Davis, lyrics by Arthur Gillespie, and music by Joe Jordan.[11] It was staged by Charles Sager, who took the role of Elder Cashingberry, with L. D. "Slim" Henderson as Jube Johnson (the Man from 'Bam) and the comedian Andrew Tribble impersonating Jube's wife. Among female cast members were Lizzie Wallace singing the hit song "Feather Your Nest," and Ethel James of Chicago making a favorable impression as Priscilla. The simple plot tells of a railway worker who wins a fortune at the race track and throws a party, but who does not tell his wife, Hester. She turns up anyway and upbraids him, predicting he will reap bad luck for mistreating her. At the next race meeting he bets on the wrong horse and loses all the money he formerly won. Reduced to poverty, he begs forgiveness of his wife, promises to be a better husband, and all ends happily. The production was a distinct hit and played to full houses for a gratifying run of three weeks. As word got around and with added promotion from Ida B. Wells-Barnett, the new Pekin attracted a more cultured audience at this production than hitherto, including curious Whites and holier-than-thou Blacks, some of whom might have come to sneer but stayed to cheer the clever performers.

In the months that followed its opening the new Pekin Theatre pursued a rigorous schedule of new productions, mostly original musical comedies and farces, with a change of show every two to three weeks.[12] This was a demanding requirement, thought necessary in order to build a theatregoing black public, to introduce new and competent actors and songsters, and to spread the word across the country of a proper professional theatre run wholly by Blacks, in which African Americans could purchase a ticket for any part of the house without restriction. Among early successes were *The Mayor of Dixie*, *Two African Princes*, *My Friend From Georgia*, *In Zululand*, *Captain Rufus*, *Count of No Account*, *One Round of Pleasure*, and *Doctor Dope*.

As interest grew, special matinée performances were arranged for show people from other cities, and there were frequent changes of personnel as company members came and went. Newcomers included Lawrence Chenault, J. Francis Mores, Charles Gilpin, the prima donnas Lottie Grady and Rosa Lee Tyler, Pearl Brown and, later, Abbie Mitchell. The previously quoted *Chicago American* caught the excitement of the period when it wrote:

> Show followed show, all of them written by colored men until now the theatre is an established success and turns 'em away two or three nights a week...Nothing of a dramatic nature has yet been attempted – the patrons of the New Pekin would rather laugh than worry. Music, fun, singing and dancing, most of it of a grade that measures up very favorably with that presented at other theatres...make up the shows.[13]

By the start of summer 1907 Motts must have realized he had over-reached his investment in the Pekin and needed to find ways to further exploit his assets. Over the coming months he explored various means to market Pekin productions at other venues, but none proved feasible. His first attempt was to send two recent productions to New York during the summer for a short two-week stay at Hurtig and Seaman's Music Hall in Harlem.[14] For the first week the Pekin company presented *Captain Rufus*, billed as a military musical comedy written jointly by producing director J. Ed. Green and Alfred Anderson with music by H. Lawrence Freeman and Joseph Jordan. The second week showed *The Husband*, a farce comedy with music, the authors being Flournoy Miller and Aubrey Lyles, who would later become celebrated for *Shuffle Along* (1921) in New York. Although both productions received useful reviews, a major if unintentional consequence of the Pekin troupe's visit was to provoke New Yorkers into questioning why, if Chicago could have its own all-colored stock company present-ing plays in its own playhouse, shouldn't New York have at least one such enterprise?[15]

Motts' second venture took the form of a press announcement in the *Indianapolis Freeman* dated 28 December 1907, listing his theatrical holdings, for example, "twenty-five original three-act musical comedies, books, lyrics, music, scenery, costumes and equipment, ready for production on any stage." He also declared that he was "in close touch with over one hundred of the highest class of performers among the colored race" and was able to engage them at a moment's notice. Finally, he proposed that if three or four men of good business standing and integrity would be prepared to invest $15,000 each, he would do likewise and they could establish colored theatres in several locations that he had already scouted. His offer obviously found no takers, for reasons that will shortly be evident.

For his third attempt to extend the reach of the Pekin beyond its home crowd, early in 1908 Motts opened the Columbia Theatre located on Chicago's north side, near Clark and Division Streets. This 1,250-seat theatre was in a white district and the wily manager explained that he had acquired the use of the playhouse in order to provide entertainment for Whites in their community, thus obviating the need for them to travel to the less sedate southside. Motts increased the size of his acting company, his intention being to extend the run of his productions by performing at two venues and rotating shows between them. Unfortunately, the experiment came too late. As reported in the *New York Age* of 2 April 1908, despite the large attendance during opening week and for some few weeks thereafter, business at the Columbia Theatre then abruptly declined, forcing Motts to close the new playhouse.

Writing of this last reversal of fortune, Edward A. Robinson cites several reasons why the Columbia experiment failed: unfavorable reports in the white press; tales of mismanagement; the influx of rural workers whose theatre tastes were very rudimentary; and an overall preference for vaudeville by Pekin audiences.[16] These were all contributing factors, in addition to the sudden incidence of 5- and 10-cent movie houses whose novelty alone provided the most menacing threat to live theatre. Yet another sign of changing times for the Pekin was the departure of some of its seasoned actors. Harrison Stewart, Marion Brooks, and J. Francis Mores all terminated their contracts during the ensuing months in order to seek other opportunities. They would later return to perform at the Pekin with visiting companies. As Robinson rightly concludes: "the Pekin's demise was beginning."

It is now time to focus on two of the Pekin Theatre's brightest stars, namely, Harrison Stewart, actor, and J. Ed. Green, manager, director, actor, playwright, and the individual chiefly responsible, under owner Motts, for the quality of productions at the theatre. Stewart, at age 24, left home in Washington, DC, in 1906 and headed for Chicago, hoping to find suitable work. Encouraged by his hometown friend William Foster, who believed in Stewart's acting ability, he auditioned at the Pekin and received a one-year contract. After a tentative start, he was asked by director J. Ed. Green to assume an important role in *Two African Princes*, replacing the experienced actor Andrew Tribble, who had resigned from the Pekin to join Cole and the Johnsons' acting company. Stewart did well in the part and when the next senior comedian left the Pekin, "all the leading comedy roles were given him" (i.e., Stewart). It was not long before the name of Harrison Stewart was a big drawing card for the little playhouse, and the management saw fit to bill the new comedian all over town.[17]

During his twenty-month stay at the Pekin, Harrison Stewart created comedy roles in twenty-six shows, of which four were farce comedies and the rest musical comedies. He also assisted in writing the lyrics or music for many of his roles. Stewart left the Pekin in spring 1908 to explore job opportunities in New York, and was selected to head the *Oyster Man* company. He replaced the veteran Ernest Hogan, for whom the musical comedy was written and who had been its star until he became ill early in the year, causing the show to be suspended. The managers decided to revive the production in the fall and selected Stewart for the lead. Asked for his views on

playing comic roles, Stewart responded in words that presage a new era for
former blackface comedians:

> I feel that the public demands new styles in comedy lines and I try to be
> as original as I can . . . I would like to make an experiment to ascertain if
> it is absolutely necessary for a Negro comedian to use cork in order to
> gain success. To be frank, I don't think there is a funny bone in me but I
> believe I know what is necessary to bring out clearly the situations which
> provoke laughter . . . you must do more than put on a ridiculous make-up
> and wear funny clothes to produce laughter.[18]

One of the truly versatile and gifted black performers at the turn of
the century was J. Ed. Green. He was only 37 years old when he died
in Chicago, on 19 February 1910. Green had been ill for the past several
months but seemed to be recovering and was actually greeted by friends
out-of-doors the day prior to his demise. He had come originally from
New Albany, Indiana, where he completed high school education before
forming in 1892 the Black Diamond Quartet, composed of himself (with
"a light baritone voice of sweet quality but limited in range") and three
of his townsmen. After a short period with the minstrels, the quartet was
engaged for the 1894/95 season to appear with the *South Before the War*
company when, in addition to singing with the quartet, Green was chosen for the part of "Young Eph," a role he performed with much credit.
Then, according to one report,[19] in the summer of 1896 Green wrote and
staged at Havelin's Theatre in Chicago the big musical production *Fred
Douglass' Reception* (1896), which was performed by the Black American
Troubadours. Green was next employed by the Oliver Scott Company,
where he proved to be such an able stage manager and interlocutor that he
was lured away by the Georgia Minstrels to serve in these positions. So far
J. Ed. Green had demonstrated multiple skills in professional theatre, as
quartet singer, budding actor, scenarist, director, and stage manager. More
would follow.

Still gathering experience in various theatre disciplines, Green teamed up
with Bob A. Kelley to write and produce the *Queen of the Jungle*, featuring
Mme. Mamie Flowers, who had appeared in Isham's original Octoroon
company in 1895. Green also stage-managed for the Black Patti Troubadours
and performed with the Smart Set Company, where he created the part of
Kane, showing additional strength as a character actor. At this time he
wrote songs and two unproduced plays. Perhaps the highlight of Green's
career prior to his appointment at the Pekin Theatre was his association

with Ernest Hogan in 1905, the first season of the *Rufus Rastus* company. Green was invited both to stage the production in New York and to appear in the role of the headwaiter, Beasley. His work was of a high order and earned the respect of several other theatre artists, such as Joe Jordan and H. Lawrence Freeman on the production team, and J. Francis Mores in the cast. Green would shortly be associated with them and others at the Pekin Theatre. It was that summer (1905), when Green was in Chicago, that Robert Motts approached him to become managing director (also titled Director of Amusements) of the new Pekin, which would be devoted to staging plays instead of vaudeville acts.

Manager Motts could not have made a finer choice and Green must have accepted with alacrity. It seemed as if his career up to that point had been a preparation for just this opportunity. He would lead the Pekin enterprise to provide entertaining and honorable black theatre, primarily for Chicago's African American community, and he was ready for the task. Only recently he had been referred to in print as "a universal favorite . . . the very successful stage manager . . . kindly but positive, commanding but not overbearing."[20] In addition to his general responsibilities, Green ensured he would be a hands-on leader. He began by writing and directing short musical farces (e.g., *Twenty Minutes From State Street*) to music composed by Joe Jordan and it became a fad among "automobilists" on the southside "to run in half-an-hour or so and watch the shows – which are uniformly good."[21] Thereafter, Green carefully chose the plays he would direct, such as *Doctor Dope* (1907), which was defined as "a legitimate musical comedy with a strikingly operatic tinge." There were others in which he would be a cast member, but seldom in the leading role.

In his second year Green announced through a press release that he was prepared to start at the Pekin a "Training School for the Stage." Instruction would cost $1.50 an hour and classes for adults would be held on Tuesdays and Fridays. The course of study would include acting, stage dancing, stage management, producing, and vaudeville. Those who completed the course would be offered an apprenticeship at the Pekin, where they could receive a weekly stipend ranging from $10 to $25. There is no record that such a training program ever materialized; the proposal is cited simply to indicate the forward thinking of J. Ed. Green, who must have realized the need for proper instruction in most so-called professional performers. It is cause for regret that Green was only able to serve as artistic head of the Pekin for a limited period, from fall 1906 to end of spring 1908. At that time circumstances conspired to force the Pekin once again into the arms of vaudeville, and Green into a new position that was less satisfying. In an obituary notice published in the *New York Age* of 24 February 1910, Lester Walton records some of Green's achievements at the Pekin Theatre:

> through his efforts the Pekin Theatre soon became one of the theatrical novelties of America and an inspiration to the colored performer. To his foresight and judgment we are indebted for such actors and actresses as Harrison Stewart, Matt Marshall, J. F. Mores, Lottie Grady, Mae White, Pearl Brown . . . and others, and such writers and promoters as Marion A. Brooks and Will Foster. It was he who discovered the young playwrights Miller and Lyles.

Walton explained that when the advent of moving picture theatres in Chicago caused the Pekin's manager to change its policy back to a vaudeville house, J. Ed. Green and Marion Brooks organized the Chester Amusement Company, operating three theatres in Chicago and acting as booking agents for several others. Walton surmised that the eventual failure of this venture had contributed to Green's physical breakdown and concluded, "J. Ed. Green was a talented actor and a versatile and productive playwright of ability, and will be greatly missed."

Robert Motts did not long survive his esteemed managing director. While he will be remembered with favor for founding the Pekin Theatre and for publicizing its achievements to most of the country, Motts seemed to think that artistic production could be turned out regularly as merchandise from a machine. He expected that the Pekin could produce a newly written play every week or every other week, which of course was impossible, even with a generous budget. He had recently turned 50 years of age when he succumbed to leukemia on 10 July 1911, some seventeen months after Green had died.

The initial success of the Pekin Theatre as a legitimate professional African American theatre proved an enormous stimulus to the spread of black theatres nationwide. Within months of its opening an announcement on the front page of the *Broad Axe* of 16 June 1906 informed readers that a colored theatre will be opened in Little Rock, Arkansas:

> The theatre will be one of a circuit comprising ten playhouses in the South. It is intended to locate the others at Hot Springs, Pine Bluff, Fort Smith, Texarkana, and possibly Malvern in this state. The theatre will be exclusively for Negroes, and white persons will be treated just as the colored element is now served – they will have to beg for tickets and take

back seats. All of the actors will be colored, and so will the stage hands. Abe Utity of Atlanta is the organizer of this unique circuit. He is a nephew of George Lederer, the well-known New York theatrical magnate.

Whether the report be factual or fraudulent (and we are inclined to the latter belief), there is no denying the fact that the reputable *Indianapolis Freeman* of 10 May 1910 listed fifty-three Colored Theatres "owned and managed by Negroes," a roster that included no fewer than seven Pekin Theatres in addition to the original. They were located in the cities of Cincinnati, Ohio; Jackson and Memphis, Tennessee; Lexington, Kentucky; Norfolk, Virginia; Savannah, Georgia; and Tulsa, Oklahoma. The list did not include the New Pekin Theatre in Louisville, Kentucky, where play-wright Letitia Lee presented an Indian musical drama in two acts in which the heroine, "Red Wing," is kidnapped by a jealous suitor and eventually rescued.[22] As for the original Chicago Pekin, it was used mainly for vaudeville shows along with the occasional musical or farce comedy brought in by a traveling company. One of the last reports on the theatre appeared in the *Indianapolis Freeman* of 25 September 1915, which confirmed that the property, "still owned by the Motts' estate, is now open as a five-cent picture house," but will likely be used eventually for charitable and beneficial purposes.

In the decade following the demise of the Pekin Theatre in Chicago, changes swept through black America. World War One drew thousands of African Americans into the segregated military, while thousands more fled the segregated South for the North, where jobs abounded. With them, jazz danced its way north to Chicago, a city that in 1918 boasted one hundred and four theatres, cabarets, and photoplay houses, offering vaudeville, comedy skits, and even minstrel shows to Blacks. Serious drama was given little attention and had few writers. Nonetheless, two efforts should be noted: poet Joseph S. Cotter Sr.'s verse play *Caleb, the Degenerate* (1901), and William Easton's second historical tragedy, *Christophe* (1914). Only *Christophe* received production, at the Lenox Casino in New York City on 3 April 1912. Pageantry had replaced tragedy on the American stage.

Pageants

Too pictorial to be a parade, too narrative to be a play, pageants – with their music, costume, dance, narration, and tableaux – reenacted historical events. The large ones were held outdoors in stadiums or sometimes passing in front of a community seated in bleachers. Over four days *The Pageant and Masque of St. Louis* (1914) used a cast of seven thousand people and played to an audience of one hundred thousand. Smaller communities presented their histories in auditoriums, seeking to learn who the new Americans were – an important quest for a nation of diverse immigrants and recently manumitted Blacks.

America's romance with pageantry had begun in 1876 with her centennial Fourth of July, but when Philadelphia's Liberty Bell rang out to mark the Constitution's one-hundredth birthday, African Americans were scarcely visible. Black residents had been asked to ride on three floats depicting their progress from slavery to freedom. While several African Americans appeared on the last float, none would ride the wagon for slavery, even when offered money to do so.[23]

Resistance to looking back at slavery days manifested itself in one of the first, if not the inaugural pageant initiated by Blacks: *The Great Cuba Pageant of 1898*.[24] In the United States in 1898, 101 Negroes were lynched. Georgia and Mississippi headed the list, with twelve and fourteen respectively, while Minnesota, where the pageant originated, had no lynchings that year. Indeed, the black population of the entire state was less than 1 percent. However, the roughly fifteen hundred Afro-Americans who lived in St. Paul were fiercely indignant that their federal government refused to protect its colored citizens from violence and death.[25] Under the leadership of Frederick McGhee, a lawyer, and John Q. Adams, editor of the black newspaper the *Appeal*, the citizens organized the Law Enforcement League of Minnesota to protect themselves, as well as African Americans throughout the United States.

The revolution of Afro-Cubans led by the "Bronze Titan" Antonio Maceo against the Spanish crown had inspired black Minnesotans to believe that the United States' support of the Cuban revolution would spill over to championing their own cause of color.[26] Victory in Cuba would bring victory at home.

The pageant, a fund-raiser for the Law Enforcement League, was advertised in the *Appeal* as "Cuba – a Drama of Freedom... with Music, Art, Drama, Comedy." The four-act event played on 3 and 4 November at the Lyceum Theater in Minneapolis, and the week following at the Metropolitan Opera House in St. Paul. The first act presented "Liberty and her maidens carrying compassion to Cuba along with flower girls and women in armor; they then sailed to Spain to plead for the island's oppressed subjects." Later acts depicted cultural life in Cuba, the victory over Spain, and finally a worldwide celebration of freedom in the new Republic of Cuba. The *Marseillaise* was sung, as was *Der Wacht am Rhein* (in German).

The Afro-American contribution included a cakewalk, then the most popular dance in the nation. J. C. Reid, a journalist, objected: "No white-man ever looked at the cakewalk unless he thought of its origin. Our unfortunate ancestors amused their masters in the hated ante-bellum days with the cakewalk." He declared: "What we want to do is to put down every-thing that was ever connected to slavery. We want to forget those days." Reid's statements attracted opposition. A public debate, "Is the Cakewalk Detrimental to the Afro-American?," drew a large crowd to the Bethesda Church in Minneapolis. Anger and shame at the memory of bondage would continue to fuel a growing objection to black depictions of slave life on stage until a half-century after emancipation.

Within their own institutions, black college pageants promoted images honoring race progress: *The Masque of Colored America, Pageant of Progress in Chicago, Culture of Color, A Constellation of Women,* and *The Milestones of the Race*. Because these spectacles contained little dialogue and minimal narration, W. E. B. Du Bois seized on the form: "It seemed to me that it might be possible . . . to get people interested in this development of Negro drama to teach on the one hand the colored people themselves the meaning of their history and their rich, emotional life through a new theatre, and on the other, to reveal the Negro to the white world as a human, feeling thing."

Working through a series of drafts, Du Bois' monumental *The Star of Ethiopia* commemorated the fiftieth anniversary of the Emancipation Proclamation and premiered on 22–31 October 1913 at the Armory in New York City. More than fourteen thousand people viewed the work of three hundred and fifty performers and musicians under the direction of Charles Burroughs, one of Du Bois' former students from Wilberforce University. Professor Freda Scott-Giles states that it was Burroughs who provided the continuity and put the pageant into stageable form as a prelude followed by six episodes that told "the tale of the oldest and strongest of the races of mankind, whose faces be Black." Each episode illustrated the gifts of the race to the world: the Gift of Iron, the Gift of Civilization, the Gift of Faith, the Gift of Humiliation (slavery), the Gift of Struggle Toward Freedom, and the Gift of Freedom. African American music and dance underscored all of these historical events.

In 1915 Du Bois restaged *The Star* in Washington, DC, at the American League Baseball Park with twelve hundred participants, including a chorus of two hundred singers.

The Superintendent of Colored Education threw his entire system into the effort, and the Colored District Militia was enlisted for the battle episodes. J. Rosamond Johnson served as Director of Music. This production was a critical and artistic success, though not a financial one. Du Bois had hoped to reproduce the pageant at least ten more times, but could only realize production twice more: with one thousand participants in Philadelphia in 1916; and with 300 participants at the Hollywood Bowl in Los Angeles in 1925. Du Bois' dreams of establishing an independent producing organization and of gaining recognition by the American Pageant Association, which studiously ignored his efforts, remained unfulfilled.[27]

Anita Bush (1883–1974) and the Lafayette Players

In Brooklyn a tailor sent his teenage daughter to deliver costumes to the Bijou, a theatre near her home. There she found the Williams and Walker company rehearsing *In Dahomey*. For Anita Bush, it was love at first sight. She persuaded her father to let her audition for the chorus (she was approaching 17). When her father asked Williams what she would be able to do, Williams replied, "She would make a pretty picture." She not only succeeded in joining the company, but traveled to England with the musical and later performed in the chorus of four other Williams and Walker shows, her final appearance being in *Mr. Lode of Koal* (1909–10). When the musical closed, Bush formed her own dance troupe, "Anita Bush and her 8 Shimmy Babies," to tour the east coast, but she injured her back in a stage accident, ending her career in dance but not in theatre.

Maria C. Downs, a Puerto Rican, in 1909 had purchased the Nickelette Theatre at 135th and Lenox and changed its name to the Lincoln Theatre. Here comics Eddie Hunter, Tom Chapelle, and Andrew Tribble kept audiences rollicking in laughter. Fats Waller played piano for the silent films. Anita Bush persuaded Downs to try an innovation: her stock company would present a "one-act playlet" entitled *The Girl at the Fort*.[28] Downs agreed. On 15 November 1915 a cast of five seasoned actors – four from Motts' Pekin Theatre in Chicago – introduced drama to the commercial stage of Harlem's theatre. Since the play was hardly more than an hour long, the matinée bill was filled out with vaudeville acts. Audiences were pleased. Downs increased her offerings: six new vaudeville acts semiweekly and sometimes a new four-act play by the Anita Bush Stock Company. Top prices were 25-cent matinées and 35-cent evenings.[29] Coupled with an open racial policy, Downs was soon able to expand her popular theatre from 300 seats to 850 and install an organ "to achieve the much needed elevation of musical taste in Harlem," for the Lincoln was known for its rowdy crowds. The balcony "gods," nicknamed the Sharpshooters, commented freely on stage action and entered into arguments with the talents. They told Jules Bledsoe in *The Emperor Jones*: "Why don't you come on out of that jungle – back to Harlem where you belong?" The Lincoln's major attractions remained jazz and blues singers – Ma Rainey, Mamie Smith, and Bessie Smith. Early on, owner Marie C. Downs asked Bush to alter her company's name from the Anita Bush Stock Company to the Lincoln Players. Bush refused and moved her company to the Lafayette Theatre to open with a sketch entitled *Over the Footlights*, with Bush, Carlotta Freeman, Charles Gilpin, Andrew Bishop, and Arthur "Dooley" Wilson. At that time the Lafayette's black comanager, Lester A. Walton, was one of its extraordinary talents.

Lester A. Walton (1882–1965) and the Lafayette Players

Born in St. Louis to a schoolteacher and the chief bellhop at the Lindell Hotel, Lester Algar Walton[30] was named after the British actor, Lester Wallach. After graduating from Sumner High School, Walton worked as a journalist for the white *St. Louis Globe-Democrat*, serving as a combination reporter for sports and drama (a mixture common in 1920s journalism). After a brief time he moved to the prestigious *St. Louis Post-Dispatch*. Popular comedian and writer Ernest Hogan then brought Walton to New York City, where he wrote lyrics with Henry Creamer and Will Vodery for *Rufus Rastus*, and its sequel, *The Oyster Man*. This early "song play" by Flournoy Miller and Aubrey Lyles told the tale of a down-and-out vaudevillian (Ernest Hogan) attempting to pay off a debt of $22 by working various service jobs at a hotel. He fails, but then inherits a fortune, lives in the hotel where he worked, and marries his true love. The sequel, originally entitled *The Man from Baltimore*, follows the Hogan-like character as an oyster vender who travels to a mythical island of splendor. It was Hogan's last show before his death in May 1909. Lester Walton had left off writing lyrics for shows, and in 1908 the *New York Age* hired him as drama editor. In this position he developed critical standards that he maintained throughout his career. He saw black theatre as a distinct movement within American theatre. He believed that racial issues were central to any black show. His reviews reflected his belief that the critic was also a cultural historian, and he opposed the unwarranted use of dialect, stereotypes, and makeup to lighten black actors, although he approved of whitening-up for white roles.[31]

Of immediate pertinence here was his persuasion in 1912 of Meyer Jarmulowsky to build the Lafayette Theatre on Seventh Avenue and 131st Street in Harlem. Because of a strong white presence in the neighborhood, there was uncertainty whether the 2,000-seat theatre would remain segregated. Martinson and Niber, two liquor dealers on the block, leased the theatre and kept it segregated, but after six months of unprofitable box office, they surrendered their lease to C. W. Morganstern, a Broadway booking agent, and Lester A. Walton took over the management, desegregated the theatre, and supplied the community with the Anita Bush Stock Company (soon to be known as the Lafayette Players).[32] For a time, Walton retained his column in the *New York Age*, where he praised the Lafayette Players' first show, *Across the Footlights* (30 December 1915). "While visiting the Lafayette Theatre, patrons can expect to see a great and meritorious effort being made to raise the standard of the colored theatrical profession; and an endeavor to prove that the Negro can do other than sing and dance."

In February 1916 the team of Walton and Morganstern broke up; Robert Levy became the new manager of the Lafayette Theatre and opened a fresh play every Monday afternoon, with daily matinées. Beginning on Tuesday, the play for the following week went into morning rehearsals. These shows, known as "tabs," were shortened versions of Broadway comedies and melodramas, sometimes using Broadway's discarded stage sets and costumes. A movie or vaudeville act usually shared the bill. This pattern became the regular routine for seven years.

"The Lafayette Players proved the first opportunity black actors had to work in full seasons of straight dramas and melodramas, sometimes altered to suit the tastes of Harlem audiences."[33] Among the some two-hundred and fifty plays the troupe would eventually perform, a few of the more famous were: *The Octoroon*, *Madame X*, *The Count of Monte Cristo*, and *Dr. Jekyll and Mr. Hyde*, the last with Clarence Muse playing the lead in white face and blond wig. Among the more than three-hundred and sixty actor-alumni who would pass through the ranks were: Charles Gilpin, Evelyn Ellis, Frank Wilson, Edna Thomas, Abbie Mitchell, and Evelyn Preer. As Jo Tanner points out in *Dusky Maidens*, a history of black women actresses in the nineteenth century, Bush deserved the title, "The Little Mother of Negro Drama."

Not everyone was pleased to see the actors always playing white roles. Lovett Fort-Whiteman, drama editor for the *Messenger* wrote:

> The theatre going public desires to see at least occasionally, the work of
> some Negro playwrights . . . Daily this desire is becoming more intense.
> And as advice to every Negro in Harlem, I say – demand, kick, agitate until
> we get the work of our playwrights produced in the Lafayette Theatre;
> do not cease, for we must see our society reflected upon the American
> stage even if we have to call a mass meeting of Harlem's theatre-goers
> and effect a boycott on the Lafayette Theatre.[34]

Nonetheless, the Lafayette Players' success can be measured by Levy's establishing a second acting company at the Howard Theatre in Washington,
DC, and soon a third at the Grand Theatre in Chicago.[35] The Lafayette
ensemble established as the Dunbar Players in Philadelphia. It is not quite
true that no black playwrights were produced. Tom Brown, an actor with
the Lafayette Players, presented his "neo-romantic" drama, *The Eternal
Magdaline* (1917), to high praise in the *Messenger* by drama editor Lovett
Fort-Whiteman.

In 1920 Anita Bush resigned from the Lafayette Players to act in the films
The Crimson Skull (1921) and *The Bulldoggers* (1923). The Lafayette troupe
remained in Harlem until 1928, when it could no longer compete with the
popularity of film, with its low admission prices. Perhaps dreaming that
they, too, might make careers in film, a number of the players moved to the
Lincoln Theater in Los Angeles, where they revived Somerset Maugham's
popular melodrama *Rain*. Starring Evelyn Preer, the drama ran for fifty-four
successive weeks. However, the company did not survive the Depression;
they took their last bows in 1932. The Lafayette Theatre's other companies
in Chicago, Baltimore, Washington, DC, and Philadelphia (the Dunbar
Players) are discussed in chapter 7.

To bring this section to a close, a brief comparison between the two
major stock companies – the Pekin Theatre of Chicago and the Lafayette
of Harlem – may provide clues to the soon burgeoning theatre of the Harlem
Renaissance.

Both stock companies employed only black actors, but their audiences
differed: the Pekin played to Blacks and discouraged white attendance.
While the majority of the Lafayette's audiences were also black, Whites
were encouraged to attend. Second, the Pekin's entire management and
artistic staff were black. The producers and directors of the Lafayette were
white. Third, although the Pekin barely survived a decade, the Lafayette
limped on for seventeen years and produced many more plays; however,
their dramas were nearly all white-authored and played for one week.

Almost all plays produced at the Pekin were written and directed by Blacks, and runs were frequently extended to accommodate demand. Both theatres gave sustained opportunities for actors to learn their craft. Indeed, some actors, such as Charles Gilpin, worked in both theatres. It is argued that the Lafayette raised audience standards. Agreed, but for European dramatic formulae. The Pekin raised its audience standards, too, but for black entertainments. As this book will show, both of these trends played out in the Harlem Renaissance, but first we must look at the second root of the Harlem Renaissance.

TOBA and other theatrical circuits

Performing in theatres similar to the Pekin, the comedian and musician Sherman H. Dudley had worked his way up through minstrelsy to vaudeville. He achieved fame in *The Smart Set* with his comedy act, "Dudley and his Mule." In 1913 he organized a black circuit for vaudevillians and by 1916 he merged with others to form the Southern Consolidated Circuit, which controlled "over 28 theatres covering the South, East, and Midwest. For the first time an actor could be contracted for eight months out of one office."[36] To meet the competition, Whites lost no time in resuscitating an older and desultory agency, the Theater Owners' Booking Association (TOBA), active roughly between 1907 and 1921. Their announced purpose: "to save the colored theatrical industry ... to offer better booking for black performers."[37] Although this circuit primarily booked black acts, its board had two black members only – T. S. Finley, owner of the Lyceum Theatre in Cincinnati, and C. H. Douglass, owner of the Douglass Theatre in Macon, Georgia. TOBA revitalized itself at almost the same time that J. A. Jackson began writing his "Page" in *Billboard*. In his first year (1920), Jackson traveled more than twelve thousand miles to acquaint himself with black show business. Not only did he review vaudeville and film, he also traveled to county fairs and circuses, a major source of employment for entertainers.[38] He saw abuses and set out to remedy them.

Producers sometimes absconded with box-office receipts, leaving the artists stranded. Blacks had little recourse. They could not join the white National Vaudeville Artists (NVA) association, and the Actors' Equity Association (AEA) admitted only a select few. In 1921 the Colored Actors Beneficial League merged with the Colored Actors Union ($5 to join). Within a year, they boasted eight hundred members and raised the dues to $10 (which might be paid in four installments.) A major goal was to secure thirty weeks' work and prevent managers from canceling contracts whenever they wished, or if the contract was voided, full salary must be paid the performer. The Colored Vaudeville Benevolent Association designated "August 2 as National Actors' Day on which all the proceeds from colored houses and contributions and gifts from all other managers are deposited in the treasury... to furnish the home that we are now building to take care of you should you become unable to work."[39]

One of the most common abuses of performers, the midnight show, required performance without additional salary. These late-night revels appealed to rowdy crowds, who demanded music, dance, and laughter sparked by bawdry. Family audiences stayed home. Jackson campaigned for family entertainment, which would build audiences for black performers who, in turn, would drop their "blue" material. He addressed all these issues on his "Page," which was reprinted in many newspapers, and his success in bringing performers and management to the negotiating table can be attributed to his reputation as an honest broker. As late as 1928, critic Theophilus Lewis bluntly stated: "The colored performer needs an organization fashioned after Equity to address the old issue of nonpayment of actors by managers. Last year that organization (Equity) collected $200,000 in back salaries which its members would have otherwise lost."[40]

Stagehands had no better protection. White unions controlled black houses. In March 1922 the International Stage Handlers and Theatrical Employees Union, which Blacks were not allowed to join, demanded that all black hands at the Lafayette Theatre be dismissed because they were not union members. If the theatre managers refused, the union would allow no further burlesque acts to appear there. To the management's credit, the Lafayette canceled all burlesque acts and proceeded with its drama schedule.[41] In a reverse situation, John T. Gibson, black owner of the Standard and Dunbar Theatres in Philadelphia, fired his black stagehands and hired white ones. He was heavily criticized by the black press.

Ethel Waters (1896–1977)

For all the hardships, TOBA and other circuits did provide stages for those who could survive the test. Ethel Waters was one. Born an unwanted child to a teenage mother, she grew up in Philadelphia, learning things about life that no young child should know. Billed as Mama Stringbean, an agile shimmy shaker, at age 17 she sang in clubs for $10 a week. Her first acting came in short melodramatic afterpieces in Atlanta at No. 81 (Decatur) Theatre.

After an appearance at Washington, DC's Howard Theatre, she moved up to Edmund's Cellar in Harlem, where some of the top talents of the day praised her clear voice and "laid-back" style. Black Swan Troubadours (Records) advertised the 25-year-old as "The World's Greatest Blues Singer." Next came a stint at the fashionable Plantation Club, after which she stepped up into the musical *Africana* (1927), then into the *Blackbird* shows, and finally to star in *As Thousands Cheer* (1933). Her talents as a dramatic actress were highly praised for her role of Hagar in *Mamba's Daughters* (1938). Her role in *Cabin in the Sky* (1940) led to a film role in 1943. Her characterization of Bernice in *The Member of the Wedding* (1950) won her the same role in the film (1952). She was nominated for an Academy Award. The next year she starred as Belulah in the television series. The last years of her life were spent with Billy Graham's Crusade.[42] Waters' rise from a nobody to a somebody was not unparalleled. In an era when no acting schools or workshops admitted Blacks, they learned their craft by taming rowdy audiences.

Billy King (1875–1951)

Some of TOBA's brightest stars, like bravura comedian, writer, and producer Billy King, by the 1940s had faded into eclipse. King, born in obscurity on a farm near Whistler, Alabama, left home to join a group of actors and soon after organized his own troupe, the King and Bush Wide-Mouth Minstrels. Richard and Pringle's Georgia Minstrels recognized his comic talents, hired him, and King honed his craft on their southern and midwest TOBA circuits. Circa 1912, he formed a stock company in Atlanta, Georgia, where he wrote his own skits and routines. In 1915 he moved his troupe to the Grand Theatre in Chicago, and during the next eight seasons (1915–23) he "kept the house in constant laughter." According to reviews, he created new material nearly every week. His programs included a short minstrel show, a blues singer, a chorus line, a dramatic soprano, and comedy sketches with titles like "Husbands-Wives" and "Nuff Sed." In March 1922 he moved his troupe of thirty to forty artists into Lincoln Gardens, where he advertised that there would be no more cabaret acts, but high class entertainment in four acts, between which there would be community dancing. He was credited with coaching girls at the ends of a chorus line to clown, a routine used by Josephine Baker to steal scenes in *Shuffle Along* and *Chocolate Dandies*.[43] Billy King and Sherman Dudley set the pace for comedy-vaudeville.

Figure 16. The Tutt Brothers: Salem Tutt Whitney and J. Homer Tutt, *c.* 1921

The Tutt brothers and the Whitman sisters

Two black vaudeville shows set records for longevity. Salem Tutt Whitney and his younger brother J. Homer Tutt[44] in 1909 created the Smart Set. Using variations of that name, for two decades they produced *George Washington Bullion*, a full-length musical farce that portrayed a tobacco plantation owner (Whitney Tutt) trying to gain entreé to society. It became their perennial hit. Below an edited quote from the *Indianapolis Freeman* (10 October 1910) indicates how the elastic plot could expand to embrace any vaudeville act:

> The Widow Dear...introduces Mr. J. Homer Tutt as Sam Cain. He is preceded by a dozen girls in a slow enchanting ensemble dance before his entrance singing "When I hear a Minstrel Band"... There might be some difficulty in surpassing this number but for the exciting entrance of Mr. Sank Sims attired in a thousand rags with the information that the train has arrived carrying George Washington Bullion (Salem Tutt Whitney) [He] is to enter in an automobile, with J. H. Woodson, the great basso, as the chauffeur and a half a dozen men in attendance. The running, yelling, wowing of a bunch of girls foretells Mr. Bullion's appearance. A few seconds later, Mr. B. is driven in, lordly decked upon a wheelbarrow laden with suit cases, etc., and is abruptly dumped on stage...Bullion

Figure 17. The Whitman Sisters: Alberta, Mable, Essie, and Baby Alice

and Cain then hold the comedy-thirsty audience at bay eight minutes
with their catchy dialogue.

Playwright Salem Tutt Whitney wrote the second longest-running black
show in America – 1904 to the 1940s – *Silas Green from New Orleans*. During those years, it toured almost exclusively in the South. Like in *George
Washington Bullion*, the actors were replaced, jokes and the specialty acts
changed, but the plot remained the same. A devoted audience bought tickets whenever the show returned, much as they did when the circus came to
town. The theme song, "Silas Green from New Orleans," was composed
by J. Homer Tutt, who wrote fifty show songs, often in collaboration. In
1922 the brothers' musical *Oh Joy* played on Broadway for four weeks. Both
Tutts played in *The Green Pastures* (1930), with Whitney as Noah. He died
in 1934.

The success of the Tutts was surpassed only by the Whitman Sisters,
whose show toured the same circuits from 1899 to 1940. Historian Bernard
Peterson declared them the highest paid act in black vaudeville. They owned
their own show and toured all the major cities in the United States. The
four sisters, Mabel (1880–1942), Alberta (1887–1964), Essie (1882–1963), and
"Baby" Alice (1900–69) were the daughters of a Reverend Alberty Allson

Whitman, who gave his young daughters dancing and singing lessons so they might accompany him on his preaching tours. Perhaps inspired by the Hyers Sisters and the Fisk Jubilee Singers, their show would eventually include Jubilee song, coon shouts, cakewalks, breakdowns, comedians, midgets, cross-dressers, dancing girls, pickaninnies, and a jazz band. "Ma" Mabel, the black female manager of the company, "created some of the best child acts in the business because parents trusted her." They never performed in low dives, but regularly played in churches, modifying their routines to fit the moral standards of the congregation. The Whitman Sisters could easily have passed for white and did sometimes on the street and on stage. Alberta (Bert) cross-dressed as a male when she and her sister Alice imitated the dances of George and Ada Walker, as well as those of Johnson and Dean. "Bert" was recognized as the best strutter in show business.

Originally known as the Whitman Sisters Novelty Company (1904), they changed their show titles several times. Many talents passed through their programs, including the young Bill Robinson, Ethel Waters, Princess Wee Wee, Willie Bryant, and Butterbeans and Susie. Sometimes the company numbered thirty performers plus a jazz band. During the 1920s the Whitman Sisters created at least nine different shows and often played in New York City. This amazing theatrical family remained largely undocumented until Nadine George-Graves published *The Royalty of Negro Vaudeville*.[45]

The decade that began in 1910 is sometimes described as a barren one for black theatre. It suffered from being sandwiched between two exceptional eras – the ebullience of the ragtime musicals and remarkable art theatres coupled with the musical extravaganzas of the 1920s. The second decade of the twentieth century gave four of its years to World War One. Nonetheless, historian Henry Sampson uncovered over one hundred black shows that toured the East and South, some to New York City.[46]

Performances between 1900 and 1920 were not literary theatre but rather popular spectacle, dance, and music – black vaudeville whose history affords us almost no scripts, leaving us to assess the work by reading newspaper reviews that were more often "puffs" than critical assessments. There is little question that this popular theatre pleased the "lower" classes. Boisterous and bawdy performances coupled with the persistence of the minstrel stereotype, sent the middle classes away to found their own art theatres. A single example of one theatre group that attempted to leave popular theatre behind was the Negro Players, also known as the Famous Colored Players and sometimes self-referenced as the Pioneer Negro Amusement Company. Founded

Figure 18. Princess Wee Wee and partner Willie Bryant, 1920s

by Henry Creamer, Alex C. Rogers, and Will Marion Cook, their initial program, *The Old Man's Boy*, set forth two purposes: to produce playlets of Negro life today, tomorrow, and yesterday; and to bring to the stage young people with talent – those who have aspired but have no opportunity. Lester Walton in reviewing their production noted that their third act was out of the ordinary for a colored show – as it gave an opportunity to show what Negroes can do along dramatic lines. There was not a musical number in the act. "The large audience at the Casino Theater (Philadelphia) showed... that it welcomed the change from slap-stick and a ridiculing of the race, to dramatic work with acting full of human interest wherein the Negro is shown as man among men, possessing a heart and finer feelings the same as others." Toward this end, Walton observed that Pekin-trained Harrison Stewart presented real evidence of legitimate acting.[47]

The US Census of 1910 listed 1,279 Negroes engaged as actors in the entertainment profession, but those who worked in the New York areas were far fewer and knew each other's talents well. For example, *The Old Man's Boy* was a direct descendant from *Rufus Rastus* and *The Oyster Man*, which had similar plots and themes, but the Hogan productions had stepped away from the formula musical. *The Old Man's Boy* took a further step by removing music and dance from act 3.

Two years later, Ridgely Torrence, a poet and Princeton graduate, took the final step toward serious drama with *Three Plays for a Negro Theatre*: "Granny Maumee," "The Rider of Dreams," and "Simon the Cyrenian." On 5 April 1917, as the United States readied to enter its first world war, Emilie Hapgood produced the dramas at the Garden Theatre in New York City, giving "a numerous and somewhat neglected race its first real chance in dramatic art." In the first play a conjure woman plots the death of the son of a man who had lynched her son; in the second, an out-of-work husband filches money from his wife; and in the third, a black man helps Christ carry his cross on the road to Golgotha. The actors included Opal Cooper, Andrew Bishop, and Inez Clough; all portrayed their characters with dialect. The leading critic of the day, George Jean Nathan, praised the acting, and listed Opal Cooper and Inez Clough among the top ten performers of the year. The accolades were considered an acknowledgment that black actors could perform serious drama, and indeed, soon Charles Gilpin would be hailed for his portrayal of Brutus Jones in Eugene O'Neill's *Emperor Jones*, and Rose McClendon would triumph as Serena in the drama *Porgy*. The so-called barren teens had opened the gates on to a more hospitable decade – the Harlem Renaissance.

7

The Harlem Renaissance

James V. Hatch

My walk will be different, my talk and my name
Nothin' about me is gonna be the same.
> Shelton Brooks, "There Will Be Some
> Changes Made"

Forty years before the Great Migration north, Republican Rutherford B. Hayes in 1877 had cut a deal with southern Democrats, who allowed him to become president by Congressional electoral vote in exchange for withdrawing Federal troops from the South. This betrayal of Reconstruction forced Blacks into a legally sanctioned "separate but equal" existence. Strange fruit hung from southern trees. The First World War opened a window to jobs in the North. Hundreds of thousands of Blacks migrated to Cleveland, Chicago, Detroit, and New York City. They came trekking North with their tales of suffering and endurance, bringing their music, poetry, and dance – all that had sustained them over the bitter years. By the thousands they came, carrying their "long and boney dreams" for freedom, for education, and packed in their bags were the stories that would become the literature, poetry, and drama of the Harlem Renaissance.

At the end of the Civil War black illiteracy exceeded 90 percent. By 1880, 30 percent had learned to read; by 1890 half the population read, and by 1910, two-thirds possessed literacy, giving them access to schools, voting, newspapers, and aspirations for wealth. Fifty years after emancipation, the younger generations were eager to distance themselves from the shame and humiliation of slavery, going so far as to challenge their ethnic designation. Articles in the press argued whether they should call themselves "Colored," "Ethiopian," "Black," "African," "Negro," or "African American."[1]

The northern middle-class Blacks resented the country manners of the new migrants. The Urban League of Detroit issued a "Dress Well Club" pamphlet and advised the southerners: "Don't carry on loud conversations or use vulgar language in street cars. Don't be rude or ugly to people on the streets. Be courteous and polite and thereby keep out of trouble."[2] Yet when migrants strove to forget the South and disguise their poverty, their compatriots accused them of trying to be white.

It was among those who carried on "loud conversations" that Langston Hughes recognized the energy of survival. "I am a Negro / Black as the night is black / Black like the depths of my Africa," wrote Hughes, who saw no reason to turn his back upon southern or African roots. Hughes argued that Blacks who strove to be like Whites, confronted a racial mountain blocking their very source of creative beauty.[3] George Schuyler, the sharp-tongued editor of the popular *Messenger*, scoffed: "Aside from his color, which ranges from very dark brown to pink, your American Negro is just plain American." Schuyler criticized the self-promotion of the Renaissance as "Negro-art hokum," created by merchants to peddle so-called differences between the races. So what was to be done? Leave ethnic distinctions behind, or emphasize cultural differences?

The 1920s had christened itself variously as the New Negro, the Negro Renaissance, the Negro Awakening, and the Jazz Age. None of the titles served, for the Negro was not "new," although opportunity was. They had not "awakened," but white America had awakened to them. The so-called Harlem Renaissance was not Harlem's, but all urban centers where Blacks had sought freedom, and finally, the Renaissance, a symbol of renewal, was a lie since most of them began their "freedom" with little, except their culture, which had been nurtured in the segregated South.

Black mothers and fathers warned their children against speakeasies and whorehouses, where the Devil's music drowned souls in alcohol and drugs. Eubie Blake's mother had forbidden him to play ragtime in the house, and even to the end of his life, Blake would not utter the word "jazz" because of its original connotations.[4] But others in order to earn a living turned to the "Devil's playground," with its "bluesy" bars, cabarets, and dance halls.[5]

While the 1930s brought the Great Depression blues, the First World War had brought good times to many black Americans. In the decade between the war and the Depression, black theatre and performance developed along three lines: the literary, written mostly by black schoolteachers and artists; the Broadway musicals, written by Blacks and Whites; and the vaudevillians, who wrote little but entertained on the circuits of the Theatre Owners' Booking Association (TOBA) (see chapter 6).

From the roughly five thousand theatres across the nation, Blacks owned or operated 157, scattered mostly throughout the South.[6] Often called "opera houses," these theatres, along with bars and the ubiquitous clubs, served as feeder stages for the "big time" in Memphis, Chicago, or New York.[7] What inspired this swelling progress of black performance? The Art Theatre Movement? Probably not, at least not to the extent the intellectuals had hoped it would.

Art theatres in black

The Art Theatre Movement (sometimes called the Little Theatre Movement) placed art in opposition to commercialism. Space does not allow for its history except to say that in Ireland Lady Gregory and William Butler Yeats had formed an art theatre, "native and poetic," where the "living language of the folk" would drive the artificial stage Irishman from the boards. In his book, the *New Negro* (1925), Alain Locke surmised that "Harlem has the same role to play for the New Negro as Dublin has had for the New Ireland." Tragedy need no longer be the property of kings; comedy need no longer be subject to artificiality. The American tours of the Irish Abbey Theatre and the Moscow Art Theatre inspired artists to see and read the plays of Chekhov and Tolstoy, Synge and Yeats, dramas that revealed the unspoiled beauty of the "folk." Brooks Atkinson writing in the *New York Times* promoted the idea: "In a country starved for folklore, the Southern negro with his natural eloquence and with the purity of his spirituals, is an inexhaustible source of material."[8]

The black Little Theatre Movement originated not among the folk but with urban intellectuals – W. E. B. Du Bois (Ph.D. Harvard), Alain LeRoy Locke (Ph.D. Harvard), Jessie Redmon Fauset (Phi Beta Kappa, Cornell), James Weldon Johnson (Honorary Litt.D. Talladega) – all of them labeled, interpreted, and promoted folk culture. Locke along with Jean Toomer designated southern Blacks as "peasants," unspoiled by urban sophistication. A general feeling prevailed that the folk plays, by dignifying the people's struggles, extended a kind of egalitarian democracy to the rural people, and that the simple lives of these oppressed people offered a deep expression of an abiding spirit.

Inspired by Ridgely Torrence's *Three Plays for a Negro Theatre*, which had received high praise from the New York reviewers, folk drama had "arrived" in black (see chapter 6).[9] What, then, was a black folk play? In 1919 Willis Richardson (1889–1977) published an essay, "The Hope of the Negro Drama." He pleaded for Negro plays by Negro authors. "I do not mean merely plays with Negro characters... There is another kind of play – the play that shows the soul of a people, and the soul of this people is truly worth showing."[10] Over his lifetime Richardson wrote forty-eight plays. Very early on, he confronted sexism in *The Deacon's Awakening* (1920), where the father of the family tries hard to keep his wife and daughter from exercising their newly acquired right to vote. His one-act folk play *The Chip Woman's Fortune* opened on 7 May 1923 at the Frazee Theatre, making it the first black drama produced on the Great White Way. A simple tale of an old woman who has secretly saved money by selling chips of firewood, the drama presented poor people living ordinary lives and speaking naturally. Richardson owed his Broadway production to Raymond O'Neil, a white director who had studied in Europe's art theatres. After serving as art director at the Cleveland Playhouse, O'Neil resigned to form a company of professional black actors in Chicago. He persuaded several of the Lafayette Players[11] to join him by promising them roles not previously available. He sought "Not to train [the actors] in imitation of the more inhibited white actors, but to develop their peculiar racial characteristics – the freshness and vigor of their emotional responses, their spontaneity and intensity of mood, their freedom from intellectual and artistic obsessions."[12] After one year of workshops and performance, O'Neil took his company on an east coast tour, where they received mixed reviews, perhaps because the critics were not familiar with genuine folk material and because they associated the company's name, Ethiopian Art Players, with minstrels. Certainly O'Neil's choice of Oscar Wilde's *Salome* and Shakespeare's *Comedy of Errors* as companion pieces for Richardson's folk play confused matters.

Alain Locke, one of the intellectual giants of the era, had been awarded a Rhodes Scholarship to Oxford University in England. Upon his return Locke became professor of philosophy at Howard University, where among his many activities he cosponsored with Montgomery Gregory the Howard Players. Much has been made of Locke's differences with Du Bois over the purpose of theatre. Locke insisted that an art theatre would serve the cause of Blacks better than a theatre of overtly presented race issues, which Du Bois preferred. True, these men did differ, but both believed that African Americans had a talent and even a proclivity for theatre, and both men did much to promote a black theatre that they hoped would be financially and culturally independent from white theatre.

In 1922 Alain Locke published "Steps Toward the Negro Theatre."[13] In it he drew the distinction between a race drama for propaganda and a Negro theatre in which art was an indigenous expression. Locke believed that to avoid "the common handicap of commercialism, race drama should become peculiarly the ward of our colleges, as new drama, as art-drama, and as folk-drama." He volunteered Howard University as a center where the wild bird called "the folk" would be given a nest in the ivory tower, much as white Appalachian folk plays had been given a home by Frederick Henry Koch at the University of North Carolina. The Howard Players announced that their purpose would be "the establishment of a National Negro Theatre where the Negro playwright, musician, actor, dancer, and artist in concert, shall fashion a drama that shall merit the respect and win the admiration of the world."[14]

High and noble aims indeed. But where were the plays? To speed the playwrights, two black periodicals, *Crisis*, edited by W. E. B. Du Bois for the National Association for the Advancement of Colored People (NAACP), and *Opportunity*, edited by Charles S. Johnson for the Urban League, announced literary contests with cash awards; in 1924 both magazines included prizes for original plays. Du Bois believed the plays should be written for black audiences.

> If a man writes a play and a good play, he is lucky if he earns first class postage upon it. Of course he may sell it commercially to some producer on Broadway, but in that case it would not be a Negro play or if it is a Negro play it will not be about the kind of Negro you and I know or want to know. If it is a Negro play that will interest us and depict our life, experience, and humor, it can not be sold to the ordinary theatrical producer, but it can be produced in our churches and lodges, and halls.[15]

On the other hand, Charles S. Johnson

> thought the *Opportunity* competition would elicit dramas which would further the movement for racial harmony. The plays were to be written by black dramatists, but these works were to affect white racial opinions. Johnson sought the approval of influential whites and, therefore, assembled play panels which were predominantly white.[16]

From 1925 to 1927 the contests awarded fifteen playwrights thirty prizes ranging from $10 to $200, encouraging authors to write.

Zora Neale Hurston (1891–1960)

Zora Neale Hurston won the *Opportunity* contest twice, first with *Color Struck* (1925), a savage portrayal of color prejudice within the race, and the next year with *The First One* (1926), an exploration of original sin when

Noah betrayed his black son, Ham. Born in the all-black town of Eatonville, Florida, where her father was mayor, Hurston had grown up surrounded by black folk and their jokes, stories, and legends – folklore that would permeate her writing career. Known primarily as a novelist and anthropologist, she wrote at least ten plays between 1925 and 1935 – among them five one-act plays, including the monologue *Sermon in the Valley* (1931), and a full-length musical entitled *Fast and Furious* (1931), to which she contributed sketches (it ran a for slim seven performances). Hurston assayed two full-length comedies, *Polk County: A Comedy of Negro Life in a Sawmill Camp with Authentic Negro Music* (1944), coauthored with Dorothy Waring,[17] and *Mule Bone* (1931) written with Langston Hughes. The latter had been scheduled for production with the Gilpin Players, but they canceled when the authors quarreled.

In 1989 George Houston Bass, artistic director of the Rites and Reason Theatre at Brown University, workshopped the *Mule Bone* script, giving it a prologue and an epilogue. Two years later, the Lincoln Center Theatre brought Bass' conception to the Ethel Barrymore Theatre, with a star cast that included Frances Foster, Arthur French, Sonny Jim Gaines, Robert Earl Jones, Paulene Myers, Leonard Jackson, Reggie Montgomery, and twenty-two others. Directed by Michael Schultz, with original score by Taj Mahal and choreography by Diane McIntyre, *Mule Bone*, after waiting sixty years, took the stage on 14 February 1991. The simple plot evolves around two best friends, Dave a Baptist and Jim a Methodist, who are contesting for the love of Daisy. Neither wins and the men leave town together. The reviews praised the production but dismissed the plot as an excuse for the show's merry laughter. Frank Rich of the *New York Times* alone lamented the conception, which he labeled "candied Disneyesque, more folksy than folk." He wished, as did others, that the playwrights had been able to complete and polish their play. Instead, Hurston used portions in her folklore book *Mules and Men* (1935).

After 1948, Hurston disappeared from publishing and few bothered to read her novels or folklore. She died in obscurity and poverty in 1960. Her unmarked grave was located in Fort Pierce, Florida, by Alice Walker, who placed a headstone there with the tribute, "a genius of the South." After Robert Hemenway's biography of Hurston appeared in 1978, her books were reprinted. Her novel *Their Eyes Were Watching God* (1937) was acclaimed a classic and used widely in college literature classes. George C. Wolfe adapted three of her short stories to the stage, entitling them *Spunk* (1990). In 1997 the Library of Congress uncovered her last "solely authored play,

Spunk (1935), an entirely unknown original script, not the same play Wolfe
had adapted from a Hurston story." A biographical play about Hurston
by Laurence Holder, *Zora* (1979), was performed first at the New Federal
Theatre and successfully revived by the American Place Theatre in 1998,
with Elizabeth Van Dyke in the title role.

Angelina Weld Grimké (1880–1958)

For entirely different reasons, another original but neglected work by a
woman playwright, Angelina Weld Grimké, still awaits its full reassessment. *Rachel* premiered at Myrtilla Miner Teachers College in Washington, DC in 1916.[18] This powerful full-length piece was commissioned
by the NAACP to counter the virulent propaganda of D. W. Griffith's
film, *Birth of a Nation* (1915). The play's protagonist, a highly sensitive woman who, after learning that her father and brother have been
lynched, and after witnessing the cruelty black children suffer in public
schools, refuses to bear children, although she loves and longs for them.
The play provoked controversy. Responding to the accusation that it proposed race suicide, Grimké countered that her main purpose had been to
move white mothers to feel empathy for the suffering of a black mother,
a woman not unlike them.[19] A careful reading of the script shows that
Grimké, succeeded in subtly portraying the psychic rape of a sentient
woman.[20]

Rachel sparked a philosophical debate that has haunted black drama up
to the present day: should plays use art for propaganda, or use art for its
own sake and thus present characters freed from delivering the playwright's
message? Du Bois generally held the former position and Alain Locke the
latter. *Rachel* uncomfortably bestrode the two, and few were pleased. Locke,
who had been an original member of the NAACP's drama committee,
resigned stating: "An utter incompatibility of point of view – something
more than a mere difference of opinion – indeed, an abysmal lack of common
meeting ground between myself and the majority of the members forces my
retirement."[21] Seven years later he expressed his view bluntly: "It is not the
business of plays to solve problems or to reform society."[22]

Although scholars have explored the subtleties of *Rachel* in numerous
journal articles, the power of Grimké's drama on stage has remained unexplored. It received only three or four productions, the second at the Neighborhood Playhouse in New York City (1917) and the third at Brattle Hall
(1917) in Cambridge, Massachusetts.[23] Grimké wrote one other play, *Maria,*

and then turned to poetry and teaching English at Armstrong High School in Washington, DC.

Plays about lynching

After the Civil War lynching became common as an ugly, usually public execution by southern white mobs. Between 1882 and 1927, 3,589 Blacks were lynched, including 76 women.[24] Excuses for the crime varied, but most involved an accusation that the black man had "insulted" a white woman, perhaps failing to step off the sidewalk to let her pass. Some were lynched for wearing their army uniforms after returning home. Victims were hung, beaten, burned, or stabbed to death. They were tortured and/or castrated before they were killed. White women and children were often present. Food was sometimes served, encouraging a picnic-like atmosphere, and revelers gathered ears or fingers of the mutilated body as souvenirs from the outing. Sometimes commemorative postcard photos were sold.[25] Ida B. Wells, a black journalist, organized women interracially to oppose lynching. In 1922 the National Council of Women, representing 13 million American women, endorsed the Anti-Lynching Crusade. In spite of these efforts, an antilynching law was never passed by the all-white, male Congress.

The history of lynching drama has been traced by Professors Kathy A. Perkins and Judith L. Stevens, who recorded sixty-nine dramas beginning with William Wells Brown's *The Escape* (1858).[26] In their anthology *Strange Fruit, Plays on Lynching by American Women* (1998), they point out that women wrote the majority of the plays, perhaps because the sexual triad of the black male–white female–white male lay at the center of so many lynchings. The dramas themselves expose a parallel triad in the lynching mentality that stereotyped black men as rapists, black women as the prostitutes (unworthy of protection), and white women as the property of white males. The realistic folk play provided a ready-made form for these dramas. The setting was usually a living room or kitchen of a poor black family. In the early plays the crime had already taken place before the curtain went up. The victim's innocence was established, and a messenger related the horror to the women of the family. Georgia Douglas Johnson (1877–1966) in *A Sunday Morning in the South* (c. 1925) placed the lynching just offstage. The family hears the mob's shouts mixed with hymns from a nearby white church. Johnson carefully constructed six lynch plays; none was ever produced in her lifetime. Randolph Edmonds (1900–83)[27] used a similar strategy in *Bad Man* (1934). The audience sees the flames and hears the shouts of the lynchers as they fight over souvenirs from the body. Mary Burrill in *Aftermath* (1919) brings a son home from the First World War to find his father has been lynched. The son leaves the house to shoot the men who did it. Using a fresh concept, May Miller (1899–1995) in *Nails and Thorns* (1933) focused the tragedy upon a white family and its collapse under the stress.[28] Only in two or three plays is the lynching averted.

The theme of Blacks fleeing the killing fields of the South was picked up by John Matheus, who taught near the coalmines at West Virginia State College. Matheus wrote about migrants in *'Cruiter* (1926), the story of a poor family leaving the homestead for wartime jobs in the North. S. Randolph Edmonds' *Old Man Pete* (1934) presented a similar migrant family, perhaps a few years later, living a middle-class life in Harlem, but at the expense of turning their backs on their "down home" parents.

Women in the Little Theatre Movement

Schoolteachers, mostly women, were the driving force in the black Little Theatre Movement. Their plays saw production on the stages of schools, churches, and lodges and were published in women's and race periodicals. All were original voices that were unwelcome in the commercial theatre, voices that "depict our life, experience, and humor." With the increasing awareness of women's history and the rise of the feminist movement in the 1970s, these African American plays were "rediscovered." Careful readings reveal that they were not the products of club women amusing themselves. The dramas confront major issues for black women: voting, miscegenation, child-rearing, patriotism, and birth control. Mary Burrill (1884–1946), a teacher at Dunbar High School, wrote a brave one-act play entitled *They That Sit in Darkness* that appeared in the *Birth Control Review* in September 1919, three years after Margaret Sanger had opened her first birth control clinic in Brooklyn. Burrill's play condemned the cycle of poverty–children–poverty. The US Supreme Court took another fifty years before it declared that women had the right not to bear children. While at Dunbar High School, Burrill influenced three of her students to become playwrights: Angelina Grimké, James Butcher, and May Miller.

W. E. B. Du Bois, after awarding prizes for the best new dramas of Negro life, took the next logical step, forming a theatre group to produce new plays. In *Crisis* of June 1926 he proposed the establishment of the Crisis Guild of Writers and Actors' (KRIGWA) Little Negro Theatre: "An attempt to establish in High Harlem, New York City, a Little Theatre which shall be primarily a center where Negro actors before Negro audiences interpret Negro life as depicted by Negro artists; but which shall also always have a welcome for all artists of all races and for all sympathetic comers and for all beautiful ideas."[29]

KRIGWA's first program in the public library's basement at 135th Street presented three folk plays, two serious dramas by Willis Richardson (*The Broken Banjo* and *Compromise*) and a comedy by Ruth Ada Gaines-Shelton, (*The Church Fight*), one of the relatively few comedies written for the black Little Theatres. Eulalie Spence (1894–1981) would soon be distinguished as a writer, actress, and director.[30] She wrote fourteen plays, none using the folk-play formula; her own background was Nevis, British West Indies. *The Fool's Errand* (1927), first produced by KRIGWA, won the Samuel French prize of $200 in the National Little Theatre Tournament. Du Bois kept the prize money to reimburse production expenses; Spence received none. The resulting dispute led to the demise of KRIGWA.[31] However, Spence's differences with Du Bois were greater than dollars. She wrote in *Opportunity* magazine that playwrights, if they wished to succeed, should avoid the "drama of propaganda if they would not meet with certain disaster." She seized upon the lynching dramas specifically. "The white man is cold and unresponsive to this subject and the Negro, himself, is hurt and humiliated by it. We go to the theatre for entertainment, not to have old fires and hates rekindled."[32] It was an old division: should the theatre entertain or teach? With so many problems facing black migrants from the South, Du Bois came down on the side of teaching.

Marita Odette Bonner[33] (1898–1971) chose both art and propaganda. Raised in Boston, the youngest of three children, she attended writing classes at nearby Radcliffe College, where she gained fluency in German, which may have been a major influence on her playwriting. After her graduation, in 1922, she moved to Washington, DC, to teach at Armstrong High School. In *Crisis* of December 1925 she published her prizewinning essay "On Being Young – a Woman – and Colored," which revealed her to be a passionate and sensitive artist. Within five years she had written more than twenty pieces of fiction (seventeen would be published in magazines), and three plays: *The Potmaker* (1927), *The Purple Flower* (1928), and *Exit, An Illusion* (1929). In 1930 she married William Occomy and the couple had three children. She continued to teach in schools and to write short stories, but no longer had she the same creative time and energy.

Figure 19. Curtain call in KRIGWA performance, Harlem, 1926

The most experimental of the playwrights, Bonner's style has been called "surreal," a manifestation of the writer's inner consciousness – her dreams placed upon the stage.[34] Her style was hers alone. Bonner's wildly experimental *The Purple Flower* called for social and political revolution in an overt manner that other writers did not dare use until the militant 1960s. Her play declared that the Leader (Dr. Washington in her day) was mistaken! Work wouldn't do it! Book learning wouldn't do it! Money wouldn't do it! Only blood could pay for blood! Marita Bonner wasn't asking "Will there be a revolution?" but "Is it time?"

As the Art Theatre Movement grew, many amateur groups met, produced one or two one-act plays, and disbanded. Schools, women's clubs, men's lodges, churches, "Y's," and settlement houses raised platforms for stages. Characters were broadly conceived and generally few in number. A production rarely boasted more than two performances, and royalties were left unpaid because they could not be paid. Among the forgotten amateur efforts is *Broken Bars*, a modern morality play by Xenia Scott-Livingston, secretary for the Urban League in St. Louis, Missouri. Performed at the Odeon Theater in early October 1921 before "a packed house, the boxes were occupied by Whites and Colored in evening dress."[35] In benefits of this kind, theatre served as the core attraction. Charity fund-raising fell to women, and by association, men considered theatre to be a woman's club activity. Women usually wrote the scripts, and when husbands refused to be cast, women often played the male parts.[36] Church congregations were ready-made audiences. One playwright who seized this opportunity was Ruth Ada Gaines-Shelton (1872–1938), who wrote for the congregation of the African Methodist Episcopal Church in Montgomery, Missouri. Her play titles reflect local interests – *The Church Fight* (1925), *The Church Mouse*, *Mr. Church*, and *Parson Dewdrop's Bride* (all undated). The art theatre and little theatre groups clearly were middle and upper class. As early as 1921, Miss Carol McCoy of the Chicago School of Expression and Dramatic Art advertised: "If your child has shown any ability whatsoever to recite, start now and have that talent cultivated." Saturday classes met in her home on Wabash Avenue.

In Harlem some amateur groups strove to become art theatres. The Acme Players, the Sekondi Players, the New Negro Art Theatre, the Dunbar Players, the National Colored Players, and the Aldridge Players[37] all lived brief lives for a year or two. Periodically, critic Theophilus Lewis abandoned hope: "Various attempts have been made to establish a little theatre in Harlem. All have failed. No art can be developed without an adequate cultural background. The vehicle of drama cannot come into existence until society has reached a certain point in its cultural development. The rose cannot precede the leaf."[38]

The Harlem Experimental Theatre (HET) budded in 1927 under the nurturing of Dorothy Peterson, Jessie Fauset, and Regina Andrews, who had opened with an ambitious program of plays in St. Philip's Parish House and later moved to the public library where KRIGWA had begun. HET, like other art theatres, produced black playwrights when a suitable script appeared. The full-length folk play, *You Mus' Be Bo'n Ag'in* (1930) by Andrew M. Burris, suited the group.[39] Burris, born in Helena, Arkansas, placed the church folks of his home town into his comedy drama; his church revival scene, though overextended, rings as one of the more authentic in black theatre. HET also relied on white drama to fill its programs. Under the direction of Regina Andrews, a librarian, actress, and playwright,[40] the company offered Calderon de la Barca's *The Little Stone House*, a Spanish comedy; Joaquin Quintero's *A Sunny Morning*, as well as Paul Green's *No Count Boy* (1924). These art theatre writers are still read and discussed, largely because they published their work. They were a brave, alert, and passionate coterie, but they remained confined to a corner of the garden.

One notable exception among the little theatres' all-too-brief lives was the Dumas Players of Cleveland, Ohio. Although they changed their name twice, they continued to perform into the millennium, a record made possible by the theatre's nesting within Karamu, a settlement house founded in 1915 by Rowena and Russell Jelliffe to ease the transition for southern Blacks migrating North. The Jelliffes began working with children, and in 1917 produced *Cinderella* with a racially mixed cast. An interest in theatre grew into an informal group known as the Dumas Players, named after the French playwright. In 1922 the then most famous black actor in America, Charles Gilpin (1878–1930), came to Cleveland, starring in Eugene O'Neill's *The Emperor Jones* (1920). Ten months earlier, Gilpin had been hailed by the New York Drama League as one of ten individuals who had best served the theatre that season. Some at the league had objected to inviting a "Negro" to the awards dinner; Gilpin compromised. He appeared, spoke, but did not join the dinner. The black press was furious, attacking Gilpin and *The Emperor Jones*. "Yet ignorant and supine Negroes, still living under the baneful influence of a slave psychology, together with their hypocritical white masters, cry, 'that's social equality.'"[41] The opinions of the angry press preceded Gilpin to Ohio, and instead of being received as an honored guest,

Figure 20. Poster advertising Charles Gilpin in *The Emperor Jones*, *c.* 1922

"Gilpin came to a very hostile Negro Cleveland. The local Negro press had helped pave the way for this hostility."[42]

> A writer of the *New York Negro World* calls attention to the fact that Charles Gilpin's play, *The Emperor Jones*, is very harmful to our people and says that it leaves an impression that the prejudiced South is prompting in various other ways. It is on the order of *Birth of a Nation* so far as the impression referred to is concerned. This is certainly to be regretted, if true.[43]

Eugene O'Neill's image of the emperor fleeing through the jungle until he is reduced to a savage by his fears displeased many Blacks. Gilpin defended the role as "a study in the psychology of fear as it works upon the mind of an ignorant man of superstitious tendencies."[44]

He considered his role to be a great advance over all previous ones offered to Blacks. He told news reporters that he had shined shoes, traveled with minstrel shows as a fortune-teller, acted with stock companies including the Pekin and Lafayette theatres, and *The Emperor Jones* was the finest role of his career. Gilpin played the Emperor for several years and never found another role to match his talents. Awarded the prestigious Spingarn Medal, he was plainly the most famous and successful black thespian in America.

Cleveland's Dumas Players were prepared to give Gilpin a cool reception. Although his speech was never recorded, we know that he did not apologize for his role in the O'Neill play, but rather looked to the future of black theatre and told the Dumas troupe to look within themselves, to see their own lives and to ape no one. He left fifty dollars on the stage apron (a considerable sum in those days), saying, "This is to say that I believe in your future." He so impressed the group, they later changed their name to the Gilpin Players. In speeches and lectures before Blacks he promulgated Booker T. Washington's "Yes, I can" philosophy, an attitude of many who still had memories of slavery. Often he repeated, "Success, thy name is preparedness. You can do it, but you must make yourself ready." Let it be said that he helped open the way for other serious actors: Paul Robeson, Rose McClendon, and Richard B. Harrison. Gilpin died of pneumonia in 1930.[45]

The Gilpin Players acquired their own theatre in 1927, which they named Karamu House (Swahili for "a place of joyful meeting.") The company sought out black playwrights, among them Langston Hughes, who had attended school in Cleveland. At least five of his plays premiered there, including the original version of *Mulatto*, which would go to Broadway (see chapter 10). In 1939 Karamu House was destroyed by fire; it was rebuilt after the Second World War – with help from the Rockefeller Foundation, the Gilpin Players acquired two theatres, a visual arts studio, a dance studio, club rooms, and exhibition halls. During the 1940s and 1950s, Karamu was nearly the only stage on which black actors could receive professional training. In the militant 1970s racial conflict divided the staff and students. White people left and with them considerable funding. By the 1990s, Karamu, under difficult circumstances, moved again toward its original goals. Among the many who trained at Karamu House were Frances Williams, Frank Marriott, Isabel Cooley, Clayton Corbin, Mildred Smith, Leonard Parker, Ivan Dixon, Ted Shine, Charles Bettis, Robert Guillaume, and Whitney LeBlanc.

Hedgerow, a white theatre founded by Jasper Deeter in 1923, must be noted for its early casting of black actors in repertory. Once a member of the Provincetown Players, Deeter left to form his own theatre in a converted mill near Moylan-Rose Valley, Pennsylvania. Here, in thirty-three years, he produced two-hundred and ten plays in a small 170-seat theatre, giving actors an opportunity to develop and practice their talents through a frequent change of bill. Hedgerow at that time was the only true repertory theatre in America.

Deeter mounted three productions of *The Emperor Jones* (1923, 1947, and 1955), casting first Wayland Rudd and later Arthur Rich in the lead. Deeter had "discovered" Rudd acting in an amateur group in Philadelphia. Gwendolyn Bennett, reviewing Rudd's performance for *Opportunity*, noted that Rudd did something "so poignant that it wrung your heart as you lived through the part with him. He seemed to give a larger futility to the role. He didn't seem so much a senseless bully caught in the toils of his own folly as a human being crushed by an insurmountable fate."[46] Rudd received equal praise for his Othello. Ellen Winsor wrote "Please allow me to send you a word of congratulation on your splendid interpretation of 'Othello.' It will stand out forever in my memory as a vivid and intense character study."[47] Sometime soon after, Rudd left for Russia; he was one of a number of Blacks who believed that the Soviet Union offered them a freedom for advancement not available in America.[48]

In 1929, for the first time in white American theatre, Deeter offered a season of "Negro" plays: *In Abraham's Bosom* (Rose McClendon, Abbie Mitchell, Richard Huey, Armithine Latimer); *The Emperor Jones* (again with Rudd); three one-acts by Paul Green; and the premiere of Samson Raphaelson's *White Man* starring Lanie Horton. In 1930 Deeter took the unconventional step of casting Blacks and Whites interracially. Edwin Anderson played the lead in Shaw's *Captain Brassbound's Conversion* and in O'Neill's *The Hairy Ape*. Hedgerow premiered Countee Cullen's *One Way to Heaven* (1936) with Goldie Erwin and Robert Watson in the lead roles of Mattie and Sam.[49]

The 1920s and 1930s should be remembered as the years that black actors – Gilpin, Rudd, and Robeson – put their stamp upon the character of Emperor Jones so impressively that white actors seldom attempted the role.[50] It would be another fifty years before the powerful interpretations of Paul Robeson, Gordon Heath, James Earl Jones, and Earle Hyman would force Whites to relinquish Othello.[51] Blacks were able to capture these roles because their portrayals were equal or superior. The time was approaching when Blacks would successfully challenge Whites for white roles. But the energy of Harlem's Renaissance performance lay in its nightclubs, bars, and dance halls – in its popular culture.

Cabarets and clubs

In the popular imagination, the most famous spot for Harlem nightlife was the Cotton Club. In 1920 the boxer Jack Johnson opened Club Deluxe on the second floor at Lenox Avenue and West 142nd Street. Three years later, the cabaret was taken over by a gangster and rechristened the Cotton Club, with a cover charge $2.50, and until 1928 Whites only were admitted.[52] The shows were slickly professional and the service impeccable. Duke Ellington's band – introduced by a radio announcer as "jungle music" – began broadcasting nightly from the club on CBS, spreading its fame across America. Cab Calloway, with his "Hi-De-Hi-De-Ho" banter, later replaced Ellington. Ethel Waters introduced "Stormy Weather" where Edith Wilson, Earl Snakehips Tucker, Avon Long, and Lena Horne played or starred. Attendances dropped off after the riots of 1935, when Whites felt Harlem to be unsafe. In 1936 the club moved downtown to Broadway and 48th Street. In the early 1990s the Cotton Club reopened on 125th Street, near the Hudson River, where it served soul food and enjoyed a quiet life with older black clientele.[53]

Built by Percy Williams in 1925, the Alhambra Cabaret and Theatre, on the corner of Seventh Avenue and 126th Street, began as a white vaudeville house where the B. F. Keith circuit occasionally booked a black act. When the Keith circuit suffered a lawsuit for refusing to sell orchestra seats to Blacks, the management and patrons changed. A $100,000 cabaret was added, which Blacks and Whites could attend on alternate nights. Florence Mills played the Alhambra in *Blackbirds of 1926* for six weeks before touring London and Paris.

The theatre customarily offered a three-in-one show: a movie, a musical revue, and a dramatic sketch. A typical week's program might read "Pepper Sauce, a show whose name indicates its temperature," coupled with a serious drama starring Miss Evelyn Ellis in *Goat Alley*. Nonracial tabs such as *Rain* prospered at the club until the Alhambra closed in 1932.

> We had thirty minutes of musical and thirty minutes of drama. We had a big band and chorus girls and at that time we had four comedians who did skits. People from downtown like Milton Berle and Jackie Gleason would come up there. They would stand in the back of the theatre and

see what we were doing and before we knew it, they were doing our skits
downtown, down on 42nd Street.[54]

Bitter memories of Whites enjoying high salaries for the material they
had stolen from black routines commonly lace black theatre history. Comics
Harold Cromer and James Cross accused Dean Martin and Jerry Lewis of
stealing their material while watching them in the clubs; when confronted
in a Hollywood bar, Lewis offered to pay Cromer and Cross for what he
had stolen from them.[55]
    The Harlem Opera House at 209 West 125th Street had been a part of
the Keith Vaudeville Circuit, but in 1922 Leo Brecher bought it and for a
time booked class acts:[56] Buck and Bubbles earned $750 for a week's work;
Pigmeat Markham $75; Bessie Smith $150. Down the block, Schiffman
and Brecher acquired Hurtig and Seamon's Burlesque, which in 1934 they
renamed the Apollo.[57] When management shifted its live shows over to
the Apollo, Honey Coles called the Opera House the "Sideshow," and
the Apollo the "Big Top."[58] As burlesque and vaudeville routines lost their
popularity, and the white population left Harlem, managers brought in top
black and white performers and provided elaborate costumes and settings.
They coupled these programs with motion pictures. Apollo hostess Vivian
Harris would begin each show with the theatre's theme song, "I Could be
Wrong But I Think You're Wonderful." The 1600-seat auditorium hosted
thirty shows each week and was the site of regular live broadcasts transmitted
on twenty-one radio stations across the country.
    Ralph Cooper's "Amateur Hour," held every Wednesday night from 11
p.m. until midnight, hosted seven or eight contestants who were judged
by audience response. Those who failed to earn approval were booed and
hooked offstage in mid-performance, but winners, such as Ella Fitzgerald,
Sarah Vaughan, and Pearl Bailey, could be awarded recording contracts.[59]
Several times over the ensuing decades the Apollo died, only to be re-
suscitated on the strength of its legends, which included a prize list of
blackface comedians in the tradition of Bert Williams, men who elicited
laughter through mask and mime. At the Apollo, Tim Moore, Johnny
Hudgins, Mantan Moreland, Pigmeat Markham, George Whilshire, and
Dusty Fletcher tickled their patrons until the 1940s, when the NAACP
demanded that they blacken up no more. Pigmeat said that without his
blackface he felt naked on the stage.[60]
    Much of the comedy reflected the anxieties of migrants; for example,
African American women could often secure domestic employment in cities

Figure 21. Comedian Johnny Hudgins, with and without blackface

where their men found no work.[61] In cartoons, large women with rolling pins waited by the door for husbands to come home broke, drunk, and late. On stage the verbal duels between husband and wife ignited laughter, and no duo in black vaudeville was more loved for their mouthy mayhem than the team of Jodie Edwards and Susie Hawthorne, known on stage as Butterbeans (1897–1967) and Susie (?–1963). Bluesy jazz with piano or banjo punctuated Susie's saucy cakewalk. Beans, with his hands in his pockets, danced the "itch" (the "heebie-jeebies"), so-named because he seemed to be scratching himself to death.[62] The couple's insults were softened by their obvious visual affection for one another.

> *Sue*: Why your eyes are crooked and your mouth is big.
> *Beans*: My money bought your cheek and also your wig.
> *Sue*: To me you look like a chimpanzee.
> *Beans*: And Sue, you look just like his sister to me.
> *Sue*: Brokedown papa, brokedown papa, your mama can't use you no more.
> *Beans*: Brokedown mama, brokedown mama, you should have been gone long ago.

White and black cognoscenti immortalized Harlem's Connie's Inn (formerly the Shuffle Inn, owned by "Connie" Conrad and George Immerman). It nestled next door to the Lafayette Theatre. The Inn, famous for its revues, most of which were staged by Leonard Harper, was also noted for "pansy entertainment," that is, flashy in-your-face cross-dressing. A 250-pound blues singer, Gladys Bentley, played the piano continuously from ten in the evening until dawn. According to Langston Hughes, "Miss Bentley was an amazing exhibition of musical energy – a large, dark, masculine lady, whose feet pounded the floor while her fingers pounded the keyboard."[63] She encouraged her audience to sing along as she changed popular song lyrics into naughty renditions. She dressed in a tuxedo on and off stage and publicly married a woman in a New Jersey civil ceremony.[64] Unashamed, unabashed, she was the incarnation of what many voyeurs hoped to find in Harlem – the sexually liberated primitive.

On 28 June 1919 black Philadelphia banker E. C. Brown and a group of investors, known as the Elite Amusement Corporation, bought the Lafayette theatre building along with the Quality Amusement Corporation, which gave them control of both the building and the acting ensemble. The new owners returned Lester Walton as manager and he expanded the Lafayette Players into four companies, the last at the Dunbar Theatre in Philadelphia. Their success inspired a black wave of theatre leasing and building in Baltimore, New York, Norfolk (Virginia), Philadelphia, Chicago, and other cities. Few actors had been able to earn a living in dramatic roles; however, the Lafayette Players and the Dunbar Players did. When Andrew S. Bishop and Cleo Desmond starred in one of their many melodramas and mysteries, fans often lined up at the box office to adore their matinée idols. The dramas were always about Whites, so the actors made up white.[65] This practice of "passing" on stage led Hubert H. Harrison to write:

> Consider what the practice implies. If Negroes were people then it would be proper that Negro audiences should get accustomed to seeing Negroes as drawing-room guests, doctors, detectives, governors, financiers, etc., in the glow of the footlights. But if folks can't be considered as people unless they are unlike Negroes, then of course, our actors should never look like Negroes.[66]

Typical of the Dunbar and Lafayette play titles were *The Good Little Bad Girl* (1922), *The Revelations of a Wife: The Naked Truth about Married Life* (1922), and *Dangerous Love* (1922). The matinée melodramas became the forerunners of twentieth-century soap operas. Later, when Lafayette's box-office receipts became slim, E. C. Brown complained in the *New York Age* that "it was inconceivable why the best known colored playhouse in the United States and located in a section populated by 150,000 Negroes was not crowded at every performance." In June 1925, Leo Brecher and Frank Schiffman bought the Lafayette. They refurbished the theatre to make it attractive to the middle class and emphasized quality entertainment with continuous performances from early afternoon until midnight, except on Friday, when a midnight show went on until 4 a.m. As time went by, movies, revues, and vaudeville edged out dramatic material.[67] In February 1929, Maria Downs sold the Lincoln Theatre to Frank Schiffman, who offered musical revues, "one-half before and one-half after the drama," but the Depression was settling in. Schiffman sold the building to the African Methodist Episcopal (AME) Church. Churches serving as bastions of middle-class literacy and moral suasion sometimes acted as havens for amateur theatricals. On their platforms, northern urbanites enacted the stories of southern migrants in a new genre they called "folk plays."

Five plays by Blacks on Broadway[68]

To recap, two little theatre plays – *The Fool's Errand* and *The Chip Woman's Fortune*, both one-acts – ran briefly on Broadway. It is not surprising, given the racism of the Great White Way, that each of the remaining three dramas has its own peculiar history, and none more unusual than Garland Anderson's *Don't Judge by Appearances*, later shortened to *Appearances* (1925).

Garland Anderson (1886–1939) was born in Wichita, Kansas, the fourth of twelve children. He completed four years of schooling before his family moved to Sacramento, California. His mother died when he was 11 and he ran away from home. After knocking about he became a bellboy and sometime switchboard operator at the Braeburn Hotel Apartments in San Francisco. Anderson reputedly never drank, smoked tobacco, nor used rude language, and for two years he studied Christian Science, admiring the possibilities it offered for controlling one's own destiny. One day, given a free ticket to the theatre by a hotel resident, he saw the moral drama *The Fool* (1922), by Channing Pollack. Immediately he realized that to deliver his own message to the world he must write a play. "At first, the idea seemed absurd... No one realized more than myself that though I wanted to write this play, I had no training in the technique of dramatic construction."[69]

In three weeks of writing, between calls at the switchboard, he had completed the story of Carl, a black bellhop, falsely accused of rape. He sent *Appearances* to Al Jolson, who gave the novice playwright a trip to New York City to seek his fortune. A backers' audition was arranged at the Waldorf; the name of Governor Al Smith appeared on the invitation. Richard B. Harrison (later de Lawd in *The Green Pastures* [1930]), read *Appearances* to six hundred guests while Anderson sat nearby in his bellhop uniform. The event raised $140, nearly enough to pay for the rental of the hall.

Anderson wrote to President Coolidge. When an appointment was refused, he went directly to the White House and persuaded the President's secretary to allow him to meet the President (possibly as part of a group). Whatever the case, it was a publicity coup. Anderson reported: "It was due in no small measure to President Coolidge's interest in my work that my play was produced in New York."

On 19 June Lester A. Sagar, manager of the Central Theatre, cast black actors Lionel Monagas, Evelyn Mason, and Doe Doe Green. The other eleven were white. It was a bold move. Broadway policy in 1925 was to have white actors play "colored" roles in blackface in order to avoid mixed casts. *Appearances* opened at the Frolic Theater on 13 October 1925, and ran twenty-three performances. Then, for two years the drama toured Los Angeles, Seattle, Chicago, and San Francisco, playing several weeks or months in each city. On 1 April 1929 the play opened again in New York City, this time at the Hudson Theater for twenty-four performances.

Critical reception to the first opening had been kind; white critics were amazed that a Negro bellhop with a fourth grade education had written the play. Four years later, they were less kind. Black critics, with their own political agenda, saw Anderson as a white creation, an image which Anderson himself did little to dispel. Undaunted, the production traveled to London in March 1930, where the black comedian Doe Doe Green (in the role of Rufus) so amused the British that he became a *succès de curiosité* and was given a billing larger than the play's title. Despite the fact that Rufus became the star, the theme of *Appearances* ("as a man thinketh, so is he") is clearly personified by Carl the bellhop. Anderson met the Queen and became a member of the international writers' organization PEN. He also met Doris Sequirra, daughter of a prominent physician, whom he later married and brought to America. She recorded their experiences as a racially mixed couple in her book *Nigger Lover*.

Presenting a black man *falsely* accused of rape by a white woman made *Appearances* a brave play in 1925. How could a white woman's virtue be inferior to that of a black man? Answer: she was not white, she was passing. Anderson wrote for white audiences, attempting to give them something better than what they usually saw of black males. That he had little or no influence on subsequent black theatre is not surprising, although he claimed to have written three other plays. To make moral judgments about Mr. Anderson and his play is perhaps to lose sight of a trait that has been typically American: the belief that persistence and personal hard work can triumph over all obstacles.

Frank Wilson (1886–1956), an actor and playwright, subscribed to the same philosophy of "Yes, I can." Left an orphan at age 8, he moved to a home for "waifs." By working at odd jobs, running errands as a hotel doorboy, he put himself through night school. At age 17 he discovered William and Walker's *In Dahomey*. Apparently, he had not known that Blacks acted on stage. "In those days...If you went to a manager and told him you were an actor, he'd immediately take you into a back room, point to the floor and tell you 'Go ahead. Act!' That was your cue to dance."[70]

By 1908 Wilson was traveling with a vaudeville act, the Carolina Comedy Four. He married, had a son, and began working in the postal service. From his experiences delivering mail in Harlem, he wrote a series of short skits for the Lincoln Theatre.[71] After making his début with the Lafayette Players in *Deep Purple* (1917), he acted with several Little Theatres while he wrote. In 1923 his full-length play, *Pa Williams' Gal*, a father–daughter comedy, starred Rose McClendon and Richard B. Harrison. Black reviewers Theophilus Lewis and Romeo Dougherty saw in Wilson their hope for a playwright portraying black folk truthfully on stage. The next year Wilson obtained a role in the Provincetown Players' production of *All God's Chillun Got Wings* (1924), starring Paul Robeson. Wilson's career took off. His big break came when he replaced Jules Bledsoe in Paul Green's folk drama *In Abraham's Bosom* (1926). On the basis of this performance he went into the Theatre Guild's production of *Porgy* (1927), playing the lead eight hundred and fifty times. Alain Locke chose Wilson's one-act *Sugar Cane* (1927) for the seminal anthology *Plays of Negro Life*. At this point, Wilson reluctantly gave up his job at the post office.[72]

Lester Walton, who had been a theatre manager, a newspaper editor, and a dramatic critic, as well as a civil service commissioner for Mayor James J. Walker, formed an all-black producing company to mount Wilson's new play, *Meek Mose*. Financier Otto Khan advanced $12,500, substantial backing for a Broadway play in those days. After a try-out at the Gibson Theatre in

Philadelphia, *Meek Mose* opened on 4 February 1928 at the Princess Theatre, a 300-seat house in New York City. The drama's thesis, "the meek shall inherit the earth," embodied the story's weakness, a humble protagonist. Mose persuades his people to leave their homes and accept a bad real estate deal. They move into a swampland filled with disease. In the third act, oil is discovered on their new land, but it is too late to save the play. Many of the cast members had been drawn from the Lafayette Players. The glitzy opening-night audience included the German impresario Max Reinhardt and the director of *Porgy*, Rouben Mamoulian. Mayor Walker attended and praised the effort. Even though spirituals embellished the play, it survived only thirty-two performances; Walton's dream of a repertory died with it. In the 1930s, Wilson rewrote the script for the Federal Theatre Project as *Brother Mose*. He acted in *The Green Pastures* and a dozen other Broadway shows. His last appearances were as the bartender in *Take a Giant Step* (1953) and several films, including *Watch on the Rhine*.

Wilson had grown up around and in the theatre and knew that it demanded not only knowledge of dramatic structure but also the crafts of acting, directing, rehearsal, rewriting, and stage technology. Few Blacks of the 1920s had an opportunity to learn these crafts by working on the stage itself. Talent and originality could sometimes compensate, as in the case of Zora Neale Hurston and Langston Hughes. Both had turned from writing stories and poetry to theatre, where they began with little experience; nonetheless, their genius carried them through. Novelist Wallace Thurman (1902–34) possessed talent, but it was scarred by deep personal conflicts. "My candle burns at both ends; / It will not last the night; / But ah, my foes, and oh, my friends / – It gives a lovely light"[73] might have been Thurman's epitaph. A *bon vivant*, a bohemian, a novelist, editor, poet, screenwriter, and playwright, he was remembered for his novel *Infants of Spring*, a biting satire of Harlem artists whom he named "the Niggerati."

In 1926 he cofounded an avant-garde literary magazine, *Fire*, "devoted to younger Negro artists." In its first and only issue, he published "Cordelia the Crude, a Harlem Sketch," a story of a 16-year-old prostitute's initiation into the trade. Three years later he would use Cordelia as his central character in *Black Belt*, later renamed *Harlem*. William Rapp Jourdan, a professional writer and friend, helped Thurman adapt the story to the stage. The three-act play concerned a southern family that did not find in New York a *city of refuge* but rather one of *refuse* – poverty, crime, and death.[74] 25-year-old Edward A. Blatt produced the play and hired 25-year-old Chester Erskin to direct. White youth set the pace, casting fifty-nine Blacks and one White, an ensemble large enough to flood the stage with naughty dancers in the rent party scenes.

When *Harlem* opened on 20 February 1929 at the Apollo Theatre on East Forty-Second Street, the white press declared it a hit. The black press was not present because they had not been given press tickets, possibly because the producers anticipated that Harlem critics would not like the pimps, whores, gamblers, bootleggers, and murderers who insured that the southern family's efforts to survive would fail.

Theophilus Lewis vigorously defended the play as "an innovation in the treatment of the Negro character on the American stage."[75] Salem Tutt Whitney, an old and respected vaudevillian, wrote in his column "Timely Topics": "All the characters . . . represent a low, mean vulgar and vicious phase of life. At no time does right have its say or virtue get its legitimate hearing. It begins low down and ends low down."[76] George Jean Nathan wrote: "with all its holes, it gets under the skin of the characters and their lives and it has all the actuality of an untouched-up photograph . . . a dozen and one vivid hints of niggerdom at its realest."[77] Walter Winchell declared it was a "chippie off the old block." John Anderson of the *Journal American* stated that people planning to go to Harlem for frolic could save the cab fare by attending the play. For a time the press reported that the city might censor the dance scenes for being too lewd. In response to growing complaints about obscenity on the Broadway stage, in 1927 New York had passed the infamous Wade Padlock Law. "Local authorities could arrest actors, lock theatres, and ban productions deemed indecent." Although it remained on the books for forty years, it was rarely invoked. However, Mayor Jimmy Walker warned *Harlem's* producers to "clean up." White audiences filled the 1,168-seat house with a top ticket price at $3. The first week's gross was $12,000. But when a second company unpacked in Detroit, the Welfare Commissioner there demanded cuts in the "dirty" dancing. In Chicago a deluge of letters followed *Harlem's* opening. Police Commissioner Russell said that attention had been called to the vile language, vulgar dancing, and the use of the word "nigger" throughout the play.

According to the *Chicago Defender*, most of the "complaints came from our people [Blacks]." Attendance dropped away to half a house, and the show closed. While some in the black press admitted that low life existed in Harlem, it was the exception, not the rule; but how were white audiences to know that? Earlier, in 1924, Thurman had written a tourist's guide to Harlem in which he covered a wide range of life, from churches to rent parties.[78]

He concluded his text: "There is no typical Harlem Negro as there is no typical American Negro. There are many different types and classes." His play spoke only of low life, but in fairness, he had had little control over the production. Rampant racism permeated Broadway theatres. As historian Doris E. Abramson observed: "Wallace Thurman exhausted himself trying to please the public, while at the same time trying to write with a New Negro honesty."[79] His dismay and isolation can be glimpsed in a letter to his partner William Rapp.

> I am fighting hard to refrain from regarding myself as a martyr and an outcast. I wish you could take my place in Negro society for about a week. Even on the train I was beset by a Pullman porter for my dastardly propaganda against the race. And here at home a delegation of church members (at my grandmother's request) flocked in on me and prayed over me for almost an hour, beseeching the Almighty to turn my talents into the path of righteousness.[80]

The cast and the producer had other problems. In late March the ensemble struck, refusing to go on until their salaries were raised from 18 to 25 dollars a week. Management complied and cut the wages of the star Isabel Washington, who played Cordelia. Additional strain came from *Show Boat*, *Blackbirds*, and *Porgy*, all with large black casts that drew audiences away from *Harlem*. It finally closed after ninety-three performances.[81] In 1934, Thurman, at age 33 died penniless in a tuberculosis hospital, his talent never fulfilled.

Black theatre critics

Generally, black theatre critics composed encomia for their brothers and sisters on stage, but they could be contentious about matters of morality. Lester Walton (1882–1965) of the *New York Age* and Sylvester Russell (?–1930) of the Indianapolis *Freeman* had wielded their vigorous pens at the turn of the century, but burgeoning performances demanded weekly columns to mark the comings and goings of vaudeville talents. Soon critics abounded. Their pages lumped sports and theatre together, often written by the same critic. Tony Langston's column in the *Chicago Defender* was a ledger for performers' whereabouts, as was Billie Jones' in the *Pittsburgh Courier*. Critics regularly published letters from vaudeville performers on the road. Jessie Fauset, as literary editor of *Crisis* (1919–26), brought a sophistication to her reviews: "With the culminating of his dramatic genius, the Negro actor must come finally through the very versatility of his art to the universal role and main tradition of drama, as an artist first and only secondarily as a Negro." As the decade ended, vigorous debates among critics, producers, and actors enlivened the pages. More serious criticism developed with F. G. Snelson Jr., Bennie Butler of the *Inter-State Tattler*, and Lucien H. White of the *New York Age*, but initially detailed criticism was rare, with two exceptions – James A. Jackson, who wrote a page for *Billboard*, and Theophilus Lewis, who for eight years (1923–30) stood guard in the press against the denigration of black culture. Lewis held to the art theatre's lodestar – theatre must be a temple of the spirit and not a market for money changers.[82]

Self-educated, Theophilus Lewis (1891–1971?) read world drama and referenced Shakespeare and Goethe as easily as he did Florence Mills. He encouraged a Negro theatre that would rival the energy and talent of the Elizabethan. He asked: "Are the Negroes in America as civilized as the people of Marlowe's England? If they are, the time is ripe for a successful Negro Little Theatre."[83] Over and over he drummed that Blacks must control their creations to harvest the benefits. He observed that 50 percent of Harlem's theatres controlled 75 percent of the patronage, and those white owners "have no knowledge of the true nature of theatre." He dismissed them as "camp followers out of touch with the refinement of even their own race." On occasion, he shared the groundlings' enthusiasm for girlie shows and low comedy. "As lasciviousness is one of my accomplishments, I naturally regard this form of entertainment as one of the most convincing signs of God's ultimate goodness to man."[84] He knew that the roots of "Negro musical theatre lay in the jook joints and cabarets."[85] At the end of the decade Lewis blamed the decline of Harlem's Art Theatres on the new migrants from the South. "People [urban Harlemites] accustomed to observe the conventions of the theatre were annoyed by an increasing horde of barbarians from Alabama and Georgia who continually crunched peanuts and coughed and blew their noses and yelled encouragement to the actors and went back and forth, to and from the toilet during performances."[86]

He encouraged repertory as necessary to achieve better acting, for how else could the craft be learned except by practice? He condemned Lew Leslie's *Dixie to Broadway*: "This show contains bits of almost everything, a few mites of which are precious, but most of which is extremely shoddy, garish, and vulgar." He criticized the managers of the Lafayette Theatre for their chorus lines of light-skinned girls when there were so many darker lovelies they might have cast. He deplored the canonization of "Massa" Paul Green and other white authors, for their exploitation of black characters.[87] His ongoing theatre polemics with George S. Schuyler, Romeo L. Dougherty, and Salem Tutt Whitney are still a pleasure to read.

In the vast territory beyond Harlem other theatres prospered, and columnist James A. Jackson reported on this larger Renaissance. As black show business grew, the national tabloid *Billboard* seized an opportunity to increase its circulation. Who better to report the expanding African American show business than James Albert Jackson (1878?–1960), a former journalist, a conservative republican, a member of Military Intelligence Service in the First World War, and a railroad detective who knew the itinerant life. As a columnist for *Billboard*, he championed vaudevillians, that band of variety artists who depended upon booking agencies that sometimes sent them on sweepingly long tours. Traveling by train, rattling along in segregated coaches coupled directly behind the steam engine that belched coal gas and dirt into the car, those actors, dancers, comedians, and aerialists who lurched to and from one-night stands in Memphis, or two nights in New Orleans, or, if lucky, a week in Chicago. For the black audiences outside of Harlem, these traveling talents were Saturday night's entertainment. In theatres segregated either by seating or by performance hours, the salaries, like their dressing rooms, were small and shabby.

The logo on Jackson's column read, "J. A. Jackson's Page in the Interests of the Colored Actor, Showman, and Musician of America," and from November 1920 to June 1925 he worked not only against the abuses of managers and theatre owners, but also against abuses by performers, many of whom never made it to the "big time" but worked only in the hundreds of small theatres known as "opera houses," that littered the South and Midwest.

As minstrelsy bled into vaudeville, individual acts no longer had the security of belonging to a troupe but instead depended upon agents to book them into venues. Chicago had nearly one hundred and fifty such agencies and New York City two hundred and fifty. For a percentage these offices arranged pay, place, and date for performances. To insure a steady flow of acts, theatre managers relied upon bookings. For the larger theatres a white circuit such as Keith-Albee's might offer sixteen to twenty acts on one bill, perhaps including one black act. A black theatre for the week's program might host eight to twelve acts, mostly song and dance.

Some not only booked road shows but, like the Pekin in Savannah, Georgia, also had their own companies, which entertained family audiences with propriety, except for the late Saturday night ramble. At the Savannah Pekin a six-piece orchestra ballyhooed in front of the theatre before show time. Prices were 25 cents for the gallery, 35 cents for the orchestra floor, and 50 cents for the side boxes. Whites were not welcome at the Pekin. Comedians wore blackface and white gloves; there was almost no stage scenery ("the stamp of poverty is everywhere visible"). Although there was an absence of profanity, many of the jokes hinged on sexual fidelity. The Savannah Pekin burned down in the summer of 1930.

The Gibson Theater, Philadelphia

In those days vaudevillians dreamed of playing the Palace Theatre in New York. Blacks dreamed of playing the Standard Theatre in Philadelphia, a house owned and managed by John T(rusty) Gibson. Born in Baltimore, Maryland, in 1878, Gibson moved to Philadelphia, working a variety of jobs until 1910, when he entered into partnership with a real estate entrepreneur, Samuel Reading, to purchase and manage the North Pole Theatre. Spurred by moderate success, in April 1913 Gibson with a corporation of "Colored Men formed the Standard Amusement Company to purchase the Standard Theatre," a segregated house. Gibson abandoned that policy, and on 17 January 1914 the "New" Standard Theatre opened with *My Friend From Kentucky*. Gibson quickly attracted a black audience by showing class acts in vaudeville, both black and white on the same bill. By March he was doing an extraordinary business, with packed houses both afternoons and evenings. The black *Philadelphia Tribune* referred to him as the "creator of the world's largest theatre owned by a Negro."[88] His weekly receipts of $12,000 attracted competition. Two black bankers, Edward C. Brown and Andrew F. Stevens, under a corporate logo – the Dunbar Amusement Corporation – undertook to build a new Dunbar Theatre in Philadelphia. They then bought the Elite Amusement Corporation (the Lafayette Theatre building in Harlem) and the Quality Amusement Corporation (the Lafayette Players organization) from Robert Levy.[89] As part of the scheme, the Dunbar Amusement Corporation offered to the general public 10-dollar shares, appealing to Blacks to elevate community taste by bringing the best to Philadelphia and to retain the profits from the ticket sales in the community. They advertised in the *Tribune*: "There are theatres conducted for colored people at a tremendous profit, unfortunately, in the vast majority of cases, these theatres are owned and operated by Jews or other white people who are getting rich from our own people."[90]

On 29 December 1919 the Lafayette Players opened the Dunbar Theatre with a comedy drama entitled *Within the Law*, starring Cleo Desmond and Andrew Bishop. Crowds were turned away from the 1600-seat house.

The drama played twice a day for an entire week. In 1920 there were already fifty-nine theatres competing in Philadelphia. Gibson's response was to cut his ticket prices below those of his competitors. He knew that the Dunbar Amusement Corporation had overextended itself by building the $500,000 Douglass Theatre in Baltimore, as well as the Renaissance Theatre in Harlem. He was right. Abruptly, in 1921, the syndicate offered the Dunbar Theatre to John T. Gibson for $120,000. He gave them $20,000 down payment in government bonds and renamed the Dunbar the Gibson. By 1928 this man who stood 5 foot 3 and weighed 110 pounds had acquired complete control of the colored theatres in Philadelphia. The Theater Owners' Booking Association appointed him their eastern representative.

There were several reasons for Gibson's successes.[91] First, his guiding, economic principle was to present quality acts worth the price of a ticket and on vaudeville programs to mix Whites and Blacks. Second, he reviewed the local acts before booking them and would mix quality dramatic pieces with vaudeville, always giving each audience something they wanted. Third, he kept excellent rapport with the *Philadelphia Tribune*, the black newspaper where James Austin and others wrote regular weekly columns that glowed with praise for the theatre's programs. Fourth, Gibson demonstrated good business sense coupled with a good-neighbor policy in the racially mixed South Street area. Finally, he catered to the growing black middle class and their desire for "culture." Then, in 1929, the stock market crashed and so did Gibson's empire. He died near poverty on 12 June 1937.

The Howard Theater, Washington, DC

At the southern hub, only one theatre on the TOBA circuit matched the glory of the Gibson – the Howard in Washington, DC. In the nation's capital only three theatres admitted Blacks: the Belasco, the Gaiety, and the Howard, owned by whites but under black management. The Howard stood in the heart of the black community and had been named after the nearby university. It became the first theatre in Washington to serve Blacks and occupied an entire city block. With an orchestra, a balcony, and eight proscenium boxes, the Howard seated about fifteen hundred persons; its dressing rooms accommodated one hundred performers. The *Washington Bee* declared: "the Howard Theatre is no doubt the finest theatre in the city... one of the prettiest theatres in the country."[92]

The former manager of the Pekin Theatre in Chicago, W. H. Smith, became the Howard's first manager. When the theatre opened, on 22 August 1910, the *Bee* noted: "the private boxes were filled with ladies of society. The

orchestra was monopolized with the social élite of Washington, gaily and
gorgeously dressed." Will Vodery directed the orchestra, and Abbie Mitchell
was the hit of the evening. In her autobiography, Ethel Waters remembered
that "For two evening performances and one matinée during the week,
they would sell tickets only to very light-colored Negroes. At those three
performances, you could see no black spots at all."[93]

Throughout the 1920s the Howard offered dramatic plays by the
Lafayette Players. In March 1922 S. H. Dudley and William Murray bought
the Howard Theatre, but by the end of the decade the theatre had become
a temple not for Thespis, but for the revivalist Elder Michaux. In 1931
the owners brought in a new manager, Shep Allen, who engaged a native
Washingtonian, the bandleader and composer Duke Ellington, to reopen
the theatre, a celebration that ran for three weeks. Jimmy Lunceford, Cab
Calloway, and Earl Hines followed, each with several return engagements.
Soloists Pearl Bailey, Sarah Vaughan, Dinah Washington, and Lena Horne
performed there. Allen introduced an amateur night contest in the style of
Harlem's Apollo. In spite of the Great Depression, attendance remained
high. "The forties brought the Supper Shows and the Presidential Birthday
Balls, for which Washington's black élite donned their finest and turned out
en masse."[94]

Dramatic plays virtually disappeared during the 1940s, with two exceptions, both imports from the Apollo in Harlem. *Tobacco Road* (1934) in
1947 starred Powell Lindsay and Estelle Hemsley, and an all-black version
of *Detective Story* (1949) featured Sidney Poitier with Hilda Haynes and
William Branch. By the sixties the "better classes" who had traditionally
patronized the Howard, moved away. Riots following the assassination of
Martin Luther King in April 1968 devastated the community. A final blow
to the theatre, mandated by racial integration in the late sixties, gave black
performers more lucrative venues in white clubs and black audiences the
option to go to them. The Howard closed in 1970. Attempts to revive it
failed.

Shuffle Along and other musicals

Blacks not only entertained themselves, but also entertained Whites. *Shuffle
Along* (1921) kicked off a series of imitations and set the style for the 1920s.
Based on an old vaudeville skit by Flournoy Miller and Aubrey Lyles, it was
first performed without music by the Pekin Stock Company in Chicago as
The Mayor of Dixie (1905); the thin plot starred the comics Miller and Lyles as

two grocery store owners running for mayor against a reform candidate who must win the election in order to marry his true love. The musical version tried out at the Howard and Dunbar theatres before arriving $18,000 in debt at Daily's Sixty-Third Street Music Hall in New York City. The show proved a hit.

Much of the show's energy flowed from Eubie Blake's music, with lyrics by Noble Sissle, who claimed that the show-stopper, "Love Will Find a Way," was the first romantic love song ever sung in a black musical comedy; on opening night, both he and Blake had been fearful that a white audience would not accept Blacks as serious lovers; however, Roger Matthews and Lottie Gee sang the ballad so tenderly that the audience loved them, opening the way for other composers to write romantic songs.[95] Vocalist Gertrude Saunders was replaced by the then unknown Florence Mills, who stopped the show every night with "I'm Craving for That Kind of Love." The audience's feet were set tapping to "If You've Never Been Vamped by a Brown Girl You've Never Been Vamped at All" and "I'm Just Wild About Harry." Over its 504 performances, *Shuffle Along* launched other careers – Josephine Baker, who wiggled and grimaced in the chorus line until she was given individual billing in the program as "Comedy Chorus Girl"; Catherina Jarboro, whose splendid operatic voice swelled the chorus from the wings because she was "too dark" to appear on stage; Paul Robeson, who sang bass in the Four Harmony Kings; and Adelaide Hall, a voice who would soon star in *Runnin' Wild* (1923) and *Chocolate Dandies* (1925).[96]

In later years *Shuffle Along 1930*, *Shuffle Along 1933*, and *Shuffle Along 1952* followed, but none with the verve of the original, which is considered the musical that changed the Great White Way to Black.[97] *Shuffle Along*, with its southern setting, had strong minstrel comedy links. Historian Allen Woll observes that white critics expected subsequent black musicals to use the same format. When the revue *Put and Take* (1921)[98] presented a less southern and "smarter" image, a *Variety* critic, Jack Lait, wrote: "A quartet hacked away in dress suits when it should have been a success in plantation jumpers. The girls' wardrobes ran to tawdry gowns and frocks when they should have been fancifully dressed as 'picks,' Zulus, cannibals or cotton pickers. There wasn't enough true colored stuff in the show until the finale."[99]

Black shows striving to be white was a regular complaint by white critics. *Strut Miss Lizzie* (1922) was thought to be too much like *Ziegfeld Follies*. A year later, *How Come?* was accused of "an unsuccessful attempt to imitate [white] Broadway musical comedy." The message was clear: "Don't stray from the minstrel image we all know and love!" Blacks faced additional

obstacles – racism, chicanery, and outright larceny infected Broadway producers and theatre owners. The houses available to black producers required
a white sponsor, or else Blacks must wait until summer, when white shows
closed to avoid the heat. Sometimes theatre owners held onto box-office
receipts, paying salaries late, if at all. Without a union, actors had to swallow
mistreatment or quit the show.[100]

Still, the lotus bloomed in the swamp. George White, producer of the
successful *Scandals of 1920*, contracted Miller and Lyles for *Runnin' Wild*
(1923), billing them as "America's Foremost Colored Comedians." This
comedy team had worked in minstrelsy, vaudeville, and the Pekin Stock
Company. Miller was tall and light and, like Bert Williams, worked in
blackface. In one of their most popular routines, Lyles, short and dark,
would challenge Miller to a boxing match.

The uncompleted thought became a trademark of their patter.

> "Who he goin' marry?"
> "He goin' marry the daughter of Mr. . . . ."
> "That's a nice girl. Lemme tell you, I heard once . . ."
> "Naw, that was her sister."[101]

George White secured fresh talent in Adelaide Hall and Bob Lee, and
most of all in Elizabeth Welch, who sang a "Charston" number. The critics
and the audiences loved the show. Soon the Charleston became the dance
craze of the Jazz Era. (Like the cakewalk, the Charleston was claimed to
have been introduced by several black dancers.)

Meanwhile, Sissle and Blake, pioneers of the Jazz Age musical, ushered
their new show, *The Chocolate Dandies* (1924), into town. Unlike *Shuffle
Along*, this time the authors had spent lavishly on costumes and sets, which
the critics admired, but *Variety* and other critics laid their curse on the show
for being too white, "and not good darky entertainment." Even the popular
number, "That Charleston Dance," could not keep the show running beyond
ninety-six performances. Trendy revues were replacing book shows. George
White inserted black dance and music in his *Scandals of 1927*: "Birth of the
Blues," "Beauties Performing the Black Bottom," and Ann Pennington in
eight poses as she "struts a new step [in that] dance up from the levee."[102]

Critic Theophilus Lewis blamed the rise of revues for a correspond-
ing decline in acting skills, because without a book or story, actors
didn't need training. He also blamed white critics for praising poor black
performances.

Producer Lew Leslie may have observed that if *Scandals* and the *Follies* succeeded without a book, why not an all-black revue? He named it *Dixie to Broadway* (1924). Leslie's formula: everyone backstage, including director, conductor, scriptwriters – white; everyone on stage – black. By the decade's end, black talents drew patrons to the box office; Whites held the power behind the curtain.

Two talents cast by Lew Leslie – Shelton Brooks and Florence Mills – deserve note. Shelton Brooks (1886–1975), born of a black mother and a Native American father, played organ for his father's church services in Ontario, Canada. At age 18 he left to find work in the clubs and theatres of Chicago. In 1911 he proved his comedic talents in *Dr. Herb's Prescription* at Chicago's Pekin Theatre. Over the next ten years he wrote a series of successful songs, including "Some of These Days" (1910) and "The Darktown Strutters' Ball" (1917). "Walking the Dog" created the dance sensation of the same name. With the Panama Amusement Company (a series of white shows adapted for Blacks), Brooks played opposite Alberta Hunter and Evelyn Preer. In 1922 he joined *Plantation Revue* and continued in Leslie's new show, *From Dover to Dixie* (1924) when it traveled to London with Florence Mills. Together they returned to New York to star in Leslie's renamed musical, *Dixie to Broadway*. Brooks proved to be one of the top comedians of the era. He died in a Los Angeles nursing home at the age of 89.

To be a legend in the theatre, one needed to exhibit a startlingly original talent, make audiences love you, then die young. This was the destiny of Florence Mills. Upon her death at age 32, at the height of her career, 150,000 filled Harlem's streets for her funeral. An airplane released a flock of blackbirds in tribute to the song she had made her own: "I'm a Little Blackbird Looking for a Bluebird." Letters, tributes, songs, and poetry poured forth. To read them, even today, one is struck by their sincerity. What magic did Florence Mills possess? We shall never know for there is no recording of her voice. Critics fumbled for words to describe her "flute-like" notes. Gilbert Seldes managed a cryptic description with "her baffling, seductive voice." Jessie Fauset exclaimed: "the superlativeness of Miss Mills' happy abandon could know no equal." Theophilus Lewis did his best:

> Florence Mills is incomparable. She is the most consummate artist I have ever seen on the musical stage. She has perfect control of both the technique of restraint and the technique of abandon...When she sings her song, "I'm a Little Blackbird Looking for a Bluebird" she lets herself

out, and – My God! Man, I've never seen anything like it. I never imagined such a tempestuous blend of passion and humor could be poured into the singing of a song. I never expect to see anything like it again, unless I become gifted with second sight and behold a Valkyr riding ahead of a thunderstorm. Or see Florence Mills singing another song.[103]

Quite clearly, when Mills sang, she broke hearts. From where had this goddess come? At the age of 8 she appeared in a Washington, DC production of *Sons of Ham*. She traveled as a child performer in vaudeville for several years, where she developed her "winsome little-girl style." Later she married U. S. Thompson, a popular dancer, and replaced Gertrude Saunders in *Shuffle Along*; Lew Leslie cast her in his *Plantation Revue*, and when the show opened in London she was "discovered." Following a triumphant tour in *Blackbirds*, she died on 1 November 1927 of a burst appendix. Playwrights of later generations attempted to write musicals around her life, but who would play the lead?

Lew Leslie crowded his revue with talent – Bill Robinson, Tim Moore, Adelaide Hall, Aida Ward, Johnny Hudgins, and Florence Mills. He paced his shows fast, sometimes not allowing encores; however his revue broke little new ground in racial image, as revealed by some show numbers in the first act – the Plantation Orchestra – Way Down South. Review – Aunt Jemima Stroll – Scene in Jungle Land – Bandanna Babies – A Gin Mill Somewhere in Harlem.

After mid-decade, a number of black musicals danced into town and died of clichés.[104] Two lived. First, *Rang Tang* (1927), a resuscitation of Miller and Lyles as the comic hustlers from *Shuffle Along*. This time Sam Peck and Steve Jenkins once again were in desperate need of money. They find a bag of diamonds in Africa. With assistance from a very stylish production, the revue lasted 119 performances. The second, *Hot Chocolates* (1929), was born as a floor show at Connie's Inn, the home of cross-dressing and daring banter. Even though some ol' southern clichés still haunted its program – "Pickaninny Land" and "Song of the Cotton Fields" – the show opened with novelty, no curtain but a porter, a doorman, and a headwaiter who invited the audience into Connie's Inn. The Chicago *Defender* noted that "It was presented with the ease, informality and lack of artificiality of a first-class night club entertainment."[105] In this, one may glimpse how much uptown clubs and downtown musicals had influenced one another. Eight female Hot Chocolate Drops clad in much of nothing, provoked eight male Hot Chocolate Drops, clad in nothing much, to a dance that might have signaled a police raid ten years earlier. The revue's first title, *Tan Town Topics*, touted as a "new tan skin revel," suggested how far "red-hot dancing" had become a show business commodity. Eighty-five performers (not an uncommonly large cast for musicals at the time) danced and sang their way through twenty-one scenes lasting three and a half hours. What sustained its length? Talent: Eddie Green, Billy Hudgins, Edith Wilson, Jazzlips Richardson, Cab Calloway with book and lyrics by Andy Razaf; music by Harry Brooks and Fats Waller. "Ain't Misbehavin'" played as a recurring theme throughout the show. The topping to this spicy tart was Louis Armstrong in his first appearance on Broadway.

Black shows abroad

Part of the élan enjoyed by Blacks in the Renaissance arose from their forays abroad. Following World War One, the "Lost Generation" fled puritan America to drown itself in the movable feast of Paris bistros. The French embraced James Europe and jazz. Josephine Baker, using her color as a *laissez-passer* and singing in French, wiggled her way into the *Folies Bergère*. Back in Harlem, Blacks repeated tales of racial and artistic freedom abroad until anecdotes became legends. The expatriate migration swelled. Palmer Hayden and Romare Bearden sketched scenes in cafés; Elizabeth Prophet and Edmonia Lewis modeled sculptures in the shadow of Rodin. Countee Cullen and Claude McKay felt themselves to be almost racially invisible as they strolled the Left Bank. In 1925 another writer, Jessie Fauset, then literary editor of *Crisis*, confessed to the *Paris Tribune*:

> I like Paris because I find something here, something of integrity, which I seem to have strangely lost in my own country. It is simplest of all to say that I like to live among people and surroundings where I am not always conscious of "thou shalt not." I am colored and wish to be known as colored, but sometimes I have felt that my growth as a writer has been hampered in my own country. And so – but only temporarily – I have fled from it.[106]

Yet language remained a barrier for comedians. The incisive and humorous idioms of black speech did not clear the high bar of translation. English-language plays confined themselves to a coterie of diplomats and expatriates. When *Blackbirds of 1929* opened with a cast of more than one hundred, the reviewer in the *Paris Tribune* noted:

Figure 22. Josephine Baker in Paris, 1920s

Although brought here by Mr. Lew Leslie primarily to appeal to the
tourist trade and the resident British and American colony, this typically
American show has caught the fancy of the French. And this is no little
compliment to the talent of the players, for they must *put over* songs
and dialogues in a language not understood by a goodly portion of the
audience.[107]

The lingua franca for black theatre abroad remained music, song, and
dance; the legends grew. Even today one may find seedy cabarets in Copen-
hagen, Hamburg, and Amsterdam named "The Cotton Club."

Soon buried in the swamp of the Great Depression, all this and so much
more seemed to have died, but it was not forgotten. Fifty years later, Broadway conjured up the nostalgic legends of the Jazz Age. *Bubbling Brown Sugar*
(1975) ran for 766 performances, using original 1920s talents – Avon Long
and Joseph Attles – in their old comic routines. *Eubie!* (1978) celebrated
the 95-year-old composer with 437 performances of his ragtime and jazz
hits, including "Memories of You." Veteran tap dancer and choreographer
Henry LeTang guided the Hines brothers through the show's intricate tap
routines. *Sophisticated Ladies* (1981) celebrated Duke Ellington with thirty-
five of his songs, but it was an unsophisticated, almost shabby production at
the Village Gate that caught the flavor of TOBA's 1927 vaudevillians, who
made one-night stands on tiny stages owned by calloused white managers.
One Mo' Time (1979), written and acted by Vernel Bagneris, used its five
actors joking, singing, dancing to the music of trumpet, piano, clarinet,
drums, and tuba. Easily the most gorgeous remake of a 1920s revue was
Black and Blue, an import from Paris. Claude Segovia and Hector Grezzoli
created much of their magic by casting legendary blues singers, Ruth Brown
and Linda Hopkins, along with fabled hoofers Bunny Briggs, Ralph Brown,
and Jimmy Slyde. A vigorous young chorus styled their way through the
"Black Bottom" and "Black and Tan Fantasy." The record holder for a nostalgic musical, *Ain't Misbehavin'*, played in 1978 and again in 1982 for a total
of 1,604 performances. Luther Henderson arranged some thirty songs by
Fats Waller, including some taken from *Hot Chocolates*.

The old comedy routines and skits held up, but only barely.[108] Time had
been kinder to music and dance, but as these would-be clones of the 1980s
passed in review they reinforced one powerful notion: black dance and
music from the 1920s remained vital enough to attract audiences in the
new millennium. George C. Wolfe and Michael John LaChiusa set out
to prove it by adapting a long poem, *The Wild Party*, written in 1928 by

Joseph Moncure March.[109] In the introduction to the original, Louis
Untermeyer noted that the story was "vulgar, brutal, cynical, ugly, sensational." He added that the plot was set in "night-clubbed, bootlegged,
sex-ridden, tabloid-jazzed New York," a perfect scenario for a Jazz Age musical. *The Wild Party* production diary by Wiley Hausam,[110] associate producer of the Joseph Papp Public Theatre, stated that, as early as September
1997, director George Wolfe had consulted Ann Douglas' history of the
Jazz Age, *Terrible Honesty, Mongrel Manhattan in the 1920s*,[111] for guidance,
a book in which Douglas had made a strong case for what she called the
"Negroization of American culture." Her subtitle, "Mongrel Manhattan,"
captured white ambiguity and dilemma: how could a hedonistic and inferior
culture [black] be so vital, attractive, and lucrative? Douglas' book flew in
the face of earlier judgments that had downplayed the value of black art in
the 1920s. In the 1920s the dour sage of Baltimore, H. L. Mencken, had
pontificated over the artistic achievements of the Negro race:

> The acceptance of the educated Negro removes his last ground for com-
> plaint against his fate in the Republic, and leaves him exposed to the
> same criteria of judgment that apply to everybody else ... So far, it seems
> to me, his accomplishments have been very modest. Even in those fields
> wherein his opportunities for years have been precisely equal to the white
> man's, he has done very little of solid value. I point, for example, to the
> field of music.[112]

Mencken then anointed Paul Whiteman and George Gershwin as "the
best jazz" artists. Turning to poetry and the novel, he found black authors
inferior to white. He concluded: "It may be that he [the Negro] has ventured
into the arts too soon – that they can flourish only in a house more solid
and stable than the one he is just moving into. It may be that his greatest
success during the next generation or two will be made, not in the arts, but
in business."[113]

Irrefutably, white participation in the Harlem Renaissance influenced
its development. On the positive side, Whites, led by Carl Van Vechten
(1880–1964), drew attention to African American life, art, and artists, vault-
ing the Negro into vogue.[114] Whites even drew the larger black community
into an awareness of their own artists. Ridgely Torrence followed closely by
Eugene O'Neill, Paul Green, and Dorothy and DuBose Heyward can be
credited with providing serious dramatic roles for Blacks. The white press
canonized Charles Gilpin, Paul Robeson, Rose McClendon, and, later,
Ethel Waters.

Seven decades after the Harlem Renaissance, many judgments had shifted. Jessie Fauset, editor of *Crisis* in 1927, had viewed *Porgy* as a great advance for the race: "Does the situation of the educated Negro in America with its pathos, humiliation and tragedy call for artistic treatment at least as sincere and sympathetic as *Porgy* received?"[115] James Weldon Johnson agreed: "The Negro performer removed all doubts as to his ability to do acting that requires thoughtful interpretation and intelligent skill. Here was a large company giving a first-rate, even performance, with eight or ten reaching a high mark. The evidence was massive and indisputable."[116] Nonetheless, after the 1930s *Porgy* was rarely performed, although Gershwin's opera *Porgy and Bess* (1935) insured the survival of Catfish Row. Whites loved the music and Blacks loved to sing it.[117] Then, in April 2001 Henry Miller directed for the Opera Company of Philadelphia a fresh interpretation, "sophisticated enough to elevate the cast from cartoonish stereotypes into complex, if weathered, human beings."[118]

What is the legacy of the Harlem Renaissance? George S. Schuyler thought the whole movement was "Negro-Art Hokum. [A]ll this hullabaloo about the Negro Renaissance in art and literature did stimulate the writing of some literature of importance... The amount, however, is very small but such as it is, it is meritorious because it is literature and not Negro literature."[119]

Nathan Irvin Huggins, in his major study of these issues, declared that "the art of the renaissance was problematic, feckless, not fresh, not real." The major reason, Huggins felt, was that Blacks, failing to identify themselves as Americans, had remained provincial, "which limits the possibility of achieving good art."[120] Houston A. Baker Jr. objected. The key question to be addressed was by whose standards do we judge?

Renaissance plays were as ephemeral as yesterday's newspaper; few are given a second life. O'Neill's *Emperor Jones* (1920) is revived occasionally as a period piece, but is it a better play than Grimké's *Rachel* (1916)? In dramatic construction, O'Neill may win, but in conveying the "truth" about Black lives Grimké easily triumphs. The issues that concerned Blacks did not always interest Whites. Occasionally, as in the *Trial of Dr. Beck* (1937), both audiences were pleased, even if for different reasons. It would seem, then, that if we listen again to Du Bois' dictum that black theatre must be *by, for, about, and near Blacks*, we may find that Huggins had a point – such a theatre is provincial. It had to be in order to serve the community for which it was designed, and by that standard the literary plays of the Renaissance should be judged.

Finally, because the music and dance of the Jazz Age came from bars, clubs, and bordellos, it stood little chance of recognition as "high art." Yet, now, in the new millennium, the Smithsonian has declared jazz a national treasure. Ken Burns produced nineteen hours of jazz documentary for National Public Television. Jazz is studied in the universities. Duke Ellington and Ethel Waters' faces stare at us from United States postage stamps. The debate may continue whether or not the Harlem Renaissance created "high art," but one verdict is already in. Professor Richard Long of Emory University summarizes it well: "The Harlem Renaissance has moved from the periphery to center in the cultural topography of the American past and, inevitably, the American present."[121] If we speak only of theatre, with its performance, music, and dance, it is now safe to say that the Harlem Renaissance ensured a place for African Americans in world culture.

8

Educational theatre

James V. Hatch and Errol G. Hill

Each one, teach one

Too often in the past when programs were planned for the relief or rescue of society's broad underclass, those acutely affected by the decision made would be the last if ever to be consulted. Fortunately, General N. P. Banks felt differently. Having in 1863, during the Civil War, liberated black folk from serfdom in Louisiana, the General gave orders that they should be canvassed to determine what they needed most as a free people. The poll established five principal items: three as negatives and two as positives. The negatives reflected on the treatment that Blacks had experienced as slaves and did not want repeated in their new condition as freemen: (i) no separation of families, (ii) no flogging, (iii) no forced labor on estates where they had been abused. The two positive responses were also revealing, especially the first: (iv) schools for freemen; and (v) fair wages for work done.[1] It was painfully clear that emancipated Blacks placed a high priority on schooling, since from early in the nineteenth century laws enacted in the southern states had made it a crime to teach slaves to read or write.

The numbers involved were staggering. At the time of the Emancipation Proclamation the Negro population in the United States was estimated in round figures to be 4.5 million, of which not more than 10 percent – or less than half a million – could read. As the freedmen of the South numbered close to 4 million, the task faced by a nation already exhausted by civil war was enormous. Three different types of organizations responded to the challenge: established religious denominations from the North; Negro religions that had formed their own churches to avoid racial discrimination; and the newly organized Freedmen's Bureau entrusted by Congress with responsibility to protect the welfare of newly freed Blacks. Appointed in May 1865 to head the bureau was General Oliver O. Howard, age 34, who had commanded a column during General Sherman's "march to the sea."[2] Commenting on the appointment, Sherman wrote to the new commissioner: "I cannot imagine that matters that involve the future of four million souls could be put in more charitable hands."

Howard opened his headquarters in Washington, DC, and, dividing the former Confederate area into ten districts, he named army officers as assistant commissioners, with the control of all matters concerning refugees, freedmen, and abandoned lands in their respective districts. Since the federal government had made no appropriation for the relief of the freedmen, the bureau would work with various benevolent organizations to accomplish its goals. Education was one of the areas where assistance was desperately needed, especially after President Andrew Johnson had vetoed a bill passed by Congress to enable the bureau "to procure land and erect suitable buildings, asylums, and schools for dependent freedmen and refugees." In this regard, northern missions were ready and able to provide relief. With the ink of capitulation hardly dry at Appomattox, the American Missionary Association flew into the South and founded a series of denominational Protestant schools.[3] There were exceptions: Lincoln University of Jefferson City, Missouri, was founded by black Civil War veterans, and the Catholics established Xavier University in Louisiana. After the Civil War the AME Zion Church fostered a number of elementary and secondary schools, confining its work at college level to one institution, Livingston College in Salisbury, North Carolina. However, New England Protestantism dominated historically black colleges and universities (HBCUs) for nearly a hundred years.

Labeled "the nursery of ministers," the new black "colleges" graduated only preachers or teachers or both. The schools, often designated as "institutes," "colleges," or "universities," began instruction at the elementary level, for the vast majority of the former slave population had never been taught to read or write. A "high school" diploma came with completion of the eighth grade, which entitled one to become a teacher: "Each one, teach one." An all-consuming passion for the long-denied education gripped the former slaves. Those who submitted themselves to the discipline of the process internalized the puritan values of their teachers, who initially were nearly all Whites. The boards of trustees, presidents, and deans of these colleges remained White until after the Second World War.[4] They controlled curricula, faculty, and student life with rigid discipline. John D. Rockefeller christened Spelman College in Atlanta with his wife's maiden name. Florence Read served as its president for twenty-seven years, reading and censoring every play produced on campus. Enforcing Rockefeller's strict Baptist morality, Read permitted no sexual innuendoes, profanity, or drinking of alcohol on stage. When Blacks gradually assumed administrative power, they were often as authoritarian as the Whites, and in many cases more so.[5]

The dispute between W. E. B. Du Bois, a product of New England schools (except for his BA from Fisk), and Booker T. Washington, a graduate of Hampton Institute, Virginia, embodied two diverse approaches to the education of former slaves. The missionary New England school teachers had brought with them the only schooling they knew – the classical study of Greek, Latin, the Bible, and mathematics. Washington, who had come up from slavery, knew that the majority of freedmen needed skills to earn a living.

> What deeds have sprung from plow and pick!
> What bankrolls from tomatoes.
> No dainty crop of rhetoric
> Can match one of potatoes.[6]

Neither New England Puritanism nor southern pragmatism embraced the theatre. The carpenters, bricklayers, and potato planters of Hampton Institute had little leisure or motive to study drama. The northern Baptists and Methodists had small tolerance for the stage, unless it was disguised as a moral lecture; nonetheless, their future ministers and teachers studied rhetoric and elocution, which included the Greek and Roman orators. The art of declamation, with its rhetorical flourishes, led to the recitation of the Bible and Shakespeare aloud.

It is often assumed that drama in HBCUs began at Howard University with the organizing of the first drama club in 1911.[7] In fact, there were at least two or three earlier beginnings. In the fall of 1895 Atlanta University appointed Mrs. Adrienne McNeil Herndon (a colored woman) as a teacher of elocution. For several summers and a final winter's leave of absence she studied at the Boston School of Expression, completing the course with distinction. Mrs. Herndon also studied at the School of Dramatic Arts in New York City. Beginning in 1900, students presented plays under her direction. The graduating class of 1905 presented *The Merchant of Venice*, initiating a tradition followed by each subsequent class: 1906, *The Taming of the Shrew*; 1907, *As You Like It*; 1908, *Twelfth Night*. In 1909 the senior class chose Sheridan's *The Rivals*, and for 1910 Mrs. Herndon chose Shakespeare's *The Tempest*. Students were familiarizing themselves with the play at the time of her death.[8] In a 1906 article on "Shakespeare at Atlanta University," Mrs. Herndon had written words that possibly touched a responsive chord in the minds of her mature students: "to interpret the depth of the human heart and to bring it into another's consciousness, one must have lived and suffered, and striven – and who among the Negro race has not received this sympathetic touch and insight as a birth-right? A more dramatic life than the one given the American Negro can hardly be imagined."[9]

By the turn of the century, dramatic readings had become acceptable to both public and denominational schools. An important start in black college theatre was made at North Carolina Agricultural and Technical College in 1907, when Mrs. Susan B. Dudley taught a course entitled "Expression and Dramatic Art." Mrs. Dudley wrote, produced, and directed several plays, including *How Shall I Go Up To My Father?* (1898), *Crusades and Crusaders* (1901), *Practical Christianity* (1907), *Land of Opportunity* (1917), and *A Christmas* (1922). In 1923 she persuaded her husband, Dr. James B. Dudley, then president of the college, to hire the celebrated actor Richard B. Harrison. Harrison had made his living by performing one-man versions of *Macbeth* and *Julius Caesar* in black colleges. At A&T Harrison founded his own Dramatic School (1922–29). He taught the "Expression and Dramatic Art" course and directed a play each summer until 1930, when he left to star on Broadway in Marc Connelly's *The Green Pastures*.[10]

Tuskegee Institute hired the Shakespearian Charles Winter Wood to teach English, drama, and public speaking, and to direct plays. Professor Wood's Tuskegee Players vie with Adrienne Herndon of Atlanta University and Richard B. Harrison of North Carolina A&T for the honor of being the first dramatic club in a southern black school, but for many decades their dramatic societies, like their counterparts in New England, would not attain curriculum status. Even Howard University, where Ernest Just, fresh from Dartmouth College, organized the Howard Players in 1911, did not include theatre in its curriculum until the 1920s.

By 1900, because of poor facilities and few teachers with college degrees, none of the southern missionary or state schools had earned national accreditation. To remedy the situation, half a dozen northern philanthropists began to channel money into scholarships, buildings, and stipends for teachers.[11] The major fund to promote theatre and speech was the General Education Board, which had been established by John D. Rockefeller in 1902. Its purpose was to work for accreditation by awarding scholarships to Blacks who would study in northern colleges and then teach in southern schools. One was Anne Cooke, a 1944 Ph.D. graduate of the Yale Drama

Figure 23. Charles Winter Wood

School. As early as the summer of 1930 while teaching English at Spelman College, she wrote and directed a pageant "dramatizing the history of the college through dialogue, music, tableaux, and dance performed by students of Morehouse and Spelman." In 1929 these two institutions had merged with Atlanta University to become a single cooperative university. In 1934, Anne Cooke founded the university's Summer Theatre. It produced four shows in six weeks; one of them, if available, would be a black play. Most were Broadway hand-me-downs or classic European (Capek's *R.U.R.*, Wilder's *Our Town*, Sheridan's *School for Scandal*). An energized University Players group "began a long history of excellent dramatic entertainment in the University Center ... as Miss Cooke selected some of the most demanding

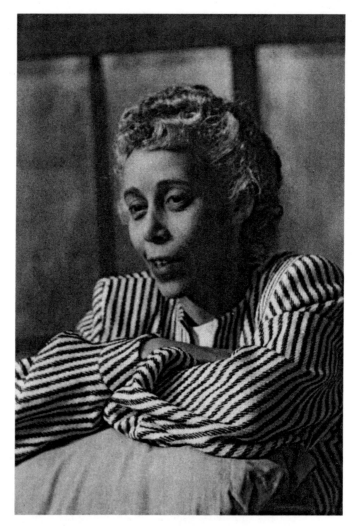

Figure 24. Anne Cooke Reid, Howard University

plays written by world famous dramatists."[12] Atlanta's Summer Theatre became an important training center for many talents: Sterling Brown, Marion Douglas, Baldwin Burroughs, Dorothy Ateca, Raphael McIver, John M. Ross, and Owen Dodson (the latter two, graduates in the 1930s of Yale University's Drama School).

Miss Cooke left Spelman in 1942 for Hampton Institute and from 1944–58 she was Professor of Drama at Howard University, but she returned to direct the Summer Theatre at Atlanta. Owen Dodson was associated with her in directing the program and later Professor Baldwin Burroughs of Spelman was in charge. The summer program was still being offered in 1974, making it the longest-running summer theatre in America.

In the early years two important movements helped change the face of black college theatre: the Art Theatre Movement, with its embrace of folk drama, and W. E. B. Du Bois' pageant, *The Star of Ethiopia*, discussed earlier. Negro colleges emulated Du Bois' achievement and throughout the 1920s presented dozens of pageants – their titles were self-explanatory: *Out of the Dark* (1924) by Dorothy C. Guinn, *Ethiopia at the Bar of Justice* (1924) by Edward J. McCoo, *By their Fruits: A Pageant of the Negro Race* (1924), and *The Milestones of the Race* (1924) by Ada Crogman. Virginia State College presented *The Teachers' Pledge* annually in the 1930s. Typically, these spectacles were written by civic leaders or faculty to celebrate race progress, women's contributions to art and learning, or the history of a college. Pageants clearly embraced civic pride, moral uplift, and respect for education. The spectacles enhanced the status of dramatics in black schools and colleges.

Willis Richardson's Broadway début of his short play *The Chip Woman's Fortune* (1921) also set a standard for black achievement. African Americans and Whites saw on stage a rural family speaking in regional dialects, struggling with poverty. As the passion for folk theatre spread across the nation, philosophy professor Alain Locke in 1922 designated Howard University as a center where "race drama becomes peculiarly the ward of our college, as new drama, as art-drama, and as folk-drama."[13] However, the university's president, J. Stanley Durkee, turned down Willis Richardson's dialect folk plays as inappropriate for Howard's students. Many African Americans did not want dialect recognized as acceptable speech, but after William Dean Howell, the literary lion of New England, had blessed Dunbar's poems, dialect became quaint and acceptable on college stages. As a response to Durkee's rejection, African American historian Carter Woodson encouraged two folk playwrights – Willis Richardson and May Miller – to publish *Negro History in Thirteen Plays* (1935), mostly based on the lives of great black leaders. Some of their protagonists spoke in a modified dialect (how could Sojourner Truth and Harriet Tubman not do so?). Black playwrights had begun to control their own history.

The second boon to college drama was the Art Theatre Movement, which swept America in the second decade of the century. W. E. B. Du Bois and Alain Locke, with others, welcomed the movement by encouraging the writing of folk plays. By 1925 it was estimated that more than three thousand amateur groups – schools, women's clubs, men's lodges, churches, and settlement houses – had built raised platforms for stages and "put on plays," usually one-acts that seldom required more than a single set. Since experienced actors were not available for amateur productions, characters were broadly conceived and generally few in number, ideal for college presentation. The Little Theatre Movement gave a facelift to the sometimes scurrilous reputation of the American stage by comparing itself to the art theatre of Europe, exemplified by the Théâtre Libre in Paris or the Moscow Art Theatre. In time, drama became more respectable and acceptable to college trustees and presidents.

By the 1930s there was general recognition that the arts should play an important role in teacher education. The Rockefeller Foundation's General Education Board awarded scholarships to artists in music, dance, theatre, and painting to obtain advanced college degrees.[14] The Julius Rosenwald Foundation sent Sheppard Randolph Edmonds on a fellowship to make an observational study of amateur drama organizations in England, Ireland, Scotland, and Wales. In March 1930 Edmonds, who was by then on the faculty at Morgan College, called together representatives from four other schools – Howard, Hampton, Virginia Union, and Virginia State College – to found the Negro Intercollegiate Dramatic Association (NIDA), to which he was elected president. Its charter listed six purposes:

1. to increase the interest in intercollegiate dramatics
2. to use dramatic clubs as laboratories for teaching and studying drama
3. to develop Negro folk materials
4. to develop aesthetic and artistic appreciation for the dramatic art
5. to train persons for cultural service in the community
6. to establish a bond of good will and friendship among the colleges

Their first major project was to quicken faculty and student interest in drama by holding an annual tournament of one-act plays at a different campus each year. In two years the association's membership grew to ten. Some felt that the competition for prizes did not promote "good will and friendship among the colleges," and eventually the tournament was changed to a festival. The creation of NIDA achieved immediate results. "Morgan College had the distinction of being the first black college to install a complete dramatic laboratory (playwriting, acting, stagecraft, directing, and technical experience), where all the work in connection with the drama was advantageously pursued."[15]

In 1936, Professor Edmonds moved to Dillard University in New Orleans, a distance too great for participation in NIDA. He assembled another cadre of black colleges[16] to form the Southern Association of Dramatic and Speech Arts (SADSA). However, the association's production of Negro plays was frustrated by a scarcity of scripts. To inspire playwrights to write "twenty- to forty-minute plays" that would have a "strong moral or religious point, or deal with a social problem or folk materials," the association offered students a production at the next festival. The association was clearly tired of seeing the "same ol' thing," for the craft of playwriting proved too time-consuming and too demanding for inexperienced students. SADSA set forth new goals that addressed class and race in a manner different from NIDA's goals in 1930:

1. Negro playwrights could write about middle-class life, not always Negro folk drama
2. Negroes might write about white life as they see it
3. more experimentation is needed
4. more plays need to be written and more need to go into the wastebasket
5. a desirable attitude should be created among Negroes toward plays of Negro life

In order to fill the void, Professor Edmonds produced his own original scripts, which he published in three volumes: *Six Plays for a Negro Theatre* (1930), *Shades and Shadows* (1934), and *The Land of Cotton and Other Plays* (1942). At least three of his plays had already become standards at black college festivals: *Yellow Death*, concerning the malaria experiments on colored soldiers during the Spanish-American War; *Gangsters over Harlem*, a contemporary melodrama; and *Nat Turner*, an historical presentation of the 1831 slave insurrection.

The nineteen member colleges of SADSA, scattered over a distance of two thousand miles, found that if they spent two days in travel and two days watching plays, no time was left for scholarship and Association business. They divided the colleges into three regions.[17] Each school was to send a play to the regional contest, where three judges would select the best plays and have them sent on to the central SADSA conference.

Sheppard Randolph Edmonds (1900–83) was the father of black educational theatre. A graduate in English from Oberlin (1926), he attended Columbia University for his MA, followed by a year at the Yale Drama School. A Rosenwald Scholarship enabled him to spend a year in Dublin and London studying drama, and it was this wide-ranging education that gave

Figure 25. Sheppard Randolph Edmonds

him the vision to establish educational theatre associations in the South. For his contribution to drama in the academy, he was fondly called "the Dean of Black Theatre." He spent his final teaching years at Florida A&M University, where an ongoing visiting scholars program was set up in his name.

Edmonds' promotion of plays of Negro life raised an issue concerning the "Purity of Southern Speech." He defended the use of dialect in his plays by stressing its authenticity as one of several elements that included "worthwhile themes, sharply drawn conflict, [and] positive characters."[18]

Figure 26. The Importance of Being Earnest, Howard University, 1951

The association faced a choice: either insist that their students adopt the pronunciation of the mainstream and speak standard English, or embrace regional speech and dialect as a worthy second language. Some colleges initiated "Better Speech Week." Regionalism never had a chance against the New England perspective of how properly to speak the Queen's English. In the 1950s the drama department of Howard University hired special teachers, in the words of Owen Dodson, to cleanse the "mushy mouths" of southern students. In that decade Howard staged fourteen European classics and four African American plays. Dialect in folk plays was tolerated, but the student actors imposed art upon nature. It was a classic struggle of the oppressed to join or reject the mainstream, a struggle that surfaced again in 1996 in the Ebonics debate of the Oakland schools in California.

Makeup, too, was put on trial. In 1941 at Tuskegee, the association watched Professor Lillian Voorhees conduct a demonstration entitled "Makeup in Sepia." Various shades of Thespian, a greaseless paint, were used to even up complexions for characters in the same play – that is, to bring a dark complexion up and a light complexion down. This was the period when both Broadway and Hollywood refused to cast Negro actors because they were "too white to be black, or too black to be white." Max Factor had not yet manufactured grease paint for amateurs in hues useful to nonwhite actors who were faced with using mixtures of minstrel black, Chinese yellow, Indian red, and Mexican brown.

English and American plays dominated college stages during the 1940s and 1950s. Very few new and suitable black plays had been written and would not be until late in the 1960s. In addition, black faculty increasingly obtained advanced degrees from northern and midwestern universities, they traveled abroad and saw theatre, and their familiarity with world drama encouraged them to mount European plays. Professor Anne Cooke of Howard stated frankly that she was preparing her students professionally to play all roles, even though in the late 1940s few parts except maids and butlers were offered to Blacks. When the actress Roxie Roker (Howard BA, 1952) became a regular on television's *The Jeffersons* in the 1970s, she expressed her gratitude to Professor Cooke for insisting on world-class theatre.[19]

Because Howard University was funded by the US Congress, it offered security in tenure and budget that attracted talented faculty. Designer and actor James Butcher (1909–94), writer and director Owen Dodson (1914–83), and director and administrator Anne Cooke (1907–) led Howard's theatre department from the mid-1940s into the 1960s, and they typically produced plays by writers such as Maeterlinck, Shakespeare, O'Neill, Sophocles, Tagore, and others – programs more classically oriented than those staged at many white colleges during the same period.[20]

On 31 August 1949 in New York Harbor, Mrs. Eleanor Roosevelt, as a trustee of Howard University, boarded the SS *Stavangerfjord* to bid the Howard troupe *bon voyage*. The three faculty members with twenty black students sailed to Norway, Denmark, Sweden, and Germany to perform Ibsen's *The Wild Duck* and Du Bose Heyward's *Mamba's Daughters*. The Howard Players gained wide international publicity. So enthusiastically were they received by their host countries that the US State Department began to routinely send artists abroad as part of its foreign policy, including the Florida A&M Playmakers, who toured seven African countries.

Thomas Pawley, a key figure in the development of black college theatre, while working on his MA (1947) and his Ph.D. (1949) at the University of Iowa, had taken a position at Lincoln University in Jefferson City, Missouri, where he taught English and speech and directed plays. Pawley recounted an incident all too typical of early educational theatre.

When I arrived at Lincoln [1940] I found that tiny Page Auditorium had a quaint stage that was raked. After I discovered the awkward stances my actors were taking (they looked as if they were leaning down stage), I began erecting a platform which eliminated the rake. There was always the danger of someone falling off the platform. When Winona Fletcher brought her Players to perform *Blithe Spirit*, the actress playing Madame Arcati got carried away, forgot the warning to be careful, and fell off the stage![21]

In 1952, to create greater campus interest in drama, Pawley initiated a summer theatre at Lincoln University, where students would produce three or four plays and take related academic work. Pawley brought in John M. Ross as technical director, along with two talented women – Lillian Voorhees, a faculty director who had served as secretary for SADSA, and Winona Fletcher, who had recently graduated from Iowa with an MA in costuming. The outdoor staging made production costly – a stage had to be built, lights brought in, and no admission fee could be charged because the theatre was open on all sides. After the summer of 1953 the program ran out of money and was discontinued until 1959, when the new air-conditioned Richardson Auditorium was opened and an admission fee could be charged. However, the summer's box office never met expenses. Lincoln's summer theatre closed in 1961.

The work of Lillian W. Voorhees deserves acknowledgment. She joined Talladega College *circa* 1928 as a speech teacher and director of the Little Theatre. By 1934 she had produced with student casts ten full-length and forty-one short plays. When Ms. Voorhees left Talladega after fifteen years' service to assume an advanced position at Fisk University, her influence on students had been profound. "Where else," a distinguished alumna wrote to her in 1961, "could I have seen the spectacle of a small white woman (in exasperation at her Negro students' peccadilloes) say 'the trouble with *our* people is that it takes us so long to make up our minds to commence to start to begin to do something.'"[22] Voorhees served as executive secretary of SADSA from 1937 to 1942. In 1943 she received her Ph.D. from Columbia University and moved to Fisk. In 1948 she became initial editor of *Encore*, the association's new annual journal. The culmination of her work was in 1957–59, when by popular vote she was elected president of the National Association of Dramatic and Speech Arts.

As membership in SADSA grew, the association turned its attention to placing drama in the college curricula by removing it from departments of English, where often untrained faculty were designated to direct the annual class play. SADSA recommended that drama be wed to the other speech arts – debate, oratorical contests, public address, and verse reading. SADSA hoped to create separate departments of speech and theatre, each with its own budget and faculty.

In 1947 Grambling State University in Louisiana did just that. Fifteen years later, after the university had opened a 212-seat theatre, the department offered liberal arts degrees in speech and theatre. Although Grambling's drama programs remained tied to speech education and pathology, the department thrived. In 1962 Grambling's Dr. Floyd L. Sandle toured Noël Coward's *Blithe Spirit* for the United Service Organization (USO), taking the play to Newfoundland, Iceland, Greenland, and Labrador. Nonetheless, theatre in most black colleges remained in the English department and play production continued as an extracurricular activity, like football or track. A major obstacle to departmental autonomy was the universities' reluctance to commit funds to a major in theatre, because students had little opportunity to earn a living in the profession. Finally, there was a feeling that the professional theatre was not made up of the "best people."

Following President Truman's order of 1948 to integrate the US Army, hope grew that segregation was ending. In 1949, SADSA sought affiliation with the American Educational Theatre Association (AETA) and discovered that to be represented on AETA's advisory council, it must be a national organization. SADSA promptly voted to change its name to NADSA, substituting the word "national" for "southern." In the spirit of the Supreme Court's 1954 decision to end school segregation, mainstream theatre organizations emphasized that they would welcome African Americans. Southern black drama teachers found that the national associations offered new opportunities for professional contacts. Fifty years after NIDA first issued its six objectives, some had been achieved and others superseded because the militant theatre of the 1960s and 1970s had opened college repertory to a wider range of performances, ones that two generations ago would have been considered low-class or vulgar. The Black Arts Movement had freed the college repertory from a dominance of European and Broadway shows.

A final but not fatal blow to black regional college drama would come in the 1990s, when arts and humanities budgets were cut. Howard University, which once set the standard for quality theatre, considered eliminating its division of fine arts. Talented students who once might have enrolled in small colleges now elected a university with its better-equipped facilities, and promising actors often chose professional schools. As black theatre students enrolled in white theatre departments, they required and demanded black faculty, a complete turnaround from 1970, when Owen Dodson retired from Howard University at the age of 59 with a record of directing and/or writing more than one hundred shows, including three productions of *Hamlet*. Dodson was unable to secure a position in a white college department. One of the early Blacks to receive tenure outside a black college was Errol Hill, who joined the Dartmouth faculty in 1968. Hill was recruited on the recommendation of Professor John Gassner of the Yale Drama School, where he had completed his doctorate in fine arts (DFA). Perhaps the capstone to this shift in racial hiring occurred when in 1968 the National Playwrights Conference of the Eugene O'Neill Memorial Playwrights Theater Center appointed Lloyd Richards as director. In 1979 Richards became dean of the Yale University School of Drama and artistic director of the Yale Repertory Theater, where in 1982 he staged the premiere production of August Wilson's *Ma Rainey's Black Bottom* (1982).

While small black colleges continued their efforts to develop aesthetic and artistic appreciation, their once special mission of theatre for the student body and community had diminished. Many Blacks turned to television, film, CDs, and cyberspace. Undergraduate drama and theatre programs could not compete with professional schools in a climate of dwindling budgets. At the approach of the millennium, seventy years of work were in danger of dissolution. Indeed, Professor Samuel A. Hay of North Carolina A&T State University published "The Death of Black Educational Theatre," a satire predicting black theatre's demise as of 2 January 2001. The causes of death were given as "inadequate budgets, lack of facilities and space, too few full-time teachers, and little school-wide interest and emphasis." The obituary went on to claim that of the 116 HBCUs, sixty-two had no theatre, and of the remaining ones, only twenty-four had one- to three-person programs that allowed two productions a year. Only two schools offered BFAs in theatre and there were no graduate programs. Using the persona of actor Richard B. Harrison, the obituary concluded: "The family members did nothing but meet and run their forever-open mouths. Now they will come bleeding all over the casket and trying to throw themselves into the grave. Frankly, they can all take a running leap if that is all the respect they can muster."[23]

Professor Hay was correct: except for a half-dozen flagship colleges, drama in southern schools had long suffered from poor facilities and inadequately trained faculty. Ironically, school desegregation had contributed to the fragility of theatre programs; however, that same desegregation also offered opportunities to upgrade faculty skills. William R. Reardon of the

University of California at Santa Barbara and Thomas Pawley of Lincoln
University, Missouri, offered black drama teachers a summer institute where
they would not only learn but would be presented with information and
scholarships to enable them to obtain advanced degrees. In 1968, with the
money from the US Office of Education, Reardon and Pawley assembled
a staff of professionals – Owen Dodson, Frank Silvera, and Ted Shine –
to produce four plays: Ted Shine's *Morning Noon and Night* (1962); Loften
Mitchell's *Tell Pharaoh* (1967); *Curtain Call, Mr. Aldridge, Sir* by Ossie Davis;
and Bernard Jackson and James Hatch's civil rights musical *Fly Blackbird*
(1960). After the program's conclusion, the directors published *The Black
Teacher and the Dramatic Arts* (1970), a seminal work of playscripts, essays,
and African American theatre bibliography. In its final report the institute
concluded:

> 1. The [drama] situation [in HBCUs] is abysmal and an insult to the
> Negro college student. 2. Administrative echelons appear guilty of some
> mental commitments hanging over from a day long gone. 3. Colleges
> are brutally understaffed administratively and are painfully personalized
> operations. 4. The colleges are incredibly divorced from reality of the
> ghetto community, which often surrounds them.[24]

The summer institute was so successful that the following year Tom
Pawley and Professor Joan Lewis of Fayetteville State University obtained
$100,000 from the Office of Education, the Office of Economic Oppor-
tunity, and the Southern Education Foundation for an institute at Lincoln
University. A company of thirty-two students (all on scholarship) and sixteen staff members met for eight weeks, attending workshops and pro-
ducing two original plays: Ted Shine's *Come Back After the Fire* and Tom
Pawley's *The Tumult and the Shouting*, the latter an original biographical
drama of an overworked, underpaid English teacher in a small black college.
The institute's program was funded a third summer at Winston-Salem,
North Carolina. Professor Juanita Oubre saw an opportunity to upgrade the
"inferior conditions which existed in National Association of Dramatic and
Speech Arts institutions." A number of participants in these three programs
later received doctorates in theatre.

Dr. Winona Lee Fletcher of Indiana University conceived a second strategy, this one aimed at black theatre students. Fletcher, born in Hamlet,
North Carolina, on Thanksgiving Day 1926, the fourteenth child of Mama
and Papa Lee, had attended the segregated Dudley High School in Greensboro and then Johnson C. Smith College at Charlotte, where she graduated

Figure 27. Production staff of Summer Theatre Lincoln, 1960. (Left to right: William T. Brown, Owen Dodson, Whitney LeBlanc, and Winona Fletcher; Tom Pawley is standing)

magna cum laude in English.[25] After receiving her MA in costume design from the University of Iowa, she became a "soldier" for NADSA, serving as executive secretary from 1958 to 1962. She had discovered her career mission: the promotion of theatre in black colleges. Elected president of the University and College Theatre Association (1979–80), she was drafted by the Kennedy Center to find ways to bring black student productions into their previously all-white college theatre festival. Conceived by producer Roger L. Stevens, the annual festival honored the best of college productions. It had opened its first bill of plays in 1969; nonetheless, it took thirteen years before Professor Fletcher could persuade black colleges to bring plays to the Kennedy Center. This she did by initiating awards open to all college students for the best full-length plays written by them on the black experience.[26] To encourage writers, Robert Nemiroff, husband of the late Lorraine Hansberry, with cosponsorship from the McDonald Corporation, established the Lorraine Hansberry Playwriting Award for full-length plays, with a first prize of $2,500 for the playwright and $750 for the producing college. In 1984 a second prize of $1,000 for the playwright and $500 for the school were added. The contest's purpose was to "insure the continuation of dramas on the black experience." From 1977 to 1996 twenty-five of the twenty-nine college winners of the Hansberry contest were black, and the majority, women. Two winners, Judi Ann Mason, who wrote *Jonah and the Wonder Dog*, and Vincent D. Smith, who wrote *Williams and Walker*, later received professional productions in New York City. Under the aegis of the Kennedy Center, Professor Fletcher published eleven of the winners in an anthology, *The Lorraine Hansberry Playwriting Award* (1996).

According to Fletcher, the Kennedy Center productions revealed that the standard for acting, directing, and playwriting in black colleges was much higher than that of the technical aspects of lighting, design, and costume. Although professors such as Carlton Molette, William Brown, and Bob West provided sound technical training in their schools, most black colleges simply did not have or did not allocate money to hire faculty trained in technical theatre, preferring the less expensive route of relying on teachers of art, home economics, and industrial education to lend a hand in play productions.

The Eden Theatrical Workshop, Colorado's first multicultural theatre, gave selected festival winners second productions of their plays. The founder and executive director, Lucy M. Walker, claimed Eden to be "the oldest continuously active theatre organization guided by an African American woman." In Denver, the theatre celebrated its thirtieth anniversary in 1993; it had mounted one hundred major and more than two hundred experimental productions.

Over the decades, some HBCU graduates became professionals; for example, Moses Gunn and Roxie Roker (actors); Judi Ann Mason, Ted Shine, and Joe Walker (writers); and Gilbert Moses and Shauneille Perry (directors). Finally, HBCUs did graduate qualified drama teachers and instilled in many other participating students an appreciation of live drama and theatre.

9

The Caribbean connection

Errol G. Hill

Apart from adjacent Canada, the Commonwealth Caribbean, historically known as the West Indies, are the closest English-speaking countries to the United States. However, being relatively small and poor, they are often overlooked in the geopolitics of the hemisphere. As a result these countries, many of them islands and littoral states in and around the Caribbean basin, tend increasingly to ally themselves with their immediate neighbors regardless of language differences, since they all share a common history of exploitative colonialism.

The 1807 ban placed by Congress on the African slave trade was promptly circumvented by southern planters, who continued to receive transshipments from the Caribbean. Border states such as Virginia also trafficked in slave labor, the presumed fecundity of Blacks having produced a profitable oversupply of slaves for sale to cotton-growing states in the Southland. In addition, free Blacks from the Caribbean found ways to move to America during the early nineteenth century and beyond. They came to northern slave-free states, many as runaways seeking work. Some came as sailors; the reader is reminded that the first known black theatre company in the United States was founded by a West Indian seaman in 1821.[1]

Yet despite the stringent economies of most Caribbean nations, there has developed a tolerance of racial difference among people to the extent that the island nations, by their very existence, stand as a corrective to the rampant prejudice that has, for well over a century, corroded the body politic of wealthy America. There are doubtless complex reasons to account for what may be termed "the American dilemma." It should simply be noted that in the Anglophone Caribbean, slavery ended thirty years earlier than in the United States; slave-owners were reimbursed by the British government for freeing their slaves; and there was no bitter civil war to further exacerbate feelings on this grievous issue. Moreover, given the demography of the region, black slaves and the indentured Asian Indians who replaced them as estate workers could hope one day to be free to elect their own government. When that day came, former masters or their descendants who could not accept the new dispensation would pack up and leave, as in fact some did. Those who stayed might jokingly admit that few Whites in such a closely knit society had not, as they put it, been "touched with the tar brush." For some period of time in the new Caribbean, the end result has been that quality of mind and of achievement, rather than skin color, are what count most among nationals.

Caribbean theatre in America has taken on different forms. There have been straight dramas and musicals set in the area, written and produced by people usually considered to be "outsiders." Such productions have provided work for black actors, including those from the Caribbean. As is indicative of Caribbean life, however, these works are seldom significant as they tend to avoid dealing with issues that daily confront people of the region. Plays of a similar nature were written and produced by Caribbean artists of an earlier time, who strove mainly to entertain, but generally native writers aspired to more fundamental concerns. The relationship between American and Caribbean theatre really began in 1755, when Lewis Hallam's Company of Comedians visited Jamaica. The troupe (which originally came from England) stayed three years on the island and returned for a longer sojourn in 1775–85, during and immediately after the American War of Independence. The ill-fated visit to Trinidad in 1839 of the African Theatre's James Hewlett provided another, regrettable, point of contact.[2]

By the mid-nineteenth century solo readers and reciters from America performed regularly in Jamaica and other islands. Then, for the first time, the compliment was returned when Raphael de Cordova, a Jamaican business executive resident in New York, began in 1858 to give highly successful public readings, often written by himself in rhymed verse. One of his most popular presentations, entitled "Broadway," described an omnibus ride along an avenue destined to glorify some of the nation's finest theatre. Blackface minstrelsy came to the islands in the 1860s and 1870s, but it was not until 1896, when the Black Patti Troubadours toured the Caribbean with their opening skit *At Jolly Coon-ey Island*, that the area was exposed to genuine African American theatre. The troubadours made a second tour of the region in 1915, by which time the company had blended its comedy routines into a unified show entitled *Lucky Sam from Alabam'* with their star soloist, Black Patti, becoming a character in the cast.

By this time reciprocity of Caribbean performers was substantial. They, too, began with music and song rather than straight drama.[3] In 1912 Lovey's Trinidad String Band visited New York studios to cut the first recordings for phonograph under the Victor Talking Machine label. This was followed in the 1920s by recordings of calypsos (also called *kaisos*) and traditional choruses sung by Sam Manning, Wilmoth Houdini, and other islanders then resident in Harlem or visiting New York for recording sessions. Music for accompaniment was provided by string bands led by noted Caribbean musicians such as Lionel "Lanky" Belasco, who had come to Trinidad as a child from Barbados, Walter Merrick of St. Vincent, and Cyril Monrose, also from Trinidad. Within a few years some of the renowned calypso singers would be sent annually to New York, where discs were cut in preparation for the oncoming carnival season back home. Among these singers were Atilla (*sic*) the Hun (Raymond Quevedo), the Roaring Lion (Hubert Charles, a.k.a. Rafael de Leon), the Growling Tiger (Neville Marcano), and Lord Beginner (Egbert Moore). While visiting the city these calypsonians would appear at Harlem nightclubs singing before both black and white audiences.

Two events of historic importance were directly related to calypso recordings in New York. The first involved a court case in which a charge of plagiarism was brought against an American music publisher and the alleged composers of a famous calypso entitled "Rum and Coca-Cola." First sung in Trinidad by Lord Invader (Rupert Grant) in 1944, the calypso was published, attributed to the American comedian Morey Amsterdam, and then recorded by the popular singing trio the Andrews Sisters. According to attorney Louis Nizer, who represented the plaintiff, 200,000 records were sold.[4] The second important event to emerge from the presence of professional calypsonians in New York was the carnival parade, organized by West Indians in 1947 and held in Harlem on Labor Day, the first Monday in September. Street disturbances in 1964 caused a suspension of the revelry, which was resumed some time later in Brooklyn, where many West Indians had relocated.

Called the West Indian American Day Carnival, the parade is now held along the spacious Eastern Parkway, which can comfortably accommodate the masquerade bands, steel orchestras, sound trucks, vendors offering West Indian dishes and drinks, and well over one million spectators. Modeled on the parent pre-Lenten festival in Port-of-Spain, Trinidad, the Brooklyn carnival lasting five days, from Thursday to Monday, has included a kiddies' carnival, steel band and calypso contests, a reggae concert, masquerade competitions for queen and king of the bands, exhibitions of Old Mas' characters, and the dancing of moko jumbies (stilt walkers), all consummated on Labor Day in brilliantly costumed bands of revelers jumping and jiving along the Parkway to the latest calypsos and other musics. It is little wonder that street carnivals emulating the Brooklyn festival have multiplied to enliven the end-of-summer holiday spirit in many cities across the United States.

Of the strictly theatre offerings, the earliest known productions showing Caribbean influence were a score of revues and musical comedies featuring the multitalented composer, lyricist, playwright, and bandleader Donald Heywood.[5] Born in Trinidad in 1901, Heywood at an early age showed promise of unusual musical ability by mastering the piano and other stringed instruments. However his father, a physician, desired that his son follow his profession and upon graduating from secondary school, young Heywood was sent to Fisk University in Nashville, Tennessee. He stayed for two years, then transferred to Northwestern University in Evanston, Illinois, for medical training. By this time he had become deeply interested in black American music and had moved to New York, having composed music for the farce *North Ain't South* (1923). It was staged at the Lafayette Theatre in Harlem by the brothers Salem Tutt Whitney and J. Homer Tutt.

Thereafter Heywood became a regular part of production teams, at times assuming full responsibility for whatever show was in production. Over the period from 1923 to 1941 he was involved in nineteen full-scale musical stage productions and an original one-act sketch. Five of his shows were classified as "touring revues," a label indicating that they comprised separate vaudeville acts strung together without a common theme or story line. For an additional nine shows Heywood wrote the music and/or lyrics, and for the remaining six productions he was responsible for book, lyrics, and music; on occasion another writer shared credit as lyricist. Mention of some of these shows in different years will illustrate Heywood's contribution to the musical comedy genre of his time.

In 1927 the musical revue *Africana*, conceived and produced by Earl Dancer, who also wrote the comedy sketches, had lyrics by Heywood and Dancer and music by Heywood. It featured a youthful Ethel Waters and was an important step in her rise to stardom. Among items in the first part of the program was a courtroom scene entitled "Jedgement Day" that required a cast of seven, after which the act closed with a cakewalk. Part 2 moved the scene from Harlem to Paris, complete with a parody of Josephine Baker, then in her heyday at a Parisian theatre, and with Heywood and

Ms. Waters dressed-up in one scene as a count and countess indulging in an "African Stomp." The production played at the Sixty-Third Street Theatre on Broadway for a respectable seventy-seven performances and ended with an out-of-town tour of several weeks.

Heywood was always on the lookout for successful New York shows that he could emulate without being slavishly plagiaristic. One such show was Lew Leslie's *Blackbirds* of 1926, the first in a series of song-and-dance revues by the white producer, using black performers who had excelled in floor shows at a Harlem nightclub that catered only to white patrons. Leslie's production ran for six weeks at the Alhambra Theatre in Harlem, was taken to Europe where it played in Paris for five months, then to London for six. The 1928 version of *Blackbirds* amassed 518 performances; but the 1930 show recorded a mere fifty-seven, due to its tired format and to the approaching economic recession. Two years later Heywood and Tom Peluso wrote music and lyrics for their new offering, *Blackberries of 1932*. With book by Eddie Green and Lee Posner, the production raised only twenty-four performances. Later that season, watching Marc Connelly's *The Green Pastures* settle securely on Broadway for over two years, Heywood produced *Ol' Man Satan*, a folk allegory with music in which a black mother tells biblical stories to her son. Despite an experienced cast led by Rex Ingram, fine acting and dancing, and clever antics the show, at the Forest Theatre in New York, survived for a mere twenty-four performances, payment of its 125 cast members constituting too heavy a financial outlay for an extended run.

In 1934, seven years after his staging of *Africana*, Heywood appropriated the same title for a new show, billed as a "Congo Operetta," that he claimed was entirely his creation: book, lyrics, and music. It was designed as a complete musical comedy, having a strong plot in which an Oxford-educated prince of the Belgian Congo returns home resolved to reform and modernize the country against the wishes of its people. The prince also announces plans to marry the mulatto daughter of a missionary, prompting a threat from his father the king to disown him. Sadly the show was denied a fair hearing by an incident that occurred on opening night at the Venice Theatre in New York. While conducting the orchestra in the overture, Heywood was attacked with an iron bar by a man who alleged he had collaborated with Heywood on writing the show but had received no credit. The fracas delayed the performance for almost an hour, casting a pall on the proceedings, about which the critics were mostly negative. The production was withdrawn after only three performances.

Heywood rebounded in 1936 with a new musical comedy in two acts having the worn title *Black Rhythm*, for which he wrote the book, lyrics, and music. The show carried a rather thin plotline about an "amateur night" in Harlem at which many specialty acts were presented. Staged by Earl Dancer and Heywood at the Comedy Theatre in New York, the musical opened on 19 December but lasted for just six performances, due partly to another uncalled-for delay when someone threw a stink bomb on stage, causing panic among performers and audience. The dancer Avon Long had a principal role in the aborted show. For his final production, *Tropicana* (1941),[6] Heywood reverted to a touring revue-type show, having in his latest offerings endured a string of reverses that tarnished his reputation as a producer while severely jeopardizing his income.

The Trinidad calypsonian Sam Manning followed Heywood in presenting black musical theatre. Manning had entertained British forces in North Africa while serving in the 1914–18 war. Some years later he migrated to the United States, where, in January 1925, he played the minor role of Rastus in John Howard Lawson's drama, *Processional*, at the Garrick Theatre in New York. Manning then became one of the vaudeville headliners at the Alhambra Theatre in Harlem and in 1926 he joined with Amy Ashwood Garvey to stage the musical comedy *Hey, Hey!*, a catchphrase from the then current Harlem Renaissance.[7] In the comedy Manning and George McClendon played two black Americans evicted from home by their respective wives. They traveled to Africa in search of true soul mates, only to find that the women made from their ribs were left behind at home. The musical was presented at Harlem's Lafayette Theatre in November 1926 for a limited run. The next year Amy Ashwood Garvey and Manning again collaborated on a second musical comedy, *Brown Sugar*, in which a brownskin girl is courted by two suitors – an Indian prince and an American mechanic – the comedy inherent in contrasting the lifestyles of the two beaux, especially when the scene shifts to India.

Partnered next with the comedian Syd Perrin, who had appeared in Leslie's 1926 *Blackbirds*, Manning traveled to Jamaica in May 1929, giving song and dance performances interlaced with comedy routines. The duo left Jamaica for Panama, Trinidad, and other Caribbean ports before returning to the United States. May 1934 found Manning in London, England, at the head of a vaudeville company called *Harlem Night Birds*, which may have been patterned on the American *Blackbirds* revue in which Florence Mills "charmed theatre-goers with her outstanding versatility."[8] While in London, Manning joined with Rudolph Dunbar in opening the Florence

Mills Social Parlour, a smart new nightclub on Carnaby Street, to honor the revered and recently deceased trouper.

When exactly Manning returned to the United States is uncertain but it was not until 1947 that he again ventured into production in New York, with *Caribbean Carnival*, a show billed as "the first calypso musical ever presented." Manning directed and, with Jamaican bandleader Adolph Thenstead, composed lyrics and music. Choreography was by Trinidad-born Pearl Primus and Claude Marchant, both of whom danced in the show. The simple plot concerned the efforts of a white photographer, played by Pamela Ward, to attend a voodoo ceremony in Trinidad. The first part consisted of different specialties leading to the ceremony, which occurred in the second part. With over fifty dancers and singers in gorgeous costumes the production was little more than an expensive revue.

After try-outs in Philadelphia and Boston, the show opened at the International Theatre on Broadway on 5 December and played for only eleven performances. Along with Manning, Primus, and Marchant, the cast featured the singer and dancer Josephine Premice of Haitian background, the calypsonian Duke of Iron (Cecil Anderson), the Trio Cubana, and others.[9] In his later career Manning, accompanied by Amy Ashwood Garvey, traveled to West Africa, where he not only performed but immersed himself in the culture of his African forebears. They visited Sierra Leone, Liberia, Nigeria, and Ghana where, in 1960, fatally afflicted with tuberculosis, Manning died and was buried. He had created, often in combination with other writers, a score of memorable songs and medleys that are his true memorial.

William Archibald was another Caribbean playwright from Trinidad who migrated to America in 1937 and became a dancer, singer, play director, and choreographer. At age 20 he enrolled at the Academy of Allied Arts in New York and studied dance under Sybil Shearer and Jose Limon, making his Broadway début as a principal in the revue *One For the Money* (1938). After appearing in several shows in Boston and New York as well as singing at the Blue Angel and other supper clubs, Archibald wrote the book and lyrics for *Carib Song* (1945), staged at the Adelphi Theatre by Mary Hunter with choreography by Katherine Dunham, who starred in the production. Also in the cast were Avon Long, Eartha Kitt, the Jamaican Elsie Benjamin, and the Dunham Dancers, among others. Dunham had spent over a year on site studying the dance, music, and folk ceremonies of the Caribbean, but apparently authenticity alone did not satisfy the critic Miles Jefferson, who found the dialogue trite, the music unoriginal, and the dances "pseudo-exotic and interminable."[10]

Over the next twelve years Archibald had four of his plays staged in New York theatres, as well as an opera, *Far Harbour* (1948), for which he wrote the libretto and also directed at Hunter College auditorium. Two of his plays were adapted from the writings of Henry James: *The Innocents* (1950), staged at the Playhouse, was taken from the short story "The Turn of the Screw," while *Portrait of a Lady* (1954) at the American National Theatre and Academy (ANTA) theatre, was dramatized from the novel of the same name. *The Innocents* was hugely successful, winning critic Brooks Atkinson's endorsement as "a perfectly wrought drama...adults can admire and enjoy."[11] Archibald also wrote the book and lyrics for *The Crystal Heart* (1957), which premiered at the Saville Theatre in London, England, and was revived three years later at the Seventy-Fourth Street Theatre in New York, directed and choreographed by the author.

Archibald's most abstract and macabre drama was *The Cantilevered Terrace* (1962). In it the author assembled a group of five close relatives and friends, who sit and talk, "speaking monologues of memory, reading aloud, attacking, suffering attacks. The talk is about love, hate, parents and children, death. The conversants decline to listen, decline to answer, decline to react [except when] they react in some context secret to them or to the playwright's mind."[12] Before the group gathers, one man asks his friend to kill his parents for him and after a while the friend agrees. Towards the end of the play the parents leave for their habitual evening walk along the cliff that overhangs the sea and the friend quietly follows. The play was directed by the author at New York's Forty-First Street Theatre. Archibald also wrote, with Truman Capote, the screenplay for *The Innocents*, for which they received in 1961 the Best Screenplay award from the Mystery Writers of America. Archibald died in New York at age 53 from infectious hepatitis.

William Archibald was one of the first Caribbean playwrights to have produced on American boards a number of straight plays that did not rely on song and dance for their interest. However, his plays did not portray Caribbean life. The next four productions, over a period of two decades (1943–63), returned to musical theatre in a Caribbean setting, not because they were more authentic but on account of the region's presumed exoticism. First of the four shows was *Early to Bed* (1943), with book and lyrics by George Marion Jr., music by Thomas "Fats" Waller, and situated in and around a Martinican brothel run by an ex-schoolteacher. Complications arise when the house is visited by celebrities and the Madam has to pretend it is really a finishing school for young ladies. Curiously, as observed elsewhere, there were only four Blacks in a primarily white-oriented cast.[13]

The production opened on Broadway on 17 June and played for 382 performances. Black critic Miles Jefferson gave the show short shrift when he called it "pictorially gorgeous but essentially dull and tasteless."[14] Even the music of "Fats" Waller was felt to be lackluster.

The second musical comedy of the period was by the novelist Truman Capote, who wrote a story that he later converted into the musical *House of Flowers* (1954). It is a good example of theatre with a Caribbean locale, having its entire production team – playwright and lyricist, composer, director, choreographer, setting, costume, and lighting designers – all highly reputable and white while the cast were all colored.[15] The West Indian island is unnamed but it could be Haiti during the Mardi Gras festival, and this time there were two competing bordellos run respectively by Mme. Fleur (whose girls were named after flowers) and Mme. Tango (whose girls had other propensities). Fleur's business was in jeopardy due to an outbreak of mumps, while her rival's house enjoyed the custom of visiting sailors. How Fleur solved her problems by routing Tango and reclaiming her patronage shaped a plot that was supposed to be entertaining.

The production occupied the Alvin Theatre on Broadway on 30 December and ran for 165 performances. Its sterling cast, led by Pearl Bailey as Mme. Fleur and Juanita Hall as Mme. Tango, included five Trinidad performers: the dancer and choreographer Geoffrey Holder and, probably a first on Broadway, a steel band ensemble of four comprising Austin Stoker, Rod Clavery, Albert Popwell, and Michael Alexander. Josephine Premice was the one person of Haitian ancestry in the cast. Critic Miles Jefferson considered the show opulent and earthy, with a simple, appealing love story; yet there were "flaws in good taste – was it necessary to show young boys working up a sexual lather in a house of ill-fame, or... having a representative of the law emerge from it buckling his suspenders and putting on his coat?"[16] In a 1968 revival, black critic Clayton Riley found the script "woefully inadequate... Capote fails to create a single character of any dimension." Premice, playing Mme. Fleur in the revival, managed "to squeeze something out of the worst lines, particularly in songs."[17]

Jamaica (1957) was the third musical of the period with a Caribbean setting. The text was by E. Y. Harburg and Fred Saidy with lyrics by Harburg. Music was in the capable hands of Harold Arlen, and Robert Lewis directed. As with *House of Flowers*, the originators, designers, and director were all white. The actors, however, due to a casting problem, turned out to be interracial, at least among the principals. The script was meant as a folk play for Harry Belafonte, whose illness caused his withdrawal from rehearsals.

Replacements were considered but eventually the part was rewritten for Lena Horne with a suntanned Ricardo Montalban as her leading man. The story line had some legitimacy for an island setting. Koli, a poor fisherman, is in love with Savannah, who wants to get to New York where life is modern and exciting. A young hustler arrives and is willing to take her there. In a dream sequence she visits the metropolis but when her brother, caught in a hurricane, is rescued by Koli, she decides to remain in Jamaica. The production at the Imperial Theatre on Broadway opened on 31 October and played for 558 performances. It proved a triumph for Ms. Horne, who was universally hailed by the critics: Richard Watts Jr. in the *New York Post* called her "one of the incomparable performers of our time." Others in the cast included Ossie Davis, Adelaide Hall, Josephine Premice – "a fresh and vastly engaging talent"[18] – with leading dancers Alvin Ailey and Christyne Lawson.

The last musical of the period under discussion was *Ballad for Bimshire* (1963). Set in Barbados (familiarly called "Bimshire"), it was significantly different from the previous three shows as the principal author, composer, and lyricist was Irving Burgie, whose mother was Barbadian and who was well acquainted with the island. Associated with Burgie in writing the script was the experienced playwright, essayist, and theatre historian, Loften Mitchell. The director was Ed Cambridge and Talley Beatty choreographed. The subject matter was likewise different from the musical's antecedents for, although merely a simple love story between a teenage girl and an American playboy, according to encyclopedist Bernard Peterson, "Scenes of island life and customs are presented . . . and important questions of colonialism, racism, and nationalism are also raised."[19] Moreover the musical, which was financed mainly by Blacks, was produced off-Broadway at the Mayfair Theatre (located in the Paramount Hotel's basement), where it opened on 15 October and played for seventy-four performances. In 1978 a revised script was produced in Cleveland, Ohio, under the title *Calalou* (*sic*).

Josephine Premice, whose parents had come from Haiti, was born in Brooklyn in 1926. She attended Columbia University and the New School for Social Research, but, primarily interested in theatre and dance, she studied with Martha Graham and Katherine Dunham. Ms. Premice started her career as a singer and dancer, appearing at The Village Vanguard and The Blue Angel for some years. She was only 17 when she appeared at New York's Carnegie Hall in a dance festival; two years later she bowed onto Broadway in *Blue Holiday* (1945), a variety show at the Belasco Theatre featuring Ethel Waters and the folk singer Josh White. From this point on and for the next thirty years, apart from periods when she lived in Europe, Ms. Premice graced the New York stage with skill and vitality, whether in musical theatre or straight drama. Apart from the musicals already mentioned,[20] other productions in which she appeared include *Mr. Johnson* (1956), an adaptation by Norman Rosten of Joyce Carey's novel on life in colonial Africa. Directed by Robert Lewis at Broadway's Martin Beck Theatre, the play featured an up-and-coming Earle Hyman in the title role. Ms. Premice was also "extremely effective in her freewheeling deliveries" in *A Hand is on the Gate* (1966), a program of selections from black poetry and folk music arranged and directed by Roscoe Lee Browne at the Longacre Theatre.[21] Off-Broadway Ms. Premice appeared in *The Blacks*, *The Cherry Orchard*, *Electra*, and was one of two actors in Philip Hayes Dean's short melodrama *This Bird of Dawning Singeth All Night Long* (1974) at the Actors' Studio, New York. She also took part in Loften Mitchell's *Bubbling Brown Sugar* (1976–77), a musical journey featuring the best-known songs of black composers, lyricists, and singers. One of her last stage appearances occurred in 1982, when she played the title role in *The Mind of Danielle Edwards* at the American Place Theatre in New York.

Through the mid-century I have focused attention on musical theatre as the medium chosen to represent the Caribbean on the American stage. It was the form used at the time to promote a touristic view of the region as comprising happy-go-lucky surf-and-sand islanders when to the natives themselves life was no less complex there than elsewhere. There was, of course, another type of theatre that more accurately reflected Caribbean life of the period, and it is time now to discuss that literary drama.

In 1951, Edgar Mittelholzer, a Guyanese living in London, England, published a bizarre novel, *Shadows Move Among Them*, about a white missionary and his two daughters who live an unconventional life of freedom in the jungle paradise of Guyana. They are visited by a mentally unstable young man who is gradually healed by the idyllic life, even as his bitter cynicism begins to infect those around him. The novel so intrigued American playwright Moss Hart that he secured permission to adapt it for the stage.[22] Under its new title, *Climate of Eden*, the dramatized version of the novel opened at the Martin Beck Theatre in November 1952 and eked out twenty performances. The major critics, respectful of veteran playwright-cum-director Hart, were divided in their reviews: "original and absorbing play...directed with force and distinction" wrote one; "fascinating and beautiful" chimed another; but "more irritating than fascinating...a repulsive lot" fumed a third; and a fourth found the tormented man "a distasteful and uncommunicative case history." When years later, in November 1978, the Reverend Jim Jones and his cult of worshippers in the Guyanese hinterland performed mass suicide, it all seemed strangely familiar to Mittelholzer readers.[23] Then, on 6 May 1965 when Mittelholzer, author of twenty-four novels and several unproduced plays, immolated himself in a field near his country home in Surrey, England, due it is alleged to "despondency over his art," a chapter closed on the life of an extraordinary Caribbean man and writer.

Errol John was another of the literary playwrights from the Caribbean to be domiciled in London. Born in Trinidad, he was cofounder (with Errol G. Hill) of the Whitehall Players and from the outset became its leading actor. In 1950 he went to England as a guest of the British Council and while there performed several roles, including Haemon in Sophocles' *Antigone* (1951) and the title role in Derek Walcott's *Henri Christophe* (1952), both directed by Hill at the Hans Crescent student center in London. The next year, when John toured England as Lester with the American Negro Theatre's production of *Anna Lucasta* and then appeared in *Cry, the Beloved Country* at St. Martin-in-the-Fields, London, his professional acting career was launched. John had also shown promise as a dramatist before leaving Trinidad and in 1957 he won the London *Observer* playwriting contest with his major play, *Moon on a Rainbow Shawl*. Set in a crowded Port-of-Spain (Trinidad) barrack yard, where a small house and several single rooms jostle each other, the play presented a motley group of characters who struggle to make a living in the post-World War Two era. It premiered in London in 1958 and was presented off-Broadway in 1962 with a sterling cast that included Vinnette Carroll in an Obie-winning performance as Sophia Adams, James Earl Jones, Cicely Tyson, Ellen Holly, and others. The play was widely produced around the world. John had an active career as a stage, television, and film actor; he continued to write scripts for the stage and television, and in 1967 he published three screenplays, but none of his later work attained the enormous and enduring success of *Moon*.

In recognition of his work with the Whitehall Players, Errol G. Hill in 1949 received a British Council scholarship to the Royal Academy of Dramatic Art in London, England. In 1953 he was appointed drama tutor in the extramural department at the then University (College) of the West Indies (UWI) in Jamaica.[24] Hill traveled throughout the Anglo-Caribbean, promoting drama and theatre through lectures, classes, summer schools, directing, and organizing relevant workshops. In all, Hill served the UWI for some eight years, first as drama tutor then as creative arts tutor, during which time he started the collection, editing, and printing of the Caribbean Plays Series that was adopted and expanded by UWI's extramural department (now the School of Continuing Studies) in Trinidad under its indefatigable director Esmond Ramesar. In 1958 Hill received a Rockefeller Foundation fellowship to the Yale School of Drama,[25] and later was given leave to accept the foundation's offer of a secondment to the School of Drama, University of Ibadan, Nigeria, from 1965 to 1967, to strengthen the faculty at an institution receiving foundation support.

As a playwright, Hill has written and produced eight one-act plays, a major folk musical comedy, and two open-air carnival extravaganzas. Of the shorter plays, *Strictly Matrimony*, a satire on society do-gooders in Jamaica, was staged in New Haven, Connecticut, in 1959, while *Dance Bongo*, a verse play centered on the ritual dance at "dead-wake" ceremonies in Trinidad, received multiple productions. It showed at New York University in December 1965; in San Francisco by the Aldridge Players/West in 1967; and by the Morehouse-Spelman Players at Spelman College, Atlanta, in 1970, with a revival for that year's Atlanta University summer theatre that featured "Plays from the Caribbean." The season included *Terminus* by Dennis Scott of Jamaica and *Malcochon* by Derek Walcott of St. Lucia. Directing the summer session was Professor Baldwin Burroughs of Spelman College, Atlanta, Georgia. Hill's major play entitled *Man Better Man* (the name of an island herb believed capable of instilling magical powers) is written in rhymed calypso verse and is about Trinidad stickfighters and an obeahman (sorcerer) who seeks to dupe them. With traditional choruses and original songs by Hill, the play was professionally produced in 1969 by the Negro Ensemble Company, New York, directed by Douglas Turner Ward.[26] Hill concluded his teaching career at Dartmouth College in Hanover, New Hampshire, where he served in the drama department from 1968 to 1989.

The 1960s and 1970s witnessed the rise of modest, independent theatre organizations; several in the New York City area provided production opportunities for playwrights of Caribbean heritage or persuasion. Examples of these entities were the Judson Poets' Theater and La MaMa Experimental Theatre Club, both formed in 1961. More important toward the end of the decade, the Negro Ensemble Company (NEC), occupying the St. Marks Playhouse, and the O'Neill Theater Centre's playwrights' conference in Waterford, Connecticut, helped promote the work of dramatists from the Caribbean. Joseph Papp's New York Shakespeare Festival (NYSF) and Public Theatre had been in existence since 1954 and, in accord with his perceived goal to bring the best theatre of all types to the culturally deprived,

Figure 28. The obeahman (Bill Cook) charms the young stickfighter (Phil Kaufman) as medium Minee Woopsa (Diane Cobb) looks on. A scene from Errol Hill's *Man Better Man*, presented at Dartmouth College, 1975

Figure 29. Derek Walcott

Papp made a special effort to open several theatre spaces he controlled to Caribbean playwrights.[27]

Renowned as a poet and recipient in 1992 of the Nobel Prize in Literature (most prestigious of his several literary awards), Derek Walcott also ranks as a major West Indian dramatist, having produced a substantial roster of plays. He is also a play director, scene designer, and serves on the faculty of Boston University. Born in St. Lucia with twin brother Roderick in 1930, Walcott by age 20 had published two slim volumes of poetry and an historical verse play, *Henri Christophe* (1950), about the self-proclaimed Haitian king who had been a slave. In 1953 he obtained an arts degree from UWI in Jamaica and, after a short period teaching at secondary schools, he became a journalist, writing mainly about the arts and theatre while continuing to compose poetry and plays. At college he had been active in the dramatic society and he maintained contact with that group and with the newly formed Federal Theatre Company that in 1957 produced at the Ward Theatre in Kingston his Greek-style play, *Ione*, about warring hill tribes on the island of St. Lucia.

These were heady times for the Anglophone Caribbean islands, which had agreed to form the West Indies Federation. Walcott was invited to write a pageant as the centerpiece of the inaugural ceremonies, to be held in April 1958 in Trinidad, host country for the Federation's headquarters. Although after four years the federal experiment failed, beginning with the withdrawal of Jamaica, Walcott's open-air pageant, *Drums and Colours*, to which member states assigned personnel, gave him regional, even international exposure. From among the pageant actors Walcott decided to form an acting company, the Trinidad Theatre Workshop (TTW), and set off on a Rockefeller Foundation fellowship to prepare for his new role as playwright and director by observing for a year the operations of small independent theatre companies in New York.[28]

Walcott's first known production in the United States was a one-acter called *Journand; or, A Comedy Until the Last Minute*, which was presented in 1962 at the Judson Poets' Theater in New York. It concerned the disposal of a coffin acquired by vagrants, one of whom imitates an act of resurrection. Next came *Malcochon; or, The Six in the Rain*, another one-acter clearly inspired by the Japanese film *Rashomon* and set on a coconut estate in St. Lucia. It was presented in 1969 by the NEC at St. Marks Playhouse in New York. This production was merely a prelude for Walcott's major play, *Dream on Monkey Mountain*, which the NEC would offer next season. Walcott has characterized the play as "a dream . . . illogical, derivative, contradictory . . . It is best treated as a physical poem with all the subconscious and deliberate borrowings of poetry."[29] The drama centers on a woodcutter, Makak, who leaves his hut in the hills and descends to the town in pursuit of a dream.

Walcott was invited to present the play in its formative stage and using his original TTW cast at the National Playwrights Conference in Waterford, Connecticut, after which it would inhabit the Mark Taper Forum in Los Angeles, under the imaginative director Michael Schultz. However, the

Actors' Equity Association (AEA) opposed the use of non-AEA actors in a professional production at the Forum, and, despite special pleading by Walcott on behalf of TTW actors, the AEA refused to budge. Actually, the play was well served by the American actors – Roscoe Lee Browne as Makak and Ron O'Neal as Corporal Lestrade. When the production moved to the St. Mark's Playhouse in March 1971 it had been finely honed and won for the NEC an Obie award as the most distinguished foreign play off-Broadway in the 1970/71 season. Other American showings took place in 1974 at the White Barn Festival Theatre in Greenwich, Connecticut, directed by Walcott, and in 1976 at the Center Stage, Baltimore, under the direction of TTW's Albert Laveau.

With *Dream* Walcott became a name to be reckoned with in literary drama in America and new productions followed. *Ti Jean and His Brothers*, a folk play in which three brothers separately contest with the Devil, was a clear favorite. The play, directed by Errol G. Hill, was staged at the Hopkins Center, Dartmouth College, in May 1971; in the summer of 1972 it was directed by Walcott himself for the NYSF, with Laveau as the Devil, when it toured the five New York City boroughs on a mobile unit. In 1974 *Ti Jean* was presented by the Courtyard Players at the Dorsch Center, St. Croix, US Virgin Islands. This group commissioned a new Walcott play that premiered under his direction in April 1977. Entitled *Remembrance*, it was meant to acknowledge the great teachers of Walcott's youth. Joe Papp's NYSF included the play in their 1978/79 New York season. The script was published with another of Walcott's popular plays, the comedic two-hander *Pantomime*, which parodies the Robinson Crusoe–Man Friday relationship. The action takes place in a gazebo on the grounds of a hotel in Tobago (Crusoe's isle) and near the edge of a cliff. The two characters are the English hotel owner and his black handyman. This play has had different productions at Chicago's Goodman Theatre in 1983, at the Arena Stage in Washington, DC, and elsewhere. Walcott directed it at his Boston Playwrights' Theatre in 1994.

There is limited discussion of Walcott's plays to productions in the United States or its Caribbean territories. In 1974, for instance, the Mark Taper Forum staged *The Charlatan* directed by Mel Shapiro and for the first time scored by the composer Galt MacDermot (who wrote the music for *Hair*). He would join the team for other shows, such as the new musical *Marie Laveau* (1979) set in New Orleans and directed by Walcott in St. Thomas, US Virgin Islands, with an American cast. Other specialized collaborators recruited by Walcott for his productions were Richard

Montgomery as set designer and Carol La Chapelle from Trinidad as chore-ographer.

Three of Walcott's productions of the 1990s were seriously flawed and one of them was aborted. In 1991 the American Repertory Theatre produced *Steel*, a tribute to the steel band movement of Trinidad, at the Hasty Pud-ding Theatre on the Harvard University campus. As so often with Walcott's premieres, the play seemed murky and not quite ready for public viewing. Then in 1994 the Arena Theatre in Washington, DC, presented Walcott's three-hour verse play *The Odyssey*, adapted from Homer. Here too, despite the use of a blind, guitar-playing, and dreadlocked narrator, the epic was somewhat "incoherent" and not helped by being staged in the round. Fi-nally, Walcott's 1998 arrival on Broadway as coauthor and lyricist with Paul Simon for the musical *Capeman* was by most accounts an $11 million flop at the Marquis Theatre, which even the skillful touch of a hastily recruited experienced American director could not redeem. Walcott, however, is a fastidious writer with a penchant for reworking his plays, whether as scripts or as productions, giving them new life and new titles. There is every hope that these latest lapses will eventually emerge in forms befitting a gifted and committed Caribbean poet and playwright.[30]

One of the more absurd incidents arising from the late 1960s black protest movement in America involved the Trinidad-born Lennox Raphael and his play *Che*, named after the Cuban revolutionary, Ché Guevara. On 24 March 1969 the actors, director, and playwright were arrested by the Public Morals Police Squad of New York City and charged on fifty-four counts of consen-sual sodomy, public lewdness, and obscenity. The off-Broadway production was shut down. The figure of United States President Lyndon Johnson sit-ting on a toilet in one scene was felt to be especially objectionable.[31] The production was reopened after a judge ruled that the play was protected under the First Amendment as political speech. Raphael claimed that ques-tionable actions in his play were merely symbolic, that they represented a strident sociopolitical protest against the war in Vietnam and other puni-tive government policies. But there is little doubt that the prurient scenes and legal proceedings were largely responsible for the play's notoriety and quite obscured any redeeming value it might have had as a vehement protest against a most unpopular and costly war.

Edgar White ranks among the more original playwrights of the Black Arts Movement during the 1960s and beyond. He was born in 1947 on Montserrat, one of the smaller Leeward Islands in the Caribbean, and was taken to New York at the age of 5, yet he identifies himself as a West Indian dramatist. White is also a fiction writer, a musician, and a composer. He gained a Bachelor of Arts degree from New York University, attended the Yale School of Drama for two years (1971–73), and has written well over twenty-five plays, most of which have been produced in the United States or in London, England. White's first production, *The Mummer's Play* (1969), was a fantasy in fifteen scenes in which a retired sculptor and a young poet – symbolic Harlem characters – discuss the plight of the black artist. It was presented at the NYSF Public Theatre, which staged the next six of White's productions, several of them one-act plays. Examples of these are *The Life and Times of J. Walter Smintheus* (1971), an allegory in which a black intellectual loses his sense of self in attempting to adopt an alien culture, and *Les Femmes Noires* (1974), which portrays vignettes from the lives of black women.

White's *The Burghers of Calais* (1971) took its title from the Rodin statuary that memorialized the slaughter of the Huguenots in the seventeenth century. White's play, however, was based on the 1931 tragedy of the nine Scottsboro Boys, who were wrongly accused and jailed for raping two white prostitutes in a railway car. Many years later White revisited this tragedy in his blues opera based on the court trial and entitled *Ghosts: Live from Galilee*. With music by Genji Ito and directed by George Ferenz, the opera was presented at La MaMa's Experimental Theatre Club on 11–28 February 1999 in honor of African American History Month. In 1975 White wrote a partly biographical play called *Lament for Rastafari*, about a West Indian family who leave their island home for London, England. Staged first at the NYSF Public Theatre, this play was also seen at the Billie Holiday Theatre in Brooklyn and in 1977 at La MaMa Experimental Theatre Club. White tested his play *The Defense* (1976) at the Eugene O'Neill Memorial Theater Center (where new plays were given staged readings for critical review under the guidance of Lloyd Richards) before bowing to the public at the New Federal Theatre in New York, with music composed by White. The plot concerns a young West Indian guard at a housing project who, troubled by nightmares of impending death, conducts a defense of his life.

White has stated that for him the best theatre is "religious" and that all his plays are rituals of one sort or another.[32] In 1987 he opted to give Barbados the world premiere of his important play *I, Marcus Garvey (and the Captivity of Babylon)*, which was directed by Earl Warner in the Frank Collymore Hall, Bridgetown, for sixteen performances. Three years later the play received a stage reading at the United Nations in New York and a production the next year by the Caribbean Arts Festival Ensemble (CAFE), who also produced

White's *The Generation* and a new play for dance entitled *Orfeo in a Night World* directed by Charles Turner. Theatre historian Mance Williams has written: "Edgar White has managed to evade the clutches of genre and ethnic categorizing." Although White has written realistic dramas on racial problems, he has also used theatre of the absurd, the *lazzi* of *commedia dell'arte*, and the presentational style of English medieval plays, all designed to focus attention on the racial condition as essentially a human condition.[33]

Another playwright from the Leeward Islands is Antigua-born Gus Edwards, who grew up in St. Thomas, US Virgin Islands. At age 20 Edwards moved to New York City to study and work in the theatre. In 1977 he became resident playwright with the NEC, which produced three of his plays in the 1977/78 season. *The Offering* (1977), depicts a young hired killer who tries without success to bribe his down-and-out mentor to commit the crime. *Black Body Blues* (1978) presented a one-time boxer and his angry brother, a dope-pusher. The pugilist works for a kind, white man whom the pusher shoots in order, as he says, to liberate his brother from a master–slave relationship. This play received a staged reading at the O'Neill Theater Centre's National Playwrights Conference in June 1977 prior to its production by the NEC the following year. *Old Phantoms* (1978) revealed the effect on his three children of a domineering father after his death and the death of their mother in childbirth. Edwards wrote several more plays, but only one of them, *Ramona* (1986), was set in the Caribbean. It portrayed a woman free of restraining inhibitions and was staged by the NEC. Edwards' dramatization for PBS Films of James Baldwin's novel *Go Tell it on the Mountain* was telecast in 1985.

Steve Carter is a playwright of Caribbean heritage whose mother came from Trinidad. He has emphasized this connection by writing a "Caribbean Trilogy" of plays among his works. Carter majored in art at the High School of Music and Art in New York, hoping to become a scene designer. He gained further design experience working for the American Community Theatre under Antigua-born Maxwell Glanville. The first play in his trilogy, *Eden* (1976), dramatized the love of a West Indian girl for an African American youth against the wishes of her authoritarian, Garveyite father. The drama was produced by the NEC, where Carter served from 1968 for thirteen years in a number of different positions, as costume designer, production coordinator, and playwright-in-residence. His drama *Eden* won an AUDELCO award for Best Play of the Year.

Second in the trilogy of plays was *Nevis Mountain Dew* (1979), set in a West Indian household in Queens, New York, where family and friends gather to celebrate the fiftieth birthday of the family head, who lives in an iron lung. As the celebrants imbibe home-brewed West Indian rum ("mountain dew"), their anxieties are exposed and the patient begs them to unplug the machine in order to release him and themselves from further agony. The NEC staged this work, which was also done at the Arena Stage in Washington, DC. In the third and final play of the series, *Dame Lorraine* (1981), members of a dysfunctional West Indian family in Harlem await the return of the only surviving son, who has been in prison for a quarter-century. As the strain of waiting mounts, feelings of love and hatred are exposed. The play was first produced at the Victory Gardens Theatre in Chicago in March 1981 and had a six-week billing at the Los Angeles Actors' Theatre in January–February 1982. Carter has spoken of an underlying tension that in his view has existed in relationships between West Indians and black Americans. He explained: "West Indians are proud; other Blacks think they're high-falutin'."[34]

Similarly, Brooklyn-born Clifford Mason revealed his Caribbean roots by writing a series of plays about Jamaica. Known also as an actor, director, teacher, and critic, Mason has been active in all of these professions. At least three of his plays deal with an affluent middle- or upper-class Jamaican family caught in a changing political climate as the island moves toward self-government and the working-class vote becomes crucially important in national elections. Examples of these plays are *The Verandah* (1978), which was produced off off-Broadway at the Gene Frankel Theatre, *Time Out Of Time* (1980), first staged by the Black Theatre Alliance (BTA) in New York and later by the New Federal Theatre in November 1986, and *Half-Way Tree Brown* (1972), for which no production is recorded. Other Jamaican plays by Mason include the farce-comedy *Captain at Cricket* (1982), staged at Brooklyn College's Gershwin Theatre in August–September 1983, which derided the bedroom affairs of an island cricketer, *Royal Oak*, played by a Caribbean theatre group at Long Island University's Triangle Theatre in June 1987, *Return to Guy's Hill* (1981) and *The Boxing Day Parade* (1983), both identified by the author as Caribbean plays but with no available production record. Together these titles represent about half the number of plays attributed to Clifford Mason.

In the mid-1970s a new organization called the Caribbean American Repertory Theatre (CART) was formed to promote on the New York stage aspiring and talented actors and playwrights from the Caribbean. Leading the group were Trinidad-born Neville Richen, artistic director, and Olivier Stephenson from Jamaica as executive director. Located initially in the heart of West Indian culture on Eastern Parkway, Brooklyn, the group began with a budget of $5,000, which was increased to $20,000 by the New York State Council for the Arts. Despite good reviews CART-sponsored shows, often performed in clubs, community centers, church halls, and occasionally in small theatres, had difficulty building a strong, supportive audience.

By the end of its fourth season, in spring 1979, CART reported successful productions of the following plays: *A Trinity of Four* and *Fog Drifts in the Spring*, two one-act plays by Lennox Brown from Trinidad; *Sweet Talk* and *Alterations* by Michael Abbensetts from Guyana, then resident in London;[35] and *Journey Through Babylon*, a ritual fantasy based on the poems of Olivier Stephenson and dealing with the experiences of a Caribbean man in New York. The production was conceived and directed by Arlene Quiyou of Trinidad. For its next season, 1979/80, CART offered two presentations. The first consisted of a pair of plays entitled *The Roomer* and *The Visitor* by Amirh Bahati (Patricia Roberts), followed by *Shango de Ima*, subtitled *a Yoruba Mystery Play*, in which gods and goddesses determine man's destiny. Written by the Cuban playwright Pepe Carril with English adaptation by Susan Sherman, the play was performed by La Mama Dance Drama Workshop and was directed by Richen.

A hiatus exists in the record of CART's activities between 1980 and 1985. Stephenson had left the organization and although Richen apparently carried on as artistic director, it is unclear whether or not his theatre work during this period was under CART's auspices. In May 1986, however, a revival occurred when CART presented a mini-festival of *Eight Plays from the Rest of America* at the New Theatre on East Fourth Street, Manhattan. The plays, all one-acts, included a reprise of *Revolution* by Stephenson and the only known production by CART of a play written by Roderick Walcott called *The Trouble with Albino Joe*. The latter was one of two plays directed by Richen; the only other director of two plays on the program being Jeffrey Anderson-Gunter from Jamaica. An actor and director, Gunter would assume control of CART for the next few years until he moved to Los Angeles and the mantel fell to a new artistic director and actor, Rudolph Shaw from Guyana. Following the one-act play festival, CART offered in October 1986 Derek Walcott's *Beef, No Chicken*, a slight and static comedy set in 1960s Trinidad. It traced a family's resistance to "industrial development" in the form of a new highway that is being constructed through their district, accompanied by illegal payments to the parties involved. In 1987 Stephenson returned briefly to straighten out affairs at CART and directed

Stafford (Ashani) Harrison's *West Indian Play*, described as "a cantankerous comedy," which played for eight performances at the Paul Robeson Theatre in Brooklyn.

With Stephenson's departure to Jamaica, Shaw became CART's executive director. A resident of Queens, New York, from where he has conducted the group's business, Shaw is a regular employee at the United Nations (UN) headquarters in Manhattan. This position has facilitated contact with influential Caribbean representatives and made possible CART's use of the UN Library auditorium for appropriate cultural events. In 1988 Shaw held a fund-raiser at the Lincoln Center Neighborhood Theatre at which excerpts from several Caribbean plays were enacted. In February the next year CART joined in presenting at the UN Library the play *Masquerade* by Ian Valz, directed by Fred Tyson. It formed part of the celebrations marking Guyana's nineteenth anniversary as a cooperative republic. In May the company revived two short plays from the "Rest of America" festival and played them at a regional high school in Aberdeen, New Jersey.

The 1990s brought a resurgent CART strengthened by the addition of Jemma Redman (Trinidad) as new artistic director. Redman arranged another "Evening with the Company" at the UN Library hall, featuring Caribbean and African American poetry and African dance. These "evenings" carried different titles.[36] They permitted cast members to express themselves creatively in settings more intimate (and less costly) than a formal theatre or a public assembly hall. One of the truly original presentations was a musical comedy monologue called *Tillie*, written and performed by the late Rita Madero of the Dominican Republic. Unmasking a Caribbean woman's quest for the American dream through marriage to an ageing, rich, white male, Ms. Madero's recital was first presented in 1990 at the Ernie Martin Theatre in New York and revived a year later at a high school in Queens. Another innovation of the new leadership was the use on its programs of nonblack plays such as Edward Albee's *The Zoo Story* and Peter Shaffer's *The Public Eye*. In 1996 Shaw directed the radio play *Sweet Karaila* by Wordsworth MacAndrew of Guyana. It examined the relationship between African and Indian Guyanese in the 1950s and was aired on FM radio on several occasions. Then, in 1998, Redman presented a staged reading at the Victoria 5 Theatre in Harlem of *To Live With Hamlet* by Ronald John of Trinidad and Tobago.

To end the decade, the century, and the millennium, CART mounted the play *My Children! My Africa!* by South African Athol Fugard at the Henry Street Settlement in Manhattan and at a high school in Queens. A debate, moderated by an old-fashioned black teacher, occurs between a black male student who aspires to become a freedom fighter and a white female student who opts for peaceful progress through education. Implicitly the question was posed: which route will the new South Africa take? CART's future was also in question. Its focus had widened; apparently it no longer concentrated strictly on Caribbean theatre.[37] Normally, CART will mount one or two plays a year to be presented, under contract, at public libraries or schools in the borough of Queens and it has promoted popular events such as a calypso evening to raise funds to meet operating expenses. For its leadership, administering the group is essentially a labor of love relieved only by the opportunity to perform.

In 1995 Anderson-Gunter formed in Los Angeles a west coast branch known as CART/West. He directed Walcott's *Beef, No Chicken* for the new group's début and won the Drama-Logue award for best director. CART/West's second production was Errol John's *Moon on a Rainbow Shawl*. It was presented at the Lee Strasberg Creative Center, where Anna Strasberg, executive director and Lee's widow, provided facilities and staff for the show, which played intermittently in the summer and fall of 1996. In spring 2000 the team performed a modern passion play, *The Rope and the Cross*, written by Easton Lee of Jamaica and directed by Anderson-Gunter. CART/West has normally comprised about a dozen core actors from the Caribbean via New York, among whom are several, such as Leon Morenzie, Austin Stoker, Claudia Robinson, and Gunter himself, who have had noteworthy careers in theatre and film.

At times playwrights would form their own acting companies, which might exist in theory only until a production gets under way, when the company would be given a name or might be used to sponsor the show. Three writers took advantage of this option. Sullivan Walker won a trip to New York in 1969 as his prize in a Trinidad talent contest. A schoolteacher with a penchant for the stage, Walker settled in Harlem, attended auditions, and was eventually cast in *A Season in the Congo* at the Harlem School of the Arts. When the production closed, Walker began to write and perform one-man shows, forming by 1973 the Caribbean Experience Theatre in Brooklyn, of which he was artistic director. From 1973 to 1985 he staged some eight productions in churches, community centers, and even at a "disco space" in Brooklyn. Among his play titles were *Black Macbeth* (1973), *Black Woman* (1974 and 1983), *The Journey*, a monologue (1977), *Two Soldiers at a Crossroads* (1978), about a Black Power uprising on a Caribbean island, *Requiem for Ah Pan Mastah* (1981), celebrating a steel band player, and *Boy Days* (1985), a series of sketches about the author's childhood in the Caribbean. Walker moved to Los Angeles "about ten years ago," where he appeared in several movies and television shows. In April 2000 he returned to New York and has been offering acting workshops at Space 24 in Manhattan, based on his experiences of the stage, television, and the movies.[38]

Paul Webster founded the Barbados Theatre Workshop about the time he produced his folk comedy *Under the Duppy Parasol* (1975), which played at the Harlem Cultural Center, then at Baruch College of the City University of New York, and later at the Billie Holiday Theatre in Brooklyn. His next play, *Sea Rock Children is Strong Children* (1982), with lyrics and music by Ricardo Cadogan, was set in a red-light district of Barbados and produced after the group had acquired a new name, the Caribbean Theatre of the Performing Arts. First presented at the Paul Robeson Theatre in Brooklyn, *Sea Rock* moved to the Billie Holiday Theatre and the New Federal Theatre in 1984. Upon Webster's untimely death, leadership of the group passed to Wayne McDonald from Jamaica, who became the new artistic director. Carlos E. Russell of Panama also formed a group to stage his plays. Called the African Diasporan Theatre, its folksy productions proved to be popular, with titles such as *Pappyshow and Monkeyshines*, *Love Lies*, and *Momma's Baby*. To those who would discredit theatre at the level suggested by these titles, Russell contends that "we reach more Caribbean people because we're attempting to tell the truth."[39]

Prolific Trinidad playwright Lennox Brown migrated to Canada in 1956 and gained a BA in journalism and an MFA in literature. He worked on a newspaper and as magazine journalist, and was a producer for the Canadian Broadcasting Corporation. He published poetry and plays in Canadian and London periodicals. In the National One-Act Playwriting Contest held in Ottawa, Brown won the first prize three times and the second prize once in the four-year period 1965–68. He also gained awards for his longer plays and has had his work produced on stage and for television. He moved to the United States prior to March 1972, when his play *A Ballet Behind the Bridge* was produced by the NEC at their St. Marks Playhouse under the direction of Douglas Turner Ward. Two brothers, one a scholar and the other a criminal, are contrasted, their essential difference being somehow a result of European colonial history as revealed in flashbacks. That summer Brown had another of his plays, *Prodigal in Black Stone*, presented in a stage reading at the National Playwrights Conference in Waterford, Connecticut. The prodigal is a West Indian who returns home to face an embittered mother after the death of his father.

In *Sisterhood of a Spring Night* (1974) shown at the Queen's College Theatre in New York, three black women living in Canada fail to find satisfying male companionship. Two of the prizewinning one-acters – *The Trinity of Four* and *Fog Drifts in the Spring* – were staged at New York's IRT Loft Theatre in 1975 and at the Billie Holiday Theatre in Brooklyn in February 1976. The former play shows how a planned revolt is betrayed by an infirm slave in exchange for freedom; the latter describes an encounter in Paris between a Trinidad taxi driver and a black American sailor that ends in murder. *Devil Mas'* (1976), a ritualized interpretation of the Trinidad carnival as a powerful antidote to church dominance, had its premiere at the Arena Theatre of Karamu House in Cleveland, Ohio, and was also produced at Dartmouth College, Hanover, New Hampshire, in 1987. *The Winti Train* (1977) played at the Billie Holiday Theatre and at the University of Hartford, Connecticut. Passengers on a train bound for Harlem are excited to participate in a Black World Festival when news spreads that two festival members plan to blow up the train. In the one-acter *The Twilight Dinner* (1977–78), played both at the IRT Loft Theatre and by the NEC at St. Marks Playhouse, two middle-aged Blacks reminisce about their militant college days and wonder whether they have had any effect on a complacent society. "I write about injustices," Lennox Brown is quoted as saying, "this is my form of protest."[40]

In the Trinidad carnival season of 1956 the Mighty Sparrow (Slinger Francisco) sang one of his most famous calypsos, "Jean and Dinah." These ladies from the city of Port-of-Spain were part of a clutch of prostitutes left stranded when American army and naval bases on the island closed at the end of the Second World War. Then in 1994 playwright Tony Hall, working with the actors Rhoma Spencer and Penelope Spencer, sought to give voice to the two women by creating a situation where they are older, poorer, and Dinah is ailing. Jean visits her on carnival morning; they revive memories but fail to relive past glories. The play, directed by Hall, was widely successful in Trinidad and overseas, despite reservations on the too-frequent use of profanity in the name of authenticity. Performances in America with the original cast and director were held in 1998 at the Goodwin Theatre of Trinity College, Hartford, Connecticut, at Colgate University in Hamilton, New York, and at the Aristocrat Manor in Brooklyn, New York, when more than two thousand people attended.

Jamaica, largest and most populous of the English-speaking Caribbean islands, has nourished a tradition of indigenous theatre since the storytelling days of the Murray family – a father and two sons – in the late nineteenth century. But when the senior Murray went to Boston to perform, the visit was aborted because he could not pay the American manager £30 (at the time about $150) in advance of bookings.[41] In the 1920s the conviction and imprisonment of Marcus Garvey in America, and his subsequent deportation back to Jamaica, may have made Jamaican theatre people reluctant to seek production opportunities in the United States. For them, London, England, was the haven of choice. West Indians went to England for higher education or professional training and, after World War Two, to help rebuild "the mother country," for which many had fought. In Jamaica, meantime, a new generation of playwrights and performers were preparing to expand their province to American as well as British audiences.

Two senior Jamaican playwrights in the century's final decades were Barry Reckord and Trevor Rhone. Reckord won a scholarship to Cambridge University in 1950 and, apart from short periods of return to Jamaica, he elected to stay in England as a teacher and professional playwright. In 1973 he was awarded a Guggenheim Fellowship in recognition of his work in drama. Of the dozen or more plays he has written and staged in England and Jamaica, several have been revised and given new titles; mostly they deal with questions of race, class, and sex. A notable feature of Reckord's playwriting is the creation of strong-willed, independent female characters. Apparently only one of his plays, *A Liberated Woman*, was actually staged in America at La MaMa's theatre in New York in 1970. It was directed by Barry's younger brother, Lloyd, who has created his own career in the theatre as an actor, director, and producer.

Lloyd Reckord attended the Bristol Old Vic Theatre School in the early 1950s and later studied theatre training at various institutions in the United States, including the Yale School of Drama. He has, in fact, directed most of brother Barry's plays in London, as well as in Jamaica, where in 1968 he established with corporate support the National Theatre Trust to provide high-quality productions of Caribbean plays, the classics, and contemporary world drama. When feasible, Lloyd, a consummate actor, would appear on stage in one of his productions. In the years 1978–81 he undertook an extensive solo tour of the United States, performing selected items of black poetry and prose from Africa, America, and the Caribbean under the title *Beyond the Blues*. He appeared at the United Nations auditorium in New York, the Eugene O'Neill Memorial Theater Center in Waterford, Connecticut; the Smithsonian Museum of African Art in Washington, DC, and at colleges and universities across the country including Dartmouth College. It is gratifying to report that after some thirty years of tenacious striving for a productive life in the theatre from his home base, Lloyd Reckord still retained the skill and persuasive powers of a seasoned actor.

Trevor Rhone is another new-era Jamaican playwright whose work has become known in the United States. Four years out of high school, Rhone enrolled in 1960 at Rose Bruford College in Kent, England, to study theatre. Upon graduation he returned to Jamaica to teach speech and drama at secondary school level and to write plays for school production. With Yvonne Brewster he founded an acting company and converted a garage into an intimate playhouse called the Barn Theatre, seating 150 patrons. There Rhone staged his own plays, amassing record numbers of performances and starting a trend for small, bare-boned playhouses in Kingston, often featuring the work of a single playwright.

At least three of Rhone's plays were presented at different venues in the United States: *Smile Orange*, a satire on the Jamaican tourist trade, played in 1972 at the O'Neill Theater Center, and then moved to the Billie Holiday Theatre. In 1978 the two-hander *Two Can Play* showed first in Gainesville, Florida; then in Manhattan at the NEC's Theatre Four in 1985; and in 1993 at the Black Theatre Festival in Winston-Salem, North Carolina. Rhone returned to this summer festival in 1995 with his play *Dear Counsellor*, self-directed as is customary with American productions of his plays. Rhone's most endearing play, *Old Story Time*, recounts a woman's desperate struggle to forge a better life for her son. With the principal roles of Pa Ben and Mama acted by revered Jamaican troupers Charles Hyatt and Leonie Forbes-Harvey, the drama was staged in 1978 at the Gusman Theatre in Miami and in 1979 at the Baird Auditorium of the Museum of Natural History in Washington, DC, to accompany a traveling exhibition.

From his play titles it would seem that Louis Marriott was primarily interested in musical theatre and revues. His offering *A Pack of Jokers*, which he directed with music by "Grub" Cooper, consisted of songs, monologues, and sketches reflecting aspects of contemporary Jamaican society. The show was already a hit at home when it arrived at the Schimmel Center for the Arts at Pace University, New York, in September 1979. Similar productions followed but were not recorded until 1992, when Marriott directed his musical comedy *Funny Business*, which told a New York audience about an unscrupulous hotelier and his questionable relationship with staff and guests. The following year brought to New York – and an equally unspecified Florida locale – *Jokers*, a compendium of the best items from several revues. *Bedward*, a nonmusical drama on the legendary Jamaican charismatic religious leader, was presented in Miami in 1985.

Because of the enormous costs involved, few authentic Caribbean plays reach Broadway and of those that do, few are successful. High expectations of success were raised for the Caribbean-inspired musical, *Reggae*, set in Jamaica and built on the twin pillars of Rastafarian belief and reggae music. Credit for the show's concept went to Michael Butler, but the book, lyrics, and music were created by Melvin Van Peebles, Kendrew Lascelles, and the Jamaican, Stafford (Ashani) Harrison. The production was booked into the Biltmore Theatre for a 27 March 1980 opening and, despite its assumed thematic popularity, the show survived a mere twenty-one performances.

Sistren, a theatre collective of working-class women, was formed in Kingston, Jamaica, in 1977 to address issues of concern to members of that social sector. Among these issues were unemployment, poverty, teenage pregnancy, and rape. Under the guidance of Honor Ford-Smith and others, the group created their plays from improvisations of lived experiences that evolved into full-length presentations. Among these were *Bellywoman Bangarang* (1978), dealing with women's rites of passage, *Nana Yah* (1980), citing incidents from the life of Nanny, a Maroon warrior, and *QPH*,[42] a memorial to 167 women who perished when fire engulfed their Kingston almshouse. Sistren traveled to rural Jamaica, other Caribbean countries, and to Europe presenting their work, but only three productions have been recorded in the United States of the same play, *Muffet Inna All A We*.[43] One production took place in New York as part of the 1985 Latino Festival, a second occurred in Washington, DC in 1987, and the third appearance was in Boston as part of the Women in Theatre festival sponsored by area universities. On this occasion, Sistren performed to good press notices at Northeastern University's Auditorium on 25–26 March 1988.

Collective creation was also the route chosen by two actresses of the Graduate Theatre Company, originally an arm of the Jamaica School of Drama, to explore their quite different and dynamic personalities. Honor Ford-Smith and Carol Lawes created a play based on the life stories of two decrepit characters. Starting in January 1987, they were joined at different points in the process by a dramaturg, a playwright, and a director. The first public viewing of their collective creation, called *Fallen Angel and the Devil Concubine*, took place in Kingston in February 1988, one year after they began the experiment. With production credited to the renamed Groundwork Theatre Company, the two-character play went to Boston for the 1989 Women in Theatre festival. This time, however, the *Boston Globe* critic was not impressed either with the playscript, which she regarded as "contrived and dramatically inert," or by a performance that relied on "speechifying and posturing."[44]

The so-called "roots" (grassroots?) drama of Jamaica is a popular form of urban theatre that usually inhabits small, rudimentary Kingston playhouses, devoid of complex stage mechanics and appealing strongly to grassroots audiences. The writers choose topics of immediate concern to their public. They produce, direct, and some act in their own plays. They tour productions to outlying towns and seek opportunities to perform in the United States, relying on Jamaican and other Caribbean immigrants and associates for their primary audience. Impressive among these writers have been Balfour Anderson, Basil Dawkins, and Ginger Knight, as well as Trevor Nairne, whose plays are produced under the banner Jambiz International. Discussion of two playwrights from this group will illustrate the genre.

Writing and producing since 1979, Ginger Knight has to his credit some fifteen or more plays carrying descriptive titles such as *Stepfather*, *Dis-A-Reggae*, *Poli-ticks*, *Part-time Lover*, *Whip-lash*, and *Higglers*. One of his most successful ventures was *Deportee*, performed in 1995 at the 700-seat Gusman Center for the Performing Arts in Miami and at the Brooklyn College Auditorium in New York, seating 2,200. A report on the Brooklyn performance was given by Knight, who, as the lead character "Mark," wants to enter the United States. Firstly, Mark convinces the immigration officer that he is a bona fide returning resident and when the officer stamped his passport a collective roar went up from the audience. However, having studied hard for the interview, Mark feels he has got through too easily and holds back to really impress the officer. "This turned to a heart-stopping kind of shock," Knight said of the audience's reaction; "they were totally devastated; they couldn't understand how anyone could ever hesitate after getting a visa... the people cuss me dog rotten... about ten patrons approached the stage and wanted to drag me away from the officer," who had become suspicious and decided to cancel the visa. Then the audience remembered a red handkerchief Mark's mother had given him in case he had immigration problems. They shouted: "take out the kerchief, wipe you face! Mark did this then flashed the kerchief in the direction of the immigration officer. Pandemonium! The show suffered another enforced break" as the flustered officer gave back the visa to roars of approval from the crowd.[45] Having chalked up nearly two hundred performances, *Deportee* had a return booking for Miami and projected visits to several more cities across the United States.

Playwright Basil Dawkins has focused mainly on relations between the sexes. Crafting his plays with care, he has employed experienced directors such as Lloyd Reckord and Keith Noel, and engaged celebrated actors such as Leonie Forbes-Harvey, Charles Hyatt, and Grace McGhie for his productions. Between 1986 and 1999 Dawkins presented five of his plays in America, mostly at the Gusman Center in Miami and in other cities as far away as Los Angeles. *Couples* (1986) was a comedy about two wives who agree to swap husbands, an arrangement that works for one couple but is disastrous for the other. *Champagne and Sky Juice* (1986) showed the effect of a change of government on a Jamaican couple who split their support between the two major political parties. *Same Song, Different Tune* (1990) deals with the sexual abuse of a village girl by a wealthy man from the city. Echoing Bernard Shaw's *Pygmalion* but with a twist, the comedy *Toy Boy* (1996) tells of a young widow whose husband dies of AIDS. Unable to attract another spouse, she takes a derelict off the street, cleans him up, finds him unusually erudite, and decides to keep him, but then has difficulty protecting him from her female friends. Finally, *Feminine Justice* (1999) put a cheat and a wife-beater in a serious motor accident. Unconscious, he meets with God, who is a woman, and pleads for another chance at life.

The Trinidad playwright Mustapha Matura, who resides in England, is another example of the diminishing importance of race in the Caribbean context. Born of an Asian Indian father and a Creole mother,[46] Matura dropped out of school at age 13, went to England in 1961, began writing seriously in 1966, and had his first full-length play staged at the Traverse Theatre in Edinburgh and the Theatre Upstairs at the Royal Court in London in 1971. That production won both the John Whiting and the George Devine awards for new playwrights. Since this auspicious launch, Matura has written well over a score of plays, mostly centered in Trinidad; he has received additional honors and writing commissions, and is considered to be a distinctive voice among the galaxy of Commonwealth writers who reside in the United Kingdom.

Since 1976 Matura's plays have been performed in the United States at regional centers and at prestigious theatres such as the Arena Stage in Washington, DC, and the Mitzie Newhouse Theatre at the Lincoln Center, New York. That year (1976) *Rum 'n' Coca-Cola*, a two-character study about calypsonians entertaining tourists out of season and hating it, was presented by the Chelsea Theatre Center at the Brooklyn Academy of Music with a three-piece steel band in attendance to enliven proceedings. In the same year *Play Mas* was staged by the Urban Arts Corps off off-Broadway and introduced a cross-section of Trinidad's complex population at carnival time. The play was later directed by Derek Walcott at the Goodman Theatre in Chicago in 1981. The Phoenix Theatre of New York presented the world premiere of Matura's *Meetings* in March 1981, and it was promptly on the boards of the Crossroads Theatre Company in New Brunswick the next year. A husband and wife, the latter an inveterate smoker, are successful businesspeople with little time for each other. The wife is promoting a new brand of imported cigarette that poisons a village. The husband leaves home as she is on the phone and coughing up blood.

By 1984 Matura had developed a novel form of transposing to a Trinidad locale, with appropriate shifts of lexicon and speech patterns, recognized classics from world drama. His first attempt was Synge's *The Playboy of the Western World*, which became *Playboy of the West Indies* with Mayaro Village replacing County Mayo in the original. The new play, commissioned and produced by the Oxford Playhouse Company in England, enjoyed repeated productions in America: in April 1988 at the Court Theatre in Chicago; then in the 1988/89 season by Washington's Arena Stage at the Kreeger Theatre; at the Crossroads Theatre in New Brunswick; and at the Yale Repertory Theatre in New Haven. The play also appeared at the Lincoln Center's Mitzie E. Newhouse Theatre, New York, in 1993.

Following this success, Chekhov's *The Three Sisters* was transformed to *Trinidad Sisters* and set in the city of Port-of-Spain during the years 1939–44, when American troops were billeted on the island. Clinton Turner Davis directed the play in 1992 for the Arena Stage, which later commissioned the first Matura play with an American setting. Titled *A Small World*, the action passes in a Brooklyn bar with the play's two characters from Trinidad. Carol, a bar owner and longtime immigrant, meets Herman Gomez, a visiting businessman and her one-time lover. As the night progresses, Carol unfolds "a lurid tale of urban horrors – drugs, racism, violence" that she has had to endure. It's a small world and there is no way out of it.[47]

Early in the 1990s two new musicals set in the Caribbean adorned the New York stage but not on Broadway. Moreover, each made an honest attempt to capture the spirit of island culture through the use of music, song, dance, and mime associated with the area. *Once On This Island* (1990), adapted from Trinidad-born Rosa Guy's novel *My Love, My Love*, was set in the French Antilles and depicted in fairy-tale fashion the love affair between a black peasant girl and a wealthy mulatto. With book and lyrics by Lynn Ahrens and music by Stephen Flaherty, the 90-minute musical, directed and choreographed with imagination by Graciela Daniele, was presented by Playwrights Horizons in midtown Manhattan. Less than a year later, Triplex Theatre in lower Manhattan staged *The Mermaid Wakes*, a collective creation by a cast of ten actors and four musicians (many of whom came from the West Indies). The troupe was led by the director and composer Elizabeth Swados, whose "exuberant pageant of singing, folk dancing and storytelling interweaves many vignettes into a tapestry of village life... one in which everyday activities, dreams and supernatural intuitions are so thoroughly interwoven as to be inseparable."[48] The fact that Disney's animated film, *The Little Mermaid* (1989) had been highly successful may well have brought parents and children out to at least one of these Caribbean musical productions.

Three of the Virgin Islands in the Caribbean – St. Thomas, St. Croix, and St. John – are defined as "unincorporated territories of the United States." Lying 40 miles east of Puerto Rico and with a total population just over one hundred thousand, these islands were purchased in 1917 from Denmark because of their strategic position on the sea-lane leading to the Panama Canal. Residents (one-third coming from other Caribbean states) speak English and hold American citizenship. Since 1971 the College of the Virgin Islands, upgraded in 1987 to a university (UVI), has staged an average of two productions a year at its Little Theatre on St. Thomas and has traveled with them to St. Croix. In 1978 the Reichhold Center of the Arts, a gift from Henry Reichhold, was built on St. Thomas, but there was no clear focus on producing Caribbean drama until a new director and playwright, David Edgecombe of Montserrat, was appointed in July 1992. By this time the Reichhold Center, which had been buffeted by hurricane Hugo in 1989, was administered by UVI. More storms were to come in 1995, 1996, and 1998, causing damage and disrupting production schedules. Nevertheless, the attempt was made not only to produce Caribbean plays but, to the extent resources permitted, to recruit a small cadre of professional actors and staff for them.

A summary of Caribbean plays staged by UVI and the Reichhold Center since 1990 would include four by Edgecombe, three of which had been earlier produced elsewhere, and *Marilyn* (1997), a world premiere that uses collective consciousness to portray the effect of a disastrous hurricane. Other playwrights featured in order of production are Derek Walcott, Steve Carter, Mustapha Matura, Alwyn Bully of Dominica, Caryl Phillips of St. Kitts and London, Trevor Rhone, and Cecil Williams of St. Vincent.[49] Announced for the summer theatre festival in the year 2000 at the Reichhold Center were

Triptych by Kendel Hippolyte of St. Lucia, *Jean and Dinah* by Tony Hall of Trinidad, and another world premiere, *Smile Native Smile* by Edgecombe.

In this chapter our primary focus has been on plays and musicals mostly by Caribbean writers who have sought to present before American audiences a view of life as they have experienced or observed it at home and abroad. While the work of playwrights has been a major concern, we are not unaware that sterling contributions to the American stage have also been made by other Caribbean theatre artists: directors, actors, musicians, and company managers. The director and designer Geoffrey Holder from Trinidad comes to mind for the extraordinary talent demonstrated in such productions as *The Wiz* (1975), *Kismet* (1978), and, in the same year, *Timbuktu*. At a different level but no less impressive is the work of actress Mizan Nunes, who was born and reared in Trinidad. At age 16 she joined her mother in the United States, graduated from Franklin and Marshall College in Lancaster, Pennsylvania, studied drama at the American Conservatory Theatre in San Francisco, and has been acting professionally since 1981. Ms. Nunes has appeared in widely different roles, from Cleopatra in *Antony and Cleopatra* (1989) for the Riverside Shakespeare Company in New York, to Gloria, the leading role in Rodney Douglas' *Ethnic Bacchanal* (1995), where, as daughter of a mixed marriage, she falls in love with an American soldier stationed in Trinidad. As Woman II in Samm-Art Williams' *Home* (1986), her performance was declared to be "simply dazzling": "she is by turns a little boy, a wino, a condescending caseworker, a pleasant bus driver, a lonely soldier, a taunting prison guard, and a big city seductress."[50]

We have attempted to make the case primarily for the Anglophone Caribbean, but it could also have been made for Francophone or Hispanic neighbors in the region. Or we could with conviction have pointed to the Caribbean's gift in the realm of dance theatre or song, or in the resurgent field of storytelling. Throughout the years, as so-called mainstream theatre has provided greater access to fine writers and performers on the periphery, American theatre has been greatly enriched and the value of cultural diversity has advanced toward universal acceptance.

10

The Great Depression and federal theatre

James V. Hatch

Look for the silver lining

Variety, the show business weekly, headlined the stock market crash of October 1929 with "Wall Street Lays an Egg" (show biz slang for an act that falls flat before an audience). Stigmatized as the "Great Depression," the 1930s could not put Humpty Dumpy together again. The great black musicals of the 1920s were no more. Fifty percent of the 350,000 Blacks in Harlem – last hired, first fired – were on relief. Harry F. V. Edward, who worked in a federal employment agency on 132nd Street and Lenox Avenue, set down his frustration in a one-act, *Job Hunters* (1931), which he published in *Crisis* magazine. Men waited in the hiring hall all day. Nearly three thousand black performers, writers, and others associated with the theatre pounded the streets. In a nation where one in four was unemployed, black and white playwrights addressed the fear, anger, and despair. Owen Dodson wrote two plays addressing poor people's desperation. The first, *The Shining Town* (1937), concerned black women who auctioned their day labor to white women at the Bronx subway station at 167th Street for as little as 10 cents an hour. His verse drama *Divine Comedy* (1938) portrayed a charismatic leader (Father Divine) luring frightened and hungry people to join his church and to surrender their property to him. Clearly, African Americans had not received the fruits of emancipation. In the Southland the penury of sharecropping circumvented the Fourteenth Amendment. In the Northland the penury of unemployment imprisoned families in the filth of city tenements. Black and white playwrights implored and warned audiences that change must come and come soon, or a great tribute would be exacted from a nation in default. Langston Hughes placed black and white workers in the same play, seeking common redress for their shared distress.

Black folk culture on Broadway

The Green Pastures (1930) employed nearly one hundred African Americans in a fantasy about a black god with black angels at a heavenly fish fry. Amid the worst depression the nation had known, this fantasy entertained audiences for five years. How had it happened? White dramatist Marc Connelly had read a book of so-called black folklore entitled *Ol' Man Adam an' His Chillun* (1928) by Roark Bradford, a southerner who claimed his book to be a "Negro preacher's vision of Old Testament Bible stories." Needless to say, many Blacks resented a play representing them as simple-minded. However, Connelly averted disaster and won the Pulitzer Prize by making two shrewd decisions: he cast Richard B. Harrison as "De Lawd," and he hired Hall Johnson to arrange the spirituals. Neither black man had had Broadway experience, but both had served long years in the theatre.[1]

Born the son of fugitive slaves in Ontario, Canada, Richard B. Harrison (1864–1935) had won prizes as a young man for his oratory and dramatic readings. Pursuing his dream to become a professional actor, he traveled to Detroit, where he studied drama and developed a one-man show interweaving readings from Shakespeare with the poems of Paul Laurence Dunbar. While touring colleges and schools he met poet Dunbar; they became close friends, and the poet acted as best man at Harrison's wedding. Dunbar then wrote a comedy of manners for Harrison entitled *Robert Herrick* (1899), which was never produced. Over the years Harrison gained a reputation for his one-man shows, and, in 1922, he persuaded North Carolina Agricultural and Technical College at Greensboro to inaugurate a summer session for teachers in the theatre arts. He remained there as a full-time faculty member until 1929, when at the age of 65 he accepted the role of "De Lawd" in *The Green Pastures*. Like Charles Gilpin in the role of Emperor Jones, Harrison's career became circumscribed by a single role; he portrayed "De Lawd" 1,657 times and then found himself too weak to play the 1,658th. Upon his death, Charles Winter Wood, who had been Harrison's understudy for five years without playing a single performance, finally stepped into the role of "De Lawd" for a six-week run. Although Wood was praised for his acting, Harrison had been so totally identified with the role that *The Green Pastures* died with him.[2]

Hall Johnson (1888–1970), the musical director of *The Green Pastures*, had exhibited an early talent for music. Born in Atlanta, the son of a minister, he graduated from Knox Institute and went on to study violin with Frederick

Hahn. In 1914 he joined James Europe's instrumental group and toured with Irene and Vernon Castle, ballroom exhibition dancers. In 1921 he played in the orchestra of Sissle and Blake's *Shuffle Along*. Then he founded the Hall Johnson Choir, whose trained voices insured that *The Green Pastures* would be a hit. Senior critic James Weldon Johnson rolled out the superlatives to describe *The Green Pastures*: "a play so simple and yet so profound, so close to the earth and yet so spiritual, that it is as high a test for those powers in the actors as any play the American stage has seen – a higher test than many of the immortalized classics."[3] Alain Locke wrote more guardedly: "*The Green Pastures* is a controversial subject, especially among Negroes. Is it a true version of the Negro's religion? By the warrant of spirituals and the characteristic Negro sermons, it is too drably realistic, and not apocalyptic enough. But it is certainly not what some have accused it of being, a white man's version of what he thinks Negro religion ought to be."[4] A virulent attack came in 1935 when in an essay entitled, "The Trouble with Angels," Langston Hughes blasted "De Lawd" and his cast for failing to stand up to management and demanding salaries commensurate with Whites.

Although the play had been a hit for years in New York and on tour, the Negro actors and singers were paid much less than white actors. And although the dramatist and his backers made more than $500,000, the colored troupers, now on tour, lived in cheap hotels and slept often in beds that were full of bugs.[5]

Johnny Logan, a baritone in the cast, attempted to organize a strike at the National Theatre just before the Washington, DC, premiere, when *no* black people were allowed in the audience. (Later a special Sunday matinée was arranged for Blacks.) When "De Lawd" failed to support Logan, the entire cast abandoned the strike leader, who was arrested and removed just before the curtain went up.[6] Bernard Schoenfeld subsequently converted Hughes' essay into a one-act for the New Theatre League, a leftist labor organization in New York.

Over the years Connelly's play has suffered critical depreciation. That which was a racial "advance" in the 1930s, was seen by 1957 as a perpetuation of stereotypes. Critic Nick Aaron Ford wrote that James Weldon Johnson's *God's Trombones* (1927) was nearer to a "genuine interpretation of the untutored Negro Christian's conception of God and the Bible." Ford's judgment proved true; Johnson's sermons are still regularly staged, while Connelly's play, following a television performance in 1957, has been left on the library shelf. However, *The Green Pastures* in its time inspired imitations. Negro spirituals were to be found in many productions, even in plays that had nonracial themes, and it probably inspired Hall Johnson to conceive *Run, Little Chillun* as a "rebuke to Connelly's play."[7]

While *The Green Pastures* was still running, Hall Johnson wrote and rehearsed his own play, *Run, Little Chillun*, a "Negro folk drama" with incidental music composed and arranged by the author. To the Renaissance Casino in Harlem Johnson summoned 175 singers for rehearsals. He could not pay them with anything but promises that if the show opened on Broadway they would have work. Two remarkable accounts describe in detail the rehearsals and how singer and actress Juanita Hall kept morale high for five months by feeding and rehearsing the cast until producer Robert Rockmore took the show downtown to the Lyric Theatre, where it ran for 126 performances.[8] Broadway was not integrated; the singers were not union; nonetheless this large cast of nonprofessionals worked as a community by teaching and looking after each other. An extended discussion of *Run, Little Chillun* is reserved for later in this chapter, when in 1938 the Federal Theatre in Los Angeles presented a revival.

Another folk play did not reach Broadway, *Heaven Bound*, a morality play. After seventy years of annual Eastertime ceremonies at Big Bethel AME Church in Atlanta, Georgia, this play is still being produced. Tapping into a near-universal fascination with the soul's journey to salvation, the story dramatizes the pitfalls and many temptations besetting everyman and everywoman on their pilgrimage to heaven. The Devil (played for fifty years by Henry Furlow) provides the comedy and drama as he intercepts pilgrims on their journey. Opening nine days before *The Green Pastures*, the premiere of *Heaven Bound*, on 17 February 1930 with a cast of thirty-four, including the choir, created a sensation. Two thousand seats at 10 cents admission sold out. The play's idea had come from Lula Byrd Jones (*c.* 1870–1940), a laundry woman and a choir member, as a way to raise money for the church. (Atlanta had 60 percent black unemployment.) The play succeeded, and in the years that followed, other churches attempted to duplicate its success. *Heaven Bound* gained national publicity from articles in *Time* and in *Theater Arts*, "as the first great American folk drama."[9]

Langston Hughes (1902–67)

In the 1930s Langston Hughes wrote about the folk but also confronted race and class issues. Born in St. Louis, he moved early in life to Cleveland,

Ohio, where he attended Karamu programs and classes. Even after he left Ohio, he kept in touch with directors Rowena and Russell Jelliffe, and the Gilpin Players gave premieres to several of his plays, including *When the Jack Hollars* (*sic*) (1936), a folk comedy about superstition among sharecroppers, *Troubled Island* (1936) also named *Emperor of Haiti*, a drama about the rise and fall of Dessalines, and *Joy to My Soul* (1937), a comedy about a con woman hustling a bachelor.

The Great Depression transformed art theatres into stages for social problems and leftist politics. Hughes saw theatre as a tool for change, a theatre championing not only African Americans, but all poor people. A glance at the provocative anthology *The Political Plays of Langston Hughes* (2000) will remind the reader of just how radical Hughes was.[10] Even as late as 1961, he had not given up his vision that theatre could make a difference in the real world of politics.

It is a cultural shame that a great country like America, with twenty million people of color, has no primarily serious colored theatre. There isn't. Karamu is the very nearest thing to it. My feeling is not only should a Negro theatre, if we want to use that term, do plays by and about Negroes, but it should do plays slanted toward the community in which it exists. It should be in a primarily Negro community since that is the way our racial life in America is still...It should not be a theatre that should be afraid to do a Negro folk play about people who are perhaps not very well-educated because some "intellectuals" in quotes, are ashamed of such material. I don't see why it [theatre] couldn't have such agit-prop plays if one wanted them or needed them...writers are starting to realize that there are so many social problems that need to be stated forcefully and strongly.[11]

Langston Hughes wrote several satiric skits. *Scarlet Sister Barry* (1938) presented a famous unnamed actress whose face was made up half-black, half-white. The setting was the "Realm of Art." Ethel Barrymore's blackface appearance in *Scarlet Sister Mary* (1930), an adaptation of Julia Peterkin's Pulitzer Prize novel, had inspired Hughes, who ridiculed Barrymore's portrayal of a "scarlet" Negro woman who bore eight illegitimate children. He not only mocked her performance but also threw a jibe or two at *Show Boat* (1927). *Em-Fuehrer Jones* (1938) trashed Eugene O'Neill's *The Emperor Jones* (1920) and also taunted Adolf Hitler with Jesse Owens' triumph over the Aryan race at the Berlin Olympics in 1936.[12]

Hughes' parodies may have been written for the Suitcase Theatre, a group that he and Louise Patterson had formed to produce *Don't You Want to Be Free?* (1937), a collage of music, poetry, and skits. The name "Suitcase Theatre" was meant to convey an absolute minimum of scenery, props, and theatre paraphernalia, an idea that Hughes may have picked up while touring in Russia (1931). Opening on 24 April 1938, the production traced American history from slavery to the 1930s, using twenty actors and eight singers. The production was "sponsored by Branch 691 of the IWO" (Industrial Workers Order, a leftist union for which Louise Patterson worked). Originating in the union's second-floor loft in Harlem, *Free* spent its second season in the library basement on 135th Street, playing a total of 138 performances. Other productions followed in Chicago and Los Angeles. Hughes himself explained why his play had not been mounted by the Federal Theatre Project (FTP) (1936–40): "I was never able to enroll in the Federal Writers Project of the WPA because I had had two small volumes of poems published and a novel, so the government presumed I was well off – not realizing that a writer cannot eat poems."[13]

Topics for Hughes' agitprop plays sprang from the events of the decade: *Scottsboro Limited* (1931), a one-act, exonerated the nine black young men who were falsely arrested for rape in Mississippi; *Angelo Herndon Jones* (1936), a one-act, concerned the communist labor organizer falsely imprisoned in Atlanta; *Blood on the Fields* (1935), a three-act drama, told of union attempts to organize the cotton pickers in California.[14]

In August 1938, Hughes used the same theme of unionizing for *The Organizer [De Organizer], A Blues Opera in One Act*, an anthem dedicated to the black cotton pickers of the South. James P. Johnson composed the music. The score, except for "The Hungry Blues," appeared to have been lost, but in June 2002 Professor James DaPogny of the University of Michigan at Ann Arbor discovered a partial score for the one-act opera that was subsequently performed at Detroit's Orchestra Hall on 3 and 11 December 2002. The opera, much like Clifford Odets' *Waiting for Lefty*, begins with workers waiting for the Organizer, the man who will lead the sharecroppers out of deadly and deadening physical slavery. Mid-play, the Organizer arrives, bringing his message. The Overseer attempts to break up the meeting, but fails in the face of worker unity. *The Organizer* was performed at Carnegie Hall in 1940 as part of an International Ladies' Garment Workers Union convention, which may have been its sole production. CBS then considered it for radio, but finally stated that it was "too controversial for us to give it an emotional treatment on an essentially dramatic show."

Hughes' *Mulatto*

In 1863, in an attempt to defeat Abraham Lincoln's bid for reelection, two journalists, David Croly and George Wakeman of the *New York World*, manufactured the word *miscegenation* for a pamphlet which they claimed had been written by abolitionist democrats.[15] The journalists' thesis: the newly freed slaves would attempt to mate with "your white daughter," thus creating an America befouled by a race of mixed-bloods – mulattos. Hughes, a descendant of mixed-race ancestry, chose to be identified with African Americans regardless of their color.[16]

Mulatto is unique among Hughes' nearly one hundred theatre pieces. It is an early play (perhaps his second) and its story is told through a conventional "well-made" play formula.[17] Possibly the conventional form was imposed by Martin Jones, the play's director, who optioned and rewrote the script, putting it into rehearsal without Hughes' participation. The plot concerns Colonel Norwood, a southern planter who has fathered three children by his slave, Cora Lewis. The youngest son, Robert, who resembles his father in feature and color, returns home from a northern education and demands to be treated like a legitimate heir to the Colonel. His assumption that he is as good as a white man angers the Colonel; they quarrel and the son strangles his father, an action for which he will be lynched. Originally Hughes had intended the play to be a tragedy of race, but director Martin Jones corrupted it by adding a gratuitous rape of the daughter. The change turned tragedy into a sex melodrama.

Mulatto opened at the Vanderbilt Theatre on 14 October 1935 to negative and mixed reviews, which ordinarily would have condemned it to a rapid closing.[18] *New York Times* critic Brooks Atkinson sympathized with the Colonel, who was killed "by a boy so cocky and impudent that he seems more like an ungrateful son than a martyr to race prejudice." Robert Garland of the *New York World-Telegram* wrote: "An attempt to dramatize an inferiority complex which is perhaps unconscious. *Mulatto* is untimely, uncalled for, and unworthy of the author."[19] In spite of negative reviews, *Mulatto* enjoyed 373 performances as a sex melodrama, giving it the longest Broadway run of any play by a Black until Abram Hill's *Anna Lucasta* (1944) and Lorraine Hansberry's *A Raisin in the Sun* (1959). *Mulatto* then toured the United States for eight months and later was produced in Italy by Italian actors, where it ran for two years. The play's Broadway success can be attributed in part to the cast, which featured a most talented actor, Rose McClendon, in the role of Cora. The composer Jan Meyerowitz so admired the drama that he adapted it into a successful opera, *The Barrier* (1950). Over the next thirty years Hughes wrote in many theatrical forms, but never again did he try a race tragedy.

Mulatto marked Rose McClendon's (1884–1936) last Broadway appearance before her death by "cancer" (an abhorrent word in the 1930s; her death certificate listed pneumonia). Unquestionably, she had been the diva of black dramatic actresses. Alexander Woolcott, critic for the *New York World*, reported: "When *Deep River* (1926) was having its trial flight in Philadelphia Ethel Barrymore, one of America's premier actresses, slipped in to snatch what moments she could of it. 'Stay till the last act if you can,' director Arthur Hopkins whispered to her, 'and watch Rose McClendon come down those stairs. She can teach some of our most hoity-toity actresses distinction.' It was Miss Barrymore who hunted *him* up after the performance to say, 'She can teach them *all* distinction.'"[20]

Born in Greenville, North Carolina, as Rosalie Virginia, McClendon and her family fled to New York City after her uncle was lynched and burned. In 1904 she married a Pullman porter and lived in Harlem. Around 1916 she attended the American Academy of Dramatic Art on scholarship and studied with Franklin Sargent for three years. In 1924 she acted in a series of plays by white authors. In *Roseanne*, she first played opposite Charles Gilpin and, in a later revival, opposite Paul Robeson. Professional triumphs followed: *Deep River* (1926); *In Abraham's Bosom* (1926); then she immortalized the role of Serena in *Porgy* (1927). This was followed by *The House of Connelly* (1931), *Never No More* (1932), and *Black Souls* (1932). After her triumph as Cora in *Mulatto*, her friend John Houseman recommended she be appointed head of the Negro Unit of the FTP in New York City, but she was already too ill to meet the challenge. Following her death, friends founded the Rose McClendon Players to continue her legacy.[21]

Many details of McClendon's life are sketchy, but Vinie Burrows in 1999 undertook a thorough search of the records and presented the actress' struggle and dreams in a widely praised one-woman show, *Rose McClendon, Harlem's Gift to Broadway*.

Porgy and Bess

Du Bose Heyward's novel *Porgy* had first been adapted into a play in 1927, before George Gershwin turned it into the "Negro opera," *Porgy and Bess*. Critics did not know if it was an opera, a musical, or something else, but they liked it. Many Blacks did not like the story for its portrayal of gambling, and fighting "niggers" in the slums of Catfish Row. Duke Ellington did not like it because Gershwin's music was too white for ghetto portrayal. Other Blacks accused the composer of plagiarizing music from the Georgia Sea Islands. Nonetheless, the music pulled heart strings and *Porgy and Bess* moved on to revival after revival, providing work for serious singers – work that Whites weren't allowed to sing, except in Germany and Russia, where initially African American vocalists were scarce and local white artists would don blackface. After Blevin Davis and Robert Breen's 1952 world tour of *Porgy and Bess* for the US Department of State, the work rose to become America's internationally acclaimed opera. A year rarely goes by without a production, and African Americans continue to find work in a story that some believe degrades the race.[22]

Negro Actors Guild

"Negro Actors Form Their Own Guild" read a headline in *Variety* on 8 December 1937. The organization had been four years in planning before New York State granted a certificate of incorporation to the Negro Actors Guild (NAG). Its officers and board of directors included nearly all the big names in black show business, with Noble Sissle as president. He explained that NAG "would function along the lines of the Catholic, Jewish, and Episcopal Actors Guilds, that is, NAG would give the actors status. Needy Negro performers had found it difficult to enroll for welfare relief because they were unable to identify themselves professionally."[23] NAG immediately launched a series of fund-raisers to assist in funeral and burial expenses of black actors. To help bring money into its treasury, membership was open to all races, and one could obtain an associate membership without being an actor. Although the organization survived until 1982, integration took a serious toll on NAG in the 1960s, when many African Americans joined the Actors' Equity Association (AEA).

Federal Theatre Project

In 1935, to cope with the continuing unemployment, the US Congress and President Franklin D. Roosevelt created the Works Progress Administration (WPA), which included the Federal Theatre Project (FTP) with its initial sixteen and later nineteen or even twenty-two Negro units, depending on how smaller projects are counted.[24] The national project director, Hallie

Flanagan, stated her immediate aim: to employ the thousands of actors, directors, and technicians in all aspects of theatre, and further, "to organize and support theatrical enterprises so excellent in quality and low in cost... that they will continue after federal support is withdrawn." After 1939 it was not to be.

In October 1935 Congress appropriated $27 million for unemployed artists, musicians, theatrical people, and writers. This figure was less than 1 percent of the $5 billion appropriated for the WPA. By March 1936, eleven thousand theatre artists at an average of $24 a week worked on payrolls in twenty-two states and performed for weekly audiences of 150,000.[25] Whites occupied the administrative and supervisory positions because, since segregation in the theatre had been so nearly total, few Blacks had been trained to teach the theatre crafts. Looked at from another perspective, self-segregated Whites were ignorant of the talents possessed by black writers, actors, directors, carpenters, and electricians. Only Ralf Coleman of Boston and Rose McClendon of New York headed black units. McClendon reportedly told Flanagan that Blacks would prefer to start under more experienced (white) directors. When McClendon became too ill to work in 1936, John Houseman became director of the New York City Project. Black playwrights, too, were scarce. When FTP published a list of sixty-three "Negro" plays, only sixteen were written by Blacks – the majority of those, one-acts. In the introduction to the list, playwright John D. Silvera wrote: "The number of plays written for Negro actors has up to now been almost negligible. We must bear in mind the fact that writing for the stage has been subjected to commercial dictation and Negro themes find little market for expression."[26] The problems faced by the new theatres can be illustrated by looking at the history of three major and three minor Negro units.

New York Harlem unit

Born on 5 February 1936, Harlem's FTP was the largest and most productive of all the black units. About 150 members were true professionals. Many of the other five hundred actors, singers, and dancers had never appeared on stage. Another 250 signed up for other theatre crafts.[27] In order to meet a variety of audience expectations, as well as making use of a large range of diverse talents, Houseman divided the unit: one group for adaptations of classic plays and a second group for plays by and about Blacks. The first production of the latter section was a revival of Frank Wilson's *Meek Mose* (1928) under a new title, *Brother Mose*, which had had a successful touring record of 325 performances two years earlier under the aegis of another agency, the Federal Emergency Relief Administration.

Wilson's second play, *Walk Together Chillun*, a dramatization laced with spirituals, concerned a labor dispute between New York State and southern Blacks brought in as strikebreakers. It managed twenty-nine performances. *Conjur' Man Dies*, a mystery by the novelist Rudolph Fisher adapted to the stage by Arna Bontemps and Countee Cullen, was a Harlem crowd-pleaser, playing to an estimated twenty thousand people before going on tour. Director Clinton Turner Davis revived the script at the New Federal Theatre in 2001.

Orson Welles headed Houseman's classics unit; his mission was to perform black adaptations of the great western dramas, an idea promoted by Hallie Flanagan, formerly head of the Vassar Experimental Theatre. Orson's first wife, Virginia Welles, suggested a Haitian setting which would parallel the story of King Henry Christophe, a tyrant who was brought down by intrigue and misrule. The adaptation was enhanced when Welles discovered that Asadata Dafora Horton, a native of Sierra Leone, had brought his dancers to the USA as a commercial venture to perform his own dance drama, *Kykundor (Witch Woman)*. Welles placed Horton's dancers and drummers in *Macbeth*, transmuting Shakespeare's witches into Haitian *mambo*, giving the drama its sobriquet, the "Voodoo Macbeth." Welles cast 137 people, crowding the stage of the Lafayette Theatre. Nat Karson provided a two-level set on which a tall, handsome mulatto, Jack Carter, in the lead with Edna Thomas as his Lady, welcomed Service Bell as the King. Canada Lee played Banquo and Maurice Ellis, Macduff. Opening 14 May 1936 to nearly universal acclaim, Harlemites flocked to see it; Whites hurrying uptown to join them.[28] By December two Nigerian members of the Dafora troupe, Norman Coker and Momadu Johnson, had written and directed their own dance drama, *Bassa Moona (The Land I Love)*. Hallie Flanagan described their piece as homesick memories of Nigeria. It played sixty-eight performances, nearly as many as *Macbeth*, but the latter toured other FTP theatres across the nation, playing to an estimated hundred thousand people.

Welles, riding his success, left the unit, and Houseman joined him after appointing a triumvirate of Blacks to direct the project: Harry Edward, Gus Smith, and Carlton Moss, all experienced artists with diverse talents. They mounted or imported at least twenty-five productions aimed at satisfying all tastes: comedies, costume dramas, children's plays, problem plays of social realism, some written by Whites, some by Blacks. *Haiti*, starring

Figure 30. Maurice Ellis as Macduff in *Macbeth*, Harlem Federal Theater Project

Canada Lee, became the unit's longest running drama, with 180 performances. William DuBois, a white southern journalist, had intended his
play to be a tirade against miscegenation, but the director refocused the
story on Toussaint L'Ouverture and Christophe's struggle for racial pride
and independence. In granting rights to his plays, the author had stipulated
that no white person should touch a black person in performance. Director

Maurice Clarke acquiesced to this demand, but at the curtain call, the cast members all held hands and took their bow united. In a less serious mode, on 22 July 1937, Cecil Mack, Milton Reddie, and Eubie Blake opened a new musical comedy that topped *Haiti's* long-run record. *Swing It*, a shipboard sailors-meet-girls romance with Eubie Blake's foot-tapping music, lasted ten months.

After Eugene O'Neill and George Bernard Shaw released all their plays to the FTP for a token $50 royalty, Shaw's *Androcles and the Lion*, an audience favorite, played in Denver, Los Angeles, and Seattle. Shaw encouraged the FTP to use black casts: "for Negroes act with a delicacy and sweetness that make white actors look like a gang of roughnecks." A dancer, Add Bates, played the lion from whose paw Androcles (Arthur "Dooley" Wilson) had once removed a thorn, and when Androcles finds himself in the Roman arena, the lion remembers him and refuses to eat his friend. Audiences loved it for 104 performances. Perry Watkins designed the costumes, as well as sets for at least three other FTP shows. In 1938 he was admitted to the scene designers' union for designing *Mamba's Daughters* on Broadway.

The Chicago Unit

In Chicago a leftist political theatre emerged from the Depression. In the early 1930s actor Lou Gilbert had founded the Negro People's Theatre, located in the Lincoln Center settlement house. Gilbert's group had toured schools and community groups reciting such works as Langston Hughes' "The Ballad of Roosevelt." In 1933, Richard Wright, Nelson Algren, Studs Terkel, Katherine Dunham, Charles Sebree, William McBride, Margaret Goss, and Jack Conroy joined the Chicago Repertory Group. As the Depression deepened, these artists determined to make their art serve the poor, both Black and White.[29]

Before the 1930s, Chicago had twenty legitimate theatres, including the Goodman School of Drama, but by 1935 only four theatres remained in business. The Chicago Negro unit, with an initial enrollment of twenty-five Blacks,[30] opened its theatre on 1 April 1936 with the musical *Romey and Julie*, an adaptation from Shakespeare by Robert Dunmore and Ruth Chorpenning. Indigenous African Americans played the Montagues and Caribbean black immigrants played the Capulets. Reviews were positive; the musical played before 2,017 patrons. However, three uninspired productions followed.[31] Richard Wright, publicist for the FTP in Chicago, lamented in his autobiography *American Hunger*:

Figure 31. Arthur Dooley Wilson as Androcles and Add Bates as the Lion, Federal
Theatre Project, 1938

FTP had run a series of ordinary plays, all of which had been revamped
to "Negro style," with jungle scenes, spirituals and all. The skinny white
woman who directed it, an elderly missionary type, would take a play
whose characters were white, whose theme dealt with the Middle Ages
[*Everyman*] and recast it in terms of Southern Negro life with overtones

of African backgrounds. Contemporary plays dealing realistically with Negro life were spurned as being controversial. There were about forty Negro actors and actresses in the theater, lolling about, yearning, disgruntled, not knowing what to do with themselves. What a waste of talent. Here was an opportunity for the production of a worthwhile Negro drama and no one was aware of it.[32]

Wright seized that opportunity and recommended to Charles DeSheim, director of the Chicago Federal Theatre Negro unit that he produce *Hymn to the Rising Sun* (1936), Paul Green's brutal drama about a southern chain gang. According to Wright, the actors were appalled. "We think this play is indecent. We don't want to act in a play like this before the American public...We want a play that will make the public love us." This fear on the part of actors who had backgrounds in vaudeville and minstrelsy was difficult to overcome.[33] The actors may have been embarrassed and repulsed by representing themselves as being whipped by a white overseer. Recent migrants simply did not wish to enact the poverty and cruelty that they had experienced in the South.[34] Also, Wright's proposal for a drama that confronted political issues sprang from Chicago's strong progressive left, which some may have resented. In any case, the state's WPA supervisor settled the argument by closing the show on the night it was to open.

In an attempt to avoid further "disapproval and open resentment," the play bureau of the FTP mailed an opinion poll to one hundred "representative Negro citizens...Thru [*sic*] this poll we hope to form a basic policy in selecting and approving plays for production. We hope to eliminate any matter that may be offensive to the races and groups that form our composite population."[35] It is not known if the memo was ever mailed, or if so, the results. The "representative" citizens included newspaper editors, doctors, lawyers, and professors, citizens of influence. Although addressed to a number of cities – Atlanta, Norfolk, Chicago, Bridgeport, Cleveland, New Orleans, etc. – the majority lived in New York City. One may conclude that the opinions of the New York City Talented Tenth mattered.

The Chicago FTP unit had no African American administrators. Then Shirley Graham (Du Bois) was appointed director; she was certainly the most qualified black woman for the job. While a student at Oberlin she had expanded her own one-act *Tom Tom* into a three-act opera to satisfy an invitation from the Theatre of Nations to present an African American opera in the Cleveland Stadium.[36] The result was an opera that shared many characteristics with ethnic pageants so popular at the time. It is probable that W. E. B. Du Bois' *Star of Ethiopia* influenced Graham's style. *Tom Tom*, directed by Ernest Lert with Jules Bledsoe singing the lead alongside a cast of five hundred actors, singers, and dancers, played on 30 June 1932 before an audience of ten thousand, and then repeated its triumph with a second performance on 9 July before fifteen thousand people. Apart from the enormity of the production, *Tom Tom* deserves attention for its theme – the continuity between African and African American life and spirit – as well as for its authenticity; Graham had worked hard to make the costumes, scenery, and the music genuine African.

> Graham did not write traditional recitative of European opera. She employed the long chant of early African American preachers. The music of the first act was inspired by African themes and rhythms over five hundred years old that were collected by her uncle, father, and brother, all of whom lived and worked in Liberia for several years.[37]

Graham lived a rich creative life. Even before the Chicago unit closed, she received a Rosenwald Fellowship and attended the Yale University School of Drama (1938–40). At this time she wrote plays: *Dust to Earth* (1938), produced at Karamu; *I Gotta Home* (1940), staged at Case Western Reserve University; *Elijah's Ravens* (1941), presented at Spelman College, Atlanta. She wrote several novels as well as a biography of Benjamin Banneker. In 1951 she married W. E. B. Du Bois and after his death in 1963 she published a memoir of her famous husband. In 1961 she became a founding editor of *Freedomways* and in the same year moved to Ghana. There she served as organizing director of state television for President Kwame Nkrumah. During this period, the US Department of State would not permit her to return to the United States, citing her membership in subversive groups. In 1977 she died in Beijing of cancer.

When Graham came to the Chicago FTP, she immediately had to confront a political decision. Theodore Ward's (1902–83) *Big White Fog* (1938) had ignited a battle with reactionary forces within and without the FTP. The play's story, based on an incident witnessed by Ward, centered around a black family in Chicago whose father, Victor Mason, has invested his life savings in Marcus Garvey's Universal Negro Improvement Association (UNIA). With Garvey's imprisonment by the federal government for mail fraud and later deportation to Jamaica, the UNIA collapsed, leaving the Mason family destitute in the Great Depression. The mother has become bitter, the slumlord brother-in-law faces bankruptcy, the daughter turns to prostitution, and the father dies from a police bullet during an attempted

Figure 32. Theodore Ward, author of *Big White Fog*, 1938

eviction from the family's home. The only hope seems to lie in the young son, who calls together his black and white communist comrades to oppose the eviction by carrying the furniture back into the house, making the curtain call a powerful emotional and political statement of populist unity in the face of capitalist racial oppression.

Speculation rumored that if Ward's play was produced, it would cause racial schism, even riots. Others averred that Blacks would despise the play because the black family did not represent the community, nor its aspirations. Harry Minturn, a former vaudevillian turned acting director of the FTP, asked Shirley Graham to hold a play reading for southside community leaders at the YMCA, perhaps to give the play preproduction publicity in the black community as much as to test the waters for an audience response. Black reaction was muted until the white director Kay Ewing remarked that the Masons were a "typical Negro family." The members of the National Association for the Advancement of Colored People (NAACP), the Urban League, and other middle-class folk attending the evening did not regard the Garveyite Mason family as typical of themselves. Nonetheless, with some script modifications, the production went ahead, opening at the Great Northern Theatre on 7 April 1938 for thirty-seven performances attended by racially mixed but majority white audiences. Then Minturn decided, probably in concert with Shirley Graham, to move the play into the black community on the southside. Rena Fraden's essay appropriately entitled "The Cloudy History of Big White Fog"[38] traces the murky political and personal conflicts that generated this misjudgment, a decision that sent a successful play at a midtown Loop theatre back into a southside "Negro high school," where it wilted at the box office after four days.

And yet the play was to be born again. The newly formed Negro Playwrights Company (NPC)[39] of Harlem premiered the play on 22 October 1940 at the Lincoln Theatre on 135th Street and Lenox Avenue. Powell Lindsay directed. The cast of thirty included a number of theatre veterans: Canada Lee, Maude Russell, P. J. Sidney, Lionel Monagas, Frank Silvera, and Hilda Offley. Setting and lighting were designed by Perry Watkins. Some downtown critics and a few black ones misjudged Big White Fog as "propaganda for communism," a damning accusation that plagued artists on the political left. Fog closed after sixty-four performances. Ward blamed the play's abrupt closure on the signing of the Stalin–Hitler pact, which had divided Poland between the Soviets and Germany, a move that alienated many Americans on the political left. Twelve years after Ward's death, in 1983, his drama was revived by Penumbra director Lou Bellamy for the Guthrie Theatre in Minneapolis. Big White Fog had entered a category reserved for very few plays – a drama unsuccessful in its own time that emerged triumphant fifty years later, possibly because the issues of the play were no longer as personal to the audience as they had been in the 1930s. Professor Vanita Vactor summarizes Big White Fog: "Although American theatre history has excluded Ward, his role is undeniable. I argue that it was Ward's Mason family, and not Lorraine Hansberry's Younger family (as dramatized in A Raisin in the Sun) that introduced the American stage to the first dramatic portrait of a Chicago urban African American family" (see note 30).

The Chicago FTP unit did produce a second artistic triumph, and a financially successful one, too: *The Swing Mikado* (1938).[40] Director Kay Ewing had begun rehearsals for a traditional Gilbert and Sullivan *Mikado* when Project Director Harry Minturn happened by a rehearsal as some of the cast were horsing around by "swinging the music" and "tapdancing unto." Minturn saw the possibilities and took over the direction and production himself. Harold Rogers wrote: "it can be said without contradiction that *The Swing Mikado* was created by the members of the production company... with Mr. Minturn acting as a wise and judicious editor."[41] He changed the location from Japan to a coral island in the Pacific. Gentry Warden arranged five songs, presenting the first two verses of each as written, then swinging the remaining verses. Many critics would complain later that the songs should have all been "jived." Choreographer Sammy Dyer with experienced assistant Hazel Davis and vocal director Viola Hill taught the chorus how to "truck and peck," a popular black dance of the time. John Pratt (later husband of Katherine Dunham) sketched and built the costumes. Nat Karson created the sets.[42]

After eight months of rehearsal, the show opened on 25 September 1938. Originally scheduled for a two-week tour locally, the opening night reviews changed the schedule radically. The audiences loved it, making it the highest grossing show in the entire Chicago FTP. By January 1939 the production had broken Great Northern Theatre's attendance records. Private theatre entrepreneurs approached the unit with offers to produce the show in New York City. These suitors brought the unit new troubles. Among the moneyed beaux, the Shuberts arrived offering to put the show on Broadway with a totally new cast, using the cast from Lew Leslie's warmed-over *Blackbirds*, who at the time were performing in Boston. Some individuals in the Chicago cast were offered a place in the New York cast. Such tactics did not succeed, but instead made for legal trouble; according to federal law, an unemployed FTP actor if offered a paying job, had to accept it. Among the other suitors, the most persistent was Mike Todd. When his bid was refused by the Chicago FTP, Todd set about creating a clone, *The Hot Mikado*. In the meantime, Minturn laid out his own plans to move the company to Broadway. Todd started a campaign to keep Chicago's *The Swing Mikado* out of New York. His argument was twofold: first, there were unemployed actors in New York who would be denied work by importing the Chicago troupe; second, the federal government had no right to compete with private enterprise (an argument heard against TVA for providing cheap electricity to the poor). Many in Congress agreed with Todd, and eventually the issue helped to fell the FTP.

On 25 February 1939, after a 22-week run before audiences numbering 154,660, *The Swing Mikado* closed in Chicago. On 1 March the cast opened at the New Yorker Theatre on 54th Street. The reviews were favorable, but they did not deter Mike Todd, who three weeks later opened *The Hot Mikado* at the Broadhurst Theater. Todd's complaint that the federal government should not compete with his production ignored his advantages. He was not limited by the WPA requirement that 90 percent of expenditures be used for salaries. Hence his costumes and sets were more glorious, and to top off the show, he hired Bill "Bojangles" Robinson to dance and sing the role of the Mikado. Reviewers cast their ballots: Todd's *The Hot Mikado* won hands down. Under political and financial pressure, the FTP sold its franchise to private investors, who moved the show directly opposite Todd's enterprise. After three weeks *The Swing Mikado* closed and the nearly one hundred actors returned to Chicago. However, the war of the *Mikado* had taken its toll. After another eighty-five performances Todd's musical, with its ensemble of 150, also closed.

In April 1939 Congress voted to terminate the entire FTP for reasons to be discussed later. Nonetheless, in three years the Chicago unit had produced fourteen shows, and there can be no question that within that time black talents had made rapid professional progress, which became the impetus for forming smaller independent companies such as the Negro People's Theatre. William Nix, the director, in a program dated 13 April 1940 announced that their production of Irwin Shaw's *Bury the Dead* "would be like a Federal Theatre Living Newspaper. Admission would be free."[43]

Seattle unit

Not until after the Civil War did the first African Americans migrate to Seattle, many via cargo ships. Some arrived during the touring days of the black minstrels, in time to see the New Georgia Minstrels, the Fisk Jubilee Singers, and Bert Williams and George Walker with *Sons of Ham* and *In Dahomey*. In 1890, on the twenty-fifth anniversary of emancipation, the small community of Blacks held its first public celebration, "Juneteeth."[44] By 1900, from Seattle's population of forty-two thousand, Blacks numbered only 286. Some worked on the docks; Seattle had become America's largest commercial seaport on the Pacific Coast. During the longshoremen's strike of 1916, employers imported four hundred Blacks from New Orleans,

St. Louis, and Kansas City as strikebreakers, creating racial turmoil. However over the next two decades the International Longshoremen's Union began to issue union cards to Blacks, so that during the strike of 1936–37 employers dared not import more Blacks as strikebreakers.[45] All of this local history would feed into the black unit's production of *Stevedore*. First, however, some background on Seattle theatre of the 1930s will provide necessary context.

In 1928 Florence and Burton James founded the Repertory Playhouse, later to be known as the Old Rep, where they produced Ibsen, Chekhov, and Shaw. After two years of using rented stages, the Jameses acquired their own theatre and a core group of ten white actors. Their initial experience with Blacks was *In Abraham's Bosom* by Paul Green. They discovered their audiences loved spirituals, and soon Burton used the singers to bridge scenes in other plays.

In 1935 the Roosevelt administration offered a Federal Theatre Project to Seattle, although its black population was just thirty-three hundred. Joe Jackson, head of the Urban League, applied to head the Negro unit but was turned down because his troupe did not have its own theatre space; subsequently, the FTP awarded Florence James the Negro unit, presumably because she managed the Repertory Playhouse. Historian Tina Redd concluded: "Given that it was a Negro unit that was being organized, the fact that no "Negroes" were included [in administration and technical aspects] is indicative of a covert racism that would continue to guide decisions regarding the unit." The director of the western region, Gilmore Brown, wrote Flanagan that the Negro Repertory Company (NRC) in Seattle had a peculiar difficulty: "They are actually having to teach dialect to many of the players in their opening production of *Porgy* [which was canceled]. This makes me wonder a little if our whole white approach to the Negro theatre question isn't wrong."[46]

Hallie Flanagan wrote that under the guidance of Burton James, the NRC chose its own plays. She reported: "The mystical naïveté, of André Obey's *Noah* [a fantasy about the building of the biblical ark] seemed to them natural; done with a chorus of Negro voices singing songs of their own people." Burton James had placed benches in the pit where Blacks sang at "the opening and closing of each scene and sometimes within the body of the scene." One may detect *The Green Pastures* revisited.

Next, *Stevedore*, an agitprop play of union busting, premiered on 14 May 1936, to a specially invited audience of labor leaders and African Americans. Cast member Joe Staton recalled the enthusiasm of union members: "Boy, those longshoremen came out there one night and they bought out that show and I'm telling you, it kind of shook us up because those guys were all for it... People became so engrossed in that last scene that they came up on stage and helped us build a barricade. That was really something!"[47]

But even for this militant drama, the scenes were bridged with a black chorus singing some work songs, mixed with "St. Louis Blues," and "Careless Love." *Stevedore*, with its integrated cast, ran for twenty-seven evenings.[48] The Jameses' sensitivity to racial image was that of liberal Whites of the 1930s.

Theodore Browne (1910–79) a graduate of City College in New York, became a mainstay for Repertory Playhouse Company (RPC), writing and adapting four of the fifteen productions that the NRC would eventually mount. His most successful play, *Natural Man* (1937), was written specifically for Joe Staton, an actor whose strong singing voice enabled him to play the legendary John Henry. Folk stories told how Henry had cut rock for the Big Ben Railway Tunnel, a 1.5-mile shaft in Virginia. Henry swung two 20 lb hammers, and in a 30-minute contest beat a steam-driven drill.[49] Subtitled "a folk opera," *Natural Man* opened 28 January 1937 at the large downtown Seattle Metropolitan Theatre.[50] Set in the 1880s in West Virginia, the contest, which Henry wins, occurs in the second scene. In subsequent scenes, Henry embarks on a series of misadventures: a casual affair with a prostitute; an arrest for a crime he does not commit; a jail sentence served in a chain gang; a camp meeting; and finally, a triumphant return to his profession as a steel-driving man.

In an interview forty years later, playwright Browne remarked that although the NRC actors had strong talents, they had no formal training, and that when he adapted Aristophanes' *Lysistrata*, he deliberately avoided any literary language that would be difficult. He also avoided "indecency" in this classic comedy, in which the women of Athens refuse all sex to their men until they stop the war. Browne's adaptation did not avoid censorship.[51] The state's WPA supervisor, Don Abel, on the strength of two complaints (one of which was from his wife), closed the show without seeing it or even consulting with the many who praised it. The theatre had sold tickets six months in advance, and the play promised to be a financial bonanza, a phenomenon all too rare for Seattle's FTP. Abel's decision to close the show was tied directly and indirectly to the race of the actors; that is, a sex comedy played by Blacks had become in the white gaze, pornographic, even though the costumes, the language, and the physical action were designed not to be provocative.[52] Browne later told the director of the Boston unit,

Ralf Coleman, that he had become very upset and angry over discrimination in the theatre, and that he was through with it. Yet in 1948, when
Howard University chose *The Wild Duck* and *Mamba's Daughters* for its tour
of Scandinavia, Browne wrote a scathing letter to the newspaper: "Instead
of fostering the culture of its own people, [Howard] is making it quite plain
that it is not interested in the culture of its own people."[53]

When WPA administrator Harry Hopkins in 1935 had first announced
the genesis of the FTP, he asked Hallie Flanagan to supervise an American
theatre "free, adult, and uncensored." Certainly he knew if Flanagan did her
job, she would face charges of political favoritism, immorality, communist
sympathies, and "boondoggling" (wasting public money). Negro Units received their share of that criticism and censorship. A final and terrible irony
happened ten years later; the demise of the James's playhouse itself. In 1948
the Canwell Committee of the Washington State legislature held hearings
and falsely accused the Jameses of communist activities. Within six months
thirty-six theatre parties canceled 6,500 seat reservations. The playhouse
closed permanently in December 1950.[54] One may prudently speculate that
the James's progressive labor agenda and mixing of Blacks and Whites on
stage contributed to the hostility of conservative lawmakers that ended a
22-year history of meaningful plays and artful theatre.

Los Angeles unit

None of the other units matched New York, Chicago, and Seattle in number or quality of productions. Los Angeles mounted seven shows (most
repeats from other units), but one triumph compensated for previous lackluster efforts – Hall Johnson's *Run, Little Chillun*. In 1933 the play had had a
successful Broadway run of 126 performances. Billed as a "folk play," it had a
choir of twenty-six and nearly as many dancers. Critics named it a musical
and even an opera. Its author and composer had organized and conducted
the choir for *The Green Pastures* (1930) before presenting his own drama of
religious conflict between "the New Pilgrims, an African religion and the
Hope Baptist Church, a fundamentalist Christian sect intolerant of all non-
Christian worship."[55] In Los Angeles a black guest director, Clarence Muse
(1889–1979), was appointed to direct the FTP production. A recent star
from the film *Hearts in Dixie* (1929) and a veteran of the Lafayette Players,
Muse would later appear in more than two hundred films. He wrote and
self-published a pamphlet entitled *The Dilemma of the Negro Actor* in 1934,
in which he traced the difficult sojourn of the black actor, who had to

accommodate two audiences, one white that "demanded buffoonery, one black that desired to see elements of real Negro life." Because white producers controlled the money, audiences seldom saw anything truthful concerning African Americans or their culture on stage. When handed the directorship of *Run, Little Chillun*, Muse saw an opportunity, at least for one show, to explore the dimensions of black talent. *Run, Little Chillun* opened at the Mayan Theatre in Los Angeles on 22 July 1938 and ran for 181 performances. Echoed through the critics' almost universal encomia, one theme persisted: the acting was natural and different from that usually seen in all-black musicals. The director had worked hard to make his art appear artless, taking his cues from his own writing: "The Negro artist is capable of translating his so-called dialects into more acceptable, understandable language without losing the richness of his characters."[56] The reviewer in the *Los Angeles Eagle* summed it up: "Those of us who witnessed the performance of *Run, Little Chillun* saw a different Negro. Not the Nordic man's idea of a Negro but the Negro as he actually is."[57]

Newark unit

Meanwhile, across the continent a theatre town long known for its vaudeville and later for its swing bands, Newark, New Jersey, hosted separate white and black units. In spite of the fact that Newark's Blacks made up nearly 9 percent of the city's population, the black unit had remained dormant until Hughes Allison submitted *The Trial of Doctor Beck* in 1937. Politically, the play was an amazing *tour de force*. Using the device of a murder mystery, Allison constructed a courtroom suspense drama in such a way that both white and black audiences agreed that color in America had the power to influence courtroom justice. The play's mulatto protagonist, Dr. Beck, marries a rich dark-skinned woman who pays his way through medical school. After graduation Beck falls in love with a light-skinned woman. His rich wife is found murdered; he is the prime suspect. The drama centers on the question: did he do it? All the evidence presented centers on Black and White hatred of dark skin, and the play condemns racism, with all its color classifications. *Doctor Beck* opened in Union City and Newark to unanimous praise. J. J. Shubert said it was the best play he had seen anywhere in the federal theatre, and his prompting moved *The Trial of Doctor Beck* to the Maxine Elliott Theatre on Broadway, where it ran for four weeks.[58] Brooks Atkinson of the *New York Times* dismissed the play with "The best that you can say of it is that its inadequacies are not conspicuous."[59] Herbert

Drake of the *New York Herald Tribune* thought better: "The situation is a difficult one to handle and it must be said that it is extremely well done in *The Trial of Doctor Beck.*" Seen from the perspective of sixty years, the play is an amazing piece of dramaturgy by a novice playwright who went on to write two more plays: *It's Midnight Over Newark* (1941), a Living Newspaper dramatization of the plight of black physicians in Newark hospitals, where they were not allowed to practice, and *Panyared* (1938; a West African term for *kidnapped*), a trilogy that traced an African prince from his sale into slavery through his descendants up to Reconstruction. Although there were plans for production, all were canceled when the FTP closed down.

Other units and productions

Blacks participated in all forms of FTP. Living Newspaper plays, which used current events, all had strong political bents. Abram Hill and John D. Silvera composed a documentary, *Liberty Deferred* (1938), tracing the history of Blacks in America from slavery to the 1930s. Because of its strong racial statements, the play was "deferred" until the FTP closed.[60] Other black units in Durham and Raleigh, North Carolina, contented themselves with children's plays: *Bluebeard* (1936) and *Hansel and Gretel* (1936). Shirley Graham (1886–1977), as musical and play director, adapted Charlotte Chorpenning's *Little Black Sambo* (1938) with great success at Chicago's Goodman Theatre. Esther Wilhelm, the woman in charge of the Buffalo FTP unit, created the Buffalo Historical Marionettes troupe and employed eight African Americans – five men and three women – who called themselves the Jubilee Singers, to perform the plays with music. The African American troupe used black and white marionettes to present *Uncle Tom's Cabin* with spirituals, and *The Life of Stephen Foster* (1937) with his music, as well as scripts about Lincoln and Washington. They performed in schools, hospitals, playgrounds, and orphanages, and also on the radio.[61]

Professor Tina Redd has documented a detailed history of Birmingham, Alabama's Negro unit, which performed under extreme racist restrictions. First, the unit's formation had to be delayed until a white unit was in place with salaries superior to Blacks. Second, no plays could challenge the complete segregation of the races, which meant that plays such as *Stevedore* could not be considered. Third, a totally white administration not only ruled and misruled, but also fought among themselves.[62] In spite of these obstacles, in the eight months between March and November 1936 the unit produced five plays. One, *Great Day* by a black man, M. Wood Morrison, "traced the history of the Negro race from 4500 BC to the present."

No FTP survey can be complete without acknowledging Ralf Coleman (1898–1976), the only Black to direct a FTP unit from its conception to its demise. Born in Newark, New Jersey, he and his brother were adopted by O. Paul Thompson, a Baptist preacher who believed the theatre to be an invitation to sin. Nevertheless, the Coleman brothers managed to enter the theatre by reciting poetry with Jubilee quartets. Circa 1921, Ralf narrated *The Open Door*, a large spectacular pageant at Symphony Hall in Boston. For a time he attended Harvard, then worked with Maud Cuney Hare and became director and actor with the Allied Art Players (1926–35). In the 1930s he helped to found and direct a community group, the Boston Negro Theatre. His Broadway début came in 1934 when he and his brother Warren played in Paul Green's *Roll, Sweet Chariot*, albeit only for seven days. The next year Warren was cast as Crown, the villain in the original *Porgy and Bess*.

When Ralf was appointed to the directorship of FTP's Boston Negro unit in 1935, he chose Frank Wilson's *Brother Mose*, a revised version of the one mounted in Harlem on 17 April that year. The federal Emergency Relief Administration sponsored the production and toured it to various units. Coleman had 170 actors, singers, and dancers to keep busy, and he had two audiences to please. His white audience enjoyed Negro folk plays, and he would produce several – *In Abraham's Bosom*, *The Man Who Died*, *At Twelve O'clock*, *Plumes* – but his black audiences did not care to see themselves represented as southern rural folk. Expressing middle-class black resentment, the *Boston Chronicle* editorialized: "The Federal Theatre is the finest chance that the Negro actor has had to experiment and endeavor to educate white audiences in accepting characterizations without seeking to penetrate through the grease paint... we must not allow either prejudiced white officials or half-baked Negro directors [Coleman] to rob us of the opportunity."[63]

The record of the Boston productions is incomplete; nevertheless, it is clear that over the four years of his administration, Coleman produced a variety of programs. On 18 October 1935 he directed his own black version of *Macbeth*, a full six months prior to Welles' New York success.[64] He remounted plays previously produced by other units – *The Trial of Dr. Beck* and *Tambourines to Glory*. He set on stage at least one original, *Cinda* by Jack Bates, a colleague from the Boston Negro Theatre. He confronted both political and sexual censorship in a city known for its puritanical repression in the literary and visual arts. In spite of opposition, he mounted the activist dock strike drama, *Stevedore* and *Bloodstream*, the story of a prison revolt by black convicts against white jailers.[65]

Coleman remained in theatre all his life. After the FTP closed, he toured professionally with *Anna Lucasta* as stage manager. In the 1950s and 1960s he continued to act and direct in amateur groups. In the late 1970s he was proclaimed by the Negro History Week Committee of Greater Boston to be "Mr. Theatre," an honor that pleased him.

In 1939 the WPA budget proposal of $875 million lay before the US Congress. The relief and employment programs that fed and housed the poor during the Depression would be extended or killed. The Senate version contained money for the federal theatre, whose share of that budget was less than 0.5 percent of the total, but the House version of the budget had none for theatre. Through its hearings the House Un-American Activities Committee vilified the theatre project by announcing (not proving) that the FTP was a "hotbed of communists." To save the larger WPA program, President Roosevelt and his administrator Harry Hopkins sacrificed the FTP. On 30 June the Federal Theatre Project closed forever. Among the eight thousand who lost their jobs that day, about 850 were Blacks. Over their four years the black units had mounted a total of seventy-five plays in one hundred separate productions. Many African Americans had received precious theatre training, backstage and on.

Within thirty days, four years of work – all the records, posters, playbills scripts, scene renderings, even marionettes – were hastily thrown into boxes and shipped to the Library of Congress, that had no space for theatre memorabilia; the library dumped the crates into an abandoned air hanger near Baltimore, where the boxes remained – forgotten – for thirty-four years. The FTP disappeared from American history until 1974, when Professors Lorraine Brown and John O'Connor of George Mason University "discovered" the FTP cache. Brown and O'Connor persuaded the Library of Congress to allow them to move the entire collection to their university, where they sorted, cleaned, and catalogued approximately 525,000 items, or 522 linear feet of shelf space. Forty-three file cabinets, hundreds of articles, and production books became available to scholars. Then, in 1992, Dr. James Billington, the new Librarian of Congress, ignoring the maxim "If it's not broken, don't fix it," demanded the return of the archives to Washington, DC. Lorraine Brown wrote:

In spite of a year and a half intense lobbying, unmarked trucks arrived on August 23 and began hauling away boxes containing the fruit of twenty years of our scholarly and archival work. That morning I stood at the library loading dock and came face to face with our utter and unmitigated defeat at the hands of an arrogant, bloated bureaucracy, clearly not accountable to anyone at our level of scholarly/artistic influence. Not a pleasant experience.[66]

George Mason was allowed to keep duplicates and any original material Lorraine Brown had collected.

In four short years, *The Swing Mikado*, *Big White Fog*, *Run, Little Chillun*, and dozens of others had proved how deep and vast was the well of black talent waiting for opportunity. The FTP proved that once the federal government established a national theatre, how fast and how far such a project could move toward promoting an end to discrimination in the arts. The decade that had begun with a white man's fantasy, *The Green Pastures*, ended with Richard Wright's bitter and compelling accusation, *Native Son*. Black playwrights had entered the arena of social criticism with a force and an authenticity never felt before on the American stage. At the beginning FTP's objective had been "to attain new aesthetic heights hitherto unexplored by the Negroes in the theatre, and thus to lay the cornerstone for the Negro Theatre of the future." The FTP's idealism continued to flow into the black theatres of the 1940s and 1950s; however, for four years the Second World War absorbed and redirected much of the theatre's energy.

II

Creeping toward integration

James V. Hatch

Some Negroes believe they should play any part for which they feel temper-
amentally suited without calling any particular attention to their colour.

Stage, November 1947

From the surprise attack on Pearl Harbor on 7 December 1941 to the
final surrender of Japan on 10 August 1945, Americans on the home front
concentrated on the "war effort," which included such diverse activities
as salvaging tin foil, conducting air raid drills, buying War Bonds, working
double shifts, rationing sugar, wearing "V" for victory insignia on lapels, and
practicing "racial tolerance," a self-discipline that the government stressed
was necessary for winning the war. On the other hand, African Americans
were expected to tolerate the segregated Armed Services, nonemployment
in war industries, and continued discrimination in housing and education.
The *Pittsburgh Courier* and the New York *People's Voice* both placed two
Vs on their newspaper mastheads: one for victory over fascism abroad and
one for victory over racism at home. Poet Witter Bynner's verse caught the
irony

> On a train in Texas German prisoners eat
> With white American solders, seat by seat,
> While black American soldiers sit apart –
> The white men eating meat, the black men Heart.

The Selective Service and Training Act of 1940 required all eligible males
from age 18 to register for the draft. To address "the religious, spiritual, welfare, and educational needs" of the new inductees, six organizations formed
the United Service Organization (USO).[1] They supported a dual racial
policy: "On the one hand, where circumstances indicated a club established
especially for Negroes was the practicable approach, separate clubs were

established and staffed by Negro personnel. On the other hand, in certain sections of the country it was possible to render most of the basic services through USO Clubs established without any particular reference to racial identity of the constituents."[2] At the peak of the USO's activity, when nearly one million Blacks were serving in the armed forces, approximately three hundred clubs were staffed by Blacks for black military personnel.

The USO Camp Shows project was set up with support from the National War Fund for the specific purpose of maintaining the morale of the armed forces. A special service division of the army, with a budget of $4 million, held the responsibility for welfare, recreation, and making liaisons with the civilian theatre organizations. Actor and director Dick Campbell, at age 38 and about to be drafted, was asked to head the all-Negro units. His first overseas program, *Porgy and Bess* with musical direction by Eva Jessye, toured the Caribbean Islands in 1943. Camp Shows, Inc. traveled to three hundred and fifty theatres. More than one-tenth of all Camp Show performers were Blacks, representing all specialties; they played before both black and white servicemen.[3] Performers and technicians were paid union salaries.[4] Most units were variety shows, consisting of musical revues with a chorus of pretty girls, a master of ceremonies, comics, tumblers, singers, and acrobats. Among the most popular of the vaudeville revues were Negro units, especially a short version of *Shuffle Along* with some of its original cast – organized by Noble Sissle (who was also a member of the Camp Shows' board).

New York City's Stage Door Canteen, an integrated club, was created by the American Theatre Wing. Carl Van Vechten, who had responsibility for managing the Canteen two nights a week, wrote to a friend that the hostesses were ordered to "dance with uniforms, not with colors." He observed that interracial dancing was frequent and unmarked, and that tables were shared by both races; by contrast, at a similar canteen in Philadelphia, the races separated themselves.[5] James McColl and Irving Berlin's *This is the Army* (1942) included a scene in the Canteen featuring the popular ballad, "I Left my Heart at the Stage Door Canteen." Its most popular act, "What the Well-Dressed Man in Harlem Will Wear," featured three black dancers – George Anderson, Marion "Spoons" Brown, and James "Stump" Cross (later of the comedy team Stump and Stumpy.)

Each military base had a Special Service officer, who promoted camp morale by organizing recreational sports, bands, and soldier theatricals written and performed by the men for their comrades. James W. Butcher from the Howard University drama department served at Fort Huachuca in

Arizona as a theatre consultant for the army's Special Services Division. At no base was educational drama more successful than at Camp Robert Smalls at the Great Lakes Naval Training Center, where Lt. Commander Daniel W. Armstrong, son of Hampton Institute's white founder, gave full support to seaman second class Owen Dodson, a graduate of the Yale School of Drama. His mission was to elevate company morale by creating plays about famous African Americans, naval history, and America's wartime allies. Dodson, with fellow-seaman Charles Sebree (former member of the Dunham Dancers in Chicago), wrote and directed eleven plays, some of which received national recognition. Their first, *Dorrie Miller* (1943), concerned the African American messman who shot down four Japanese planes at Pearl Harbor; *Everybody Join Hands* (1943) dramatized China's role in the war; and *Freedom the Banner* (1943) praised America's then ally, the Soviet Union. For this last play, Dodson received severe criticism from his commander and was discharged for "an asthmatic condition."[6]

The USO also booked "colored" tent shows, such as *The Bronze Manikins*, that traditionally toured the southwest, playing country and state fairs and carnivals on "Colored Day" (a fair day set aside for Blacks in the South and southwest.) A husband and wife team, Charles and Vivian Taylor, advertised their show as *Club Ebony*. Charles and his preteen daughter June danced, while the mother, under her maiden name Vivian Henderson, conducted the orchestra. On occasion, Pigmeat Markham and Baby Slade toured with the Taylors.[7]

Overseas, most teams were allocated by the number of performers that the planes could carry, and units were designated as red, white, and blue. Fox-Hole Units (Blue Circuit) were five people or fewer sent to war areas to perform on the top of jeeps. Larger units might be sixteen (White Circuit) or even thirty-two (Red Circuit).[8] During 1943 and 1944 the Red Circuit and the White Circuit were dissolved and replaced by the Victory Circuit, which comprised 168 entertainers in four different units.[9] Black performers touring the military bases in America and overseas were generally segregated in performance, although on special occasions they shared programs with Whites. An all-black concert and opera unit headed by the soprano, Caterina Jarboro, appeared in Italy. Several other concert voices – Paul Robeson, Marian Anderson, Dorothy Maynor, Muriel Rahn, and Aubrey Pankey – toured home bases, but they were never on the payroll of USO Camp Shows. When the war ended in 1945, one of Director Campbell's Berlin units entertained generals Eisenhower, Montgomery, and Zukov. At the apex of the war, Campbell had sixty-five units with more than three thousand artists performing all over the world.[10] African American troupers traveled an aggregate of more than five million miles and performed approximately ten thousand times over four years. The war had ended three years before President Harry Truman ordered the integration of the Armed Services.

Civil rights dramas

From the end of the Second World War to the beginning of the McCarthy period (1945–50), the American professional theatre produced twenty shows on civil rights issues, nine of them on Broadway. Off-Broadway and out-of-town shows displayed a wider array of moral stances, ranging from gentle persuasion of *Florence* (1949) by Alice Childress and the religious fervor of *Trial by Fire* (1947) by George Dunne to the activism of *Earth and Stars* (1946) by Randolph Edmonds.[11]

While musicals dominated commercial theatre in the 1940s, four dramas about African Americans addressed the nation's racial dilemma. The first, Richard Wright's *Native Son* (1941), opened at the St. James Theatre on Broadway on 24 March 1941. Wright's novel had firmly laid the responsibility for Bigger's brutality on the doorstep of white America, but in adapting the novel to the stage, Paul Green, a southern folk dramatist, had insisted that Bigger take some responsibility for the murders he had committed. John Houseman and Orson Welles preferred Wright's original concepts and discarded the modifications made by Green, which had softened Bigger's character. When Green saw the play he was angered and later published his own version. Canada Lee[12] created the role of Bigger Thomas, receiving near unanimous praise from the critics. The production ran for 114 performances before touring major US cities and returning to New York to run for an additional eighty-four performances before closing, in part because of America's declared war on 7 December 1941, which had refocused the nation's attention.

The second civil rights drama, *Strange Fruit* (1945), set in a small Georgia town, had been adapted from Lillian Smith's controversial novel. Staged by José Ferrer, the play featured 23-year-old Jane White as Nonnie, a black girl made pregnant by a white boy played by Mel Ferrer. Other Blacks in the cast were Juano Hernandez, Edna Thomas, Alonzo Bosan, Ken Renard, and Dorothy Carter. Robert Earl Jones played the lynch victim. The play lasted for sixty performances, in part because Eleanor Roosevelt wrote enthusiastically about it in her syndicated column, "My Day."

Figure 33. Perry Wilson and Canada Lee in *On Whitman Avenue,* 1946

After the Allies defeated Germany and Japan in 1945, black soldiers returned home to segregated housing. *On Whitman Avenue* (1946), a civil rights drama on discrimination in the renting and sale of housing, starred Canada Lee, this time playing a decorated war hero trying to move his family into a white neighborhood. Abbie Mitchell, Augustus Smith, and Peter Morell played the members of Lee's family. Margo Jones from Dallas, Texas, directed the drama, which was written by Maxine Wood. In response to unenthusiastic reviews, Eleanor Roosevelt observed in her weekly column that the American people were in a period of retrogression and did not want to be reminded of their shortcomings. With Roosevelt's help and that of Langston Hughes, the play remained alive for 148 performances.

The war's end propelled yet another play about a black veteran returning home to the South. *Deep are the Roots* (1945), written by Arnaud D'Usseau and James Gow, was directed by Elia Kazan and starred Barbara Bel Geddes and Gordon Heath; the play ran for 477 performances before moving to London, England. Evelyn Ellis, who had played the mother in *Strange Fruit,* played the maid. The drama became one of the very few civil rights dramas to return money to its investors.

The second drama on the Great White Way written by an African American during the 1940s, following *Native Son,* was *Our Lan'* (1947) by

Figure 34. Soviet Union production of *On Whitman Avenue*, 1947

Theodore Ward. A costume drama, *Our Lan'*, which is set on the Georgia coast at the end of the Civil War, relates the attempt by newly freed slaves to claim and keep the 40-acre plots of land promised by the federal government. When the federal army threatens to take the land back, the Blacks determine to fight, although they are certain to lose. *Our Lan'* opened at Henry Street Settlement House in New York on 18 April 1947; enthusiastic reviews spurred Associated Playwrights and the Theatre Guild to move the play to Broadway, where it was poorly directed by Eddie Dowling and Edward R. Mitchell. It closed after forty-one performances.

In 1948, the Actors' Equity Association (AEA) withdrew all performers from the National Theatre, the only major commercial house in Washington, DC, demanding the management drop its 112-year-old policy of excluding Negroes from the audience. Marcus Heiman, a New Yorker and president of the corporation operating the National Theatre, refused to integrate because he claimed other businesses in the capital had not. The strike lasted eighteen months, indirectly encouraging theatregoers and drama critics to attend performances at Howard University. On 20 November, Fredrik Haslund, then Norway's delegate to the United Nations, attended Anne Cooke's production of *The Wild Duck* at Howard University. The novelty of Ibsen played by African Americans intrigued him, and he invited Anne Cooke, James Butcher, and Owen Dodson to bring twenty-four actors to Scandinavia for a ten-week tour. In Norway, Denmark, Sweden, and Germany critics praised the Howard Players. One critic called the Howard *Wild Duck* "a freshly vacuumed Ibsen." The Germans preferred *Mamba's Daughters*; one critic commented that many of the younger members of the audience were disappointed that not all the actors looked coal black or chocolate brown. Several Howard students on that tour went on to professional careers – Shauneille Perry, Graham Brown, Zaida Coles, and Marilyn Berry.

The Fair Employment Practices Committee, which insured Blacks would be hired in the defense industry during the war, had no direct jurisdiction over commercial theatre, and yet the 1940s can be viewed as initiating some modest progress toward integration. Harold Rome's revue *Call Me Mister* (1946) dramatized the problems of returning veterans. He cast three Blacks – Bruce Howard, Alvis Tinnin, and Laurence Winter – in roles other than "spear carriers" (walk-ons). Winters sang "Goin' Home Train," and in the number "Red Ball Express" took center stage to relate how black war heroes had returned home to be denied jobs. After 734 performances, William Warfield took over the roles for the tour.[13]

Black musicals

In the 1940s significant black employment on Broadway remained mostly in shows with all-black casts. The decade began with *A Cabin in the Sky* (1940), a show that seemed to have been inspired by *The Green Pastures* (1930), the highly popular fantasy about "darky heaven." In *Cabin*, Joe Jackson (Arthur "Dooley" Wilson) is tempted by the devil (Rex Ingram) to be unfaithful to his wife Petunia (Ethel Waters). Her husband's greatest temptation was the dancing demon Georgia Brown (Katherine Dunham). For 155 performances Joe barely made it safely through the Pearly Gates. The book, lyrics, music, direction, and choreography were all by Whites. In 1944, MGM filmed *Cabin*, casting, among others, Lena Horne, Louis Armstrong, Willie Best, Butterfly McQueen, Mantan Moreland, and the Hall Johnson choir.

Carmen Jones opened three years later, on 2 December 1943, and ran for 502 performances, making it the longest running all-black musical of the 1940s.[14] Based on Georges Bizet's opera, *Carmen* (1875), author Oscar Hammerstein II revamped the lyrics and moved the Spanish setting to South Carolina during the Second World War. Producer Billy Rose immediately faced a casting problem: where to find experienced African Americans with trained opera voices who could carry the roles eight times a week? The lead role of Carmen was to be played alternately by Muriel Rahn (wife of Dick Campbell) and Muriel Smith, a 20-year-old student at the Curtis Institute in Philadelphia. The critics loved the show, but there would be trouble in paradise.

Muriel Rahn's AEA contract read that she would sing the role of Carmen for four performances a week. It permitted her to play more, but she was not required to do so. When alternate Carmen Smith contracted laryngitis, Rahn sang the role on twelve nights straight in Boston, but once on Broadway she refused to continue to substitute for Smith unless she received further compensation. According to the columnist David Quirk, as well as Muriel Rahn's husband and manager, Dick Campbell, the producer Billy Rose, was "a vicious squeezer." The show grossed as much as $57,000 a week for one and a half years. Rose's expenses for one week, including cast, crew, orchestra, and theatre, totaled $14,000. He paid Muriel Rahn $250 a week and Muriel Smith, $150.[15] When Smith became ill and lost her voice, Campbell would not let his wife go on unless Rose doubled her salary to $500 a week. If Rose declined, the show with its 135 people would be out of work. Campbell refused to budge. Leigh Whipper of the Negro Actors Guild (NAG) pleaded with Campbell not to close the show.

Equity sided with Whipper. Campbell's job as director of the USO camp shows was threatened. Channing Tobias, then chairman of the NAACP, told Campbell that the day had to come for black people to bargain for their talent. Although Smith was still ill, Rose forced her to go on. She could not sing, but read Carmen's lines. Rahn returned to the show for a time and Rose hired Inez Matthews as an understudy to assume the role. Producer Rose later established the Billy Rose Collection at the Lincoln Center for the Performing Arts, and at other times promoted opportunities for Blacks; however, his treatment of Muriel Rahn was disgraceful.

St. Louis Woman (1946), based on Arna Bontemps' novel *God Sends Sunday* (1931) and dramatized in collaboration with Countee Cullen, originally premiered in November 1931 with the Gilpin Players at the Karamu Theatre in Cleveland and was revived there in 1935. Eleven years later, on 30 March 1946, the curtain rose at Broadway's Martin Beck Theatre, this time with Harold Arlen's music and lyrics by Johnny Mercer, but not without conflict. Walter White, head of the NAACP, condemned *St. Louis Woman* before it opened because its prostitutes, gamblers, and murderers were all Black. Lena Horne turned down an invitation to play the lead; Ruby Hill played it instead. Rehearsals were fraught with tension when Rouben Mamoulian, director of *Porgy and Bess* fame, asked the cast to get down on their knees and wave their hands in the air, but the cast resented the 1920s darky image. Rex Ingram played Bigelow Brown, the villain, and Harold Nicholas (of the Nicholas Brothers) played Little Augie, the jockey who finally wins the race and gets the girl. Even though Pearl Bailey as a barmaid had only two songs in the show ("Legalize my Name" and "Tired"), her performance won her the 1946 Donaldson Award as the best newcomer on Broadway. In her biography *The Raw Pearl*, Bailey expressed regret that the songs had stereotyped her as a bar girl. The musical sang and danced its way through 115 performances.[16]

Although all-black or all-white musicals dominated the 1940s, some dramas used racially mixed casts. Upon reading *Cry, the Beloved Country* (1948), the playwright Maxwell Anderson found a parallel between South Africa's racism and America's own apartheid. He adapted the Alan Paton novel into the musical *Lost in the Stars* (1949) and persuaded Kurt Weill, the German-Jewish composer of *Three Penny Opera* (1928), to write the music. With Rouben Mamoulian directing, the Playwrights Company produced the musical for a modest budget of $90,000. The critics liked the cast, especially Todd Duncan, who had starred in *Porgy and Bess*. Other Blacks included in the racially mixed cast were Gertrude Jeannette, Julian Mayfield,

William Marshall, and Warren Coleman, but the critics were lukewarm in their praise of the script – a story of racial murder. The critics failed to find parallels between the racism in South Africa and that in the USA. *Lost in the Stars* closed after 281 performances and then toured fourteen cities, but recouped only half its investment, a fiscal fact not lost on Broadway producers of the 1950s.

A happier mixed-cast musical, *Finian's Rainbow* (1947) by E. Y. Harburg, Fred Saidy, and music by Burton Lane, became the civil rights success of the decade, running for 725 performances. The authors' marriage of an Irish tale of leprechauns with a pot of gold provided enough levity to lighten the subplot, a racial satire on the all too real Mississippi Senator Theodore Bilbo. African Americans William Greaves, Maude Simmons, Augustus Smith, and others played minor roles as singers and dancers in the chorus.

Beggar's Holiday (1946), an update of John Gay's *Beggar's Opera* (1728), brightened Broadway for 108 performances. Unique among musicals, it boasted not only a mixed-race cast but also a racially mixed orchestra, with music by Duke Ellington and Billy Strayhorn, as well as Dunham Dancers Archie Savage and Tommy Gomez. Produced by Perry Watkins and John R. Sheppard, race played no part in the story itself.[17]

The Equity Library Theater (ELT), sponsored by the AEA, regularly provided tested scripts for its members to perform, and often cast black actors. P. J. Sidney played the treacherous Raja in William Archer's *The Green Goddess* (1946). An all-black cast in John Galsworthy's British drama, *Justice*, included Milton Wood, Charles Swain, Lew Peterson, and Vivienne Baber. *Stevedore* from 1934 lived again with a mixed cast. The Blackfriars, a Catholic brotherhood, produced *A Young American* (1946) about a young black concert pianist; Louis Peterson, a recent graduate from the Yale Drama School played the pianist. *Trial by Fire* (1947), a California civil rights drama by the Reverend George H. Dunne, starred William Marshall and Paulene Myers. Only ELT and Blackfriars employed nonracial casting.

Although many African Americans launched promising careers in the 1940s, most were confined to all-black shows. Two artists both surnamed Smith – Elwood and Mildred – appeared in Broadway shows; both had talent and both discovered, after fifteen years of small roles, that they could not make a living as actors. In *Home is the Hunter* (1945), Elwood Smith began his career as a newly discharged veteran returning from Europe with fascist convictions. The critics blasted the play. In spite of an inauspicious beginning, Smith found a spot in the all-black musical *St. Louis Woman*, and then off off-Broadway in the Blackfriars' *City of Kings*, as the Peruvian saint,

Martin de Porres, possibly the only role of depth he would ever play. In 1952 he appeared in the prestigious if obscure and exotic revival of *Four Saints in Three Acts*; two years later, in *Finian's Rainbow*, then in the Broadway comedy *No Time for Sergeants* (1955). He directed *A Medal for Willie* at Club Baron and appeared in two television plays, *Light in the Southern Sky* (1958) and *The Bitter Cup* (1961). His final recorded performance came as a policeman in the civil rights musical *Fly Blackbird* (1962).

Mildred Joanne Smith's career began in a short-lived drama, *Men to the Sea* (1944), and after the disastrous all-black *Lysistrata* (1946), she again found work in Broadway's *Beggar's Holiday* (1946). In 1948 she was cast in four plays that closed early, including *Set My People Free*. She ended her career in 1949 in a poor play, *Forward the Heart*, about a maid who is loved by a blind war veteran.[18] In seeming contrast, the career of a third Smith, Muriel, achieved more success than most actors, black or white. In her very first audition she captured the title role of *Carmen Jones* (1943), which she played for three years. After brief splashes in a series of soon-closing shows – *Our Lan'*, *The Cradle Will Rock*, *Sojourner Truth*, and *Hypolytus* – she found a home as Lady Thiang in the revival of the *King and I* (1953–56). In London she sang the role of Bloody Mary in *South Pacific*, and the lead in a revival of *Carmen Jones* (1956). Her career ended with two films, *The Crowning Experience* (1960) and *Voice of the Hurricane* (1964). She is quoted as saying: "Since I have been in the profession it has been my deliberate purpose and intention to steer away from any parts that might be considered stereotype."[19] But a glance over the show titles in which she and the other Smiths worked indicates how tightly all their talents were confined by race. In 1947 the British journal *Stage* commented: "Never in a single year have so many Negro artists crossed the Atlantic to play in London." However, they still were unable to secure any roles not marked "colored."

Yet, within these restrictions several individuals delivered bravura performances. In 1947, John Marriott broke free of servant roles to play Joe Mott, a barfly who, like the white alcoholics in *The Iceman Cometh*, lied to himself about the things he would still achieve. In the person of Joe Mott, O'Neill had given John Marriott a role with humanity. Marriott continued to work until 1976, in roles that offered little challenge to his talents. Others praised for their work in the postwar period were Ethel Waters in *The Member of the Wedding* (1949) and Juanita Hall in *South Pacific* (1943). Canada Lee appeared as Caliban in *The Tempest* (1945) and as Daniel de Bosola in *The Duchess of Malfi* (1946), a role he played in whiteface. Although he made several films, including *Lifeboat* (1944), Lee's career collapsed in the 1950s

Figure 35. Paul Robeson

when his name appeared on the US Attorney General's list of subversives. The FBI under the direction of J. Edgar Hoover named Lee an "outstanding Communist Party fellow traveler." In 1949, Lee called a press conference to declare: "I am not a Communist or a joiner of any kind. Call me a Communist and you call Negroes Communists." In spite of his denial he was "whitelisted" from roles in film and theatre. He died in 1952, but the theatre tradition from which he sprang had not.

Paul Robeson's (1898–1976) theatre career cannot be separated from politics and should not be. A Phi Beta Kappa scholar, an all-American football end, a graduate of Columbia Law School, a linguist who spoke seven or eight languages, a concert singer, a fearless spokesman for equality, and gifted with one of the most distinguishable voices ever heard in the theatre, Robeson with his tall, muscular stature sounded like a *man* and looked like a *man*. For black people, he was their Joe Louis of the stage. Unbeatable.

Robeson's stage career began by taking over Charles Gilpin's role in *Emperor Jones* (1923) and then in the Provincetown Players' 1925 production of Eugene O'Neill's *All God's Chillun Got Wings*. Threats of riot were heard in the streets because in the play Robeson kissed the hand of his white wife. In 1928 London audiences loved him when he sang "Ol' Man River" in *Show Boat*, a triumph he repeated in New York in 1930. He returned to

London to play *Othello* (1930), *The Hairy Ape* (1931), and *Stevedore* (1933). He made several films in England and then traveled to the Soviet Union in 1934, where he received such a warm welcome that he became a frequent visitor and an outstanding international spokesman for the oppressed.

In 1943, fourteen months before his *Othello* opened in New York, the director Margaret Webster brought her actors – José Ferrer, Uta Hagen, and Paul Robeson – to try-out at Brattle Hall, Cambridge, Massachusetts. Robeson would become the first black man to play Othello on Broadway, an honor that created a prodigious anticipation in New York. He had previously played the role in London in 1930 with Maurice Browne as Iago and Peggy Ashcroft as Desdemona. When the tragedy opened at the Shubert Theatre, a critic reported that Robeson's voice "filled the lines organ-like, with full meanings, deep music and great passion."[20] All the critics agreed that Robeson's voice was magnificent, but some complained that he was too restrained in the role, perhaps because of his concern that he invest the African general with dignity rather than primitive passion. The production set a record run for a Shakespeare play on Broadway, 296 performances, a record that still stood on the centenary of Robeson's birth, in 1998.

His Othello would become the pinnacle of his theatre career. He could not have known that the Cold War with the Soviet Union would bring a wave of oppression down on the artists in America. Fascism had been defeated in Germany but not in America. The political right, determined to roll back the power of the unions, resumed its attacks on communism, particularly the Soviet Union, where Robeson had been so popular. In April 1948, Robeson had spoken in Paris at a conference for world peace and declared that if there were a war with the Soviet Union, the American Negro would not fight its former US ally. Continuing his concert tour, he told an audience in Oslo that "only in Russia could the Negro artist straighten his shoulders and raise his head high." When he returned home, a mob of American patriots stoned him at the Peekskill concert.

In a downpour of unverified personal and political calumnies calculated to suppress all political dissent, the US Attorney General created a list of organizations considered to be communist or communist fronts. Senator McCarthy, reelected in 1953, was chairman of the Senate's permanent investigation subcommittee. From that platform, he destroyed careers by branding actors, writers, and directors as subversives, which made producers afraid to hire them. Some theatre artists, such as Elia Kazan, when summoned before McCarthy's committee named colleagues as communists or sympathizers. Kazan continued to work and received an Oscar in 1999 for his "lifetime achievements." Others defied McCarthy. Some artists went to prison for refusing to name names. Playwright Lillian Hellman stood firm, telling McCarthy that she would not cut her conscience to fit the fashion of the times. For African Americans the era was doubly dangerous. Always on the edge of unemployment, many black professionals became cautious about supporting liberal causes or being seen in "political" plays. Robeson refused to sign an oath disavowing communism; the State Department withdrew his passport. His singing and acting career came to an end. In 1958 the Supreme Court declared the loyalty oath unconstitutional, and Robeson published his biographic statement of belief, *Here I Stand*. Welcomed abroad, he tried to resume his concerts, but he no longer had his former energy. Exhausted, he returned home and then two years later his wife Eslanda died. In 1973 friends and patriots celebrated his seventy-fifth birthday at Carnegie Hall, but he was too ill to attend. In a message to the gathering he described himself as "dedicated as ever to the worldwide cause of humanity for freedom, peace and brotherhood." He died in Philadelphia in 1976. Three decades later, the United States still denied Robeson's genius by refusing to issue a postage stamp with his image.

The Harlem art theatres of the 1920s had given birth to political theatres of the 1930s. Tenacious troupes in the tradition of the African Grove, they persisted in mounting plays for their own edification. In the companies discussed below, note the idealism expressed in their founding. When Congress had killed the FTP, the Negro Playwrights Company (NPC) knew that if they were to pursue racial and economic justice, they would have to provide their own stage. NPC's initial organizer, Abram Hill (1914–86), had graduated in English from Lincoln University.[21] Hill had a long apprenticeship in theatre. The son of a railway fireman from Atlanta, Georgia, at age 7 Hill appeared in a Morehouse College Theatre production. In 1925 the family moved to New York City, where Hill graduated from De Witt Clinton High School and attended the City College of New York for two years. In 1936 he secured a job in drama with the Civilian Conservation Corps (CCC), for whom he directed plays with young men ages 16 to 25. For the next two years Hill shuttled between his job directing for the CCC and working for a BA at Lincoln University in Pennsylvania, where he had studied theatre under Professor J. Newton Hill. After graduation in 1938, Hill returned to New York and joined the FTP as a script reader. While serving in this capacity, he wrote two plays, *Stealing Lightning* and *Hell's Half-Acre*, the latter produced by the Unity Players of the Bronx, which helped him to obtain a Theresa Helbrun scholarship at the New School for Social Research to study playwriting with John Gassner and Erwin Piscator. Within a year, Hill completed a social satire which he gave to actor-director Dick Campbell of the Rose McClendon Players. With some revision, *On Strivers' Row* ran for sixteen performances. With the founding of the American Negro Theater (ANT) in 1940, Hill became its director and produced the play as the theatre's first major effort; it ran for a 101 performances. So popular did *Strivers' Row* become that ANT revived it twice, once as a musical.

Hill's comedy, with its theme similar to Molière's *Bourgeois Gentleman*, has continued to delight college and community audiences. Although it is doubtful that Hill had read *In Dahomey* (1902), the Van Striven family of *On Strivers' Row* are dramatically "kissing cousins" to the Lightfoot family of *In Dahomey* – they both live in a chichi neighborhood; they both have a daughter they wish to place in high society; they both are surrounded by a greedy entourage; and in both plays a party-crashing and jive-talking hustler embarrasses the families by his low-class behavior. Finally, in both plays young true love wins out over family pretense, demonstrating to the audience that all's well that ends well.

On 5 May 1940, Abram Hill called together a band of playwrights – Hughes Allison, Theodore Ward, Powell Lindsay, Theodore Browne, Langston Hughes, and George Norford – to organize the Negro Playwrights Company as a nonprofit group. They set down their ideals:

> Harlem can possess a theatre that reflects all the grace and the beauty and the truth of our daily life, a theatre that gives voice to the best that men have thought and believed, that boldly and honestly deals with the major problems of the world, and that depends upon the deepest interests and aspirations of the race for its dignity and inspiration.[22]

They rented and reopened the Lincoln Theatre in Harlem, an old vaudeville house on 135th Street where the Anita Bush Players had been born. For their first and only production they chose Theodore Ward's carefully crafted *Big White Fog*, which the FTP had premiered in Chicago in 1938.[23] The play survived sixty-four performances. Then Stalin signed a pact with Hitler to invade and divide Poland. Ward's play closed, a casualty of the anti-Soviet feelings in America. The NPC, which had been closely associated with the left, collapsed too.

The NPC masthead had never included Abram Hill's name; he had resigned and assembled yet another group, who felt the theatre should embrace a larger artistic philosophy than the more political agenda of NPC. "As a director and a playwright," Hill wrote, "I have tried to bring a balance in the Negro theatre. Most of the big-time commercial productions on race themes have dealt with only about 10 percent of the Negro people, as a rule the exotic lower depths. All I am trying to do is introduce a few of the other types who run the gamut from professionals, middle class, and everyday Dicks, Toms, and Harrys."[24]

American Negro Theater

Hill again assembled some theatre friends – Fred O'Neal, Howard Augusta, James Jackson, Virgil Richardson, Claire Leyba, Jefferson D. Davis, Vivian Hall, Austin Briggs-Hall, Stanley Green, and Kenneth Manigault. They had no money so they took up a collection and discovered that they had just 11 cents. According to Hill, they mailed out eleven postcards inviting others to the next meeting. By the third or fourth meeting they had thirty people attending. They named themselves the American Negro Theater; the acronym ANT was much liked as a metaphor for the communal, hardworking theatre the group hoped to build. After a series of conferences, on 5 June 1940 the group declared itself to be the founding body of the organization and was later designated to be its executive committee. Arguably ANT became the most important, self-contained black theatre troupe between the demise of the African Company in 1823 and the birth of the Negro Ensemble Company (NEC) in 1967.

Their constitution drew upon Du Bois' dictum that theatre should be *by, about, for*, and *near* African Americans, and stated in its preamble that Blacks brought a special gift and style to the American stage. The 30-page document reflected the ideals of the FTP:

> A people's theatre is a very valuable institution. It provides the finest outlet for class emotions that can be organized. It serves as a spur to citizen ambition, provides a partly self-supporting source of work and income, and a healthy kind of occupational therapy on a national scale for thousands.
>
> Unhappily, we have been trained to think of the theatre mostly in terms of commercial enterprise that is too expensive when it is worthy, and too cheap and boring when it is not. We know it too frequently as an investment for gambling show men, or as a playground for dilettantes and escapists who are unable to withstand the hard realities of life.
>
> We need a people's theatre which shall in effect be a national theatre. The people who want a theatre will have to organize it and pay a part of the expense for both its creation and support. Realizing the reluctance

of the people to assume this responsibility, the essential burden of stimulating the development of such a project rests upon the shoulders of those individuals who are willing to assume this obligation; those who feel sincerely the call in a genuine quest for the content of theatre art, and by their talent, industry, and profound respect for a theatre they shall create. (American Negro Theatre Constitution, 1940)

Taking his cue from the Rose McClendon Players, who had occupied a stage in the public library on 124th Street, Hill approached the librarians on 135th Street. They granted ANT the use of their basement stage. To raise funds, ANT immediately produced *Hits, Bits and Skits*. The basement theatre held 150 seats. ANT charged 49 cents admission. *On Strivers' Row* had succeeded with the Rose McClendon Players, so Hill immediately put his play into rehearsal. It ran for five months. In March 1941, after adding Don Burley's lyrics, J. P. Johnson's music, and choreography by Leonard Harper, Hill moved *Strivers' Row* to the Apollo Theatre as a musical, where it ran for one week.

ANT's dream was to enlist a subscription audience. Initially their patrons came from outside Harlem, but by the second year, after a vigorous campaign with Harlem organizations to buy tickets, two-thirds of their audience were local. By the third year, 90 percent came from Harlem. By the time they produced *Anna Lucasta* in 1944, they had a following of five thousand.[25] Rarely has a community theatre production achieved such a dichotomy of results as ANT's mounting of *Anna Lucasta* in 1944. Hill had had the play in his drawer for two years. The saga of a Polish family in Pennsylvania whose daughter is a waterfront prostitute had not appealed to him. The story was mean, sad, and grim. However, when Hill reread the script, he saw possibilities to make it an African American family and to lighten the story, turning it into a comedic drama. He contacted the original author, Philip Yordan, a Hollywood screenwriter, who gave Hill *carte blanche* to change the script anyway he liked. Hill rewrote the play, and it opened on 16 June 1944, with Hilda Simms in the lead, and ran for five weeks.[26] Nine New York newspaper dailies came to review the show. They raved. Producers quarreled over who would get the play. Yordan and Hill signed a Dramatists Guild contract making Hill coauthor. He would receive 5 percent author's royalties. As the originating producing company, ANT would receive 5 percent of all first-class productions worldwide, including Broadway. ANT would also enjoy 2 percent of all subsidiary rights. This was not to be.

Figure 36. Hilda Simms in *Anna Lucasta*, American Negro Theatre, 1944

The show closed for the summer in preparation for an autumn Broadway opening. The producer, John Wildberg, insisted on bringing in Harry
Wagstaff Gribble (1891–1981), who had directed *Johnny Belinda* (1940).
Gribble rewrote the last act. The play opened at the Mansfield Theatre
on 30 August 1944 and ran for 957 performances, setting a record for a black
play. Two other companies toured, one to London, the other to major cities
in the United States. Two films were made. The first with a white cast was
a box-office failure; the second, in 1958, with Eartha Kitt and Sammy Davis
Jr. was a hit. However, ANT never benefited from the bonanza. The two
copies of the Hill – Yordan – Wildberg contracts filed with the Dramatists
Guild could not be found. They had inexplicably vanished. In 1974, thirty

years later, Hill still refused to say what he thought had happened to the contracts because he could be sued for slander.

Hill had to renegotiate his entire contract. At first Wildberg, according to Hill, refused to discuss it. "Yordan said, 'Don't worry. He'll take care of you.' That went on all summer of 1944."[27] Just before the Broadway opening, Hill threatened an injunction. Wildberg said he would pay 2 percent of the Broadway production. Hill took it before the ANT committee and explained it. Eight members of ANT were in the Broadway show. Three of them were on the committee. They were also under contract with Wildberg, who offered no additional rights from a possible movie and no radio rights. He offered only 2 percent of the Broadway show. The committee voted to accept it. Consequently, ANT received royalties ranging from $200 to $250 a week for about two years. Hill asked for money for rewriting the script. The producer said Hill's percentage was included in the 2 percent for ANT. Hill claimed his "lost" contract called for 10 percent of the writing share. He battled for six months. The producer offered Hill $1,500. Hill's lawyer fought. They offered $15,000. Then $22,000. Finally, the producer said, instead of money, they'd produce Hill's drama about a prizefighter, *Walk Hard*, on Broadway, which ANT had produced in Harlem for a six-week run. Hill decided that rather than risk losing everything if *Walk Hard* failed, he would accept a flat fee of $25,000 for his writing efforts. This happened a year after the show had opened. Hill claimed the play and the two film versions had grossed $80 million. "Yordan got 10 percent down the line – three to ten million dollars. We [ANT] would have had a minimum of $300,000. Yordan had producer's rights too. We were the first to produce it [*Anna Lucasta*] four or five years after Yordan wrote the original play."[28]

Distinguished professionals who began with ANT include Alvin Childress, who left for Hollywood to play in the television series *Amos 'n' Andy*. His wife, Alice Childress, whose complexion was too fair for commercial black roles, turned to playwriting and her career will be addressed later in this chapter. Earle Hyman, who played the romantic lead in *Anna Lucasta*, emerged as an exceptional actor, capturing classic roles in *The Cherry Orchard*, *Pygmalion*, *Death of a Salesman*, *Long Day's Journey into Night*, *The Master Builder*, *Othello*, and *Hamlet*. He was also honored by the Norwegian government for his performances of Shakespeare and *The Emperor Jones* in the Norwegian language. Theatre critic Edith Oliver, after seeing Hyman in the Roundabout Theatre production of *Othello*, observed: "Earle Hyman is said to have performed Othello more often than any other living actor. His distinguished performance is like no other I've ever seen. He acts without rhetoric and recitation, so that even the great speeches are never allowed to become set pieces; they seem fresh and spontaneous."[29]

Fred O'Neal, who cofounded ANT, divided his time between assisting Hill in running the organization and developing his own talent as an actor. He was elected manager and made things work for five years while acting in *On Strivers' Row*, *Christophe*, *Tin Top Valley* (as a hillbilly white man with a blond wig), and *Anna Lucasta*. He stayed with ANT to its demise. O'Neal (1905–92) went on to play in a dozen films, twice that number of television dramas, and as many Broadway and off-Broadway productions. He assumed the vice-presidency of the AEA and finally its presidency in 1964–73.

Another fine talent, Ruby Dee (born Wallace 1924), came to ANT as a sophomore from Hunter College in New York City because the faculty could find no roles for her. ANT cast her in *Three's a Family*, *Walk Hard*, and *On Strivers' Row*. Her first Broadway show was *South Pacific* (1943), followed by *Jeb* in 1946, when she worked with Ossie Davis (born 1917). Dee then played Anna, the lead in the touring company of *Anna Lucasta*, with Ossie Davis as Rudolf, the romantic lead. They married in 1948. Over the years, although each had separate writing and acting assignments, Davis and Dee often played in the same shows. Dee created the role of Ruth Younger in *A Raisin in the Sun* (1959), and was joined by Davis when he replaced Sidney Poitier as the male lead. In 1961, Davis wrote *Purlie Victorious* and they both starred in the Broadway production. From 1971 to 1976 they worked on the radio series *Ossie Davis and Ruby Dee Hour*. Both had film careers, Davis directing as well as acting. Both appeared in Spike Lee's film *Do the Right Thing* (1989). Dee also wrote *Glow Child and Other Poems* (1972) as well as her own one-woman show, *My One Good Nerve* (1998). Ossie Davis delivered the eulogy at the funeral of Malcolm X, which remains a high-water mark in composition and rhetoric, a splendid tribute to the dead hero. Their service in civil rights and labor causes coupled with their careers in film, theatre, and television brought them respect and honor far beyond the brief tribute here.[30]

Davis and Dee were not ANT's only famous pair. Sidney Poitier and Harry Belafonte shared the same acting classes. In order to become members, all apprentices had to be trained in the disciplines of stagecraft, choreography, and speech. Acting classes were directed by Osceola Archer. According to Hill, the legend that Poitier was rejected initially because of his West Indian accent is not true. Fred O'Neal did tell him that if he expected to play all kinds of roles with all kinds of speech patterns, he would have to rid himself of his accent. He did. His break came when he performed with Canada Lee in *Cry, the Beloved Country*. His early career lay entirely in theatre, including the Broadway role of Walter Lee in *A Raisin in the Sun*. In 1968 he directed Louis Gossett and Cicely Tyson in an integrated comedy, *Carry Me Back to Morningside Heights*, his farewell to live theatre. Shifting to Hollywood, Poitier's fame grew steadily – acting, directing, producing in more than fifty films, including *Guess Who's Coming to Dinner* (1967) and *Buck and the Preacher* (1972), in which he costarred with Harry Belafonte, whose first professional recognition had come as a calypso singer. Belafonte's early training with ANT, as well as at the New School for Social Research with Erwin Piscator, did not bring him Broadway roles as it had for Poitier. Instead, much of Belafonte's early professional life centered on musical appearances in variety television shows; he received an Emmy Award for *Tonight with Belafonte* (1959) and a Grammy Award in 1960.

Why did such a successful company as ANT come to an end? Twenty-five years after its demise, Abram Hill assessed that *Anna Lucasta* had destroyed them. "A division occurred. The Broadway group with its publicity and salaries included some who had not been with ANT from the beginning. The group who didn't get to Broadway resented those who did because they felt they too had contributed to the success of the others."[31] "Community" had dropped out of community. Each member of the original organization had pledged to a sincerity of purpose and a willingness to sacrifice their individual attainment for the greater good of the group. Further, if any of them did become commercially successful from ANT's productions, they would return 1 or 2 percent of their salaries. Only Fred O'Neal and one or two others fulfilled their pledge. Most of those who became professionals did not return to ANT to perform.

The Rockefeller Fund for General Education awarded ANT $9,500 for the 1944/45 season, enabling salary payments for the first time. Previous to that, the theatre never made enough money to pay its people any more than the car fare. A year later Rockefeller awarded ANT a second grant of $11,000. Plans were put forward to build a new theatre for $250,000. The library on 135th Street had told ANT that they would have to move. Newspaper critics always wrote of how hot, crowded, and hard the seats were. The library felt it was negative publicity for them. For four years the library had paid the lighting bill when ANT was unable to pay its rent.

ANT moved to the Henry Lincoln Johnson Elks Lodge on 126th Street. Rent and electricity cost from $250 to $400 a month. They searched for a theatre building to buy, but found none they could afford, so they continued at the Elks Lodge, where they produced a series of plays by white authors. The primary reason for this may have been a dearth of black playwrights; also, perhaps ANT hoped to draw some white patronage to the second floor of 126th Street. *Home is the Hunter* (1945), *The Peacemaker* (194?), and *Tin Top Valley* (1947), all by white writers, were artistic and audience failures. Black playwrights did no better, with *Meet Miss Jones* (*Sugar Hill*, 1947) by Miller and Lyles, and Abram Hill's adaptation of Gorky's *The Lower Depths* (*A Long Way from Home*, 1948). Kenneth White's *Freight* (1949), with Maxwell Glanville, William Greaves, and Sidney Poitier, moved to Broadway for one week. Osceola Archer, Audrey Beatrize, and Bessie Powers attempted the Irish folk drama *Riders to the Sea*, but these women of considerable talent were unable to transfer the Irish culture to Harlem. An announcement in a program for the 1947 season stated that all training classes had to be suspended for "lack of funds." To help pay the rent, ANT's admission was raised to $1.20 and then to $1.80, with the best seats at $2.50.

ANT's demise stemmed from several sources. From 1945 to 1948 the cost of production and supplies had skyrocketed. Hill's original vision had been that ANT would become self-sustaining within five years. The quality of shows declined. Feeling within the organization grew bitter, and Hill was blamed because productions were not up to standard. He was spending 90 percent of his time not in directing and writing, but in conference. "I couldn't stand all the acrimony. They didn't want any show that did not have a Broadway potential. We had nearly three hundred members. Women came in looking for Hilda Simms roles; guys looking for Poitier roles."[32]

Hill came to believe that it was not possible in America to sustain an ethnic theatre without a crutch, that is, without grants and funding from government and private foundations. "As long as we have inequities in our society, we, as an ethnic group, will have to rely more and more upon ourselves and not anybody else."[33] Hill had articulated black theatre's dilemma: equity in arts funding would not exist until there was equity in society itself, and, in the meantime, black theatre must rely on itself to survive. August Wilson would wrestle with this same dilemma at the millennium. Hill resigned in February 1948. The company limped on until 1951.

The records of productions by ANT vary because some tallies count student productions. From 1940 to 1948, Abram Hill counted eleven originals. In addition to those already mentioned, the list includes Theodore Browne's *Natural Man* (1941), the John Henry legend,[34] and Owen Dodson's *Garden of Time* (1945), a poetic adaptation of the Medea legend placed in the South. Other standard works include: *You Can't Take It With You* (1946), in which

Figure 37. Bill Greaves and Sadie Brown in *The Garden of Time*, by Owen V. Dodson, American Negro Theatre, 1945

Sidney Poitier turned in a rousing portrayal of the Russian ballet dancer; Sean O'Casey's *Juno and the Paycock* (1946), in which both Poitier and Harry Belafonte played, as they both did in *Days of Our Youth* (1945); *Starlight* (1942) featured Ruby Dee; *Three's a Family* (1944) presented Hilda Simms, Jacqueline Andre, Fred O'Neal, and Alice Childress. While ANT still attracted reviewers from the major New York dailies, the plays of the latter years were all by white authors and few of them were originals.[35]

The American Negro Theatre survived for eleven years and holds an honored place in theatre history. All those associated with the company, either as trainees, actors, or members, cannot be listed here; many, like Roger Furman, who had begun a career as a scene designer with ANT, continued to work in the theatre profession.[36]

Langston Hughes and political theatre

Langston Hughes was never a member of ANT, but perhaps as much as anyone, he carried the art theatre banner, founding one group in Chicago and another in Los Angeles. From its origins as a pueblo in 1781, Los Angeles had had a black presence. By 1940 the census counted 75,000 African

Americans, most living in the Central Avenue ghetto, which extended southward toward Watts. Prior to the Second World War the city had segregated swimming pools, restaurants, and parks. Black men worked as manual laborers and women as domestics. The Japanese attack on Pearl Harbor abruptly opened thousands of jobs in the defense industry, enabling Blacks to buy homes and attend the theatre. In Los Angeles, and indeed in the entire west, there had been no permanent black theatre for "the presentation of the problems, achievement, and beauties of Negro life." Locating his New Negro Theatre (NNT) in Gray's Musart Theatre at 4068 South Central Avenue, Langston Hughes conceived it as an instrument "to promote social justice and to fight fascist oppression." Plans were made for a constitution making NNT a permanent theatre with an executive board and a charter membership. It "would be funded by Theatre Patrons, Subscribing Patrons, and Organizing Patrons – some Patrons contributing $5.00 annually,"[37] and it would produce plays by both Blacks and Whites.

Don't You Want to Be Free?, following its success in New York City, opened in March 1939. Admission was 35 cents and some Hollywood names attended, notably Hattie McDaniels and Clarence Muse, the latter participating as guest director. The play ran twice weekly for six months during the spring and summer seasons on a triple bill with two satirical skits by Hughes.[38] However, when he returned to Los Angeles, Hughes announced that *Don't You Want to Be Free?* would be replaced with *De Organizer*, a "blues opera" with music by James P. Johnson. It never happened. Instead, in October 1940, Hughes sent NNT a draft of *Cavalcade of the Negro Theatre* (1940), a pageant inspired by the FTP writers project. Produced for the Chicago American Negro Exposition on 4 July through 2 September 1940, *Cavalcade* satisfied neither Hughes nor his cowriter Arna Bontemps, because the history was lost in "a sort of glorified Spirituals to Swing with plenty of pretty girls, fast dancing and good singing."[39] There were no further notices of impending NNT productions in Los Angeles.

In its short four-year life, the FTP had left a rich legacy of idealism and appreciation of theatre as a tool for democracy. In the 1940s the art and community theatres of Chicago resembled those in Harlem insofar as the founders and members embraced democratic idealism. Many were middle-class university graduates or had worked with the Art Institute's Goodman Theatre. Original black plays were few. In August 1941, to premiere his new play *The Sun Do Move* (1941), Hughes founded the Skyloft Theatre in the Windy City. Based in the community house of the Good Shepherd Congregational Church at 5120 South Parkway, Skyloft offered classes in stagecraft, acting, and scenic design. The Reverend Horace Clayton and his wife Irma were personal friends of Hughes, who stayed with them while he directed his own play.[40] After Hughes left, Helen Spaulding, a graduate in theatre from Northwestern University, became director and membership grew to more than two hundred. In 1945 Hughes reported to Arna Bontemps that the Skyloft Players had split into two separate camps. Among the many actors who worked at Skyloft, the name of James Edwards stands out. Edwards captured three Broadway roles in the 1940s as well as several in television and film, including *Home of the Brave* (1949), *The Caine Mutiny* (1954), and *Nat Turner* (1960).

Following the tenure of the Pekin Theatre (1904–11), Chicago's black community theatres had been confined to churches and settlement houses. The personnel in these art theatres drifted from one group to another. Harris B. Gaines Jr. had begun with the Negro People's Theatre in 1939. When that group expired in 1940 he founded the United Theatre League, which performed skits and sketches for trade unions and civic groups, such as the Urban League and the Chicago Negro Press Club. After one year, this organization, too, collapsed. Gaines then enlisted in the navy and after the war joined the Chicago Negro Art Theatre (CNAT) at 708 East Forty-Seventh Street, where, on 23 April 1946, he produced his original play, *The Life We Live*. A group of "progressive minded people who were interested in producing plays that had artistic and social meanings" had organized CNAT on 28 September 1945. Although these art theatres confronted social issues, many of their productions paralleled white community theatre bills with the popular plays *Craig's Wife* and *Death Takes a Holiday*.

Two years after President Truman signed an order integrating the armed forces, in 1948, communist North Korea invaded South Korea. Truman ordered the military to the South's defense. The Korean War (at first called a "police action") lasted three years and actively enforced racial integration in the armed forces. The war also unleashed a search for "subversives" in the film industries, theatre, and in broadcasting, as well as in the State Department, where individuals were identified as communists and homosexuals. The era would become associated with the senator who led the attack, Joseph McCarthy. It was a bitter irony that the senator's hit man, Roy Cohen, and the FBI's director, J. Edgar Hoover, were closet homosexuals.

In 1947, before McCarthy began his witch hunt, a cadre of former ANT members, along with musicians and painters in New York, had formed the Committee for the Negro in the Arts (CNA). They defined themselves as "dedicated to the integration of Negro artists into all forms of American culture on a dignified basis of merit and equality." Harry Belafonte, Sidney Poitier, Alice Childress, Vinie Burrows, Maxwell Glanville, and Clarice

Taylor were central members, and their purpose was to secure employment in mainstream theatre for minority artists, an objective which the cultural critic Harold Cruse denounced, because he saw integration as a loss of power for Blacks, an argument that was still a burning issue in the diversity controversy of 1998. A member of CNA, Ruth Jett, recalled:

> There was not one Black at the Metropolitan Opera, not one behind the cameras in the television stations that were just coming into being. When our Committee first started, we held a series of open hearings, and a number of fine singers were presented at Town Hall to convince people that there were singers of operatic quality. The visual arts suffered from the same exclusion. Jacob Lawrence was probably one of the few artists who had representation in a downtown gallery, and African Americans in the theatre were confined to servant roles.[41]

The committee determined to open an alternative theatre of their own. In 1949, CNA moved into Club Baron, located at 132nd Street and Lenox Avenue in Harlem, where it would produce plays for the next four years. For a minimal fee the cabaret's owner, Johnny Baron, gave the committee the use of its stage, a room next to the bar. The CNA program initially ran three nights for three weeks, and admission was $1.20 and $1.80. In between productions performers such as Frank Silvera gave readings and Harry Belafonte sang folk songs.

Beginning on 18 September 1950 with three one-acts, CNA produced *Grocery Store* by Les Pine, a play about voting rights, and two pieces by Alice Childress – *Florence* and *Just a Little Simple* (1950), an adaptation of Langston Hughes' stories *Simple Speaks His Mind*, not to be confused with Hughes' own 1937 musical adaptation he named *Simple* or his later 1956 adaptation *Simply Heavenly*. Childress transposed Hughes' Simple character into her own musical, *Just a Little Simple*. Donald McKayle and Elizabeth Williams choreographed movement to music composed by Robert Lissauer; John Proctor directed. In a scene entitled "When a Man Sees Red," Simple and the Bartender exchange charges:

> *Bartender*: You better be careful or they'll have you up before the Un-American Committee.
> *Simple*: I wish that old Southern Chairman would send for me. I'd tell him "Your Honery, I wish to inform you I was born in America, I live in America and long as I have been black, I been an American. Also I was a Democrat, but I didn't know Roosevelt was going to die. How come you don't have any Negroes on your Un-American Committee?

At the beginning of the twenty-first century, such dialog may seem innocuous, but in 1950 it could cost one a career.

From 1940 to 1948 Alice Childress (1916–94) had worked as an actor, a technician, and a teacher with the ANT, and in 1950 she directed plays at Club Baron: "The greatest experience of my life," she later declared, for there she learned her craft as a writer. From her grandmother, with whom she lived as a child, she had acquired an appetite for education (reading two books a day in the library) and a passion for integrity. In later years, producers offered her contracts "under the table," if she would ignore her union contract with the Dramatists Guild; she resolutely refused. She said that if her plays were to have misrepresentations of society and humanity in them, the errors would be her own and not those of producers. Eleven times her plays were optioned for Broadway, and each time never performed because she would not compromise. These options included *Wedding Band* (1966), a play about a black–white love affair based on her ancestors in South Carolina. When some found the subject "offensive," she replied: "If a racist society cannot stand what its playwrights have to say, it will suffer for it." In later decades, *Wedding Band* became her most produced play.

Childress' eighteen dramas were nearly always about the poor and mostly about women. She observed that the theatre rarely represented the people she respected most – ordinary people. "I always deal with those who know the condition they're in, who don't like it, but cope on a day-to-day basis. These people have been missing from drama." These are the characters who appear in *Florence* (1949), her first play, which concerns a black mother who wishes to dissuade her daughter from leaving the South to seek an acting career; the mother changes her mind after meeting a white woman in a Jim Crow waiting-room. For *Trouble in Mind* (1956), a drama about a black actress who refuses to play a stereotypical role, Childress received an Obie, the off-Broadway award for the best original play that season.

In 1952, CNA produced Childress' *Gold Through the Trees*, which spoke of racism in South Africa. In her essay "For a Negro Theatre," she wrote: "We need a Negro people's theatre, but it must be powerful enough to inspire, lift, and eventually create a complete desire for the liberation of all oppressed peoples."[42] It was the oppressed that she wrote about in *Wine in the Wilderness* (1969) for National Educational Television. The play dramatized class and gender conflicts nearly a full decade before other writers took up the subject. Master of the well-made play form, Childress became one of the most skilled craftspeople writing for the stage.

William Branch's *A Medal for Willie* (1951) was a drama in the tradition of the black veteran who had fought abroad and died for freedoms he did not have at home. Branch turned down an offer from a white producer to option the play when it involved rewrites the playwright could not accept. Instead, he gave it to CNA. The plot directly confronted racism. Willie Jackson's mother is to receive the medal for her son's brave death, but faced with the contradictions of racism, she refuses to accept the medal from the military general who is presenting it in public ceremony. The cast included Clarice Taylor, Julian Mayfield, Roger Furman, and Maxwell Glanville. The play ran for four months. Ironically, the morning after the play opened Branch was inducted into the army.

The last hurrah of CNA at Club Baron came in the summer of 1953, when Maxwell Glanville and Ruth Jett presented a bill of one-act plays under the title Burlap Summer Theatre. *Soul Gone Home* featured Frances Foster and Franklin Thomas. *Pot Luck* starred Isabel Sanford and Elwood Smith. *The Other Foot* by Julian Mayfield featured Carrie Carver, Roger Furman, and Louise Stubbs. Maxwell Glanville staged the plays, and production supervision was credited to Howard Augusta.

The CNA formed a professional alliance with three other theatres: the Harlem Showcase, the Elks Community Theatre, and the Penthouse Theatre. They called themselves the Council on Harlem Theatres (CHT). The alliance began by issuing a resolution noting the failure of the Broadway theatre to deal with African Americans in a truthful dramatic way and exhorting the representative groups to produce plays by black playwrights within the Harlem community. Their stated purposes were (i) to mutually support local drama groups by sharing actors, scenery, mailing lists, and audiences, (ii) to create a calendar that would prevent conflicts of production scheduling, and (iii) to agitate and press for the production of plays that reflected the Negro culture in its true light.[43]

A glance over Harlem's community theatres reveals that a core of ANT veterans were responsible for most of the work. These people shared more than a love of theatre; they shared an idealism that theatre could make a better world, a concept they had carried over from the days of the FTP. Such an individual was Loften Mitchell, a playwright who, with the help of the librarian Regina Andrews, founded the People's Theatre. There Mitchell produced his own plays: *The Cellar* (1947) and *The Bancroft Dynasty* (1947). In 1952 the company presented another Mitchell agitprop piece, *The Shame of the Nation*, about the Trenton Six, who were wrongly accused of murdering a white shop owner and his wife. With the success of this play, the People's

Theatre moved to 290 Lenox Avenue and became known as the Harlem Showcase Theatre. They lasted four years.

Another ANT alumna, Gertrude Jeannette, founded the Elks Community Theatre (Negro Arts Players) located on the second floor in the Elks Lodge at 15 West 126th Street (the once home of ANT in the late 1940s). Here she directed her own play *This Way Forward* (1952), a comedic drama about a city woman who moves to a prejudiced rural community in order to establish a high school. Jeannette had studied acting under Osceola Archer and pursued a successful acting career on Broadway, beginning with *Lost in the Stars* (1949). At Elks, Maxwell Glanville directed Ossie Davis' first play, *Alice in Wonder* (1952), which was later expanded into a full-length script, *The Big Deal*. This saw production at the Yugoslav Hall on Forty-First Street, New York City on 6 March 1953, when it was staged by the New Playwrights Company. The drama concerned a black TV producer, who, during the McCarthy period, has to choose between loyalty to his friends and keeping his job.[44] The Elks Community Theatre's final production was a group of one-act plays in 1952.

In contrast to a political agenda, general director J. Hugo Forde and executive coordinator Sheldon B. Hoskins of the Penthouse Theatre made their preferences clear in a 1948 theatre program, "Night must fall": "We are interested in the presentations of artistic and cultural activities and *will not be a party to any political issues.*" The Penthouse Theatre occupied the fourth floor of the Mount Zion Lutheran Church at 421 West 145th Street in New York City. Organized in July 1947, the group advertised themselves as "a group of young amateur Negro actors." Paramount among their aims was to provide opportunity for interracial casting which would be done "according to ability, not race or types."[45] Information gleaned from their programs suggests that Penthouse Theatre remained a completely black ensemble. Their nonpolitical stance may have stemmed from their desire to dissociate themselves from those in the CHT.[46]

Out of the postwar theatre ferment some unity emerged. In 1953, eighty-five actors, dancers, choreographers, and a variety of entertainers joined with Lester Walton to form the Coordinating Council for Negro Performers. From 1954 to 1955 they mimeographed an eight-page newsletter, the *Negro Theater Spotlight*, available for a $1.25 subscription. Their thrust was to present lists of qualified black performers to television producers, who otherwise would not be aware of them. They also monitored programs to detect discrimination and reported the guilty to the media. They invited major network executives to the Harlem YMCA to remedy the absence of colored actors, but the white executives absented themselves and little progress was made.

Many of the actors, playwrights, and directors from these grassroots organizations found the beginnings of a professional career, although the theatres themselves did not survive the mid-1950s.[47] Several forces militated against the community theatres. Television was coming to New York. (Even motion picture houses suffered from low attendance.) The promise of integration seemed at last to be arriving in the military, and in 1948 the Supreme Court had struck down housing covenants. The success of the Birmingham bus strike led many Blacks to think of black theatre as a segregated theatre. The 1940s had not introduced integration in the theatre, but that decade had provided work for African Americans on and off Broadway. Ironically, as we shall later show, when the theatre did begin to integrate in the 1950s, Blacks had fewer roles. Then, too, theatre production had become expensive. The unions pressured some Harlem theatres to hire union stagehands, although those same unions would not admit Blacks. To pay an AEA actor the minimum of $25 a week required twenty paid audience admissions. The single union stagehand at Club Baron made $16. These "small" salaries were just enough to sink the already fragile budgets. When off-Broadway producer Stella Holt mounted Langston Hughes' *Simply Heavenly* (1957) with a cast of seventeen, she was forced to drop several AEA actors because the revenue from her small house could not meet the demands of union salaries.

Finally, the climate of fear created by McCarthy had driven both artists and audiences away from protest theatre. This, coupled with the death of Canada Lee, the stoning of Paul Robeson at Peekskill, and the Korean War, all contributed to sapping the last energy that had been created by the FTP. It would be another decade before LeRoi Jones would raise the battle cry of racial and political unity in the theatre, and then, not for a progressive left, but for a segregated black artistry. One of the few white theatres to integrate casts was the Greenwich Mews Theatre located at 141 West Thirteenth Street in Greenwich Village. In 1952 the Mews hired Stella Holt as its director. Legally blind from the age of 13, she had graduated from Cornell University in English and did graduate work in sociology at New York University. Her approach to theatre she labeled "experimental," casting all her shows according to talent, not race. Claudia McNeil, Diana Sands, and Gilbert Price were some whose careers she encouraged. The Greenwich Mews Theatre was sponsored by the Village Presbyterian Church and the Brotherhood Synagogue. They gave Holt authority to change the theatre from a membership company to an independent, and by 1965 Holt and her companion Frances Drucker had produced thirty-four shows – eight of which were written by black playwrights.

The first was Bill Branch's *In Splendid Error* (1954), in which Frederick Douglass disputed with John Brown the use of violence in freeing slaves and the wisdom of forming guerrilla bands to spark a slave uprising in the South. Brown insisted on carrying out his plan and attacked Harper's Ferry. Douglass realized that Brown had committed himself to a "splendid error" but later acknowledged, "Let every man work for the abolition of slavery in his own way. I would help all and hinder none." The play ran nine weeks, and critics generally praised the production and the fine performance of William Marshall as Douglass, although the authoritative *New York Times* critic, Brooks Atkinson, confessed that he had never heard of Frederick Douglass; neither had Bruce Catton, the Civil War historian. Branch received a Guggenheim in 1958 and went on to write several successful television shows, winning the Robert E. Sherwood Television Award for *Frontiers of Faith*, a religious-oriented show. His television documentary *Still a Brother/Inside the Negro Middle Class* in 1968 was nominated for an Emmy. Branch continued to write plays, edit play anthologies, and held a variety of positions, including a professorship at Cornell University.

Greenwich Mews' next triumph, Alice Childress' *Trouble in Mind* (1955), starring Hilda Haynes and Clarice Taylor, ran for ninety-one performances. The plot: a liberal white director casts a black actress to play the mother of a lynch victim. The mother's character had been written as a mammy stereotype, and the actress refuses to play the role as written. The director is forced to confront his own racism. Brooks Atkinson wrote that the play was well worth a trip downtown. *Trouble* has remained a popular play in colleges and small theatres. D. J. R. Bruchner of the *New York Times* found that the 1998 Negro Ensemble production on Theatre Row in Manhattan still had the power to make one feel its anger and humor. Alice Childress' play possessed the art to contain her uncompromising idealism. She insisted that Blacks must articulate their own point of view:

> Most of our problems have not seen the light of day in our works, and much has been pruned from our manuscripts before the public has been allowed to glimpse a finished work. It is ironic that those who oppose us are in a position to dictate the quality and quantity of our contributions. To insult a man is one thing, but to tell him how to react to the insult adds a great and crippling injury.[48]

Encouraged by the stage success of Childress and Branch, and inspired by the successful court case initiated by the Reverend Joseph DeLaine of Clarendon County, South Carolina, an action that ultimately resulted in the Supreme Court declaring segregated school inherently unequal, Loften Mitchell wrote the Reverend's struggle into *A Land Beyond the River*. Opening on 3 March 1957 at the Greenwich Mews, the drama ran for more than a year before touring. In part, the play's strength stemmed from its close adherence to the facts and to the heroic engagement of the Reverend DeLaine himself. In 1957 the AME Church reported:

> In retaliation, the enemies of Christian democracy burned DeLaine's house to the ground. His wife and relatives were deprived of their positions as schoolteachers. Economic sanctions were forced upon them. For safety his Bishop transferred him to Lake City, South Carolina. There his enemies burned his church and Bible. They fired shots at him and he left town making his home in New York City where he found asylum.[49]

Mitchell had grown up in Harlem, but graduated in 1943 with a BA from Talladega College in Alabama. After serving in the navy for a year, he enrolled in John Gassner's playwriting class at Columbia University. Mitchell considered himself an "agitprop" writer who promoted black culture and history. He wrote plays based on black theatre personalities – Bert Williams, Florence Mills, Ethel Waters – and the musical *Bubbling Brown Sugar* (1976), which presented a series of attractive black theatre moments from 1910 to 1940. Based on a concept by Rosetta LeNoire, who produced the script at her AMAS Theatre, the play ran for a year before moving to the ANTA Theatre on Broadway, where it ran 766 performances before touring America and Europe. Mitchell was also the author of the first extensive history of African American Theatre – *Black Drama* (1967).

Aside from Langston Hughes' *Jericho-Jim Crow* (1963) and *Prodigal Son* (1965) discussed elsewhere, other black plays produced by Greenwich Mews included Bill Gunn's first play, *Marcus in the High Grass* (1960), which was severely panned; William Hairston's *Walk in Darkness* (1963), the story of a black GI in Europe who marries a white girl, ended tragically.

When Josephine Baker returned triumphant from Paris for a US tour, it was celebration time. No one admired her solo performances at the Strand Theatre more than critic Miles Jefferson, who found the rest of the season "empty."

Besides being smoothly bedecked in the creations of Dior, Molyneux and Jacques Fath, which she displayed with undulating walk, proud, but not snobbish, she exuded a warmth belying the continental chill of sophistication one was inclined in advance to associate with her name. The sensational wardrobe, the "horse-tail" coiffure and the stylish capering were merely appurtenances to a generous goodwill with which she was undoubtedly born. After all, this is what distinguishes the true artist from the charlatan.[50]

Jefferson's report smacks of the delicious savoring Blacks experienced when one of the race bested Whites at their own game. On 16 October 1950, Baker was a guest at the Stork Club. Others at her table were served dinner, but her order was "forgotten." Furious at this insult, she made her grievance known to the press. Columnist Walter Winchell labeled Baker a communist, a Nazi sympathizer, and an anti-Semite. She left America, not to return until a quarter of a century later.

Two years after reviewing Baker, critic Jefferson thrilled again to a second lady in a solo program, *At Home with Ethel Waters* (1953). He praised Waters but seemed saddened by the singer's ageing.

[Her] voice no longer has the old rich ring and volume of the early years, but style and artistry compensate for this lack. And such relatively minor complaints as her overwhelming and sometimes distracting avoirdupois and questionable taste in the selection of her wardrobe, did little to rob the performance of the sunny and completely beguiling authority which has established Miss Waters as a queen in the field of popular entertainment.[51]

A report to the Actors' Equity Association by Fred O'Neal, chairman of the executive board of the Negro Actors Guild, pointed out that over a six-and-a-half-month period during the 1951/52 season, only thirteen Blacks had parts in Broadway plays. These thirteen actors amounted to less than 2 percent of the total 692 players used in the forty-nine shows. In support of O'Neal's claim, Miles Jefferson noted that *My Darlin' Aida*, an adaptation of the opera *Aida* to a southern town, initially had no Blacks in its major roles, but under pressure, William Dillard was given the role of Aida's father, although his daughter was cast as white.[52]

All-black musicals, so popular in the 1940s, dwindled to a few revivals in the 1950s, and the only one written by a Black was a resuscitation, the 30-year-old *Shuffle Along* (1921). *The Green Pastures* was resurrected briefly with William Marshall as De Lawd. *Four Saints in Three Acts* (1934), the "high art" opera conceived by Gertrude Stein and Virgil Thomson, opened again and vanished quickly. Stalwarts *Porgy and Bess* and *Carmen Jones* were trotted out again, but big box office came from the new trend in touting black cabaret stars in white musicals – Pearl Bailey as a slave in *Arms and the Girl* (1950), then later as a bordello madam in *House of Flowers* (1954), and then as Mehitabel the cat in *Shinbone Alley* (1957); Lena Horne starred as the love interest in *Jamaica* (1957), and Sammy Davis Jr. danced, sang, and joked as a cabaret entertainer in *Mr. Wonderful* (1956). Triumphing over poor reviews, Davis touted his own show to success; he also touted *Mister Johnson* (1956), a Broadway adaptation of Joyce Carey's novel about a young African clerk, played by Earle Hyman, who aspires to be a British gentleman. While the acting of Earle Hyman, Ruth Attaway, and Josephine Premice was widely praised, the script was not. Black Americans perceived the African as a "handkerchief head" and refused to book theatre parties; the production closed early. However, in the next two seasons Hyman was cast in seven plays, including the role of Vladimir in Samuel Beckett's *Waiting for Godot* (1957), a role he would play in three subsequent productions. Director Herbert Berghof had correctly perceived that Beckett's tragicomedy of endless waiting was an apt metaphor for African Americans. Rex Ingram, Mantan Moreland, and Geoffrey Holder played the other roles for a limited run.[53]

America's "good neighbor" policy of the late 1940s and early 1950s was reflected in Hollywood films and on the Broadway stage. Led by the young Nelson Rockefeller and his brother David of Chase Bank, the American government had set out to ease the history of the United States as a colonial exploiter, by presenting a new face, the friendly good neighbor, albeit still a big brother. Symbolically, New Yorkers renamed Sixth Avenue, the Avenue of the Americas. In films, Carmen Miranda or Fred Astaire muted cries of revolution from banana republics by dancing the samba, conga, and carioca with the locals. In the same decade, black people on Broadway imported the Latin dancing mania from the Caribbean.

In the 1940s two choreographers trained in anthropology reintroduced African influences. In 1935 Katherine Dunham traveled to Haiti to record the island's black dance. What she learned appeared on Broadway in 1943 when she brought her Chicago company to New York in *Tropical Revue*, and again two years later in *Carib Song* (1945). At nearly the same time, dancer and choreographer Pearl Primus, who had sailed to Monrovia to study African dance, introduced her African program at the Young Men's Hebrew Association (YMHA) and then at Café Society. Primus made her

Broadway début with *African Ceremonial* in 1944 at the Belasco Theatre, with a program derived from African and Haitian dances. The choreography of both these women, along with their dances, would eventually change the dance style of the American musical, as evidenced in the work of George Balanchine, Jerome Robbins, and Bob Fosse. However, these black influences did not receive formal recognition from critics until scholars Brenda Dixon Gottschild and Jacqui Malone[54] published their dance histories in the 1990s. In the meantime, Americans were treated to *Blue Holiday* (1945), *Caribbean Carnival* (1947), *House of Flowers* (1954), and *Jamaica* (1957), all studiously avoiding race issues. But change was on the way.

Two serious dramas, both about adolescents reaching maturity, came to Broadway in the 1950s. The first was *Mrs. Patterson* (1954) by Charles Sebree, an African American, in collaboration with playwright Greer Johnson, and the second, *Take a Giant Step* (1953), by Louis Peterson, a black graduate of the Yale Drama School. In 1949, Charles Sebree, a dancer, easel painter, and scene designer with ANT, had written *The Dry August*, a play about a young black girl who dreams of growing up to become a rich white woman. That story became the basis for *Mrs. Patterson* (1954), "a play with music." The role of the girl gave Eartha Kitt her final boost into stardom. "Her scintillating gamin personality threw light in many a dark corner of the play," declared Miles Jefferson.[55] Sharing the stage lights were the veterans Ruth Attaway as Teddy's mother and Avon Long as Mr. D, the devil.

The second drama, *Take a Giant Step* (1953) by Louis Peterson, presented an adolescent, Spencer, played by Louis Gossett, coming of age in a white community. His "giant step" is into black manhood, with all its attendant problems of white racism. Harold Clurman wrote in *The Nation*:[56] "the particular color, immediacy and urgency of its feeling – a kind of emotional frankness, a wry naïveté and a rough goodness of heart that smack of something truly native, original in tone and unmistakably lived." Yet the audience did not respond at the box office. The producers ran an ad in the *New York Times*: "To the New York Theatregoer: We've got a hit! – Where are you?" The play closed after seventy-six performances. Revived off-Broadway three years later, it ran for 264 performances. *Take a Giant Step* launched the careers of two young leads, Louis Gossett and Bill Gunn.[57] For the first time, Broadway audiences watched middle-class black people living "normal" lives. While neither play had a long Broadway run, Peterson's family drama may have taken a small giant step in preparing the way for Lorraine Hansberry's triumph, *A Raisin in the Sun* (1959).

A comparison of the adolescent Spencer in *Take a Giant Step* with Bigger Thomas in *Native Son* a dozen years earlier, throws some light upon America's changing racial attitudes. Bigger had attended grammar school; Spencer is in high school and planning for college. Bigger's father has disappeared; his mother works as a maid; they live on social welfare in a slum. Spencer has a brother in college, a grandmother and mother who nurture him, and a father who serves as disciplinarian. Bigger has three black friends but they seem to fear him. Spencer's friends are all white and they abandon him in adolescence. Bigger is nearly inarticulate when he speaks with white people. Spencer is highly articulate. Bigger has no dreams he dare pursue. Spencer dreams of being like his brother Mack, with an education, and of finding love. In brief, although Spencer is confronted by white racism, he is able to deal with it. Bigger, eviscerated by poverty and ignorance, copes only through violence. White people in 1940 read the novel and attended *Native Son* the drama, but when *Giant Step* appeared, they did not support the play. Was it because Spencer was not a black and violent victim? Six years later, *A Raisin in the Sun* confronted Whites for an acknowledgment that a black family could be fully human, "just like us." Indeed, its impact was so great that twenty years later many white Americans assumed that Hansberry's play was the first black family drama.

The dearth of black roles on the professional stage led some to create their own, as Charles Gilpin and Richard Harrison had done at the turn of the century, when they had toured black colleges with solo performances of poetry and dramatic readings. In the 1950s two women, Paulene Myers and Mercedes Gilbert, often played maids in Broadway shows, such as Gilbert in *The Searching Wind* (1944) and Myers in *Anniversary Waltz* (1954), but even these minor parts might be scarce. In order to buy groceries and pay the rent, both actresses, independently, turned to solo performances in schools and community organizations. Although Mercedes Gilbert (1889–1952) had débuted on Broadway in 1927 with *The Lace Petticoat*, she had to turn to touring in 1941 in her own *One-Woman Theatre*. Paulene Myers' first Broadway play was *Growing Pains* in 1933. Reading the poetry of Paul Laurence Dunbar and Langston Hughes, she toured alone with *The World of My America*. Aufbau, the critic for the *New York Courier*, wrote: "Miss Myers proves to be an uncommonly gifted actress. Her emotional range is wide and she manages to hold the audience's interest throughout the entire program, a very difficult task indeed for one woman alone on stage."[58] In the 1990s performance artists rediscovered that hard truth.

The only quality role for black males in the 1950s on the professional stage was Othello, played separately by Earle Hyman – Shakespeare Guild Festival Company (1953) – and William Marshall – New York Shakespeare Festival (1958). Although reviews praised Hyman as "a performer of consummate skill [who] can move with force and distinction in any company,"[59] the commercial stage endowed neither Hyman nor Marshall with the name recognition it gave Josephine Baker and Ethel Waters. While the "sexual allure" of black women was played up in publicity, black male sexuality was played down. Black females gained romantic roles in opera long before their male counterparts. A black man's "sexual allure" could only be displayed in the boxing ring. It would not be until the 1980s and 1990s that the black male singer and actor could attract large white audiences.

For these reasons and others, African American audiences held a distrust of the commercial theatre, which had so often insulted them. When in the summer of 1952 Frank Schiffman, owner of the Apollo Theatre in Harlem, offered *Detective Story* (1952) with Sidney Poitier and *Rain* with Nina Mae McKinney, Blacks stayed away in such numbers that Schiffman proclaimed that Harlem had no interest in serious drama. Why should they? Downtown, they saw themselves portrayed either as servants in white plays, or comics in all-black musicals; uptown, live commercial drama had been killed since the 1930s, when Schiffman closed the Harlem Opera House on 125th Street and changed the Lafayette and Apollo theatres into movie and vaudeville houses.

Nonetheless, Juanita Hall, believing African Americans could be lured to Broadway by using star names such as Josephine Baker, opened an agency in Harlem's Hotel Theresa. She offered to assist those wanting tickets for a good show, who had neither the time nor convenience to approach a downtown box office. Alas, as will be seen later, it would take more than box-office convenience to integrate the audiences, even on the more "liberal" west coast, where Nick Stewart achieved some success in attracting white audiences. Born and raised in New York City, Stewart had run errands for the Hoofers' Club in Harlem. He gradually developed his own comedy act around a character he called Nicodemus, a clown who is afraid of ghosts and rolls his eyes in the tradition of Stepin Fetchit, but Stewart claimed that Nicodemus "was more a clever character." Stewart played Nicodemus in two Broadway shows, *Swingin' the Dream* (1939) and Irving Berlin's *Louisiana Purchase* (1940).

In 1940 Stewart moved to Los Angeles, where he was cast in the television series *Amos 'n' Andy* as the character Lightnin'. From the money he saved, he and his wife Edna opened their first theatre in 1950, a converted garage at Washington and Jefferson Boulevards, which they named the Ebony Showcase Theatre. It was a small house seating just 100, and its first play, *Anna Lucasta*, ran for weeks to sold-out audiences. In the cast were Alvin Childress, Eddie Banks, and James Edwards. Stewart followed his first success with *Three Men on a Horse* and *A Streetcar Named Desire* with James Edwards, who had had three Broadway roles. "In the fifties, if you were a New York actor coming to the West Coast, Ebony Showcase Theatre and the Actors Studio in Hollywood were the only places you might be able to work."[60]

In 1956 Stewart took over a movie theatre on Crenshaw Boulevard, where he produced *Lost in the Stars*, but even with the publicity of the author, Maxwell Anderson, attending the production, the Ebony Showcase lost money. The Stewarts did not abandon their enterprise. Eight years later, they acquired the Metro Theatre on Washington Boulevard near La Brea, an area on the border between the white and black communities, where Whites from Hollywood and from the Fairfax area would not feel unwelcome. Stewart converted the 1000-seat Metro into an intimate 250-seat house with a thrust stage, and opened with *Purlie Victorious*, followed by *The Odd Couple*, in which he himself played Felix.

In the 1950s there had been criticism from the black community that black theatre was *ipso facto*, segregated. Following the integration of the armed forces and the success of the Birmingham bus strike, audiences had aspirations of full integration into the American mainstream. Stewart said in an interview: "Even black people said that they hoped they'd seen the last of the black theatre. The newspapers – the critics said, 'What do you need a black theatre for?' I'm suspicious of the press. I think to a great extent, they try to discourage a black theatre."[61]

In the early 1960s Stewart wrote his own musical, *Carnival Island*, which featured the young Micki Grant, future author of *Don't Bother Me, I Can't Cope* (1970). But his greatest success came in the early 1970s when he produced *Norman, Is That You?* about a father who discovers his son is gay, a farce that had failed on Broadway. The cast was black except for the son's lover. The play ran for seven years and attracted the same audiences that would later support the Urban Circuit plays of the 1980s. John Amos played the father, a role which led to television roles and a movie. Among others who worked at the Ebony Showcase were Al Freeman, Juanita Moore, and Frank Silvera.

After the Watts riots in 1965, Whites grew fearful of going to West Adams and South Central Avenue; the Ebony Showcase audience changed from white (Jewish) to black. By the early 1970s Stewart was caught in the double bind. The white audience had disappeared, but Stewart steadfastly refused to do what he called "violent plays" of the Black Arts Movement. "I produce shows that say something, that have humanity and deal with universal problems."[62] Except for a federal Comprehensive Employment Training Act (CETA) grant to support a youth workshop, Stewart also avoided grants, fearing his theatre would come to rely on funding that would eventually be withdrawn. In 1980 Mayor Tom Bradley presided over the thirtieth anniversary of the Showcase, an amazingly long run for a small professional theatre.[63] In 1997 the National Black Theatre Conference gave Nick Stewart a lifetime achievement award. He died of natural causes at the age of 90.

Looking back

A glance at a sour incident in 1952 provides perspective on the rife discrimination faced by black actors. In a three-page letter, AEA actress Milroy Ingram wrote to Fred O'Neal in his official position, a carefully documented accusation that Stella Adler, arguably the most popular teacher working outside the Actors' Studio, discriminated against Negroes, first by excluding them from her classes, then by mocking them to her students, and finally, by threatening any of her students who attempted to enroll Blacks. Ingram concluded her letter:

> Miss Adler is head of the ANTA [American National Theatre and Academy] workshop and I feel that her racist views and actions make her position there an untenable one and wholly out of keeping with the avowed principles of the ANTA. Moreover, I feel that Equity (in view of its whole past and present position on the Negro question) cannot continue to lend support to an institution in which such opposing views [opposed to Equity's] are perpetuated. I urge that some positive action be taken to insure the integration of Negroes into the theatre workshop of ANTA and to insure that we have an opportunity to participate in every phase of ANTA's work from training to production. In line with this, if Miss Adler cannot be made to change her present attitude on the Negro as reflected in her classes, she must be removed from this position.[64]

Racial discrimination in the theatre was not banished in the 1950s, but attempts were made. Near the end of the decade, on a Monday afternoon at the Majestic Theatre, the AEA, the Dramatists Guild, and the League of New York Theatres sponsored an "Integration Showcase 1959." Diahann Carroll welcomed the audience with the song "Love Makes the Stage Go Round," followed by a scene from Ben Jonson's *Volpone* in which a cast of fourteen was completely integrated. Other scenes followed from *Tea and Sympathy*, *Room Service*, and *The Caine Mutiny Court Martial*, demonstrating conclusively that if the acting was good, color did not matter. Donald McKayle choreographed an integrated ballet called *Games*. Songs and scenes from Leonard Stillman's *New Faces* filled out the afternoon. On the program cover, beside a handsome painting of a Renaissance actor of color were printed these words: "We call upon all responsible creative elements of the theatre arts to grant freedom of choice to cast aside preconceptions regarding the casting of Negro artists...in all forms of American entertainment." That was 1959. Clinton Turner Davis addressed these same issues in a like manner in the 1990s.

Harold Cruse, in his *The Crisis of the Negro Intellectual* (1967), resurrected a serious question, as well as others that had dogged black theatre since its commercial beginnings: wouldn't integration result in a loss of black power? was integration desirable or possible? what was the relationship between the economics of the theatre and its culture? for whom should the black playwright write? The black militants of the 1960s had their own answers.

12

From Hansberry to Shange[1]

James V. Hatch

Black Art initiates, supports, and promotes change. It refuses to accept values laid down by dead men.

Maulana Ron Karenga

Bob Dylan's "The times they are a-changin'" became a theme song of the 1960s. Woodstock Nation's Love-In promised peace and joy. San Francisco's Haight-Ashbury beckoned young souls to flower power. The Living Theatre stripped off its clothes and declared "Paradise Now." War would be no more. Poverty, no more. The shibboleth of the flower children: "Don't trust anyone over thirty." The Age of Aquarius had arrived, or so it seemed.

In 1965 Congress created agencies to develop and promote a broadly conceived national policy of support for the arts and humanities. For the first time since the New Deal of the Roosevelt era, federal money was awarded directly to artistic talents, this time dispensed by the National Endowment for the Arts (NEA). The National Endowment for the Humanities (NEH) supported many who either wrote about the arts or who maintained the arts in libraries and museums. Additionally, state and city governments funded theatres, dance groups, poets, and musicians. Matching grants totaling $2.5 million encouraged philanthropies to support the arts. The regional theatres outside of New York City received a quarter million. Long the dream of serious artists, companies sprouted up from Louisville to Minneapolis, from Atlanta to Seattle. Lorraine Hansberry and Ntozake Shange serve as "playwright bookends" for an era that radically changed the history of African American theatre.

Centuries of war, poverty, and racial segregation were not easily dismissed. Martin Luther King – murdered. Malcolm X – murdered. John Kennedy and his brother Robert – murdered. President Nixon and his staff manipulated the war in Vietnam to linger on and on. Heroin and cocaine from southeast Asia flooded the nation. The civil rights movement splintered into black and white factions. The funding for the War on Poverty dried up, as did much of the money from the NEA, which increasingly directed funds, not to small community groups, but to large, established institutions. By 1976 the Age of Aquarius and its flower children had withered, replaced by the American bicentennial celebrations and President Nixon's diversionary hoopla about protecting the environment. Nonetheless, the years between the Broadway productions of *A Raisin in the Sun* (1959) and *For Colored Girls Who Have Considered Suicide/When the Rainbow is Enuf* (1976) had produced a second Renaissance of African American poetry, dance, music, and theatre.

Following the Second World War, the military, and then schools and transportation, gave access to all races. In 1957 television changed America's racial climate by broadcasting film footage of nine children entering Little Rock High School under the protection of federal troops. Many Whites who had had little contact with Blacks no longer accepted the myth that black Americans enjoyed their second-class citizenship.

In 1962 Hansberry had written but had not published a "Prospectus for the John Brown Memorial Theatre of Harlem."[2] Hansberry's new and ideal theatre would be dedicated to the aspiration and culture of African American people. It would use their cultural heritage and turn its back upon commercial theatre and turn away from "impotent and obscurantist efforts of a mistaken avant garde" (i.e., the Theatre of the Absurd). It would welcome all artists of grand imagination and skills.

The appearance of *A Raisin in the Sun* (1959) at the Ethel Barrymore Theatre on Broadway clearly indicated that the McCarthyism of the early 1950s was giving way to the integration of the 1960s. The play's production under the direction of Lloyd Richards had been exceptionally well done. Hansberry's art had pulled the critics empathically into the Younger family. The struggle of Walter Lee to become the man of the family, Beneatha's dream of becoming a doctor, Mama's vision of owning a home in suburbia, all resonated in middle America, and possibly resonated so loud that the political and economic systems that caused the problems were overlooked.

For reasons of theatre history, as well as politics, *A Raisin in the Sun* (1959) is considered a watershed drama. It marked the first appearance of a black woman dramatist and a black director on Broadway. It was the first black play to capture a national audience in theatre and film. Hansberry became the youngest American and the first Black to win the New York Drama Critics Circle Award. *Raisin* launched careers for nearly every actor in the play – Sidney Poitier, Claudia McNeil, Ruby Dee, Glynn Turman, Diana Sands, Ivan Dixon, Louis Gossett, Lonne Elder III, and Douglas Turner Ward, and it played 530 performances, eclipsing the record set by Langston Hughes' play *Mulatto* (1935). Columbia Pictures bought the rights for a film.[3]

Hansberry's play was the foster child of two earlier Chicago plays: Theodore Ward's *Big White Fog* (1938), which ended with an eviction, and Richard Wright's *Native Son* (1941), which was set in a rat-infested slum. All three plays clearly demonstrated that racism caused poverty, which in turn caused crime and mental and physical illness, leading to family disintegration. Hansberry's drama was set solidly in this tradition. Theatre historian Margaret Wilkerson, Hansberry's authorized biographer, declared *A Raisin in the Sun* to be the herald of black militant theatre of the 1960s and 1970s.

Not everyone praised the play. The young LeRoi Jones attacked *Raisin* as a bourgeois document, but later reversed himself.[4] Harold Cruse dubbed *Raisin* a middle-class soap opera designed for white people to fantasize that the Younger family was just like theirs.[5] To Hansberry's annoyance, white critics praised the play for what it did *not* do: it did *not* preach, it did *not* grind an axe. The critics' negative compliments praised *Raisin* while condemning black drama that spoke out directly against racism.[6] Hansberry's play demonstrated that corrupt capitalism held the Younger family in bondage, and that it used racism to divide working people. How was it, then, that the white critics had failed to hear her indictment?[7]

Hansberry's next play did not back away from controversy. When *The Sign in Sidney Brustein's Window* (1964) opened at the Longacre Theatre on 15 October 1964 the audience expected to see black characters confronting the race problem. They didn't. The protagonist was a Greenwich Village Jewish lawyer (Hansberry was married to Robert Nemiroff, a Jew), and she had set out to portray a rainbow family in much the same fashion as she had created a broad spectrum of Blacks in *A Raisin in the Sun*. The reviews were mixed. The play had only one African American. Black reviewers criticized Hansberry for not writing a black play because Blacks had so few opportunities for professional production. White critics attacked *Brustein* for having little plot and using the stage as a cocktail hour to discuss social problems. Attendance was poor, but friends and motion picture personalities kept the play open for 101 performances until the author's death of cancer at age 34.

Death did not end Hansberry's career. Her husband adapted *Les Blancs*, an incomplete script. This anticolonial drama opened at the Longacre

Theatre on 15 November 1970 with a rainbow of humanity seldom seen on stage. The English-educated son of an African chief returns to his village to find his younger brother has become an alcoholic and his older brother has been ordained a priest. A homosexual doctor, the wife of a white mission-ary, a well-intentioned white liberal journalist, and an African revolutionary leader who is posing as a faithful servant to a white military commander make up the cast, from which Hansberry wove a scathing indictment of colonialism and its missionaries. Critical reception was cool, and the play closed after forty performances.

In 1971, Nemiroff with Harry Belafonte produced *To Be Young, Gifted, and Black: A Portrait of Lorraine Hansberry in Her Own Words*. It ran at the Cherry Lane Theatre off Broadway for 380 performances. Originally conceived in 1967 as a script for radio station WBAI, the posthumous play was a collage of speeches, articles, and scenes from her work.

Another unrevised play, *The Drinking Gourd* (1961), had been commis-sioned by NBC-TV; however, Hansberry's examination of slavery, silhou-etted against civil war capitalism, was apparently too penetratingly severe for television's family entertainment policy. Set in the 1850s, *Drinking Gourd* revealed how the economics of slavery destroyed even the best of human intentions. The script was never televised but was staged in 1974 at the Harlem Community Center for the Arts. A number of colleges and com-munity productions followed.

Hansberry's final triumph was her husband's production of *Raisin* (1973) as a musical. Directed by choreographer Donald McKayle, the adaptation ran at the 46th Street Theatre for 847 performances and received the Tony Award[8] for the best musical that season. It ran parallel with *Purlie*, the musical adaptation of Ossie Davis' *Purlie Victorious* (1961), which ran for 688 performances. Audiences attended both musicals in twice the numbers that had attended the plays.

In spite of the success of *A Raisin in the Sun*, other serious plays with racial themes were scarce in the early 1960s. *The Long Dream* (1960), an adaptation by Ketti Frings of Richard Wright's novel, closed quietly. In 1962, Diahann Carroll played a black fashion model in love with white pho-tographer Richard Kiley. Richard Rodgers, the show's lyricist, informed the press that *No Strings* "has absolutely nothing to do with any racist angle."[9] *New York Times* critic Howard Taubman praised Peter Feibleman's *Tiger Tiger Burning Bright* (1962) as a play "about the human condition. There is no preachment or propaganda. Nor is there a cry from the heart that the trials and sorrows of this family are especially Negro...They are wrestling with problems that could scorch the lives of any family."[10] In the early 1960s these commercial efforts exploited racism but did not confront it.

The Greenwich Mews Theatre confronted racial problems with *Walk in Darkness* (1963) by William Hairston and *The Cool World* (1960) by Warren Miller and Robert Rossen, both of which sympathetically revealed the unfocused lives of gang members in Harlem. Athol Fugard's *Blood Knot* (1963) received the most plaudits, viewing race problems at a distance – in South Africa. Fugard's plays – *Boesman and Lena* (1969), *Sizwe Bansi is Dead* (1974), *The Island* (1974), *Master Harold... and the Boys* (1982) – continued to remain popular; it may have been reassuring to white Americans that racial segregation was not theirs alone. Before 1964 race issues, if not absent from the theatre, were nonconfrontational. All-black shows in the decade of the civil rights movement both pleased and displeased the integrationists. While the shows proved that African Americans could play white roles they were still segregated, and none led to casting actors nonconventionally, an issue to be taken up in the 1980s.

Another diversion that kept "the problem" off stage was the *Carmen Jones* tradition of adapting white musicals for black stars. The most popular were Sammy Davis, starring in a musical adaptation of Clifford Odets' *Golden Boy* (1964), Robert Guillaume as Nathan Detroit in *Guys and Dolls* (1976), and Pearl Bailey and Cab Calloway in *Hello Dolly!* (1964), an adaptation of Thornton Wilder's *The Matchmaker* (1954). In the latter, Carol Channing had opened the show, but to keep it running, David Merrick replaced the Whites with an all-black cast.

By the mid-1970s Blacks themselves were adapting white musicals. It had been assumed that *The Wizard of Oz* (1939 film) could not be remade because the American psyche had canonized Judy Garland in the role of Dorothy. On 5 January 1975 the black version opened to mixed reviews, including a negative one from the *New York Times*; it seemed a self-fulfilling prophecy that "somewhere over the rainbow" was reserved for white people. Many assumed *The Wiz* to be doomed; however, the producer, Twentieth Century-Fox, wooed black suburban and church audiences with television and radio ads, designating *The Wiz* as a satire that white critics did not understand. Bus loads of African Americans arrived at Broadway's Majestic Theatre. The musical was not a remake of the Garland version, but a genuine black cultural event with music by Charlie Smalls, choreography by George Faison, and costumes and direction by Geoffrey Holder.[11] *The Wiz* ran for 1,672 performances, winning seven Tony Awards (including best musical) and five Drama Desk Awards. Although the movie did not fare as well, in part because Stephanie Mills as Dorothy was replaced by a much too glamorous Diana Ross, the lesson had not been lost on Broadway producers: African Americans would pay Broadway prices to see something of themselves on stage.

In 1978, Geoffrey Holder directed and choreographed a second musical adaptation starring Eartha Kitt. This time, an African version of the operetta *Kismet* (original 1953), renamed *Timbuktu*, played 221 performances at the Mark Hellinger Theatre; the company toured for a year. In both musicals, Holder's flamboyant costumes brought to the American stage the spectacle of the Caribbean carnival. Eartha Kitt returned to Broadway after serving time in Turkey. Trouble had begun in 1968 when Lady Bird Johnson invited Kitt to a White House tea to discuss rising juvenile delinquency in America. Speaking from her own experience, the performer told the President's wife that the millions being spent on the Vietnam War should be redirected to help the poor in the nation. The result of her confrontation with the First Lady was, not only to find herself "whitelisted," but under surveillance by the FBI and the CIA, all of which destroyed her career in America, as the career of Paul Robeson had been. For a time Kitt lived in Istanbul and introduced the West to popular Turkish music. Not until 1978, however, was she able to return from Europe and find work in Geoffrey Holder's Broadway musical *Timbuktu* (1978).

A Raisin in the Sun's successful encounter with racial issues inspired other civil rights pieces, including the Chicago musical *Kicks and Company* (1962), written by Oscar Brown Jr. in collaboration with Robert Nemiroff. Lorraine Hansberry directed this story about the Devil working against the civil rights movement. It closed in Chicago. C. Bernard Jackson and James V. Hatch wrote *Fly Blackbird* (1960), a musical inspired by the college student sit-ins in Greensboro, North Carolina. Produced first in Los Angeles, the musical moved off-Broadway and was awarded an Obie for Best Musical Off-Broadway in 1962.[12]

Dedicated "to the dead children of Birmingham," James Baldwin's drama *Blues for Mister Charlie* (1964) was based loosely on the murder of the boy Emmett Till by white men in Mississippi; the play's militancy challenged conventional stereotypes of southern Blacks and Whites. Although it closed after 146 Broadway performances, the drama over the next thirty years became a standard for black colleges and is considered by some to be equal to Baldwin's earlier drama *Amen Corner* (1954).

Amateurs, too, used civil rights themes in the theatre. Ann Flagg, a teacher in West Virginia public high schools, became director of the Children's Theatre at Karamu in Cleveland. She wrote *Great Gettin' Up Mornin'* (1963), a one-act about a family preparing for their daughter's first day in a previously all-white school; the play won the National Collegiate Playwriting Contest and was later televised on CBS.

Perhaps the most successful of the civil rights plays was Ossie Davis' *Purlie Victorious* (1961), a satire of southern plantation stereotypes, which played Broadway for 231 performances, starring Davis as a young preacher and Ruby Dee as his wife. A decade later the script was adapted into the musical *Purlie* (1970). Part of the musical's success was its use of traditional gospel, a style the civil rights movement had made familiar to white audiences during the 1960s.

Gospel plays

Spirituals, the progenitors of the gospel play, had made their commercial début with the Fisk Jubilee Singers in 1871. Soon minstrelsy cashed in on the vogue, and in the 1890s Black Patti sang spirituals along with selected opera arias. From the 1920s into the 1940s Marian Anderson and Roland Hayes, after singing German lieder, climaxed their concerts with two or three spirituals, a tradition continued by Simon Estes into the 1990s.

In dramatic form, the gospel play combined spirituals and biblical parables with pageantry – a series of key moments held together by scripture, music, and spectacle in which the minister bridged dramatic sketches with narration. Gospel plays employed local talent from church choirs and rarely used original music. The plots were simple, usually a Bible story already known to the audience. The transition of spirituals in church to the concert stage and finally on to the Broadway stage culminated with the Hall Johnson choir in *The Green Pastures* (1930). White audiences flocked to hear what they believed to be the authentic African American celebration of God. In the same decade black churches performed "folk" plays written by and for their own congregations. The most popular and long-lasting of these was *Heaven Bound* (1930), performed at Big Bethel AME Church in Atlanta, Georgia (see chapter 10).

In the 1960s the increasing popularity of gospel musicals may have been inspired, in part, by the theatrical style of black ministers in the civil rights movement. Certainly, the voices and delivery of Martin Luther King, Ralph

Abernathy, and others on national television and radio, and on records, introduced the black sermon to a broader segment of Americans. Langston Hughes capitalized on gospel's popularity with four musicals: *Black Nativity* (1961), which opened off Broadway and then toured Europe for two years; *The Gospel Glow* (1962),[13] which Hughes described in the program notes as "the first Negro passion play depicting the life of Christ from the cradle to the cross"; and Hughes' third musical, *Tambourines to Glory* (1963), which featured the Devil in a comic melodrama about two women and a storefront church in Harlem. The primary audience for all these shows had been African Americans. As the 1960s progressed, however, the form flourished with white audiences, too.

In *Jericho-Jim Crow* (1963), Hughes reintroduced an important theme into the gospel play: a civil rights history of segregation, a form which soon developed into another popular format – the cavalcade of African American history on stage. Loften Mitchell's *Tell Pharaoh* (1967) used traditional music to trace the black man's journey from Africa to the present. Mitchell also coauthored, with John Oliver Killens, *Ballad of the Winter Soldiers* (1964); more of a pageant than a play, it dealt with freedom fighters throughout history. Josephine Jackson and Joseph A. Walker used the music-cum-narrative format for their *The Believers* (1968), with choral songs and narrative. The same team produced *Ododo* (1968) at the Afro-American Studio in Harlem. In Washington, DC, Howard University celebrated its centenary with a similar epic, *Til Victory is Won* (1965) by Owen Dodson and composer Mark Fax. This play was revived at the Kennedy Center in 1970.

Vinnette Carroll, who founded the Urban Arts Corps in a downtown loft in Manhattan, began by producing and directing *Trumpets of the Lord* (1963), an adaptation of James Weldon Johnson's *God's Trombones* (1927), a stylized Negro sermon. Ms. Carroll nurtured performer, writer, and composer Micki Grant and took her revue *Don't Bother Me, I Can't Cope* (1972) to Broadway, where it ran for 1,065 performances at the Edison Theatre and then toured. In the show's lead, Carroll had cast Alex Bradford, a popular gospel singer. As its title suggests, the theme presented African Americans and others struggling to exercise their civil rights. Winner of two Drama Desk awards as composer and performer, Micki Grant also collected an Obie, two Outer Critics' Circle Awards, and a Grammy Award. The team of Carroll, Grant, and Bradford went on to write *Your Arms Too Short to Box with God* (1975), which played first at the Festival of Two Worlds in Spoleto, Italy. When it opened on Broadway at the Lyceum Theatre in 1976, Delores Hall received

Figure 38. Micki Grant, author of *Don't Bother Me, I Can't Cope,* 1970

a Tony Award for her gospel singing. A second company toured sixty-six cities as late as 1995, a record twenty years.

The Gospel at Colonus (1983), an adaptation of Sophocles' *Oedipus at Colonus,* was clearly an anomaly that reached far beyond Humanities 101. Lee Breuer and musician Bob Telson had wedded the ancient Greek myth of man's primal sin to the ritual of the black Pentecostal sermon of Christian redemption. The production used the J. D. Steels Singers and the Institutional Radio Choir of Brooklyn, with Morgan Freeman in the dual role of Oedipus and the Preacher and with the five Blind Boys of Alabama as alternate personae for the role of Oedipus. African Americans filled all the roles. So gripping was the performance that when the scenery caught fire at the Brooklyn Academy of Music during the 15 December 1983 performance, the audience refused to leave until the fire was extinguished and the performance concluded. After a long world tour, the musical came to Broadway's Lunt-Fontanne Theatre in 1988.

In the last three decades of the twentieth century, gospel musicals became commercial, often with original music. The genre reached it peak with *Godspell* (1971) and *Jesus Christ Superstar* (1971), the latter starring Ben Vereen as Judas Iscariot. By the late 1980s, the white audience's passion for gospel waned. Both Broadway gospel shows *Sing, Mahalia, Sing* (1986) and *Truly Blessed* (1990) closed early.

Vy Higginsen, former disc jockey and accountant representative for *Ebony* magazine, targeted a new audience of working-class people who rarely bought tickets to expensive Broadway shows. Using gospel music, and booking theatre parties through the churches, Higgensen and Ken Wydro staged *Mama, I Want to Sing* (1980), a musical whose entire plot lay in its title. In a small theatre on the edge of Harlem their show ran for eight years and grossed more than $25 million in its first five years. Higgensen then took the show on the road as far as England and Japan. Soon, other producers copied her production style: a few good gospel singers playing characters familiar to church congregations, a slight story with minimal scenery, and dramatic lighting to create a revival atmosphere. Through these new mini-companies, gospel music underwent a second theatrical revival. Advertising only in black newspapers and on black music stations, these shows reached an audience that Broadway never had attracted and became the big moneymakers on the "urban circuit" of the 1980s and 1990s (see chapter 13).

The rise of small nonprofit theatres

The militant theatre of the 1960s sprang from the civil rights movement, which brought America's attention to the exorbitant price paid for racial segregation and discrimination. Dr. Kenneth Clark of New York's City University published *Youth in the Ghetto: A Study of the Consequences of Powerlessness and a Blueprint for Change*, which clearly outlined the causes of despair in central Harlem, an area of 3.5 square miles with a 94 percent black population. Of the 31,000 students in the community's elementary and junior high schools, at least 50 percent had been designated as educationally retarded. The rate of juvenile delinquency was twice that of adjacent city communities, and one major cause was no jobs. Dr. Clark proposed a series of remedies, which he named HARYOU, an acronym for Harlem Youth

Opportunities Unlimited. President Kennedy and the Congress funded the programs, initially under Dr. Clark's direction.

HARYOU used community boards to provide job training, educational and social service programs, as well as money for arts and culture. Taught by practicing artists, five thousand young people participated in a full range of classes and workshops in graphic, plastic, and performing arts; the last included stagecraft, playwriting, play production, dance, and music (both vocal and instrumental). Classes met twice a week for three to four hours and members received a stipend, not unlike the Federal Theatre Project of the 1930s, although that politically controversial model was never mentioned.

In New York City skilled teachers abounded. Roger Furman, Robert Macbeth, and Hazel Bryant, to name just three, used the HARYOU initiative to found theatre companies. The not-for-profit status established by Congress and the IRS in 1954 had previously been the domain of established churches, large foundations, museums, and libraries, but now with the aid of Volunteer Lawyers for the Arts, small theatre groups acquired a tax-exempt 501(c)3 status, making them eligible to receive gifts of money from corporations, foundations, and individuals, money that the donors could partially deduct from their taxes.

Under President Johnson's "war on poverty," theatre groups thrived. Federal funding for the arts was often allocated as a job retraining measure.[14] The NEA created a separate arena for minorities named Expansion Arts. The first to take advantage of the new support programs were existing theatres, those founded by the older Harlem generation trained in the 1940s and all "graduates" of ANT: Osceola Archer, Charles Griffin, Gertrude Jeannette, Rosetta LeNoire, and Roger Furman.

Born in 1924, Furman bridged both the older ANT and the Black Arts Movement. In 1964 he was appointed field supervisor of the HARYOU Arts and Culture Program, and with a budget of $43,000 he established a summer community program at the YMCA auditorium, which he named the New Heritage Repertory Theatre. Columbia University awarded him a grant to teach young Blacks and Puerto Ricans the technical aspects of theatre. In 1969, after using various public schools for residencies, his company renovated a loft on 125th Street and installed a 110-seat theatre. A multitalented man, Furman acted, directed, designed, wrote plays, and became a founding member of the Black Theatre Alliance (BTA).

Furman's senior, the actress Gertrude Jeannette had studied acting under Osceola Archer at ANT. Concurrent with a successful Broadway career,[15] Jeannette established the Elks Community Theatre, where she produced two of her own plays, *This Way Forward* (1951) and *A Bolt from the Blue* (1952). In 1968 she founded the HADLEY Players, a group that distinguished itself by its longevity, by successfully combining standard plays with originals, and by attracting a community-based audience for three decades.

A third "graduate" of ANT, Rosetta LeNoire (born Burton in 1911), began her stage career with the FTP productions of *Macbeth* (1936) and *Bassa Moona* (1936). She then joined her uncle, Bill Bojangles Robinson, in Mike Todd's *Hot Mikado* (1939) and enrolled at the American Negro Theater, where she played Stella in *Anna Lucasta* (1944). LeNoire in 1968 founded her own company, the AMAS Repertory Theatre, "in reaction to the racial tension and reverse attitude of separation." As more and more black theatres were organized, many produced only "black" plays. "I thought it was going in the wrong direction," said LeNoire.[16] AMAS (Latin for "you love") swam against the current, using interracial casting in all its shows. Ms. LeNoire's career in theatre, television, and film extended over sixty years.

After President Kennedy's assassination in 1963, a political struggle developed between Dr. Kenneth Clark, founder-director of HARYOU, and Harlem's senior politician, Adam Clayton Powell; the two quarreled over how and to whom the federal money would be given. When in 1968 Robert Kennedy was killed, Dr. Clark lost a powerful ally and resigned from HARYOU. Friction and quarrels among the politicians, gangsters like "Bumpy" Johnson, the artists, and the administrators crippled the programs, which had begun to produce strong works by youth in painting, photography, theatre, and dance. Subsequently, many of the younger talents moved out to create their own improvised stages with works for, by, and about themselves.

Between the years 1961 and 1982 nearly six hundred new African American theatres were established across the nation.[17] A younger generation had emerged – at first, presenting traditional forms – realism, musicals, and gospel plays, and nearly all of it in New York City. But as the sixties progressed, realism gave way to the absurd; the one-act play replaced the full-length script; the black Broadway musical was supplanted by rituals comprised of poetry, music, and dance on college and community stages. Wedding words, sound, and motion, the Black Arts Movement was born and with it a renewed interest in African motifs.

As more Haitian and African drummers immigrated to the United States, and more African Americans made their *hadj* to Africa, the authenticity of theatrical rituals improved. Schools for drumming opened. The

African Cultural Center on 125th Street in Harlem, founded by Nigerian Babtunde Olatunji, became seminal. From the time of his arrival in 1950 to his return to Lagos in 1981, Olatunji propagated authentic African culture through classes, television appearances, and concerts across the nation.

For party-time, young Americans watched Chubby Checker on TV and danced the Twist, the Watusi, and the Funky Chicken, but on stage many of the African and quasi-African dances derived eclectically from the work of Katherine Dunham, Pearl Primus, and a choreography improvised from generic modern dance – à la Martha Graham. A visible source of neo-Africanisms for the stage arrived after the UNESCO-sponsored First World Festival of Negro Arts in Dakar in 1966. African Americans returned from Senegal wearing African cloth and costume. Clothing merchants caught the trend quickly and sold dashikis by the thousands. Kente cloth, real and simulated, draped the arms and necks of students. On stage, pharaonic styles dominated. Eleven years later, when the Second World Black African Festival of Art and Culture (FESTAC) convened in Lagos-Kunda, Nigeria, (1977), the iconography had shifted from the Nile to the Niger.[18]

The publication of Jahnheinz Jahn's *Muntu* in 1961 gave English-speaking readers a door into Bantu philosophy – *Muntu, Kintu, Hantu, Kuntu, Nommo*. The creative power of the word reverberated in performances. Three young men from Harlem, known as The Last Poets,[19] borrowed the Black Power rhetoric of Stokely Carmichael and Rapp Brown to chant a seminal style for the rap of the 1980s. Backed by drums, Abiodun Oyewole, Alafia Pudim, and Omar Ben Hassen sang and rapped their original verses, which were at once witty and cutting ("Niggers Scared of Revolution"). Their four albums – the first issued in 1969 – set the tone of militancy marching in irony to the news of the Birmingham bus strike (1955), the Greensboro sit-ins (1960), the murder of Malcolm X (1965), and the assassination of Martin Luther King (1968), and, concomitant with the violence, a new generation of stand-up comics and monologists emerged.

Racial humor bopped out of the pool halls, beauty salons, up from the kitchen and off the streets into the theatre as a business. In the late 1950s and early 1960s stand-up black comics – Dick Gregory, Moms Mabley, Redd Foxx, and later Richard Pryor – along with white comics Lennie Bruce and Shelley Berman, brought race and sex jokes out of the bars and into nightclubs, on to records, and, finally, on to television. Playing before racially mixed audiences, the comics uttered the unutterable aloud ("nigger"), a word shocking enough to evoke laughter from both Whites and Blacks. Prior to that, black comics who made jokes about race before black audiences had relied heavily on in-group humor.

Moms Mabley (*c.* 1897–1975), born Loreta Mary Aiken, had traveled the TOBA circuit in a number of revues before appearing on Broadway in *Blackberries* (1932) and *Swingin' the Dream* (1939). In the 1960s she signed a record contract before being cast on television as Bill Cosby's mother. Alice Childress wrote her story into a play called *Moms* (1987). Clarice Taylor, who starred in the lead, claimed that she had written a portion of the script; Taylor had a legal falling out with Childress over the rights to the play. Nonetheless, Moms Mabley remained the funniest female comic of the late twentieth century. Dick Gregory, who began as a $5-a-show comic, within two years was earning $6,500 a week. He cleared the path for Richard Pryor, Eddie Murphy, Sinbad, and a host of talented younger comedians. Literary poets – Amiri Baraka and Sonia Sanchez – moved their words off the page, rapping and chanting.

Absurdist theatre and the Black Arts Movement

The third defining force for the black arts theatre burst upon America's intellectuals, black and white, when Jean Genet's *The Blacks* opened on 4 May 1961 at the St. Marks Playhouse on Manhattan's Lower Eastside, where it ran for 1,408 performances. Although many African Americans objected to the play's thesis – if Blacks came to power, they would be as oppressive as Whites – for three years the production provided dozens of black actors with regular paychecks, and the play's absurdist style, combined with its confrontational stance, awakened and aroused American playwrights, preparing the intellectual stage for Edward Albee's *Zoo Story* (1960) and *The Death of Bessie Smith* (1961).

In turn, Albee's absurdist style attracted Adrienne Kennedy to his playwrights' workshop at the Circle in the Square, where she wrote *Funnyhouse of a Negro* (1962). After a workshop production, Albee produced her play at the East End Theatre in the same year as LeRoi Jones' *Dutchman* (1964). The two one-act plays shared Obie awards for 1964 as the best off-Broadway dramas of the season. Both plays clearly exhibited the influence of the absurdist movement. Kennedy continued to create in the absurdist style – *The Rat's Mass* (1966) and *The Owl Answers* (1965). Her objects and characters embraced multiple people and ideas, sometimes simultaneously, creating the effect of nightmares; however, as in a dream, behind her kaleidoscopic vision hovered a literal story. The "funnyhouse" was the madhouse of racism;

the mulatto woman, who occupies the center of the drama, is torn between the paradoxes of black and white, past and present, flesh and spirit. The role was originally created by Billie Allen. Adrienne Kennedy, like her literary ancestor Marita Bonner, attempted to resolve the contradiction between everyday life and our wildest dreams, one of the major goals of the surrealist movement of the 1920s.[20] After nearly two decades of confinement to the ivory towers, in 1995 a retrospective of seven Kennedy plays was presented at the Joseph Papp Public Theater by the Signature Theatre Company. Critics declared Kennedy to be a major American playwright.

Black militant theatre

Ed Bullins dabbled in the absurdist style for his first play, *How Do You Do* (1965), produced by the San Francisco Drama Circle. However, two years later he denounced absurdism as an attempt "to perpetuate and adapt the white man's theatre, to extend western reality and finally to *rescue* his culture and have it benefit his needs."[21] Edgar White's sometimes absurdist plays are among the most original of the Black Arts Movement; however, his work was not subjected to anything like a retrospective or even extensive criticism (see chapter 9). In a different "revolutionary" vein, one of the more "absurd" incidents centered on Trinidadian-born Lennox Raphael and his play *Ché* (1969), named after the Cuban revolutionary. On 24 March the actors, director, and playwright were arrested by the Public Morals Squad and charged on fifty-four counts of consensual sodomy, public lewdness, and obscenity. The play was closed. The figure of President Johnson sitting on the toilet was especially reprehensible to many. Raphael claimed that the play's actions were symbolic and a sociopolitical protest against the war in Vietnam and other policies. (The play's characters, along with Ché Guevara, included the Son of King Kong, a Nymphomaniac Nun, and the President of the United States.) The play was reopened after a judge ruled the defendants not guilty.

The sixties generation boiled with righteous anger. Chicago's Student Nonviolent Coordinating Committee (SNCC) in their pamphlet "We Want Black Power" inveighed: "We must fill ourselves with hate for all white things." SNCC was not alone. The Black Panther Party founded in Oakland, California, in 1966 proclaimed: "We must destroy both racism and capitalism." In his one-act, *Dutchman* (1964), LeRoi Jones vented his frustration. Borrowing his title from "The Flying Dutchman," the story of a sea captain doomed to sail forever, the drama depicted a violent interracial encounter on the New York subway. The play became one of the most produced in America. When performed at Howard University, Owen Dodson, the director, deleted all the profanity because he thought it would offend the university's conservative, church-oriented audiences. On opening night, following the performance, playwright Jones took the stage and recited the words that Dodson had expunged. When compared to white theatre presentations such as *Hair* and *Paradise Now*, African American plays seldom employed nudity; however, their overloading of profanity defeated the intended impact and denied playwrights subtlety and precision of expression.

Following *Dutchman's* initial success, Jones quickly presented three more militant one-acts: *The Baptism*, *The Toilet*, and *The Slave*, all produced in 1964 and all sharing nonrealistic elements. In 1965, Jones abandoned commercial theatre and moved to Harlem, where he founded the Black Arts Repertory Theatre School (BARTS). Here he produced his *Experimental Death Unit 1* (1965), a one-act in which black militants murder two white homosexuals and a black prostitute who has befriended them. Anti-gay rhetoric combined with racism ("white faggots") was not unknown in the poetry and plays of the period. BARTS' policy was to allow no white people into its building. Self-segregation, coupled with Baraka's call for armed revolution, caused the administrators of HARYOU/ACT to cancel BARTS' funding. An allied group of radical young men, the Revolutionary African Movement (RAM), threatened HARYOU's administrator Julian Euell with violence if he did not reinstate BART's funds. Charles Patterson, a militant member of RAM, shot Larry Neal, the arts and culture editor of *Liberator* magazine, wounding him in the leg. Later, Neal reported, "LeRoi Jones at that time had all these strange sick cats who had found a way to get their personal lives mingled with the idea of revolution and struggle, and who really became a very oppressive force in the community."[22] A Harlem numbers' boss, Ellsworth Raymond "Bumpy" Johnson (the inspiration for the movie *Shaft* [1971]), "cooled" RAM's "oppressive force," but too late. BARTS closed down, and Baraka moved to Newark.

LeRoi Jones discarded his "slave" name for Imamu Amiri Baraka. He then founded Spirit House in Newark, New Jersey, where he wrote and produced a number of plays, including his own *Slave Ship* (1967), a ritual drama about the middle passage of African people to America. Other plays in similar revolutionary modes found production at Spirit House, which generated spin-offs. Yusef Iman, whose *Praise the Lord, but Pass the Ammu-nition* (1967) was produced by Baraka's theatre, became founder and director of the Weusi Kuumba Troupe in Brooklyn, where he produced several of his own plays.

Four one-acts produced commercially by Woodie King Jr., first at the Chelsea Theatre Center at the Brooklyn Academy and then at Tambelli's Gate Theatre in Manhattan, were published in 1970 as *Black Quartet*. They included Ben Caldwell's *Prayer Meeting; or, The First Militant Minister* (1967), a satire on politically conservative preachers, Ed Bullins' *Gentle-man Caller* (1969), a satire reconceiving the image of Aunt Jemima, Amiri Baraka's trial of a middle-class father, *Great Goodness of Life (A Coon Show)* (1967), and Ron Milner's family tragedy of lost dreams, *The Warning – A Theme for Linda* (1969).

In the late 1960s and early 1970s black nationalism reached its apogee. The raised fist, internationalized by black athletes at the 1968 Olympic Games in Mexico City, became the symbol of Black Power. Maulana Karenga (Ronald McKinley Everett) created Kwanzaa and disseminated the seven African values taken from Swahili. He and Baraka both believed that revo-lution could not come until black people rejected the cultural values of the dominant society ("Back to Black" or "Kawaida"). The Black Panther Party espoused a different interpretation, believing that power must come from social and economic changes, not cultural change.

As the most articulate and outspoken of the new theatre militants, Baraka demanded theatre that would "commit black people to their own liberation and instruct them about what they should be doing. Black theatre should be of itself an act of liberation."[23] Baraka wanted theatre to be as necessary to the community as black music. He believed that critics should share the same value system as the artists they criticized. Finally, Baraka believed that he who paid the fiddler called the tune. Their theatre could not be culturally self-determining unless it was financially self-sustaining. Otherwise, white capitalism would use the black stage to prevent the liberation of black people. After several years in the forefront of the cultural nationalist movement Baraka turned left and became a Marxist/Leninist, believing that racism could best be confronted and defeated by Blacks and Whites uniting in class struggle. From this period, his representative plays are *The Motion of History* (1975) and *What Was the Relationship of the Lone Ranger to the Means of Production* (1979).[24] The second leading militant playwright of the era was Ed Bullins.

Ed Bullins and the New Lafayette Theatre

Born in 1936 on Philadelphia's northside, Ed Bullins began his writing career in 1959 at the City College of Los Angeles, where he was introduced to the new black militancy when he met Ron Karenga, the founder and leader of US (as opposed to "them"), an Afrocentric group. Bullins moved to San Francisco in 1964, and the next year the drama circle at the Firehouse Repertory Theater, encouraged by Kenneth Rexroth, produced Bullins' experimental one-acts, *How Do You Do* (1965), *Dialect Determinism* (1965), and *Clara's Ole Man* (1965), giving his plays their first serious attention. Following a stormy political falling out with the cultural group Black Arts/West (1967–69), Bullins accepted an invitation from Robert Macbeth to join the New Lafayette Theatre in Harlem as resident playwright (1968–73).

Improvising on the lives of his characters, Bullins initiated a play structure analogous to that of jazz. His plays, more than those of any other playwright, established the cultural life of black "street people" as the central thrust of the Black Arts Movement; he placed in his characters' mouths an urban speech that had not been heard on the American stage. His best full-length work in this genre includes *In the Wine Time* (1968), *Goin' a Buffalo* (1966), and *In New England Winter* (1971). In these dramas Bullins presents a range of young males who deny to themselves and others the affection they so desperately need. The young man in *A Son Come Home* (1968) after ten years returns home to his mother, only to leave again after he is unable to love or be loved. More than any other playwright, Bullins captured the delicate balance of humanity in ghetto youth. If directors and actors fail to discover and project this humanity, the characters may be perceived as hustlers, often cruel and unreliable. Such a controversy surrounded the production of *The Duplex* in 1972 at the Lincoln Center. Although directed by a black director, Gilbert Moses, Bullins denounced and picketed the production, calling it a minstrel show. Apparently Bullins objected to the absence of ritual, which left the characters afloat in a Lincoln Center naturalism, which in turn allowed the white audience to view characters as stereotypic card-playing, wine-drinking, sex-driven Blacks. The 1969 premiere of *The Electronic Nigger* at the American Place Theatre created protest over the playwright's use of the "N" word on the marquee.

Bullins became the most prolific and most produced playwright of the period. His controversial subjects and original style of drama made him the recipient of three Obie awards, a New York Drama Critics Circle Award, a Drama Desk–Vernon Rice Award, two Guggenheim fellowships, four

Rockefeller Foundation playwriting grants, and two NEA playwriting fellowships. Richard Schechner, editor of the *Drama Review*, gave over the 1968 summer issue of the journal to Bullins to publish anything he wished. Included in this historic issue were several writers who would lead the new movement: Larry Neal, Ben Caldwell, LeRoi Jones, John O'Neal, Sonia Sanchez, Marvin X, Ronald Milner, Woodie King Jr., Bill Gunn, and Henrietta Harris. Their essays, plays, manifestos, and energy initiated a national call for a new African American theatre. A bibliography published in the same issue listed only twelve books with black plays, five of which were self-published. However, within five years, Bullins, Baraka, and Hansberry were able to accomplish what few other playwrights had: they published all their major plays and became subjects of biographies.

Bullins influenced a number of playwrights, particularly those working at the New Lafayette Theatre: Martie Charles, J. e. (*sic*) Franklin, Neil Harris, OyamO, Sonia Sanchez, and Richard Wesley, who was the managing editor of New Lafayette's *Black Theatre, A Magazine of the Black Theatre Movement* (1968–72), an inspirational publication with a subscription list of eight thousand, mostly young African Americans, across the nation.

No group symbolized the new black theatre more dramatically than the New Lafayette Theatre (NLT) of Harlem, founded by Robert Macbeth as a direct outgrowth of his participation in HARYOU. Born in 1934 in Charleston, South Carolina, and educated at Morehouse College, Macbeth had begun his career as a professional actor, director, and playwright before he founded NLT in 1967 at the site of the old Lafayette Theatre in Harlem. In his first season, before the theatre burned down, Macbeth directed two plays – Ron Milner's *Who's Got His Own* and Athol Fugard's *Blood Knot*. A year later, with a grant from the Ford Foundation of $450,000, Macbeth put together a company of musicians, stage technicians, actors, and playwrights – forty artists – all on salary for fifty weeks a year. Their mission: "To show black people who they are, where they are, and what condition they are in." Toward this end, Ed Bullins became playwright-in-residence and Macbeth his director.

In the five years of the ensemble, they produced seven Bullins plays and four rituals, the latter composed of music (jazz and blues), dance, poetry, and lighting designs to enhance the *mise-en-scène*. The title of the first ritual, produced in 1969, embraced the theatre's mission: *A Ritual to Bind Together and Strengthen Black People So That They Can Survive the Long Struggle That is to Come*. Because the rituals were conceived as uniting black people in their common struggle with racism, NFT banned white reviewers from

its productions for one year. When the Ford Foundation stopped funding
NLT, Macbeth lifted the ban and invited the Bertolt Brecht specialist Eric
Bentley, who found the New Lafayette's production of *The Psychic Pretenders*
important because it attempted "to raise the consciousness" of the black
community. If the community of Harlem came to know how and why it
had become "a ghetto," the people would unite to change their psychic
and social conditions. Bentley also raised a key question: "Why doesn't
the ghetto itself support ghetto theaters?" Part of the answer lay with the
Harlemites, whose experience had been with television, film, and a theatre
of realism – stories and characters they recognized, even if by stereotype.
The NLT's rituals were not ones the Harlem audience could easily enter.
Professor Rhett S. Jones has suggested that "Black theatre has not been
consistently successful in attracting black audiences because it refused to
create and maintain familiar figures, plots, rituals, and environments that
will meet the African American need for a predictable orderliness. When
African Americans attend a baseball game or a Sunday service, they know
what to expect."[25]

In his book *Black Theatre in the 1960s and 1970s*, Mance Williams defined
the dilemma. As the militant theatre moved away from European forms
and the Theatre of the Absurd, audiences of white intellectuals abandoned
black theatre. A new black audience had to be won. When the black theatre
rejected traditional European aesthetics and the bourgeoisie church, they
were left with a philosophy of black nationalism expressing itself through
spectacle. The collages of poetry, dance, and music evolved into rhetorical
ritual, but not a dramatic form in which the audience felt safe. In retrospect,
in spite of efforts to teach their unity philosophy in the local schools, the
NLT group failed to make themselves an integral part of the community or
to present plays in a genre familiar to the audience.

During the early 1970s ritual theatre became a staple in colleges, where
black studies departments encouraged evocations of mother Africa through
costumes and drums. Woven into the rituals were elements of Afrocentric
mysticism, manifesting itself in iconographic pharaohs, pyramids, and the
Nile. Unlike the standard play, a ritual could substitute lighting for scenery,
but more importantly, rituals could be constructed by juxtaposing music and
poetry in a linear fashion; the difficult craft of the well-made play of realism
could be circumvented. Many writers employed the history-cum-nostalgia
formula, but it worked best as spectacle that spotlighted music and dance.

On occasion, these celebrations of African American history and culture succeeded commercially, as did *A Hand is on the Gate* (1966). This

narration-of-history format fell between a musical revue and a slightly plot-ted book-musical. Conceived and directed by Roscoe Lee Browne, *Gate* de-manded talented performers – Gloria Foster, James Earl Jones, Josephine Premice, Moses Gunn, Cicely Tyson, Leon Bibb, and Ellen Holly – to hold their audience with a series of bravura performances. Browne him-self embodied qualities of the Renaissance gentleman – twice US indoor 1,000-yard champion – a former teacher of French and English at Lincoln University, he had come into the theatre playing a variety of roles at the New York Shakespeare Festival; over seven summers he performed in *Titus Andronicus* (1956), *King Lear* (1962), and *The Winter's Tale* (1963). Recognized for a resonant voice coupled with precise diction, Browne was able to com-mand many classic roles: *Tartuffe* (1967), *Volpone* (1967), and his memorable enactment of the African Babu in the off-Broadway production of *The Old Glory: Benito Cereno* (1964). Browne has appeared in four Derek Walcott plays and two August Wilson dramas. His creation of *The Hand is on the Gate*, originally entitled *An Evening of Negro Poetry and Folk Music*, remains his single writing and directing credit in the 1960s. His many awards included the Helen Hayes Award for distinguished work in the theatre.

Negro Ensemble Company (NEC)

The average American theatregoer in the 1970s, if asked to name a black theatre group, would probably have mentioned the Negro Ensemble Com-pany (NEC). Not only was it early in the field, but by touring it achieved a national and international reputation. In 1968, NEC's first season played to a 25 percent black audience. The company attracted African American subscribers, and Blacks made up 68 percent of the audience for the next twenty years. NEC would become a major factor in changing the color of audiences.

An article written by Douglas Turner Ward for the *New York Times* of 14 August 1966 had asked why there was no theatre in America for black talents. McGeorge Bundy, then head of the Ford Foundation, read the article and a year later awarded a total of $1.2 million to establish the Negro Ensemble Company, for the production of plays that would "concentrate primarily on themes of Negro life... whatever the source."

In 1968 actor and director Robert Hooks, administrative director Gerald Krone, and artistic director, playwright, and actor Douglas Turner Ward rented the second floor of St. Mark's Playhouse on Second Avenue

Figure 39. Douglas Turner Ward, founder and director of the Negro Ensemble Company

(a location easily accessible for white and black audiences). There they began an impressive program of actor-training and workshops in playwriting, with three or four major productions a year plus a schedule of season-within-a-season plays.[26] NEC used black actors almost exclusively, and after the first production, Peter Weiss' *The Lusitanian Bogey* (1968), playwrights of color wrote the scripts for all its fifty major productions, as well as dozens and dozens of workshop presentations.

In the late 1960s the term *Negro* fell from fashion and was replaced by *Black*; however, the NEC retained its title and bore criticism from members of the New Lafayette Theatre and others, who charged that it catered to Whites and occupied the position of an Uncle Tom. Nonetheless, NEC out-lived nearly all its rival companies. During its twenty-year halcyon period, the company harvested an impressive list of awards and honors, including a Pulitzer, a Tony, three Drama Desk Awards, and a dozen Obies. The NEC's policy of producing only original plays developed several professional play-wrights: Joseph A. Walker, Douglas Turner Ward, Paul Carter Harrison, Gus Edwards, Samm-Art Williams, Steve Carter, and Charles Fuller. Al-though the company produced plays by Alice Childress and Pearl Cleage, women playwrights were rare, while the men received repeated productions, a process required in order to develop the skills of the craft. In spite of a "works-in-progress" program for new writers, the relative "closed" circle of main-stage writers contributed to the company's decline.

The NEC toured Europe and Australia, as well as cities in the continental United States. The company never owned its theatre building. After it lost its original stage at St. Marks Place, it moved to the 55th Street Theatre in Manhattan. Eventually the organization suffered the fate of most companies that rented theatre space; they became homeless and, as a consequence, NEC had increasing difficulty in maintaining a regular production schedule with a subscription audience. Production became irregular, at various venues. Susan Watson Turner, daughter of the founder, mounted Joseph A. Walker's drama *The Absolution of Willie Mae* (1999) under the NEC logo on Theatre Row for a short run in the late 1990s. In fairness, it should be pointed out that neither the private sector nor the government agencies ever encouraged theatre artists to own their theatre space. When the grants ended, so did the theatre companies, a lesson that some companies of the 1980s and 1990s took to heart. Meanwhile, black theatre had awakened in the South.

Free Southern Theatre (FST)

In October 1963, Gilbert Moses, Doris Derby, and John O'Neal at Tougaloo College Drama Workshop in Jackson, Mississippi, christened themselves the Free Southern Theatre (FST) (1964–80) and set forth their goals, which were as original as they were brave. Into the small towns of Mississippi and Louisiana the FST brought plays that were the theatre arm of SNCC's civil rights campaign to register voters. In a greatly abbreviated form, here were their major goals:

1. to establish a legitimate theatre in the deep South
2. to stimulate creative and reflective thought among Blacks
3. to provide opportunity for black involvement in the theatre
4. to develop a form that is unique to black people, like blues and jazz
5. to evolve social awareness into plays written for a black audience
6. to open up a new area of protest in the present to struggle for freedom[27]

Beginning with a company of three Blacks and five Whites, the FST toured rural Mississippi and Louisiana presenting Martin Duberman's *In White America* (1963) and Samuel Beckett's *Waiting for Godot* (1952). In the latter, the white master (Pozzo) held the rope around the neck of his black slave (Lucky). Because this image "shocked the black audiences out of comprehension," Pozzo was later played in whiteface. With some consultation with Richard Schechner of Tulane University, Moses and O'Neal then set up an actor-training workshop, and within two years the company, including administrators, had grown to twenty-three. By 1966 all the actors were black.

FST soon learned that the urban scripts of Baraka and Caldwell were inappropriate for their churchgoing audiences, in whose buildings they frequently performed. The company began to write its own skits; most of their pieces preached self-pride and liberation to their rural patrons, many of whom were witnessing a live stage performance for the first time.[28] The organization struggled to pay its actors $35 a week, which brought a nine-month budget to $59,000. Because no admission was charged, fund-raising became a necessity. FST traveled to New York City. The civil rights movement was at its height and foundations and wealthy individuals supported FST. But in reply to the observation that FST would always be losing money (foundations did not like to support groups that were always in deficit), O'Neal responded that foundations would "have to change their minds." However, deficit spending had its limits. Nine years after its founding, FST began to charge a small admission.

When *Life Magazine*'s theatre editor Tom Prideaux wrote a review of FST's production of *Roots* (1966), he gave the theatre national attention and attracted white northern volunteers, who soon outnumbered the southern Blacks. Gradually Whites dropped out, the last one, Murray Levy, business manager and actor, left in 1968. A black actress, Seret Scott, then studying theatre at New York University, took leave of school with the understanding that she would receive credit for acting with FST. The university later reneged on that agreement, but after a year of touring in the south, Scott did return to New York in Gilbert Moses' production of *Slave Ship* (1969), which played first at the Chelsea Theatre Center, then at the Brooklyn Academy of Music, and finally at Theatre-in-the-Church at Washington Square, before leaving on a tour in 1970 of France, Switzerland, and Italy. In the first section of the play the actors spoke only Yoruba. The audience looked directly into the belly of the ship, which rocked. European audiences received the production enthusiastically.

Gil Moses elected to remain in New York. Multitalented, he composed music with Archie Shepp for Baraka's *Slave Ship* (1970) and then directed Ed Bullins' *The Taking of Miss Janie* (1975). Both plays won Obie awards. Moses also earned a Tony nomination and a Drama Desk Award for his direction of Melvin Van Peebles' *Ain't Supposed to Die a Natural Death* (1971).[29]

Because of financial problems at home, FST moved to New Orleans, where they hoped to access more money from the black middle class; however, this move alienated part of the company, who saw FST as abandoning the rural poor. Playwright and activist Kalamu ya Salaam along with Tom Dent formed their own organization, Blkartsouth, which for a time served as an umbrella for the theatre. But financial problems persisted. Even with help from celebrities – Arthur Ashe, Julian Bond, Jules Irving – and money from national organizations and philanthropies, FST still struggled to pay its debts. Their home state of Louisiana finally granted them $3,000 in 1977, fourteen years after their founding. While FST continued to espouse the raising of black consciousness, John O'Neal, a former field secretary for SNCC, believed that consciousness would best be addressed by focusing on black history. In 1978, FST presented Theodore Ward's[30] *Candle in the Wind* (1967), a biohistory of Charles Caldwell, a black politician from Mississippi during the Reconstruction period. O'Neal also wrote his own pre-civil war history drama of Blacks, *Where's the Blood of Our Fathers?* (1973), which asked the question: did black folk sit idly by waiting for Massa Lincoln to set them free?

John O'Neal, who had remained with FST, in the 1980s toured his own one-man show *Don't Start Me to Talking or I'll Tell Everything I Know: Sayings from the Life of Junebug Jabbo Jones* (1980). O'Neal advertised his monologue as "a new start for FST, Junebug Productions, Inc." Ten years later he toured his third Junebug show, *Ain't No Use Goin' Home, Jodie's Got Your Gal and Gone* (1990). "These lively and irreverent plays were constructed partly from folklore and oral histories."[31] The ensemble days of FST had come to an end.

Woodie King Jr. and the New Federal Theatre (NFT)

In 1960 to 1961, Woodie King, David Rambeau, Clifford Frazier, Richard Smith, and Ron Milner[32] borrowed $950 from eight investors for one year to rent a badly maintained building located at 401 East Adams, Detroit, for $50 a month. The building had been a barbershop with marble floors, so they had to build a platform in order to install fifty seats. It would become the only people's theatre in the heart of the black community. Named Concept East Theatre (CET), the company in its first season produced nine plays (six originals), including Ron Milner's first play, *Life Agony* (1961), an early version of *Who's Got His Own* (1965). In its first five years, CET produced thirty-five plays and published three issues of *Black Theater Arts Magazine*.

In 1971 CET moved to its second location, the abandoned Salesian High School at 60 East Harper. In 1972 they merged with Ron Milner's company the Spirit of Shango Theater. Their most successful production came the following year, with Baraka's *Slaveship*, the 150-strong cast of which played to capacity houses for fourteen weeks. The next year a fire closed the theatre. Even though CET obtained a CETA grant to pay the salaries of six staff members, including a new artistic director, Von H. Washington, there was no money for production and the company disbanded in 1978, but not before it had provided training for both playwrights and actors, a number of whom went on to professional work.[33]

Woodie King left Detroit in 1964 to travel as an actor to New York City with Malcolm Boyd's play *A Study in Color*. When the company returned to Detroit, King remained in the Big Apple to pursue a theatre career. In 1970 he founded the New Federal Theatre (NFT), named after the progressive FTP of the Roosevelt era. NFT's first season included a production of J. e. Franklin's *Black Girl* (1971), which toured eighty-five universities and colleges. NFT did not purchase its own space, but instead secured a home at Henry Street, a settlement house with an auditorium. Here King developed Milner's *What the Wine-Sellers Buy* (1973), which moved uptown to the Vivian Beaumont Theatre at the Lincoln Center. A decade later King produced Milner's *Checkmates* (1988) on Broadway, starring Denzel Washington and Ruby Dee. He also staged important revivals: Hughes Allison's FTP play *The Trial of Dr. Beck* (1937) and Phillip Yordan's ANT play *Anna Lucasta* (1944). King's list of triumphs includes the original production of Shange's *For Colored Girls Who Have Considered Suicide/When the Rainbow is Enuf* (1976). Between 1970 and 1999 the NFT produced more than 160 plays, most of them originals. King became the most prolific and the most successful of all African American producers. In 2000, Wayne State University, King's *alma mater*, awarded him an honorary doctorate in humanities.

In 2001 the Frederick Douglass Center celebrated its thirtieth anniversary. Located in Upper Manhattan, it was founded in 1971 by Fred Hudson and Hollywood screenwriter Budd Schulberg.[34] The Frederick Douglass Center's steady growth stemmed, in part, from its liaisons with the Writers Guild of America, East, the Ethical Cultural Society, the Schomburg Center and the Manhattan Neighborhood Network (with its four public access channels). The center made good use of celebrity women, who gave scholarships, taught classes, and appeared on panels and at awards ceremonies.[35] The center focused on classes in writing – novels, screenplays, fiction, poetry, radio, and journalism. Fully 90 percent of the enrollment was African American and 50 percent was female. In the year 2000, Fred Hudson received the Governor's Arts Award from George Pataki on behalf of the center.

Farther uptown in Harlem, Ernie McClintock in 1966 combined his Afro-American Theatre with a school that offered actors a five-term curriculum of ten-week workshops in singing, karate, makeup, movement, yoga, speech, and black theatre history. To enable inexperienced actors to free their talents, he evolved his jazz acting technique, a process which allowed actors to contribute to a production in much the same manner as a musician contributed to a jazz ensemble. As McClintock's classes and company grew, he moved his studio three times to larger spaces before securing a "permanent" home for it at 415 West 127th Street, a two-story building that had once been a brewery. Using a pool of talent from his classes, he mounted three to six productions a year. The choice of shows ranged from *Shango de Ima: A Yoruba Mystery Play* (1976) to *Equus* (1982). McClintock then moved to Atlanta.

Women playwrights and directors

Although the most prolific period of black playwriting in America began with Lorraine Hansberry and ended with Ntozake Shange, very few women playwrights came to prominence during the 1960s and 1970s. Both Hansberry and Shange received recognition from the white community: Hansberry for writing a great "Negro play," and Shange for her perceived attack upon the chauvinism of males. True, during the 1960s assertive black manhood had taken center stage; consequently, women wrote fewer plays than men did, perhaps a tacit acknowledgment that they had little chance of production. After attempting careers as performers and discovering very few opportunities New York black women established their own companies – Marjorie Moon (Billie Holiday Theatre); Cynthia Belgrave (Acting Studio); Hazel Bryant (Richard Allen Center); Vinnette Carroll (Urban Arts Corps). Carroll insisted upon a place at the table: "They told me that I had one-third less chance because I was a woman; they told me I had a third less chance again because I was black, but I tell you, I did one hell of a lot with that remaining one-third."[36] Beginning her career as an actress and director, in 1962 Vinnette Carroll carried Langston Hughes' *Black Nativity* to the Spoleto festival in Italy, then toured the show to seven European countries and then to Australia and New Zealand. Hoping to duplicate the success of *Black Nativity* in Europe, Carroll persuaded Stella Holt of the Greenwich Mews Theatre to produce Hughes' gospel-song play, *Prodigal Son* (1965). After nearly one hundred performances at the Greenwich Mews, in the autumn of 1966 a British producer offered the cast of fifteen a tour of Holland, Germany, Belgium, and France. Principals were to receive $175 a week and the chorus $125, but by 3 January the producer had not paid the cast for several weeks. The cast "sat in" on the stage of the Champs Elysées Theatre. The *gendarmes* were called; the cast and musicians were forcibly removed.

Back home in America, Carroll, finding no theatre work, created opportunities for herself and for other minority talents. In 1967, as director of the Ghetto Arts Program for the New York State Council on the Arts, she established the Urban Arts Corps, where classes in professional dance, acting, and theatre crafts trained hundreds of young artists, including Jonelle Allen, Marvin Felix Camillo, and Sherman Hemsley. Carroll, politically astute, was a fighter. When in 1971 producer Roger L. Stevens announced he would use a white director for the South African musical *Lost in the Stars*, Carroll fired off a blistering public letter that concluded: "I suppose it is naïve to think that white folks have passed the point where their instincts tell them to throw pennies in the street and command Niggers to dance!"[37]

For more than eleven years from her loft-theatre on West 20th Street in Manhattan, Carroll produced more than one hundred plays, two of which became hit musicals on Broadway: Micki Grant had come to the Big Apple from Los Angeles with the civil rights musical *Fly Blackbird* (1962); she remained to star in her own civil rights musical, *Don't Bother Me, I Can't Cope* (1972). The theme was positive and upbeat. Compared with Van Peebles' dour view of racial inequities, it was clear that audiences preferred to accent the positive. Carroll's second Broadway success, *Your Arms Too Short to Box With God* (1975), ran for 429 performances before touring and returning in 1980 to Broadway for another 149.[38] She died on 5 November 2002.

Equally determined to make a place for black theatre in America was Hazel Bryant. At the age of 24 Bryant came to New York from her home in Baltimore and discovered that American opera had no place for a black soprano who had studied at the Mozarteum in Salzburg. Not one to give up a dream, Bryant in 1968 founded the Afro-American Total Theatre (named after Richard Wagner's concept of a reunification of the arts.) Here she wrote and produced four of her own plays, all with music. *Black Circles'Round Angela: A Documentary Musical* (1970) and *Sheba* (1973) were produced at the Brooklyn Academy of Music. Beginning in 1970, Bryant coordinated the

Figure 40. Hazel Bryant, founder and director of the Richard Allen Center, New York City

Annual Festival of Community and Street Theatre at the Lincoln Center. This should not be confused with her founding of the *Black Theatre Festival USA, An Arts Revival at the Lincoln Center* (1979), which brought together eleven black theatre and dance companies from nine cities, one of her major accomplishments. To help call attention to her company, on 22 December 1982 she presented Langston Hughes' *Black Nativity* at the Vatican before Pope John Paul II.

Bryant worked in "borrowed" theatres; in 1976 she leased two floors from the Empire Hotel across from the Lincoln Center and named her theatres the Richard Allen Center for Culture and Art (RACCA). Here her work ranged from the *The Confession Stone*, a poetic retelling of the Easter story by Owen Dodson, to the highly acclaimed all-black *Long Day's Journey into Night* (1981). At RACCA Bryant worked closely with playwright and director Kathleen Collins (1942–88), a graduate from the Sorbonne in Paris. Bryant's cadre included Bill Gunn (1930–89), actor, playwright, and Emmy winner (1972), whose vampire film *Ganja and Hess* won international acclaim at the Cannes Film Festival in 1975, and Duane Jones (1937–88), who had attended the Sorbonne, been nominated for an Emmy, and regularly acted and directed plays for Bryant, Collins, and Gunn. These four artists held fast to their vision that theatre should offer more than images of urban poverty and despair. Their deaths in the 1980s, all within five years of one another, proved a great loss to African American theatre.[39]

Other women wrote consistently and honestly about their gender. For a time China Clark became a staff writer for television's *Bill Cosby Show*.[40] Gertrude Greenidge wrote more than thirty plays, including *Ma Lou's Daughters* (1974), the story of a woman who must confront her own mulatto daughter, the child of a rape. Between 1971 and 1981 P[atricia] J[oann] Gibson also wrote nearly thirty works, including television dramas. Gibson was awarded an NEA playwriting grant and two Audience Development Committee (AUDELCO) awards. J. e. Franklin, after her initial success with *Black Girl* (1971), wrote a series of ten-minute plays she called *Gray Panthers* (1990), because they focused on African American elders whose folk wisdom had forged an enduring value system. Anthologies of women's plays did not appear until the 1980s and 1990s.

Community theatres

When the grants dried up, companies found they could no longer pay salaries or the rent. A microcosm of the battles faced and won by small urban theatres can be seen in the surge of new companies that had sprung up in Queens and Brooklyn, New York. Franklin A. Thomas had grown up in Bedford-Stuyvesant. Trained in theatre by Osceola Archer at ANT, he would later become the first black president of the Ford Foundation, a position he used to revitalize a severely depressed neighborhood by establishing the Bedford-Stuyvesant Restoration Corporation. The $6 million unit covered one square block and eventually included a supermarket, an ice-skating rink, and the 218-seat Billie Holiday Theatre, which opened in May 1972 and became the hub of the corporation's cultural and recreational activities. Thomas' concept was to expose the second largest black community in America to the arts while providing an outlet for local talent. Under executive director Marjorie Moon, the theatre built a community audience by placing Bedford-Stuyvesant citizens on the theatre's board. Its Theatre for Little Folk (ages 3 to 13) brought parents and siblings to programs that ranged from *Hip Rumpelstelzkin* to *African Dancing and Drumming and the Seven Principles of Blackness*. Plays written by local talent sold seats. Weldon Irvine's *Young, Gifted and Broke* (1977) ran for a record seventy-seven sold-out performances. Among its alumni, the theatre listed the film actor Samuel Jackson, actor and playwright Samm-Art Williams, whose drama *Home* (1979) ran for 279 performances on Broadway, and Debbie Allen, choreographer of Oscar shows. Moon invited other theatre companies to share the space, a policy that provided funds while keeping the theatre in use. However, an annual budget of $230,000 in 1974 dollars was difficult to raise. Ten years later, the budget had doubled to nearly $500,000, and in spite of success, the budget was still difficult to raise. Part of the solution was to produce shows for $35,000 to $40,000 and charge $13 for a ticket, as compared to Broadway's $75 or $100. But Moon's was not the only new company in Bedford-Stuyvesant.

"One never forgets how Bedford-Stuyvesant Theatre looks," wrote reviewer Barbara Walker. "Painted black, draped with three huge paintings, the theatre seems to be the only thing that represents some sort of life. All the other buildings are either torn down or badly rundown. Pieces of broken glass, dog shit, empty wine bottles, turned-over garbage, seem to be the only form of scenery the neighborhood has."[41] Yet, in what commonly was described as the worst ghetto slums of Brooklyn, three small community theatres grew: Bed-Stuy Theater founded by Delano Stewart in June 1968, the Bedford Stuyvesant Street Academy created by director Thomas Turner with playwright Pat Singleton in 1970, and the Brownsville Laboratory Theatre incorporated by Sister Lubaba (Yvonne Madison) and her husband James, with administrator Cecil Cummings in 1970. All three shared black community audiences who suffered poverty, drug infestation, and crime. All three believed that their community had its own culture, one worthy of being placed upon the stage, where it might see and understand itself.

Black Theatre Alliance (BTA)

The growth of the black theatre movement created the need for a support network. The first of these facilitators was the Black Theatre Alliance

(BTA). In the fall of 1969, Hazel Bryant had been one of four black theatre directors that the New York Council on the Arts sponsored for a technical training workshop at the Columbia University School of Drama.[42] The four directors soon discovered that they all faced similar problems. Substantial money had been given by the Ford Foundation and the Rockefeller Foundation to the NEC and the NLT. With no more large grants available, small companies could not buy lighting instruments, controls boards, and costumes. The solution? To share resources, both physical and administrative. Delano Stewart suggested they formalize the arrangement into a nonprofit corporation, the Black Theatre Alliance (BTA) (1970–82). BTA invited three more theatres into their group – Sister Lubaba Lateef's Brownsville Laboratory Theatre, Buddy Butler's Theatre Black, and Ernie McClintock's Afro-American Studio Theatre.

Once the BTA had obtained its not-for-profit status it became eligible for philanthropic gifts. While the New York State Council on the Arts could not award grants to cooperatives, it did fund individual talents and companies. Beginning its first year with $15,000, BTA's budget grew to $150,000 in four years, which enabled it to hire Joan Sandler as executive director and to issue small loans to member companies. The BTA conducted workshops in management and technical theatre, and provided a place where small theatres could share common problems, exchange information, launch a joint program for audience development, and publish a quarterly newsletter.

To increase its visibility, the BTA held its first theatre festival in 1971 at the St. Mark's Playhouse. Because the stage was the home of the Negro Ensemble Company, BTA presented plays only on nights the theatre was dark; the festival lasted five weeks. Its success recruited new members, and BTA grew to sixteen companies, all New York-based. The following year BTA presented their second festival at the Billie Holiday Theatre in Brooklyn. Two more festival years followed. The final one, held at the Lincoln Center in New York City, attracted twenty-one companies. Mayor Beame, in honor of the festival, declared November 1974 Black Theatre Month. By 1980, BTA members, counting dance companies, had grown to more than seventy-five. The alliance moved into a building on the newly renovated Theatre Row on West 42nd Street, whose facilities included a small theatre as well as rehearsal and office space. BTA's 1979 budget had grown to $468,000, half of which came from the federal CETA program. Then President Reagan turned thumbs down on the arts and CETA collapsed. BTA's debts totaled $90,000, including two months' back rent.[43] Brooke Stephens became BTA's fourth executive director; she had attended Harvard Business

School and knew how to handle money, but she had no money to handle. Ironically, while Playwrights Horizons, the Harold Clurman Theatre, and others on Theatre Row were creating new and positive images, the BTA fell into arrears and dissolved. However, one of their inspirations lived on.

In 1975 Woodie King Jr. of the NFT met with the BTA to establish a black touring circuit, the National Black Touring Circuit.[44] His twofold plan was to make existing black theatre productions available to larger audiences, and to develop a viable mechanism for participating theatres to share the profits. The plays would be provided by the touring members. Realizing that half of America's black population lived in its cities, King set up a black subscription audience in four cities: Washington, Philadelphia, Chicago, and Detroit. Each would receive four plays a year, played by star professionals. At first, the touring circuit faced a handicap; traditional subscription audiences were white. But after six years of hard work and planning, King, along with Shauneille Perry and Gloria Mitchell, had raised $500,000, enough to launch their dream. Using AEA actors, small casts, and rigorously budgeted productions, the touring circuit opened at the Terrace Theatre, John F. Kennedy Center for the Performing Arts in Washington, DC, in 1980. Twenty years later, the circuit continued to tour its plays into the millennium.

Frank Silvera Writers' Workshop (FSWW)

Other fresh and bold projects emerged. As late as 1973, there still was a paucity of well-crafted plays by and about African Americans. Garland Thompson, a director and playwright from the west coast, approached Joan Sandler of BTA about forming a workshop for playwrights, a place where the authors could hear their scripts read aloud by professional actors, and have them criticized by a sympathetic but professional audience. Thompson named it after Frank Silvera, an actor and director he had much admired in Los Angeles, who had founded the Theatre of Being, and who had brought James Baldwin's play *The Amen Corner* (1965) to Broadway. On 22 October the first full-length script was read. Using Monday night and Saturday afternoon for readings and discussion of new plays, the FSWW by 1977 was giving hearings to more than ninety new works each year. During the first years, Thompson borrowed and rented space for the readings – the Harlem Performance Center, City College of New York, Pace College, St. Marks Playhouse, the Martinique Hotel. Then, with assistance from the

NEA and the New York State Council on the Arts, FSWW acquired its
own space on the corner of 125th Street and St. Nicholas Avenue in Harlem,
where it remained for the next twenty years. From this process more than
seventy-five off off-Broadway productions were mounted. Simultaneously,
a sister organization was growing – the Audience Development Committee.
(AUDELCO).

AUDELCO

For theatre to prosper in a community, attendance must become a habit,
in the same manner people attend a season of baseball or the high school
basketball games. While African Americans in Harlem had ritualized attendance at the Apollo Theatre to hear music and listen to their favorite
comics, they did not turn to the Apollo for plays or go downtown to Broadway theatres. All that changed with the Black Arts Movement, when it
became possible to attend a different play or performance every night of the
week. The little theatres were there, the plays were there, but the audience
often was not.

In 1972, Vivian Robinson, a social reporter and theatre critic for the
Amsterdam News, set out to fill the empty theatre seats with African
Americans. On 1 April 1973 she founded the Audience Development Committee (AUDELCO). By the year following, 548 members paid $5 apiece
to receive her newsletter advertising plays by and about black people. Using
vouchers from the Theatre Development Fund, she offered theatre parties
at reduced prices.[45] Knowing that the major New York critics rarely recognized black talent with the Tony or Drama Desk awards, AUDELCO
established its own annual theatre prizes. The members voted for their fa-
vorites and each November, *à la* the Academy Awards, AUDELCO in an
annual gala acknowledged the best acting, directing, writing, as well as the
arts of set and costume design. As theatre attendance grew, so did the pres-
tige of AUDELCO. Soon, actors began to list the awards on their résumés
and agents began to pay attention. When Vivian Robinson died, in 1996,
AUDELCO had presented more than four hundred awards to African
Americans for outstanding theatre endeavors.

White organizations, too, began to acknowledge the black presence. The
Actors' Equity Association, fifty years after its formation in 1913, had enrolled only 4 percent actors of color, but in 1952 it elected Frederick O'Neal as
vice-president. In 1964, through pressure and a petition led by Hilda Simms,
it elected O'Neal to its presidency. In that position, he fought for integrated

casting. Because of O'Neal's work, in 1973 the American Theatre Association's Black Theatre Program during its New York convention honored Paul Robeson's achievements. The AEA then commissioned Richmond Barthé to sculpt a bronze head of Robeson, which on 23 April 1976 was placed in the Library and Museum of the Performing Arts at the Lincoln Center, an important gesture toward recovering the actor's reputation, which had been soiled by the malice of the Un-American Activities Committee.

Six who did survive

In 1926, when W. E. B. Du Bois set forth his famous criteria for Negro theatre as being *"by, for, about,* and *near* us," he envisioned a community theatre, usually performing in borrowed space (halls, libraries, churches, schools). The audiences lived nearby and knew the actors. Finances were always a problem, and most groups collapsed after two or three productions. Forty years later, community theatres had changed, but the central cause of failure remained fiscal. A brief glance at theatres in six selected cities reveals similar if differing survival stories.

Baltimore's Arena Players (not to be confused with the Arena Theatre in Washington, DC) celebrated their forty-fifth season of dramatic productions in 1998. The founding father and visionary, Samuel H. Wilson Jr., died in 1995, but not until he and his friends (some of whom had been associated with the original Baltimore KRIGWA group) had seen their theatre through several moves from church to gymnasium to recreational hall. In 1969 in an economically depressed area, Arena bought for $10,000 the building that had been St. Mary's Episcopal Church. Over the next six years the players moved the stage from the second floor to a two-thirds arena house on the ground floor. Along with a new 314-seat theatre, they added classrooms, rehearsal spaces, a Youtheatre (ages 13 to 18), a children's theatre, and an art gallery. Their first program of plays in 1953 began with William Saroyan's *Hello Out There* and Thornton Wilder's *Happy Journey.* Every season saw at least six shows on the boards. In 1992 the plays presented were all by African Americans, as were nearly all the audience. Church and school groups were bused in to the Mount Vernon district, a developing middle-class neighborhood. In 1997 the Arena Theatre had grown to 150 active members and boasted a million-dollar facility. It owned the land and its building.

In New Orleans, an old Catholic church housed the Dashiki Theatre, an auditorium seating 150 people in folding chairs. From center stage hung a large electric bingo sign, which had to be incorporated into every production design (no performances on Saturday nights, Bingo Night!). With a group of his former students from the Players Guild, Dr. Ted Gilliam, assistant professor of drama at Dillard University, founded the Dashiki in 1968. They began by producing five plays a season, but by 1982 pulled back to three – all from the African Diaspora. Dashiki's resident playwright, N[orbert] R. Davidson Jr., contributed new plays to each theatre season. His play about Malcolm X, *El Hajj Malik: The Dramatic Life and Death of Malcolm X*, a collage of poetry, chants, slides, music, dancers, and dramatic narration, premiered in 1968. After Ed Bullins published it in *New Plays from the Black Theatre* (1969), Davidson's script was widely produced by young Blacks because of the originality of its staging and the pertinency of its subject. Expanding in 1973, Dashiki enrolled forty-two teenagers in the Ethiopian Youth Workshop to produce their own original dramas.

In 1965, C. Bernard Jackson, Dr. J. A. Cannon of UCLA, and Josie Dotson founded the Inner City Cultural Center (ICCC) in Los Angeles, which occupied a series of venues before nesting (with a mortgage) in their own space on Vermont Avenue, one of the city's poorer districts. Executive Director Jackson had the foresight to purchase an old Masonic Hall on the edge of Hispanic, Black, Asian, and White neighborhoods, which was a strong motivation for ICCC to cast all its productions multiculturally.

For their first year *Tartuffe*, *The Glass Menagerie*, *The Seagull*, and *A Midsummer's Night's Dream* were chosen and directed by Andre Gregory with a largely white staff. The second year Jackson set out to find a distinguished academic of color, someone acceptable to the Office of Education and to the NEA, who had placed inordinate pressure upon the ICCC to show that minority artists could succeed in the classics. He found Owen Dodson of Howard University. Over a six-week period, 25,000 high school students were bused to the center to see Jean Anouilh's *Antigone*. For many in the audience, it was their first trip to "the inner city," where they saw actors cast without regard to color. Bernard Jackson knew the center was a test case. "We had to achieve within an area that was considered extraordinary for Blacks to achieve in. We had to prove ourselves; we had to be better than *they* were at what they did."[46] Under Dodson's direction, Adolph Caesar played Creon; Susan Batson as Antigone won the Los Angeles Drama Critics Circle Award for best actress.

When the ICCC's building was damaged by earthquake, Jackson purchased the Ivar Theatre in Hollywood, where the organization pursued its original mission to train minority youth in the theatre arts and to present

Figure 41. C. Bernard Jackson, founder and director of the Inner City Cultural Center, Los Angeles

plays that had relevance to their lives. However, when Bernard Jackson died in 1995, the Ivar was lost to its mortgage and the ICCC had no home. Their best-known "graduate" was George C. Wolfe, who became artistic director of the Joseph Papp Public Theater.

Further south along Los Angeles' Vermont Avenue, Vantile Whitfield, a.k.a. Motojicho (Swahili, "fire eyes"), in 1964 built a 100-seat theatre and christened it the Performing Arts Society of Los Angeles (PASLA). In addition to mounting play productions, Whitfield, with the assistance of Warner Brothers animator Frank Braxton, started a film workshop for the youth of Watts. PASLA received commendations from both the city and county of Los Angeles. Partially as a result of this recognition, in 1970 Whitfield became Director of Expansion Arts, a division of the NEA targeted for minority programs.

The Black Arts Movement arrived in Seattle in April 1961 with a production of *A Raisin in the Sun*, which inspired actor and stage manager Douglas Q. Barnett to found three theatre companies successively: the first two – Ebony Stage Productions and Theatre Black – were short-lived. The third, the New Group Theatre, sustained itself by touring productions to schools, churches, and universities and by forming a liaison with the local antipoverty agency, the Central Area Motivation Program. In 1969, Barnett acquired his own theatre space and renamed his group Black Arts/West, after the then defunct San Francisco Black Arts/West Theatre. Jason Bernard, a proponent of the Grotowski acting method, conducted improvisation workshops. Lorna Prim Richards conducted modern and African dance classes, which eventually expanded to include beginning ballet. At its peak, dance enrolled between 100 and 150 students. In 1968, R. G. Davis' *Minstrel Show* (1968) toured Seattle. Inspired by the pseudo-minstrel's format and its ability to address local issues, Barnett and Black Arts/West created their own minstrel show, *Da Minstrel Show* (1968), followed by a second topical play, *Days of Thunder, Nights of Violence* (1968–70). Over the next four years, Black Arts/West produced more than thirty-one plays.[47]

Workshopping *Ain't Supposed to Die a Natural Death* (1971) with Gilbert Moses brought Black Arts/West national publicity and more funding, which became a mixed blessing. Black Arts/West's dependency on grants rather than earned income led umbrella organizations to exert paternalistic political and artistic control. Barnett resigned in 1973. The new project director Buddy Butler opened the season with the Broadway success *The River Niger* (1972) and managed the theatre through 1977. Black Arts/West collapsed in 1980 but its important legacy came a decade later with the reawakening of ethnic theatre in Seattle.

Even well-managed community theatres, white or black, seldom live beyond eight to ten years because administrators tire or retire, the best actors move on to professional roles, funds dry up, and – unless the theatres own their property or have roots in larger organizations – higher and higher rents shut them down. From the turn of the century settlement houses and cultural centers located in African American neighborhoods served as venues for theatre groups.

The South Side Settlement House on Wabash Avenue in Chicago, founded during the WPA days, acquired a new home on Michigan

Avenue named the South Side Community Art Center. When it opened in 1941, Mrs. Roosevelt came to bless it. Here Gwendolyn Brooks, Elizabeth Catlett, Charles White, and John Biggers studied. In 1966 this arts settlement opened a wing for the performing arts and initiated its stage with two plays by the "older" generation – *Florence* (1949) by Alice Childress and *Whole Hog or Nothing* (1952) by Theodore Ward. The next year South Side Community Performing Arts (SSCPA) leased the Louis Theatre, an old 548-seat movie house in the heart of the ghetto. After renovation, some members wished to present contemporary plays; however, Theodore Ward, as executive director of SSCPA, had obtained the money for the remodeling. He chose to open the theatre with his own 1947 Broadway drama, *Our Lan'*, in spite of protest that the play was out of step with the new direction of Black Power.

As internal strife at the South Side grew, a husband and wife team, Francis and Val Gray Ward (no relation to Theodore) called their friends together in 1968 to form the Kuumba (Swahili "to create") Workshop. For performance space, they pioneered rituals in churches, schools, and even taverns. The essential components were improvisation, audience involvement, and teaching – don't use dope, don't drink, gamble, or use violence against others. In 1974 Kuumba moved to an old warehouse once used by Al Capone during the 1920s. In 1978, in order to obtain its tax exempt status, the workshop changed its name to Kuumba Community Theatre, even though many of their projects and efforts were other than theatre, such as panels on exploitation movies, aid to the starving of Ethiopia, and a national tribute to Gwendolyn Brooks. After ten years Kuumba moved to the Civic Opera House in the West Loop. In 1993, Kuumba, under the auspices of Malcolm X College, celebrated its twenty-fifth anniversary.

In New York City another successful wedding of theatre and settlement occurred at Upper Manhattan's Union Settlement Community Center, an interfaith church. There in 1966, Mical Whitaker's East River Players found a home in the James Weldon Johnson Theatre Arts Center. With the security of knowing his theatre's rent would be paid, Whitaker produced plays as varied as *Amen Corner*, *Threepenny Opera*, and *Simply Heavenly*, using multiethnic casting for a multiethnic audience. After a theatre life of fourteen years, Whitaker in 1981 returned to his home to teach in Mitter, Georgia; the East River Players drifted and died.

Earlier, the Harlem Children's Theatre Company (HCTC) had invited Whitaker to produce an original script, *The Liberation of Mother Goose* (1974) by Aduke Aremu (Gwen Jones), who had founded the company in 1970.

Working with ages 4 to 17, HCTC advertised itself as the only professional black children's company in America. Their skills in acting, singing,
and dancing brought them to television, and their company performed at
FESTAC in 1977, the international theatre festival in Lagos-Kunda, Nigeria.

For many years, the best playwrights, black and white, did not write for
children, an audience they thought capable only of fairy tales and Christmas
pageants. Because the main thrust of a settlement house was to improve opportunities in slum neighborhoods, children's theatres fitted logically into its
programs. In Boston, the New African Company founded by Jim Spruill
and Gus Johnson, incorporated in 1970 under the wing of the Theatre
Company of Boston, flourished until the mid-1980s until President Reagan's financial cutbacks closed many black theatres, cutbacks necessitated by
Reagan's Savings and Loan Bank scandal, which cost the nation billions of
dollars. In 1994 the New African Company resurfaced with Lynda Patton's
Ol' Sis Goose, the tale of a goose put on trial for swimming on the wrong
side of the lake. Kelsie E. Collie of Howard University also crusaded for
juvenile performance, by writing more than a dozen children's plays, which
he produced.

Black theatres in the universities

College student sit-ins of 1961 spurred young Blacks to demand their full civil
rights, and when that access was slow in coming, many, led by the rhetoric of
Stokely Carmichael and Rapp Brown, joined the Black Power Movement.
Offstage, they demanded black autonomy and the establishment of black
studies departments. Onstage, they applauded the new plays that taught
pride in Blackness, plays like Carlton and Barbara Molette's *Rosalee Pritchett*
(1970), where black, middle-class striver Rosalee is raped by soldiers from
the white National Guard who, she had insisted, were in town to protect
her against black rioters.[48] Many on black faculties felt that the Black Arts
Movement, with its profane and racially charged rhetoric, was a denigration
of the humanities, a kind of reverse racism. The militants responded: "If
you're not part of the solution, you're part of the problem." There was
little room for compromise. Ron Milner in his play *Monster* (1969) has one
of the students accuse the bourgeois faculty of complicity in maintaining
the status quo; the solution, the students must assassinate the dean of the
college.

The establishment of black studies divisions on white campuses took
one of three academic forms, but all affected the quality and longevity of

black theatre. They ranged from a "department" where black professors sat on college-wide committees and participated in deciding college policies, to a "program," which might have its own separate curriculum and staff; however, its relation to the rest of the university was peripheral, with no academic power to control tenure or budget. Between these two was the "division," where black studies could be lodged within a traditional department, perhaps in English, history, or even in speech and theatre. Black theatre lodged as a "division" depended upon its host department for budget, faculty, and space. A prickly relationship with an indigenous drama department would be an invitation for conflict and neglect. In sum, black theatre's tenure on many campuses depended upon the racial and academic power of black studies, which in turn owed its existence to the continuing militancy of the students. When this constituency graduated, the colleges often reduced or eliminated black courses and staff.

In the fall of 1970 George Bass at Brown University began with fifty undergraduate and graduate students. With a budget of $3,000 ($1,800 from the student caucus and $1,200 from Bass himself), he built Rites and Reason, a theatre to celebrate black culture. Joining forces with Professor Rhett Jones of the Afro-American Studies Program and History Department, Bass used original research from students and others to create a series of plays exploring and celebrating black history, a dramaturgic program of research, writing, and productions that brought the Providence community into collaborative engagement with the playwrights. In five years, Bass, with grants from the NEA, engaged two hundred students and community people.

An example of a different structure but still a successful nesting was the Kuntu Repertory Theater in the Department of Black Community Education Research and Development at the University of Pittsburgh. In 1974 Dr. Vernell A. Lillie established Kuntu, a Bantu word meaning "way." In 1976 Kuntu produced *Homecoming* by a then unrecognized playwright, August Wilson. That script later became the basis for *Ma Rainey's Black Bottom.* Kuntu recruited veteran director and actor Allie Woods and, with resident playwright Rob Penny, Kuntu celebrated its twentieth-fifth anniversary in 1999/2000.

Theatre departments had to satisfy angry students and at the same time appease trustees and faculty. A case in point: Howard University's budget depended upon US Congressional appropriation. When in 1964 the Confederate flag was draped over the marquee to advertise *Purlie Victorious,* the administration ordered the students to remove the flag because it might offend some members of Congress. Students pressured faculty to produce militant plays. No more *Hamlet* or *Long Day's Journey into Night* but instead a program that would include *El Hajj Malik* or *Niggers*. When older faculty at Howard (Anne Cooke, James Butcher, and Owen Dodson) retired, the young lions painted the interior of the Ira Aldridge Theatre black to symbolize their new pride. Not all college programs changed so radically, but most were forced to allow for younger and blacker voices.

A severe but not fatal blow to black college drama would come in the 1990s when legislators and administrators cut the budgets of the arts and humanities. Howard University, which once set the standard for quality theatre, considered eliminating its division of fine arts. Nonetheless, fifty years after the Negro Intercollegiate Dramatics Association had first issued its six objectives (see chapter 7), the Black Arts Movement freed the colleges from a dominance of European and Broadway shows. Drama teachers in increasing numbers joined national associations, which expanded provincial horizons.[49]

Black theatres in prisons

While touring companies as well as community groups had often performed plays in prisons for convicts, the 1960s and 1970s saw the development of theatre groups within the prisons, motivated in part by the increasing population of young black males as well as the shower of government money coming under the rubric of rehabilitation programs.[50] In 1967 Akila Couloumbis, a Greek American, with actress Beverly Rich founded Theater for the Forgotten in New York City using AEA actors who worked for no salary. Couloumbis discovered early that prison inmates preferred African American plays. By 1973 the project had grown to three hundred performances a year by three companies funded by the New York State Council on the Arts, the Corrections Department, and the Rockefeller and Mellon Foundations. Gradually, inmates were able to build sets and perform themselves. Success allowed some to rehearse outside in various colleges. Some inmates were even paid. In 1974 a drama workshop for youngsters aged 14 to 16 was established at the Spotford Juvenile Center in the Bronx.

Another prison program evolved from the Elma Lewis School of Fine Arts in Roxbury, a suburb of Boston, Massachusetts. The school, established in 1950 in a six-room apartment, enrolled twenty-five students to learn dance, theatre, and art. By 1973 the school had enrolled more than eight hundred students and was housed in the National Center of Afro-American Artists Complex. Lewis established the Technical Theatre Training

Program in nearby Norfolk Prison, where inmates performed their own plays. She published a history of these experiences along with several plays written by prisoners, *Who Took the Weigh? Black Voices from Norfolk Prison* (1972).[51]

Street theatres

Street Theatre, with its potential to reach people directly, to raise their consciousness and "to free their minds from the slavery of white/capitalistic media," became a wing of black activism. Politicians and government officials liked it for its potential to defuse rebellion through art, music, dance, and language, instead of fire. Street theatre developed in two forms: mobile theatre (plays and companies that came from *outside* the community) and local street theatre (groups that developed from *within* the community.) The theatre that came from outside was sometimes called guerrilla theatre (unannounced, unexpected, and without a permit), or if it were planned and announced, it was an experimental group whose roots often derived from radical European dramatic traditions. In that sense, it might be said that guerrilla and experimental groups were the theatres of university students – The Living Theatre, San Francisco Mime Troupe, Bread and Puppet Theatre, and so forth. The NEA gave money to these theatres in much greater largess than they gave to neighborhood companies. To remedy this inequity, to help theatres in ghettos and rural areas, in 1970 the NEA created a division of expansion arts and appointed as its director Vantile Whitfield, who stated: "I personally feel that the theatre presently in this country is new-European, and that we don't have American Theatre yet. The important contribution that we can make is that American Theatre will embrace everybody."[52] Street theatre was born, which is not to say that it had not existed prior to 1970, but national funding for it had not. For eight years under Whitfield's leadership, Expansion Arts, starting out with a staff of one and a budget of $375,000, grew to a staff of twelve and a budget of more than $8 million that funded more than six hundred arts groups per year nationally. In 1996 Congress, led by Senator Jesse Helms of North Carolina, eliminated its programs.

Most street companies shared similar obstacles. The first hurdle was obtaining a permit to perform. Mike Malone of the Black Repertory Theatre, before applying for a permit in the nation's capitol, had to have a petition from the target community showing 50 percent support. Forms were sent about ten days in advance to the local police precinct for each location.

The workshop discovered that follow-through was seldom smooth, and they might arrive to find that the police had not yet closed off the street. Ostensibly, a street theatre group had to be invited to play in a given location or they might find themselves thrown out, as was a company from the New York Shakespeare Festival in 1964, when they played in Brownsville, Brooklyn, without consulting the local block association. The Free Street Theatre run by the Illinois Arts Council was often required to have a local neighborhood sponsor whose responsibility it would be to obtain the right forms and signatures.

As part of the federal government's efforts to abort another Watts or Newark riot, budgets often included token salaries. Administrators and technicians might be paid $10 per performance, while the actors would receive $5. Established groups such as the Public Theatre's Shakespeare Company could do five shows a week for four weeks with a budget of $19,000 – administrators receiving $150 per week. The Free Street Theatre of Chicago, a group formed by the Goodman School of Drama and the Illinois Arts Council, paid their performers $125 per week. When federal poverty funds were cut, the groups disbanded. By 1996 Expansion Arts was totally eliminated.

Families in jeopardy

In the 1960s serious dramas written by Blacks presented several families driven dysfunctional by racism, even though white people never appeared on stage. Unlike the family in Hansberry's *A Raisin in the Sun* (1959), who at the final curtain are united against racism, several stage families in the early 1960s continued to self-destruct. Lonne Elder III's *Ceremonies in Dark Old Men* (1965) examined the disintegration of Russell B. Parker and his sons, who turned to fencing stolen property, running numbers, and bootleg whiskey in order to make a living. Nominated for the Pulitzer Prize in drama, it was telecast by ABC in 1975 and won the Christopher Television Award. Two domestic tragedies written by Ron Milner focused on the paternal legacy of anger left to wives and children. Woodie King Jr. directed Milner's *Who's Got His Own* (1965) and later *The Warning – A Theme for Linda* (1969) at the American Place Theatre. *Black Girl* (1969) by J. e. Franklin and directed by Shauneille Perry portrayed the failure of a young woman to break away from her destructive family; the play won the 1971 Drama Desk Award. No playwright presented the bitter anguish driving families to madness better than Philip Hayes Dean. In his *The Owl Killer* (1971), a working-class father evicts his son and daughter from their home after years of mistreatment and deprivation. Dean's *The Sty of the Blind Pig* (1971), produced by the NEC, won the Drama Desk Award and was selected by *Time* magazine as one of the ten best plays of the year.

Richard Wesley's *The Past is Past* (1973) presented a son confronting his father, who had deserted his mother before the son was born. Directed by Lloyd Richards at the Billie Holiday Theatre in Brooklyn, it won the AUDELCO Award in 1974. The ruptured family was also treated comically in *Five on the Blackhand Side* (1969) by Charlie Russell. A would-be middle-class family is driven apart when they find and conceal stolen cash; when they lose the money, they are reunited. Judi Ann Mason exploited a similar idea in her comedy *Livin' Fat* (1974). The mad family theme appeared in Ted Shine's full-length drama *Morning Noon and Night* (1962), where the matriarch maid systematically poisons her enemies. A similar character reappears in Shine's *Contribution* (1969), a "wicked" comedy in which the "good darky" grandmother poisons her employers. Joseph A. Walker's *The River Niger* (1972), a melodrama, focuses on a Harlem father's struggle to be the traditional male head of his family. Produced on Broadway, it received a Drama Desk Award and a Tony Award for best play, and ran for four hundred performances.

James Baldwin's family play, *Amen Corner* (1955), had traveled a long road before Frank Silvera blew the dust off an old copy he may have acquired after the Howard University production in 1955.[53] He rented the 80-seat Robertson Theatre in Los Angeles and founded his "Theatre of Being." Having studied at the Actors' Studio in 1950, Silvera brought his own version of the "method" to his actors, asking them to go behind the words in the script and bring their personal experience to the role. Three hours long, *Amen Corner* soon found its churchgoing audiences and moved to the Coronet Theatre, where it ran for one year. *Amen Corner* remained popular with black audiences because of its family conflict in a church setting. Margaret, the minister of a small storefront church, struggles to bring her son up in the ways of the Lord as opposed to the ways of the boy's father, a jazz musician. Riding on the drama's Los Angeles success, in April 1964 Silvera moved it into the Ethel Barrymore Theatre in New York, where it received mixed reviews. On the positive side, the play established Beah Richards nationally as a dramatic actress. On the other hand, Vantile Whitfield, the set designer, and Gertha Brock, wardrobe mistress, became the first two African Americans to work a Broadway show without having to join the unions. The United Scenic Artists Association (USAA) simply waited for the show to close, as it did in three months, secure in the knowledge that no white producer would hire Blacks for another Broadway show.

Black and commercial

Better luck blessed actor and playwright Charles Gordone, who won the Pulitzer Prize in Drama, the first ever awarded an African American, for his *No Place to be Somebody* (1967). Set in a bar, the play presented the owner, Johnny Williams (played by Nathan George), as a hustler who tries to hoodwink his way out of a small-time Mafioso swindle and is shot. Costarred in the cast was Ron O'Neal, who would later achieve fame in blaxploitation films. Gordone angered some African Americans when he declared that he was "not a black militant writer" because he was "part Irish, part Indian, part French, and part nigger." The play ran for a total of 312 performances. Gordone wrote other scripts, but none achieved *No Place's* recognition. He died in 1995. Richard Wesley's play *The Mighty Gents* (1977), whose original title was *The Last Street Play* (1974), concerned an ageing street gang's refusal to accept the reality that they had become surplus people in American society. Morgan Freeman's Broadway performance was highly praised, but the show closed after nine performances. By the 1980s black dramas (and drama generally) disappeared from Broadway; musicals offered better returns on investment.

Melvin Van Peebles placed two musicals on Broadway within seven months of each other. *Ain't Supposed to Die a Natural Death* (1971) had a bitter and garish look at ghetto street life, and was subtitled "Tunes from Blackness." The play's director, Gilbert Moses, along with Douglas Q. Barnett of Black Arts/West, had workshopped the script for eight weeks in Seattle.

> On a hot humid night in August of 1971, prior to the Broadway opening, Black Arts/West presented the inaugural production of, *Ain't Supposed to Die a Natural Death* (1971). We presented three free productions to the community, all of which were jam-packed and over 90 percent Black. The closing Saturday night performance was the most emotional I'd ever witnessed. The bag lady's speech was given a searing reading that brought the audience to its feet. Our only regret was that since Gilbert used the workshop to put the poems into their final play/musical structure, that we [Black Arts/West] deserved a credit in the Broadway production to let the world know that we did it first![54]

The Broadway production began with the "Star-Spangled Banner." Some Whites stood up; many Blacks did not. The play won a Drama Desk Award, ran for 325 performances, and was the most militantly political black work to appear on Broadway that season. Van Peebles' second musical *Don't Play Us Cheap* (1972) set an entirely different mood, a comedy in which two demons enter the bodies of a rat and a roach. Avon Long, Esther Rolle, and Joe Armstead starred in the original, which managed 164 performances.

Black producers and critics

In 1965, Maria Cole, widow of Nat King Cole, bankrolled *Amen Corner*. She joined, along with Melvin Van Peebles, a shortlist of black producers – Charles Blackwell, Ossie Davis, Dick Campbell, Vinnette Carroll, Woodie King Jr., Ken Harper, Frank Silvera, and Ashton Springer Jr. – who had produced an off off-Broadway drama by Ray Aranha, *My Sister, My Sister* (1973), which won Drama Desk Awards for playwriting and acting (Seret Scott). Encouraged by his accolade, Springer turned to the musical *Bubbling Brown Sugar* (1976), which made money, and to *Eubie!* (1978), which lost money. *Eubie!* grossed around $100,000 a week, just enough to cover weekly expenses. Ashton Springer admitted that out of fifty or so investors in his shows, only one Black invested sizably. Union rules required producers to have extensive knowledge of working hours, defined duties, and the obligatory bonds held by the AEA. Because Springer did not know he had to inform his investors about cost overruns, he was hit with a $100,000 lawsuit by the Attorney General of New York. In another example of cost overruns, *The Wiz* (1975), budgeted at $650,000, spent $1,165,000 because of road expense and publicity. On the other hand, Vinnette Carroll and Woodie King Jr. were able to bring down rehearsal costs by initially staging their shows in their own small theatres for as little as $7,000. Most importantly, investors' money had a direct influence as to which plays reached the stage, perhaps as much influence as critics had on which plays would run for a profit.

In the 1960s black critics rarely received assignments to review white plays, but when white critics writing about militant black shows found the music too loud or inappropriate, the acting undisciplined, the plays too propagandistic, they seldom acknowledged that Whites were not the audience the playwright had in mind.

After a time, some newspapers hired black reviewers – Clayton Riley, Townsend Brewster, Larry Neal, Peter Bailey, and Barbara Lewis – whose reviews sometimes appeared alongside a review of the same play by a white critic. After three or four years, when militant plays waned, black critics disappeared from white newspapers.

Theatrical unions

The Actors' Equity Association wrote into their 1962 contracts, "The actor shall not be required to perform in any theater or other place of performance where discrimination is practiced because of race, color or creed." The AEA's stand on integration pulled black members away from the Negro Actors Guild (NAG). The election of Frederick O'Neal as president of the AEA and his active promotion of integrated casting for union shows, sealed NAG's doom. After a legal dispute in 1977 that divided the guild, NAG died in 1982. Throughout the 1960s the roles for Blacks increased only slightly in the areas where race was not thematically necessary.

The unions for costume, lighting, and stage design were slower to integrate. Lorraine Hansberry, when a student at the University of Wisconsin, confided to her adviser that she wished to become a scene designer. He discouraged her because she would be unable to find a job. Although Perry Watkins had been admitted into the USAA for *Mamba's Daughters* (1939), other African Americans were ignored, not examined, or were failed.

The story of Blacks backstage was neglected until 1981, when Professor Kathy A. Perkins at the University of Illinois, a professional lighting designer, undertook to collect the history. She discovered that during slavery, many black women had learned dressmaking and blackmen carpentry. These skills had been passed through families, who found their way into costume and stage design in the 1920s. In other instances, visual artists such as sculptor Meta Vaux Warrick Fuller (1877–1968) had turned their talents to costume design, as did painter Charles Sebree, who conceived and executed sets and costumes for the American Negro Theatre (1940–49). Professor Perkins mounted an exhibition entitled "Onstage: A Century of African American Stage Design" (1995) at the New York Public Library for the Performing Arts at the Lincoln Center. The hundred pieces included costumes, posters, set renderings, and lighting plots. The exhibition opened an abundant history of talented African American designers. In costume and makeup, there had long been a need for color considerations because the gels of stage lights, designed for white skin, changed the hues on makeup worn by Blacks.[55] In 1953, Louise Evans became the first African American woman to be admitted to USAA for costume design. She had begun her training at the Art Institute in Chicago. Gertha Brock, costume designer and seamstress for many shows, including *Ceremonies in Dark Old Men* (1965), had long declared that white designers usually did not know how to fashion clothes to adorn black bodies.

The stagehands unions were even more difficult to enter, as jobs were often passed down from father to son. However, in the 1970s the federal government included clauses regarding racial parity in shops that received federal funds, which may explain the appearance in 1974 of an advertisement by the International Alliance of Theatrical Stage Employees in New York's black newspaper the *Amsterdam News*: "UNIONS: State Employees Local #1, IATSE. 254 W. 54th Street; Organization apprenticeship test for stagehands. Age 17–31, April 21 thru 25 1974; One must sign up for the test. and bring birth certificate, photo 2X2 Soc. Security card and $20.00."[56]

Since the early 1920s, Local No. 1 had created a separate local No. 1-A for African Americans, whose members could only work in houses that were predominately black. In 1955 the two locals merged. Two years later producer David Merrick "asked the union to provide five black stagehands for his show *Jamaica* (1957). Told that was impossible, Merrick threatened the union with publicizing its delaying tactics and suddenly the leaders found the requested workers."[57] In 1968, of the fourteen hundred members, twenty were Black and six Puerto Rican. In 1996, the USAA, with more than twenty-two hundred members, had enrolled thirty African Americans.

During the 1960s and 1970s some minority designers obtained union cards. Among them was Geoffrey Holder, whose *The Wiz* (1976) startled audiences with its splendor. Edward Burbridge designed Richard Wesley's *The Mighty Gents* (1978) on Broadway, and Felix E. Cochren designed scenery for *A Soldier's Play* (1981). William H. Grant III credits Bernard Jackson with starting him on a lighting design career at ICCC in Los Angeles. "Jack gave me tremendous freedom to try things. He was a risk taker and he instilled that in me. I owe my entire career to him."[58] Grant moved on to become one of a very few who were able to cross over and design for white shows. The *grande dame* of African American costume during these decades unmistakably was Judy Dearing, who won seven AUDELCO Awards for her designs for shows produced by the New Federal Theatre and the Negro Ensemble Company, including *A Soldier's Play*, which won the Pulitzer Prize in 1982. She died in September 1995.

Personnel in box offices and other front offices changed little. Even ushers of color did not appear until the 1980s. However, when George C. Wolfe became artistic director at the Joseph Papp Public Theater, people of

color suddenly appeared in all technical and business capacities, extending
a policy that Joseph Papp had begun.

Blacks in classics

Following the practice of Ira Aldridge, black actors continued to play the
classics in the 1960s, where they suffered fewer slings and arrows from
outraged critics. James Earl Jones won praise for capturing roles other than
Othello, a role he played in five productions. Like Frank Silvera ten years
earlier at the Delacorte Theatre in Central Park, Jones played the title role in
King Lear (1962), supported by Ellen Holly and Rosalind Cash as his wicked
daughters. As early as 1966 *New York Times* critic Stanley Kauffmann in a
syndicated article asked:

> Must Negro actors be confined to plays about Negroes or to Negro char-
> acters in otherwise white plays? All art lives by convention which means
> factual unreality for the sake of larger truth. Now theatrical convention
> is being extended so that the actor who is best for the role – in ability,
> temperament and physique – can be engaged, regardless of color.[59]

James Earl Jones conceived an all-black *Cherry Orchard* (1972), himself
playing the role of Lopahin, the merchant. Produced by Joseph Papp, the
cast included Gloria Foster, Ellen Holly, and Earle Hyman, all of whom
were highly praised. In 1977, Jones portrayed Oedipus for a three-week run
at the Cathedral of St. John the Divine. Critic Barbara Lewis reported
that "His words eject piercingly into the air ahead of him, resounding with
full echoes and surprising clarity. His energy and presence have a crackling
wit and a volatile imagination."[60] Although critics anointed Jones *the* black
classic actor (competing for the title with Earle Hyman, who had played
twenty-five roles in nineteen plays of Shakespeare), newcomers to that élite
cadre of performers were not always welcome.

In 1979, Joseph Papp formed the Shakespearian Repertory Troupe, made
up entirely of Black and Hispanic actors. Papp said that the new company
was not created as a gesture of reverse racism. "I got tired of token casting."
The company's thirty-six actors essayed *Julius Caesar* (1979) under director
Michael Langham, who cast all the experienced Shakespearians – Earle
Hyman, Robert Christian, Arthur French – in minor roles. The lead actors,
although experienced in "kitchen-sink drama," as Morgan Freeman called
it, had not been trained to speak iambic pentameter naturally and without
bombast. The critics almost unanimously agreed that the mixture of Black

and Hispanic regional accents seriously interfered with the audience's belief that the actors were citizens of Rome. Even black critics found the accents "bothersome." Papp pleaded for more time, stating that he did not expect the company to happen overnight. He employed speech teachers and pushed on with the next show, *Coriolanus*. Except for Morgan Freeman, whose work was widely applauded, the company again suffered for abusing the ears of its audience. "Apart from ragged speaking, there is a ragged standard of performance," wrote the *New York Times'* critic.[61] Black critic Lionel Mitchell blamed the director, but conceded that *Coriolanus* "was dreadful."

Papp's Black and Hispanic company brought protests from Asian Americans who wanted Papp to fund an Asian company. Other black theatre companies accused the Public Theater of white hegemony. Why should the theatre's money, which would soon be a budget of more than $2 million, not be given to black repertory companies already in existence? The Public Theatre's experiment with ethnic repertory stopped until the 1990s when George Wolfe, without calling attention to it, successfully integrated black actors in classic roles.

Although it may have been difficult to see immediate results from Papp's efforts, he had seriously and successfully introduced onto America's stages the concept of black actors playing nonblack roles. Variously called nontraditional, multiracial, or color-blind casting, the concept gradually made its way into the 1980s and 1990s, and much of that continuing impetus can be attributed to Papp's efforts, and those of his successor, George C. Wolfe, a man who realized Papp's dream of an American theatre.

This chapter closes as it began, with a woman playwright who changed black theatre. Ntozake Shange (Paulette Williams) in the "foreword" to her book *Three Pieces*, wrote:

As a poet in american theater / i find most activity that takes place on our stages overwhelmingly shallow / stilted & imitative, that is probably one of the reasons i insist on calling myself a poet or writer / rather than a playwright / i am solely interested in the poetry of the moment, the emotional and aesthetic impact of a character or a line. For too long now afro-americans in theater have been duped by the same artificial aesthetics that plague our white counterparts / "the perfect play."[62]

When Shange published her poems under the title *for colored girls who have considered suicide/when the rainbow is enuf* with the Shameless Hussy Press in 1975, there was no subtitle identifying the collection as a "choreopoem," a term which critic Neal A. Lester defined later as "a theatrical expression that combines poetry, prose, song, dance, and music – those elements that outline a distinctly African American heritage."[63] Shange rejected European aesthetics and embraced the African (living with opposition without the necessity of closure, repetition as intensification, both of which reflected the traditional African life more than the European linear view, which demanded a beginning, middle, and end.)

How, then, did Shange's "choreopoem" differ from the poetry, music, and movement that had danced across African American stages for a decade? First, as noted earlier, black women writers had received fewer productions than the men. Second, Shange's poetry revealed for the first time on stage unexpressed experiences held in the hearts by many black women. Finally, her work appeared during the rise of the white feminist movement, and much of the box-office support Shange received came from women. Initially, Shange had read her poems in San Francisco bars with choreographer Paula Moss, who improvised dance to Shange's poetry. Then, in the summer of 1975 they performed the poems in several New York lofts and bars. Theatre director Oz Scott suggested they use seven women to correspond to the colors of the rainbow. Woodie King saw the show at Demonte's Bar in East Village and brought it to the Henry Street Theatre, where from November 1975 to June 1976 the choreopoem was staged and restaged. Then Joseph Papp took the show to the Public Theater. In September 1976 the piece moved to the Booth Theatre on Broadway, where Tarzana Beverly won the Tony Award for her performance of the Lady in Red. The play ran for 747 performances, creating sharp and often acid controversy.

Women, black and white, supported the play. *Cue* magazine wrote "This fierce and passionate poetry has the power to move a body to tears, to rage, and to an ultimate rush of love."[64] Many black men disagreed, finding the choreopoem an attack upon them. Abiodun Oyewele, one of the original Last Poets, wrote a corrective view entitled *Comments* (1977), which was performed at the Harlem Performance Center to a standing-room only crowd. Some black women attacked Shange's play as divisive. "The African community witnessed a deadly enemy highlighting the problems occurring between African men and women. The play was not meant to create healthy dialogue between the sexes, but was presented in such a psychotic manner as to foster animosity . . . and divide the African family," said Angela Jackson, who, in a rebuttal to Shange, wrote her own play entitled *Shango Diaspora: An African-American Myth of Womanhood and Love* (1982). Bonnie Wright attempted to write a final chapter to the male–female conflict with her play *No Colored Girls/No Colored Boys Allowed* (1990). Produced by the Afrikan

Women's Repertory Theatre, it opened at the Café Ariel Theatre in New York with the message that misunderstandings occur "when women and men refuse to communicate with each other." A still later reaction came from Keith Antar Mason, founder and director of the Los Angeles Black Repertory Company. Written in a style similar to Shange's, Mason in 1991 premiered his full-length poem *for black boys who have considered homicide when the streets were too much*. His title embraced his thesis, making the angst and precarious lives of teen males manifest.

Repeatedly, Ms. Shange found herself defending *for colored girls*, denying that it was "revengeful" toward black men and saying that she only wanted to be honest about her own experience of frustrated tenderness. White audiences would not connect Beau Willie's act of throwing his children from a window to the violence he had endured in Vietnam and the rejection he received when he returned home. Neal A. Lester came to Shange's defense: "In *for colored girls*, Shange manages to transform personal pains associated with race and gender into a public celebration of black women's potential for selfhood and self-determination in a racist and sexist society."[65]

Shange's choreopoem had become the opening volley of a turbulent decade examining black male–female relations. Michele Wallace's book *Black Macho and the Myth of the Superwoman* (1979) set off a second volley of heated exchanges. Journalist Tony Brown called the period "the marketing of black male inferiority."[66] Julia and Nathan Hare brought out a journal *Black Male/Female* (1979–82), which addressed the key conflict issues. As the 1980s progressed, the controversy left the public eye. Ntozake Shange's play had begun to bring the genders into balance. She went on to write about other issues.

In 1972 the National Black Political Convention (NBPC) in Gary, Indiana, drew three thousand delegates and five thousand observers. Amiri Baraka chaired the two-day event and sought to unify the diverse spectrum of African American activists into a single party capable of wielding national political power ("Unity without uniformity"). When the convention proposed resolutions critical of Israel and busing for school integration, the NAACP and King's civil rights coalition withdrew. The NBPC found itself splintered – Whites from Blacks, women from men, middle class from working class. The Black Arts Movement drifted, losing its funding. Theatre groups disbanded. Nonetheless, its excitement, its creativity, its writers, actors, and companies had created an era more fecund than the Harlem Renaissance. Even though the great majority of companies collapsed within a few years, black theatre had changed American theatre forever. Black playwrights had placed on the stage a variety of African Americans never seen before, characters who reflected the nation's population more accurately. Writers had moved from the racial periphery of theatre toward the center; they were now considered skillful and worthy of commercial and college venues. Racial attitudes and issues, previously restricted to segregated black audiences, now played to all audiences, and the old stereotypes gradually muted. These changes brought black patrons to the box office, and producers began to plan their plays and advertising to attract them. The movement had created respect and influence internationally.

Women playwrights began to achieve parity by writing more plays using female and feminist issues. Other minorities took courage and inspiration from black theatre to form Asian American, Native American, Hispanic American, and Chicano American theatres. Cross-cultural or nonracial casting began to emerge and would become an important issue in the 1980s. The arts, and theatre in particular, enjoyed an increasing recognition in the black community. And finally, black theatre scholarship found respectability in academia and publication burgeoned (see appendix).

Although criticism and theory could not keep pace with the flood of plays and production, unshackled debate crowded the pages of journals. Coming down heavily on the side of nationalism, Addison Gayle in *The Black Aesthetic* (1971) edited a collection of essays covering theory, music, poetry, fiction, and drama, nearly all of them promoting cultural nationalism. A professor at the City University of New York, Gayle believed that "art must be functional and relevant to the lives of black people." Owen Dodson, professor of theatre at Howard University, took a humanist approach. He wrote in his essay "Playwrights in Dark Glasses": "So many of our Negro playwrights are so saturated with the idea of Negro oppression, which of course they should be, that they have left out the lasting power, the universality of their art."[67] Debates were brisk and sometimes virulent, but they stimulated the movement to ask key questions: what is black theatre? does it have a separate aesthetic? who is its audience? who should write its criticism? what is theatre's fundamental purpose?

Larry Neal became the critic who best framed questions and found answers. He caught the mood and ideas of the time in his essay "The Black Arts Movement" (1968). Born in Atlanta in 1937, Neal was a graduate of Lincoln University in Pennsylvania. With Amiri Baraka, he coedited the seminal anthology *Black Fire* (1968). For a time he served as educational director for the Black Panther Party and directed the Commission on the Arts and Humanities in Washington, DC. A playwright and intellectual, he attempted to instill a sense of aesthetics into cultural nationalism. He believed that if the messages of the revolution were to raise black consciousness, then they must capture and hold the audience. Neal correctly perceived that the propaganda of Nation-Time, after its initial shock, would eventually tire the theatregoer. Before his death from a heart attack in 1981, he became the leading theoretician and black cultural critic of his time.

On 10 October 1976 an article entitled "The Black Theater Audience Grows" by Paul Delaney appeared in the Sunday *New York Times*. It quoted black producer Ashton Springer: "It is more than phenomena, almost unbelievable that there are seven black-oriented productions on Broadway today." The article pointed out that black musicals on tour[68] were often SRO and that older and middle-class Blacks were buying tickets as never before. This explosion of color Delaney attributed to the *end* of the militant era in black theatre. Yes, the times they were a-changin', but if there had been no militant era, would there have been black musicals on Broadway in such numbers? In the same year *New York Times* critic Mel Gussow exclaimed: "The theatre district could almost be named the Great Black Way." However, almost exactly ten years later, Gussow in the Sunday *New York Times* realized that "progress, such as it is, is deceptive." It is principally limited to musicals, to classics and to individual performances which have broken through to public consciousness.

Quoted in the same article, Ossie Davis shared Gussow's opinion that the promises of the 1960s had collapsed in the 1980s. "It's a miracle that we're still here at all. What sustains us in this mad adventure is the feeling that, from the inside, there is a light at the end of the tunnel."[69] As the final chapter of this book will show, for some there would be light; for others, the dark was light enough.

13

The millennium

James V. Hatch

Here Comes Everybody
James Joyce, *Ulysses*

In the final decades of the century tides of race and gender swept through theatre. Women claimed greater roles in writing and directing; gays and lesbians demanded their turn on the stage; the number of talented and trained actors burgeoned; performance artists toured widely; black directors and playwrights attracted national attention; black play festivals sprang up in major cities; scholars began to debate which plays should be in "the canon"; the August Wilson–Robert Brustein confrontation initiated debate over multicultural theatre, color-blind casting, and the diversity movement; white theatres produced more black plays; direct government support of the arts withered, and some theatres survived by paying as much attention to finance as they paid to art. Finally, the hip-hop generation developed a theatre culture of its own.

The reign of Ronald Reagan (1980–88) seriously crippled arts funding as well as that of social programs – both important subsidies for minority theatres. James A. Michener named the 1980s "the Ugly Decade." Indeed, by the 1990s the Republican Congress, led by Senator Jesse Helms of North Carolina, threatened to abolish the National Endowment for the Arts altogether. The NEA survived the knife but abolished Expansion Arts, a division within the NEA established to award funds to minority arts organizations. Like a rock thrown into a pond, Reaganomics sent shock waves through state art councils and corporate donors. What the government programs had given, the government took away. For example, the McCree Theatre of Flint, Michigan, originally created through the Comprehensive Employment Training Act (CETA) and the Model Cities Programs, and further developed through the Department of Housing and Urban

430

Development, discovered in 1985 that basic grants that had created and sustained it were no longer available. C. Bernard Jackson, executive director of Inner City Cultural Center in Los Angeles put it bluntly:

> There are the "not-so-good times" and the "downright-bad times," like now – times which began making their presence felt in the early 1980s with federal cutbacks and which continue to grow worse as available fund offerings from city, county and state prove highly competitive and grossly inadequate, some even call them "insulting."[1]

During the decade, Jackson's ICCC had twice attempted to acquire its own theatre building: the first, an ageing Masonic Hall, they lost to the earthquake; the second, the Ivar Theatre in Hollywood, they lost to the bank. Los Angeles with its patina of hospitality to the arts, doled out $1.53 per capita, compared to New York's $8.87 per capita; however, the Big Apple had scant reason to boast. The year after the Negro Ensemble Company won a Pulitzer for *A Soldier's Play*, their funding was cut by $50,000. In the 1985/86 grant carnage, Woodie King's New Federal Theatre lost $70,000, nearly forcing it to close.

Hip-hop performance artists

The scarcity of funding and venues contributed to the proliferation of one-man/woman, low-budget performance artists who labeled themselves the "hip-hop generation." They anointed themselves with two missions – destroying old stereotypes and creating new and real images of African Americans.[2] Given these responsibilities, race and gender satire emerged as a major genre. Using break dancing, rap, DJ-ing, and music as an integral part of performance, young artists abandoned realism and launched experiments in a number of styles, often substituting personal anecdotes for story continuity.[3] Catherine Igwu, editor of *Let's Get It On*, an anthology of black performance art, described the elements:

> [Performance art] incorporates and uses a range of media. It is incessantly concerned with images of the moment; any cultural symbol, reference or icon is appropriated and subverted; the world is up for grabs. Process, context and site are significant, as is the direct and unmediated interaction between the artist and the viewer. The raw and naked exposure of the artist is bound up with the live presence of the viewer. The experience is invariably ephemeral, the only evidence following the event, existing in the memories and the imaginations of both artist and audience.

Some of these elements had surfaced in the happenings of the 1960s, but a comparison with hip-hop performance of the 1990s reveals both similarities and contrasts. Happenings originated with visual artists and were embraced by white university students, who joined the flower children of the Woodstock generation. Their crusades centered on sex, drugs, racism, and the Vietnam War – their music: the Beatles, Bob Dylan, Jimi Hendrix, Janis Joplin, and an army of folk singers.

By contrast, the hip-hoppers of the 1980s and 1990s came bopping out from the mean streets of the South Bronx, a black army of break-dancers, graffiti artists, disco DJs, B-boys, and angry rappers whose work focused on drugs (new ones), race, prison population, colonialism, sex, and violence – their celebrities: 2 Live Crew, Ice-T, Queen Latifah, and Tupac Shakur.

In the sixties capitalism had commodified dashikis, earrings, and Altarmaster peace symbols. In the 1980s and 1990s it sold the hip-hoppers $200 sneakers, gold chains, and beltless, oversized pants – patterned after the prison clothing on Rikers Island, where belts were denied to prisoners. Greg Tate, writer for *Village Voice*, defined the style: "Hip-Hop is reverse colonialism / Hip-Hop is the perverse logic of capitalism used by an artform / Like capitalism, Hip-Hop has no morals, no conscience, and no ecological concern for the scavenged earth or the scavenged American minds it will wreck in its pursuit of new markets."[4]

Contrary to Hippie and Yippie proclamations of the sixties that the revolution would not be televised, and contrary to Greg Tate's pronouncement that hip-hop did not live on YO! MTV Raps,[5] business did digitalize and commercialize the new performance arts. Time Warner's CD sales soared into the millions. Ice-T, L. L. Cool J, and Ice Cube copped roles in Hollywood films. Following Michael Jackson's conquest of Music Television (MTV), disaffected white youth ("wiggers,"[6] a slurring of "white nigger") identified with black hip-hop much as the nineteenth-century's young "wage slaves" had identified with minstrelsy.[7] Soon, Latin and Caribbean youth appropriated rap to their own needs, and hip-hop theatre found its home with those who felt disenfranchised "because of race or economic background or simply being young."[8] In the 1990s rap could be heard in many Asian, South American, and African languages, wherever alienated youth could find a turntable and a microphone. Kim Cook, theatre director of Theatre Artaud in San Francisco, produced his own script, *One Size Fits All*, interweaving stories of four impoverished teenagers living in Haiti, Indonesia, Yugoslavia, and the United States. In the fall of 1999 newsletter *Tha Skit*, subtitled "Hip-Hop Drama News," appeared its central message:

hip-hop theatre would continue to grow because it spoke to youth worldwide.[9] After being refused an NEA grant at age 46, Pope L[ancaster], who once worked with Mabou Mines, vowed to crawl from the feet of the Statue of Liberty, on to a ferry, then on to 207th Street where Manhattan meets the Bronx. He estimated his performance would take five years. A review of this "performance" (which has yet to be completed) appeared in *Art News*, perhaps indicating that the border between the visual arts and the theatre was melding again.

Performance artists of the early 1970s had conceived an alternative vision of America. Idris Ackamoor, codirector of Cultural Odyssey in San Francisco, returning from an African sojourn, declared: "I was set upon a path to combine the art forms of music, dance and theater into a unified whole. I was awed by how African art was informed with a merging of the spirit... the flowing of the various art forms into one."[10] Ackamoor, a multi-instrumentalist, tap dancer, director, and producer, had joined Rhodessa Jones in San Francisco's North Beach in a double-bill performance, *The Beginning of the Second Earth* (1979). Jones had been dancing, singing, rapping in her adaptation of *Gorilla, My Love* (stories by Tony Cade Bambara), and had performed *The Legend of Lily Overstreet* (1979) in which an erotic nude dancer challenges female reticence concerning exhibitionism. Much of her work became autobiographical. She once claimed that theatre had saved her life. In 1986 the California Arts Council invited her to teach dance/movement in a women's prison. Jones named her venture the Medea Project: Theater for Incarcerated Women. Discovering that many of the women could not read well, she adapted classic Greek myths – those of Medea, Persephone, and Sisyphus – to express and address their problems. Her play, *Big Butt Girls, Hard-Headed Women* (1991), a variant of the "Ugly Duckling" fairy tale, used testimonials (monologues) based on interviews with the incarcerated. Jones rejected the "feminist" label of white, upper-class women and instead renamed herself a "womanist." One of twelve children born into a family of migrant farm workers, Rhodessa Jones understood welfare and working women.

In 1992 the Medea Project went public; seven years later, on 21 January 1999, Jones' *Slouching Towards Armageddon* opened in San Francisco's Lorraine Hansberry Theatre, a 300-seat auditorium. The entire two weeks sold out. "The Rockefeller Foundation gave her money to develop this performance with women in the jail around the subject of race and racism." Jones told her audience that "she started the workshop by asking the women two questions: what was their first memory of race; and if they could take a pill and change their race, their gender, their entire being, what would they choose to become."[11]

Over ten years, she wrote or directed ten plays, three with her brother Bill T., including *The Blue Stories* (1993), which premiered at the National Black Theatre Festival in Winston-Salem, North Carolina. Her other work was seen at La MaMa Experimental Theatre Club in New York City, as well as in Europe and Japan.

Her brother, Bill T., had majored in theatre and dance at the State University of New York, Binghamton, where he met Arnie Zane, who became his partner and lover. Together until Zane's death from AIDS in 1986, they created a number of new and provocative dance pieces. As if in anger at the loss of his partner, Bill T. went on to develop a confrontational style. Dancing, singing, and using monologue, he agitated, incensed, and captivated his audiences. HIV positive, Jones conducted a series of Survival Workshops in which he addressed young people suffering from cancer and other terminal diseases. "Now everything I do," he said, "everything for me is the last time. I see myself almost as a historical presence. Too much so, in a way. Because I'm constantly thinking, 'You will remember that dance. It will be yours, and I will be gone.'" In his program titled *Last Night on Earth* (1994), he sang "The River Jordan is deep and cold, chills the body but warms the soul."[12]

During the same period Keith Antar Mason, founder and director of the Hittite Empire, an ensemble based in Santa Monica, California, had become one of the more confrontational rebels of the 1980s. Using a variety of media, his "live" works" included *Black Folks and Heroes*, *Sexual Illegals*, and *Icarus Looking Back*. Calling himself an Africentric ritualist, he performed new works internationally, in London, Mexico City, and Anchorage, Alaska. His short plays were not for the sentimental or the faint-hearted. Like the theatre of Artaud, Mason used cruelty, an in-your-face style much like the "gangsta rappers," to lay bare the brutal truths of race and violence in America. His style left the audience with a gut feeling that the future held little promise for black youth, who were not about to sit down and quietly await the apocalypse.

Mason's views were shared by Robbie McCauley, the author and performance artist, who said: "I like the concept of speaking the unspeakable." The form and flow of McCauley's performance pieces stemmed from music; the process of her work emerged from her experience as an actor; she had played the Lady in Red in *For Colored Girls*, Joan Little in Ed Bullins' *The Taking of Miss Janie*, as well as roles in Adrienne Kennedy's *Cities in Bezique*.

Born in 1942 in Norfolk, Virginia, and growing up in Georgia, McCauley had heard the tales of black women dragged out of their cabins into the dirt, and "being done it to" by sons of slave masters as their ritual passage into white manhood. *Sally's Rape* on this theme received the Obie award for best American play in 1992. McCauley's work, informed by history, viewed rape as related to race, class, and gender. Her performance works often included slides, live music, video, and film.[13] Her approach was best revealed in her statement: "I prefer when people say, 'You made me think; I disagreed with you, but I was moved to think.'"

Dance as theatre performance

In the 1980s African American dance and theatre coalesced in new and political ways, giving traditional dance and theatre an edge it had seldom exhibited. Two ensembles stand out: Donald Byrd's The Group and Jo Zollar's Urban Bush Women (UBW). When Zollar created UBW in 1984 she did not start out to create a feminist company, but over the next five years the male dancers left her ensemble while the original women stayed.[14]

Breaking customary distinctions between dance and theatre, Zollar introduced into her programs "hauntingly poetic rants," dialogs, news items, songs, as well as improvisation suggested by the audience. Zollar asked her dancers to recite nursery rhymes and narrate folk tales. Jennifer Dunning of the *New York Times* stunned the troupe with a rave review of their first performance, which gave the company instant attention.[15]

In their next two shows, *Lipstick* examined women inscribing their bodies to create desire, and *Girlfriends* explored the joy women experienced when entertaining each other. These pieces caused UBW to be labeled a feminist theatre, even though the company explored other issues, as in *Shelter*, "an unsentimental commentary about homelessness and the destruction of life on that giant home called Earth."[16] In 1989 the troupe suffered from state and national funding cuts. They turned to touring. In 1994 they received the forty-third annual Capezio Award, and the company grew to ten dancers. In their most ambitious project they joined the David Murray Octet in *Crossings* (1999), which began with the Underground Railroad and continued to explore the legacy of slavery and resistance down to the present day.

Like Zollar, Donald Byrd's visions ranged from pure dance to dance theatre, from classical ballet to jazz dance and combinations of both. Much of his thematic emphasis fell on social concerns, such as issues of isolation, community, race, culture, and gender. In the summer of 1994 at the

Atlanta Black Arts Festival, Donald Byrd/The Group performed four original numbers: *Life Situations*, *An Annotated Tale*, and *Bristles*, with *Sentimental Cannibalism* as an afterpiece. Byrd's *The Minstrel Show* (1991) merged dance and theatre. In the person of Bones, some dancers shouted out minstrel conundrums and received racial answers from others in the person of Tambo. The program included an interlude in which Byrd asked the audience to tell their favorite racist jokes while dancers executed minstrel dance routines to jazz. Jennifer Dunning of the *New York Times* named Byrd's creation "an intense evocation rather than overt protest." From his beginning in 1976 to the decade of the 1990s, Byrd created more than eighty works; he commissioned original music and frequently involved collaborations with artists in other fields.

Byrd was not alone in giving provocative performances, as indicated by the following report:

> The Department of African American Interpretation and Presentations in Colonial Williamsburg performed an eighteenth-century estate auction involving the sale of four slaves.
>
> The Event, which attracted more than two thousand spectators, was widely covered in the regional and national media, chiefly because the Virginia branches of the National Association for the Advancement of Colored People (NAACP) and the Southern Christian Leadership Conference (SCLC) protested the performance before, during, and after the presentation.[7]

The audience was mostly white, giving rise to the question: how can one realistically recreate a racist historical event without reempowering its racism? As will be noted later, the Wooster Group had stumbled into a similar difficulty in its reanimation of minstrelsy.

Gay and lesbian performance

In January 1969 the police raided Stonewall Inn, a gay bar in Greenwich Village. Tired of harassment, the gays fought back, throwing rocks and bottles. Known later as the Stonewall Rebellion, the incident marked an important date for liberation, creating the impetus for a number of theatres dedicated to gay plays and performance that presented images other than the stereotypic effeminate male. Like the black women marginalized by the white feminist movement, Blacks felt they were not so much excluded by gay Whites as ignored. In addition, many black males felt oppressed by the homophobic rhetoric in black churches.

In San Francisco three gay males – Djola Bernard Branner, Eric Gupton, and Brian Freeman (an eight-year veteran of the San Francisco Mime Troupe) – were determined to address homosexual issues by establishing Pomo Afro Homos (Postmodern Afro-American Homosexuals):

> We decided then and there to keep it simple and limit the group to just the three of us. The initial goals were to do something fun, and to do something challenging. We didn't want to do the Empowerment Hour, and we didn't want to be just silly. We didn't want this to be *the* show about Black Gay Life. We wanted it to be *a* show about black gay life.[18]

Their first revue of twelve sketches, *Fierce Love: Stories from Black Gay Life* (1991), included "Men on Mens," a satire on the two gay males in television's *In Living Color*, a program which itself was less a satire than an affirmation of the effeminate image. The Pomo Afro Homos took on the difficult task of mocking a satire, but their cabaret audiences got the point and applauded them enthusiastically. PAH was the first gay group to be funded by the NEA through Expansion Arts.

Their second revue, *Dark Fruit* (1991), originated as a response to a Robert Mapplethorpe photographic exhibition. PAH objected to seeing the black male in the photographs as a plaything of Mapplethorpe. In *Dark Fruit*, actor Brian Freeman represented Mapplethorpe in the person of Dr. Dobson, a white sexologist who manipulates black males for his own sexual agenda; however, the play raised its own issue of political correctness: if Whites were no longer permitted to blacken up, then should Blacks "whiten" up? The question, if not settled, was deferred when white audiences responded positively.

Carrying their shows to the Joseph Papp Public Theater and to the Lincoln Center, PAH received enthusiastic receptions, but neither in 1991 nor in 1993 could the gay troupe gain a venue at the National Black Theatre Festival (NBTF), a biennial event held in Winston-Salem, North Carolina, the stomping ground of conservative Senator Jesse Helms. PAH claimed that NBTF had banned them because they were gays. In 1995, original founding PAH member, Djola Bernard Branner, did finally obtain a venue in Winston-Salem for his solo performance, by identifying his sponsoring organization as the Southeastern Center for Contemporary Art. In 1999 Brian Freeman became artist-in-residence at the Joseph Papp Public Theater, where he wrote, directed, and acted in *Civil Sex*, a play about the sexual politics of civil rights leader Bayard Rustin.

PAH compared their struggle to that of the gay Irish, who yearly demanded inclusion in New York's St. Patrick's Day Parade and yearly were
denied. Had not Irish and black heterosexuals indulged in homophobia
with a pronounced contempt for "faggots"? Had not both black and Irish
men suffered discrimination and harbored feelings of inferiority? Had not
both countered fear of being labeled effeminate by pursuing macho images
as prizefighters and football players? The Pomo Afro Homos demonstrated
through their performances that manhood need not be defined as hetero-
sexual only.

Using similar themes, Wayne Corbitt examined the sexual politics of
family in his play *Crying Holy*. First performed at Josie's Cabaret and Juice
Joint in San Francisco, the play's 40-year-old HIV-positive protagonist
returned to his southern home "to rest in the bosom of his family," only
to discover that his relatives do not want to know about his condition. His
revelation: blood relatives are no longer his family. He has to create new kin
among his friends.

Shirlen Holmes, a lesbian playwright, concurred. "I knew I could not
count on my family for its support, but my friends were there. The greatest
disappointment of all was the lack of acceptance by black theatre companies, [which] are least likely to produce works that present gays and lesbians honorably, if at all." To explain black homophobia, Holmes claimed:
"In our churches, temples and mosques we learn that God is homophobic
and therefore we must be also." She described her work as Pride Plays,
which "are like Cayenne pepper: they makes you mad but wakes you
up [sic]."[19]

Rapping on stage

In the 1980s and 1990s hip-hop and rap could be found everywhere. Ifa
Bayeza (Wanda Celeste Williams, Ntozake Shange's sister) used a black
griot to rap upon the actions of the many characters in *Homer G. and
the Rhapsodies in the Fall of Detroit*, a two-hour musical first performed
as a work-in-progress at the Sorbonne in Paris. When *Homer G.* (1996)
débuted at the Lorraine Hansberry Theatre in San Francisco on the occasion
of the theatre's fifteenth anniversary, the playwright described it as an
"experimental serial work." Critic John Williams assessed the play as being
"as postmodern as anything written by Adrienne Kennedy and as wry with
acerbic humor as anything by Ishmael Reed."[20] For *Homer G.*, Ms. Bayeza
received a $10,000 award from the Kennedy Center Fund.

Bring in 'Da Noise, Bring in 'Da Funk (1995), George C. Wolfe's history
of black improvisational dance, presented hip-hop as the most recent avatar
of black dance's phoenix-like rebirths. *Funk*, a word originally referring to
body odor, over the years had ameliorated to mean a grassroots culture, a
black ethos undiluted by European or middle-class tastes. Wolfe described
the show's title:

> The words "Noise" and "Funk" work in tandem with one another. Noise
> is the outlet, the release, the expression of self. Savion Glover dancing or
> Michael Jordan on the courts or some sixteen-year-old kid doing spoken
> word poetry – they are each bringing in 'da Noise. And Funk is the texture,
> the history, the grit and grease that's churning underneath. For example,
> if Bessie Smith singing the blues is her bringing in 'da Noise, then slavery,
> lynchings, lost love and oh, say collard greens are some of the textures
> that make up 'da Funk that's underneath.[21]

Wolfe wove the rap lyrics of Reg E. Gaines into an art labeled "tap/rap,"
(tap dancing informed by hip-hop and funk rhythms).[22] Choreographed
by Savion Glover, the theatre resounded with youth's energy, talent, and an
in-your-face insouciance as Gaines rapped through a history of black dance.

> Be boppin
> toe tappin
> Hip-hoppin
> crackin–snappin
> . . .
> Cuz when you bring 'da noise
> You gots to bring 'da funk.

Margo Jefferson of the *New York Times* declared the show "as dance,
as musical, as theater, as art, as history and entertainment, there's nothing
Noise/Funk cannot and should not do." Her statement encompassed Wolfe's
expansive definition of theatre. From where had his genius come?

George C. Wolfe was born on 23 September 1954 in Frankfurt, Kentucky.
His father, Costello, had been a writer for the army newspapers during the
Second World War and later had worked as a clerk for the state government
of Kentucky. Wolfe's mother, Anna, taught in schools and earned a doctorate
at Miami University. As a child, Wolfe directed plays in high school; he
describes himself as "Probably a neurotic child, very spoiled. If I didn't
want to do a thing, I wouldn't do it." Wolfe attended Pomona College in
Claremont, California, where in 1976 Professor Angela Davis appended an

Figure 42. George C. Wolfe

evaluation note to George C. Wolfe's semester project – a study of black stereotypes in film: "I have read bad papers, good papers, even excellent ones. Beyond that, there are those rare instances when a student creates something of such insight and such beauty that I hesitate even to classify it as a 'paper.' Your study, in my opinion, is one of those unique creations." In retrospect, Wolfe's paper might be considered his initial exploration for his play, *The Colored Museum* (1986), a revue that would change the face of African American theatre.

After graduating from Pomona College, Wolfe joined the Inner City Cultural Center in nearby Los Angeles, where director Bernard Jackson and administrator Josie Dotson recognized his talents and provided him with a stage to write and direct his own plays. In 1979 he came to New York City "to starve. I had been practicing," Wolfe said. He enrolled in New York

University's dramatic writing program, and after a year he added musical theatre in order to meet professional music producers and directors.[23] Wolfe supported himself by teaching acting at the Richard Allen Center and at New York's City College, where he directed his own play, *The Coming of Nabuku* (1982), a "Japanese theatre–Caribbean cartoon." *Nabuku* would serve as a rough draft for Wolfe's direction of *The Tempest* (1995), a carnival interpretation produced at the Delacorte Theatre in Central Park. In 1985 Playwrights Horizons produced Wolfe's *Paradise*, a satire mocking the role western colonial greed had played in destroying the beauty of the natural world. The critics blasted the play as though they personally had been attacked. Their culture had been.

From 1980 to 1984, Wolfe worked at the Hatch-Billops Collection, an archive of African American theatre. This exposure may have become his second inspiration for *The Colored Museum*, which in 1986 premiered at the Crossroads Theatre Company of New Jersey. Within six months, Joseph Papp brought the play to the Public Theater. In the words of Frank Rich of the *New York Times*: "George C. Wolfe says the unthinkable, says it with uncompromising wit and leaves the audience, as well as a sacred target, in ruins. The devastated audience, one should note, includes both Blacks and Whites. Mr. Wolfe is the kind of satirist, almost unheard of in today's timid theater, who takes no prisoners."[24]

What had Wolfe done in *The Colored Museum*? In a series of "exhibits" the revue attacked the regency of basketball stars, the exploitation of slavery, the exoticism of miscegenation, the banality of the mammy stereotype, the superficiality of *Ebony* magazine, the drug legacy of Vietnam, the fear of homosexuality, the tyranny of black hair styles, the beatification of *A Raisin in the Sun*, the Josephine Baker legend, and teenage pregnancy. The most outrageous of his parodies, which came in the center of the revue, was a comic caricature of black males who saw themselves as victims of "the man" (Bigger Thomas in *Native Son*; Walter Lee Younger in *A Raisin in the Sun*; Beau Willie in *For Colored Girls*). To add insult to injury, Wolfe satirized the most sacred image in African American theatre, "Big-Mama-on-the-couch," the mother who dominated her family in the names of love and survival. For this and for using the word *colored*, Wolfe was roundly abused by Blacks; nonetheless, his wit and theatrical inventiveness enabled laughter to triumph. African American theatre had been reborn with an edge, having no self-pity, no stereotypes, and a style that shunned realism. The immediate reaction: "Everybody was very threatened and hostile, particularly what I call the guardians of black culture. The self-appointed guardians applied their simplistic minds so as to dismiss it [*The Colored Museum*], in large part because of jealousy, because here I was this new Negro and I had not sprung forth from them."[25]

The Colored Museum launched Wolfe into the most frenetic and creative years of his life. Beginning with *Spunk* (1989), an adaptation of three stories by Zora Neale Hurston, Wolfe then wrote and directed *Jelly's Last Jam* (1991), a musical based on the life of New Orleans jazz musician Jelly Roll Morton. In the same year he was chosen to direct Tony Kushner's two-part drama of politics and homosexuality, *Angels in America*, making him the first black director of a major white Broadway play. In 1993 the board of the Joseph Papp Public Theater appointed Wolfe as artistic director; he promptly initiated a broad multicultural program of new plays, dedicated to a venerable vision – to hold the mirror up to nature, which he interpreted to mean, in part, "here comes everybody." His only caveat: everybody had to come with truth, clarity, and the artistic talent to astonish. He was not shy: "Humility is tremendously overrated. Reality and racism are gonna try and humble you, so there's absolutely no reason in the world for you to do it to yourself."

Wolfe gave his actors a strong sense of style, something that had been missing in many black shows. For the *Caucasian Chalk Circle* (1990), he relocated Brecht's play in Haiti and introduced a puppet sequence. In *Jelly's Last Jam* he created an arrogant and unsympathetic protagonist in the character of Jelly Roll Morton, a bold move for a commercial Broadway musical.[26] At the time he acquired the leadership of the Joseph Papp Public Theater, its public funding had been cut by one-third. Ticket sales accounted for only 10 percent of its annual $9 million budget. Papp had made up deficits by moving *Chorus Line* and *The Pirates of Penzance* to Broadway. Wolfe, too, moved his *Funk, Tempest*, and *On the Town* to Broadway. The latter show lost money and when *The Wild Party* closed after it failed to win any Tony Award in 2000 Wolfe came under attack in the press for the loss of $14 million on two shows. In November 2000 the Public Theater's governing board appointed Fran Reiter, a former deputy to the mayor, to oversee business operations. She was dismissed from the post a year later.[27]

In the first four years of his tenure at the Public Theater, Wolfe nurtured several talents. Reggie Montgomery, who had come from the ICCC, created in *The Colored Museum* a prototype, Miss Roz, a gay male rapper. Equally talented, Danitra Vance (1959–94) had been the first black woman on television's *Saturday Night Live*. Two years later, Wolfe cast her in *The Colored Museum* as the slave ship stewardess; she won an Obie for her performance in Zora Neale Hurston's *Spunk* (1990). At the Public Theater in 1991 Vance, wearing a taped X where her breast had been removed in a mastectomy, played her last solo performance in her own piece *Danitra, Live and in Color!* (1991). She recited the "funny" things people say to sick people: "I thought you were dead." "Why don't you have the other one removed?" "How are you?" She received the Independent Spirit Award and died the next year of cancer.

Unlike other performance artists, Anna Deavere Smith did not exploit her own life and personality. At age 43, after teaching and performing in colleges, she had developed a virtuosity for impersonation. Coupling this gift with a bent for social-issue documentary, she created a TV-news style delivery.[28] Her first piece to attract national attention, *Fires in the Mirror*, derived from a riot in Crown Heights, Brooklyn, after the car in a Jewish Lubavitcher rebbe's motorcade hit and killed a black child named Gavin Cato. In the riot that followed, a Jewish scholar from Australia, Yankel Rosenbaum, was stabbed and killed. The black man accused of his murder was found innocent in a New York court, but was later retried in federal court and found guilty. The driver of the rebbe's car escaped to Israel and was never tried. These events of uneven-handed justice ignited the racial fires that had been smoldering in the community for several years.

Smith took her tape recorder to Crown Heights and spoke with Blacks and Whites, Jews and non-Jews, women and men, old and young to ascertain the causes of the riot and what should be done to heal the community. She translated and edited her twenty-nine recordings into monologues for *Fires in the Mirror*. According to Smith, the fire images in the title represented the many small, dormant social fires that can flare up as a result of high-speed friction. The mirror was the stage, reflecting the fires back to the audience.

Smith used only small props, caps, jackets, and scarves. With these, she appropriated the style employed by television news, which audiences were already accustomed to accept as trustworthy. Her technique promoted a climate of reflection, which at once entertained by its virtuosity and led to reassessment of the passions that had sparked the riot. For her performance she won an Obie, the Drama Desk, and the Lucille Lortel Award and was runner-up for the Pulitzer Prize in Drama.[29] The media anointed Smith spokeswoman for race relations. Magazines and television talk shows clamored for her. George C. Wolfe directed *Fires* for American Playhouse on PBS.[30]

Gordon Davidson of the Mark Taper Forum commissioned Smith to create a sister performance piece based on the Los Angeles rampage that had ignited a riot when a "not guilty" verdict acquitted the Los Angeles police who had brutally beaten Rodney King, a black man. *Twilight Los Angeles 1992* wove together twenty-six personal cameos – taken from 175 interviews, including Koreans speaking their own language. In March 1994, Wolfe brought *Twilight* to the Public Theater and after an enthusiastic reception, moved it to Broadway's Cort Theatre, but Smith's cameos on a larger stage did not sustain an audience. In March 2000 *House Arrest*, vignettes of American Presidents from Teddy Roosevelt to Bill Clinton opened at the Public Theater. Race surfaced as one of several subthemes in a progression that traced the public's curiosity and access to the personal lives of the presidents.

Smith had created her own genre of theatre – a community documentary of many voices. Her plays may have been so unique to time, place and to their creator and performer that productions could not be mounted without their author, although Smith said she would like to see another actor in her roles "on alternate nights." She also noted that an American audience might not accept a white actor playing the black roles as readily as they accepted fair-complexioned Smith in white roles. She received the first appointment as artist-in-residence to Harvard University's newly formed Institute on the Arts and Civic Dialogue (1997), whose mission was

> to explore ways in which the arts can enhance public discussion of vital social issues. Activities will include: development of up to four independent works of art, group discussions and guest speakers, seminars, and workshops for participants and selected guests, collaborative research, master classes, public forums, and media projects.[31]

The institute enjoyed an initial funding of $1.5 million and the joint sponsorship of the W. E. B. Du Bois Institute for Afro-American Research directed by Henry Louis Gates Jr. and the American Repertory Theatre headed by Robert Brustein. The three-year experiment closed in 2000 with indeterminate results. In another role, Smith refereed the Wilson–Brustein Cooper union debate, an event to be discussed later.

In a different mode and mood, the Joseph Papp Public Theater mounted four experimental plays by Suzan-Lori Parks: *The America Play* (1993), *Venus* (1996), *In the Blood* (1999, with some Brecht-like songs in a contemporary adaptation of Hawthorne's *Scarlet Letter*), and *Top Dog/Under Dog* (2001);

for the 2003 season a rewrite is scheduled entitled *Fucking A.* "It's just that those structures [i.e., conventional structures] never could accommodate the figures which take up residence inside me," said Parks.[32] A hallmark of Parks' dialogue is repetition and revision ("rep and rev"), in the style of Gertrude Stein in the 1920s. Avant-garde producer Richard Foreman directed *Venus*, a play based on Saartje Baartman, a South African woman known in Europe as the Hottentot Venus, a woman who by European standards possessed very large buttocks. Author Parks made no attempt to present Baartman as a victim, but focused on European reactions to the African, who was displayed as a freak. "It's about show business, showing yourself, being in a show."[33] Many in Parks' audiences found the subject of *Venus* objectionable and the form difficult to follow. The "rep and rev" dialogue seemed to breathe like "a patient etherized upon a table," its life breath laboring in a weariness just this side of death. Drama critic Abiola Sinclair wrote: "*Venus* is not absurdist, it's insulting and absurd."[34]

In an essay entitled "An Equation for Black People Onstage," Parks pleaded for writers to eschew defining black characters as an absence of, or in opposition to, Whites. That, she argued, "would reduce Blacks to one way of being. Instead, we should endeavor to show the world and ourselves our beautiful and powerfully infinite variety."[35] She won recognition and prizes: two NEA awards in playwriting, grants from Rockefeller, Ford, New York State Council on the Arts, New York Foundation for the Arts, Whiting Foundation, and in 1990 an Obie for Best New American Play, *Imperceptible Mutabilities in the Third Kingdom*, and a Pulitzer Prize for *Top Dog/Under Dog* in 2002.

In yet another vein, producers and writers revisited blackface minstrelsy. "We wear the mask, that grins and lies" fumed poet Paul Laurence Dunbar. "Why should the world be overwise in counting all our tears and sighs?" Why indeed? The Wooster Group in New York City in its 1981 production of *Route 1 & 9* juxtaposed Thornton Wilder's *Our Town* (1938) against a reconstruction of a Pigmeat Markham comedy routine. Performed by four white actors in blackface, the piece generated a widely reported racial controversy.[36] Because of the blackface segment, the New York State Council on the Arts cut Wooster's funding by 43 percent. Wooster called several public forums and appealed the cut, but the moneys were not restored. Comments by the director and one of the actresses provide a glimpse of how successfully the racist history of blackface had eluded both white women. Kate Valk:

"The blackface gives me a lot of pleasure. It's the most fun I've ever had."
Elizabeth LeCompte, the director of the Wooster Group, explained her
attraction. "Blackface offered a physical mask, as well as the throwaway
vaudeville style and the 'non-acting' we had explored in porn films for
Nayatt School. The structure of set-up and delivery offered a verbal mask
that was interesting to me. The jokes offered a cultural mask and seemed
extremely simple but were like parables. They seemed so elemental, so
basic. There's no ironic play or psychologizing. They're very simple situations, that kind that I've always been attracted to."[37]

In 1987 the Wooster Group revived the piece, and again the New York
State Council cut its funding. For their subsequent production, they chose
Eugene O'Neill's *The Hairy Ape*, this time calling the blackface, "sootface."
In donning the mask that "grins and lies," the mask itself is a satire that will
not be mocked.[38]

In 1993, twenty-five hundred people attended the Friar's Club annual
"roast," where black actress Whoopi Goldberg with her white partner, television star Ted Danson, made up in blackface, white mouth, and red wig,
delivered a series of raw sexist and racist "jokes," which shocked the audience, including the then mayor of New York, David Dinkins. Goldberg's
subsequent rebuttal: "I suppose we ain't ready to make fun of how stupid
we act 'cause the person next to us a different color. I wonder when we
do be ready for that."[39] On 6 October 2000 filmmaker Spike Lee accepted
Goldberg's challenge by releasing the film *Bamboozled*, a blackface satire on
racism. Lee premised that if Whites sponsored a blackface minstrel show on
national television, Americans, black and white, would accept its racism as
chic, a fun fad with a number of profitable spin-offs. The black "messenger"
who delivered the racist performance from the platform of artistic freedom
would be rewarded with grants, fellowships, and sales of his or her art to
a white public, who would justify their consumption with "a nigger hisself
did it."

With the approach of the millennium, both Blacks and Whites exploited
racist images on stage and off. In-your-face gangsta-rap lyrics used a numb-
ing repetition of "nigger," making millions of dollars for Time Warner, the
record owners, and, by its repetitive use, granting permission to popular
youth culture to use the word without penalty, but the epithet continued to
exercise its own deadly power. Three white men in Hillsborough, Florida,
kidnapped Christopher Wilson from outside a shopping mall, took him to
a field, doused him with gasoline, and set "the nigger" on fire. Private James
Norman Burmeister II, a white paratrooper at Fort Bragg, shot two

anonymous "niggers," murdering the couple to fulfill an initiation ritual
into the Aryan Nations. Three white males in Texas dragged "a nigger" behind their pickup truck until his head came from his body. While America's
ethnics had excised minstrelsy's "Kike," "Shenee," "Kraut," "Wop," "Chink,"
"Greaser," and "Mick" from the lips of popular culture, the "n-word" continued to make money; blackface remained a dangerous and widely mis-
understood vehicle, allowing the "nigger" ghost to hover over the theatre,
inside and out.[40]

Women playwrights take the stage

Following the success of Shange's *Colored Girls* in 1976 many women, in
numbers as never before, turned to playwriting and production. Several
carved out careers. Poet and playwright Pearl Cleage described herself as
"a third-generation black nationalist and a radical feminist. The primary
energy that fuels my work is a determination to be a part of the ongoing
worldwide struggle against racism, sexism, classism, and homophobia."[41]
After publishing several books in the early 1970s, Cleage turned to playwriting. The Alliance Theatre of Atlanta commissioned Cleage to write
Flyin' West (1992), a portrayal of the strength and loyalty of black frontier
women in Nicodemus, Kansas, an all-black town which is now a National
Historic Site. Directed by Kenny Leon, the Alliance's artistic director, the
drama brought Cleage national recognition at the Crossroads Theatre and
the Kennedy Center, where *Flyin' West* starred Ruby Dee. The talented duo
of Leon[42] and Cleage proved itself again when the Alliance Theatre produced *Blues for an Alabama Sky* (1995), a play set during the Great Depression
in Harlem. Cleage stated: "I purposefully people my plays with fast-talking,
quick-thinking black women...It is my firm belief that exposing my audiences to these African American Nationalist Feminist Warriorwomen,
innocently ensconced within the framework of the well-made play, will
quicken the swelling of our ranks."[43]

  Glenda Dickerson, in a career ranging over more than two decades,
devoted much of her directing talents to women's works – *Black Girl* (1972),
Daughters of the Mock (1978), *A Season to Unravel* (1978). Winnie Mandela,
wife of the South African leader, inspired Dickerson to create *Every Step I
Take* (1986). While a director and writer at Rutgers University she produced
Womanwords, a Cabaret of Scenes and Songs Celebrating Women (1989), a piece
inspired by Maxine Hong Kingston's *The Woman Warrior*. Two years later,
with Breena Clarke, she wrote *Re/Membering Aunt Jemima* (1991), which

premiered in 1992 at the Lorraine Hansberry Theater in San Francisco. The authors developed the show and brought it to the National Black Arts Festival in 1994 with a subtitle: *A Menstrual Show*. They employed the old minstrel format of malapropisms, puns, and conundrums.

Using a different format, Aishah Rahman, a CETA artist with the Black Theatre Alliance and a director of the playwrights workshop at the New Federal Theatre, rejected the European critical term, "absurd," but described her work as being in the tradition of the " 'jazz aesthetic' which acknowledges the characters' various levels of reality. They have triple consciousness of the unborn, the living and the dead. Jazz may be discussed primarily as an articulation which has a specifically African-American historical framework from which it flows."[44]

Rahman's play, *The Mojo and the Sayso* (1989), explored the "accidental" shooting of 10-year-old Clifford Glover by a white policeman. The parents try to escape the pain and guilt of their son's death, the mother by drowning in religion, the father by building an automobile in the living room of their home. At the final curtain they get into the car and drive off into the future. The play won for Rahman the Doris Abramson Playwriting Award in 1989.[45]

Because African Americans had been so systematically omitted from the chronicle of American history, plays of biography served to recover, rectify, and preserve their heroes. As early as the 1920s historian and educator Carter Woodson had pressed playwrights to dramatize the lives of black heroes.[46] With a similar goal, musicians Anthony Davis and his brother Christopher approached their cousin, Thulani Davis, to write the libretto for an opera about Malcolm X. A playwright and novelist, Ms. Davis had written several original off-Broadway pieces before adapting *The Caucasian Chalk Circle* (1990) for George C. Wolfe's Haitian interpretation.

Ms. Davis noted a problem faced by those who write about black historical figures: how much would it be necessary to explain to Whites in the audience? She discovered that many young Blacks knew little more about Malcolm X than Whites did. A related question was how much black vernacular to use? Davis selected very few of Malcolm's phrases, using only the vernacular needed in the hope that the opera would work as theatre. Beverly Sills, general director of the New York City Opera, contracted to produce *X: The Life and Times of Malcolm X* at the Lincoln Center, but she soon discovered a number of Jewish foundations that traditionally funded opera at City were refusing money, because they saw the historical Malcolm X as a black Muslim militant. Sills turned to the black community for help, and, on 28 September 1986, the opera premiered before a racially mixed audience with an all-black cast of thirty-one. The authors vociferously denied that their piece was a "jazz opera," but the critics had never before seen an opera that allowed for improvisation within the text. Thulani Davis insisted she was making serious claims for a place in the operatic tradition, that X was more than a "black" opera; it was an American one.

Over the years, Vinie Burrows has constructed a series of one-woman shows to recite the great literature of the world. Her work as Permanent Representative to the United Nations for an international women's organization included actual testimonies of women from four continents. As would be expected, her earliest works were drawn from the literature of the theatre: Shakespeare, Molière, O'Casey, Hughes and colleagues. In 1971 the AEA presented the Paul Robeson Award to Vinie Burrows for a thirty-year theatre career championing "Universal brotherhood of humankind and the artist's responsibility to the profession and the greater society." A social activist, Burrows spoke before the United Nations Commission on the Status of Women during its thirty-eighth assembly. In many celebrations of 8 March (International Women's Day), her one-woman show, *Sister, Sister*, has played in Brussels, Geneva, Prague, Dusseldorf, and many cities in the US. In 1999 her bravura performance of 1930s actress Rose McClendon premiered at the Henry Street Settlement in New York to an enthusiastic reception.

In the century's final decade, several women writers benefited from the diversity programs in white theatres. A younger generation dramatist, Kia Corthron in *Come Down Burning* (1993), explored the grim realities of abortion, welfare, and social survival in the rural mountains of the South. Produced by the American Place Theatre in New York, the story accorded dignity to women when society had denied it. In *Cage Rhythm* (1994), Corthron produced a real/surreal voyage into a women's prison. She taught at Rikers Island prison as part of Manhattan Theater Club's Van Lier Playwriting Fellowship.[47] Corthron's drama *Force Continuum* (2001) examines three generations of African American police officers. Premiering off-Broadway at the Atlanta Theater Company, the play, said *New York Times* critic Ben Brantley, "has the overall effect of an exceptionally eloquent and even-handed piece of journalism. It could be so much more."[48] Nonprofit theatres have commissioned nine of her fifteen plays.

Cheryl L. West, too, crossed over into diversity theatres – the Goodman Theater of Chicago, the Cleveland Playhouse, the Seattle Repertory Theater, and the Manhattan Theatre Club. A former human services counselor, her first major play *Before it Hits Home* (1989), premiered at the Arena Stage in Washington, DC. The story, similar to Wayne Corbitt's *Crying Holy*, involves a man with AIDS, who discovers he must create a new family to replace the one which no longer wants him. *Jar the Floor* (1996), a comedic drama, plunges into women's issues across three generations of mother–daughter relations. The often acerbic critic John Simon praised the off-Broadway production: "She writes not as a political agitator but only as a playwright and human being."[49]

Kathleen McGhee-Anderson's *Oak and Ivy* (1999), titled from Paul Laurence Dunbar's first collection of poems (1892), crossed over at the Arena Stage in Washington, DC. The story of Dunbar's marriage to poet Alice Ruth Moore, a strong feminist, created drama. The union was poetic (he had fallen in love with her photo in a newspaper), but poetry was not the glue to hold their union together. The *Washington Post* praised Arena's production and attributed its success to director Charles Randolph-Wright, a bright talent who followed his success with *Oak and Ivy* by directing his own play, *Blue* (2000), which concerned a well-to-do South Carolina family that the writer calls "upwardly dysfunctional." Phylicia Rashad remained in the lead when it moved to the Roundabout Theatre off-Broadway.[50]

Many poets have failed to negotiate the theatre's distinct requirements. Rita Dove, Poet Laureate of the United States and consultant-in-poetry to the Library of Congress, accepted that challenge. "The question always intrigued me: Why did we find meaning in Greek tragedies?"[51] In part, Dove found the answer in her own adaptation of Sophocles' *Oedipus Rex* to a South Carolina plantation of the 1820s, when the colored baby of a slave-owner's wife is sold away, only to return twenty years later, as her lover. *The Darker Face of the Earth* (1994) premiered at the Oregon Shakespeare Festival in 1996. The following season, Ricardo Khan directed Dove's play at Crossroads. Donna Seaman for the American Library Association called the play "brilliant, potent, and repercussive." Others thought the play more literary than dramatic.

"Yes-I-Can" stories usually trace an individual's rise from obscurity to fame. Dr. Endesha Ida Mae Holland's journey *From the Mississippi Delta* (1986) chronicled her own life from prostitution in Greenwood, Mississippi, to her intellectual awakening during the civil rights movement, to the completion of her doctorate in American studies in 1985. The play premiered at Buffalo's Ujima Theatre Company and was picked up by New York City's Henry Street Settlement and the NEC. Originally directed by Ed Smith, an alumnus of the New Lafayette Theatre Company, the play was nominated for the Pulitzer Prize.

Marcia L. Leslie led her audiences on a similar discovery of merit when she confronted two fictional stereotypes: the mammy and the mulatto mistress. In a courtroom drama, *The Trial of One Short-Sighted Black Woman vs. Mammy Louise and Safreeta Mae* (1998), the play defends the two women against facile condemnation by white liberals and "politically correct" African Americans who never really know why the women had been stereotyped initially.

The rise of black arts festivals

In the first half of the twentieth century performance venues shifted from county fairs in the South and Midwest, which had once hosted a variety of entertainments side by side with exhibitions of farm animals, canned preserves and quilting. During fair week, at least one day would be set aside for black attendance.[52] As rural communities lost population, and as highways and automobiles made travel easier to reach the state fair, with its greater variety, many county fairs shrank and dissolved.

When towns and small cities lost industry to technology or overseas competition, they turned to marketing their cultural histories in a new kind of fair – the arts festival. In the summer of 1999 the Internet listed more than two thousand multicultural festivals, performances, exhibits, and so forth. Blacks accounted for a sizable number. Birmingham, Alabama, celebrated its Annual Heritage Festival; Muscle Shoals hosted the W. C. Handy Music Festival; Chicago attracted audiences to its Gospel Festival; and Texas declared Juneteenth a legal holiday and joined Jacksonville, Florida, in attracting tourists to commemorate the day that Freedom came. In the decade of the late 1980s two enterprising southern cities – Atlanta, Georgia, and Winston-Salem, North Carolina – launched their own black arts festivals. Both cities developed similar formats: they would hold the festival in the summer; invite well-known celebrities; organize events around a popular theme, such as "family values" or "Harlem Renaissance"; involve the entire city; give the festival an international flavor by inviting African theatre and dance companies; present awards to "living legends"; and finally, demonstrate that local businesses could make money.

Initially, Atlanta had two perceived advantages: its population of 650,000, of which 50 percent was black, and a promotional reputation as "the city too busy to hate." With a black mayor and a progressive-minded business community, the chairman of the Fulton County Commission, Michael Lomax, dreamed of a national black arts festival as a showcase for all the fine arts. For the week of 30 July–7 August 1988, Lomax imported top black talent, past and present, including the Copesetics, Urban Bush Women, George Faison's production of *The Wiz*, and the NEC's production of Charles Fuller's historical Civil War drama, *Sally*. Locally, Atlanta-based Jomandi Theatre revived Marsha A. Jackson's *Sisters*. With Coca-Cola and AT&T leading the pack, Atlanta raised $600,000 from local corporations, enabling the festival to present fifty-three out of sixty-five events free to the public. By 1994, forty major corporations contributed to Atlanta's Black Arts Festival. New marketing ideas included "Friends of the Festival," who received priority for tickets to the premier cultural events. To bolster the festival's image in theatre, Avery Brooks (Commander Sisko of *Star Trek*'s starship *Enterprise*) was appointed artistic director for the 1994 festival. Four years later a more experienced administrator, Dwight Andrews, took command.

The second city, Winston-Salem, North Carolina, had a smaller population of 150,000, but was home of R. J. Reynolds Tobacco Company. Here Leon Larry Hamlin initiated his own festival, the National Black Theatre Festival, in 1989, but in lieu of exhibiting all the fine arts, Hamlin concentrated on theatre. In 1979 he had founded the North Carolina Black Repertory Company (NCBRC), soliciting memberships for his theatre guild at fees ranging from $10 to $100. Within two years he had 500 subscribers. By the third year, funding sources were coming to him in the same way they had come to the Negro Ensemble Company or to Black Arts/West (Seattle) when news of their success reached the media.

In the course of his struggle to build a theatre company, Hamlin discovered that wherever he went, black theatres shared similar problems of funding, community support, and financial management. "The fragmentation and isolation of black theatre... allows damaging myths to surface unanswered. Public and private funding sources are oftentimes misled by such myths."[53] In February 1989 Hamlin, in a shrewd move, sent announcements to black theatres across the nation that NCBRC would host "The first national black theatre festival in America."[54] Believing there were perhaps fifty or sixty black companies, he discovered nearly two hundred and fifty, of which forty were active. He mused, "Here we were in the same businesses, and we didn't even know each other." He offered the ensembles funds for travel if "they would execute a letter of support for the festival immediately."[55] He secured sixteen reputable African American Companies.[56]

As a further inducement, Hamlin announced that each festival night would feature a celebrity who would "mingle with the crowd."[57] To this package, he added workshops to address major issues, such as "The Effects of Non-Racial Casting in Black Theatres Today." Then he rented booths to marketers of arts, crafts, and books. Deliberately or not, Hamlin had begun to replace the functions of educational theatre conventions. R. J. Reynolds Tobacco Company headed his sponsors' list, followed by two-dozen others, donating $300,000 toward the budget of $750,000.[58] Twenty thousand visitors attended to watch thirty-one performances. It was estimated that the festival generated between $4 million and $5 million for the local economy.[59] In 1997 the celebrities list had grown longer; Hamlin's advisory board boasted forty-five national celebrities from film, television, and the universities. "Six days and nights of fun for the family."[60] In his original letter to theatre companies, Hamlin had set forth ten goals, promising to address "the concerns and problems faced by black theatres, and to discover answers." He promised to formulate strategies, including long-range financial planning. His critics did not fail to note that these goals had become secondary to an emphasis on celebrity. Yet, it was those very celebrities who helped bring 30,000 people to the festival.

The arts celebrations in Atlanta and the theatre galas in Winston-Salem, both energized black theatre, providing it with international recognition. Both festivals survived a decade and grew. Both served as an opportunity for networking among the companies, and both addressed, if not resolved, the ever-present question of black theatre survival.

August Wilson, playwright

As sometimes happens, an innovator appears unannounced and unforeseen. Born Frederick August Kittel on 27 April 1945 in Pittsburgh, Pennsylvania, August Wilson had attended the Central Catholic High School until age 15, when he dropped out. His German-American father had abandoned his family, and August rejected the name Kittel, taking his mother's maiden name, Wilson.

An avid reader in the "Negro Section" of the Pittsburgh Public Library, he discovered Ralph Ellison, Langston Hughes, and James Baldwin. At age 18 he enlisted in the army. Upon his discharge in 1965, 20-year-old Wilson bought a $20 typewriter. He attempted to write militant poetry in the popular style of the Black Arts Movement, but failed to find his own voice. With Pittsburgh playwright Rob Penny, Wilson founded Black

Horizons Theatre (1968–70), where they produced Amiri Baraka's *Four Revolutionary Plays*. In 1976 Kuntu, a group at the University of Pittsburgh, produced Wilson's play *Homecoming*, which became the root for *Ma Rainey's Black Bottom*. The following year a Pittsburgh friend, Claude Purdy, later to become director of Alabama's Shakespeare Festival, suggested to Wilson that he fly to St. Paul, Minnesota, and develop his poems into a play. At about the same time Wilson's discovery of the recordings of Bessie Smith and the art of Romare Bearden led him to find his own voice and articulate his own blues.

In 1982, the Eugene O'Neill Theater Center accepted a rewrite of *Ma Rainey*. Two years later Lloyd Richards, having succeeded Brustein as dean of the Yale Drama School, directed the play for the Yale Repertory and then on Broadway, where it won the Drama Critics Circle Award. Actors Theresa Merritt and Charles Dutton received Tony Awards. Wilson's career was launched.

Wilson became a long-distance runner, chronicling decade by decade Blacks who had left the South to become urban dwellers in the North. By 1998 he had completed seven of his projected ten plays. *Fences* (1987) won for its author a Pulitzer Prize and a Tony Award. The star performers, James Earl Jones and Mary Alice, captured Tony Awards. Wilson's second Pulitzer came with the fifth installment of the ten-play series *The Piano Lesson* (1990). Inspired by Romare Bearden's collages, the parallels between Wilson's and Bearden's lives could not be missed. Both were born of German-American fathers, both had grown up black in Pittsburgh. Bearden's collage, "The Piano Lesson," had captured the blues of migrant families and demonstrated that the past was not past; rather, the ancestors and the legacy of slavery still burdened, and sometimes inspired, the living. Wilson told an interviewer, "I think *Piano Lesson* is my best play."[61] In contrast, Wilson's nemesis, the critic Robert Brustein, considered *The Piano Lesson* the "most poorly composed of Wilson's four produced works."[62] Brustein's misjudgment had highlighted a critical distinction between Eurocentric and Afrocentric aesthetics: the African American experience was not factorable into Brunetière's nineteenth-century well-made play formula. Hence the vital importance of a black director like Lloyd Richards, who would direct seven of Wilson's Broadway plays. "Lloyd is unquestionably the major influence in my life," Wilson said. "His abilities have enabled me to write. And the faith he had in me made everything fall into place."[63]

With his début as director of *A Raisin in the Sun* (1959), Richards had acquired an international reputation, but his greatest contribution to American

Figure 43. August Wilson and Camille Billops

theatre came from his thirty-three years as artistic director of the National Playwrights' Conference at the Eugene O'Neill Theater Center, where he oversaw the development of nearly five hundred plays by 362 black and white playwrights, many of whom had gone on to win Pulitzer Prizes, Tony Awards, Oscars, and Emmys. Upon his retirement from the NPC, Richards observed that the plays he received were better because authors "sit in front of the [TV] box. They learn the form of storytelling. They learn the form of drama."

In 1993, President Clinton awarded Richards the National Medal of Arts. Richards' appointment as dean of the Yale Drama School and artistic director of the Yale Repertory Theatre (1979–91) had placed him in a position to mentor the younger Wilson, who was still learning his theatre craft. Scholar Sandra G. Shannon in her study *The Dramatic Vision of August Wilson*[64] notes that both men had grown up in cities (Richards in Detroit), both had known men whose dreams had been scuttled by poverty, men like those in Wilson's *Fences*, men who collected garbage for a living when they had dreamed of playing professional baseball.

At the heart of Wilson's first full-length play *Jitney* (1979), a group of ageing black males, all gypsy cab drivers, fight despair and defeat, sustained by the brotherhood of their common entrapment. The scarcity of women in his casts moved an interviewer to ask Wilson why he did not write more parts for women. He replied, "I'm a man, so naturally that's what I know best."[65] Directed superbly by Walter Dallas, *Jitney* premiered (officially) at the Crossroads Theatre as part of their twentieth anniversary celebrations. To a degree Wilson and Richards invented a new try-out system, replacing the old road towns of New Haven and Buffalo with black theatres, as well as with the League of Resident Theatres (LORT) establishments across the nation. *Jitney* never came to Broadway, but opened off-Broadway at the Union Square Theatre (2000) and closed after a year's run, perhaps to make way for Wilson to work on *King Hedley II*, which premiered at the Virginia Theatre on 2 May 2001 and closed a few weeks later. Some thought the play miscast; others, overwritten.

Professor Shannon notes that the people in Wilson's plays, although victimized by their situations, were not victims, but survivors. His people plucked joy from their sad lives by drawing upon what the poet Owen Dodson called their "ancestors' long and boney dreams." Employing a loose poetic narrative of naturalism, Wilson's plays effused an African spirituality. His characters did not don Kente cloth or take African names, but in a more dramatic connection to the past, they retold and relived the stories of their families and friends. Wilson invoked an African spirituality without naming it. Nowhere does the playwright address the power of the African American past more directly than in *Joe Turner's Come and Gone* (1988), a drama in which the ancestors of the past have an influence on the stage action. It may be Wilson's most profound play.

No white characters were invited into his stories. White audiences were privileged to glimpse working-class people living in a self-contained black world, although white racism, like a pressure cooker, hissed and bubbled somewhere off stage. Finally, Wilson's greatest contribution to American theatre may have been his ability to present black people as beautiful and extraordinarily heroic in their everyday lives.

National Black Theatre Summit, 1998

In March 1998, August Wilson addressed the issues of survival by calling for the National Black Theatre summit, "On Golden Pond." Dartmouth College, where Wilson was playwright-in-residence, offered to host the event, but the story had begun earlier. Like many battles, this one began with a routine shot. White critic Robert Brustein, who was also director of the American Repertory Theatre at Harvard University, had complained that Wilson's plays were "weakly structured, badly edited, prosaic, and overwritten."[66] Wilson countered by calling Brustein "a sniper, a naysayer, and a cultural imperialist," adding that the black experience was unique and "we cannot allow others to have authority over our cultural and spiritual products."[67]

From his theatre column in the *New Republic*, Brustein lamented that funding sources (possibly referring to the Lila Wallace grants for creating audience diversity) were using sociological and not aesthetic criteria as a basis for support. Wilson countered in a speech at the eleventh biennial Theatre Communications Group Conference, pointing out that white aesthetics did not allow for black aesthetics. Wilson's rebuttal, "The Ground on Which I Stand," was published in *American Theatre* magazine. Anna Deavere Smith then arranged for a face-to-face debate in a public forum. That confrontation played at Town Hall on 27 January 1997, to a standing-room only audience. While the evening itself turned out to be something without much drama, the disagreements remained large. Wilson called for black artists to explore their own culture with their own expression. Brustein called for theatre without consideration of culture or color; one focused upon common aesthetic principles. The debate ultimately centered on funding problems. Wilson pointed out that of the sixty-six members of LORT, only Crossroads was black. Since then, the Freedom Theatre of Philadelphia became a member and Crossroads closed, a topic taken up later in this chapter. What did this mean for the survival of black theatres? Some facts and figures are necessary.

LORT theatres – Alabama Shakespeare Festival, American Repertory, Goodman, Guthrie Theatre, Lincoln Center, Mark Taper Forum, and Old Globe Theatre, to list a few – were major theatre houses that annually employed 20 percent of AEA's actors, compared to Broadway and touring shows, which employed 26.5 percent. Since 1992, some seven thousand union actors had worked in LORT theatres, earning between $440 and $592 a week. Authors earned 10 percent of the gross; set designers, $3,000 to $6,000, and directors, $5,000 to $9,000. Crossroads had been the only black theatre that could afford to pay those salaries.[68] Meanwhile, among an estimated eleven hundred nonprofits, most had budgets under $500,000.[69]

Because of their large subscription audiences, LORT theatres served (informally) as launching pads for many Broadway-bound shows, and as a conduit for touring shows that did not make it to Broadway. Their white subscription audiences would subscribe to see a black play if it had been Broadway approved; consequently, even though LORT theatres might present one black play a season, most black professionals could not make a living in LORT theatres. Funding sources rewarded LORT members for using black actors in nonblack roles and for casting traditional white plays with all-black casts. Hence, Wilson's observation, that the money supported white institutions and white plays, not black.

Furthermore, Wilson argued that producing a Eurocentric playwright – Shakespeare or Arthur Miller – with an all-black cast not only stripped black actors of their ethnicity, but denied a black playwright an opportunity for production. Some theatre artists and critics, both black and white, were dismayed by Wilson's position. Was not racial integration in theatre arts what Blacks had been pressing for since the 1940s? How long and how hard had black actors struggled to be cast as Macbeth, Ophelia, or Willie Loman? The situation seemed to be analogous to school integration. Once black children entered white schools, black schools closed, black teachers lost jobs, and students no longer learned black history. Still, was not Wilson taking a step backward? Yes and no, came the answers. Yes, there was a separate African American culture; no, it was not receiving the share of funds it so desperately needed to survive.

Brustein had some support from Blacks. Eugene Nesmith, actor, director, and theatre professor at the City College of New York, wrote in *American Theatre* that an undesignated black Renaissance had indeed blossomed in the 1980s and 1990s: the culture of African Americans had taken center stage. In one year, August Wilson's *Fences* (1987) and Toni Morrison's novel *Beloved* had taken Pulitzer Prizes. These had been followed by Morrison's and Walcott's Nobel Prizes in literature, and Henry Hampton's six-part documentary on the civil rights movement, *Eyes on the Prize*, had aired on national television. George C. Wolfe had been appointed to the directorship of the Joseph Papp Public Theater. Margo Jefferson had become a *New York Times* regular cultural critic. Led by Wynton Marsalis, the Lincoln Center finally recognized jazz as American classical music. Spike Lee's films had captured national audiences. Cornell West and Henry Louis Gates had been appointed professors at Harvard and received national consideration for their opinions. Digesting these accomplishments, Nesmith concluded that it was not a time for separation of the races, but rather a time for complete social integration in the theatre. "We are headed in the direction of diversity and multiculturalism. We cannot allow the myth of race to impede our progress on that road."[70]

To address these various points of view, August Wilson, along with Dartmouth professors Victor Walker and William W. Cook, called for a colloquium. Funded by the Rockefeller and Ford Foundations, as well as by

Dartmouth College itself, they invited forty-five consultants – playwrights, corporation administrators, lawyers, and critics – to a "Summit on Golden Pond," where they sequestered themselves for five days to investigate how to build audiences, encourage playwrights, and publish their plays. Importantly, they addressed not only questions of aesthetics and legal problems, but also financial planning. On the sixth day, an enthusiastic audience of three hundred turned up at the college campus in Hanover to hear the summit's results. Two immediately emerged. First, the Amos Tuck School of Business Administration at Dartmouth would reserve two or three spaces in business education for minority theatre managers.[71] The school also planned to begin consulting with black theatre groups about their financial problems. Second, Dartmouth expressed an interest in establishing the African Grove Institute for the Arts (AGIA), to proclaim and promote black theatre and its artists on a global scale.

The impetus for AGIA had originated, at least in part, from the final and inspirational chapter in Professor Samuel A. Hay's *African American Theatre: A Historical and Critical Analysis*, in which Hay traced the difficult histories of black theatre movements from the African Grove Theatre (1821–23) to 1990. Hay analyzed the causes for failures and found that lack of black unity and poor financial planning headed the list. In calling for the summit, founders Wilson, Walker, and Cook set a structure in motion which they felt would resolve basic confusion about how to proceed. Dartmouth College had made a long-term commitment to AGIA. Residency fellowships were established at the Getty Institute in Los Angeles. Theatre historian Errol Hill was the first to be nominated. The future for black theatre appeared to have brightened.[72]

In New York City, some who had not been invited to the Golden Pond summit formed their own "empowerment" group. In their seminar, Barbara Ann Teer of National Black Theatre stated: "The way grants are going in this country, social action, social change, all that is no longer *in vogue*, and nobody is going to address social, cultural or economic change. We must begin to develop our own entrepreneurial skills." Toward keeping small theatre groups alive, Ruby Dee and Ossie Davis established a foundation in 1998 to "help relieve some of the financial stress and to encourage community theatres." Ossie Davis estimated that 75 percent of African American artists in television and movies still came from community theatres. The initial contributions to the foundation totaled more than $300,000.[73]

The following summer Wilson assembled the second Golden Pond summit at the Atlanta Black Arts Festival, where he made clear that the movement was *not* one of racial separatism, but a demand that black theatre funding be made equitable with white. He emphasized that black culture was not a subculture, but a complete culture in itself, with its own philosophy, religion, mythology, and history. African Americans had brought valuable insight into the human condition, a resource that America could ill afford to ignore, and "our humanity is not open to negotiation."[74]

Black theatre representatives present at Atlanta agreed and called for unity and problem-solving. Although "diversity" remained a contentious issue ("diversity won't develop black playwrights"), most theatre representatives concurred that black theatre must acquire its share of public moneys, which would enable it to "stop begging, and start building."

It was off stage that Wilson elected to confront issues of diversity and cross-racial casting. The playwright had long opposed nontraditional casting, reasoning that African Americans were being asked to deny their blackness in order to participate in society. Douglas Turner Ward shared Wilson's objections for an additional reason. To cast a black actor, James Earl Jones for instance, as Big Daddy in *Cat on a Hot Tin Roof*, was to diminish the play's depiction of a racist society and a family whose wealth and power were based on the exploitation of Blacks.[75] These objections had come to the fore in June 1996 at the biennial Theatre Communications Group conference at Princeton University, where Wilson declared, "Color-blind casting is an aberrant idea...a tool of cultural imperialists. To mount an all-black production of a...play conceived for white actors...is to deny us our humanity, our own history, and the need to make our own investigations from the cultural ground on which we stand as black Americans.... We need those misguided financial resources to be put to better use." Color-blind casting, he noted, did not increase productions for black playwrights. Not all African Americans agreed. Nontraditional casting had its own history, which dated back to the AEA's Non-Traditional Casting Project (NTCP) in 1959 (see chapter 11).

In 1986 director Clinton Turner Davis and Harry Newman resurrected and reanimated the AEA project by inviting five hundred producers, actors, and directors to a "nontraditional casting" festival, where they watched eighteen scenes ranging from *The Crucible* and *Macbeth* to *The Philadelphia Story* and *The Importance of Being Earnest*. All roles were played by ethnic minorities and women, "where race, ethnicity, or gender were not germane to the character or to the development of the play." Those performances at the Shubert Theatre in New York demonstrated that good acting decreases awareness of race, while poor acting intensifies it.

THE MILLENNIUM 461

Multiethnic casting was an idea whose time had come. Within five years, roles for minority actors increased 87 percent. In 1992 the American Express Company gave $150,000 for the Artist Files Online program to make résumés and photos of minority actors available to theatres across the nation via the computer network. By 1997 seventeen hundred projects had consulted NTCP's five thousand files. NTCP expanded its vision to include the handicapped. For its contribution to the theatre, in 1997 the program received an Obie and a Drama Desk Award.

Although interracial casting had been practiced since the Harlem Renaissance, in the 1970s C. Bernard Jackson exerted a west coast influence over color-blind casting. From his founding of ICCC in 1965 until his death thirty years later, the center's productions were cast for talent; race was not a consideration. As early as 1968, Jackson's *Our Town* received some puzzled reviews from the critics, who discovered that Grovers Corners was not all white (*LA Times* critic Dan Sullivan excepted). When the young writer and director George C. Wolfe and administrator John C. Thorpe apprenticed at ICCC in the 1970s, they came away with a vision of cultural diversity, a stage reflecting the larger world.

Both men then migrated to New York. In 1989 Thorpe founded the Network of Cultural Centers of Color (NCCC), a booking and touring organization parallel to the white League of Resident Theatres. Its purpose: "to nurture, support, and promote collaborations among its members to bridge barriers of cultural and geographic isolation." By its tenth anniversary in 1999, NCCC had grown to have contacts with nearly three hundred and fifty cultural groups of color, reaching out as far as Hawaii, Brazil, and the Philippines. Thorpe had proposed a separate NEA for minorities because "we ascertain that if people of color actually received a return on their arts tax dollar, it would be so much greater than what organizations receive now." Unlike August Wilson, who asked for a bigger share of the funding pie, Thorpe believed that Blacks must ask for their own pie. "What's amazing about American culture," said Thorpe, "is that it can assimilate everything about you except you."[76]

Diversity or cross-color casting

In the 1990s some theatres had no history of diversity while others had thirty-year traditions. Certainly the most well-known theatre of diversity was Ellen Stewart's La MaMa Experimental Theater Club in New York City. From its first production of Tennessee Williams' *One Arm* in 1962,

La MaMa provided theatre space to creative artists regardless of race. Although Stewart was born African American in Alexandria, Louisiana, and although her seasons sometimes included Adrienne Kennedy, Ed Bullins, or Andre De Shields, she deliberately projected and carefully nurtured an international image. Recipient of many, many awards, including a $300,000 MacArthur Fellowship in 1985, Ellen Stewart might be regarded in contemporary theatre as the "mother of diversity."

Some saw "diversity" as a code word for "affirmative action." Under pressure from equal opportunity employment legislation, some theatres cast people of color as tokens. Others fully integrated their season's plays and their casts. For example, both Wynn Handman of the American Place Theatre and George C. Wolfe of the Joseph Papp Public Theater insisted upon diversity, although Wolfe rejected the term along with its connotations. "The need to come up with a term to express the inclusion of people is based on the absurd fact that in America, European culture is held up as the only true legitimate culture... If you are not telling the stories of all the different people in this country, then you can't call yourself an American theatre."[77] In the Joseph Papp tradition, Wolfe's productions used mixed casts – the Vanessa Redgrave production of *Anthony and Cleopatra*, and Wolfe's own *Macbeth*, starring Angela Bassett and Alec Baldwin. An example from the Midwest, the Mixed Blood Theatre Company of Minneapolis from its founding in 1976 defined itself as ethnically diverse – Asian, Black, Latino, and Native American. In Detroit the Repertory Theatre had cast interracially since 1957. By the late 1980s several Detroit companies added a black play to their season.

The issue of diversity was tried out under several rubrics: "color-blind casting," "nonconventional casting," "nontraditional casting," "cross-racial casting," "cultural diversity," and "multiculturalism." Zelda Fichandler of Washington's Arena Stage, an advocate, declared: "Multiculturalism will be the theater's single most important issue of the 1990s."[78] Part of her enthusiasm stemmed from Arena's $1 million grant from NEA, $200,000 from the Ford Foundation, and $100,000 from the Meyer Foundation, all the money targeted toward Arena's Cultural Diversity Program to place minorities at all levels of administration, technology, and performance.

But developing an audience to accept diversity in casting required exposure. In 1977, Earle Hyman was cast as Uncle Ben in an otherwise all-white *Death of a Salesman*. Mel Gussow asked: "Why has Willy a black brother? A more understandable approach to casting was taken some seasons ago at the Center Stage in Baltimore. There all the Lomans were black."[79] When

Tim Bond left the integrated ensemble of the New Group Theatre in Seattle to work as associate artistic director for the Oregon Shakespeare Festival, he took several actors of color with him. In an interview with theatre critic Misha Berson, Bond admitted that some patrons of the Shakespeare Festival still objected to black or female actors in the traditional roles of white males. "You don't look for a resolution. You just hope for communication," said Bond.[80]

It must be added that Seattle's second largest theatre, ACT (A Contemporary Theatre), since its founding in 1965 by Gregory A. Falls had had a policy of using minority actors, but they imported them from New York and Los Angeles. In 1997, ACT broke with the past and cast Pearl Cleage's *Blues for an Alabama Sky* with entirely local talent.

As has been noted, when the acting is superb, the audience is able to suspend their knowledge of an actor's race and gender. At the turn of the millennium an outstanding example of superior "diversity" talent manifested itself in the career of Karen Kandel. Kandel left the English department of Queens College in New York City to accept her first role in Elizabeth Swados' *Runaways* (1978). Over five years, Lee Breuer of Mabou Mines worked with her and unfettered her talent in the gender-reversal role of Edgar/Edna in his *Lear*. Her work was soon recognized with two Obie awards. Kandel's talents were brought to full maturity in an "aural *tour de force*," Breuer's *Peter and Wendy*, where she not only played Wendy but also created and sustained seven voices, male and female, for all the play's puppet characters for more than 150 minutes. Hers was the play's single voice. Lee Breuer's work should not be confused with that of Brad Brewer, who in 1973 founded the Brewery Puppet Troupe with four black puppeteers – Glenngo A. King, Darren Brown, Martin Brown, and Brad Brewer – known internationally as the "Crowtations," a singing quartet of rod puppets where skills and art ranked with the Jim Henson creations.

Diversity played out in Seattle

In Seattle diversity issues played out in all their complexity. In 1978 at the University of Washington, Rubén Sierra collected eleven actors to produce Miguel Piñero's *Short Eyes* (1974). Its reception encouraged Sierra to found the New Group Theatre, colloquially known as the Group. Its announced mission: to present contemporary theatre works primarily by American playwrights employing and developing minority theater artists in all facets of production and avoiding stereotypes. Within ten years the Group had built an audience of 85,000 by selecting provocative bills of social and political plays. The Ford Foundation awarded Sierra $162,775 for his "commitment to multiracial theatre and casting without regard to ethnic persuasion." The leveraging power of this grant was to encourage other Seattle arts organizations use minority artists; it worked, perhaps too well.

The Group left its secure home at the University of Washington to renovate and move into Center House, a 192-seat theatre in the prestigious Seattle Center. Funding organizations flocked to help – the Lila Wallace Reader's Digest Theatre for New Audiences, the Pew Charitable Trust, and the National Arts Stabilization Fund, this last to build a working capital reserve over five years to ensure the long-term fiscal health of the theatre. Yet, five years later, in 1998, notwithstanding the strong initial funding, the Group died. What had happened?

A brief recapitulation of the Seattle Repertory Theatre's diversity history will give insight into the dilemma. Founded in 1964, the Rep, Seattle's major theatre, had no black actors or technicians, a fact that had motivated Douglas Barnett to found Black Arts/West. Originally, Barnett had assumed that the Rep would eventually include minority actors. When it did not, Barnett along with theatrical associate Keve Bray met with Stuart Vaughan, Seattle Rep's then artistic director, to express their dismay.[81] According to Barnett, Vaughan stated in the starkest of terms that, since they were a classical repertory company performing Molière, Shakespeare, Greek tragedy, and so forth, there was no place for black or minority actors in his company. Furthermore, he could not think of a single black actor who had the skills for the classics except Roscoe Lee Browne, who, if hired, would have to perform in whiteface. Outraged, Bray and Barnett filed a discrimination lawsuit against the Seattle Rep, citing Title VI of the 1964 Civil Rights Act, which forbade giving federal funds to any institution that practiced discrimination in their hiring practices. The echo came bounding back: the Seattle opera, symphony, and Rep had all failed to hire talent of color.[82]

The Rep dismissed Stuart Vaughan and replaced him with Allen Fletcher, who promptly employed Beatrice Winde, Juanita Bethea, and Jason Bernard. Word about the lawsuit spread; other all-white companies benefiting from federal money hurried to hire minority actors. This was in the late 1960s. The Rep hired a few token minority actors and continued to produce a mostly European program, but it received multicultural funds to create diversity. Thirty years later, in 1991, its only black actor,

Wendell Wright, resigned claiming: "I wasn't getting good parts for the coming season. I was a token. I'm not going to spend a whole year playing the third soldier from the left or fourth townsperson from the right [crowd scenes]. The Rep gets community funding. Its work ought to fairly reflect the community."[83] August Wilson, a resident of Seattle, pointed out that large theatres with white subscription audiences received funds to produce a single black play in their season and to hire several African American actors. Small black theatres got little or no moneys. As Wilson observed in Atlanta, while some Blacks were working in the mainstream, the diversity policy was bankrupting small black theatres, and those were the stages black playwrights had depended upon for production. In the example of Seattle, when the New Group's funds and part of its program were redirected to the Seattle Repertory Theatre, the Group collapsed.

Nationally, the problem replicated. In 1996 the Mark Taper Forum empowered L. Kenneth Richardson to assemble a symposium of African American directors, actors, and writers (the Blacksmyths) to address the diversity dilemma. Tim Bond proposed that the larger regional theatres cooperate with black theatres in productions and audience promotion.[84] The argument did not settle the Seattle paradox or the Mark Taper Forum dilemma. Power must be shared equally. Too many small theatres had gone under.

As the year 2000 came to an end, the Screen Actors Guild, which had been tracking minority hiring since 1992, released casting data reports for both prime-time and theatrical performances. African Americans comprised 14.1 percent of all roles in 1999, a slight increase from the 13.4 in 1998. Latino and Asian employment also rose. Theatrical entertainments slowly but steadily were moving toward the reality of "our American scene."[85]

The Chitlin' Circuit

Henry Louis Gates Jr. in a February 1997 *New Yorker* article called attention to the "Chitlin' Circuit," theatres that once had thrived between the late 1930s and the mid-1960s by booking musical talents such as Nat King Cole or the Ink Spots.[86] Before integration diverted black audiences to white theatres, black clientele had filled the Apollo Theater in Harlem. When Gates applied "Chitlin' Circuit" to the touring gospel shows of the 1990s, Professor Beverly Robinson objected; she rechristened the touring companies the "Urban Circuit."

The roots of this genre had originated in the black church and its preachers who evoked vocal response from their congregations. These rituals passed into gospel plays, first within the church and later on the commercial stage. Urban Circuit comedies exploited that oral tradition in which audiences vocally advised the characters on stage on what actions to take.

This tradition was revived in the late 1980s and developed into a gold mine. *Beauty Shop* (1987) by Shelly Garrett grossed $33 million. "My show is strictly pure entertainment. I don't want to teach anybody anything," asserted the author.[87] Some detractors denigrated the plays. Theatre critic Chris Jones described Garrett's play as "a loud and raucous comic affair set in a hair salon. *Beauty Shop* consists mainly of wild sexual banter among assorted stereotypical hair stylists (there's a gay man, a large woman, a sexy tease) and their gossiping customers. Much of the dialogue consists of deadpan insults and one-liners."[88] Nonetheless, with top ticket prices at $35 (half the price of Broadway's loge and orchestra seat), *Beauty Shop* had sold 21 million tickets, making it the all-time box-office grosser in black theatre history. Garrett followed his coup with *Fake Friends*, a gospel extravaganza, *Beauty Shop Part II*, *Barber Shop*, and *Laundromat*. All the shows featured gospel singing to attract church audiences. Producer Woodie King Jr. pointed out that not all the big money earned on the Urban Circuit went into black pockets:

> In the so-called urban circuit, a black guy will write the play, star in the play, direct the play, and the show will gross $600,000 in Philadelphia, but he makes only $50,000, and the actors make only $300 a week. What happened to the other $500,000? That's where we run into the problem. The man who owns the theatre says, "I like your show. I'll pay you fifty grand and pay all the other people and expenses." The theatre owner may then spend $100,000 promoting to a black audience. The black guy has nothing to do with the radio spots, nothing to do with the flyer that goes into the churches. All he knows is that his picture's on it and his name remains on the show; the white guy's name [theatre owner and producer] is nowhere to be seen. Then the black guy decides "I'll produce it myself," but he doesn't have a theatre or any of the promotional apparatus.[89]

Garrett's "success" attracted competitors, who were not theatre artists but investors and money managers. An accountant, Kevin Fontana, wrote and produced *Whatever Happened to Black Love?* (1990). David Talbert, a business-based entrepreneur from Las Vegas, wrote and produced *He Say,*

She Say, But What Does God Say?, and Slivy Edmonds Cotton founded WCT (Wild Crazy Things) Productions, a touring company. Their plays all had happy endings; all used gospel singers, but few AEA actors; all had casts under nine or ten, sometimes as few as three; all promoted themselves in church programs and on black radio and video; all encouraged audience participation; many used celebrities for a single evening's performance. From a typical production budget of $200,000 nearly half would be slated for advance publicity aimed primarily at salaried women between the ages of 36 and 54. If successful, the gross for one night ranged between $25,000 and $45,000.

In 1998 television and Hollywood film climbed onto the chitlin' band-wagon and made a pitch for MTV audiences. The producers of Terry McMillan's profitable *Waiting to Exhale* launched a second film *How Stella Get Her Groove Back*, starring Whoopi Goldberg and Angela Bassett, the latter as a wealthy, 40-year-old account executive pursued by a handsome 20-year-old Jamaican medical student. Aimed directly at the salaried con-sumer female, the film elicited laughter, tears, and fantasies of true love, wealth, and materialism. After a disappointing box office, the film was sold to television. A clear message emerged from the Atlanta panel: black the-atres, if they were to succeed, must master aggressive marketing as MTV video, sports, and the Urban Circuit had.

The Urban Circuit's financial bonanza created envy and widened the century-old division between high art and popular black entertainment, a division that extended back to the New England missionaries who had founded and ruled southern black colleges for nearly a century. They had ingrained in their students a disdain for popular (immoral) entertainments. At the Atlanta Theatre Festival, David Talbert reported that those "hincty" attitudes still divided "high" arts from popular entertainment. For example, he had rented a theatre from a black company in California and, to the astonishment of the owners, filled its 250 seats night after night. The resident company then accused Talbert of not producing "art" because too many people were coming to the theatre.

Throughout history ephemeral popular theatre has entertained broadly while the aim of art and university theatres has been to preserve and nurture theatre of "lasting value." Even before the Harlem Renaissance black theatre had had two audiences. While the middle class (mostly schoolteachers) wrote plays to instruct, the majority of African Americans preferred to spend their money laughing, crying, and shouting to the TOBA performers at the Lincoln Theatre in Harlem.

One producer at the Atlanta Panel told his listeners that he could create an audience for *He Say, She Say, But What Does God Say?*, but he'd have trouble bringing that same audience to a play entitled *Seven Guitars* by August Wilson, who had averred that the Chitlin' Circuit had something that might offer the seeds for a future black theatre. A look at the most successful theatres may shed some insight into how class agendas influence what is produced.

Long-term survival

How many black companies from the 1960s and 1970s survived to the year 2000, and how did they do it? The histories selected here represent a wide geographical spread, but their experiences are shared. The omission of other long-lived theatres has been either a concession to space or because the theatres are presented elsewhere; for example, the New Federal Theatre of producer Woodie King is certainly a supreme example of survival, and much of his story is told in chapter 12.

The years approaching the millennium brought professional black theatre to Texas, a state with a 40 percent black and brown population. Although Margo Jones' Theatre '47 in Dallas and Houston's Alley Theatre had long held national acclaim, people of color were seldom seen on most professional stages. Paul Winfield's appearance in Fugard's *Message from Aloes* in 1982 may have marked the first time a Black performed on stage at the Dallas Theater Center. Blacks attempting to finance their own companies met serious roadblocks. In 1984 not one black theatre in Dallas was able to qualify for any of the city's $3 million arts budget because an operating budget of $200,000 or more was required. Corporations employed similar dodges; they would not fund a theatre unless it had a salaried chief executive officer, which excluded most small groups. Subsequently, in an attempt to acquire arts funding, two or three theatres banded together to form the Black Arts Council.

Houston, Texas

"The oldest and most distinguished professional theatre in the Southwest devoted to the African American Experience was the Ensemble Theatre of Houston."[90] In 1997 it celebrated its twentieth anniversary by occupying a new $4 million complex with three theatres. Founder George Hawkins had not lived to realize his dream of a black theatre on Main Street, but after his death in 1990, the artistic direction of Eileen J. Morris fulfilled Hawkins' vision. How had Ms. Morris erected a $4 million complex? The answer included eighteen foundations, thirty-five corporations, an audience that was 65 percent African American, and a full-time staff of seven, including a technical director. Over the years Morris persisted in producing five annual fund-raising shows, including the Christmas show *Black Nativity*. Woodie King, New York producer, pronounced the Ensemble one of the top fifteen black theatres in America. Morris' next goal was to become a full AEA theatre, like her white neighbors, Theatre Under the Stars and the Alley.[91] In 1999 Morris moved to an administrative position at Kuntu Theatre in Pittsburgh.

San Francisco, California

In California, three black theatres in the Bay Area of San Francisco survived for more than two decades: the Lorraine Hansberry, a professional theatre downtown; the Oakland Ensemble, which primarily served Blacks; and the Berkeley Black Repertory (BBR), a community group established in 1964 by two schoolteachers from Vicksburg, Mississippi, Nora and Birel Vaughn. "The Group," as they called themselves, "put on plays" in the Down Memorial United Methodist Church, where Birel directed the choir. Nora acted. In 1967 the Vaughns moved their Group to South Berkeley, where they converted a small space into a 99-seat theatre. Their audiences were 70 percent black, with a scattering of Whites and Asians. Their first production, *Purlie Victorious*, was followed by two Langston Hughes audience-pleasers, *Mulatto* and *Tambourines to Glory*.

The San Francisco Foundation gave BBR its first grant, but the Vaughns remained skeptical: what if they grew to depend upon grants and then the largess stopped? They had operated successfully from box-office sales and from Sunday "buy-outs" (renting the theatre to social clubs and fund-raisers). For them, *community* remained the key word, drawing support from socially committed black women, such as members of the Phyllis Wheatly Club. In 1977 BBR created a new arts program in which five playwrights could see their work and hear audience comment. In the same season, on the main stage for four weekend performances, the BBR produced five plays by established writers. In the 1970s admission was $1; in the 1990s, a top ticket cost $20.[92] On 11 October 1987 BBR moved again, this time into a new 250-seat house built upon land rented to them by the City of Berkeley for $1. The Vaughns had asked for a larger house of 750 seats, so they might have greater income. The city refused because BBR was incorporated as a community theatre and because it must remain a non-AEA house. Nonetheless, on occasion AEA actors waived their salaries because the BBR had become a showcase and conduit for television and film roles. Mona Scott, the founders' daughter, while finishing her Ph.D. at Stanford, took over grant writing. When her parents died, she became the producing director. The theatre's annual budget never exceeded $180,000, and in 1998 general admission was still pegged at $12. In 1984 the Lorraine Hansberry Theatre of San Francisco gave BBR a twenty-year service award, but trouble came in 1998 when some members of the City Council attempted to evict BBR from its theatre by voiding its rental contract with the city. The community fought back with such vigor that, at the time of writing, BBR had retained its space although threats by some City Council members continue.

Oakland, California

The Oakland Ensemble emerged in 1972. Benny Sato Ambush obtained nonprofit status for the ensemble and took over the artistic directorship for the next twenty years. They began with a 99-seat auditorium lodged in an old house in West Oakland. Ken Ellis then designed a new home at the Alice Arts Center, a theatre-in-the-round that could be converted to a thrust stage with 500 seats; however, it did not qualify the ensemble for membership in LORT, whose rules required 750 seats or more.

In 1982, when the ensemble's budget was $586,000, they signed a "Bay Area" contract to employ five to seven AEA actors. Twelve years later, in 1994, when Zerita Dotson became producing director, the budget had been halved to $260,000. The box-office proceeds became less than half the budget. A season ticket for a "super patron" cost $250, of which only $100 was ticket cost. Gradually the repertory of five or six shows a year shrank to three. A highlight of the theatre's history came in 1996, when Roger Smith premiered his one-man show, *Huey Newton*, at the ensemble. The Black Panther Party's history after thirty years had returned to its original home in Oakland.[93]

Detroit, Michigan

In an interview published in 1988, Detroit theatre producer Maggie Porter estimated that "since the 1960s, eighteen Black theatre companies have died." The cause: failure to sustain an audience. Porter's own theatre, Harmonie Park Playhouse and Actors' Lab, survived into the 1990s. Established in 1980, Harmonie claimed to be the only black theatre in Michigan residing in an independent, permanent, performing, and administrative space occupied and controlled solely by the theatre. But Harmonie was evicted from its home in 1992 by "urban renewal."[94]

In 1989 two Wayne State graduates, Gary Anderson and Michael Garza, founded Plowshares Theatre Company. Within five years they had become "Michigan's only professional African American theatre company." Plowshares' success resulted from several policies. Although committed to producing African American plays almost exclusively, it advertised to diverse audiences, establishing relationships with civic, educational, and cultural groups, including the Meadow Brook Theatre on Oakland University's campus, where they coproduced OyamO's *I Am a Man* (1994), a labor play about the Memphis garbage strike.[95]

Artistic director Gary Anderson initiated the New Voices Play Development Program, a three-year pilot project to encourage new works for Plowshares. Up to six new scripts were to be chosen and given staged readings in the summer Festival of New Plays, and $1,000 was to be awarded to the best play. In figuring his company's budget, Anderson carefully avoided an overdependence upon any single revenue: 8 percent from individual contributions, 14 percent from local government, 23 percent from community support. The company reached an agreement with the new Museum of African American history to perform in their 317-seat theatre. Plowshares would dramatize African American historical exhibits for visitors.[96] The theatre's growth paralleled an agreement with the AEA to use two actor members in each production plus a stage manager. In 1997 the *Detroit Free Press* nominated Plowshares for thirteen theatre excellence awards. Plowshares won three major awards that season, including Best Play for its production of Eugene Lee's *East Texas Hot Links*. In the light of Porter's statement that eighteen black theatres had died since the 1960s, it seemed that Plowshares might live.

St. Paul, Minnesota

In the state of Minnesota, the Hallie Q. Brown Community Center, an umbrella social service agency in St. Paul, provided Penumbra Theatre with its first 135-seat theatre. Its artistic director and founder, Lou Bellamy, said that Penumbra's racial "isolation" in the Midwest gave it distinction – Minnesota

had only sixty thousand Blacks in the entire state. Following ten successful years, the company expanded into a 265-seat house in the Community
Center's Martin Luther King Building. Penumbra, which had been established in 1976, originally around a core of twenty actors, became Minnesota's
only African American professional theatre. Perhaps its uniqueness helped
its initial survival, but its longevity lay in a vision, as well as careful planning
by Bellamy, who framed Penumbra's mission to increase public awareness
of the significant social contributions that African Americans had made.[97]
A Penumbra season typically linked classic black plays (*A Raisin in the
Sun*) with historical pieces (*Flyin' West*) with contemporary topics (*Canned
Goods*). In addition, it invited performance artists such as Robbie McCauley
and Jo Zollar to create a sense of experimental excitement and to alert audiences to alternate worlds of theatre. Each year's program would include a
musical as well as Langston Hughes' *Black Nativity*, a perennial and financial sugar plum for black theatres.

Penumbra's operating budget for the 1998/99 season of six plays swelled
to nearly $2 million, and rarely did the theatre derive more than 50 per-
cent of its budget from box-office sales. In addition to meeting core AEA
salaries, over the years Bellamy hired about one hundred actors, choreographers, dancers, directors, and administrators to augment productions,
"more black theater professionals than all the other professional theaters
in Minnesota combined."[98] In 1982, Penumbra's Cornerstone Playwriting
contest attracted the then novice writer, August Wilson, who won the contest with a satire, *Black Bart and the Sacred Hills* (1982). In 1984, Wilson's
Jitney became Cornerstone's maiden production. Over the years Penumbra
produced more of Wilson's plays than any other theatre in the world.[99]

Wilson offered this tribute:

> We are what we imagine ourselves to be, and we can only imagine what
> we know to be possible. The founding of Penumbra Theatre enlarged
> that possibility. And its corresponding success provokes the community
> to a higher expectation of itself. I became a playwright because I saw
> where my chosen profession was being sanctioned by a group of black
> men and women who were willing to invest their lives and their talent in
> assuming a responsibility for our presence in the world and the conduct
> of our industry as black Americans.[100]

While Penumbra saluted all artists of color, it focused on black. Twenty
years passed before Bellamy was able to convince his giant neighbor, the
Guthrie Theater, to invite Penumbra to produce a black play, *Big White Fog*
(1938), for their audiences. Accolades from the "experiment" encouraged

Guthrie to ask Bellamy to direct Rita Dove's adaptation of the Oedipus myth, *Darker Face of the Earth* (1994), for production in 2000.[101]

St. Louis, Missouri

Nearly a thousand miles down the Mississippi River, Ron Himes, "The Father of Black Theatre in St. Louis," in 1976 founded the St. Louis Black Repertory, the largest African American performing arts organization in Missouri. Like the entrepreneurs of the Urban Circuit, Himes entered theatre via business school, but when he graduated he abandoned his plan to get an MBA; instead he turned to Webster University to pursue a master's degree in directing. After renting a hall and mounting *The Brownsville Raid*, he was offered a theatre space in the community center attached to the Greely Presbyterian Church. In 1981 he opened his first theatre season with *The Black Musical Review*, featuring excerpts from *The Wiz* and *Bubbling Brown Sugar.*

"We packed people in," Himes said. "There were two hundred seats in the space, and we were selling three hundred tickets a night. All of a sudden we caused a big buzz. We were really drawing a large black audience at a time when other theatres were saying black people didn't go to theatre."[102]

Producing five shows a season and using adult theatre classes, Himes built a core company where "everybody did everything – directing, acting, lighting." The company became the community cultural center. Attracting community and corporate sponsorship, "Black Rep" moved into the Grandel Square Theatre, a new 471-seat house and opened with August Wilson's *The Piano Lesson.*

Steve Callahan's radio review reveals some reasons for the company's successes:

> The Black Rep just gets better and better! They've opened *Blues for an Alabama Sky* by Pearl Cleage. Don't miss it – it's theatre at its very best. For years the Black Rep has astonished me with their musical productions; however, I've sometimes neglected their straight plays. Should I be ashamed to have assumed that their dramas tend to deal with specialized issues? That they speak more to a black audience than to me? If so it's a tiny shame, and one that I'm sure I share with thousands of white theatregoers in St. Louis.[103]

"Black Rep" reached an annual audience exceeding fifty thousand. The summer of 1999 saw Himes direct *Never Lost a Passenger, the Story of Harriet Tubman*, an opera sung by children and accompanied by the St. Louis

Symphony Youth Orchestra. In addition to its six main-stage productions
each season, the "Black Rep" offered touring shows, residencies, workshops
in drama and movement for children and adults, a professional intern program, and an education program that included student matinées and a free
Noonday Series during lunch hour for discussions with artists of the main-
stage productions.

Chicago, Illinois

Chicago's ETA Creative Arts Foundation in its thirty-year history claimed
never to have had a deficit. Incorporated in April 1971 as a nonprofit organization, it provided professional training in the performing and technical arts for youth and adults. In 1979 founder and president Abena Joan
Brown had purchased an old factory for $35,000 and by 1988 she had built
a 200-seat theatre. ETA became "Chicago's leading performing and cultural arts complex in the African American community, as well as the only
African American owned and managed facility of its kind in the city."[104]
It may be the first African American cultural and performing arts institution to establish a $1.5 million endowment to insure its survival. By the
end of 2001, ETA planned to have $15 million collected for its expansion
programs.

Governed by a twenty-six member board, ETA involved more than five
hundred volunteers for the myriad tasks required to operate a large organization that brings more than ninety thousand people in one year to
participate in its programs: Reader's Theatre, an art gallery, an arts in education program, a playwrights discovery initiative, as well as main-stage
and children's productions. From 1971 to 2001 ETA produced more than one
hundred and thirty main-stage and fifty children's plays. In 1994, a typical
year, four new playwrights – the poet Afaa Michael Weaver, Songodina Ifa-
tui, the late Frances DeVore-Harrison, and Phyllis Curtwright – received
commissions for workshops and productions. All but 2 percent of ETA's
shows were originals. Abena Brown's creative business acumen provided
the foundation with imaginative fund-raising: in 1999, it sold sweepstake
tickets at $10 each; first prize, a 1999 Ford Escort.

New Brunswick, New Jersey

On the east coast, Crossroads Theatre, the same age as Penumbra, was born
in 1977 in New Brunswick, New Jersey. Like the NEC of the late 1960s,

Crossroads had been conceived by energetic young artists with a dream supported by the Ford Foundation. Its mission was fourfold: to provide a professional environment for black theatre artists; to educate and to promote public interest in and support of professional theatre; to present honest and positive portrayals of black life, culture, and art; and to uphold the highest standards of artistic excellence.[105]

Ricardo Khan and L. Kenneth Richardson, two graduates of the Mason Gross School of the Arts at Rutgers University, in association with Louise Gorham (who left early on), approached Eric Krebs of the George Street Playhouse in October 1978 with plans to found a regional black theatre in New Brunswick, an economically depressed town of forty thousand. Their stage on the second floor of a rundown former factory seated 132 people. Beginning with a $50,000 grant from CETA, they put twenty-two people on staff and mounted their maiden show, *First Breeze of Summer.* For its first performance, they sold seven $2 tickets, even though the play had previously won an Obie for best play. Khan and Richardson began an aggressive campaign to create new audiences, black and white. Sales improved.

In 1980 Crossroads bid farewell to the George Street Playhouse, which had umbrellaed their CETA grants. They soon acquired the distinction of being the only theatre in New Jersey drawing a multicultural audience on a steady basis. Whites made up between 25 and 30 percent. Their initiatives took several forms. First, Khan believed that original scripts would help Crossroads capture a diversified audience. A "New Play Rites" program and an associate artists program would provide a "home" for playwrights, actors, and technical personnel, where they could develop new work for African American theatre. Eventually the program included Leslie Lee, Emily Mann, Denise Nicholas, Ntozake Shange, George C. Wolfe, and director Harold Scott. In 1982 CBS and the Foundation of the Dramatists Guild selected Crossroads as one of five theatres nationwide to participate in their New Play Program, a $20,000 contest to promote the production of more original plays by regional theatres. The five theatres were inundated with scripts from five thousand hungry authors. Crossroads chose George C. Wolfe's *The Colored Museum* (1985), a play which had already been turned down by five theatres. Premiered at Crossroads in 1986, the revue was picked up by Joseph Papp at the Public Theater and parlayed into a production in Public Television's Great Performances, where millions saw it nationally. Crossroads received the National Governors' Association Award for Distinguished Service in the Arts. In 1988, L. Kenneth Richardson was

dismissed by the Board of Trustees for "personal issues and health," leaving
Khan solely in charge as artistic director.[106]

An important initiative to develop audiences came in 1985, when Sydné
Mahone, literary manager, became director of play development. "When
I arrived at Crossroads, they had produced three plays by black women
and since then the number is over twenty."[107] In 1991 the women's company *Sangoma* came to fruition with the premiere of *The Mother Project*,
a collaborative work developed by *Sangoma's* members under the direction
of Sydné Mahone. In 1994 the Theatre Communication Group published
her anthology, *Moon Marked and Touched by Sun: Plays by African-American
Women*.

Ten years of hard work had paid off. First, bolstered by a $1.25 million
budget, Crossroads became an AEA regional theatre. Second, it had
achieved world-class status through a string of acclaimed seasons highlighted by more than two-dozen premieres. Third, the subscriber base had
grown by more than three thousand. Fourth, support from public and private sources had increased, and fifth, media recognition rose again in 1991
when Leslie Lee's *Black Eagles*, a drama about the Tuskegee airmen of World
War Two, was seen and publicly hailed by President George Bush, General
Colin Powell, chairman of the Joint Chiefs-of-Staff, and civil rights matriarch Rosa Parks. Bill Cosby hosted five sold-out performances. In 1985 the
Ford Foundation awarded Crossroads $233,000.[108] Box-office sales rarely
covered more than 40 percent of the budget. Sixty percent of ticket sales
came from African Americans; however, with a dependency on grants, bad
news follows good.

On 8 November 1990, Ricardo Khan in a public letter appealed for funds.
He wrote: "Last month we found out that our annual State Arts Council
grant, like those of most other arts organizations in New Jersey, was reduced
by 50 percent. For all groups, I am sure that this was painful. For us, though,
the cut of $302,000 was devastating." The cut came just as the company
was leaving its century-old former garment factory for a new, $4 million,
264-seat facility in the heart of the New Brunswick Cultural Center, a
symbol of the city's revitalization in which Crossroads had played a key role.
The city had contributed major funding toward the new facility, and it did
not let Crossroads die. Instead in 1998 Crossroads celebrated its twentieth
anniversary with an "official" premiere of August Wilson's *Jitney* (1979).
Until 1999 Crossroads was the only black theatre to belong to the League of
Resident Theatres. In the spring of 1999 it was awarded the Antoinette Perry
(Tony) Award for regional theatre that had displayed a continuous level of

artistic achievement contributing to the growth of theatre nationally."[109] But then, as in a tragedy, a dramatic reversal of fortune befell. On 11 September 2000 reporter David J. Harris of New Brunswick's *Home News Tribune* broke the story. Burdened with nearly $2 million in debts, Crossroads would cancel its 2000/01 season of plays; 1,492 subscribers would probably not receive their refunds, although they might be given passes to the George Street Theatre next door. What had happened?

General manager Deborah Stapleton reported that financial trouble had begun in 1991 when Crossroads moved site to 7 Livingston Avenue. Operating costs had increased by $300,000 a year. Crossroads did not own their theatre, but rented it from the Cultural Center, a nonprofit umbrella organization, and in 1994 the rent was $90,264. Debts mounted; employees were furloughed. Finally, veteran director Hal Scott replaced artistic director Khan, who had returned to his native Trinidad, promising to return to help fund-raise for a "turnaround plan." In the meantime, Crossroads' major funding sources withheld their money until the theatre's finances could be reorganized.[110] In the winter of 2001 the New Jersey State Council on the Arts agreed to give the theatre $100,000. Crossroads was to hire a new artistic director and other "qualified individuals." It was hoped that the theatre would be able to reopen its doors for a series of fund-raising performances.[111] Committed to realizing this dream, Rhinold Ponder became new president of the Crossroads. After nearly two years, Ponder through negotiation reduced the 2 million dollar debt to 1.4 million. Plans were then laid to reopen Crossroads with "An Evening of Comedy with Moms Mabley," written by and starring Clarice Taylor, to be followed by three other small productions through the spring of 2003. However, two days before the new lease was to take effect, Ponder backed out of the agreement with the Cultural Center and resigned his position as president of Crossroads' board. To avoid eviction, an appeal was sent to New Jersey Governor McGreevey. At the time of writing, the rest is silence. Crossroads' initial successes may have contributed to its downfall by assuming that present debts would be met by future revenues. Freedom Theatre of Philadelphia seems to have had a better plan.

Philadelphia, Pennsylvania

Established in 1966 by John Allen Jr. and Robert E. Leslie, Freedom Theatre advertised itself as "the nation's largest and Pennsylvania's oldest African American Theatre." In 1982 the theatre had purchased the house, which was located at 1346 North Broad Street in a mansion built in 1855 by the actor Edwin Forrest. Classifying itself as a small professional theatre and a performing arts training program, Freedom Theatre presented more than 150 performances a year.[112] The founders had focused their energies upon youth, enrolling about three hundred a year in their performing arts training school. In its 25-year history, the program schooled more than ten thousand students. In 1998, with an enrollment of nine hundred, 98 percent graduated from high school, and 85 percent went on to higher education. More than five thousand people participated in its outreach program. With this record, the theatre was able to raise $10 million from corporate sponsors and government grants for renovation and construction of a new 299-seat theatre, as well as eleven apartments for visiting artists. In 1996, Governor Tom Ridge awarded Freedom Theatre a $250,000 grant "for educational services and programs through the state's Alternative Education fund."

When founder John Allen Jr. died in 1992, Walter Dallas took over the artistic directorship. Dallas was a graduate of Morehouse College in Atlanta and of the Yale Drama School, and his world premiere production of Wilson's *Seven Guitars* (1995) at the Goodman Theatre in Chicago was nominated for a Pulitzer Prize and hailed by *Time Magazine* as one of the top ten best theatre events of 1995. His stage adaptation of the film *Cooley High* (1996) broke all box-office attendance records in Freedom's 33-year history. In 1996 a Ford subsidiary, the Working Capital Fund, awarded Freedom Theatre a series of grants totaling $425,000 plus access to a $1.25 million loan pool. Previously, in the sixties the Ford Foundation had given money to the Negro Ensemble Company and to the New Lafayette Theatre for artist training and for production. While the money lasted, the theatres prospered. In the 1980s Ford refocused its policy toward teaching theatre personnel how to manage money, "to avoid the pain and risk of growing too fast." In the 1990s Ford reported that its mission with minority organizations was "to develop a judicious process for making decisions about their direction and future. The troupe planned its repertory season much like a financial adviser builds a diversified investment portfolio. It doesn't shy away from producing tough plays by little-known writers," but it offsets the risks by casting a star or two or rounding out the season with certain hits.[113]

In 1998 Freedom Theatre's revenues for earnings and contributions exceeded $4 million. After expenses, there remained a surplus of $11,000, making the theatre, if not unique, certainly a special category. Freedom became the second black theatre to join LORT, giving it an additional power

base. Nonetheless, four years later, in 2002, Freedom Theatre found itself
in serious financial trouble.

New York City

Although approximately 112 experimental black and white theatres were
founded in New York City during the late sixties, the National Black Theatre
(NBT) was one of only a few to survive into the 1990s. Founder Barbara
Ann Teer had abandoned a professional Broadway career because the Great
White Way offered her roles that gave her spirit no nourishment. She
envisioned a theatre where Blacks would control and bring validation to a
group suffering from the negative effects of cultural hegemony, a theatre
that would embrace the dual heritage of being African and American by
combining the elements of the black Pentecostal church with the Yoruba
ceremonial rites of Nigeria. In 1968 she chose 125th Street in Harlem for a
theatre that would "raise the level of consciousness through liberating the
spirits and strengthening the minds of its people." This education of African
American consciousness was to evolve through five cycles of increasing
self-awareness: the Nigger, the Negro, the Militant, the Nationalist, and
the Revolutionary. Theatre performers and the audience undertook this
spiritual journey together.

A Revival (1969) written by Charlie Russell, author of Five on the Blackhand Side (1969), remained in NBT's repertory for five years. The Street
and the Temple – a two-part liberation – intermingled audience and the
actors in mutual interaction. A Revival informed both the spirit and the
mind. "We are only 11 percent of the population of the United States," Teer
informed the audience/congregation, "but we drink more than 49 percent of
the scotch and 25 percent of the grape soda; we spend $200 million on suits
and $8 million on ties." Audiences were mostly black, although everyone
was welcome. Richard Schechner, after attending a performance, indicated
that he had never felt threatened by being the only White present.

The great test of Teer's tenacity came when her theatre building burned
down. She and the members of NBT built a new one. She had seen very
early on that to survive in community theatre meant owning the land
and the building, and if possible owning other income property that
would feed the theatre. Teer launched a bed-and-breakfast residency for
tourists and others who wished to attend one of America's unique theatres.
In spite of all these efforts, the NBT found itself in debt as it entered the
millennium.

A summary of eleven survival strategies

In 1973 the Black Theatre Alliance counted 139 "professional" theatres around the nation. In 2001 it was estimated that no more than fifty existed. The theatres that survived into the 1980s and 1990s shared common traits. First, the founders with artistic visions remained in control for at least ten and often for twenty years. Second, the leadership possessed a vision that planned for the future, understood budgets and financial planning. Third, all the theatres claimed dedication to black culture, playwrights, and actors; however, they welcomed Whites at the box office. Fourth, all the theatres had roots in their surrounding communities to the extent that many functioned as community centers, offering classes in the arts. Fifth, several directors expressed an intention to educate the audience, that is, to bring them new experiences. Toward this end discussions after performances with the actors and director were common. Sixth, all the theatres produced at least one play per season celebrating black history.[114] Seventh, most theatres produced original plays, fostered playwriting contests, and presented readers' theatres. Eighth, most companies sought additional income through touring productions. This in turn gave them national and even international recognition. Ninth, the ensembles either owned their own space or worked under an umbrella organization, such as a community center, that provided rent stability. Tenth, four of the theatres reached agreements with the AEA to use at least some union actors and stage managers. Finally, most theatres made use of celebrities, particularly their own "graduates"; however, the primary focus remained on their own black community. Stanley Williams of the Lorraine Hansberry Theatre of San Francisco dissented: "As a black theatre artist, I did not want to be located in a neighborhood that was predominantly black. I want the whitest audience possible to see our work."[115] While no theatre supported itself entirely from box-office receipts, all built predominantly black subscription audiences.

On the slippery side, most organizations still depended upon government grants and the largesse of corporations and foundations. Although several theatres in the 1990s for the first time ended the season with budget surpluses, for many, bankruptcy always hovered near. Some worried that economic survival had been achieved at the sacrifice of spirit, that the rush to join the American stock market economy had taken a serious toll on the soul of black theatre, that black theatre's historic concern with oppression had shifted too far toward mindless television comedy and the deadly violence of film. But then hadn't serious drama always been the underdog when it competed with popular entertainment? And finally, hadn't the plays of August Wilson, Ntozake Shange, Adrienne Kennedy, and others kept black theatre's soul alive?

Final thoughts

A thoroughly integrated American theatre history has yet to be written, although the third volume of this Cambridge series took long steps in that direction. The authors of this book devoutly hope that the materials assembled here will make it possible for future scholars to write about American Theatre without either ignoring the contributions of African Americans or relegating them to token paragraphs.

While racism has continued to deny Blacks access to money, stages, recognition, the old nemesis had grown weaker as black consciousness and confidence has grown. African American performance, literary and popular, celebrated the year 2000 with an astounding history of "We're still here and more alive than ever!"

The authors are pleased to have offered something of black theatre's record.

Appendix: theatre scholarship 2002

James V. Hatch

Because we of black theatre history have never been integrated into American theatre history, keeping our own histories and bibliographies has been a necessity. From Hilda Lawson's theatre treatise in 1939 to the year 1960, fewer than twenty black dissertations had been written, but by 1975 there were a hundred, and two decades later nearly three hundred. In the early 1970s black theatre research became academically respectable, releasing a flood of criticism and anthologies. Almost no collection of black plays had been published since the 1930s, but in the late 1960s and early 1970s more than thirty collections of plays appeared, three times the number published earlier. Among the first was William Couch's *New Black Playwrights* (1968). Bullins and Baraka followed with anthologies of their own plays, and four other anthologies joined theirs: William R. Reardon and Thomas Pawley, *The Black Teacher and the Dramatic Arts* (1970), a seminal book in bibliography; Darwin Turner, *Black Drama in America* (1971); Clinton Oliver and Stephanie Sills, *Contemporary Black Drama* (1971); and William Brasmer and Dominick Consolo, *Black Drama* (1970). Only three anthologies survived into the millennium: Lindsay Patterson, *Black Drama* (1971); Woodie King and Ron Milner, *Black Drama Anthology* (1972); and *Black Theater USA* (1974) edited by Ted Shine and James V. Hatch.

Soon black women edited their own play collections by gender: Sydné Mahone, *Moon Marked and Touched by Sun* (1994); Kathy A. Perkins, *Black Female Playwrights* (1989); Elizabeth Brown-Guillory, *Wines in the Wilderness* (1990); Margaret Wilkerson, *Nine Plays by Black Women* (1986); and Kathy A. Perkins and Roberta Uno, *Contemporary Plays by Women of Color* (1996). Women also entered the market with collections organized by genre: Pamela Jackson, *Black Comedy: Nine Plays* (1997); Winona Fletcher, *The Lorraine Hansberry Playwriting Award* [Plays] (1996); and

Kathy A. Perkins and Judith Stephens, *Strange Fruit* (women's dramas about lynching, 1998).

Texts of contemporary dramas burgeoned: Woodie King Jr. and Ron Milner, *New Plays for the Black Theatre* (1989); Woodie King Jr., *The National Black Drama Anthology* (1995); Paul Carter Harrison, *Totem Voices* (1989); Eileen Joyce Ostrow, *Center Stage: 21 Contemporary Black-American Plays* (1981). The Negro Ensemble published *Classic Plays* (1995) from its past repertoire followed by William Branch's *Black Thunder* (1992) and *Crosswinds* (1993); Harry J. Elam and Robert Alexander published *Colored Contradictions* (1996), an anthology from the more avant garde writers. Author anthologies joined the parade: *New/Lost Plays by Ed Bullins* (1993), *Three Plays by August Wilson* (1991), and *Adrienne Kennedy in One Act* (1988).

In the 1980s anthologies of black history plays claimed attention. Errol Hill's *Black Heroes: 7 Plays* was published in 1989. Alain Locke and Montgomery Gregory's *Plays of Negro Life* (1927) was reissued. Christine Gray reedited Willis Richardson's *Plays and Pageants from the Life of the Negro* (1930). Forgotten or ignored plays from the Renaissance were born again in James V. Hatch's and Leo Hamalian's *The Roots of Black Drama* (1993), and *Lost Plays of the Harlem Renaissance, 1920–1940* (1996). Importantly, Leslie Sanders and Nancy Johnson edited Langston Hughes' *The Plays to 1942* (2002).

Doris Abramson had traced the production histories of plays in her *Negro Playwrights in the American Theatre, 1925 to 1959* (1967). In that same year Loften Mitchell published *Black Drama, The Story of the American Negro in the Theatre*, which remained the only general history book for three decades. Bill Reed's *Hot From Harlem: Profiles in Classic African-American Entertainment* (1998) provided rich anecdotal material on black music, dance, and theatre, particularly in Los Angeles. James Haskins' *Black Theater in America* (1982), along with his many biographies of stars and their famous venues, for example, *The Cotton Club* (1977), did much to popularize the rich heritage, particularly for young people. In the final decades of the century black theatre histories reinterpreted the underreported past. Many questions that had haunted the African Company from the 1820s were answered by George A. Thompson Jr.'s *A Documentary History of the African Theatre* (1998), a brilliant model for theatre scholarship. A wealth of hidden history emerged in Errol Hill's *Shakespeare in Sable: A History of Black Shakespearean Actors* (1984). In like manner, Professor Jo A. Tanner's *Dusky Maidens* reintroduced a host of black actors who had "disappeared" from the chronicles of nineteenth-century stages. These texts documented the talents and courage of James Hewlett, Morgan Smith, Laura Bowman, Inez Clough, and so many more. David Krasner's *Resistance, Parody, and Double Consciousness in African American Theatre, 1895–1910* (1997) presented a refreshing interpretation of the ragtime musicals and the performances of Ada (Aida) Walker, her husband George, and Bert Williams.

Minstrelsy emerged from its restless grave largely due to Eric Lott's *Love and Theft, Blackface Minstrelsy and the American Working Class* (1993), which sparked a number of reinterpretive studies: Dale Cockrell's *Demons of Disorder* (1997), William J. Mahar's *Behind the Burnt Cork Mask* (1999), and Annemarie Bean and colleagues' *Inside the Minstrel Mask* (1996), to name only three. Henry T. Sampson's diligence in examining hundreds of old black newspapers for his two books *Blacks in Blackface* (1980) and *The Ghost Walks* (1988) must be noted, for he recorded evidence of neglected black performance from minstrelsy through the Harlem Renaissance, including data about theatre people and events that had long been "forgotten."

One scholar in particular deserves mention for assembling the basic data on which history must rely: Bernard Peterson Jr. (1927–2000), a retired librarian living in Elizabeth, North Carolina, annotated nearly every playwright, theatre, musical, and play, as well as many, many actors. His five bibliographies have made black theatre research possible. Other contributors of bio-bibliography include Edward Mapp and Allen Woll. These texts and others encouraged the offering of survey courses in black theatre history.

Although criticism and theory could not keep pace with the flood of plays and production, unshackled debate crowded the pages of journals. Debates were brisk and sometimes virulent, but they stimulated the posing of key questions: what was Black Theatre? did it have a separate aesthetic? who was its audience? who should write its criticism? what was theatre's fundamental purpose?

A book by Paul Carter Harrison, *The Drama of Nommo* (1972), provided an original examination of the Afrocentric theories that lay behind black drama; a second book with wider philosophical approaches was Carleton W. and Barbara J. Molette's *Black Theatre: Premise and Presentation* (1986). Samuel A. Hay's *African American Theatre, A Historical and Critical Analysis* (1994) examined basic questions and issues by tracing the parallels and contradictions in black theatre from the African Theatre in the 1820s to the 1990s. Woodie King Jr.'s *Black Theatre: Present Condition* (1981) laid out a comprehensive plan for survival in the 1980s. Another important text, *Drumbeats, Masks, and Metaphor* (1983) by Geneviève Fabre, placed the theatre of the 1960s and 1970s in a sociological context. One of the early books to confront the struggle of playwrights in terms of "creating a national literature" was Leslie Sanders' *The Development of Black Theater in America: From Shadows to Selves* (1988). Sanders saw the problems of African American writers to be similar to those artists of color in neo- and postcolonial countries, where the writers were forced to redefine themselves by using the language and theatre of the oppressor. The reexamination of black theatre in the nineteenth century forced a reinterpretation of the twentieth. These much-needed studies provided a historical continuity.

The final decades of the twentieth century saw a renewed interest in the past. The Harlem Renaissance evoked several cultural summaries: Nathan Huggins' *Harlem Renaissance* (1971); Bruce Kellner's *The Harlem Renaissance. A Historical Dictionary for the Era* (1984); Jervis Anderson's *This Was Harlem* (1981); David Levering Lewis' *When Harlem Was in Vogue* (1981); and Richard Long's *Grown Deep: Essays on the Harlem Renaissance* (1998). A valuable reprint was Anthony D. Hill's editing of the *Pages from the Harlem Renaissance, A Chronicle of Performance* (1996), a republication and interpretation of J. A. Jackson's theatrical columns from *Billboard*, a unique record of black performances from 1920 to 1925. David Krasner's *A Beautiful Pageant, African American Theatre, Drama, and Performance in the Harlem Renaissance, 1910–1927* provided insights neglected by others.

Professor Lorraine Brown of George Mason University recovered the Federal Theatre Project archives (1935–39) and was most generous in sharing her discoveries. Important black theatre studies emerged from the archives: E. Quita Craig's *Black Drama of the Federal Theatre Era* (1980) and Rena Fraden's *Blueprints for a Black Federal Theatre 1935–1939* (1994). A third book contained photos of some black productions: John O'Connor and Lorraine Brown's *Free, Adult, and Uncensored: The Living History of the Federal Theatre Project* (1978). Glenda E. Gill published *White Grease Paint on Black Performers: A Study of the Federal Theatre* (1988).

Errol G. Hill brought many issues together in his seminal collection of critical and historical essays, *The Theatre of Black Americans* (1980). Publishers also reaped profits from other critical studies: Stephen R. Carter's *Hansberry's Drama* (1995), Deana Thomas' *Barbara Ann Teer and the National Black Theatre* (1998); Sandra G. Shannon's *The Dramatic Vision of August Wilson*; and Neal Lester's *Ntozake Shange, a Critical Study of the Plays*. Harry J. Elam Jr. and David Krasner's *African American Performance and Theater History* (2001), an anthology, covered a wide range of history and performance arts by recognized authorities, as did Annemarie Bean's

A Sourcebook of African-American Performance: Plays, People, Movements (1999).

In general, theatre autobiographies suffered the reputation of being promotional ("And then I played..."). Even many of the biographies written as "told to" suffered from self-promotion, with few objective evaluations. As the century neared its end, an increasing number of critical biographies and autobiographies graced the shelves. Among them were Sidney Poitier's *This Life*, Ruby Dee and Ossie Davis' *In This Life Together*, Samuel A. Hay's *Ed Bullins, a Literary Biography* (1997), James V. Hatch's *Sorrow is the Only Faithful One: The Life of Owen Dodson* (1993), and Gordon Heath's *Deep are the Roots* (1992). Eric Ledell Smith wrote a well-researched biography, *Bert Williams* (1992). Nadine George-Graves' *The Royalty of Negro Vaudeville* (2002) provided the first biographical history of The Whitman Sisters.

Following the *Drama Review*'s "Black Theatre" issue in 1968, a flood of black arts and theatre journals appeared, led by the New Lafayette Theatre, whose journal *Black Theatre* (1968–72), reaching an estimated eight thousand subscribers, became the most influential. A host of bulletins, newsletters, and reviews published short plays and theatre articles; some were white, some black, but nearly all were subsidized by universities or government funding: *Black Dialogue*, *Black Creation*, *Black Lines*, *Callaloo*, *Obsidian*, *Scripts*, and *Theatre*. From Washington, DC, came *Black Stage* (1973–74); from the Inner City Cultural Center in Los Angeles came *Neworld* (1975–80). Every April (1968–74), *Black World* (formerly *Negro Digest*) published a theatre issue devoted to essays and plays by critics and artists. Beginning in the 1970s, the Black Theatre Alliance published its *Newsletter*, reporting the activities of production groups. Each week the New York *Amsterdam News* published a half-page of current black performances and shows. The deluge of print resulted in black theatre becoming *au courant*, particularly with young people and students, much as black films would become in the 1990s. Many college-age African Americans who had never considered writing, acting, or directing in the theatre seized upon the latest theatre issues, many of which were funded more by enthusiasm than planning; consequently publications often disappeared after one or two issues. Nonetheless these journals provided inspiration and confirmation that a new era had dawned. In a word, theatre not only absorbed the energy from the civil rights movement, it helped sustain it.

Two black journals emerged: *Black Masks*, with Beth Turner as editor and publisher, furnished scholars of contemporary theatre with ten issues a year from 1984 to 2003. Black Theatre Network (BTN) published *BTNews*.

The philosophical roots of BTN lay in the Negro Intercollegiate Dramatic Association, which was founded in 1930 by Professor Randolph Edmonds.[1] Evolving through a series of black college drama associations, Black Theatre Network officially began in 1986. Thirteen years later it published *Black Theatre's Unprecedented Times*, 124 pages documenting a new and vital vision for black theatre across America. So-called mainstream theatre journals, too, sought out articles about black drama and performance. Black theatre has not only survived, the "fabulous invalid" has given vital transfusions of talent and energy to American theatre.

Notes

Introduction

1. Natalie Angier, "Do Races Differ? Not Really, Genes Show," *New York Times*, 22 August 2000, Science Times section, p. F1. Dr. Venter and National Institute of Health scientists working on the human genome say apparent differences among people dissolve when one looks beneath the skin.

2. Journalist-historian Lerone Bennett Jr. puts the figure lost to Africa at roughly 40 million, made up as follows: 20 million taken to the New World; another 20 million died during capture, after capture, on ships, and on plantations. See his *Before the Mayflower: A History of Black America*, 5th edn (Harmondsworth: Penguin, 1984), p. 29.

3. ibid., p. 31.

4. ibid., p. 32. Quotation attributed to Mary Wilhelmina Williams.

5. Germán Arciniegas, *Caribbean: Sea of the New World*, trans. Harriet De Onís (New York: Alfred A. Knopf, 1946), pp. 26–27.

6. ibid.

7. A contract awarding exclusive rights to import African bondsmen into colonies for the nation that held it. The contract was held successively by Portugal, Holland, France, and England. Spain was barred by papal bull from transporting slaves from Africa but in return was given large areas of the New World to be colonized.

8. Several new colonies changed hands frequently as the fortunes of European governments waxed and waned. The Windward Islands of Grenada, St. Vincent, St. Lucia, and Dominica were fought over by France and England; both Jamaica and later Trinidad were governed by Spain and conquered by the English. The classic and only successful overthrow of a colonial regime by its black slaves took place in St. Domingue, which was renamed Haiti. After French duplicity removed its trusting black leader, Toussaint l'Ouverture, and attempts to subdue the rebellion failed, the country was denied help by wealthier nations as a form of punishment. It remains one of the poorest independent black nations on earth.

9. Sylvia Wynter, "Bernardo de Balbuena: Epic Poet and Abbot of Jamaica, 1562–1627," *Jamaica Journal* 3 (September 1969): 3, p. 5.

10. The treasure in gold and pearls, which was calculated at 150,000 ducats, was reportedly stolen by the pirate Giovanni da Verrazano (nicknamed Juan Florentin).

It had been sent to Charles V of Spain, who was elected Holy Roman Emperor in 1519. The emperor ordered Verrazano hanged when he was captured.

11. One source indicated that the emperor rejected Spanish sovereignty and conversion to the Christian faith by tossing to the ground the Bible handed to him by a priest.

12. The late 1960s to early 1970s was a period of great unrest on American college campuses. At Dartmouth white students had destroyed symbolic shanties placed on the college green in support of divestment in South Africa. The show had opened but black students decided to withdraw from the production as one form of protest. In a tense discussion with the faculty director (Errol G. Hill), the students eventually agreed to perform on one condition: that in the very next show involving Blacks, they would no longer be the victims. In their own words: "We will no longer be losers, we must win." In 1972 Genet's *The Blacks* seemed to satisfy their demand.

13. A similar displacement of Native Americans from their traditional homelands to less hospitable "reservations" would occur with the expansion of the English colonies of North America, especially after they won independence from Britain in 1776 and became the United States of America.

14. In 1998 a hereditary paramount chief of the Lokono Arawaks published an article in the *Barbados Advocate* asserting that "in 1492 there were ten Amerindian tribal nations in the West Indian islands." Four were Arawak clans: the Lokono (not Lucayo), the Shiba-Lokoni (not Ciboney), the Taino, and surviving remnants of Taim. They mostly inhabited the Bahamaian islands, and also Hispaniola, Cuba, Jamaica, and Puerto Rico. In addition there were six Karifuna Carib clans whose lands stretched from eastern Puerto Rico to Trinidad and Tobago. See "Last Arawak Princess Buried in Barbados," *Barbados Advocate*, 23 March 1998, p. 9.

15. *Caribs* is said to be a misnomer given by Europeans, the correct name for this group being *Karina* for men and *Karifuna* for women. See Lennox Honychurch, *The Dominica Story: A History of the Island* (Dominica: Dominica Institute Press, 1975), p. 19. Present-day descendants of exiles in Belize, Central America, call themselves the *Garifuna*.

16. Sylvia Wynter, "New Seville and the Conversion Experience of Bartolomé de Las Casas," *Jamaica Journal* 17 (May 1984): 2, pp. 25–32. It should be noted that as early as 1502 the new governor of the Indies had recommended the introduction of African slave labor while in 1511 the Dominican priest Antonio Montesinos had openly preached against slavery in any form.

17. Prior to the seventeenth century black Africans imported to tropical America averaged fewer than two thousand. By the eighteenth century the figure had risen to more than sixty thousand a year. See Daniel C. Littlefield, "The Atlantic Slave Trade: An Overview," in *Encyclopedia of African-American Culture and History*, vol. v, ed. Jack Salzman, David Lionel Smith, and Cornel West (New York: Macmillan Library Reference, 1996), p. 2472.

18. It can justly be called the 350-year Holocaust of African people, and there is still no memorial.

19. Some historians give the headroom allowed below deck as an incredible 15 inches.

20. Presumably deaths occurred from sickness, suicide, and revolt. Conditions were much worse in the nineteenth century, when the trade moved to East Africa where slaves were cheaper and "slaving captains said they could make a profit on the voyage

if they landed half of their cargo alive." See Daniel P. Mannix in collaboration with Malcolm Cowley, *Black Cargoes: A History of the Atlantic Slave Trade, 1518–1865* (London: Longmans, Green, 1963), p. 247.

21. See the program for the fifth anniversary season of the Chelsea Theatre. It contains a short glossary of Yoruba terms for the benefit of the audience.

22. See Littlefield, "Atlantic Slave Trade," p. 2472.

23. Quoted in Robert F. Engs, *Freedom's First Generation: Black Hampton, Virginia, 1861–1890* (Philadelphia, PN: University of Pennsylvania Press, 1979), pp. 86–87. See also *Richmond (VA) Dispatch*, 25 February 1865.

1 Slavery and conquest: background to black theatre

1. "Slavery" in *Black Women in America: A Biographical Encyclopedia*, ed. Darlene Clark Hine, 2 vols. (Brooklyn, NY: Carlson, 1993), pp. 1045–1070.

2. Lerone Bennett Jr., *Before the Mayflower: A History of Black America*, 5th edn (Harmondsworth: Penguin, 1984), p. 442.

3. In the two hundred years from 1663 to 1864 there were "at least 109 slave revolts" that occurred on land and some 55 mutinies on slave ships between 1699 and 1845. See C. Eric Lincoln, *The Negro Pilgrimage in America* (New York: Bantam, 1969), p. 159.

4. Quoted in Garry Wills, *Inventing America: Jefferson's Declaration of Independence* (New York: Doubleday, 1978), p. 67.

5. The presumed inferiority of Blacks apparently did not deter Jefferson from an on-going intimate relationship with the slave woman Sally Hemings, who bore his children.

6. See *New York Times*, 17 May 1999, p. A12, and 14 May 2000, p. I16.

7. See George Varga, "Jefferson's Sallygate gets an off-Broadway Show," *San Diego Union-Tribune*, 27 January 1999, Lifestyle section, p. E-6.

8. Towards the end of the eighteenth century owners of slaving vessels based in Liverpool made annual profits amounting to £300,000; those who supplied the "trade goods" used in exchange for slaves cleared an additional £140,000.

9. The Trinidad scholar C. L. R. James, while researching for his book on the Haitian revolution entitled *The Black Jacobins* (1938), wrote a play named after the black slave leader *Toussaint l'Ouverture* (1936). It was presented by the London Stage Society in March 1936 for two performances at the Westminster Theatre, with the American actor Paul Robeson in the title role.

10. John Hope Franklin and Loren Schweninger, *Runaway Slaves: Rebels on the Plantation* (Oxford: Oxford University Press, 1999). From an excerpt in *American Visions* (August/September 1999): pp. 18–25.

11. It is possible that the breeding of black bondsmen could have been encouraged in Virginia and other states, in order to supply the perceived need of cotton-growing southern states for additional slave labor.

12. Ironically, the Haitian slave uprising may have been inspired as much by the American revolution of 1776 as by the French version of 1789. It is known that a group of black Haitians participated on the side of America in 1776, among them Henri Christophe, who succeeded Dessalines as king of Haiti.

13. See Herbert Aptheker, *American Negro Slave Revolts*, 5th edn (New York: International Publishers, 1983).

14. The role of Yale University faculty, alumni, and students in a successful attempt to free the Africans is documented in a permanent exhibit, which was installed in 1996 in the vestibule of Battell Chapel, New Haven. It forms part of the Connecticut Freedom Trail. See *Yale Alumni Magazine* (November 1997): p. 80.

15. Lerone Bennett Jr., *Pioneers in Protest* (Harmondsworth: Penguin, 1968), pp. 170–177. Three of the men were left in the farmhouse as a rear guard.

16. James V. Hatch, ed., *Black Theatre USA: Forty-five Plays by Black Americans, 1847–1974* (New York: Free Press, 1974), p. 587.

17. First published in *Negro History in Thirteen Plays*, ed. Willis Richardson and May Miller (Washington, DC: Associated Publishers, 1935).

18. In addition, according to the *Los Angeles Times* of 10 March 1985, Gordon Davidson of the Mark Taper Forum staged *Harriet, the Woman Called Moses* by Scottish-born Thea Musgrave. The musical consisted of "authentic period tunes, folksongs, and spirituals [woven] into a romantic portrait of Harriet Tubman."

19. On some Caribbean islands runaways would form viable communities, such as the "maroons" of Jamaica, who retreated to secure mountain plateaus from where they would carry out raids on the plantations below. Often the government would be forced to accept the status quo and reach a peace pact with the leaders of the maroons.

20. Evarts B. Greene and Virginia D. Harrington, *American Population Before the Federal Census of 1790* (New York: Columbia University Press, 1993).

21. Colin A. Palmer, "The First Passage, 1502–1619," in *To Make Our World Anew: A History of African Americans*, ed. Robin D. G. Kelley and Earl Lewis (Oxford: Oxford University Press, 2000), pp. 46–47.

22. Loren Schweninger, "The Free Slave Phenomenon: James P. Thomas and the Black Community in Ante-Bellum Nashville," *Civil War History* 22 (1976): 4, pp. 293–307.

23. Schweninger (ibid.) explained that even upper-class white aristocrats opposed educating Blacks, who they felt might forge passes to escape or might be planning revolt. He reported that at "about 1837 a free Negro teacher...was taken out by white toughs and whipped nearly to death. Such occurrences were common."

24. ibid., p. 303.

25. Errol G. Hill, ed., *The Theatre of Black Americans*, 2 vols. (1980; reprinted in one volume, New York: Applause Theatre Books, 1987).

26. ibid., pp. 30–44.

27. ibid., pp. 45–60.

28. ibid., pp. 89–98.

29. ibid., pp. 99–111.

30. ibid., pp. 13–29.

2 The African Theatre to Uncle Tom's Cabin

1. In the records Brown was always referred to simply as "Mr. Brown." Scholars seeking his full name came up with different combinations until it was finally established by historian George A. Thompson Jr. in his *Documentary History of the African*

Theatre (Chicago, IL: Northwestern University Press, 1998). We are indebted to this work for many facts reported in this chapter and acknowledge Mr. Thompson's continuing generosity in sharing his ongoing research.

2. According to an article of 1860 by Dr. James McCune Smith, who was at the time a youth in the city. But Thompson suggests that the Grove might have been in existence for only one or two years before it was closed by the city authorities. See Herbert Marshall and Mildred Stock, *Ira Aldridge: The Negro Tragedian* (1958; reprinted, with an introduction by Errol G. Hill, Washington, DC: Howard University Press, 1993), p. 31; Thompson, *Documentary History*, p. 6.

3. The Colley Cibber version, which was very popular at the time.

4. Marshall and Stock, *Ira Aldridge*, p. 31.

5. *National Advocate*, 29 September 1821, p. 2. Noah's critiques were mostly couched in the language of ridicule, which makes their reliability questionable.

6. Samuel Hay, *African American Theatre: An Historical and Critical Analysis* (Cambridge: Cambridge University Press, 1994), pp. 6–14.

7. Hay (ibid., pp. 8–10) argues that Brown may have deliberately chosen to open his theatre with *Richard III*, knowing that the Park Theatre would be offering the same play on its reopening and had engaged the English actor Junius Brutus Booth, who had recently migrated to America, for the lead. Hay also alleges that Stephen Price, in league with Sheriff Noah, was determined to close down the African Theatre, whose growing popularity with both black and white audiences reduced box office income at the Park.

8. Equivalent to 12.5 pennies.

9. Kean had played in New York in the spring of 1821 and there had been mention in the newspapers of his impending return. See *Commercial Advertiser*, 10 August 1822, p. 2.

10. It is possible that the name "American Theatre" on the printed notice was either a printer's error or a deliberate act of subversion by a detractor.

11. Thompson, *Documentary History*, pp. 92–96.

12. *Commercial Advertiser*, 17 August 1822, p. 2. The entire episode is covered in Thompson, *Documentary History*, pp. 99–112.

13. Thompson, *Documentary History*, pp. 90, 112.

14. ibid., p. 124.

15. "The History of Tom and Jerry," *London Era*, 27 March 1870, p. 11.

16. The text was published in England in 1819 and in New York in 1820, when it was marked "as performed at the New-York Theatre." The play was also staged in Philadelphia when Mr. Wallack – probably James – and his brother Henry Wallack both played leading roles.

17. Playbill information reproduced in Thompson, *Documentary History*, p. 136. Despite the announcement Thompson suggests, in a letter to author Hill dated 2 September 1998, that Brown may not have actually written a playscript but instead have dictated the story line to Hewlett and other cast members, who then developed the action and dialogue through improvisation under Hewlett's direction.

18. I. E. Kirby and C. I. Martin, *The Rise and Fall of the Black Caribs of St. Vincent* (Kingstown, Saint Vincent and the Grenadines: St. Vincent and the Grenadines National Trust, 1972), p. 10.

19. As early as 1769, British commissioners reporting on the continuing strife between English settlers and Black Caribs recommended to the Lords of Trade and Plantations that it would be very dangerous to allow the Caribs to remain in their present state, as it is difficult to gain access to them "for the purpose of executing justice." According to the commissioners, the Caribs harbored slaves of the settlers, sheltered vagabonds and deserters from the French, and, in case of war with France, would distress the settlers and attempt to conquer the country. See ibid., p. 27.

20. Hay, *African American Theatre*, p. 239 n. 22. In a lecture titled "Mr. Brown of the African Company in New York," held in Baltimore 18 April 1985, Hay suggested that Brown might well have been one of the Black Caribs.

21. Thompson, *Documentary History*, p. 130.

22. H. P. Phelps, *Players of a Century: A Record of the Albany Stage*, 2nd edn (Albany, NY: J. McDonough, 1880), p. 56.

23. *Klinck's Albany Directory* for 1823 and T. V. Cuyler's *Albany Directory* for 1824 and 1825. State Street, a main artery in the city, was intersected by Market; the Columbian Hotel at 559 South Market could not have been more than a few blocks away from Brown's residence.

24. Thompson, *Documentary History*, pp. 150–151.

25. *Nottingham and Newark Mercury* (England), 22 May 1830. Copied from a report entitled "The Negroes of New York" in *Family Magazine*. Excerpt furnished by Professor Bernth Lindfors of the University of Texas at Austin. Professor Lindfors has generously shared with us his research on Ira Aldridge.

26. *Tatler* 260 (4 July 1831): p. 11. Item contributed by Professor Lindfors.

27. *New York Evening Post*, 2 June 1830, p. 2; and Thompson, *Documentary History*, pp. 45, 192. The substance was most likely nitrous oxide, also known as "laughing gas."

28. Thompson, *Documentary History*, p. 207. By 1837 Hewlett's fame, or infamy, had reached other parts of the country. When the Marigny Theatre for "people of color" was founded in New Orleans, the *Times-Picayune* of 4 February 1838 advised the manager "to send for Hewlett, the colored tragedian, and open with 'Othello, or, the Jealous Nigger.'" Reference kindly furnished by Professor Tisch Jones of the University of Iowa.

29. After the African Theatre closed, Hewlett advertised his solo performances claiming that he had worked at the Coburg Theatre in London. No evidence has been found to support this claim.

30. *Port-of-Spain Gazette* (Trinidad), 13, 17, and 24 December 1839; *Times* (London), Sunday, 29 March 1840. Initial reference furnished by Professor Lindfors.

31. *New York American*, 27 April 1826, p. 3, col. 1.

32. Thompson, *Documentary History*, pp. 75–80.

33. "Ira Aldridge," *Anglo-African Magazine* 1 (January 1860): pp. 27–32. Aldridge may not have wanted to advertise his appearances with the African Theatre. His father wished him to become a preacher and did not approve of his son's interest in the theatre.

34. Aldridge had worked backstage as dresser for Henry Wallack, James' brother, when the former played at the Albany Street Theatre in May 1821, the Park Theatre being rebuilt at the time.

35. *Times* (London), 11 October 1825; *Globe*, 11 October 1825; and *Drama*, November 1825.

36. *Theatrical Observer* 1480 (2 September 1826): p. 1.

37. Bernth Lindfors, "The Signifying Flunkey: Ira Aldridge as Mungo," *International Journal of Black Expressive Culture Studies* 5 (fall 1993): pp. 1–11.

38. Marshall and Stock, *Ira Aldridge*, p. xvii.

39. In his essay "'Nothing Extenuate, Nor Set Down Aught in Malice': New Biographical Information on Ira Aldridge," Bernth Lindfors suggests that Aldridge was kept off the London stage for most of his career because his humble origins were known there and his intimacies with white women were greatly resented. See *African American Review* 28 (1994): 3, pp. 457–472.

40. Marshall and Stock, *Ira Aldridge*, p. 125–126.

41. *Globe*, 11 April 1833; *National Omnibus and General Advertiser*, 19 April 1833, p. 29.

42. Marshall and Stock, *Ira Aldridge*, pp. 213–214.

43. ibid., p. 311.

44. *Negro Heritage* 1 (1962): 23, p. 92.

45. With the possible exception of Charleston, South Carolina, where early playbills for some theatres stated: "People of Color cannot be admitted to any part of the House." See James H. Dormon Jr., *Theater in the Ante-Bellum South, 1815–1861* (Chapel Hill, NC: University of North Carolina Press, 1967), p. 233 and n. 11.

46. Edward Ingle, "The Negro in the District of Columbia," *Johns Hopkins University Studies in Historical and Political Science*, 11th series (March/April 1893): pp. 47–48.

47. Lyla Hay Owen and Owen Murphy, *Créoles of New Orleans: People of Color* (New Orleans: First Quarter Publishing, 1987), p. 102; Dormon, *Theater in the Ante-Bellum South*, p. 236.

48. Thompson, *Documentary History*, p. 209. Professor Tisch Jones of the University of Iowa furnished material on the Marigny Theatre.

49. Reprinted in *Frederick Douglass' Paper* (continuation of *North Star*), 3 June 1853. We assume the arrest took place some time in the previous month.

50. Q. K. Philander Doesticks [Mortimer Neal Thomson], *Doesticks: What He Says* (New York: E. Livermore, 1855), pp. 313–322. Since no other reference to this theatre has been found, we conclude that humorist Thomson based his article on the African Theatre, whose existence remained in public memory. Reference furnished by George Thompson Jr.

51. ibid., pp. 316–322.

52. Thomas D. Pawley, "The First Black Playwrights," *Black World* 21 (April 1972): pp. 16–25.

53. Bernard L. Peterson Jr., *Early Black American Playwrights and Dramatic Writers: A Directory and Catalog of Plays, Films, and Broadcasting Scripts* (Westport, CT: Greenwood Press, 1990), p. 173. For an English translation of Séjour's one-act comedy "The Brown Overcoat," see James V. Hatch and Ted Shine, eds., *Black Theatre USA: Plays by African Americans*, revised and expanded edn (New York: Free Press, 1996), pp. 25–34.

54. William Edward Farrison, *William Wells Brown: Author and Reformer* (Chicago, IL: University of Chicago Press, 1969), p. 294.

55. Hatch and Shine, *Black Theatre USA*, p. 36.

56. Doris E. Abramson, review of *The Escape; or, A Leap for Freedom. Educational Theatre Journal* 24 (1972): pp. 190–191.
57. The play *Clotield: The President's Daughter*, written by Pearl M. Graham, was based on Wells Brown's novel, *Clotel; or, The President's Daughter: A Narrative of Slave Life in the United States* (London: Partridge and Oakey, 1853). It examined the life of the elder of two sisters, the alleged daughters of Thomas Jefferson by a slave owned by John Graves. In the novel Clotel chose to drown herself in the Potomac in order to escape being captured and returned to slavery. "Clotield" in Graham's title was apparently a misnomer. It was the name of the last known slave ship to transport Blacks to America, its cargo having been off-loaded at Mobile, Alabama, in 1859.
58. *Cleveland (OH) Gazette*, 22 November 1884.
59. Rosemary L. Cullen names fifteen such plays, beginning with Bickerstaffe's *The Padlock*, first performed in the United States by Lewis Hallam at the John Street Theatre in New York in 1769, and ending with *Uncle Tom's Cabin* in 1852. See *The Civil War in American Drama Before 1900: Catalog of an Exhibition, November 1982* (Providence, RI: Brown University Press, 1982), pp. 1–10.
60. Robert Montgomery Bird, "The Gladiator," in *Dramas from the American Theatre, 1762–1909*, ed. Richard Moody (Cleveland, OH: World Publishing, 1966), p. 254. The role of Spartacus was played by the American actor Edwin Forrest.
61. Florence Polatnick, "An Historical Perspective," in *Showcasing American Drama: Uncle Tom's Cabin*, ed. Vera Jiji (Brooklyn, NY: Humanities Institute, Brooklyn College, 1983), p. 17.
62. Moody, *Dramas from the American Theatre*, p. 350.
63. In "The Origins of Uncle Tom's Cabin," Charles Nichols contends that the chief source for Stowe's novel was Richard Hildreth's *The Slave; or, Memoirs of Archy Moore* (1836), and cited a number of parallels. See his article in *Phylon* 19 (1958): 3.
64. The conspiracies were led by three black slaves and one free white male. Their names and dates are Gabriel Prosser in 1800, Denmark Vesey in 1822, Nat Turner in 1831, and John Brown in 1859. They were all convicted and hanged, along with certain of their associates. The two mutinies took place on the *Amistad* in 1839 and the *Creole* in 1841. Public appeals for a general revolt by slaves were made in Boston by David Walker in an antislavery pamphlet published in 1829 and by Henry Highland Garnet in 1843 in a speech to the American Anti-Slavery Convention.
65. J. C. Furnas, *Goodbye to Uncle Tom* (New York: W. Sloane Associates, 1956), p. 271. The "coon songs" were not so designated until much later in the nineteenth century.
66. George C. D. Odell, *Annals of the New York Stage*, vol. XII, *1882–1885* (New York: AMS Press, 1970), p. 164. By the end of 1852 London had eight productions running, including an "equestrian drama on the subject" at Astley's Amphitheatre in November and a pantomime version at the Drury Lane Theatre in December. See Harry Birdoff, *The World's Greatest Hit: Uncle Tom's Cabin* (New York: S. F. Vanni, 1947), pp. 148–149.
67. Furnas, *Goodbye to Uncle Tom*, p. 283.
68. Quoted in Herbert Aptheker, ed., *A Documentary History of the Negro People in the United States*, vol. II (1951; 4th paperback edn, New York: Citadel Press, 1968), p. 655.
69. ibid., p. 657.

70. *Indianapolis Freeman*, 24 September 1892.
71. W. E. B. Du Bois, *The Souls of Black Folk: Essays and Sketches* (1903; reprinted Greenwich, CN: Fawcett Publications, 1961), pp. 146–147.
72. Alain LeRoy Locke, ed., *The New Negro* (1925, reprinted New York: Atheneum, 1969), p. 5.
73. ibid., pp. 30–31.
74. ibid., p. 155.
75. *New York Herald Tribune*, 29 May 1933.
76. ibid., 29 October 1936.
77. Thomas Wentworth Higginson, *Black Rebellion; A Selection from Travellers and Outlaws* (1889; reprinted New York: Arno Press, 1969), p. 55.

3 The Civil War to The Creole Show

1. Francis G. Peabody, *Education for Life: The Story of Hampton Institute* (Garden City, NY: Doubleday, 1918), p. 4.
2. Although 1 January 1863 is generally accepted as the date on which black slaves were freed in America, it was really the beginning of a process not legally completed until December 1865. Even so, Lincoln's declaration in January 1863 did not reach Texas until 15 June of that year. Curiously, most formerly enslaved Blacks chose "Juneteenth" as the date to celebrate the end of chattel slavery.
3. For Civil War data I am mostly indebted to Lerone Bennett, Jr., *Before the Mayflower: A History of Black America*, 5th edn (Harmondsworth: Penguin, 1984), pp. 187–213.
4. S. Morgan Smith, *A Critical Review of the Late Speech of Charles O'Conor, "Negro Slavery Not Unjust"* (Philadelphia: n.p., [1865?]).
5. William Norris, "New Light on the Career of S. Morgan Smith," *Black American Literature Forum* 18 (fall 1984): 3, p. 118.
6. ibid.
7. The sudden change of climate, the absence of a comforting spouse, and the care of their infant son were too much to bear. There is no word of what happened to the child, who might have been placed in a home for orphans.
8. The Chevalier St. George was a colored man born in 1717 on the island of Martinique, French West Indies, of a liaison between a Black and an aristocratic White. Sent to France at an early age, he received a first-class education and excelled in everything he undertook, as violinist, composer, playwright, actor, swordsman, etc. He died in 1799.
9. Morgan Smith would hope to find work during the summer at one of the popular London playhouses. Possibly he would also be able to visit his son.
10. See James M. Trotter, "Paul Molyneaux," *New York Globe*, 28 April 1883. A good part of our data comes from this article. Although we have traced no family connection, it is of interest that "America's first great boxer" was a Black named Tom Molyneux, whose dates are 1784–1818.
11. ibid.
12. P. A. Bell's first appearance in a play. He may have been related to George W. Bell and, substituting for him in an emergency, acquitted himself well except for the

dying scene, when, according to a reviewer, he took ten minutes to expire. George Bell did perform in the 31 December revival.

13. *San Francisco Pacific Appeal*, 21 and 26 November and 31 December 1870.

14. *San Francisco Pacific Appeal*, 1 April 1876, p. 2.

15. See "California Theatre," *San Francisco Pacific Appeal*, 31 December 1870, p. 2.

16. See Errol G. Hill, "The Hyers Sisters: Pioneers in Black Musical Comedy," in *The American Stage: Social and Economic Issues from the Colonial Period to the Present*, ed. Ron Engle and Tice L. Miller (Cambridge: Cambridge University Press, 1993).

17. Extract from manuscript copy 34821, Rare Book Room, Library of Congress, Washington, DC.

18. *Los Angeles Times*, 21 February 1890.

19. *Portland (OR) Oregonian*, 22 April 1879, reprinted in *San Francisco Pacific Appeal*, 8 May 1879.

20. The diamonds were insurance against disaster and could be pawned to bail out a company if it were stranded on the road.

21. *St. Paul (MN) Western Appeal*, 23 May 1891. There were several companies of Nashville Students, a name made popular by association with the Fisk University Singers from Nashville, Tennessee. The troupe referenced was formed and managed in the 1890s by P. T. Wright, who died in March 1898 at age 40.

22. The drama was also entitled *The Slave's Escape* or *Escape from Slavery* in various issues of the press.

23. See "Sam Lucas' Theatrical Career Written by Himself in 1909," *New York Age*, 13 January 1916.

24. Anna Madah had two further marriages: one to Harry Stafford, stage manager, master of transportation, and electrician for Isham's *Octoroons*, and the other in retirement to the chiropodist Dr. Fletcher. Emma Louise remarried once, to actor Walter Espy, after the death of Freeman.

25. The records reveal one other marriage ceremony on stage: that of Jodie "Butterbeans" Edwards and Susie Hawthorne in a Greenville, South Carolina, theatre on 15 May 1917, for which the couple received a fee of $50.

26. Henry T. Sampson, *The Ghost Walks: A Chronological History of Blacks in Show Business, 1865–1910* (Metuchen, NJ: Scarecrow Press, 1988), p. 199.

27. Eileen Southern, ed., *African American Theater: "Out of Bondage" (1876) and "Peculiar Sam; or, The Underground Railroad" (1879)* (New York: Garland, 1994), p. 52.

28. See *San Francisco Argonaut*, 5 April 1879, and *Chicago Inter-Ocean*, 21 March 1889.

29. See *New York Age*, 14 April 1888, for a list of leading characters. A review of the 1888 staging, published in the *Boston Herald* and reprinted in the *Cleveland Gazette* of 17 March, credited James H. W. Howard with authorship of the drama. Howard had in fact written and published in 1886 a narrative with a similar title, namely, *Bond and Free: A True Tale of Slave Times*.

30. *New York Globe*, 29 March 1884.

31. The Francophone names may well have belonged to Arneaux's actor friends, who had also joined the troupe.

32. *New York World*, 2 January 1887, p. 12.

33. *New York Freeman*, 7 November 1884.

34. Quoted in William J. Simmons, *Men of Mark: Eminent, Progressive, and Rising* (Cleveland, OH: O. G. M. Rewell, 1887), p. 489.
35. See reviews and correspondence in *New York Freeman*, 6 November 1886, 5 and 12 February 1887; *Cleveland Gazette* of 20 November 1886, 5 and 19 February 1887.
36. Why was Richard III popular with Blacks? Possibly because he was double-faced, as they had to be to survive; he also represented victory for the underdog at a time when Blacks began to experience their "winter of discontent" as Reconstruction ended; and there was genuine interest in comparing various character portrayals by British and American actors.
37. In most instances, only the author and title of a play are given in the press notice, except in the case of a production, when an additional short report may be offered.
38. *New York Age*, 31 December 1887 and 30 November 1889.
39. *New York Age*, 14 April 1888; *St. Paul (MN) Western Appeal*, 28 April and 20 October 1888.
40. *Cleveland Gazette*, 4 February 1888.
41. *Cleveland Gazette*, 29 September 1888.
42. *New York Age*, 22 September 1888; *Indianapolis Freeman*, 23 March 1889.
43. Davis, Strange, and Wood were all accomplished actors and monologists of Shakespeare's plays. For a fuller treatment than is possible here, see Errol G. Hill, *Shakespeare in Sable: A History of Black Shakespearean Actors* (Amherst, MA: University of Massachusetts Press, 1984).
44. *Washington (DC) Bee*, 21 July 1883.
45. *Cleveland Gazette*, 6 January 1884.
46. The fair was open for six months, from May 1 to October 31. Eventually a controversial Colored American Day was held on 25 August and presided over by Frederick Douglass, who had been appointed by the Haitian government to manage its exhibition pavilion. After the fair the antilynching activist Ida B. Wells published an 81-page booklet entitled *The Reason Why the Colored American is Not in the World's Columbian Exposition: The Afro-American's Contribution to Columbian Literature* (Chicago: n.p., 1893).
47. *Colored American Magazine*, September 1902.
48. See Hill, *Shakespeare in Sable*, pp. 57–61.
49. *Report on the Population of the United States at the Eleventh Census, 1890* (Washington, DC: Government Printing Office, 1897), part 2, table 82, p. 355. The report further revealed that close to 1 million "Negro persons" were attending school during the census year.
50. When in 1916 composer Harry Burleigh published a collection of spirituals under the title *Jubilee Songs of the United States of America*, his object was "to preserve them in harmonies that belong to modern methods of tonal progression without robbing the melodies of their racial flavor." See Eileen Southern, *The Music of Black Americans: A History* (New York: W. W. Norton, 1971), p. 287.
51. Interviewed by the critic Sylvester Russell for the *Indianapolis Freeman*, 7 October 1905, on the use of the word *coon* in popular songs, Bob Cole found its use to be "very insulting and must soon be eliminated." Asked why he had named his own comedy *A Trip to Coontown*, Cole replied obliquely that "the day had

passed with the flowing tide of revelations." See Sampson, *Ghost Walks*, pp. 349–350.

52. ibid., p. 71.

4 American minstrelsy in black and white

1. In 1834, when Jamaica emancipated its slaves, many black families carried their masters' Irish names. They then emigrated to the United States. Others married and intermixed with the Irish in Boston, New York, Baltimore, and Cincinnati.

2. Leni Sloan, "Irish Mornings and African Days on the Old Minstrel Stage," *Callahan's Irish Quarterly* 2 (1982): p. 3.

3. With great fanfare and publicity, the Rainer family quartet from Austria billed themselves as "Tyrolese Family Minstrels" and toured widely on the east coast from 1839 to 1843.

4. Examples of Virginny farces are *Oh Hush! or; The Virginny Cupids* (1833), *The Yankee Peddler* (1834), and *The Virginny Mummy* (1835).

5. A description of the Virginia Minstrels' historic performance can be found in Hans Nathan, *Dan Emmett and the Rise of Early Negro Minstrelsy* (Norman, OK: University of Oklahoma Press, 1962), pp. 118–122.

6. Thomas W. Talley, *Negro Folk Rhymes* (New York: Macmillan, 1922), p. 232. Equally arresting is Talley's reference to "Possum up the Gum Stump." We know that English comedian Charles Mathews parodied actor Ira Aldridge's New York performance of "Possum" in 1822. Whether that event allegedly seen at the African Theatre is true or not, Mathews' naming of the song suggests that southern rural songs were known in the North as early as the 1820s, and their influence passed into white minstrelsy.

7. Dale Cockrell, *Demons of Disorder: Early Blackface Minstrels and their World* (Cambridge: Cambridge University Press, 1997), pp. 15–16.

8. William J. Mahar, "'Backside Albany,' and Early Blackface Minstrelsy: A Contextual Study of America's First Blackface Song," *American Music* 6 (1988): 1, pp. 1–88. Hopkins Robinson in 1815 blackened up to sing "Backside Albany," recounting the Battle of Lake Champlain and prompting the audience to laugh at the British naval defeat in the war of 1812. One must ask, why was the British defeat funnier when sung by a white actor in blackface? Earlier claims that Andrew Allen was that actor are contradictory and confusing.

9. Eric Lott, *Love and Theft: Blackface Minstrelsy and the American Working Class* (Oxford: Oxford University Press, 1993), p. 69.

10. *Narrative of the Life of Frederick Douglass* (1845) sold 30,000 copies by presenting a vivid account from childhood to his escape from bondage.

11. W. T. Lhamon, Jr., "Ebery Time I Wheel About I Jump Jim Crow: Cycles of Minstrel Transgression from Cool White to Vanilla Ice," in *Behind the Minstrel Mask*, ed. Annemarie Bean, James V. Hatch, and Brooks McNamara (Middletown, CN: Wesleyan University Press, 1996), p. 277.

12. The rise of white fear of competition, rebellion, and retribution came ironically as the proportion of New York Blacks dwindled from nearly 8 percent at the beginning of the century to less than 3 percent in the 1830s.

13. Brenda Dixon Gottschild, *Digging the Africanist Presence in American Performance: Dance and Other Contexts* (Westport, CT: Greenwood Press, 1997), p. 97.

14. Marian Hannah Winter, "Juba and American Minstrelsy," *Dance Index* (1947), p. 31.

15. Marshall Stearns and Jean Stearns, *Jazz Dance: The Story of American Vernacular Dance* (New York: Macmillan, 1968), p. 45. Lane's handbill suggests other mercurial performances given by Michael Jordan on the basketball court, Muhammad Ali in the ring, and Tiger Woods on the golf course as examples of the African aesthetic of "cool."

16. Winter, "Juba and American Minstrelsy," p. 38.

17. Jacqui Malone, *Steppin' on the Blues: The Visible Rhythms of African American Dance* (Urbana, IL: University of Illinois Press, 1996), p. 54. In contemporary times Malone's observations might be verified by Savion Glover's tap styles in George C. Wolfe's *Bring in 'Da Noise, Bring in 'Da Funk* (1996), and his dancing in Spike Lee's film *Bamboozled* (2000).

18. An early performance was at the Varieties Theatre in New Orleans, when the manager demanded a lively march for the drill team of forty female Zouaves. The orchestra conductor selected "Dixie," a nickname for New Orleans as well as for the $10 bill with a large "Dix" printed on the side issued by a bank in New Orleans.

19. Howard L. Sacks and Judith Rose Sacks, *Way up North in Dixie* (Washington, DC: Smithsonian Museum Press, 1993), pp. 159–160.

20. In 1997 the Virginia legislature voted that Bland's song no longer be the official anthem of the state.

21. Karen Linn, *That Half-Barbaric Twang: The Banjo in American Culture* (Urbana, IL: University of Illinois Press, 1991), pp. 43–44.

22. Harry Reynolds, *Minstrel Memories: The Story of Burnt Cork Minstrelsy in Great Britain from 1836 to 1927* (London: Alston Rivers, 1928), pp. 201–202.

23. Linn, *That Half-Barbaric Twang*, p. 45. Linn suggests that the enduring appeal of southern plantation ideology with the "darky" and his banjo offered a nostalgic alternative to the violent images of the Wild West and the materialism of the industrial North. In any case, by the end of the nineteenth century the guitar, with its possibility for harmonic chords, had replaced the banjo.

24. The bones should not be confused with the "jaw bone," an instrument of African origin, which was played by clicking a stick over the jawbone teeth from a mule or horse. The popular minstrel song "De Ole Jaw Bone" was of black origin.

25. Henry Louis Gates, Jr., "A Black Lecture on Language," in *The Signifying Monkey: A Theory of Afro-American Literary Criticism* (Oxford: Oxford University Press, 1988), pp. 94, 95.

26. Published sheet music of the 1820s and 1830s reveals a high rate of borrowing from immigrants' speech, black and white, because Americans found humor in their struggle with language. As the number of dialect songs grew, authenticity in transcription diminished. The same pattern held for black speech. For an opposing view as to whether black dialect in minstrel skits was racist, see William J. Mahar, *Behind the Burnt Cork Mask: Early Blackface Minstrelsy and Antebellum American Popular Culture* (Urbana, IL: University of Illinois Press, 1999), pp. 59–100.

27. The early printed speeches found in white skits, stump speeches, and dialogues were apparently borrowed from a variety of sources: immigrant and regional dialects, manufactured malapropisms, general American English from the lower classes, and African phonology. The latter, in turn, stemmed from three forms: West African pidgin English; plantation Creole; and American black English vernacular, a form developing from the days of slavery. William J. Mahar, "Black English in Early Blackface Minstrelsy: A New Interpretation of the Sources of Minstrel Show Dialect," *American Quarterly* 37 (1985): p. 261. The appreciation of black English had to wait for the publication of stories and novels by Charles Chestnut and Zora Neale Hurston, as well as the plays of Willis Richardson and, more recently, August Wilson.

28. Shane White, "A Question of Style: Blacks In and Around New York City in the Late Eighteenth Century," *American Folklore* 102 (1989): 403, p. 30.

29. David Krasner, *Resistance, Parody, and Double Consciousness in African American Theatre, 1895–1910* (New York: St. Martin's Press, 1997).

30. Sexual boasting, however, survived in folklore toasts until the late twentieth century, when rap lyrics placed it near the top of the commercial music chart.

31. Anna Cora Mowatt's *Fashion* (1845) ridiculed the *nouveau riche* who substituted manners for morals; her main comic device was an illiterate blackfaced servant named Zek.

32. Robert C. Toll, *Blacking Up: The Minstrel Show in Nineteenth-Century America* (Oxford: Oxford University Press, 1974), pp. 198, 275.

33. Booker T. Washington, *A New Negro for a New Century; an Accurate and Up-to-Date Record of the Upward Struggles of the Negro Race* (Chicago, IL: American Publishing House, 1900).

34. Although some notices and reviews can be uncovered in the *New York Globe* and the *Indianapolis Freeman*, most coverage appeared in white periodicals, particularly the trade paper, the *New York Clipper*.

35. Jack Shalom, "The Ira Aldridge Troupe: Early Black Minstrelsy in Philadelphia," *African American Review* 28 (1994): 4, pp. 653–657.

36. ibid.

37. Colonel W. Higginson, *Army Life in a Black Regiment* (1870; reprinted East Lansing, MI: Michigan University Press, 1960).

38. Apparently they were still without surnames; Lee advertised them as John, James, Stephen, Pompey, Julius, Josh, Ginger, and Master Neil.

39. Henry T. Sampson, *The Ghost Walks: A Chronological History of Blacks in Show Business, 1865–1910* (Metuchen, NJ: Scarecrow Press, 1988), p. 30.

40. *New York Globe*, 26 May 1883.

41. Sampson, *Ghost Walks*, p. 264.

42. Toll, *Blacking Up*, p. 201.

43. *Norwich (CT) Bulletin*, 15 March 1884.

44. Reynolds, *Minstrel Memories*, pp. 161–164.

45. According to minstrel historian Colonel T. Allston Brown, Brooker and Hicks listed themselves as proprietors. *New York Clipper*, 22 September 1912.

46. *Hamburger Nachrichten*, 11 February 1870.

47. Richard Waterhouse, *From Minstrel Show to Vaudeville: The Australian Popular Stage, 1788–1914* (Kensington, Australia: New South Wales Press, 1990), pp. 52–53.

48. In the next generation, Harlem Renaissance entertainers adorned their handbills with résumés of performances before royalty. Later generations entertained the Pope at the Vatican, a venue that impressed the folks at home.

49. *New York Clipper*, 2 September 1872.

50. Tom Fletcher, *One Hundred Years of the Negro in Show Business* (New York: Burdge and Company, 1954), p. 71.

51. *Seattle Herald*, 5 September 1881.

52. The Fisk Jubilee story was retold in the musical *Train is Comin'* (1998) by McKinley Johnson, produced by the St. Louis Black Repertory Company. The eleven singers used thirty songs from the era.

53. We are indebted to Sandy Graham's unpublished paper "Spirituals in Minstrel Shows," 1996, HBC.

54. George Bailey Sansom, *The Western World and Japan: A Study in the Interaction of European and Asiatic Cultures* (New York: Alfred A. Knopf, 1950), p. 280. Apparently minstrel shows by navy men were not all that rare. In 1897 the Naval Minstrels from the USS *Monterey* performed at the Seattle Theatre, and in 1911 the crew of the USS *Pennsylvania* performed at the same theatre for the Moose Lodge.

55. Sampson, *Ghost Walks*, pp. 30–31.

56. Waterhouse, *From Minstrel Show to Vaudeville*, p. 76.

57. Eileen Southern, who relied heavily upon Ike Simond's *Reminiscences*, names the members of his troupe, which included musicians.

58. Toll, *Blacking Up*, p. 212.

59. Booker T. Washington, "Interesting People: Bert Williams," *American Magazine* 9 (1910): pp. 600–604.

60. *Music and Drama*, 7 June 1888.

61. Sampson, *Ghost Walks*, pp. 73–74.

62. *Redding (CA) Daily News*, 16 September 1896.

63. During and after the Civil War the arming of African Americans had been opposed by Whites who maintained that Blacks were incapable of military engagement. Possibly some of the rumors had been inspired by New England Election Day antics by local militias. In any case, the Union forces remained reluctant to provide guns to Blacks until the North had suffered terrible battle losses. When finally armed, Blacks proved brave and capable warriors; however, the myth of cowardice and incompetence remained on the white minstrel stage.

64. After minstrelsy dissolved, African Americans continued the tradition of marching bands in their black colleges. The marching and dancing Grambling University band promoted as much pride as its football team. One may also speculate that the high-stepping drum majors of the 1870s carried their strutting into the cakewalk of the 1890s.

65. Twenty years later, Bert Williams used the drum routine in the first act of *In Dahomey* (1902).

66. Henry T. Sampson, *Blacks in Blackface: A Source Book on Early Black Musical Shows* (Metuchen, NJ: Scarecrow Press, 1980), pp. 401–402.

67. The following were among the terms offered by the Middletown, Connecticut, Opera House to the Haverly minstrel show "The Blackbirds of the Nation" for Tuesday, 11 March 1884: the Opera House would furnish a license, stagehands, ushers, stage furniture, and properties in-house, bill posting and distributing, newspaper advertisements, ticket sellers, advance sales, billboard, twenty-five straight-back chairs, and assistance in moving all baggage in and out of theatre. The Haverly Minstrels would furnish orchestra, brass band, perishable properties, door tenders, tickets, and all printing necessary for the proper advertisements of entertainment. Haverly was to receive 75 percent of the gross and the Opera House would receive 25 percent. A $50 to $75 deposit was required of the company to hold the date. Kit Clarke, "Haverly Minstrel Press Book," 1883–84 (HRHC).

68. *New York Clipper*, 9 May 1873.

69. W. C. Handy, *Father of the Blues* (New York: Macmillan, 1941), p. 44.

70. Sampson, *Ghost Walks*, p. 277.

71. ibid., p. 190.

72. Sacks and Sacks, *Way up North in Dixie*, p. 127. The Zouaves had become popular during the Civil War, when they fought on the Union side. After the war many militia drill teams from lodge societies adopted the uniform. A case in point, the Blacks formed the Mount Vernon Zouaves and paraded in honor of the Fifteenth Amendment's ratification in 1870. Later, Zouaves were added to Wild West shows.

73. Sampson, *Ghost Walks*, p. 195.

74. *Seattle Intelligencer*, 16 February 1902.

75. Sampson, *Ghost Walks*, p. 458.

76. *Pacific Commercial Advertiser*, 17 March 1900.

77. Jim Magus, *Magical Heroes: The Lives and Legends of Great African American Magicians* (Marietta, GA: Magus Enterprises, 1995). The biographies of many black magicians, including the first, ventriloquist Richard Potter (1783–1835), and women prestidigators Ellen E. Armstrong and Madame Sapphirra, are found here.

78. The *Freeman* of 3 October 1903 stated: "the work of Cooper the ventriloquist justified any and all claims that had been made for him." On 27 February 1909, *Variety*, a white publication seldom friendly to colored talent, stated incorrectly that Cooper was the first colored ventriloquist of record. The remainder of *Variety*'s review was condescending. A positive biographical sketch can be found in Stanley Burns, *Other Voices: Ventriloquism from BC to TV* (privately published, 2000).

79. Sampson, *Ghost Walks*, p. 287.

80. Reynolds, *Minstrel Memories*, p. 206.

81. When Haverly returned to the United States in 1881, the company divided into Haverly's Colored Minstrels and Callender's United Colored Minstrels. Again, Hicks lured the troupe away from Callender, and, in turn, lost it again, this time to Charles and Gustave Frohman, who bought Haverly Colored Minstrels and merged it with Callender's to form Callender's Colored Minstrel Carnival.

82. *New York Age*, 15 August 1915.

83. *New York Clipper, c.* 1887.

84. Hosea Easton (banjo), Billy Saunders (end man), and O. T. Jackson (tenor) rejoined Hicks in Australia.

85. Very possibly this play was Tom Taylor's *Ticket-of-Leave (Man)*, a four-act mid-Victorian melodrama.
86. Sampson, *Ghost Walks*, p. 279.
87. *Owl* (Cape Town, South Africa), 28 August 1897.
88. Sampson, *Ghost Walks*, p. 133.
89. Denis Martin, *Coon Carnival: New Year in Cape Town: Past to Present* (Cape Town, South Africa: David Philip Publishers, 1999). Black theatre history could benefit from a study comparing South African Coon Carnival, Jamaican Jonkonnu troupes at Christmas, New Orleans masking at Mardi Gras, and Ghanaian concert salons.
90. Sampson, *Ghost Walks*, p. 201.
91. *New York Clipper*, 4 November 1871.
92. In 1893 at the Chicago World's Fair, Mahara's Minstrel Carnival hired Leroy Bland (no relation to composer James Bland) to impersonate Black Patti, the opera star.
93. Sampson, *Blacks in Blackface*, p. 434.
94. ibid.
95. ibid.
96. ibid.
97. Sampson, *Ghost Walks*, p. 183.
98. Stearns and Stearns, *Jazz Dance*, p. 88.
99. Dewey Markham, "Pigmeat," interview by Tony Bruno, tape recording, 18 April 1972, in *Artist and Influence* 13 (1994).
100. *Evening Post*, 31 August 1899.
101. *Indianapolis Freeman*, 17 March 1906.
102. When M. B. Curtis abandoned his company of fifty, leaving them stranded in Australia, it was Hogan who held them together. Initially, the American consul sent the troupe to Auckland, where it was arranged that they would sail to Honolulu. They were delayed for several weeks because the steamship company refused to book passage for the troupe. Hogan brought suit against the Canadian Australian Royal Mail Steamship Company and won a judgment of $2,250. He also reorganized the minstrel company into Hogan's Afro-American Minstrels, whose management he shared with the magician Carl Dante. They performed in Honolulu to rave reviews.
103. *Indianapolis Freeman*, 29 December 1906. He may have been the inspiration for the De Dion poster of the period that featured a black chauffeur driving with a white woman beside the Mediterranean Sea.
104. Sampson, *Ghost Walks*, p. 245.
105. ibid., p. 275.
106. *Pacific Commercial Advertiser*, 17 January 1902.
107. *St. Louis (MO) Star*, 7 May 1904, quoted in Sampson, *Ghost Walks*, p. 318.
108. Sampson, *Ghost Walks*, p. 385.
109. Bill Reed, *"Hot from Harlem": Profiles in Classic African-American Entertainment* (Los Angeles, CA: Cellar Door Books, 1998), p. 54. Another report of his death placed it in 1949 and possibly not by fire.
110. Brander Mathews, *A Book about the Theater* (New York: Scribner's Sons, 1916), pp. 219–233.

5 New vistas: plays, spectacles, musicals, and opera

1. Henry T. Sampson asserts that productions of this period gave black actors an opportunity to play dramatic roles and credits "the brilliant Billy McClain" as an agent for change. See his *The Ghost Walks: A Chronological History of Blacks in Show Business, 1865–1910* (Metuchen, NJ: Scarecrow Press, 1988), p. 71.

2. ibid., pp. 94, 97, and 99.

3. ibid., p. 92.

4. Robert W. Rydell, *All the World's a Fair: Visions of Empire at American International Expositions, 1876–1916* (Chicago, IL: University of Chicago Press, 1984), p. 66.

5. Robert Muccigrosso, *Celebrating the New World: Chicago's Columbian Exposition of 1893* (Chicago, IL: Ivan R. Dee, 1993), p. 146. There were other days at the fair reserved for specific ethnic groups.

6. At the opening night's performance reviewed in the *Freeman* of 9 September 1893, Dessalines was played by William H. Barker, whose performance was judged as "fair" and lacking spirit. However, the playscript published in 1893 by J. W. Burston carried several pictures of Scottron as Dessalines in appropriate costume and settings with matching captions. I presume that the experienced actor Scottron replaced Barker early in the run.

7. Robert J. Fehrenbach, "William Edgar Easton's *Dessalines*: A Nineteenth-Century Drama of Black Pride," *CLA Journal* 19 (September 1975): 1, pp. 75–89.

8. Some say in New Bedford, Massachusetts.

9. *Indianapolis Freeman*, 21 November 1896. One coauthor was probably G. F. Richings, who wrote *Evidences of Progress Among Colored People*, 12th edn (Philadelphia, PN: G. S. Ferguson, 1905). He may have helped to recruit the racially integrated cast.

10. Reported in the *Washington (DC) Colored American*, 14 February 1903, and credited to the *Denver Exchange*. The report gives a play synopsis by acts, a critique, and a detailed list of cast and characters.

11. Lacking proof of a stage production for *The South in Slavery*, it must be assumed that the author converted the script into his new passion play *The Negro*, to be discussed presently.

12. *Indianapolis Freeman*, 14 January 1899, p. 5.

13. I am indebted to Professor John Graziano of the Graduate Center of City University, New York, for factual details in the ensuing discussion.

14. Stuart Berg Flexner, *I Hear America Talking: An Illustrated History of American Words and Phrases* (New York: Simon and Schuster, 1976), p. 54.

15. At the time Blacks were not permitted to own guns and some carried a razor as a form of protection.

16. Eileen Southern, *The Music of Black Americans: A History* (New York: W. W. Norton, 1971), p. 314.

17. There is confusion about this date. According to Miss Irwin's capsule biography in *Who's Who on the Stage 1908* (ed. Walter Browne and E. De Roy Koch [New York: B. W. Dodge, 1908]) she became a star in *The Widow Jones* (1895–96) when "she began the coon-song singing which has added materially to her popularity." During the next season she was successful as a star in *The Swell Miss Fitzwell* (1896–97), and in the following season (fall 1897) she appeared in *Courted into Court*. Even

so, Gerald Bordman in *American Musical Theatre: A Chronicle* (Oxford: Oxford University Press, 1978) reports that Miss Irwin was a big hit in two songs "added to the play," one of which was Hogan's "All Coons." Possibly she did not actually perform the song on stage until the second season (fall 1898).

18. See Roger Allan Hall, "Black America: Nate Salsbury's Afro-American Exhibition," *Educational Theatre Journal* 29 (March 1977): 1, pp. 49–60.
19. *Boston Sunday Herald*, 14 July 1895, p. 10.
20. *Washington (DC) Post*, 27 October 1895, p. 19.
21. ibid.
22. See program for performance of *Darkest America* at the New Park Opera House in Erie, Pennsylvania, 5 February 1897.
23. *Pottsville (PN) Miners Journal*, 27 November 1897. Quoted in Sampson, *Ghost Walks*, p. 137.
24. Henry T. Sampson, *Blacks in Blackface: A Source Book on Early Black Musical Shows* (Metuchen, NJ: Scarecrow Press, 1980), pp. 61–62.
25. *Indianapolis Freeman*, 3 July 1897.
26. Sampson, *Blacks in Blackface*, pp. 64–65.
27. R. W. Thompson, "The Mirror Up to Nature," *Indianapolis Freeman*, 19 December 1896.
28. Sampson, *Blacks in Blackface*, p. 380; Allen Woll, *Black Musical Theatre: From Coontown to Dreamgirls* (Baton Rouge, LA: Louisiana State University Press, 1989), p. 12.
29. I again acknowledge the generosity of Professor Graziano, biographer of Mme. Jones, for sharing with me his ongoing research.
30. In June 1899, Mme. Matilda S. Jones obtained a divorce from her husband, David P. Jones, at Providence, Rhode Island, on the grounds of nonsupport. The press notice stated they had been married for five years. See Sampson, *Ghost Walks*, p. 179.
31. Mme. Jones did not appear at the controversial Colored People's Day but instead sang at a later date at the Women's Pavilion.
32. Professor Graziano explained that Mme. Jones' public appearances that summer were at outdoor gardens seldom covered by newspaper critics.
33. The company changed directors quite often. Among others who served in that capacity after Cole and Hogan were J. Ed. Green, Salem Tutt Whitney, and Tim Owsley.
34. The Philippines were newsworthy at the time as a result of the 1898 Spanish-American war, when Spain abandoned claims to Puerto Rico, Cuba, Guam, and the Philippines.
35. See Sampson, *Ghost Walks*, pp. 242–243, 323, and 423.
36. Rosamond Gilder *et al.*, eds., *Theatre Arts Anthology* (New York: Theatre Arts Books, 1950), pp. 227–233.
37. *Indianapolis Freeman*, 27 November 1897, p. 3.
38. Tom Fletcher, *One Hundred Years of the Negro in Show Business* (New York: Burdge and Company, 1954), p. 103.
39. *Huntsville (AL) Daily Mercury*, 18 and 19 January 1887.
40. *Indianapolis Freeman*, 4 March 1899, p. 4.

41. *St. Louis (MO) Globe-Democrat*, 28 November 1897.
42. *New York Herald*, 23 January 1897.
43. Dunbar was fast becoming recognized as a major poet of the race, celebrated for his "negro dialect verses." He was also known as a novelist and short-story writer when he died in 1906, at the early age of 34.
44. *New York World*, 20 June 1905.
45. Thomas L. Riis, "'Bob' Cole: his Life and his Legacy to Black Musical Theater," *Black Perspective in Music* 13 (fall 1985): 2, pp. 135–150.
46. ibid., p. 137.
47. Worth's Museum was located at Fourth Avenue and Thirtieth Street.
48. Riis, "'Bob' Cole," p. 138.
49. I am indebted to Dr. Jewel Plummer Cobb, research scientist, president of the California State University at Fullerton, and a relative of Bob Cole, for supplying photocopies of the clippings and other papers.
50. In the Cole family papers, sister Carriebel affirmed that the real reason for the separation was Johnson's excessive drinking. Riis suggests that Cole had already met the talented Johnson brothers from Florida and could foresee a promising future for himself in musical theatre as a member of their team.
51. Among white leading ladies in musical comedy to use Johnson, Cole and Johnson songs at this time were Anna Held singing "The Maiden with the Dreamy Eyes," Mary Cahill reveling in "Under the Bamboo Tree," and Lillian Russell offering "The Maid of Timbuctoo."
52. See reviews in *New York Age*, 23 August 1906; 13 June, 1 August, and 31 October 1907.
53. See reviews in *Indianapolis Freeman*, 23 March and 5 October 1907; *New York Telegraph*, 5 June 1907.
54. The finale of the show was a rousing song and chorus called "The Old Flag Never Touched the Ground" written by Cole and the Johnsons as a tribute to the 54th Massachusetts Regiment that in 1863 lost the battle for Fort Wagner, South Carolina, but kept the flag flying at the cost of several lives. See Benjamin Brawley, *Negro Builders and Heroes* (Chapel Hill, NC: University of North Carolina Press, 1937), pp. 117–119.
55. *New York Telegraph*, 30 May 1908. At this time brother James Weldon Johnson was posted overseas in the consular service. Cole might well have been spurred by intimations of mortality. In the fall of 1908 George Walker suffered a partial stroke and in a few months was forced to retire from the stage.
56. *North American, Philadelphia Times, Philadelphia Inquirer*, all dated 15 September 1908.
57. Despite their success, Cole and Johnson were still denied access to first-class theatres by their managers and by booking agencies. Was there a conspiracy to keep them out?
58. Cole was apparently diagnosed as suffering from paresis, a symptom of advanced syphilis for which there was at the time no known cure. The family papers include a letter from Cole's sister Dora to Dr. Albert Reed explaining the family's fruitless search to get her brother admitted to a New York sanatorium.

59. Some sources say Antigua, British West Indies. His mother was Antiguan and when in 1918 Williams applied to become a naturalized American he reported that he was born in the Bahamas.

60. See Christopher Reed, *"All the World is Here!" The Black Presence at White City* (Bloomington, IN: Indiana University Press, 2000), p. 160. The author claims that Williams and Walker were at the Chicago World Columbian Exposition – as was Will Marion Cook – listening intently to the music of the Dahomians. But Williams and Walker recalled substituting for the late arriving Dahomians at the San Francisco Midwinter Fair, which followed the Chicago World's Fair. See Walker's article "The Real 'Coon' on the American Stage," *Theatre* (August 1906): p. 224. It is unlikely they were in Chicago during the world's fair, which closed on 31 October 1893; nor has it proved possible to construct a logical itinerary with dates for Williams and Walker's cross-country trip.

61. Quoted in Eric Ledell Smith, *Bert Williams: A Biography of the Pioneer Black Co-median* (Jefferson, NC: McFarland, 1992), p. 21. We are indebted to this work for many of the factual details concerning the productions of Williams and Walker.

62. John Koster and Rudolf Bial managed a popular vaudeville house at Sixth Avenue and 23rd Street. They kept a saloon and allegedly skirted laws against serving alcohol in a theatre.

63. *New York Dramatic Mirror*, 7 November 1896. Quoted in Smith, *Bert Williams*, p. 25.

64. *New York Dramatic Mirror*, 27 February 1897, p. 17.

65. Usually book by J. A. Shipp, lyrics by Paul Laurence Dunbar and/or Alex Rogers, music by Will Marion Cook, directed by Shipp, choreographed by Aida Overton Walker, and additional leading players such as Abbie Mitchell Cook, Lottie Williams, R. Henri Strange, and Hattie McIntosh.

66. *New York Mail and Express*, 19 February 1903, p. 6.

67. Smith, *Bert Williams*, p. 231.

68. "Aida Overton Walker at the Pekin Theatre," *Chicago Defender*, 1 November 1913, p. 8.

69. This may have been deliberate in order to blunt criticism of influential Blacks who opposed the "Back to Africa movement."

70. See Russell's reviews in the *Indianapolis Freeman* as follows: "Williams and Walker Opening," 27 September 1902; "'In Dahomey' A Howling Success," 25 October 1902; and "'Dahomey' In New York," 4 April 1903.

71. Selected for the birthday celebration of the young Prince of Wales, the show was performed on a specially constructed stage in Buckingham Palace gardens.

72. *Sunday Dispatch* (London), 20 May 1903. Cited in Sampson, *Ghost Walks*, p. 296.

73. Smith, *Bert Williams*, p. 90.

74. ibid., p. 92. Walker's insistence on securing first-class theatres on tour was prompted by his belief that their shows deserved no less. He wanted to prove that the black performer was as good as any other and deserved to be treated equally with the best. See Ann Charters, *Nobody: The Story of Bert Williams* (New York: Macmillan, 1970), p. 94.

75. The role of lawyer Blackstone was obviously written for George Walker, whose decision to play the subordinate part of Bud Jenkins raises questions. Had a rift

with Williams developed? Or had Walker sensed symptoms of his then incurable illness?

76. Smith, *Bert Williams*, p. 95. Ann Charters explains that though Walker's wife (Aida Overton) "was beautiful and genuinely talented," he liked variety in love and conducted legendary and open affairs with other women, black and white. See her *Nobody*, p. 89.

77. *Boston Guardian*, 14 January 1911, p. 2.

78. Booking a black show into a first-class house was always problematic: (i) with segregated audiences, too few places were available in the gallery where Blacks were seated; (ii) Whites in the rest of the house would resist having Blacks seated near them; (iii) where first-class theatres were not well patronized their owners preferred to turn them into second-class houses, thus reducing the number of high-priced tickets for the burgeoning black theatre.

79. *New York Age*, 14 August 1913, p. 6. The performance at the City Auditorium in Richmond, Virginia, had the largest audience of the tour. The white reserved section was so overcrowded that many sat with the colored people – an unprecedented occurrence. See Smith, *Bert Williams*, p. 169.

80. Leon Errol, who paired with Williams in the *Follies* of 1910 and 1912, reported that all the authors ever did "was to indicate in a certain point in the manuscript...'a comedy number by Errol and Williams.'" See Charters, *Nobody*, p. 120.

81. ibid., p. 133.

82. Book and lyrics by Walker DeLeon, music begun by Sigmund Romberg but mostly composed by Will Vodery; produced by Al Woods, an associate of the Shubert Company.

83. Smith, *Bert Williams*, pp. 217–219.

84. Mabel Rowland, ed., *Bert Williams: Son of Laughter; a symposium of tribute to the man and to his work, by his friends and associates* (1923; reprinted New York: Negro Universities Press, 1969), pp. 168–169.

85. ibid., pp. ix and xi.

86. Most helpful in this summary of African Americans in opera through the 1930s have been the following studies: Eileen Southern, *The Music of Black Americans: A History* (New York: W. W. Norton, 1971); Eileen Southern, *Biographical Dictionary of Afro-Americans and African Musicians* (Westport, CT: Greenwood Press, 1982); Eric Ledell Smith, *Blacks in Opera: An Encyclopedia of People and Companies, 1873–1993* (Jefferson, NC: McFarland, 1995); Bernard L. Peterson Jr., *Profiles of African American Stage Performers and Theatre People, 1816–1960* (Westport, CT: Greenwood Press, 2001).

87. Hewlett's reputation as a soloist may have been established by earlier performance at the African Grove tea garden, which generated the African Theatre.

88. See documents 13, 26, and 33 in George A. Thompson Jr., *Documentary History of the African Theatre* (Chicago, IL: Northwestern University Press, 1998), pp. 70, 82, and 93 respectively.

89. Of this interregnum in what was a fairly regular schedule of performances Eileen Southern writes: "The company toured briefly but staged most of its productions in New York and surrounding areas." See Southern, "Drury, Theodore," *Biographical Dictionary*, p. 115.

90. ibid.
91. Kwame Anthony Appiah and Henry Louis Gates Jr., eds., *Africana: The Encyclopedia of the African and African American Experience* (New York: Basic Civitas Books, 1999), p. 1460.
92. Southern, *Biographical Dictionary*, p. 30.
93. ibid., p. 173. This writer was privileged to attend a concert performance by Mr. Hayes in Trinidad and can vouch for his purity of tone and effortless delivery.
94. Sterling Stuckey, "The Cultural Philosophy of Paul Robeson," *Freedomways* 11 (1971): 1, p. 81.
95. Paul Robeson Jr., "Paul Robeson: Black Warrior," *Freedomways* 11 (1971): 1, p. 26.
96. Southern, "Robeson, Paul," *Biographical Dictionary*, p. 323.
97. Bernard L. Peterson Jr., *A Century of Musicals in Black and White* (Westport, CT: Greenwood Press, 1993), p. 156.
98. Southern, "Still, William Grant," *Biographical Dictionary*, p. 359.
99. Langston Hughes and Milton Meltzer, *Black Magic: A Pictorial History of the Negro in American Entertainment* (Englewood Cliffs, NJ: Prentice-Hall, 1967), p. 147.

6 The struggle continues

1. John E. Bruce, *The Blood Red Record: A Review of the Horrible Lynchings and Burning of Negroes by Civilized White Men in the United States, as Taken from the Records* (Albany, NY: Argus Company, 1901). Reprinted in Herbert Aptheker, ed., *A Documentary History of the Negro People in the United States*, vol. 11 (1951; 4th paperback edn, New York: Citadel Press, 1968), pp. 800–803.
2. James Weldon Johnson, *Black Manhattan*, chapter 12 (New York: Alfred A. Knopf, 1930), pp. 126–127. James Weldon and his brother, J. Rosamond Johnson, were partners of Bob Cole and James had written lyrics for some of the songs used in their shows.
3. In 1955 the "fiendishly mutilated body" of a 14-year-old Chicago boy missing on a visit to Mississippi was found in the state's Tallahatchie River. In a hard-hitting denunciation of such crimes, Louis E. Burnham published in December that year a pamphlet which states: "if all the rivers, swamps and woodlands of the Southern countryside could recount the tales of the tens of thousands of Negro bodies thrust into watery graves . . . their story would be too horrible for decent humanity to hear." Reprinted in *Freedomways* 2 (winter 1962): 1.
4. James Weldon Johnson, *Along This Way: The Autobiography of James Weldon Johnson* (Harmondsworth: Penguin, 1933), pp. 317–318.
5. Ida B. Wells was born a slave in Holly Springs, Mississippi, in 1862. She lost both parents to yellow fever in the 1878 epidemic and became a certified teacher in Memphis, Tennessee, at age 22, but was dismissed for criticizing the school board. In 1892, when she denounced in her own newspaper the lynching of three Negro businessmen, an angry mob destroyed her press and threatened to lynch her. She moved north and continued her crusade against lynching in the United States and on visits to Britain. In 1895 Ms. Wells married a Chicago newspaper man and civil

rights activist, Ferdinand L. Barnett. See Alfreda M. Duster, ed., *Crusade for Justice: The Autobiography of Ida B. Wells* (Chicago, IL.: University of Chicago Press, 1970).

6. Aptheker, *Documentary History*, vol. II, p. 798. Excerpted from the *Cleveland Gazette*, 9 April 1898.

7. Ida Forsyne, interview by Cassandra Willis, tape recording, February 1972, HBC.

8. J. E. Hawkins, "The Negro and Chicago, Past and Present," *Chicago Whip*, 8 May 1920. Article continued in issues of 15, 22, and 29 May 1920, and 5 June 1920.

9. Many have asked why was the name "Pekin" chosen? Firstly, there is a city in Illinois called "Pekin." According to the Tazewell County Genealogical Society located in that city, it was named by the wife of Major Cromwell in 1829, the year it was surveyed, "we suppose after the celestial city of that name," i.e., the Chinese capital city of Peking, now called Beijing. A second theory is that the American city was so named because it lies "directly straight through the earth" from the Chinese city.

10. *Chicago American*, 7 October 1906, as quoted in "Only Afro-American Theatre in World," *New York Age*, 18 October 1906.

11. As advertised in the weekly *Salt Lake City (Utah) Broad Axe*, 24 March 1906, p. 4. But in *A Century of Musicals in Black and White* (Westport, CT: Greenwood Press, 1993), Bernard L. Peterson Jr. credited Flournoy E. Miller and Aubrey Lyles with authorship of the script "originally" while Joe Jordan and Will H. Vodery were given credit "originally" for the music.

12. Later shows would run for three weeks instead of two, and popular productions such as *In Zululand* would be revived with new songs replacing some of the original ones.

13. *Chicago American*, as quoted in *New York Age*, 18 October 1906.

14. In his review of the production Lester A. Walton refers to the theatre as the "Harlem Opera House." The question why manager Motts would send two productions to New York in the summer for a one-week showing of each remains a mystery. Did Motts expect someone to buy the shows?

15. The Anita Bush Stock Company would be one of the first such resident black theatre groups in New York City when in 1914 it opened at the Lincoln Theatre in Harlem with the play *The Girl at the Fort*. Several former Pekin (Chicago) players formed part of the company, which transferred to the Lafayette Theatre and was later reconstituted under Charles Gilpin as the Lafayette Players. See Henry T. Sampson, *Blacks in Blackface: A Source Book on Early Black Musical Shows* (Metuchen, NJ: Scarecrow Press, 1980), pp. 120–123.

16. Edward A. Robinson, "The Pekin: The Genesis of American Black Theater," *Black American Literature Forum* 16 (winter 1982): 4, pp. 136–138.

17. "Harrison Stewart," *New York Age*, 9 July 1908.

18. ibid.

19. Peterson, *A Century of Musicals*, p. 137. This item is not mentioned in Green's obituary notices in the *New York Age* of 24 February 1910 or the *Indianapolis Freeman* of 26 February 1910.

20. "A Favorite Performer and Stage Manager," *Indianapolis Freeman*, 15 September 1906.

21. "Only Afro-American Theatre in World," *New York Age*, 18 October 1906.
22. "New Pekin Theater," *Indianapolis Freeman*, 14 November 1908.
23. David Glassberg, *American Historical Pageantry: The Uses of Tradition in the Early Twentieth Century* (Chapel Hill, NC: University of North Carolina Press, 1990).
24. Labor historian David Reihle uncovered the long-forgotten pageant and set forth the complex forces that entered into the making of the *Great Cuba Pageant*. All material in this summary is taken from his article "Three Hundred Afro-American Performers' The Great Cuba Pageant of 1898: St. Paul's Citizens Support the Struggle for Civil Rights," *Ramsey County History* 33 (winter 1999): 4, pp. 15–20.
25. The militant awareness of St. Paul's citizens was reflected in their social organizations: the Nat Turner Lodge, no. 2 of the Knights of Pythias; the John Brown Memorial Association; and the Toussaint l'Overture Dramatic Club.
26. America declared war on Spain on 21 April 1898 ostensibly because of the destruction of the battleship *Maine* in the Harbor of Havana. The war lasted barely three months and resulted in Cuban independence and the American acquisition of the Philippines. Mrs. Jeff Davis, wife of the Confederate president, saw the war "as an expedition on behalf of the 'miserable mulatto race.'"
27. The larger history of this pageant, from which this material is taken, may be read in Freda Scott-Giles, "Introduction to *The Star of Ethiopia*," in *Black Theatre USA: Plays by African Americans*, revised and expanded edn, ed. James V. Hatch and Ted Shine (New York: Free Press, 1996), pp. 87–88.
28. *Indianapolis Freeman*, 27 November 1915. The players in addition to Anita Bush were Carlotta Freeman, Charles Gilpin, Arthur "Dooley" Wilson, and Andrew Bishop.
29. Richard Newman, "The Lincoln Theatre," *American Visions* 6 (August 1991): 4, pp. 29–32.
30. Walton would serve not only as a songwriter and a journalist for black and white newspapers, but also as a theatre manager, a United States diplomat to Liberia, a trustee for the Colored Vaudeville Benevolent Association, a director of publicity for the Colored Division for the Democratic National Commission, and a PR man for Black Swan Records and the promotion of Ethel Waters; he produced Frank Wilson's *Meek Mose* (1928) on Broadway with the dream of establishing a black Broadway repertory company. See chapter 7 below. The variety of eminent positions held by Walton invites comparison to the parallel life of James Weldon Johnson.
31. The summary of Walton's life and critical standards is taken from Paul Nadler, "The Life of Lester A. Walton" (unpublished paper, City University of New York, 1991).
32. John Gilbert Monroe, "A Record of the Black Theatre in New York City: 1920–29" (Ph.D. dissertation, University of Texas at Austin, 1980).
33. Nadler, "Life of Lester A. Walton."
34. *Messenger* 1 (November 1917): 11, p. 30.
35. We owe much of our information on the Lafayette Theatre and its players to Mary Francesca Thompson, "The Lafayette Players 1915–1932" (Ph.D. dissertation, University of Michigan, 1972).
36. Henry T. Sampson, *Blacks in Blackface: A Source Book on Early Black Musical Shows* (Metuchen, NJ: Scarecrow Press, 1980), p. 49.
37. For a detailed account of the TOBA, see: Bernard L. Peterson Jr., *The African American Theatre Directory, 1816–1960: A Comprehensive Guide to Early Black Theatre*

Organizations, Companies, Theatres, and Performing Groups (Westport, CT: Greenwood Press, 1997); Sampson, *Blacks in Blackface;* Anthony D. Hill, *Pages from the Harlem Renaissance: A Chronicle of Performance* (New York: P. Lang, 1996). Hill's book also contains the best biography of J. A. Jackson.

38. A glance at Jackson's "Page" of 21 October 1922 reveals a world of diverse talent.

39. Charles A. Barry, "CAU Facts," *Chicago Defender,* 29 October 1921. See also "Colored Actors Union" pamphlet and Hill, *Pages from the Harlem Renaissance,* pp. 104–105.

40. Theophilus Lewis, "Along the Lines of Equity," *Inter-State Tattler,* 24 August 1928.

41. William E. Clark, "White Stage Hands Attack Colored Employees in Harlem," *New York Age,* 18 March 1922, p. 6.

42. Ethel Waters recorded her experience as an evangelist with the Reverend Billy Graham in her second autobiography, *To Me it's Wonderful* (New York: Harper and Row, 1972).

43. Sampson, *Blacks in Blackface,* pp. 94–96. Although King became a major figure on the TOBA, very little research has been done on his amazing life. The scripts he wrote may have been lost. In all likelihood, many of them were never committed to paper.

44. Sampson, *Blacks in Blackface,* p. 100. "When Whitney started out with the Pugsley Brothers, Louis, the manager of the company, could not remember Salem or Tutt, so he told him he would add Whitney to his last name which he could easily remember as it was the name of a very famous white concert basso, Myron W. Whitney."

45. Nadine George-Graves, *The Royalty of Negro Vaudeville: The Whitman Sisters and the Negotiation of Race, Gender, and Class in African American Theatre, 1900–1940* (New York: St. Martin's Press, 2000). The authors acknowledge their debt to her book.

46. Sampson, *Blacks in Blackface,* p. 457.

47. Walton, "The Negro Players," *New York Age,* 15 May 1913.

7 The Harlem Rennaissance

1. J. A. Rogers, "What are we, Negroes or Americans?" *Messenger* 8 (August 1926): p. 237–238, 253.

2. Nancy J. Weill, *The National Urban League, 1910–1940* (Oxford: Oxford University Press, 1974). Schools of elocution attempted to wash southern dialect from the mouths of migrants. Howard University offered instruction in pronunciation and diction well into the 1960s. For a century, acquiring standard speech remained the royal road to economic freedom. For plays and comments dealing with class prejudices, see: Zora Neale Hurston, *Color Struck*; Randolph Edmonds, *Old Man Pete*; Theophilus Lewis, "Lowdown Theater."

3. Langston Hughes, "The Negro Artist and the Racial Mountain," *Nation* 122 (23 June 1926): pp. 167–172.

4. The wall between God's and the Devil's music remained unbreached until God's music marched out of the church and danced into minstrel shows and later into recording studios.

5. In March 1926 the Savoy opened as the most opulent dance hall in Harlem; it held up to seven thousand dancers at any one time.

6. Major houses for black shows not discussed in this chapter include Douglass and Colonial theatres in Baltimore; Grand, Avenue, Star, and Regal in Chicago; Ella B. Moore in Dallas; Globe in Jacksonville, Florida; Lincoln in Los Angeles (where the Lafayette Players presented their final performance in 1932); Attucks and Lincoln in Norfolk, Virginia; and Pershing in Pittsburgh. See Henry T. Sampson, *Blacks in Blackface: A Source Book on Early Black Musical Shows* (Metuchen, NJ: Scarecrow Press, 1980).

7. Mary Francesca Thompson, "The Lafayette Players 1915–1932" (Ph.D. dissertation, University of Michigan, 1972), p. 177.

8. Brooks Atkinson reviewing *Harlem*.

9. Susan Curtis, "Three Plays for a Negro Theatre," in *The First Black Actors on the Great White Way* (Columbia, MO: University of Missouri Press, 1998).

10. *Crisis* 19 (November 1919): pp. 338–339.

11. Among the Lafayette Players chosen by O'Neil were Evelyn Preer, Sidney Kirkpatrick, Laura Bowman, Solomon Bruce, Arthur Ray, and Charles Olden.

12. For an enlightening discussion of the troupe's history, see Addell Austin Anderson, "The Ethiopian Art Theatre," *Theatre Survey* 33 (November 1992). The concept that Blacks possessed a "primitive" character, which if given training would translate into great art, was held not only by white Americans, but also by Europeans. Scottish director Hamish Cochrane came to Harlem and formed a Shakespeare company. Baron Eugene Van Grona founded the Negro American Ballet to "provide an outlet for the deeper and more intellectual resources of the race." Max Rheinhardt, too, held these opinions. In yet another example, Anne Wolter, a white woman who had a studio in Carnegie Hall, declared that "Harlem is the greatest mine of dramatic talent in the world," and to prove it she organized the Ethiopian Art Theatre in 1924.

13. *Crisis* 25 (December 1922): pp. 66–68.

14. Gregory Montgomery, "A Chronology of the Negro Theatre," in *Plays of Negro Life*, ed. Alain Locke (New York: Harper Brothers, 1927), pp. 409–423.

15. W. E. B. Du Bois, "Paying for Plays," *Crisis* 25 (December 1922): p. 7.

16. Addell Austin Anderson, "Pioneering Black Authored Dramas: 1924–27" (Ph.D. dissertation, Michigan State University, 1986). Contest winners included Eloise Bibb-Thompson, Marita Bonner, Randolph Edmonds, Zora Neale Hurston, Georgia Douglas Johnson, John Matheus, May Miller, Willis Richardson, Eulalie Spence, and Frank Wilson.

17. *Polk County* was given a concert reading cosponsored by the Library of Congress and Arena Stage on 11 and 12 December 2000.

18. Original title: *Blessed are the Barren*.

19. Angelina Weld Grimké, "'Rachel' the Play of the Month, The Reason and Synopsis by the Author," *Competitor* 1 (January 1920): p. 51.

20. No other writer would articulate this subtle level of insight until Adrienne Kennedy's *Funnyhouse of a Negro* (1963) followed by Dael Orlandersmith's *Yellow Man* (2002).

21. Alain LeRoy Locke, letter of resignation, *c.* 1916, Moorland-Spingarn Manuscript Division, Howard University.

22. Alain LeRoy Locke, "*Goat Alley*," *Opportunity* 1 (February 1923): p. 30. In "Art or Propaganda?: A Historical and Critical Analysis of African American Theoretical

Approaches to Drama, 1900–1975" (Ph.D. dissertation, City University of New York, 2002), Henry Miller surmises that the successful rise of Garvey's UNIA exacerbated the philosophical differences between Locke and Du Bois.

23. Possibly the last production of *Rachel* was by Professor Tisch Jones at Spelman College in 1990.

24. The NAACP's *Thirty Years of Lynching in the United States* (1919; reprinted New York: Arno Press, 1969) reported 4,761. It is probable that many were never reported.

25. Jim Allen, *Without Sanctuary: Lynching Photography in America*. This exhibition of seventy photographs opened in New York City in January 2000. The photographs are on permanent loan to Emory University. Barbara Lewis explores the theatrical aspects of lynching in "From Slavery to Segregation: on the Lynching Trail" (Ph.D. dissertation, City University of New York, 2000).

26. Kathy A. Perkins and Judith L. Stephens, *Strange Fruit, Plays on Lynching by American Women* (Bloomington, IN: Indiana University Press, 1998). These two women researched where no one had gone before. The result is a startling collection of facts, scripts, letters, and production histories.

27. For an extended discussion of Edmonds' contributions to black theatre, see chapter 10.

28. Tracy Mygatt's *The Noose* (1929) used a similar collapse of a white family.

29. Crisis Guild of Writers and Artists (KRIGWA), *Krigwa Theatre Program*, May 1926.

30. A schoolteacher, she is credited by Joseph Papp, founder of the New York Public Theatre, with "scrubbing" his tongue of its Brooklyn accent. Eulalie Spence, interview by Ernest Wiggins, tape recording, 22 August 1973, HBC.

31. S. Randolph Edmonds, "The Negro Little Theater Movement," *Negro History Bulletin*, January 1949, pp. 82–84. Edmonds surmised that KRIGWA failed because, first, it was too loosely organized, and second, the directors lacked any technical training.

32. Eulalie Spence, "A Criticism of the Negro Drama as it Relates to the Negro Dramatist and Artist," *Opportunity* (June 1928): p. 381.

33. Marita Bonner had more or less disappeared from black theatre history. Thanks to the dedicated scholarship of Professor Joyce Flynn at Harvard, we have a record of Bonner's life and collective works.

34. Few black playwrights have ventured outside realism – Jean Toomer, Adrienne Kennedy, Aishah Rahman, and Edgar White. According to Shauna Vey in "Marita Bonner: American Dramatist" (unpublished research paper, Ph.D. Program in Theatre, City University of New York, 1992), Bonner may have read or seen the German expressionistic play *From Morn to Midnight* (1917) on stage in Boston and/or O'Neill's *The Emperor Jones* (1920).

35. "Urban League Dramatic Club Presents Play," *Chicago Defender*, October 1921.

36. Another example is *Africanus* by Eloise Bibb-Thompson, scheduled for a Los Angeles production in January 1922. The play's director, Miss Olga Gray-Zacsck, claimed to have acted Shakespeare with the Symphony Musical Drama Company of Detroit.

37. For histories of black Little Theaters in New York City, see John Gilbert Monroe, "A Record of the Black Theatre in New York City: 1920–29" (Ph.D. dissertation, University of Texas at Austin, 1980). A partial list of theatres in the 1920s and

1930s not discussed in this history includes: Dallas Negro Players of Dallas, Texas; Tramarden Players and New Faces Guild, Washington, DC; Neighborhood Players, Atlantic City, New Jersey; Roxanne Players, Detroit, Michigan; Civic Theatre Guild, Columbus, Ohio; Monumental Theatre Guild and Adam and Eve Production Company, Baltimore, Maryland; Boston Players, Boston, Massachusetts; Dixwell Players, New Haven, Connecticut; Olympian Players, Pittsburgh, Pennsylvania; Community Theatre, Richmond, Virginia; Aldridge Players, St. Louis, Missouri; New Orleans Little Theatre Guild and People's Community Theatre, New Orleans, Louisiana.

38. Theophilus Lewis, "Along the Lines of Equity," *Inter-State Tattler*, 24 August 1928. On a more optimistic day, Lewis held another opinion: "If I am right, those ardent souls who have consecrated themselves to the creation of Negro drama are bound to succeed. They have only to work, suffer, lie, swindle, pray, and sweat blood for five years or so and the victory is won." "Harlem Little Art Theatre: Commendable Venture That Should Have the Support of All," *New York Amsterdam News*, 27 February 1929.

39. The Gilpin Players of Karamu Theatre, Cleveland, mounted a second production on 25 February 1931. The play may never have been performed again, possibly because of its attack on religious hypocrites.

40. *Climbing Jacob's Ladder* (1931) and *Underground* (1932) were both written under the pseudonym Ursala Trelling, which she used in order to avoid any apparent conflict between the presentation of her plays and her directorship of the group.

41. Theophilus Lewis, "Charles Gilpin and the Drama League," *Messenger* 3 (March 1921): 3, pp. 203–204.

42. Reuben Silver, "A History of the Karamu Theatre of Karamu House, 1915–1960" (Ph.D. dissertation, Ohio State University, 1961). This dissertation is the major authoritative work for Karamu's early years.

43. *Cleveland (OH) Gazette*, 9 April 1921.

44. In Washington, DC, Gilpin had been greatly distressed by the Howard Players' reception of his portrait of the emperor. "The poor creature's heart [Emperor Jones] is wrung with fear, his body writhing in pain and his soul lost in despair. And the Washington audience laughed. It is, in my idea, emblematic of a childish mentality that our race audience are given to greeting great emotional climaxes with laughter instead of reverent awe." Lucien White, "Dramatic Appreciation Lacks Proper Racial Comprehension," *New York Age*, 7 January 1922.

45. Certainly the contradictions and obstacles of Gilpin's life deserve a full biography, if not a play. A concise and informed summary of Gilpin's life is John Gilbert Monroe, "Charles Sidney Gilpin: The Emperor Jones" (master's thesis, Hunter College, New York, 1974).

46. Gwendolyn Bennett, *Opportunity*, n.d., p. 271.

47. Ellen Winsor to Wayland Rudd, 22 April 1930, copy HBC.

48. Ten years later Eugene Gordon reported in the *Daily Worker* that Rudd had returned with a new play entitled *Andy Jones*, an adaptation of Angelo Herndon's book about his struggle for justice in the Alabama coal mines. The article included a synopsis of the play and claimed that *Andy Jones* had been published in *International Literature*.

Langston Hughes also wrote a one-act, *Angelo Herndon Jones* (1936), which was produced by the Harlem Suitcase Theatre in May 1938.

49. The American Negro Theatre produced Countee Cullen's *One Way to Heaven* on 18 November 1943. The authors are indebted to Gail Cohen, project director of the Hedgerow Theatre Collection, for the Hedgerow Theatre's history. Ms. Cohen has placed the Hedgerow papers at Boston University.

50. Lawrence Tibbitt played the role in Gruenberg's opera version *Emperor Jones* at the Metropolitan Opera House in New York in 1933.

51. The last major White to attempt the role may have been Laurence Olivier, who enacted the general's passionate distress by lolling his tongue out of his mouth in the film version.

52. Francis Ford Coppola's film *The Cotton Club* (1984) exploited the mythology of the famous nightspot, conjuring its legendary glamour with a nostalgia of jazz, gangsters and prohibition booze; however, the film authenticated little of the club's history.

53. Bruce Kellner, *The Harlem Renaissance: A Historical Dictionary for the Era* (Westport, CT: Greenwood Press, 1984).

54. Edna Mae and Vivian Harris, "Sirens, Sweethearts, and Showgirls of the Stage and Silver Screen," interview by Delilah Jackson, tape recording, 4 February 1990, *Artist and Influence* 10 (1991): p. 75.

55. Harold Cromer, interview by Delilah Jackson, tape recording, 20 February 1999, in *Artist and Influence* 13 (1994): pp. 37–64.

56. The Harlem Opera House had been built by Oscar Hammerstein in the fashionable German neighborhood near the polo ground. His theatre showed legitimate plays produced by the Shuberts. The turn of the century saw a demographic shift, with Germans giving way to immigrant Jews and Italians.

57. The Apollo Theatre on East 42nd Street and the Apollo, a Minsky burlesque house on 145th Street, should not be confused with the one on 125th Street.

58. The legend that Ella Fitzgerald's first performance won the amateur contest at the Apollo is in error. Her début in 1934 at age 16 was at the Harlem Opera House.

59. The fabulous invalid's history of the Apollo from the 1960s to its demise parallels that of the Howard in Washington, DC. When many of the swing-era black clubs closed, the Apollo prospered by featuring rhythm and blues revues, gospel stars, and comedians such as Moms Mabley and Pigmeat Markham. By the 1970s, civil rights had given black entertainers access to better-paying stadiums and arena venues, and the Apollo could no longer afford top acts. The theatre closed its doors in 1977 but opened and closed them again. Then, phoenix-like, it opened again in the 1990s.

60. Dick Gregory and his generation of stand-up comics voiced the unspoken; they were wordsmiths who depended on irony, quips, and allusions to the contradictions of racism. Their mime, relative to the older comics, was minimal, Richard Pryor excepted.

61. In white plays, the black matriarch rules the kitchen while her idle husband suffers her tyranny. Willis Richardson's *The Idle Head* (1927) concerns a struggling washerwoman and her idle son who steals a valuable pin.

62. White audiences never appreciated the team as much as black folks, but both races enjoyed the verbal fisticuffs of Kingfish and Sapphire in *Amos 'n' Andy* radio, as both races later enjoyed the television series *The Honeymooners*.

63. Langston Hughes, *The Big Sea* (New York: Hill and Wang, 1963), p. 65.

64. James Wilson, "Bulldykes, Pansies, and Chocolate Babies" (Ph.D. dissertation proposal, City University of New York, 1998; HBC).

65. A legendary moment at the Lafayette Theatre was Clarence Muse's entrance in white makeup and blonde wig as Dr. Jekyll. The audience, which knew Muse to be very dark-skinned with black features, went wild.

66. Hubert H. Harrison, "Are Negro Actors White?" *Crusader* 4 (April 1921): 2, p. 25.

67. In 1936 the Federal Theatre took over the Lafayette Theatre for the John Houseman and Orson Welles production of the "Voodoo" Macbeth. When the Federal Theatre ceased operations in 1940, the building became a church. In 1967 it again became a theatre when Robert Macbeth directed Fugard's *Blood Knot* and Ron Milner's *Who's Got His Own*. A year later, the theatre burned down. The New Lafayette Theatre was erected in its place. This theatre closed in 1973 and was used intermittently by various groups, including the Harlem Cultural Council.

68. Freda Scott-Giles, "Five African-American Playwrights on Broadway, 1923–1929" (Ph.D. dissertation, Program in Theatre, City University of New York, 1990).

69. Garland Anderson, "How I Became a Playwright," in *Anthology of the American Negro in the Theatre*, compiled by Lindsay Patterson (Washington, DC: Publishers Company, 1967), p. 85.

70. Anderson, "Pioneering Black Authored Dramas: 1924–27," p. 181.

71. *Confidence, Race Pride, Colored American, The Good Sister Jones, The Frisco Kid, Back Home Again*, and *Happy Southern Folks*.

72. Bob Sisk, "Frank Wilson, Actor Still a Postman," *New York World*, 9 October 1927, p. 181.

73. Edna St. Vincent Millay (a contemporary of Thurman), "First Fig," in *A Few Figs from Thistles, Poems and Sonnets* (New York: Harper and Brothers, 1928).

74. Scott-Giles, "Five African-American Playwrights," pp. 213–268, and Doris Abramson, *Negro Playwrights in the American Theatre, 1925–1959* (New York: Columbia University Press, 1969), pp. 32–43.

75. Theophilus Lewis, "If this be Puritanism," *Opportunity* (April 1929): pp. 132–3.

76. Salem Tutt Whitney, "Timely Topics," *Chicago Defender*, 13 April 1929.

77. Quoted in Abramson, *Negro Playwrights*, p. 41.

78. Wallace Thurman, *Negro Life in New York's Harlem*, Little Blue Book 494 (Girard, KN: E. Haldeman-Julius Publications, 1924).

79. Abramson, *Negro Playwrights*, p. 43. Several times Thurman had tried to purchase an orchestra seat to see his own play and was told there was none, although he could obtain one in the balcony.

80. ibid., p. 42.

81. Thurman and Rapp wrote only one other play, *Jeremiah the Magnificent*, a satire about Marcus Garvey. It was never produced.

82. Lewis' most insightful theatre essays are found between 1923 and 1930 in the *Messenger, Inter-State Tattler*, and *New York Amsterdam News*.

83. Theophilus Lewis, "Trailing the Spotlight," *Inter-State Tattler*, 25 January 1929.

84. "Lowdown Theater," *Messenger*, 7 March 1927, p. 85.
85. Zora Neale Hurston, "Characteristics of Negro Expression," in *The Negro: An Anthology*, ed. Nancy Cunard (London: Frederick Ungar, 1934), pp. 29–31. *Jooks* were small roadside "shacks" where working-class black folks could find liquor, music, and dancing. The American word *jukebox* possibly originated from *jooks*, which in turn derived from the Wolof *dzug*, "to misbehave, to lead a disorderly life" and Bambara *dzuga*, "wicked."
86. "The Harlem Sketch Book," *New York Amsterdam News*, 12 November 1930, p. 11.
87. In reviewing Ethel Barrymore's blackface performance in *Scarlet Sister Mary* (1930), Theophilus Lewis wrote this assessment: "If all the bad features of all the bad plays ever written were combined in one play and if twenty-one members of a cast of twenty-five were without doubt the worst actors to be found in Christendom, the result might be a play as banal as *Scarlet Sister Mary*." *Amsterdam News*, October 1930.
88. *Philadelphia Tribune*, 7 April 1914.
89. Hit shows from the Lafayette Players in Harlem toured the circuit: the Howard Theatre in Washington, DC; the Avenue Theatre in Chicago; the Colonial Theatre in Baltimore; and the newly built Dunbar Theatre in Philadelphia.
90. *Philadelphia Tribune*, February 1919.
91. Christopher Rushton, "Motivations of a Little Giant" (unpublished paper, Ph.D. Theatre Program, City University of New York, 1993).
92. Bettye Gardner and Bettye Thomas, "The Cultural Impact of the Howard Theatre on the Black Community," *Negro History* 55 (October 1970): 4, p. 254.
93. Ethel Waters with Charles Samuels, *His Eye is on the Sparrow* (Garden City, NY: Doubleday, 1951), pp. 106–107.
94. ibid.
95. Noble Sissle, interview by James Hatch, tape recording, 7 March 1972, HBC.
96. For a full telling of the plot, as well as details of the songs and singers, consult Bernard L. Peterson Jr.'s *A Century of Musicals in Black and White* (Westport, CT: Greenwood Press, 1993) and Allen Woll's *Black Musical Theatre: From Coontown to Dreamgirls* (Baton Rouge, LA: Louisiana State University Press, 1989).
97. The next year Gilda Gray, a star in the *Ziegfeld Follies of 1922*, sang "It's Getting Dark on Old Broadway." The lyrics included "Ev'ry café now has the dancing coon / Pretty choc'late babies / Shake and shimmie ev'rywhere / Real dark-town entertainers hold the stage."
98. The title *Put and Take* was a term borrowed from the game of shooting craps [unattested].
99. Quoted by Lester A. Walton from *Variety*, 26 August 1921, in *New York Age*. *Put and Take* (1921) had toured for a year as *Broadway Rastus*, which had been seen in various versions since 1915.
100. See Woll, *Black Musical Theatre*, for anecdotes of white villainies in Broadway theatres.
101. Spike Lee used Miller and Lyles routines in his film *Bamboozled* (2000).
102. "Art Impressions of George White's Scandals" (1927), a 32-page souvenir program.
103. *Messenger* 7 (January 1925): p. 62.

104. Florenz Ziegfeld's *Nine O'Clock Follies* (1920) and George White's *Scandals* (1920) introduced the paper-thin flapper models of the decade. The producers had taken a burlesque-style entertainment and adorned it with girls attired in skimpy costumes. The very next year the Grand Theatre in Chicago promoted its *Darktown Scandals of 1921*. Four black revues followed, using "Creole" in their titles as if bowing back to *The Creole Show* (1890–97). Rumors persisted that the "chlorines" (dancers with dyed blond hair) were so light-skinned that some of the women *were white passing for black* – and some were.

105. "Greatest Dancing Revue to Hit the Gay White Way is Likely to Outdo 'Black-birds,'" *Chicago Defender*, 29 June 1929, p. 7.

106. Pierre Loving, "We're in Paris because...," *Paris Tribune*, 1 February 1925. Reprinted in Hugh Ford, ed., *The Left Bank Revisited: Selections from the "Paris Tribune," 1917–1934* (University Park, PN: Pennsylvania State University Press, 1972), p. 47.

107. "*Blackbirds* May be Hit of Summer Season in Paris," *Paris Tribune*, 10 June 1929. Reprinted in Ford, *Left Bank Revisited*, p. 236.

108. The history of black comedy and its comedians, along with many examples of their routines, can be found in Mel Watkins, *On the Real Side* (New York: Simon and Schuster, 1994).

109. John Moncure March, *The Wild Party* and *The Set-Up* (both New York: Covici, Friede, 1928).

110. Wiley Hausam, "*The Wild Party* Production Diary: September 1997," The Public Theater, 29 April 2002, http://www.thewildparty.net/wp.b.d.1997.sep.html

111. Ann Douglas, *Terrible Honesty: Mongrel Manhattan in the 1920s* (New York: Farrar, Straus, and Giroux, 1995). Douglas provides convincing evidence of how warmly and quickly Whites (Jews in particular) embraced black music, dance, and lifestyles, but occasionally she is overly generous, as when she writes that Eddie Cantor in the film *Kid Millions* "with conspicuous good nature, takes a backseat to Harlem's fabulous tap duo [i.e., the Nicholas Brothers]." Not so. Either ignorance or arrogance must have led Cantor to present himself on the same stage with two of the most skilled dancers of the time. The film shows clearly that Cantor dropped out of the dance sequence because his own performance was so obviously inferior.

112. H. L. Mencken, "Hiring a Hall," *New York World*, 17 July 1927.

113. Quoted in Charles Scruggs, *H. L. Mencken and the Black Writers of the 1920s* (Baltimore, MD: Johns Hopkins University Press, 1984).

114. Certainly, the outstanding white promoter of black talent was Carl Van Vechten. In 1926 he published ten articles and five book reviews concerning Negro music, theatre, and literature. To the publisher Alfred A. Knopf he introduced Langston Hughes as well as Countee Cullen, Rudolph Fisher, Walter White, and Gordon Taylor. At his swank Central Park West apartment, black artists met influential Whites as well as one another. His novel *Nigger Heaven* (1926) created a scandal and many denounced Van Vechten as "merely a literary faddist capitalizing upon a current vogue and popular demand." In the retrospect of seventy years, his placement of the James Weldon Johnson collection at Yale's Beinecke Library made a major contribution to preserving the ephemera of the Harlem Renaissance and more than compensated for any misjudgments he may have made.

115. "The Negro in Art: How Shall he be Portrayed?," *Crisis* (June 1927).
116. James Weldon Johnson, *Black Manhattan* (New York: Alfred A. Knopf, 1930), p. 212. Soon cast in other shows were Frank Wilson, Evelyn Ellis, Jack Carter, Georgette Harvey, Rose McClendon, and Leigh Whipper.
117. A parallel view might be taken of white Marc Connelly's *The Green Pastures* (1930), which Connelly adapted from *Ol' Man Adam an' His Chillun* by Roark Bradford, a white southerner. Racism blinded Whites so that they accepted as truth the notions that Blacks were naïve people who believed in heavenly fish fries. To Whites, Connelly's play was a fantasy based in reality.
118. *Philadelphia Magazine* (April 2001): p. 185.
119. George S. Schuyler, "Views and Reviews," *Pittsburgh (PN) Courier*, 4 January 1936.
120. Nathan Irvin Huggins, *Harlem Renaissance* (Oxford: Oxford University Press, 1971), pp. 308–309.
121. Richard Long, "From Periphery to Center," in *Grown Deep: Essays on the Harlem Renaissance* (Winter Park, FL: Four-G Publishers, 1998), p. 1.

8 Educational theatre

1. Dwight Oliver Wendell Holmes, *The Evolution of the Negro College* (1934; reprinted New York: AMS Press, 1970), p. 29.
2. ibid., pp. 34–35. It took two years for Congress to pass the bill creating the Bureau of Refugees, Freedmen, and Abandoned Lands.
3. Four Negro religious denominations established colleges in the South to help educate the new freedmen. The African Methodist Episcopal (AME) Church, then the largest black religious body, was among the first to respond when in 1863 it purchased Wilberforce University in Tawana Springs, Ohio, and two years later founded Payne Theological Seminary on the Wilberforce campus. Between 1870 and 1886 this church established six more colleges in different states, including Allen University in Columbia, South Carolina; Morris Brown College in Atlanta, Georgia; and Shorter College in Little Rock, Arkansas. In 1931–32 a total of 1,277 students at the college grade were enrolled in these institutions. The Colored Methodist Episcopal Church founded four colleges: Lane College in Jackson, Tennessee, 1878; Paine College in Augusta, Georgia, 1992; Texas College in Tyler, Texas, 1894; Miles Memorial College in Birmingham, Alabama, 1902. The aggregate enrollment was 745. "The Negro Denominations," ibid., chapter 10.
   The American Missionary Association also founded a series of denominational schools – Tillotson College, Tougaloo College, Fisk University, Spelman Seminary, Straight University, and Talladega Institute, to list but a few. The American Baptist Home Mission Society supported Virginia Union University; Shaw University; Benedict College; Arkansas A&M; and Normal College at Pine Bluff, Arkansas. The Methodist Episcopal Church established Bennett College; Clark University; Shaw University in Holly Springs, Mississippi; the Centenary Biblical Institute (Morgan College); and Rust College. The Presbyterians established the Scotia Seminary, Barber-Scotia College, Biddle University, Tillman Seminary, and Johnson C. Smith University. The Episcopal Church established St. Paul's Normal and Industrial Institute and St. Augustine's College. There were others.

4. For a personal account of the freedman's passion for education, see Booker T. Washington's autobiography *Up from Slavery* (1901). To appreciate the conflict generated by the internalization of English literary values over black folk values, see Adrienne Kennedy's plays *Funnyhouse of a Negro* (1964) and *The Owl Answers* (1964).

5. For an authentic stage rendering of black college life in the early part of the century, see Thomas D. Pawley, "The Tumult and the Shouting," in *Black Theater USA: Forty-five Plays by Black Americans, 1847–1974*, ed. James V. Hatch and Ted Shine (New York: Free Press, 1974). The classic portrait of a black college administrator is found in Ralph Ellison, *Invisible Man* (1953).

6. Joseph S. Cotter Sr., "Dr. Booker T. Washington to the National Negro Business League" (1909?), in *The Vintage Book of African American Poetry*, ed. Michael S. Harper and Anthony Walton (New York: Vintage Books, 2000).

7. Floyd L. Sandle, "The Negro in the American Educational Theatre: An Organizational Development, 1911–1964," Ph.D. dissertation, Louisiana State University, 1959.

8. "Theater at Atlanta University," *Atlanta University Bulletin*, 4 (1974): 2, pp. 17–24.

9. Adrienne Herndon, "Shakespeare at Atlanta University," *Voice of the Negro*, pp. 482–486.

10. We are indebted to Professor Samuel A. Hay of North Carolina A&T State University for providing at our request the information contained in this paragraph.

11. As late as 1916 there were only sixty-seven Negro public high schools with fewer than twenty thousand students. Eighty-five percent of southern Negro students were enrolled in the first four grades. To remedy the problem, the George Peabody Fund (1867) gave the first $1 million; the John F. Slater Fund (1882) gave another million to church and private institutions; the Anna T. Jeanes Fund (1905) provided teachers and supervisors of teachers with salaries; the General Education Board (Rockefeller, 1902) gave $315 million, much of it toward scholarships for Blacks who would go south to teach; and the Julius Rosenwald Foundation built more than five thousand rural schools and gave teachers advanced training.

12. "Theater at Atlanta University," p. 22.

13. Alain LeRoy Locke, "Steps Toward the Negro Theatre," *Crisis* 25 (December 1922): pp. 66–68.

14. Among the recipients were Warner Lawson (music), Katherine Dunham (dance), Lois Mailou Jones (painting), and Anne Cooke, Owen Dodson, and James W. Butcher (theatre).

15. Allen Williams, "Sheppard Randolph Edmonds: his Contributions to Black Educational Theatre" (Ph.D. dissertation, Indiana University, 1972), pp. 124–125.

16. The members included Florida A&M, Alabama State University, Alcorn A&M, Lane College, LeMoyne-Owen College, Morehouse College, Morris Brown College, Prairie View A&M, Shorter College, Spelman College, Talladega College, Tougaloo College, Southern University, Wiley College, Dillard University, Winston-Salem State Teachers College, Atlanta University, Fisk University, and Tuskegee. These were later joined by Bethune-Cookman College, Leland College, Paine College, Texas College, Bennett College, Grambling State University, Tennessee A&I, Lincoln University of Missouri, Langston University, Kentucky State

College, Arkansas AM&N, and Xavier University of Louisiana. In 2002 more than one hundred schools were listed on the Internet as HBCUs.

17. The regions were the Southwestern, the South, and the Southeastern.

18. Randolph Edmonds, *Six Plays for a Negro Theatre* (Boston: Walter H. Baker, 1934).

19. Roxie Roker, interview by James V. Hatch, tape recording, 18 October 1985, HBC.

20. Others were important to SADSA but space does not permit the inclusion of their stories: Joseph Adkins, L. C. Archer, Richard Barksdale, J. P. Cochran, W. Drury Cox, Gladys Forde, Elizabeth Gordon, Arthur Clifton Lamb, John Lovell Jr., Gladys D. Maddox, Barbara and Carlton Molette, Francis Perkins, Thomas E. Poag, Floyd Sandle, Alfonso Sherman, M. B. Tolson, Beatrice Walcott, Allen Williams, and many more.

21. Thomas D. Pawley to Errol Hill, 28 April 2000, HBC. We are indebted to Pawley for verifying the data in this chapter.

22. Maxine D. Jones and Joe M. Richardson, *Talladega College: The First Century* (Tuscaloosa, AL: University of Alabama Press, 1990), pp. 115, 133, and 284 n. 64.

23. Samuel A. Hay, "The Death of Black Educational Theatre, 94, Stirs Huge Controversy," *Black Theatre News* 9 (fall 1998): 1, pp. 27–28.

24. William R. Reardon and Thomas D. Pawley, eds., *The Black Teacher and the Dramatic Arts: A Dialogue, Bibliography, and Anthology* (Westport, CT: Negro Universities Press, 1970), pp. 8–9.

25. Winona Lee Fletcher, interview by James V. Hatch, tape recording, 8 May 1995, in *Artist and Influence* 14 (1995): pp. 107–118. The subsequent data was taken from this interview.

26. Vera Roberts, "ACTF Perspective – A Festival Profile," in *American College Theatre Festival Tenth Anniversary Program*, 1978.

9 The Caribbean connection

1. By this date the indigenous South American Indian peoples – Taino-Arawaks and Caribs – except for isolated bands living in impenetrable forests, had either fled the islands or been exterminated by European settlers. Some few Carib descendants had become gentrified.

2. See chapter 2 for a discussion of Hewlett's Trinidad visit.

3. Eulalie Spence, born in Nevis in 1894, was one of the pioneer West Indian playwrights to migrate to America with her family in 1902. Although she wrote a number of short plays, had them produced, and won prizes, only one of them, *La Divina Pastora* (1929), about a blind woman seeking a cure from the saint, was set in the Caribbean.

4. Louis Nizer, *My Life in Court* (New York: Pyramid Books, 1961), p. 269. The Roaring Lion alleges that the Andrews Sisters' recording "sold half a million copies in a jiffy," and that Lord Invader received $75,000 "for his share of the royalty." See Lion's book, *Calypso from France to Trinidad: Eight Hundred Years of History* (San Juan, Trinidad: General Printers, c. 1985), pp. 85, 107.

5. See the Donald Heywood clippings file at the Library of the Performing Arts, Lincoln Center, New York City.

6. Not to be confused with Talley Beatty's *Tropicana* (1952).

7. Amy Ashwood was Marcus Garvey's Jamaica-born secretary and first wife, to whom he was married in New York for some two years before they were divorced. His second wife, another Jamaican, was also named Amy (Jacques Garvey). The staged comedy could be seen as a parody of the "Back to Africa" movement, as Garvey was at the time incarcerated in an Atlanta jail for mail fraud.

8. *Trinidad Guardian*, 6 February 1978, p. 8.

9. Some details taken from Ray Funk, "Kaiso Newsletter," no. 29, 6 November 1999, Fairbanks, Alaska.

10. *Phylon*, 2nd quarter (1946): pp. 187–188.

11. *New York Times* obituary notice, 29 December 1970.

12. Review by Michael Smith in the *Village Voice*, 25 January 1962.

13. Bernard L. Peterson Jr., *A Century of Musicals in Black and White* (Westport, CT: Greenwood Press, 1993), p. 119.

14. *Phylon* 6 (1945): 1.

15. Peter Brook (director), Harold Arlen (music and part lyrics), Herbert Ross (choreographer), Oliver Messel (sets and costumes), Jean Rosenthal (lights).

16. *Phylon* 16 (1955): 3, pp. 304–305.

17. *Black Liberator*, March 1968, pp. 20–21. The late 1960s and early 1970s witnessed a period of black militancy unsurpassed in America.

18. According to her *New York Times* obituary of 17 April 2001, p. 42, Ms. Premice was in the original cast of *House of Flowers* but left the production before it moved from Philadelphia to Broadway. She did appear in an off-Broadway revival of the musical in 1968.

19. Peterson, *Century of Musicals*, p. 24.

20. *Caribbean Carnival* (1947), *House of Flowers* (1954 and 1968), *Jamaica* (1957).

21. *Tuesday Magazine* (November 1966): p. 27.

22. Hart had a long and enviable career as a playwright and director. He wrote many successful plays, several in collaboration with George S. Kaufman, and had won both the Pulitzer Prize for playwriting and the Tony Award for directing.

23. Jones led more than nine hundred followers, mostly American and including children, to the People's Temple he had constructed in Guyana. The suicide occurred when police threatened to raid the temple following the murder of an American congressman and four associates who had visited Jones Town to investigate charges of religious coercion.

24. The UCWI began in 1948 as a college in special relationship with the University of London, England. It became a full degree-granting university in 1963. Hereafter it will be referred to as the University of the West Indies (UWI).

25. During his 1958–62 tenure at Yale, Hill completed requirements for the BA, the MFA, and course study for the degree of Doctor of Fine Arts (DFA), which was awarded in 1966 on completion and acceptance of his dissertation.

26. Productions of *Man Better Man* in academia occurred at the Yale School of Drama in April 1960, Federal City College in Washington, DC, in 1972, Dartmouth College, Hanover, New Hampshire, in 1975, and Long Island University in New York in 1986, among others.

27. Barbara Lee Horn, *Joseph Papp: A Bio-Bibliography* (Westport, CT: Greenwood Press, 1992), p. 27. The author cites Papp's belief "that a theater with the highest professional standards could attract, and should be made available to, a broadly

based public." In 1968 Papp opened the Other Stage to workshop new writers for his major Public Theatre productions.

28. Among managing directors whose work Walcott observed in New York were José Quintero at the Circle in the Square Theatre and Stuart Vaughan at the Phoenix Theatre.

29. From "A Note on Production" in Derek Walcott, *Dream on Monkey Mountain and Other Plays* (New York: Farrar, Straus, and Giroux, 1970), p. 208.

30. For Walcott's work with the Trinidad Theatre Workshop see Bruce King, *Derek Walcott and West Indian Drama* (Oxford: Clarendon Press, 1995).

31. Along with Ché Guevara, the other characters were the Son of King Kong, a Nymphomaniac Nun, and the United States President.

32. *Guardian* (London), 27 November 1978, p. 10.

33. Mance Williams, *Black Theatre in the 1960s and 1970s* (Westport, CT: Greenwood Press, 1985).

34. *Berkeley (CA) Calendar*, 10 January 1982.

35. *Sweet Talk* won the George Devine Award in London for its "grinding authenticity" in depicting a Guyanese gambler living in London with his invalid wife.

36. They were also called "Echoes from the Diaspora" or "On a Bigger Plantation." The first title refers to stories of Caribbean and African immigrants in the United States. The second dealt with the African American struggle from slavery to the present time.

37. Rudolph Shaw, executive director of CART: "We want New York to see people from the African Diaspora as major contributors to world civilization." *New York Daily News*, 12 October 1999.

38. Clem Richardson, "Giving Back is Artist's Goal" in *New York Daily News*, 30 October 2000, p. 3. See also Meredith Ebbin, "Subway Scene Boosts Actor's Career," *Bermuda Sun*, 17 November 1989.

39. Olivier Stephenson, "Evolution of Caribbean Theatre," *New York Amsterdam News*, 18 January 1992, p. 19.

40. Jojo Chintoh, "Lennox Brown: A Black Canadian Dramatist," *Black Images* (Toronto) 1 (January 1972): 1.

41. Errol G. Hill, *The Jamaican Stage, 1655–1900* (Amherst, MA: University of Massachusetts Press, 1992), pp. 204–210.

42. For Queenie (a scarred survivor), Pearlie (who died a year earlier), and Hopie (a victim) of the fire that occurred at the Alms House on 20 May 1980 in Kingston, Jamaica.

43. Meaning "Little Miss Muffet" frightened by a spider is in all of us women. Set in a tenement yard, the play explores the effects of social and sexual violence against women – in the home, the workplace, and the media.

44. Patti Hartigan, "Women in Theater: Variations on a theme," *Boston Globe*, 31 March 1989, p. 40.

45. Howard McGowan, "'Deportee' Scores Big in New York," *Gleaner* (Kingston, Jamaica), 28 June 1995.

46. The term *Creole* originally referred to a white European born in the West Indies. Around the mid-twentieth century, if not earlier, its meaning shifted to denote a person born in the Caribbean of mixed race that might include white ancestry.

47. *New York Times*, 21 February 1994, pp. C13, C17.

48. *New York Times*, 25 February 1991, p. C14.
49. Play titles are *Heaven* (1991), *Coming Home To Roost* (1994), and *Kirnon's Kingdom* (1999) by Edgecombe, Walcott's *Ti Jean and His Brothers* (1993), Carter's *Pecong* (1994), Matura's *Play Mas* (1996 and 2000), Bully's *Nite Box* (1993), Phillips' *Hotel Cristobel* (1997), Rhone's *Smile Orange* (1997), and Cecil Williams' *I Don't Want to Bathe* (1997).
50. Quoted in *Miami Herald*, 9 January 1986, p. 6B. The performance was held at a Library Auditorium in Fort Lauderdale, Florida.

10 The Great Depression and federal theatre

1. Marc Connelly, *Voices Offstage: A Book of Memoirs* (Chicago, IL: Holt, Rinehart, and Winston, 1968), pp. 166–177.
2. Walter C. Daniel, *"De Lawd": Richard B. Harrison and The Green Pastures* (Westport, CT: Greenwood Press, 1986), pp. 64–69.
3. James Weldon Johnson, *Black Manhattan* (New York: Alfred A. Knopf, 1930), p. 218.
4. Alain LeRoy Locke, *The Critical Temper of Alain Locke: A Selection of his Essays on Art and Culture*, ed. Jeffrey C. Stewart (New York: Garland, 1983), pp. 206–207.
5. Langston Hughes, "The Trouble with Angels," in *New Theatre and Film 1934 to 1937*, ed. Herbert Kline (San Diego, CA: Harcourt Brace Jovanovich, 1985), pp. 121–126.
6. ibid.
7. Leslie Catherine Sanders, *The Development of Black Theater in America: From Shadows to Selves* (Baton Rouge, LA: Louisiana State University Press, 1988).
8. The first article is in *New York American* (April 1933), p. 5m. The second source is in a typed article written by Walter Price and sent to historian Oliver M. Sayler, HBC.
9. Gregory D. Coleman, *We're Heaven Bound! A Portrait of a Black Sacred Drama* (Athens, GA: University of Georgia Press, 1994), p. 3.
10. Langston Hughes, *The Political Plays of Langston Hughes*, introduced and with analyses by Susan Duffy (Carbondale, IL: Southern Illinois University Press, 2000). A companion volume of Hughes' nondramatic political writings is *Good Morning Revolution: Uncollected Social Protest Writings*, ed. Faith Berry (New York: Lawrence Hill, 1973).
11. Langston Hughes, interview by Reuben and Dorothy Silber, Karamu Theatre, 1961, in *Political Plays of Langston Hughes*, pp. 107–128.
12. Other satirical skits were *Limitations of Life* (1938), in mockery of the film *Imitations of Life*, and *Little Eva's End* (1938), a send-up of *Uncle Tom's Cabin*.
13. Langston Hughes to Louise Patterson, 15 April 1984, Emory University.
14. Bibliographers of Hughes' plays show that he often retitled his scripts. *Blood on the Fields* had been *Blood on the Cotton* and was later revised to *Harvest*.
15. Croly and Wakeman chose to ignore the visible fact that southern white males had already created a race of mulattos by mating with slave women. The Spanish word *mulatto* meant a mule, the product of a donkey and a horse. In the years following the Civil War, state laws defined who was a "Negro" – Louisiana declared anyone with

one-sixteenth Negro blood to be a Negro and, further, its laws forbade interracial marriage. See Dion Boucicault's play *The Octoroon* (1859) for a dramatic playing-out of this thesis.

16. In two short stories, "Red-headed Baby" and "Father and Son," Hughes addressed the difficulties of being racially mixed in America, as he did in his poem "Cross," the original title of *Mulatto*. Leslie Sanders in *Development of Black Theater in America* has observed that the specific idea for a play on this subject probably came to Hughes while he was staying with the director Jasper Deeter at the Hedgerow Theatre in Rose Valley, Pennsylvania. There he watched the rehearsals of Paul Green's *In Abraham's Bosom* (1927), a Pulitzer Prize-winning three-act drama that presented a self-righteous man who resembled Hughes' own father in that he disliked poor black people and found white people intolerable. Apparently angered by Green's play, Langston Hughes created a young mixed-blood protagonist who identified as Black and insisted that he was entitled to all the rights which Whites enjoyed, even if he had to die for them.

17. The "well-made" play was defined by Ferdinand Brunetière (1849-1906) as "the spectacle of a will striving toward a goal and conscious of the means it employs." None of Hughes' many later dramas followed the formula so closely.

18. In May 1935, five months before *Mulatto* opened, Harlem had erupted in riot in part because nearly all the white businesses in Harlem refused to hire Blacks.

19. Jay Plum, "Accounting for the Audience in Historical Reconstruction: Martin Jones' Production of Langston Hughes' *Mulatto*," *Theatre Survey* 36 (May 1995): 1, pp. 5-19. I am grateful to Plum for his insights into the play and its audience.

20. Johnson, *Black Manhattan*, p. 207.

21. The distinguished ensemble included Dick Campbell, Muriel Rahn, George Norford, Ed Cambridge, Fred Carter, Viola Dean, Ruby Dee, and Ossie Davis, Sidney Easton, Rosamund Johnson, Billy King, Canada Lee, Helen Martin, Loften Mitchell, Fred O'Neal, Dorothy Paul, P. J. Sidney, J. Homer Tutt, Christola Williams, Perry Watkins, and Leigh Whipper. Their 1939 program included three original plays by African Americans: Ferdinand Voteur's *A Right Angle Triangle*, George Norford's *Joy Exceeding Glory*, and Arthur Clifton Lamb's *Black Woman in White*.

22. Anthony Tommasini proposes that the George and Ira Gershwin estate remove its stipulation that the opera be performed only by black casts, allowing white singers in the roles. "All-Black Casts for 'Porgy'? That Ain't Necessarily So," *New York Times*, 20 March 2002, Arts section, p. E1.

23. "Negro Actors Form Guild," *New York Times*, 12 November 1937.

24. The first Negro Units created were in Atlanta, Birmingham, Boston, Chicago, Cleveland, Durham, Hartford, Los Angeles, Newark, New York City, Oakland, Oklahoma City, Peoria, Philadelphia, Raleigh, and Seattle.

25. *The Federal Theatre Project Collection: A Register of the Library of Congress Collection of US Work Projects Administration Records on Deposit at George Mason University*, 1987. Credit for organizing this amazing collection must first go to Professor Lorraine Brown of George Mason University. Without her dedication, persistence, acumen, and love of the project, the material for this and many other histories of the FTP

could never have been written. It must also be noted that Professor Brown gave special attention and effort to preserve the histories of black units.

26. Irwin A. Rubinstein, *A List of Negro Plays*, pub. no. 24-L (New York: National Service Bureau, March 1938). Eleven plays by Blacks were listed in the December 1938 catalogue published in Los Angeles, and their quality had considerably improved.

27. Jo Tanner, "Classical Black Theatre: Federal Theatre's All-Black 'Voodoo *Macbeth,'" American Drama and Theatre* 7 (winter 1995): 1, p. 52.

28. A legend tells that the Dafora drummers put a curse on Percy Hammond, an acerbic white critic who panned Welles' *Macbeth*. Hammond died the next day.

29. Lou Gilbert, interview by James V. Hatch, tape recording, 13 January 1977, HBC.

30. Vanita Vactor, "A History of the Chicago Federal Theatre Project Negro Unit: 1935–1939" (Ph.D. dissertation, New York University, 1998).

31. Other plays were Lew Payton's *Did Adam Sin?* (4 April 1936), Marie Merrill's adaptation of *Everyman* (28 May 1936), and Will Jackson's *Burning the Mortgage* (August and October 1936).

32. Richard Wright, *American Hunger* (1944; reprinted New York: Harper and Row, 1977), pp. 166–177.

33. The following year the Chicago group did produce four Paul Green one-acts, mostly comedies.

34. Hallie Flanagan, national director of the FTP, refuted Wright's assessment in her book *Arena: The History of the Federal Theatre* (New York: Duell, Sloan, and Pearce, 1940):

> After performing in a deeply religious *Everyman*, the Negroes were ready to open with Mr. Green's play, which they felt to be equally serious drama... The closing of this play [by the state's WPA administrator] caused the resignation of the company's director, Mr. DeSheim, and such demoralization and timidity on the part of the Negro group that it was months before we finally got them to face another audience.

Flanagan then went on to relate New York City's enthusiastic reception of *Hymn to the Rising Sun*. Flanagan received much of her information second hand from white administrators, and she wrote her book a year after FTP closed and four years after the event. Also, it was to FTP's advantage to conceal conflicts involving race. This is reflected again in Flanagan's assessment of Ward's *Big White Fog*: "Unlike the version of the play produced by the Negro Playwrights Company in New York in 1940 this script carried no political definition." Theodore Ward's testimony, coupled with a reading of the script, refutes her assessment. Rena Fraden, *Blueprints for a Black Federal Theatre, 1935–1939* (Cambridge: Cambridge University Press, 1994), pp. 112–115.

35. This typed, undated office memo from the FTP archives was probably written in 1937 or 1938, after several plays had elicited criticism. The memo is signed "Laurence," and a list of one hundred names and addresses is attached.

36. In 1930 the *Cleveland Plain Dealer* invited thirty-six nations to participate in the "Theatre of Nations." Productions staged by these various groups were presented in the Little Theatre of Public Hall designed and built for such a movement. In this series the Gilpin Players gave *Roseanne*. Because of the size of Graham's pageant, it was presented in the stadium.

37. John Cullen Gruesser, *Black on Black: Twentieth-Century African American Writing about Africa* (Lexington, KT: University Press of Kentucky, 2000), p. 63. The sketches for the costumes as well as other aspects of the *Tom Tom* production are filed at HBC.
38. Rena Fraden, "The Cloudy History of *Big White Fog*: The Federal Theatre Project, 1938," *American Studies* 29 (spring 1988): 1, pp. 5–27.
39. See chapter 11 for a history of the Negro Playwrights Company.
40. *The Swing Mikado* has been the subject of several studies; however, the most useful and recent is Vactor, "Chicago Federal Theatre Project."
41. ibid.
42. Because Nat Karson designed several black shows, some researchers have mistakenly listed him as black.
43. Negro People's Theatre program for *Bury the Dead*, produced at the Lincoln Center, 700 East Oakwood Boulevard, Chicago, 13 April 1940, HBC.
44. Esther Hall Mumford, *Seattle's Black Victorians: 1852–1901* (Seattle, WA: Ananse Press, 1980), p. 166. The Colored Sons of Enterprise, numbering 150, left Seattle on a special train to Maple Leaf. "The Queen City String Band furnished the music. There was dancing and an abundance of chicken, turkey, ice cream, and lemonade."
45. Quintard Taylor, *The Forging of a Black Community: Seattle's Central District, from 1870 through the Civil Rights Era* (Seattle, WA: University of Washington Press, 1994). The authors are indebted to Tina Redd's article "*Stevedore* in Seattle: A Case Study in the Politics of Presenting Race on Stage," *American Drama and Theatre* 7 (spring 1995): 2.
46. Gilmore Brown to Hallie Flanagan, 20 February 1936, Regional Correspondence, RG69, National Archives. Quoted in Fraden, *Blueprints for a Black Federal Theatre*, pp. 177–178. Burton James also taught "Negro dialect" to Joe Jackson, head of the Urban League.
47. Elvamari Alexandria Johnson, "A Production History of the Seattle Federal Theater Project's Negro Repertory Company: 1935–1939" (Ph.D. dissertation, University of Washington, 1981).
48. Redd, "*Stevedore* in Seattle," p. 85.
49. Theodore Browne, *Natural Man* (1937).
50. In a subsequent 1941 production by the American Negro Theater in Harlem the music was not used. In this period two other plays about John Henry were produced, both by Whites, including the 1940 Broadway musical version starring Paul Robeson.
51. In an interview with Lorraine Brown, Theodore Browne related that he had come to Seattle in 1935 and taken up the trade of barber while acting with the NRC. He claimed that he had written or adapted *Swing, Gates, Swing* (1936), an improvised vaudeville musical, and *An Evening with Dunbar* (1938), a collage of music and poetry built around Dunbar's life. Both were produced by the NRC. Theodore Browne, interview by Lorraine Brown, 22 November 1975, George Mason University; copy of transcript and tape recording, HBC.
52. Ron West, "Others, Adults, Censored: The Federal Theatre Project's *Black Lysistrata* Cancellation," *Theatre Survey* 37 (November 1996): 2, pp. 93–113. The author shows that local cinemas in Seattle regularly and publicly advertised burlesque and nude

"girlie" flicks, and that the owners of these cinemas pressured Abel to close the NRC's smash hit because they saw it as box-office competition.

53. Clipping from the scrapbook of Owen Dodson, n.d., n.s., manuscript division, Moorland-Spingam Research Center, Howard University.

54. Over the Repertory's twenty-three seasons, more than half a million theatre patrons were entertained at more than three thousand performances in 196 productions. For a two-part summary of the Burtons and the playhouse, see Chet Skreen, "Today's Seattle Theater Owes a Lot to the 'Old Rep,'" *Seattle Times Magazine*, Sunday, 30 January 1977, pp. 8–12, and Chet Skreen, "Canwell Probe Brought Final Days for 'Old Rep,'" *Seattle Times Magazine*, Sunday, 6 February 1977, pp. 4–6.

55. The beauty of the singing was said to have been the inspiration for using Blacks in Gertrude Stein and Virgil Thomson's *Four Saints in Three Acts* (1934).

56. Clarence Edouard Muse, *The Dilemma of the Negro Actor* (Los Angeles: privately printed pamphlet, 1934; Emory University).

57. *Los Angeles Eagle*, 23 July 1938.

58. John O'Connor and Lorraine Brown, eds., *Free, Adult, Uncensored: The Living History of the Federal Theatre Project* (Washington, DC: New Republic Books, 1978), p. 22.

59. Brooks Atkinson, "The Trial of Doctor Beck," *New York Times*, 10 August 1937. This otherwise perceptive critic was not known for his acute perception on racial matters.

60. Paul Nadler, "Liberty Censored: Black Living Newspapers of the Federal Theatre Project," *African American Review* 29 (winter 1995): 4, p. 620. Ward Courtney submitted his documentary *Stars and Bars* to the black unit of Hartford, Connecticut. A Yankee in the play's opening scene announces that African Americans have done "pretty well" in Connecticut since the state abolished slavery in 1784. The remainder of the play, using incidents past and present, demonstrated the contrary. The play ends with Blacks and Whites marching off to confront Hartford's mayor. It was never produced. Converse Tyler, a supervisor of the National Service Bureau's playreading department in New York, wrote that it was a shame that the documentary was confined to Hartford, which limited its possibilities for production in other cities. He concluded that "once suggested changes were made, the play 'should be of considerable interest.'"

61. The Buffalo Historical Marionettes' "Negro unit" was not an official unit listed among the FTP's famed collection of all-black acting companies. Beth Cleary, "Refiguring Race, Representing Race: The Jubilee Singers of the Buffalo Historical Marionettes" (paper presented at "Pedagogy and Theater of the Oppressed," a conference held at the City University of New York, 1999; HBC).

62. Tina Redd, "Birmingham's Federal Theater Project Negro Unit," in Harry J. Elam Jr. and David Krasner, ed., *African American Performance and Theater History* (New York: St. Martin's Press, 2001), pp. 271–287.

63. Fraden, *Blueprints for a Black Federal Theatre*, p. 163.

64. Because the US Congress appropriated Federal Theatre funds in October 1935, the same month Coleman opened his *Macbeth*, it is possible that it, too, was sponsored by the Emergency Relief Administration.

65. I am grateful to Professor Lorraine Elena Roses of Wellesley College for sharing her research: "The Search for Black Boston's Lost Cultural Riches" (talk and slide show presented at the Ford Hall Forum, Dorchester, MA, 1999).

66. Lorraine Brown, "Library of Congress Takes Back Federal Theatre Project Archive," *New Federal One* 19 (October 1994): 3.

11 Creeping toward integration

1. The Young Men's Christian Association, the Young Women's Christian Association, the National Catholic Community Service, the National Jewish Welfare Board, the Salvation Army, and the National Travelers Aid Association.

2. *Negro Year Book, An Annual Encyclopedia of the Negro*, 1947, p. 380. In 1943 forty-two states and the District of Columbia had one or more USO operations primarily for Blacks. The exceptions were North Dakota, Minnesota, Vermont, Maine, Connecticut, and West Virginia. *Negro Handbook*, 1944, p. 136.

3. *Negro Handbook*, 1946–47, p. 256.

4. "The Theatre and the Armed Forces," *Theatre Arts* 27 (March 1943): 3.

5. Bruce Kellner, ed., *Letters of Carl Van Vechten* (New Haven, CN: Yale University Press, 1987), p. 202.

6. When Dodson returned to New York City, his reputation as a writer and director had preceded him. The Negro Labor Victory Committee hired him to write and stage a pageant in Madison Square Garden to promote black and Jewish participation in unions and to emphasize their support of the Allies in their war against fascism. On 26 June 1944 an estimated twenty-five thousand people paid 50 cents or $1 to see *New World A-Coming*, starring Canada Lee, Abbie Mitchell, Josh White, and Will Geer. Duke Ellington's orchestra played and Pearl Primus danced.

7. Audrey June Taylor, interview by James V. Hatch, tape recording, 11 March 1984, HBC.

8. In the early days the Red Circuit had sixty-eight entertainers, including Noble Sissle, Eubie Blake, Avis Andrews, Butterbeans and Susie, Al Sears orchestra, lines of chlorines, Emory Evans, and various dance and novelty teams. The White Circuit boasted such names as Lee Norman and his orchestra, Herbie Cowans orchestra and the Peters Sisters, Victoria Vigal, Al and Billie Richards, and Fetaque Sanders, a magician. Black artists who toured the Blue Circuit of early days included Minta Cato, Garner and Wilson, Ann Lewis, and Vance and Lowry.

9. During the latter part of 1944 a unit of six members, headed by Chauncey Lee with Cora Green, Dave and Witty, Dodo Proctor, and Lillian Thomas, toured North Africa, Persia, and the Far East. In another unit, headed by Alberta Hunter, were Taps Miller, the Three Rhythm Rascals, and Mae Gandy; they were flown into the China-Burma-India area. The first black Hospital Circuit unit went on tour 15 January 1945 and included Miller and Lee, Fetaque Sanders, the three Spenser Sisters, Little Jessie James, Audrey Thomas, Martha Please, "Honey Boy" Thompson, and Eubie Blake.

10. Dick Campbell, interview by Tony Bruno, 1 March 1972.

11. Paul Nadler, "American Theatre and the Civil Rights Movement, 1945–1965" (Ph.D. dissertation, City University of New York, 1996), pp. 22–23.

12. Canada Lee was christened Leonard Lionel Cornelius Canegata.

13. Hollywood's 1951 version released by Twentieth Century-Fox with Betty Grable circumvented casting a Black by using Lebanese-born Danny Thomas.

14. Dorothy Dandridge and Harry Belafonte starred in Otto Preminger's film version of *Carmen Jones* (1954).

15. Campbell, interview.

16. Other all-black shows were *Harlem Cavalcade* (1942), *Run Little Chillun* (1943 revival), *Porgy and Bess* (1952 revival), *Anna Lucasta*, (1944), *Blue Holiday* (1945), and *Carib Song* (1945). Only Jackie Robinson's dancing kept *Memphis Bound* (1945), a jazz version of *HMS Pinafore*, running for thirty-six performances. Three stars in *Lysistrata* (1946) – Etta Moten, Rex Ingram, and Fredi Washington – could not sparkle enough to save the wretched production of the Greek classic.

17. Some other mixed-cast shows were *Harriet* (1943), *On the Town* (1944), *Bloomer Girl* (1944), *The Hasty Heart* (1945), *Show Boat* (1946 and 1948 revivals), *Jeb* (1945 Broadway début of Ossie Davis), *Set My People Free* (1948), *The Iceman Cometh* (1946), *Home of the Brave* (1946), and *The Respectful Prostitute* (1946). Tennessee Williams cast Gertrude Jeannette in a minor role in *A Streetcar Named Desire* (1947). Once when asked why he didn't use more Blacks in his southern stories, Williams reportedly replied that he never felt he knew Blacks well enough to write about them.

18. Broadway and Hollywood had two solutions for staging black–white love affairs: present one of the lovers as passing for white or make one of the lovers blind. See *Patch of Blue* (1965) with Sidney Poitier and the blind white girl, Elizabeth Hartman.

19. Rosey E. Poole, "The Negro Actor in Europe," *Phylon* 14 (1953): 3, p. 260.

20. Owen Dodson, *The People's Voice*, 19 September 1942.

21. While studying with Erwin Piscator of the New School for Social Research, Abram Hill and John Silvera wrote a history of black struggles for freedom entitled *One Tenth of a Nation* (later *Liberty Deferred*, 1938). The FTP never produced it. Hill decided he would establish his own theatre.

22. Theodore Ward, Negro Playwrights Company program for *The Big White Fog*.

23. See history of *The Big White Fog* in chapter 10. For a detailed account see Rena Fraden, "The Cloudy History of *Big White Fog*: The Federal Theatre Project, 1938," *American Studies* 29 (spring 1988): 1, pp. 5–27.

24. "Introduction to 'Walk Hard,'" in James Hatch and Ted Shine (ed.), *Black Theatre USA: Plays by African Americans* (first edn, New York: Free Press, 1974), p. 437.

25. Abram Hill, interview by Michele Wallace, tape recording, 19 January 1974, *Artist and Influence* 19 (2000): p. 120.

26. The original cast included Earle Hyman, Lionel Monagas, Alvin Childress, Letitia Tool, Alberta Perkins, Fred O'Neal, Betty Haynes, John Proctor, Alice Childress, Martin Slade, Billy Cumerbatch, and Buddy Holmes. Canada Lee replaced Monagas for the Broadway production.

27. Hill, interview.

28. Hill, interview.

29. Edith Oliver, "The Theatre Off-Broadway," *New Yorker*, 11 February 1978.

30. For further reading, see Ossie Davis and Ruby Dee, *With Ossie and Ruby* (New York: William Morrow, 1998).
31. Hill, interview.
32. Hill, interview.
33. Hill, interview.
34. For an account of the original production, see "Seattle Unit," chapter 10.
35. All playwrights were white. *Henri Christophe* (1945) by Dan Hammersmith, *Angel Street* (1946) by Patrick Hamilton, *The Late Christopher Bean* (1947) by Sidney Howard, *Rope* (1947) by Eugene O'Neill, *The Show Off* (1947) by George Kelly, *The Washington Years* (1948) by Nat Sherman, *Sojourner Truth* (1948) by Katherine G. Chaplin, *Almost Faithful* (1948) by Harry Wagstaff Gribble, *The Fisherman* by Jonathan Tree, and *Skeleton* (1948) by Nicholas Bela.
36. ANT's most prominent members included Claire Leyba, Maxwell Glanville, Austin Briggs-Hall, Hilda Haynes, Gordon Heath, Robert Earl Jones, Helen Martin, Isabel Sanford and Clarice Taylor. Many founded other theatres. In 1954 Roger Furman founded the Harlem Experimental Theatre Group, not to be confused with the 1929 Experimental Theatre. Its first and only productions were three one-act plays, including an original script entitled *Oklahoma Bear* by Charles Griffin. In the 1960s Furman's New Heritage Theatre trained young Blacks in technical stagecraft.
37. Joseph McLaren, *Langston Hughes* (Westport, CT: Greenwood Press, 1997), p. 159.
38. For three months during the fall the theatre was to mount Hughes' *Soul Gone Home* (1937) on a triple one-act bill with Georgia Douglas Johnson's *Fred Douglass Leaves for Freedom* (*Frederick Douglass*, 1935), and Vincent William's *Maybe Someday* (n.d.). Fannin Saffore Belcher Jr., "The Place of the Negro in the Evolution of the American Theatre, 1762–1940" (Ph.D. dissertation, Yale University, 1940), p. 407.
39. ibid.
40. Skyloft actors appeared weekly on WBBM radio on *Democracy USA*, a feature dramatizing the lives of outstanding Blacks such as Paul Robeson and Gwendolyn Brooks (a series parallel to Roi Ottley's *New World A-Coming* on New York's WMCA). The Chicago program ran for two years. The series writer, Robert Lucas, won the Skyloft playwriting prize for *Tell 'em How We Died* (1945), a war play. Lucas had worked for Hughes in the Federal Writers Project *The Negro in Illinois* and later dramatized Arna Bontemps' novel *Black Thunder*.
41. Ruth Jett, interview by James V. Hatch, tape recording, 15 March 1988, *Artist and Influence* 17 (1998): p. 111. Typical of this integration-through-achievement philosophy was that of the National Negro Opera Foundation, founded in 1941. Its aim, in part, was to "afford the Negro the opportunity for the fullest expression in cultural development . . . and to open wide the door. The National Negro Opera Foundation has always worked inter-racial inter-cultural, having engaged members from the best local symphonic orchestras." *Ouanga* program, Metropolitan Opera House, 27 May 1956.
42. Alice Childress, "For a Negro Theatre," *Masses and Mainstream* (February 1951): pp. 61–64.
43. The prime movers of this group were Maxwell Glanville, Alice Childress, Ruth Jett, Sylvester Leaks, and William Coleman. Loften Mitchell, *Black Drama: The*

Story of the American Negro in the Theatre (New York: Hawthorn Books, 1967), pp. 144–145.

44. Actors in the Elks Community Theatre ensemble included Ruby Dee, Esther Rolle, Charles MacRae, Frances Foster, Howard Augusta, Ed Cambridge, and Isabell Sanford. Other playwrights produced included Julian Mayfield, Roger Furman, Charles Griffin, and Alice Childress.

45. Penthouse Theatre program, 15 July 1948.

46. Carrie Miller, critic for the *Amsterdam News*, observed that the biggest problem facing Negro theatre groups was that of finding and keeping suitable male lead talent. Miller stated that in the Penthouse production of *Dangerous Corner* the female cast far outweighed the males in dramatic intensity. "Backstage," *New York Amsterdam News*, 22 November 1947. Between 1947 and 1953 Penthouse produced a musical comedy *The New Teacher* (1948) by Sheldon B. Hoskins, *Outward Bound* (1948) by Sutton Vane, *Night Must Fall* (1948) by Emlyn Williams, *Papa Never Done Nothing – Much* (1948) by E. P. Conkle, *Antigone* (1949) by Jean Anouilh, *Ghosts* (1950) by Ibsen, and *Death Takes a Holiday* (1953) by Alberto Casella.

47. Typical of dreams of community theatre was the McKinley Square Players, which in February 1945 mounted a production of *Arsenic and Old Lace* in a small auditorium in the Bronx. Three veteran actors led the cast – Abbie Mitchell, Tom Fletcher, and Avon Long. Younger talent supported their efforts: Ruby Dee and William Greaves. They announced their season's program as: "*Blind Alley, The Last Mile, The Cat and the Canary, Anna Christie, Ghosts,* and other fine plays." It never happened, but the very list evokes a sigh of admiration for their dream, which no doubt had been inspired by the success of ANT.

48. Bowling Green University Theater program, *Trouble in Mind*, 5 March 1978.

49. "These are They," *AME Church Review* 83 (October/December 1956).

50. Miles Jefferson, "Empty Season on Broadway, 1950–51," *Phylon*, 3rd quarter (1950/51): p. 130. Jefferson wrote perceptive reviews in *Phylon* about black performance on- and off-Broadway from 1944 to 1957 under the title "Blacks on Broadway."

51. "At Home with Ethel Waters," *Phylon*, 3rd quarter (1953/54): p. 253.

52. "Integration," *Equity* (June 1952). A similar disenfranchisement occurred in 1999 when the major television networks cast no Blacks in significant roles in the fall season's shows. A second adaptation of Verdi's *Aida* came to Broadway on 23 May 2000. Heather Headley played the lead opposite Adam Pascal.

53. A few years later the Free Southern Theatre produced Beckett's play for prison audiences.

54. See Brenda Dixon Gottschild, *Digging the Africanist Presence in American Performance: Dance and Other Contexts* (Westport, CT: Greenwood Press, 1996) and Jacqui Malone, *Steppin' on the Blues: The Visible Rhythms of African American Dance* (Urbana, IL: University of Illinois Press, 1996), respectively.

55. "More Spice than Substance," *Phylon*, 3rd quarter (1955): p. 303.

56. Harold Clurman, *Nation* (October 1953).

57. Other Blacks in the two productions were Beah Richards, Godfrey Cambridge, Frances Foster, Hilda Haynes, Rosetta LeNoire, Fred O'Neal, Estelle Hemsley, Jane White, Paulene Myers, Estelle Evans, Maxwell Glanville, and Frank Wilson.

58. "Paulene Myers Show Scores at Greenwich Mews Theatre," *New York Courier*, 8 October 1966.
59. *New York Times*, 30 October 1953.
60. Actors sometimes referred to the Ebony Showcase as "the plantation," meaning that even with its small salaries, the Showcase provided work when there was nothing else. Jay Loft-Lynn, interview by James V. Hatch, tape recording, 25 March 1975, HBC.
61. Nick Stewart, interview by Margaret Wilkerson, tape recording, 24 November 1971, HBC.
62. ibid.
63. David Colker, "Ebony Keeps Black Theater Alive in LA," *Los Angeles Herald Examiner*, 16 October 1981.
64. Milroy Ingram to Fred O'Neal, 1952.

12 From Hansberry to Shange

1. Theatre artists in the black arts movements of the 1960s and 1970s were legion; however, because of space limitations, the many are represented by those who led, who were artistically innovative, or who represented many others by example. Many playwrights and actors who are omitted here can be found in Bernard L. Peterson Jr.'s bibliographies.
2. Steven R. Carter, *Hansberry's Drama: Commitment and Complexity* (Urbana, IL: University of Illinois Press, 1991), pp. 12–13. Hansberry's outline reflected ideals similar to those set down in the KRIGWA's 1926 manifesto as well as in the ANT constitution of 1940.
3. Ben Keppel writes, "*A Raisin in the Sun* symbolized a change not only in black theatre concept but also the manner of its arrival. Produced on Broadway by Philip Rose, a songwriter, and Daniel J. Cogan, an accountant; neither had any prior experience in theatrical production . . . and [the play] was financed by 147 individual investors who had contributed an average of just $250." *The Work of Democracy* (Cambridge, MA: Harvard University Press, 1995), p. 207.
4. Amiri Baraka, "A Critical Reevaluation: *A Raisin in the Sun*'s Enduring Passion," in *A Raisin in the Sun*, ed. Robert Nemiroff, expanded 25th edn (New York: New American Library, 1987), pp. 9–20.
5. Harold Cruse, *The Crisis of the Negro Intellectual* (New York: William Morrow, 1967), p. 278.
6. Ossie Davis, *Purlie Victorious*. This comic satire received praise for being light-hearted and not preachy. Jones' *Dutchman* (1964) and Baldwin's *Blues for Mister Charlie* (1964) were both designated as being for black audiences because of their strong protest messages.
7. Brecht, in this instance, may have been proven right. The audience's tears were for the characters and not the issues. An analogous phenomenon would happen two decades later with Shange's play *Spell 7*.
8. Antoinette Perry Award, American Theatre Wing.

9. Allen Woll, *Black Musical Theatre: From Coontown to Dreamgirls* (Baton Rouge, LA: Louisiana State University Press, 1989), p. 244.

10. *New York Times,* 23 December 1966.

11. The book's author, William F. Brown, was a white man.

12. *Village Voice* annual Off-Broadway Awards.

13. The original title, *The Gospel Glory: A Passion Play,* was changed so as not to be confused with Hughes' *Tambourines to Glory.*

14. The programs included the Comprehensive Employment Training Act (CETA), Urban Renewal, Model Cities, Open Space and Neighborhood Development, and Office of Economic Opportunity.

15. Jeannette's Broadway career included *Lost in the Stars* (1949), *The Long Dream* (1960), *The Amen Corner* (1965), *The Skin of Our Teeth* (1975), and *Vieux Carré* (1977).

16. Rosetta LeNoire, interview by George Brooker, tape recording, 15 June 1992, HBC.

17. Andrzej Ceynowa, "Black Theaters . . . 1961–1982," *Black American Literature Forum* 17 (summer 1983): 2, pp. 84–93.

18. Evidence of the transition can be seen in the pages of *Black Theatre* (1968–72), whose covers and illustrations reveal the trend away from George Ford's romantic Pharaonic images of the 1960s and toward the Bantu masks and abstractions by Ademola Olugebefola in the 1970s.

19. They took their name from K. William Kgositsile's poem "The Last Poets."

20. "Surrealism and Blues," *Living Blues* 25 (January/February 1976).

21. Ed Bullins, "The So-called Western Avant-garde Drama," *Liberator* 7 (December 1967): 12, pp. 16–17.

22. Larry Neal, interview by James V. Hatch, tape recording, 24 January 1974, HBC.

23. Amiri Baraka, interview by Mike Coleman, "What is Black Theatre?" *Black World* 20 (April 1971): 6, pp. 32–36.

24. In a 1971 Marxist pamphlet, *Literature and Ideology,* Mary Ellen Brooks denounced Baraka and Bullins as reactionaries. "These dramatists are trying to mobilize political support for the decadent imperialists by saying that the possibilities for change do not exist." Ironically, in the same year Catholic Sister Kathryn Martin, SP, in her article "On Black Theatre of Revolution" (*Today's Speech,* 1972) justified the violence in the plays of Baraka and Bullins. After quoting Matthew 10:34, "I have come not to bring peace, but a sword," Sister Martin claimed that the Theology of Revolution and the Theatre of Revolution both affirmed the black man's struggle for freedom.

25. Rhett S. Jones, "Orderly and Disorderly Structures," *Black American Literature Forum* 25 (spring 1991): 1, pp. 43–52.

26. The original company included Frances Foster, Michael Schultz, Edward Burbridge, Marshall Williams, Clarice Taylor, Ed Cambridge, Rosalind Cash, Arthur French, Denise Nicholas, William Jay, Allie Woods, Norman Bush, David Downing, Judyann Elder, Moses Gunn, Hattie Winston, and Esther Rolle.

27. William Owens, "The Free Theatre Company," 18 February 1997, http://www.bobwest.com/ncaat/frsouth.html. The summary used here is abstracted from a document by Gilbert Moses and John O'Neal, *General Prospectus of a Free Southern Theatre.*

28. Most of the agitprop skits were written by John O'Neal, Gilbert Moses, Tom Dent, Sharon S. Martin, and Kalamu ya Salaam.

29. For a time Moses wrote and directed films in Hollywood. He died of bone cancer in 1995.

30. In 1977 Theodore Ward was awarded a Rockefeller Playwriting fellowship-in-residence with the FST.

31. Dan Hulbert, "In 'Ain't No Use,' Junebug Takes Aim at Role of Blacks in Military," *Atlanta Journal and Constitution*, Sunday, 4 March 1990.

32. Milner later founded the Langston Hughes Theatre in Detroit.

33. Kathy Ervin Williams, "Concept East Theatre: 1962–1976" (unpublished paper, NCAAT, 1987), has provided the data and history for CET. Among those who worked in the company were playwrights Jean Rosenbaum, Herschel Steinhardt, Bill Harris, and Ron Milner.

34. The New York center was named after the Frederick Douglass House for Writers, which Budd Schulberg had created after the 1965 riots in the Watts section of Los Angeles, California.

35. Grants came from the Rockefeller, Sherman, and Jerome foundations, as well as from the NEA and the New York State Council on the Arts. Supporters of the center included Jackie Onassis, Terry McMillan, Pamela Johnson, Karen Jones Meadows, China Clark, P. J. Gibson, and Rita Dove.

36. Juanita Karpf, "Vinnette Carroll," *Notable Women in the American Theatre: A Biographical Dictionary* (Westport, CT: Greenwood Press, 1989), pp. 81–82.

37. Vinnette Carroll to Roger L. Stevens, 7 December 1971, copy HBC.

38. In February 1979 the landlord evicted Carroll from her theatre so that he might use the space himself. Subsequently, Carroll moved to Fort Lauderdale, Florida, where she secured $669,000 in state and local grants to establish a new 250-seat theatre in a renovated Methodist church that she rented for $1 a year.

39. Collins wrote *The Midnight Hour* (1981), *Only the Sky is Free* (1985), and *When Older Men Speak* (1986). Her award-winning films included *The Cruz Brothers and Mrs. Malloy* (1980) and *Losing Ground* (1982). Gunn's plays include *The Forbidden City* (1989) and *Black Motion Picture Show* (1975).

40. China Clark's best-known plays were *Perfection in Black*, staged as a work-in-progress by NEC in 1971, and *In Sorrow's Room*, produced at the Henry Street Playhouse, New York City, in 1974.

41. Barbara Walker, "Community Theatre," *Black Creation* 3 (summer 1972): 4, pp. 21–22.

42. The four were Delano Stewart of the Bed-Stuy Theatre, Roger Furman of the New Heritage Repertory Theatre, Hazel Bryant of African American Total Theatre, and Edward Taylor of the Afro-American Singing Theatre.

43. Bill Castleberry, "Black Theatre Alliance Closes Down," *Uptown* (summer 1981): p. 34.

44. Originally the tour theatres included Boston's National Center for Afro-American Artists, Newark's African Revolutionary Theater, Karamu House of Cleveland, Spelman College Drama Program of Atlanta, Concept East Theatre of Detroit, DC Black Repertory of Washington, and the Free Southern Theatre of New Orleans. None of these was in the final circuit.

45. To help with the AUDELCO mailings, Robinson chose a board of like-minded women: Mary Davis, Renee Chenoweth, Winifred Richardson, and Doris Smith.

46. C. Bernard Jackson, interview by James V. Hatch, tape recording, 16 October 1985, HBC.
47. The plays ranged from the topically militant – Caldwell's *Prayer Meeting, or The First Militant Minister* (1967) and Bullins' *The Electronic Nigger* (1968) – to pointed symbolism – Walcott's *Dream on Monkey Mountain* (1971) and Harrison's *Great MacDaddy* (1972).
48. *Rosalee Pritchett* was later performed by the Negro Ensemble Company (1971).
49. The National Association of Dramatic and Speech Arts (NADSA), the Black Theatre Association, the National Conference on African American Theatre, the Black Theatre Network, and the National Black Theatre Festival.
50. While most prison theatres were for incarcerated males, in the 1980s women outside began working with their sisters in prison, using theatre as an agent for gender understanding and expression.
51. As the prison population became increasingly African American, more theatre workshops were formed. Rozier Brown founded Inner Voices at Lorton Virginia's prison. Working with as many as seventy men, whose sentences ranged from two years to life, Brown was able to present 180 performances outside the prison in the Washington, DC area. Some prison companies were multicultural. In 1971 Marvin Felix Camillo and the Ossining Street Theatre began a workshop with male inmates at the Bedford Correctional Facility in New York. Five years later, Camillo was able to employ those and other ex-prisoners in a group called The Family. In the same period, while working part-time at Sing Sing as an actor-in-residence, Camillo had met Miguel Piñero, who was writing a play he called *Short Eyes* (prison slang for a child molester). In 1974 Camillo directed *Short Eyes* at the Riverside Church; Joseph Papp saw it and moved the production to his Public Theatre. After winning the New York Drama Critics Circle Award and two Obies, The Family toured Holland and Germany. The actors' wages escalated from $45 a week to $500, and they returned to perform and conduct workshops in prisons and other institutions. Camillo died from injuries received in an auto accident in 1988.
52. "Funding," *Theatre Crafts* 6 (March/April 1972): 2, pp. 13, 35–36.
53. Actor Silvera had played crossover roles in films – Mexicans, Chinese, Portuguese, an Irish seaman and many more. Disgusted and alienated from Hollywood, he placed a full-page advert in *Variety* denouncing the racist policies of the film industry.
54. Douglas Q. Barnett, interview by James V. Hatch, tape recording, 1 October 1997, in *Artist and Influence* 17 (1998): pp. 1–27.
55. Barbara and Carlton Molette were among the first to publish the techniques for makeup and lighting on shades of dark skin.
56. *New York Amsterdam News*, 14 April 1974.
57. Woll, *Black Musical Theatre*, p. 221.
58. William H. Grant III, *Black Masks* 12 (June/July 1997): 4, pp. 5–6, 15.
59. Stanley Kauffmann, "Revolution in the Theater: Negroes Play White Roles," in *Louisville (KY) Courier-Journal*, 31 July 1966.
60. Barbara Lewis, "'Oedipus Rex' King James Version," *Encore American and Worldwide News*, 4 April 1977, p. 39.
61. Richard Eder, "Frustrated General," *New York Times*, 15 March 1979.

62. Ntozake Shange, *Three Pieces* (New York: St. Martin's Press, 1981), p. ix.
63. Lester A. Neal, *Ntozake Shange: A Critical Study of the Plays* (New York: Garland, 1995), p. 3.
64. Marilyn Stasio, "Tell it, Sisters!" *Cue* (June 1976).
65. Neal, *Ntozake Shange*, pp. 267–268.
66. Tony Brown, "Black Men, Black Women," *Black Journal*, television broadcast, PBS-TV, 27 February 1977.
67. Owen Dodson, "Playwrights in Dark Glasses," *Negro Digest* 17 (6 April 1968): pp. 31–36.
68. Shows on tour included *Raisin, Bubbling Brown Sugar, Don't Bother Me I Can't Cope, Your Arms Too Short to Box with God, Guys and Dolls,* and *For Colored Girls.*
69. Mel Gussow, "Blacks in the Theater: Progress is Deceptive," *New York Times,* Sunday, 3 August 1986.

13 The Millennium

1. Tony Preston, "C. Bernard Jackson: in the Face of Adversity," *Black Masks* 4 (summer 1988): 9, pp. 6–8.
2. Rapper Chuck D defined hip-hop as "the term for urban-based creativity and expression of culture. Rap is the style of rhythm-spoken words across a musical terrain." Chuck D, "The Sound of Our Young World," 29 September 1999, Rapstation, 29 May 2002, http://www.rapstation.com/inside_the_rhyme/terrordome/ terrordome990929.html. *Rapper's Delight* (1979) is considered by many to have been the first major commercial rap record. However, *The Last Poets*, issued in 1969, shows that the style existed a decade earlier.
3. Some claimed that this personal element could be traced back to the slave narratives, oral and written, stemming from an African tradition. However, Ricardo Khan, founder and director of Crossroads Theatre, pointed out that his black audiences had to be reintroduced to the single performance style. "We've done a lot of performance art, which is totally new to black folks." Stephen Coleman, "Crossroads Marks the Spot," *Black Masks* 7 (August/September 1991): 6, pp. 5–6.
4. "What is Hip-Hop?," in *Rap on Rap*, ed. Adam Sexton (New York: Bantam, Doubleday, Dell, 1995), p. 19.
5. MTV (Music Television) brought dance and music performances by Michael Jackson, Prince, and Madonna, to name the top three, to a vast audience of teenagers.
6. The wonder of "wiggers" parodied itself; white performance artist Danny Hoch in *Jails Hospitals Hip-Hop* (1999) portrayed himself in front of a mirror practicing black speech and gesture. "I know I ain't black to you but I can take your culture, soup it up, and sell it back to you."
7. In refutation of Tom Frank's charge that dissident performance art is commodified and sold back on markup, Professor Beth Cleary of Macalester College defended performance art: "If the form of the event defies commerce-driven formulas of storytelling and 'resolution,' if it asks the audience to make meaning out of ambiguities and challenges to norms, there is practice of possibility. There is what the radical Brazilian theater director Augusto Boal calls 'rehearsal for revolution.'" Beth Cleary, "The Flashing Signs of Community," *Spectator* (September 1999).

540 NOTES TO PAGES 432–443

8. Prince Gomolvilas, "Theatre Discovers Hip-Hop, Giving Voice to Young People," *Callboard* (November 1999).
9. Rickerby Hinds, "Stalkin' the Stage, Hip-Hop Drama," *Tha Skit* 1 (1999): 1.
10. Idris Ackamoor, "Black Performance Art at the Turn of the Century: A Personal History; Cultural Odyssey," *Black Theatre News* 8 (spring 1998): 3, pp. 13–14.
11. Rhodessa Jones, *Let's Get It On: The Politics of Black Performance* (Seattle, WA: Bay Press, 1995).
12. Elizabeth Kaye, "Bill T. Jones," *New York Times Magazine*, 6 March 1994, pp. 30–33.
13. McCauley's major work divided into four genres: site-specific pieces involving community collaboration – works involving three communities in different cities, which centered on their own histories; collaborations with thought music – five pieces working with poets, dancers, visual artists, and musicians; sedition ensemble pieces – five works cowritten with musician Ed Montgomery; and the family series – four pieces that used her personal family stories, including *Sally's Rape*.
14. The women of UBW: Terri Cousar, Anita Gonzales, Christina Jones, Christina King, Robin Wilson, and Viola Sheely. Sheely, who was credited as principal dancer and cofounder of the company, died unexpectedly on 27 July 1999.
15. Jawole Willa Jo Zollar, interview by Jennifer Donaghy, tape recording, April 1989, HBC.
16. Jennifer Dunning, *New York Times*, 12 May 1994.
17. Bruce McConachie, "Slavery and Authenticity: Performing a Slave Auction at Colonial Williamsburg," *Theatre Annual* 51 (1998).
18. Suzan-Lori Parks, *Theatre Forum* 3 (spring 1993).
19. Shirlene Holmes, "Working with Pride: The Drama of Writing Black Gay and Lesbian Plays," *Black Theatre News* 8 (spring 1988): 3, p. 17.
20. John Williams, "Hip-Hop Homer," *American Theatre* (May/June 1996): pp. 6–7.
21. George C. Wolfe to James V. Hatch, 23 July 1998, HBC.
22. George C. Wolfe to James V. Hatch, 30 August 1999, HBC.
23. Wolfe received his MFA from New York University in musical theatre and dramatic writing.
24. Frank Rich, "Stage: *Colored Museum*, A Satire by George C. Wolfe," *New York Times*, 3 November 1986.
25. George C. Wolfe, "I Just Want to Keep Telling Stories," interview by Charles H. Rowell, *Callaloo* 16 (March 1993).
26. The Broadway musical *Dreamgirls* (1981) dealt seriously with the careers of the (thinly disguised) Supremes. Although the musical was written and produced by Whites, the talent and the story were black. Did this make it a black musical? Perhaps, but more importantly, it brought black material into mainstream Broadway musicals. (See Allen Woll, *Black Musical Theatre: From Coontown to Dreamgirls* [Baton Rouge, LA: Louisiana State University Press, 1989].) In *Jelly's Last Jam* Wolfe integrated black talent, story, and creation (the producers were white) into the Broadway tradition.
27. Robin Pogrebin, "Public Hires Director to Oversee Finances," *New York Times*, 14 November 2000. Within a year Reiter was dismissed.
28. In 1979 Smith began her public performance series with *On the Road: A Search for American Identity*; its segments included *Voices of Bay Area Women* (1988), *Gender*

Bending (1989), *On Black Identity and Black Theatre* (1990), and *Identities, Mirrors, and Distortions I* (1991). In 1992 she added *Fires in the Mirror* and the next year, *Twilight: Los Angeles, 1992* (1993), based on the Los Angeles rebellion that pitted Koreans against Hispanics and Blacks.

29. One-woman quick-change artistry, popular at the turn of the century, had continued its tradition in the careers of Mercedes Gilbert, Paulene Myers, and later, Vinie Burrows.

30. Richard Stayton, "A Fire in a Crowded Theatre," *American Theatre* (July/August 1993). Earlier, when George Wolfe had been "artistic associate" with the Public Theatre, he had commissioned *Fires in the Mirror* for Smith.

31. Announcement letter from Kati Mitchell to James V. Hatch, 24 November 1997, HBC. The institute's concept shadowed George Bass' Rites and Reason workshops at Brown University.

32. Suzan-Lori Parks, "Elements of Style," in *"The America Play" and Other Works* (New York: Theatre Communications Group, 1995), pp. 231–245.

33. Suzan-Lori Parks, interview by Tom Sellar, *Theatre Forum* 9 (summer 1996): pp. 37–39.

34. Abiola Sinclair, "Notes on Venus," *New York Amsterdam News*, 4 May 1996. In 1999 Parks wrote a loose adaptation of Hawthorne's *The Scarlet Letter* that played at the Public Theatre briefly. Renamed *Fucking A*, a "futuristic otherworldly tale" that focused on Hester the Abortionist, the play was scheduled to reopen at the Public in 2003.

35. Suzan-Lori Parks, "An Equation for Black People Onstage," in *"The America Play" and Other Works*.

36. David Savran, ed., *Breaking the Rules: The Wooster Group* (New York: Theatre Communications Group, 1988).

37. ibid.

38. At a May 1996 conference at Club Med Village in Senegal at which some seven hundred delegates on sub-Saharan development attended – among them two African Americans, US Secretary of Commerce Ronald H. Brown and the Reverend Jesse Jackson – a minstrel skit was presented by the employees of the club, including two white males in blackface. A $5 million lawsuit was filed against Club Med and American Express for "shock, humiliation, anger and outrage."

39. Karen Grigsby Bates, "Whoopi! There it Ain't – and Other Bad Jokes," *Emerge* (December/January 1994): pp. 69–70.

40. A successful appropriation of minstrelsy opened in New York City on 21 October 1999 with *Minstrel Show or The Lynching of William Brown*, a drama by Max Sparber. Based on an actual 1919 lynching in Omaha, Nebraska, two minstrel men were required by the court to report what they saw, which according to critic Les Gutman was "a horrific, compelling, masterful story." As the twentieth century came to its end, lynching became an academic theatre study under the rubric "performance art."

41. Pearl Cleage, "Artistic Statement," in *Contemporary Plays by Women of Color*, ed. Kathy A. Perkins and Roberta Uno (New York: Routledge, 1966), p. 46. Cleage's plays include *Puppetplay* (1981), which premiered at the Just Us Theatre in Atlanta and then at the Negro Ensemble Company in New York. Wider recognition came

with her one-act *Hospice* (1983), which won five AUDELCO Awards for outstanding achievement off-Broadway.

42. When Cleage's directing partner, Kenny Leon, graduated from Clark College in 1978, his family expected him to become a lawyer or minister, but under the influence of Spike Lee and Samuel Jackson he turned to theatre and was named an NEA directing fellow. Leon became the artistic director of Atlanta's Alliance Theatre Company and initiated a program to employ black actors and designers, courting a black audience to attend Alliance's productions.

43. Perkins and Uno, *Contemporary Plays by Women of Color*, pp. 46–47.

44. Aishah Rahman, "*The Mojo and the Sayso*, Aishah Rahman," in *Moon Marked and Touched by Sun*, ed. Sydné Mahone (New York: Theatre Communications Group, 1994), pp. 283–284.

45. A recipient of Rockefeller Foundation and the New York Foundation for the Arts fellowships, Rahman was awarded tenure in Brown University's creative writing program. Her plays have focused on women: *Lady Day, A Musical Tragedy* (1972) concerned Billie Holiday and *Unfinished Women Cry in No Man's Land While a Bird Dies in a Gilded Cage* (1977) dealt with the fantasies of unwed mothers. A biographical play, *Tales of Madame Zora* (1986), was based on the life of Zora Neale Hurston.

46. Despite the increased publication of black plays since the 1960s, only one anthology fills this need: Errol G. Hill, ed., *Black Heroes: Seven Plays* (New York: Applause Theatre Books, 1989). The heroes are Dessalines, Frederick Douglass, Marcus Garvey, Martin Luther King Jr., Paul Robeson, Nat Turner, and Harriet Tubman.

47. Kim Tooks, "Kia Corthron: Staying on Track," *Black Masks* 13 (May/June 1998): 1, pp. 5–6.

48. Ben Brantley, "Social Detectives for Life's Confusions," *New York Times*, 9 February 2001, p. E15.

49. John Simon, "Fête de Famille," *Fashion Magazine*, 30 August 1999.

50. At Arena Stage, Randolph-Wright enjoyed associate artist status and had three shows on the boards within one year, the third a freshly reconceived *Guys and Dolls*. For *Tartuffe* at the American Conservatory Theater in San Francisco, Randolph-Wright recast Molière's 1664 satiric comedy with a 1950s black family in South Carolina. Entitled *Blue* and starring Phylicia Rashad, his play moved to off-Broadway's Roundabout Theatre in 2001.

51. Rita Dove, *The Darker Face of the Earth*, play program, Crossroads Theatre Company, 4 October 1997.

52. A description can be found in Toni Morrison's novel *Beloved*.

53. Larry Leon Hamlin, publicity release from North Carolina Black Repertory Company, 25 February 1989.

54. Hamlin either ignored or was not cognizant with Black Theatre Festival USA, an arts revival at the Lincoln Center in 1979.

55. Larry Leon Hamlin, letter from North Carolina Black Repertory Company, 25 February 1989.

56. They included the Negro Ensemble Company, Penumbra, Jomandi, Just Us, Freedom Theatre, Carpetbag, and Crossroads.

57. Celebrities invited: Ruby Dee, Roscoe Lee Browne, Ossie Davis, Lou Gossett Jr., James Earl Jones, Cicely Tyson, and Oprah Winfrey.

58. Among them American Express, Cadillac, Coca-Cola, Nabisco, Nations Bank, PepsiCo, Sara Lee, US Airways, and Wachovia.

59. In 1991 NBTF hosted fifty-one performances by twenty companies. In 1993 forty celebrities, thirty companies, and a Readers Theatre of New Plays were introduced. In 1995 Miami's Teatro Avante presented the first non-English play, *La Noche de los Asesinos*. The festival had become an international attraction.

60. NCBRC Professor Linda Norflett of North Carolina A&M supervised the educational series, a conglomerate of five programs including the Youth Celebrity Project, which gave young people opportunities to meet the famous, and an international colloquium. Fifteen new plays were showcased in the New Performance in Black Theatre, a reader's theatre. Workshops and seminars expanded along with the vendors' market and art exhibits. The package even embraced a golf tournament with a $360 registration fee – green fees and a golf cart included. In a decade Hamlin had built an industry for the town of Winston-Salem and a national image for black theatre.

61. David Savran, ed., *In Our Own Words: Contemporary American Playwrights* (New York: Theatre Communications Group, 1988).

62. Robert Brustein, "The Lessons of 'The Piano Lesson,'" *New Republic* 202 (22 May 1990).

63. N. Graham Nesmith, "A Stage Champion's Summertime Good-Bye," *New York Times*, Sunday, 18 July 1999.

64. Sandra G. Shannon, *The Dramatic Vision of August Wilson* (Washington, DC: Howard University Press, 1995).

65. August Wilson, *Spotlight* 16 (n.d.): 3.

66. Simon Saltzman and Nicole Plett, "August Wilson Versus Robert Brustein," 22 January 1997, US 1 Newspaper, 29 May 2002, http://www.princetoninfo.com/wilson.html

67. August Wilson, "The Ground on Which I Stand," keynote address at Theater Communications Group, Princeton University, 26 June 1996.

68. In 1991 Crossroads' budget was $2.5 million, but by 2000 the theatre was bankrupt.

69. An exception among the smaller producing units was the Roundabout Theatre Company in New York, with an annual budget of $20 million.

70. Eugene Nesmith, "What's Race Got to Do with It?" *American Theatre* (March 1996): pp. 12–17.

71. Eileen Morris evaluated her experience of the Amos Tuck School of Business Administration thus: "Tuck gave me, an artist, the opportunity to be in an environment filled with artists that were very supportive, positive, creative and inspiring." Morris, "Theatre's Duality, Art and Industry," pp. 93–94.

72. When August Wilson's *Jitney* opened in New York City on 8 April 2000, AGIA used the occasion for a fund-raiser, selling tickets at $300 and $500, hoping to raise $100,000. AGIA's stated purpose was to "provide leadership, technical assistance, and resources for research acquisition of capital, policy initiatives and advocacy to insure the integrity of Black Theatre practice and protection of intellectual property." AGIA fund-raising letter.

73. "Ossie and Ruby Still Making Black History," *Intermission* (February 1999).
74. August Wilson, keynote address at the Atlanta Black Arts Festival, 11 July 1998.
75. *New York Times*, 28 August 1988.
76. John C. Thorpe, "On the Cutting Edge," *Black Masks* 10 (February/March 1994): 2, pp. 5–6.
77. "New Traditions," *NTCP Newsletter*.
78. *Atlanta Constitution*, 25 November 1990.
79. Mel Gussow, "'Salesman' Given in Stamford," *New York Times*, 3 March 1977.
80. Misha Berson, *Seattle Times*, 6 June 1998.
81. Stuart Vaughan had been artistic director of the Phoenix Theatre in New York City, where he had produced several classics including Dion Boucicault's *The Octoroon*.
82. Douglas Q. Barnett, interview by James V. Hatch, tape recording, 1 October 1997, in *Artist and Influence* 17 (1998): pp. 1–27.
83. "Black Actors are Fed Up with 'Token Roles,'" *Seattle Post Intelligencer*, 30 July 1991.
84. In 1995 the Guthrie in Minneapolis invited Penumbra's Lou Bellamy to direct *Big White Fog* in its theatre.
85. Stephanie Ernst, "Minority Actors Land More Roles."
86. Henry Louis Gates Jr., "The Chitlin Circuit," *New Yorker*, 3 February 1997, pp. 44–55.
87. Shelly Garrett, comment made on a panel at the National Black Arts Festival in Atlanta, Georgia, 4 August 1999.
88. Chris Jones, *Chicago Tribune*, 2 February 1996.
89. Woodie King Jr., interview by Barbara Lewis, tape recording, 14 February 1999, in *Artist and Influence* 18 (1999): pp. 55–68.
90. Founded in 1976 by a professional actor, George Hawkins, the Ensemble's hard struggle toward self-sufficiency began with two storefront locations, years of touring regional colleges and secondary schools, a young performers program for youth (175 students in 1998), a summer program taught by professionals, featuring dance, music, creative writing, and cultural studies. Publicity brochure 1998.
91. In 1981 the Jubilee Players in Fort Worth acquired nonprofit status, and by 1993 Jubilee had raised the capital to renovate a downtown theatre. In 1996 the players produced a seven-show season consisting of 170 performances involving more than a hundred local artists and technicians.
92. With the onslaught of AIDS in 1986, BBR signed a ten-year contract with the Alameda Country Department of Public Heath to dramatize methods of HIV Prevention. The company toured rest homes and prisons, venues where confined people were unable to see live theatre.
93. The ensemble introduced into five or six public schools a free twenty-week drama program called Life Issues, in which students wrote scripts that director Zerita Dotson classified as sociodramas. These plays were then presented in programs called StageFest. From 1978 to 1980 Professor Sandra Richards was artistic director.
94. "Theatre Arts," *Craft Arts Quarterly* 3 (fall 1988): 3.
95. The United Auto Workers asked Elsie Bryant, director of the Labor Studies Center at the University of Michigan, to conduct a symposium on worker culture. Bryant found six people who would tell their personal stories for Workers' Lives, Workers' Stories (1982). The company wrote its own scripts and presented itself as a readers'

theatre. The following year, the Michigan Council for the Humanities toured the show and paid the director a salary. From 1983 to 1987 the group performed about twenty-two times a year for different union locals and workers' conferences, earning salaries that were paid by the unions.

96. "Detroit's Plowshares: A New Home for a Bold Theatre," *Black Theatre News* 6 (fall 1997): 1.

97. Penumbra celebrated its twentieth anniversary in 1997.

98. Breena Clarke, "Minnesota's Penumbra Theatre Moves into the Light," *Black Masks* 7 (August/September 1991): 6, pp. 7–8, 19.

99. Penumbra's productions of Wilson's plays include the seldom seen *Black Bart* and *Malcolm X*. *Jitney*, one of Wilson's first plays, was never attempted on Broadway but played for more than a year at a theatre on Union Square.

100. August Wilson, "Twenty Years Running: Penumbra's Victory," publicity letter, 1996.

101. In 1997 more than sixty corporations and foundations, including the cereal giant, General Mills Company, plus hundreds of individuals, donated money and services. A highlight was the Bush Foundation's two-year grant of $200,000 for a "Regional Arts Development Program," and Northwest Area Foundation's three-year grant of $880,000 for "staff development, increased marketing and development initiatives, and facilities upgrades." Penumbra ended its 1997 season with assets of $24,388, a rare bottom line for any nonprofit. In 1999 the Minnesota State Legislature voted $2.25 million to build Penumbra its own theatre.

102. "The Father of Black Theatre in St. Louis," *Intermission* (October 1997).

103. Radio program, KDHX FM88, St. Louis, Missouri, August 1998.

104. "Fact Sheet," ETA Creative Arts Foundation, 1998.

105. "Crossroads Theatre Company – A History," publicity mailer, 1992.

106. "Khan: 'Lee Richardson's Dismissal was not a Power Play,'" *New Brunswick (NJ) Home News Tribune*, Arts and Entertainment section, Sunday, 6 November 1988.

107. Barbara Seyda, "Divine Testimonies," *Drama Review* 40 (spring 1996): 1 (T149).

108. The National Endowment for the Arts, the New Jersey State Council on the Arts, AT&T, the Geraldine R. Dodge Foundation, American Express, and the Kennedy Center for the Performing Arts supported Crossroads.

109. Khan had assembled a talented staff: literary manager Sydné Mahone and grants managers Deborah Stapleton and Pamela Faith Jackson. Khan made judicious use of celebrities, and perhaps most important, he made New Brunswick residents feel that Crossroads was their own community theatre.

110. This data was taken from a series of articles published on 3–6 October 2001 by Laurie Granieri, staff writer for the *New Brunswick (NJ) Home News Tribune*.

111. Linda Bean, "Crossroads Theatre Receives Funds: Expects to Raise Curtain This Summer," *Daily Diversity News and Views*, 7 February 2001, Diversityinc.com, 7 July 2001, http://www.diversityinc.com/insidearticlepg.cfm?submenuID = 080&ArticleID = 2423

112. "Freedom Theatre Fact Sheet," promotional packet, Philadelphia's Freedom Theatre, 1998.

113. Christopher Reardon, "The Arts Mean Business," *Ford Foundation Report* 30 (winter 1999): 1. Walter Dallas welcomed the change. "Looking at the theater

as a business was a big shift for me. On one level, I always knew that if we didn't get certain grants or sell enough tickets that we wouldn't have a theater." WCF helped to stabilize Freedom Theatre's budget, making it possible to bring in Barbara Silzle as director of artistic initiatives, Donald O. H. Brown as managing director, and Cynthia Hart as director of operations.

114. Every Christmas many black theatres produced Langston Hughes' *Black Nativity*, in the same manner that national television stations produce Dickens' *A Christmas Carol*. SRO performances helped to balance the budget.

115. Judith Lewis, "Eye on Tomorrow," *American Theatre*, November 1990. The Lorraine Hansberry Theatre is located in the former YMCA building on San Francisco's Union Square.

Appendix: theatre scholarship 2002

1. The lineage includes SADSA (Southern Association of Dramatic and Speech Arts); NADSA (National Association of Dramatic and Speech Arts); the American Theatre Association's Afro Asian Theatre Project; NCAAT (National Conference of African American Theatre); BTA (Black Theatre Association), and BTN (Black Theatre Network).

Bibliography

Books

Abramson, Doris. *Negro Playwrights in the American Theatre, 1925–1959.* New York: Columbia University Press, 1969.

Appiah, Kwame Anthony, and Henry Louis Gates, Jr., eds. *Africana: The Encyclopedia of the African and African American Experience.* New York: Basic Civitas Books, 1999.

Aptheker, Herbert. *American Negro Slave Revolts.* 5th edn. New York: International Publishers, 1983.

Aptheker, Herbert, ed. *A Documentary History of the Negro People in the United States.* Vol. II. 1951. 4th paperback edn. New York: Citadel Press, 1968.

Arciniegas, Germán. *Caribbean: Sea of the New World.* Translated by Harriet De Onís. New York: Alfred A. Knopf, 1946.

Bennett, Lerone, Jr. *Before the Mayflower: A History of Black America.* 5th edn. Harmondsworth: Penguin, 1984.

Bennett, Lerone, Jr. *Pioneers in Protest.* Harmondsworth: Penguin, 1968.

Birdoff, Harry. *The World's Greatest Hit: Uncle Tom's Cabin.* New York: S. F. Vanni, 1947.

Bordman, Gerald. *American Musical Theatre: A Chronicle.* Oxford: Oxford University Press, 1978.

Brawley, Benjamin. *Negro Builders and Heroes.* Chapel Hill, NC: University of North Carolina Press, 1937.

Bruce, John E. *The Blood Red Record: A Review of the Horrible Lynchings and Burning of Negroes by Civilized White Men in the United States, as Taken from the Records.* Albany, NY: Argus Company, 1901.

Burns, Stanley. *Other Voices: Ventriloquism from BC to TV.* Privately published, 2000.

Carter, Steven R. *Hansberry's Drama: Commitment and Complexity.* Urbana, IL: University of Illinois Press, 1991.

Charters, Ann. *Nobody: The Story of Bert Williams.* New York: Macmillan, 1970.

Cockrell, Dale. *Demons of Disorder.* Cambridge: Cambridge University Press, 1997.

Coleman, Gregory D. *We're Heaven Bound! A Portrait of a Black Sacred Drama.* Athens, GA: University of Georgia Press, 1994.

Connelly, Marc. *Voices Offstage: A Book of Memoirs.* Chicago, IL: Holt, Rinehart, and Winston, 1968.

Cruse, Harold. *The Crisis of the Negro Intellectual.* New York: William Morrow, 1967.

Cullen, Rosemary L. *The Civil War in American Drama Before 1900: Catalog of an Exhibition, November 1982*. Providence, RI: Brown University Press, 1982.

Cuyler, T. V. *Albany Directory*. 1824.

Cuyler, T. V. *Albany Directory*. 1825.

Daniel, Walter C. *"De Lawd": Richard B. Harrison and The Green Pastures*. New York: Greenwood Press, 1986.

Davis, Ossie, and Ruby Dee. *With Ossie and Ruby*. New York: William Morrow, 1998.

Doesticks, Q. K. Philander [Mortimer Neal Thomson]. *Doesticks: What He Says*. New York: E. Livermore, 1855.

Dormon, James H., Jr. *Theater in the Ante-Bellum South, 1815–1861*. Chapel Hill, NC: University of North Carolina Press, 1967.

Douglas, Ann. *Terrible Honesty: Mongrel Manhattan in the 1920s*. New York: Farrar, Straus, and Giroux, 1995.

Du Bois, W. E. B. *The Souls of Black Folk: Essays and Sketches*. 1903. Reprinted, Greenwich, CN: Fawcett Publications, 1961.

Duster, Alfreda M., ed. *Crusade for Justice: The Autobiography of Ida B. Wells*. Chicago, IL: University of Chicago Press, 1970.

Edmonds, Randolph. *Six Plays for a Negro Theatre*. Boston: Walter H. Baker, 1934.

Engs, Robert F. *Freedom's First Generation: Black Hampton, Virginia, 1861–1890*. Philadelphia: University of Pennsylvania Press, 1979.

Farrison, William Edward. *William Wells Brown: Author and Reformer*. Chicago, IL: University of Chicago Press, 1969.

Flanagan, Hallie. *Arena: The History of the Federal Theatre*. New York: Duell, Sloan, and Pearce, 1940.

Fletcher, Tom. *One Hundred Years of the Negro in Show Business*. New York: Burdge and Company, 1954.

Flexner, Stuart Berg. *I Hear America Talking: An Illustrated History of American Words and Phrases*. New York: Simon and Schuster, 1976.

Ford, Hugh, ed. *The Left Bank Revisited: Selections from the "Paris Tribune," 1917–1934*. University Park, PN: Pennsylvania State University Press, 1972.

Fraden, Rena. *Blueprints for a Black Federal Theatre, 1935–1939*. Cambridge: Cambridge University Press, 1994.

Franklin, John Hope, and Loren Schweninger. *Runaway Slaves: Rebels on the Plantation*. Oxford: Oxford University Press, 1999.

Furnas, J. C. *Goodbye to Uncle Tom*. New York: W. Sloane Associates, 1956.

George-Graves, Nadine. *The Royalty of Negro Vaudeville: The Whitman Sisters and the Negotiation of Race, Gender, and Class in African American Theatre, 1900–1940*. New York: St. Martin's Press, 2000.

Gilder, Rosamond, *et al.*, eds. *Theatre Arts Anthology*. New York: Theatre Arts Books, 1950.

Glassberg, David. *American Historical Pageantry: The Uses of Tradition in the Early Twentieth Century*. Chapel Hill, NC: University of North Carolina Press, 1990.

Gottschild, Brenda Dixon. *Digging the Africanist Presence in American Performance: Dance and Other Contexts*. Westport, CT: Greenwood Press, 1996.

Greene, Evarts B., and Virginia D. Harrington. *American Population Before the Federal Census of 1790*. New York: Columbia University Press, 1993.

Gruesser, John Cullen. *Black on Black: Twentieth-Century African American Writing about Africa*. Lexington, KN: University Press of Kentucky, 2000.

Handy, W. C. *Father of the Blues*. New York: Macmillan, 1941.

Hatch, James V., ed. *Black Theatre USA: forty-five Plays by Black Americans, 1847–1974*. New York: Free Press, 1974.

Hatch, James V., and Ted Shine, eds. *Black Theatre USA: Plays by African Americans*. Revised and expanded edn. New York: Free Press, 1996.

Hay, Samuel. *African American Theatre: An Historical and Critical Analysis*. Cambridge: Cambridge University Press, 1994.

Higginson, Colonel W. *Army Life in a Black Regiment*. 1870. Reprinted East Lansing, MI: Michigan University Press, 1960.

Higginson, Thomas Wentworth. *Black Rebellion; a Selection from Travellers and Outlaws*. 1889. Reprinted New York: Arno Press, 1969.

Hill, Anthony D. *Pages from the Harlem Renaissance: A Chronicle of Performance*. New York: P. Lang, 1996.

Hill, Errol G. *Shakespeare in Sable: A History of Black Shakespearean Actors*. Amherst, MA: University of Massachusetts Press, 1984.

Hill, Errol G. *The Jamaican Stage, 1655–1900*. Amherst, MA: University of Massachusetts Press, 1992.

Hill, Errol G., ed. *The Theatre of Black Americans*. 2 vols. 1980. Reprinted in one volume, New York: Applause Theatre Books, 1987.

Hill, Errol G., ed. *Black Heroes: Seven Plays*. New York: Applause Theatre Books, 1989.

Holmes, Dwight Oliver Wendell. *The Evolution of the Negro College*. 1934. Reprinted New York: AMS Press, 1970.

Honychurch, Lennox. *The Dominica Story: A History of the Island*. Dominica: Dominica Institute Press, 1975.

Horn, Barbara Lee. *Joseph Papp: A Bio-Bibliography*. Westport, CT: Greenwood Press, 1992.

Huggins, Nathan Irvin. *Harlem Renaissance*. Oxford: Oxford University Press, 1971.

Hughes, Langston. *The Big Sea*. New York: Hill and Wang, 1963.

Hughes, Langston. *Good Morning Revolution: Uncollected Social Protest Writings*. Edited by Faith Berry. New York: Lawrence Hill, 1973.

Hughes, Langston. *The Political Plays of Langston Hughes*. Introduction and analyses by Susan Duffy. Carbondale, IL: Southern Illinois University Press, 2000.

Hughes, Langston, and Milton Meltzer. *Black Magic: A Pictorial History of the Negro in American Entertainment*. Englewood Cliffs, NJ: Prentice-Hall, 1967.

Johnson, James Weldon. *Along This Way: The Autobiography of James Weldon Johnson*. Harmondsworth: Penguin, 1933.

Johnson, James Weldon. *Black Manhattan*. New York: Alfred A. Knopf, 1930.

Jones, Maxine D., and Joe M. Richardson. *Talladega College: The First Century*. Tuscaloosa, AL: University of Alabama Press, 1990.

Jones, Rhodessa. *Let's Get It On: The Politics of Black Performance*. Seattle, WA: Bay Press, 1995.

Kellner, Bruce. *The Harlem Renaissance: A Historical Dictionary for the Era*. Westport, CN: Greenwood Press, 1984.

Keppel, Ben. *The Work of Democracy*. Cambridge, MA: Harvard University Press, 1995.

King, Bruce. *Derek Walcott and West Indian Drama*. Oxford: Clarendon Press, 1995.

Kirby, I. E., and C. I. Martin. *The Rise and Fall of the Black Caribs of St. Vincent*. Kingstown, Saint Vincent and the Grenadines: St. Vincent and the Grenadines National Trust, 1972.

Krasner, David. *Resistance, Parody, and Double Consciousness in African American Theatre, 1895–1910*. New York: St. Martin's Press, 1997.

Lincoln, C. Eric. *The Negro Pilgrimage in America*. New York: Bantam, 1969.

Linn, Karen. *That Half-Barbaric Twang: The Banjo in American Culture*. Urbana, IL: University of Illinois Press, 1991.

Locke, Alain LeRoy. *The Critical Temper of Alain Locke: A Selection of his Essays on Art and Culture*. Edited by Jeffrey C. Stewart. New York: Garland, 1983.

Locke, Alain LeRoy, ed. *The New Negro*. 1925. Reprinted New York: Atheneum, 1969.

Lott, Eric. *Love and Theft: Blackface Minstrelsy and the American Working Class*. Oxford: Oxford University Press, 1993.

Magus, Jim. *Magical Heroes: The Lives and Legends of Great African American Magicians*. Marietta, GA: Magus Enterprises, 1995.

Mahar, William J. *Behind the Burnt Cork Mask: Early Blackface Minstrelsy and Antebellum American Popular Culture*. Urbana, IL: University of Illinois Press, 1999.

Malone, Jacqui. *Steppin' on the Blues: The Visible Rhythms of African American Dance*. Urbana, IL: University of Illinois Press, 1996.

Mannix, Daniel P., in collaboration with Malcolm Cowley. *Black Cargoes: A History of the Atlantic Slave Trade, 1518–1865*. London: Longmans, Green, 1963.

March, John Moncure. *The Wild Party*. New York: Covici, Friede, 1928.

March, John Moncure. *The Set-Up*. New York: Covici, Friede, 1928.

Marshall, Herbert, and Mildred Stock. *Ira Aldridge: The Negro Tragedian*. 1958. Reprinted with an introduction by Errol G. Hill, Washington, DC: Howard University Press, 1993.

Martin, Denis. *Coon Carnival: New Year in Cape Town: Past to Present*. Cape Town, South Africa: David Philip Publishers, 1999.

Mathews, Brander. *A Book about the Theater*. New York: Scribner's Sons, 1916.

McLaren, Joseph. *Langston Hughes*. Westport, CN: Greenwood Press, 1997.

Mitchell, Loften. *Black Drama: The Story of the American Negro in the Theatre*. New York: Hawthorn Books, 1967.

Moody, Richard, ed. *Dramas from the American Theatre, 1762–1909*. Cleveland, OH: World Publishing Company, 1966.

Muccigrosso, Robert. *Celebrating the New World: Chicago's Columbian Exposition of 1893*. Chicago, IL: Ivan R. Dee, 1993.

Mumford, Esther Hall. *Seattle's Black Victorians: 1852–1901*. Seattle, WA: Ananse Press, 1980.

National Association for the Advancement of Colored People. *Thirty Years of Lynching in the United States*. 1919. Reprinted New York: Arno Press, 1969.

Nathan, Hans. *Dan Emmett and the Rise of Early Negro Minstrelsy*. Norman, OK: University of Oklahoma Press, 1962.

Neal, Lester A. *Ntozake Shange: A Critical Study of the Plays*. New York: Garland, 1995.

Nizer, Louis. *My Life in Court*. New York: Pyramid Books, 1961.

O'Connor, John, and Lorraine Brown, eds. *Free, Adult, Uncensored: The Living History of the Federal Theatre Project*. Washington, DC: New Republic Books, 1978.

Odell, George C. D. *Annals of the New York Stage*. Vol. XII, *1882–1885*. New York: AMS Press, 1970.

Owen, Lyla Hay, and Owen Murphy. *Créoles of New Orleans: People of Color*. New Orleans: First Quarter Publishing, 1987.

Peabody, Francis G. *Education for Life: The Story of Hampton Institute*. Garden City, NY: Doubleday, 1918.

Perkins, Kathy A., and Judith L. Stephens. *Strange Fruit, Plays on Lynching by American Women*. Bloomington, IN: Indiana University Press, 1998.

Perkins, Kathy A., and Roberta Uno, eds. *Contemporary Plays by Women of Color*. New York: Routledge, 1966.

Peterson, Bernard L., Jr. *The African American Theatre Directory, 1816–1960: A Comprehensive Guide to Early Black Theatre Organizations, Companies, Theatres, and Performing Groups*. Westport, CT: Greenwood Press, 1997.

Peterson, Bernard L., Jr. *A Century of Musicals in Black and White*. Westport, CT: Greenwood Press, 1993.

Peterson, Bernard L., Jr. *Early Black American Playwrights and Dramatic Writers: A Directory and Catalog of Plays, Films, and Broadcasting Scripts*. Westport, CT: Greenwood Press, 1990.

Peterson, Bernard L., Jr. *Profiles of African American Stage Performers and Theatre People, 1816–1960*. Westport, CT: Greenwood Press, 2001.

Phelps, H. P. *Players of a Century: A Record of the Albany Stage*. 2nd edn. Albany, NY: J. McDonough, 1880.

Reardon, William R., and Thomas D. Pawley, eds. *The Black Teacher and the Dramatic Arts: A Dialogue, Bibliography, and Anthology*. Westport, CT: Negro Universities Press, 1970.

Reed, Bill. *"Hot from Harlem": Profiles in Classic African-American Entertainment*. Los Angeles, CA: Cellar Door Books, 1998.

Reed, Christopher. *"All the World is Here!" The Black Presence at White City*. Bloomington, IN: Indiana University Press, 2000.

Reynolds, Harry. *Minstrel Memories: The Story of Burnt Cork Minstrelsy in Great Britain from 1836 to 1927*. London: Alston Rivers, 1928.

Richardson, Willis, and May Miller, eds. *Negro History in Thirteen Plays*. Washington, DC: Associated Publishers, 1935.

The Roaring Lion (Rafael de Leon). *Calypso from France to Trinidad: Eight Hundred Years of History*. San Juan, Trinidad: General Printers, *c.* 1985.

Rowland, Mabel, ed. *Bert Williams: Son of Laughter; a symposium of tribute to the man and to his work, by his friends and associates*. 1923. Reprinted Westport, CT: Negro Universities Press, 1969.

Rydell, Robert W. *All the World's a Fair: Visions of Empire at American International Expositions, 1876–1916*. Chicago, IL: University of Chicago Press, 1984.

Sacks, Howard L., and Judith Rose Sacks. *Way up North in Dixie*. Washington, DC: Smithsonian Museum Press, 1993.

Sampson, Henry T. *Blacks in Blackface: A Source Book on Early Black Musical Shows*. Metuchen, NJ: Scarecrow Press, 1980.

Sampson, Henry T. *The Ghost Walks: A Chronological History of Blacks in Show Business, 1865–1910*. Metuchen, NJ: Scarecrow Press, 1988.

Sanders, Leslie Catherine. *The Development of Black Theater in America: From Shadows to Selves*. Baton Rouge, LO: Louisiana State University Press, 1988.

Sansom, George Bailey. *The Western World and Japan: A Study in the Interaction of European and Asiatic Cultures*. New York: Alfred A. Knopf, 1950.

Savran, David, ed. *Breaking the Rules: The Wooster Group*. New York: Theatre Communications Group, 1988.

Savran, David, ed. *In Our Own Words: Contemporary American Playwrights*. New York: Theatre Communications Group, 1988.

Scruggs, Charles. *H. L. Mencken and the Black Writers of the 1920s*. Baltimore, MD: Johns Hopkins University Press, 1984.

Shange, Ntozake. *Three Pieces*. New York: St. Martin's Press, 1981.

Shannon, Sandra G. *The Dramatic Vision of August Wilson*. Washington, DC: Howard University Press, 1995.

Simmons, William J. *Men of Mark: Eminent, Progressive, and Rising*. Cleveland, OH: O. G. M. Rewell, 1887.

Smith, Eric Ledell. *Bert Williams: A Biography of the Pioneer Black Comedian*. Jefferson, NC: McFarland, 1992.

Smith, Eric Ledell. *Blacks in Opera: An Encyclopedia of People and Companies, 1873–1993*. Jefferson, NC: McFarland, 1995.

Smith, S. Morgan. *A Critical Review of the Late Speech of Charles O'Conor, "Negro Slavery Not Unjust."* Philadelphia: n.p., [1865?].

Southern, Eileen. *Biographical Dictionary of Afro-American and African Musicians*. Westport, CT: Greenwood Press, 1982.

Southern, Eileen. *The Music of Black Americans: A History*. New York: W. W. Norton, 1971.

Southern, Eileen, ed. *African American Theater: "Out of Bondage" (1876) and "Peculiar Sam; or, The Underground Railroad" (1879)*. New York: Garland, 1994.

Stearns, Marshall, and Jean Stearns. *Jazz Dance: The Story of American Vernacular Dance*. New York: Macmillan, 1968.

Talley, Thomas W. *Negro Folk Rhymes*. New York: Macmillan, 1922.

Taylor, Quintard. *The Forging of a Black Community: Seattle's Central District, from 1870 through the Civil Rights Era*. Seattle, WA: University of Washington Press, 1994.

Thompson, George A., Jr. *Documentary History of the African Theatre*. Chicago, IL: Northwestern University Press, 1998.

Toll, Robert C. *Blacking Up: The Minstrel Show in Ninteenth-Century America*. Oxford: Oxford University Press, 1974.

Thurman, Wallace. *Negro Life in New York's Harlem*. Little Blue Book 494. Girard, KN: E. Haldeman-Julius Publications, 1924.

Van Vechten, Carl. *Letters of Carl Van Vechten*. Edited by Bruce Kellner. New Haven, CN: Yale University Press, 1987.

Walcott, Derek. *Dream on Monkey Mountain and Other Plays*. New York: Farrar, Straus, and Giroux, 1970.

Washington, Booker T. *A New Negro for a New Century; an Accurate and Up-to-Date Record of the Upward Struggles of the Negro Race*. Chicago, IL: American Publishing House, 1900.

Waterhouse, Richard. *From Minstrel Show to Vaudeville: The Australian Popular Stage, 1788–1914*. Kensington, Australia: New South Wales Press, 1990.

Waters, Ethel. *To Me it's Wonderful*. New York: Harper and Row, 1972.

Waters, Ethel, with Charles Samuels. *His Eye is on the Sparrow*. Garden City, NY: Doubleday, 1951.

Watkins, Mel. *On the Real Side*. New York: Simon and Schuster, 1994.

Weill, Nancy J. *The National Urban League, 1910–1940*. Oxford: Oxford University Press, 1974.

Williams, Mance. *Black Theatre in the 1960s and 1970s*. Westport, CT: Greenwood Press, 1985.

Wills, Garry. *Inventing America: Jefferson's Declaration of Independence*. New York: Doubleday, 1978.

Woll, Allen. *Black Musical Theatre: From Coontown to Dreamgirls*. Baton Rouge, LA: Louisiana State University Press, 1989.

Wright, Richard. *American Hunger*. 1944. Reprinted New York: Harper and Row, 1977.

Articles

Abramson, Doris E. Review of *The Escape; or, A Leap for Freedom*. *Educational Theatre Journal* 24 (1972): pp. 190–191.

Ackamoor, Idris. "Black Performance Art at the Turn of the Century: A Personal History; Cultural Odyssey." *Black Theatre News* 8 (spring 1998): 3, pp. 13–14.

Anderson, Addell Austin. "The Ethiopian Art Theatre." *Theatre Survey* 33 (November 1992).

Anderson, Garland. "How I Became a Playwright." In *Anthology of the American Negro in the Theatre*, compiled by Lindsay Patterson. Washington, DC: Publishers Company, 1967.

Angier, Natalie. "Do Races Differ? Not Really, Genes Show." *New York Times*, 22 August 2000, Science Times section, p. F1.

"At Home with Ethel Waters." *Phylon*, third quarter (1953–54): p. 253.

Baraka, Amiri. "A Critical Reevaluation: *A Raisin in the Sun*'s Enduring Passion." In *A Raisin in the Sun*, edited by Robert Nemiroff. Expanded 25th edn. New York: New American Library, 1987.

Baraka, Amiri. "What Is Black Theatre?" Interview by Mike Coleman. *Black World* 20 (April 1971): 6, pp. 32–36.

Barnett, Douglas Q. Interview by James V. Hatch. Tape recording, 1 October 1997. *Artist and Influence* 17 (1998): pp. 1–27.

Bates, Karen Grigsby. "Whoopi! There it Ain't – and Other Bad Jokes." *Emerge* (December/January 1994): pp. 69–70.

Bird, Robert Montgomery. "The Gladiator." In *Dramas from the American Theatre, 1762–1909*, edited by Richard Moody. Cleveland, OH: World Publishing Company, 1966.

Brown, Lorraine. "Library of Congress Takes Back Federal Theatre Project Archive."
    New Federal One 19 (October 1994): 3.
Brustein, Robert. "The Lessons of 'The Piano Lesson.'" *New Republic* 202 (22 May
    1990).
Bullins, Ed. "The So-called Western Avant-garde Drama." *Liberator* 7 (December 1967):
    12, pp. 16–17.
Castleberry, Bill. "Black Theatre Alliance Closes Down." *Uptown* (summer 1981): p. 34.
Ceynowa, Andrzej. "Black Theaters . . . 1961–1982." *Black American Literature Forum* 17
    (summer 1983): 2, pp. 84–93.
Childress, Alice. "For a Negro Theatre." *Masses and Mainstream* (February 1951):
    pp. 61–64.
Chintoh, Jojo. "Lennox Brown: A Black Canadian Dramatist." *Black Images* (Toronto)
    1 (January 1972): 1.
Clarke, Breena. "Minnesota's Penumbra Theatre Moves into the Light." *Black Masks* 7
    (August/September 1991): 6, pp. 7–8, 19.
Cleage, Pearl. "Artistic Statement." In *Contemporary Plays by Women of Color*, edited by
    Kathy A. Perkins and Roberta Uno. New York: Routledge, 1966.
Cleary, Beth. "The Flashing Signs of Community." *Spectator* (September 1999).
Coleman, Stephen. "Crossroads Marks the Spot." *Black Masks* 7 (August/September
    1991): 6, pp. 5–6.
Cotter, Joseph S., Sr. "Dr. Booker T. Washington to the National Negro Business
    League" (1909?). In *The Vintage Book of African American Poetry*, edited by Michael
    S. Harper and Anthony Walton. New York: Vintage Books, 2000.
Cromer, Harold. Interview by Delilah Jackson. Tape recording, 20 February 1999. *Artist
    and Influence* 13 (1994): pp. 37–64.
Curtis, Susan. "Three Plays for a Negro Theatre." In *The First Black Actors on the Great
    White Way*. Columbia, MO: University of Missouri Press, 1998.
"Detroit's Plowshares: A New Home for a Bold Theatre." *Black Theatre News* 6 (fall
    1997): 1.
Dodson, Owen. "Playwrights in Dark Glasses." *Negro Digest* 17 (6 April 1968): pp. 31–36.
Du Bois, W. E. B. "Paying for Plays." *Crisis* 25 (December 1922): p. 7.
Edmonds, Randolph S. "The Negro Little Theater Movement." *Negro History Bulletin*
    (January 1949): pp. 82–84.
Ernst, Stephanie. "Minority Actors Land More Roles." *New York Times*, 28 August 1988.
"The Father of Black Theatre in St. Louis." *Intermission* (October 1997).
Fehrenbach, Robert J. "William Edgar Easton's *Dessalines*: A Nineteenth-Century
    Drama of Black Pride." *CLA Journal* 19 (September 1975): 1, pp. 75–89.
Fletcher, Winona Lee. Interview by James V. Hatch. Tape recording, 8 May 1995. *Artist
    and Influence* 14 (1995): pp. 107–118.
Fraden, Rena. "The Cloudy History of *Big White Fog*: The Federal Theatre Project,
    1938." *American Studies* 29 (spring 1988): 1, pp. 5–27.
"Funding." *Theatre Crafts* 6 (March/April 1972): 2, pp. 13, 35–36.
Funk, Ray. "Kaiso Newsletter," no. 29, 6 November 1999, Fairbanks, Alaska.
Gardner, Bettye, and Bettye Thomas. "The Cultural Impact of the Howard Theatre on
    the Black Community." *Negro History* 55 (October 1970): 4, p. 254.

Gates, Henry Louis, Jr. "A Black Lecture on Language." In *The Signifying Monkey: A Theory of Afro-American Literary Criticism*. Oxford: Oxford University Press, 1988.

Gates, Henry Louis, Jr. "The Chitlin Circuit." *New Yorker*, 3 February 1997, pp. 44–55.

Gomolvilas, Prince. "Theatre Discovers Hip-Hop, Giving Voice to Young People." *Callboard* (November 1999).

Grimké, Angelina Weld. "'Rachel' the Play of the Month, the Reason and Synopsis by the Author." *Competitor* 1 (January 1920): p. 51.

Hall, Roger Allan. "Black America: Nate Salsbury's Afro-American Exhibition." *Educational Theatre Journal* 29 (March 1977): 1, pp. 49–60.

Harris, Edna Mae, and Vivian Harris. "Sirens, Sweethearts, and Showgirls of the Stage and Silver Screen." Interview by Delilah Jackson. Tape recording, 4 February 1990. *Artist and Influence* 10 (1991), p. 75.

Harrison, Herbert. "Are Negro Actors White?" *Crusader* 4 (April 1921): 2, p. 25.

Hawkins, J. E. "The Negro and Chicago, Past and Present." *Chicago Whip*, 8 May 1920. Article continued in issues of 15, 22, and 29 May 1920, and 5 June 1920.

Hay, Samuel A. "The Death of Black Educational Theatre, 94, Stirs Huge Controversy." *Black Theatre News* 9 (fall 1998): 1, pp. 27–28.

Herndon, Adrienne. "Shakespeare at Atlanta University." *Voice of the Negro* (1961): pp. 482–486.

Hill, Abram. Interview by Michele Wallace. Tape recording, 19 January 1974. *Artist and Influence* 19 (2000): p. 120.

Hill, Errol G. "The Hyers Sisters: Pioneers in Black Musical Comedy." In *The American Stage: Social and Economic Issues from the Colonial Period to the Present*, edited by Ron Engle and Tice L. Miller. Cambridge: Cambridge University Press, 1993.

Hinds, Rickerby. "Stalkin' the Stage, Hip-Hop Drama." *Tha Skit* 1 (fall 1999): 1.

Holmes, Shirlene. "Working with Pride: The Drama of Writing Black Gay and Lesbian Plays." *Black Theatre News* 8 (spring 1988): 3, p. 17.

Hughes, Langston. "The Negro Artist and the Racial Mountain." *Nation* 122 (23 June 1926): pp. 167–172.

Hughes, Langston. "The Trouble with Angels." In *New Theatre and Film 1934 to 1937*, edited by Herbert Kline. San Diego, CA: Harcourt Brace Jovanovich, 1985.

Hurston, Zora Neale. "Characteristics of Negro Expression." In *The Negro: An Anthology*, edited by Nancy Cunard. London: Frederick Ungar, 1934.

Ingle, Edward. "The Negro in the District of Columbia." *Johns Hopkins University Studies in Historical and Political Science*, 11th series (March/April 1893): pp. 47–48.

"Integration." *Equity* (June 1952).

"Ira Aldridge." *Anglo-African Magazine*, 1 (January 1860): pp. 27–32.

"Irwin, May." In *Who's Who on the Stage 1908*, edited by Walter Browne and E. De Roy Koch. New York: B. W. Dodge, 1908.

Jefferson, Miles. "Empty Season on Broadway, 1950–51." *Phylon*, third quarter (1950/51): p. 130.

Jett, Ruth. Interview by James V. Hatch. Tape recording, 15 March 1988. *Artist and Influence* 17 (1998): p. 111.

Jones, Rhett S. "Orderly and Disorderly Structures." *Black American Literature Forum* 25 (spring 1991): 1, pp. 43–52.

Karpf, Juanita. "Vinnette Carroll," *Notable Women in the American Theatre: A Biographical Dictionary*. Westport, CT: Greenwood Press, 1989.

Kaye, Elizabeth. "Bill T. Jones." *New York Times Magazine*, 6 March 1994, pp. 30–33.

"Khan: 'Lee Richardson's Dismissal was not a Power Play.'" *New Brunswick (NJ) Home News Tribune*, Arts and Entertainment section, Sunday, 6 November 1988.

King, Woodie, Jr. Interview by Barbara Lewis. Tape recording, 14 February 1999. *Artist and Influence* 18 (1999): pp. 55–68.

Lewis, Barbara. "'Oedipus Rex', King James Version." *Encore American and Worldwide News*, 4 April 1977.

Lewis, Judith. "Eye on Tomorrow." *American Theatre* (November 1990).

Lewis, Theophilus. "Charles Gilpin and the Drama League." *Messenger* 3 (March 1921): 3, pp. 203–204.

Lewis, Theophilus. "If this be Puritanism." *Opportunity* (April 1929), pp. 132–133.

Lhamon, W. T., Jr. "Ebery Time I Wheel About I Jump Jim Crow: Cycles of Minstrel Transgression from Cool White to Vanilla Ice." In *Behind the Minstrel Mask*, edited by Annemarie Bean, James V. Hatch, and Brooks McNamara. Middletown, CT: Wesleyan University Press, 1996.

Lindfors, Bernth. "'Nothing Extenuate, Nor Set Down Aught in Malice': New Biographical Information on Ira Aldridge." *African American Review* 28 (1994): 3, pp. 457–472.

Lindfors, Bernth. "The Signifying Flunkey: Ira Aldridge as Mungo." *International Journal of Black Expressive Culture Studies* 5 (fall 1993): pp. 1–11.

Littlefield, Daniel C. "The Atlantic Slave Trade: An Overview." In *Encyclopedia of African-American Culture and History*, vol. v, edited by Jack Salzman, David Lionel Smith, and Cornel West. New York: Macmillan Library Reference, 1996.

Locke, Alain LeRoy. "*Goat Alley*." *Opportunity* 1 (February 1923): p. 30.

Locke, Alain LeRoy. "Steps Toward the Negro Theatre." *Crisis* 25 (December 1922): pp. 66–68.

Long, Richard. "From Periphery to Center." In *Grown Deep: Essays on the Harlem Renaissance*. Winter Park, FL: Four-G Publishers, 1998.

"Lowdown Theater." *Messenger*, 7 March 1927, p. 85.

McConachie, Bruce. "Slavery and Authenticity: Performing a Slave Auction at Colonial Williamsburg." *Theatre Annual* 51 (1998).

Mahar, William J. "'Backside Albany' and Early Blackface Minstrelsy: A Contextual Study of America's First Blackface Song." *American Music* 6 (1988): 1, pp. 1–88.

Mahar, William J. "Black English in Early Blackface Minstrelsy: A New Interpretation of the Sources of Minstrel Show Dialect." *American Quarterly* 37 (1985): p. 261.

Markham, Dewey "Pigmeat." Interview by Tony Bruno. Tape recording, 18 April 1972. *Artist and Influence* 13 (1994).

Martin, Sister Kathryn, S. P. "On Black Theatre of Revolution." *Today's Speech* (1972).

Millay, Edna St. Vincent. "First Fig." In *A Few Figs from Thistles, Poems and Sonnets*. New York: Harper Brothers, 1928.

Montgomery, Gregory. "A Chronology of the Negro Theatre." In *Plays of Negro Life*, edited by Alain Locke. New York: Harper Brothers, 1927.

"More Spice than Substance." *Phylon*, third quarter (1955): p. 303.

Morris, Eileen. "Theatre's Duality, Art and Industry." In *Black Theatre's Unprecedented Times*, edited by Hely Manuel Perez. Gainesville, FL: Black Theatre Network, 1999, pp. 93–94.

Nadler, Paul. "Liberty Censored: Black Living Newspapers of the Federal Theatre Project." *African American Review* 29 (winter 1995): 4, p. 620.

"The Negro in Art: How Shall he be Portrayed?" *Crisis* (June 1927).

Nesmith, Eugene. "What's Race Got to Do with It?" *American Theatre* (March 1996): pp. 12–17.

Newman, Richard. "The Lincoln Theatre." *American Visions* 6 (August 1991): 4, pp. 29–32.

"New Traditions." *NTCP Newsletter* (1959).

Nichols, Charles. "The Origins of Uncle Tom's Cabin." *Phylon* 19 (1958): 3.

Norris, William. "New Light on the Career of S. Morgan Smith." *Black American Literature Forum* 18 (fall 1984): 3, p. 118.

Oliver, Edith. "The Theatre Off-Broadway." *New Yorker*, 11 February 1978.

"Ossie and Ruby Still Making Black History." *Intermission* (February 1999).

Palmer, Colin A. "The First Passage, 1502–1619." In *To Make Our World Anew: A History of African Americans*, edited by Robin D. G. Kelley and Earl Lewis. Oxford: Oxford University Press, 2000.

Parks, Suzan-Lori. "Elements of Style." In *"The America Play" and Other Works*. New York: Theatre Communications Group, 1995.

Parks, Suzan-Lori. Interview by Tom Sellar. *Theatre Forum* 9 (summer 1996): pp. 37–39.

"Paulene Myers Show Scores at Greenwich Mews Theatre." *New York Courier*, 8 October 1966.

Pawley, Thomas D. "The First Black Playwrights." *Black World* 21 (April 1972): pp. 16–25.

Plum, Jay. "Accounting for the Audience in Historical Reconstruction: Martin Jones' Production of Langston Hughes' *Mulatto*." *Theatre Survey* 36 (May 1995): 1, pp. 5–19.

Polatnick, Florence. "An Historical Perspective." In *Showcasing American Drama: Uncle Tom's Cabin*, edited by Vera Jiji. Brooklyn, NY: Humanities Institute, Brooklyn College, 1983.

Poole, Rosey E. "The Negro Actor in Europe." *Phylon* 14 (1953): 3, p. 260.

Preston, Tony. "C. Bernard Jackson: In the Face of Adversity." *Black Masks* 4 (summer 1988): 9, pp. 6–8.

Rahman, Aishah. "*The Mojo and the Sayso*, Aishah Rahman." In *Moon Marked and Touched by Sun*, edited by Sydné Mahone. New York: Theatre Communications Group, 1994.

Reardon, Christopher. "The Arts Mean Business." *Ford Foundation Report* 30 (winter 1999): 1.

Redd, Tina. "Birmingham's Federal Theater Project Negro Unit." In *African American Performance and Theater History*, edited by Harry J. Elam Jr. and David Krasner. New York: St. Martin's Press, 2001.

Redd, Tina. "*Stevedore* in Seattle: A Case Study in the Politics of Presenting Race on Stage." *American Drama and Theatre* 7 (spring 1995): 2.

Reihle, David. "Three Hundred Afro-American' Performers' The Great Cuba Pageant of 1898: St. Paul's Citizens Support the Struggle for Civil Rights." *Ramsey County History* 33 (winter 1999): 4, pp. 15–20.

Riis, Thomas L. "'Bob' Cole: his Life and his Legacy to Black Musical Theater." *Black Perspective in Music* 13 (fall 1985): 2, pp. 135–150.

Robeson, Paul, Jr. "Paul Robeson: Black Warrior." *Freedomways* 11 (1971): 1, p. 26.

Robinson, Edward A. "The Pekin: The Genesis of American Black Theater." *Black American Literature Forum* 16 (winter 1982): 4, pp. 136–138.

Rogers, J. A. "What are we, Negroes or Americans?" *Messenger* 8 (August 1926): p. 237–238, 253.

Schweninger, Loren. "The Free Slave Phenomenon: James P. Thomas and the Black Community in Ante-Bellum Nashville." *Civil War History* 22 (1976): 4, pp. 293–307.

Seyda, Barbara. "Divine Testimonies." *Tulane Drama Review* 40 (spring 1996): 1 (T149).

Shalom, Jack. "The Ira Aldridge Troupe: Early Black Minstrelsy in Philadelphia." *African American Review* 28 (1994): 4, pp. 653–657.

Simon, John. "Fête de Famille." *Fashion Magazine*, 30 August 1999.

Skreen, Chet. "Canwell Probe Brought Final Days for 'Old Rep.'" *Seattle Times Magazine*, Sunday, 6 February 1977, pp. 4–6.

Skreen, Chet. "Today's Seattle Theater Owes a Lot to the 'Old Rep.'" *Seattle Times Magazine*, Sunday, 30 January 1977, pp. 8–12.

"Slavery." In *Black Women in America: A Biographical Encyclopedia*, edited by Darlene Clark Hine. 2 vols. Brooklyn, NY: Carlson, 1993.

Sloan, Leni. "Irish Mornings and African Days on the Old Minstrel Stage." *Callahan's Irish Quarterly* 2 (1982): p. 3.

Spence, Eulalie. "A Criticism of the Negro Drama as it Relates to the Negro Dramatist and Artist." *Opportunity* (June 1928): p. 381.

Stasio, Marilyn. "Tell it, Sisters!" *Cue* (June 1976).

Stayton, Richard. "A Fire in a Crowded Theatre." *American Theatre* (July/August 1993).

Stuckey, Sterling. "The Cultural Philosophy of Paul Robeson." *Freedomways* 11 (1971): 1, p. 81.

"Surrealism and Blues." *Living Blues* 25 (January/February 1976).

Tanner, Jo. "Classical Black Theatre: Federal Theatre's All-Black 'Voodoo *Macbeth*.'" *American Drama and Theatre* 7 (winter 1995): 1, p. 52.

"Theater at Atlanta University." *Atlanta University Bulletin* 4 (1974): 2, pp. 17–24.

"The Theatre and the Armed Forces." *Theatre Arts* 27 (March 1943): 3.

"Theatre Arts." *Craft Arts Quarterly* 3 (fall 1988): 3.

"These are They." *AME Church Review* 83 (October/December 1956).

Thorpe, John C. "On the Cutting Edge." *Black Masks* 10 (February/March 1994): 2, pp. 5–6.

Tommasini, Anthony. "All-Black Casts for 'Porgy'? That Ain't Necessarily So." *New York Times*, 20 March 2002, Arts section, p. E1.

Tooks, Kim. "Kia Corthron: Staying on Track." *Black Masks* 13 (May/June 1998): 1, pp. 5–6.

Varga, George. "Jefferson's Sallygate gets an off-Broadway Show." *San Diego Union-Tribune*, 27 January 1999, Lifestyle section, p. E-6.

Walker, Barbara. "Community Theatre." *Black Creation* 3 (summer 1972): 4, pp. 21–22.

Walker, George. "The Real 'Coon' on the American Stage." *Theatre* (August 1906): p. 224.

Washington, Booker T. "Interesting People: Bert Williams." *American Magazine* 9 (1910): pp. 600–604.

West, Ron. "Others, Adults, Censored: The Federal Theatre Project's *Black Lysistrata* Cancellation." *Theatre Survey* 37 (November 1996): 2, pp. 93–113.

"What is Hip-Hop?" In *Rap on Rap*, edited by Adam Sexton. New York: Bantam, Doubleday, Dell, 1995.

White, Shane. "A Question of Style: Blacks In and Around New York City in the Late Eighteenth Century." *American Folklore* 102 (1989): 403, p. 30.

Williams, John. "Hip-Hop Homer." *American Theatre* (May/June 1996): pp. 6–7.

Winter, Marian Hannah. "Juba and American Minstrelsy." *Dance Index* (1947), p. 31.

Wolfe, George C. "I Just Want to Keep Telling Stories." Interview by Charles H. Rowell. *Callaloo* 16 (March 1993).

Wynter, Sylvia. "Bernardo de Balbuena: Epic Poet and Abbot of Jamaica, 1562–1627." *Jamaica Journal* 3 (September 1969): 3, p. 5.

Wynter, Sylvia. "New Seville and the Conversion Experience of Bartolomé de Las Casas." *Jamaica Journal* 17 (May 1984): 2, pp. 25–32.

Government publications

The Federal Theatre Project Collection: A Register of the Library of Congress Collection of US Work Projects Administration Records on Deposit at George Mason University. Washington, DC: Library of Congress, 1987.

Report on the Population of the United States at the Eleventh Census, 1890. Washington, DC: Government Printing Office, 1897.

Rubinstein, Irwin A. *A List of Negro Plays*, publication no. 24-L. New York: National Service Bureau, March 1938.

Dissertations, unpublished papers, and presentations

Anderson, Addell Austin. "Pioneering Black Authored Dramas: 1924–27." Ph.D. dissertation, Michigan State University, 1986.

Belcher, Fannin Saffore, Jr. "The Place of the Negro in the Evolution of the American Theatre, 1762–1940." Ph.D. dissertation, Yale University, 1940.

Clarke, Kit. "Haverly Minstrel Press Book, 1883–84". HRHC.

Cleary, Beth. "Refiguring Race, Representing Race: The Jubilee Singers of the Buffalo Historical Marionettes." Paper presented at "Pedagogy and Theater of the Oppressed," a conference held at the City University of New York, 1999. HBC.

Graham, Sandy. "Spirituals in Minstrel Shows." Unpublished paper, 1996. HBC.

Johnson, Elvamari Alexandria. "A Production History of the Seattle Federal Theater Project's Negro Repertory Company: 1935–1939." Ph.D. dissertation, University of Washington, 1981.

Lewis, Barbara. "From Slavery to Segregation: on the Lynching Trail." Ph.D. dissertation, City University of New York, 2000.

Miller, Henry. "Art or Propaganda?: A Historical and Critical Analysis of African American Theoretical Approaches to Drama, 1900–1975." Ph.D. dissertation, City University of New York, 2002.

Monroe, John Gilbert. "Charles Sidney Gilpin: The Emperor Jones." Master's thesis, Hunter College, New York, 1974.

Monroe, John Gilbert. "A Record of the Black Theatre in New York City: 1920–29." Ph.D. dissertation, University of Texas at Austin, 1980.

Nadler, Paul. "American Theatre and the Civil Rights Movement, 1945–1965." Ph.D. dissertation, City University of New York, 1996.

Nadler, Paul. "The Life of Lester A. Walton." Unpublished paper, City University of New York, 1991.

Price, Walter. Typed article sent to historian Oliver M. Sayler. HBC.

Roses, Lorraine Elena. "The Search for Black Boston's Lost Cultural Riches." Talk and slide show presented at the Ford Hall Forum, Dorchester, MA, 1999.

Rushton, Christopher. "Motivations of a Little Giant." Unpublished paper, Ph.D. theatre program, City University of New York, 1993.

Sandle, Floyd L. "The Negro in the American Educational Theatre: An Organizational Development, 1911–1964." Ph.D. dissertation, Louisiana State University, 1959.

Scott-Giles, Freda. "Five African-American Playwrights on Broadway, 1923–1929." Ph.D. dissertation, program in theatre, City University of New York, 1990.

Silver, Reuben. "A History of the Karamu Theatre of Karamu House, 1915–1960." Ph.D. dissertation, Ohio State University, 1961.

Thompson, Mary Francesca. "The Lafayette Players 1915–1932." Ph.D. dissertation, University of Michigan, 1972.

Vactor, Vanita. "A History of the Chicago Federal Theatre Project Negro Unit: 1935–1939." Ph.D. dissertation, New York University, 1998.

Williams, Allen. "Sheppard Randolph Edmonds: his Contributions to Black Educational Theatre." Ph.D. dissertation, Indiana University, 1972.

Williams, Kathy Ervin. "Concept East Theatre: 1962–1976." Unpublished paper, NCAAT, 1987.

Wilson, August. "The Ground Upon Which I Stand." Keynote address at Theater Communications Group, Princeton University, 26 June 1996.

Wilson, August. Keynote address at the Atlanta Black Arts Festival, 11 July 1998.

Wilson, James. "Bulldykes, Pansies, and Chocolate Babies." Ph.D. dissertation proposal, City University of New York, 1998. HBC.

Internet, radio, and television

Bean, Linda. "Crossroads Theatre Receives Funds: Expects to Raise Curtain This Summer." *Daily Diversity News and Views*, 7 February 2001, Diversityinc.com, 7 July 2001. http://www.diversityinc.com/insidearticlepg.cfm?submenuID=080&ArticleID=2423

Brown, Tony. "Black Men, Black Women." *Black Journal*, television broadcast, PBS-TV, 27 February 1977.

D, Chuck. "The Sound of Our Young World." 29 September 1999. Rapstation, 29 May 2002. http://www.rapstation.com/inside_the_rhyme/terrordome/terrordome 990929.html

Hausam, Wiley. "*The Wild Party* Production Diary: September 1997." The Public Theater, 29 April 2002. http://www.thewildparty.net/wp.b.d.1997.sep.html

Owens, William. "The Free Theatre Company." 18 February 1997. http://www.bobwest.com/ncaat/frsouth.html
Radio program. KDHX FM88, St. Louis, Missouri, August 1998.
Saltzman, Simon, and Nicole Plett. "August Wilson Versus Robert Brustein." 22 January 1997. US 1 Newspaper, 29 May 2002. http://www.princetoninfo.com/wilson.html

Unpublished interviews

Browne, Theodore. Interview by Lorraine Brown. 22 November 1975. George Mason University; copy of transcript and tape recording, HBC.
Campbell, Dick. Interview by Tony Bruno. 1 March 1972.
Forsyne, Ida. Interview by Cassandra Willis. Tape recording, February 1972. HBC.
Gilbert, Lou. Interview by James V. Hatch. Tape recording, 13 January 1977. HBC.
Jackson, C. Bernard. Interview by James V. Hatch. Tape recording, 16 October 1985. HBC.
LeNoire, Rosetta. Interview by George Brooker. Tape recording, 15 June 1992. HBC.
Loft-Lynn, Jay. Interview by James V. Hatch. Tape recording, 25 March 1975. HBC.
Neal, Larry. Interview by James V. Hatch. Tape recording, 24 January 1974. HBC.
Roker, Roxie. Interview by James V. Hatch. Tape recording, 18 October 1985. HBC.
Sissle, Noble. Interview by James Hatch. Tape recording, 7 March 1972. HBC.
Spence, Eulalie. Interview by Ernest Wiggins. Tape recording, 22 August 1973. HBC.
Stewart, Nick. Interview by Margaret Wilkerson. Tape recording, 24 November 1971. HBC.
Taylor, Audrey June. Interview by James V. Hatch. Tape recording, 11 March 1984. HBC.
Zollar, Jawole Willa Jo. Interview by Jennifer Donaghy. Tape recording, April 1989. HBC.

Letters

Brown, Gilmore. Letter to Hallie Flanagan, 20 February 1936. Regional Correspondence, RG69, National Archives.
Carroll, Vinnette. Letter to Roger L. Stevens, 7 December 1971. Copy HBC.
Hughes, Langston. Letter to Louise Patterson, 15 April 1984. Emory University.
Ingram, Milroy. Letter to Fred O'Neal, 1952.
Locke, Alain LeRoy. Letter of resignation from NAACP Committee on the Drama, c. 1916. Moorland-Spingarn Manuscript Division, Howard University.
Mitchell, Kati. Announcement letter to James V. Hatch, 24 November 1997. HBC.
Pawley, Thomas D. Letter to Errol Hill, 28 April 2000. HBC.
Winsor, Ellen. Letter to Wayland Rudd, 22 April 1930. Copy HBC.
Wolfe, George C. Letter to James V. Hatch, 23 July 1998. HBC.
Wolfe, George C. Letter to James V. Hatch, 30 August 1999. HBC.

Newspapers and periodicals

African American Review
American Visions
Atlanta Constitution

Atlanta Journal and Constitution
Barbados Advocate
Berkeley (CA) Calendar
Bermuda Sun
Black Liberator
Black Masks
Black Theatre
Boston Globe
Boston Guardian
Boston Sunday Herald
Chicago American
Chicago Defender
Chicago Inter-Ocean
Chicago Tribune
Cleveland (OH) Gazette
Colored American Magazine
Commercial Advertiser
Crisis
Denver Exchange
Drama
Evening Post
Family Magazine
Frederick Douglass' Paper (continuation of *North Star*)
Freedomways
Freeman (Indianapolis)
Globe (London)
Guardian (London)
Hamburger Nachrichten
Huntsville (AL) Daily Mercury
Indianapolis Freeman
Inter-State Tattler
Gleaner (Kingston, Jamaica)
Globe (Toronto)
Klinck's Albany Directory, 1823.
London Era
Los Angeles Eagle
Los Angeles Herald Examiner
Los Angeles Times
Louisville (KY) Courier-Journal
Messenger
Miami Herald
Music and Drama
Nation
National Advocate
National Omnibus and General Advertiser
Negro Handbook

Negro Heritage
Negro Year Book, An Annual Encyclopedia of the Negro
New Brunswick (NJ) Home News Tribune
New Orleans (LA) Times-Picayune
New York Age
New York American
New York Amsterdam News
New York Clipper
New York Daily News
New York Dramatic Mirror
New York Evening Post
New York Freeman
New York Globe
New York Herald
New York Herald Tribune
New York Mail and Express
New York Telegraph
New York Times
New York World
North American
Norwich (CT) Bulletin
Nottingham and Newark Mercury (UK)
Opportunity
Owl (Cape Town, South Africa)
Pacific Commercial Advertiser
Paris Tribune
The People's Voice
Philadelphia Inquirer
Philadelphia Magazine
Philadelphia Times
Philadelphia Tribune
Phylon: The Atlanta University Review of Race and Culture
Pittsburgh (PA) Courier
Portland (OR) Oregonian
Port-of-Spain Gazette (Trinidad)
Pottsville (PN) Miners Journal
Redding (CA) Daily News
Richmond (VA) Dispatch
St. Louis (MO) Globe-Democrat
St. Louis (MO) Star
St. Paul (MN) Western Appeal
Salt Lake City (Utah) Broad Axe
San Francisco Argonaut
San Francisco Pacific Appeal
Seattle Herald
Seattle Intelligencer

Seattle Post Intelligencer
Seattle Times
Spotlight
Stage (London)
Sunday Dispatch (London)
Tatler
Theatre Forum
Theatrical Observer
Times (London)
Trinidad Guardian
Tuesday Magazine
Variety
Village Voice
Washington (DC) Bee
Washington (DC) Colored American
Washington (DC) Post
Yale Alumni Magazine

Theatre programs

"American College Theatre Festival Tenth Anniversary Program," 1978.
"Art Impressions of George White's Scandals," 1927.
The Big White Fog, Negro Playwrights Company, New York City.
Bury the Dead, Negro People's Theatre, Lincoln Center, Chicago, 13 April 1940. HBC.
Crisis Guild of Writers and Artists (KRIGWA), *Krigwa Theatre Program*, May 1926.
The Darker Face of the Earth, Crossroads Theatre Company, 4 October 1997.
Darkest America, New Park Opera House, Erie, Pennsylvania, 5 February 1897.
Fifth Anniversary season, Chelsea Theatre, Brooklyn, New York.
Ouanga, Metropolitan Opera House, New York City, 27 May 1956.
Penthouse Theatre, New York City, 15 July 1948.
Trouble in Mind, Bowling Green University Theater, 5 March 1978.

Pamphlets and promotional materials

"Colored Actors Union" pamphlet.
"Crossroads Theatre Company – A History," publicity mailer, 1992.
Ensemble Theatre of Houston publicity brochure, 1998.
"Fact Sheet," ETA Creative Arts Foundation, 1998.
"Freedom Theatre Fact Sheet," Philadelphia's Freedom Theatre, 1998.
Hamlin, Larry Leon. Letter from North Carolina Black Repertory Company, 25 February 1989.
Hamlin, Larry Leon. Publicity release from North Carolina Black Repertory Company, 25 February 1989.
Muse, Clarence Edouard. *The Dilemma of the Negro Actor*. Los Angeles: privately printed pamphlet, 1934. Emory University.
Wilson, August. "Twenty Years Running: Penumbra's Victory." Publicity letter, 1996.

Index

Abbensetts, Michael, 294
Abbott, George, 59
Abel, Don, 328, 530
Above the Clouds, 86
Absolution of Willie Mae, The, 397
absurdist theatre, 388–389, 394, 448
Abyssinia, 89, 169–170
Academy of Music, Halifax, Nova Scotia, 157
Academy of Music, Lynn, MA, 71
Academy of Music, New York City, 80
Academy of Music, Philadelphia, PA, 81, 139, 148, 180
accents (*see* dialect)
Ackamoor, Idris, 433
Acme Players, 225
Across the Continent, 126
Across the Footlights, 204
ACT (A Contemporary Theatre), 463
Actors' Equity Association, 207, 289, 344, 449, 469, 470; and black theatres, 470, 471, 472, 476; employment figures, 367, 457; Non-Traditional Casting Project, 460–461; O'Neal, Frederick, 354, 367, 373, 408; promotes integration, 341, 374, 422; racism, 206, 373; strikes, 174, 341
Adelphi Hall, 78–79, 80, 179
Adkins, Joseph, 523
Adler, Stella, 373
admission (*see* ticket prices)
AETA (*see* American Educational Theatre Association)
affirmative action, 462
Africa, dance, 21, 95, 368–369, 387; depicted on stage, 77, 137, 166, 169, 277, 377; influence on American theatre, 21–22, 368–369, 386–387,

394; language, 398, 501; music, 101, 500; religion, 7, 294
African Ceremonial, 368
African Company (*see* African Theatre)
African Diaspora Theatre, 297
African Dwarf Tommy (Thomas Dilward), 112, 120
African Grove Institute for the Arts (AGIA), 459, 543
African Grove, 26, 459, 509
African Methodist Episcopal Church (*see* AME Church)
African Roscius, *see* Aldridge, Ira
African Theatre (African Company, American Theatre), 26, 29, 32, 38, 177, 273, 274
Africana (1927), 208, 276
Africana, A Congo Operetta (1934), 277
Africanus, 515
Afrikan Women's Repertory Theatre, 426
Afro-American Opera Company, 179
Afro-American Studio Theatre, 406
Afro-American Theatre, 401
Afro-American Total Theatre, 402
Aftermath, 189, 222
AGIA (*see* African Grove Institute for the Arts)
agitprop plays, 311, 312, 327, 362, 366
Ahrens, Lynn, 304
Aida, 179, 181, 182
AIDS, 303, 434, 438, 449, 544
Aiken, Loreta Mary (*see* Mabley, Moms)
Ailey, Alvin, 282
Ain't Misbehavin', 251
Ain't Supposed to Die a Natural Death, 398, 412, 420–421
Alabama Shakespeare Festival, 454, 457

Black Male/Female, 427
Black Masks, 486
Black Musical Review, The, 473
Black Napoleon (John Walcott Cooper), 122
Black Nativity, 382, 401, 403, 469, 472, 546
Black One Hundred, 122
Black Panther Party, 387, 389, 428, 470
Black Patti Troubadours, 132, 147, 149–150, 166, 196, 274, 506 (see also Jones, Sissieretta)
Black Quartet, 391
Black Rhythm, 278
Black Souls, 314
black studies departments, 414–415
Black Swan Troubadours, 208
Black Swan (see Greenfield, Elizabeth Taylor)
Black Teacher and the Dramatic Arts, The, 270
Black Theater Arts Magazine, 399
Black Theatre, 486, 536
Black Theatre Alliance (BTA), 385, 405–407, 448, 480, 486, 537
Black Theatre Association, 538
Black Theatre Festival, Winston-Salem, NC (see National Black Theatre Festival)
Black Theatre Festival USA, New York City, 403, 542
Black Theatre Network (BTN), 486, 538
Black Thunder, 533
Black Trilby Company, 118–119, 120, 154
Black Vesta Tilley (Florence Hines), 129, 145
Black Woman, 296
Black Woman in White, 527
Black World (Negro Digest), 486
Blackberries of 1932, 277
Blackbirds, 208, 230, 239, 248, 249, 277, 325
blackface, 96, 156, 196, 204, 231, 235, 242, 311; before minstrelsy, 96; first used, 499; in the 1990s, 445–446, 541; in the Caribbean, 274; in South Africa, 128; in Uncle Tom's Cabin 1933, 59; minstrelsy, 91, 92, 94; worn by Blacks, 108, 129, 130, 162, 173, 246; worn by Whites, 185, 315, 519
Blackfriars, 344
Blacks, The, 283, 388, 489
Blacksmyths, 465
Blackville Jubilee Singers, 124
Blackville Twins, The, 75, 128
Blake, Eubie, 215, 245, 246, 319, 531
Bland, James, 101
Bledsoe, Jules, 181, 182, 203, 236, 322
Blithe Spirit, 267, 268

Blkartsouth, 399
Blood Knot, 379, 393, 518
Blood on the Fields, 312, 526
Bloodstream, 333
Blue, 450, 542
Blue Angel, The, 279, 282
Blue Holiday, 282, 532
Blue Stories, The, 434
Blues for an Alabama Sky, 447, 463, 473
Blues for Mister Charlie, 380, 535
Boesman and Lena, 379
Bohee brothers (James and George), 102–103, 114, 124
Bohee, May, 118
Bolt from the Blue, A, 386
Bombastes Furioso, 36
Bond, Tim, 463, 465
bones (musical instrument), 103, 500
Bonner, Marita Odette, 223–225, 389, 514
Bontemps, Arna, 317, 343, 358, 359
Booth Theatre, 426
Booth, Edwin, 61, 81, 86
Booth-Barrett Amateurs, 86
Boris Godounov, 182
borrowing of material (see copying)
Bosan, Alonzo, 338
Boston Negro Theatre, 332
Boston Players, 515
Boston Playwrights Theatre, 289
Boston Symphony, 182
Bound by an Oath, 86
Bowery Amphitheater, 93
Bowman, Laura, 514
Boxing Day Parade, The, 293
Boy Days, 296
Bradford, Alex, 382
Bradford, Joseph, 71
Bradford, Roark, 308
Branch, William B., 17, 244, 361, 365
Branner, Djola Bernard, 437
brass bands, 117, 122
Brathwaite, William Stanley, 59
Brattle Hall, 220, 347
Bray, Keve, 464
breakdown (dance), 94, 143, 211
Brecher, Leo, 231, 234
Breen, Robert, 315
Breuer, Lee, 383, 463
Brewer, John W. (Black Eddie Foy), 121–122
Brewster, Townsend, 421

Vesey, Denmark, 16, 96, 495; depicted by
    S. Randolph Edmonds, 16
Victoria 5 Theatre, 295
Victoria Theatre, Hammerstein's, 131, 172
Victory Gardens Theatre, 293
Vietnam War, 290, 380, 389, 427
Vieux Carré, 536
Village Gate, 251
Village Vanguard, 282
violence, against Blacks, 104, 186–188; against
    black performers, 119, 131, 187, 346, 347; in
    Black Arts Movement plays, 373, 389
Virginia Essence (dance), 99, 111, 125
Virginia Jubilee Singers, 127
Virginia Minstrels, 94
Virginia State College, 261
Virginian Mummy, The, 43
Visitor, The, 294
Vivian Beaumont Theatre, 400
Vodery, Will H., 155, 203, 244, 509, 511
Voelckel, Rudolph, 147, 149, 150, 157
Vogel, John W., 145
Voice of the Hurricane (film), 345
Volpone, 374, 395
voodoo, depicted in theatre, 184, 279
Voodoo, 184
"Voodoo" Macbeth, 317, 386, 518, 528
Voorhees, Lillian, 265, 267
Voteur, Ferdinand, 527

Wade Padlock Law, 238
wages, American Negro Theatre, 355; *Carmen
    Jones*, 342; Federal Theatre Project, 316, 326;
    Free Southern Theatre, 398; *Green Pastures,
    The*, 309; Gregory, Dick, 388; Harlem Opera
    House, 231; minstrel performers, 118–119, 125,
    130; Penumbra Theatre, 472; *Prodigal Son*
    European tour, 402; *Short Eyes*, 538; street
    theatre, 418; union members, 364, 457, 472;
    USO performers, 336; vaudeville performers,
    131, 162, 207; Williams and Walker, 170, 176
Waiting for Godot, 368, 397, 534
Waiting for Lefty, 312
Walcott, Beatrice, 523
Walcott, Derek, 284, 287–290, 294, 304, 305, 525
Walcott, Roderick, 287, 294
walk around (dance), 94, 133, 152
Walk Hard, 353, 354
Walk in Darkness, 366, 379
Walk Together Chillun, 317

Walker, Aida (Ada) Overton, 129, 161, 166, 168,
    169, 171, 211, 508
Walker, Alice, 219
Walker, George, 76, 89, 104–105, 119, 129, 132,
    150, 155, 160, 161, 163–171, 187, 211, 507
Walker, Joseph A., 272, 382, 396, 397, 419
Walker, Lucy M., 272
Walker, Sullivan, 296–297
Walker, Victor, 458
walking the dog (dance), 247
Wallace, Lizzie, 192
Wallace, Michele, 427
Wallack, Henry, 492, 493
Wallack, James, 41, 492
Waller, Thomas "Fats," 202, 251, 280
Walton, Lester A., 132, 233, 236, 237, 363;
    biography, 203–204, 239, 512; criticism, 159,
    162, 198, 213
War, 65
Ward Theatre, 89, 288
Ward, Aida, 248
Ward, Douglas Turner, 285, 297, 377, 395, 396,
    460
Ward, Pamela, 279
Ward, Theodore, 63, 349, 399, 413, 533, 537
    (*see also Big White Fog*)
Ward, Val Gray and Francis, 413
Warden, Gentry, 325
Warner, Earl, 291
Warning – A Theme for Linda, The, 391, 418
Washington Years, The, 533
Washington, Booker T., 116, 228, 257
Washington, Denzel, 400
Washington, Dinah, 244
Washington, Fredi, 532
Washington, Isabel, 239
Washington, Von H., 400
Watch on the Rhine, 237
Waters, Ethel, 207–208, 211, 230, 252, 276, 282,
    342, 345, 366, 367, 371
Watkins, Perry, 319, 344, 422, 527
Watson, Robert, 229
Watts, Maggie, 78
WCF (*see* Working Capital Fund)
WCT (Wild Crazy Things) Productions, 467
Weaver, Afaa Michael, 474
Webb, B. Franklin, 89
Webster, Paul, 297
Wedding Band, 361
Weisberger Hall, 183